November

E.A.   Stadtgesichter   Richter 6/05

Christopher Woodall

NOVEMBER

A NOVEL

 DALKEY ARCHIVE PRESS

Frontispiece and front cover image is from Petra Wildenhahn's lithograph *Stadtgesichter*, used with the artist's permission.

Library of Congress Cataloging-in-Publication Data
Names: Woodall, Christopher J.
Title: November : a novel / by Christopher Woodall.
Description: First edition. | Victoria, TX : Dalkey Archive Press, 2016.
Identifiers: LCCN 2015014831 | ISBN 978-1-62897-111-8 (softcover : acid-free
    paper)
Subjects: LCSH: Blue-collar workers--France--History--20th century--Fiction.
Classification: LCC PR6123.O5278 N69 2015 | DDC 823/.92--dc23
LC record available at http://lccn.loc.gov/2015014831

Partially funded by a grant from the Illinois Arts Council, a state agency

Dalkey Archive Press publications are, in part, made possible through the support of the University of Housotn-Victoria and its programs in creative writing, publishing, and translation.

Dalkey Archive Press
Victoria, TX / McLean, IL / Dublin
www.dalkeyarchive.com

Printed on permanent/durable acid-free paper

CONTENTS.

I am not yet born; provide me
With water to dandle me, grass to grow for me, trees to talk
   to me, sky to sing to me, birds and a white light
     in the back of my mind to guide me.

From 'Prayer before birth' (1945) by Louis MacNeice.

It is well understood that for us, surrealists, the interests of thought cannot cease to go hand in hand with the interests of the working class, and that any threat to freedoms, any obstacle to the emancipation of the working class and, even more, any armed attack on it is felt by us as an attempt to poison thought.

From *Qu'est-ce que le surréalisme* (1934) by André Breton.

BOOK ONE. ARRIVING.

In which one man receives an unwelcome phone call, another over-sleeps, a third gets a date with a girl, a fourth a long-awaited smile from his wife, while a fifth invokes and then experiences a vision. These men, and others besides, are brought safely to the factory where they work. We are on the continent of Europe, in the town of Grandgobier. It is the evening of Tuesday 9 November 1976, when nobody famous gave up the ghost and no great war began or ended. For all that, things never stopped happening.

*

1. Tomec, Sarah, Mathieu, Jacques.

In pursuit of clarity, some pray, some drink, some fast, some dance, some mortify the flesh: Tomec stripped naked and made for his evening shower much earlier than he needed to, luxuriating in its steam, adopting beneath the pelting water the meditative pose of the male primate. His broad feet were slightly splayed, his right hand tugged gingerly at his sore, limp penis, while his left hand, instead of supporting his chin, scratched insistently away at its stubble – more neurotic than thoughtful, more rodent than Rodin. After a moment, he resumed soaping himself, wincing childlike.

Tomec wanted to put pictures to an account he had been reading of the death of Virgil. He needed to see the event in order to paint it and to paint it in order to sculpt it. First he would conjure into existence the foggy, muddy quayside in Brundisium to which the Roman poet was supposedly brought by ship, and its throng of people, animals and detritus. That much ought to be easy.

Gripping a bar of soap in his left hand, his arms fell to his sides, and his head tipped back. His mind felt dull and grey, his limbs weary. He blew out his cheeks and opened his eyes so wide that his crows' feet flattened to feint lines. Staring into the water that the aluminium showerhead was shooting like needles into his face, he marshalled a miscellany of features from the faces of childhood friends and later acquaintances, half-remembered family, and the men he saw each night at work. He passed them in review: eyes, noses, chins, foreheads, cheeks, mouths and ears. From such scraps might a multitude be furnished. But the fog failed to lift.

Tomec's belly distended, his penis wagged, and an uneven stream of urine was mixed with the water, turning the shower tray a billowing yellow that darkened then faded, darkened then faded. Within Tomec's mind something distinct was stirring: a shuffling of feet, a promise of people. He longed to stare into the faces of the crowd. He wanted to take possession.

Tomec's skin relaxed, his wrinkles grew back their steep sides, and a smile leapt from eyes to dimpling cheeks. Upon his imagination there now advanced images of the 'surf of people' that lapped around the Roman poet as he was borne shoulder-high from the ship. The 'brooding mass-beast' was emerging from that winter's evening gloom, its innumerable heads looming into focus, submitting to Tomec's gaze. Each shape grew just sharp enough to suggest a temperament, an occupation, the sketch of a past, a character sufficiently sheathed in living skin to be loathed or liked, admired or scorned.

Where have these forms come from? Tomec wondered as he peered at the fading figments. My own life? Drawn from features I have robbed from my friends, family or clan? There isn't one of these creatures I would call my own.

Rubbing the soap to foam on his hairy belly, the naked man broke into a long guffaw. Clan indeed! Family! All such ties are long since buried in the northern, barbarian reaches of this feud-frozen continent, far enough from ancient Brundisium. And what a pitiful, scurvy mob it was that met the poet's dying gaze on that wintry quayside!

Settling the soap on a ledge, Tomec tried again, beckoning clumsily, half-closing his eyes: show yourselves, come now! I want each one of you so neat and sharp I can smell your breath, read your fetid lives from your faces. I want to know your appetites, thrill to the filthiest of your inclinations. If once I can grip their faces vice-like in the eye of my mind, I know I can draw them, nail them to the board, sculpt the swine. If for one instant, I could pluck Virgil's eyes from his skull and glimpse that crowd I swear I would immortalize it before I die.

Tomec peered straight ahead, then down at the knuckles of his toes clawing at the corrugated white enamel. The current swirled his sparse brown hair into a monk's mop, while the neon light picked out stray white strands. Glancing up again as if alerted by some sound, Tomec caught the faces advancing through the steam toward him, stumbling upon the squint of his mind's eye, clearer now than before, appearing both hostile and, in spite of the man's vaudeville of invitation, still shambling. He chuckled as he soaped as he saw. I have visions, he muttered. It is about time. I am a man possessed!

And possessing? he wondered, snagged like a fish hooked from a river, thrashing airborne on a barbed word, while time swerved and stopped.

For down the contingent corridor, in a space that served as studio, kitchen and bedroom, Sarah sat naked, straight-backed and cross-legged on a mussed bed, sipping from a glass of green tea, taking care not to ingest the leaves and lemon flotsam that bobbed on its surface. Her brow was knit, her breath short and her lips pursed, as if to bestow a kiss: she too was on the brink of some revelation.

In a corner, on the floor, a gramophone grated with modern opera. While the instruments crescendoed and faded and the voices plummeted, soared, and in one case merely droned, emotion set the young woman's chestnut curls swaying. She turned and gazed as the arm rose from the disc's centre and with a clicking and a clanking travelled to its edge, dithering before it dropped back onto vinyl, adding the crackle of nominal silence to the machine whirr. The music began again and the woman brushed away a tear. *Einziger, ewiger, allgegenwärtiger und unvorstellbarer Gott . . .* , the voice intoned. God, unique, eternal, ever-present . . . Sarah frowned. A thought was struggling to be born.

What remains of Moses's visionary passion and Aaron's slick oratory once God has quit the scene? Like siblings who lose the engine of their rivalry when their parent dies, how can Moses remain the seer and Aaron the crowdpleaser once God is dead or dethroned by incredulity? Or does God, like the dead parent, linger, a curmudgeonly vestige, breathing fusty life into the conflict and clash of sons? Sarah's head was beginning to pound. A sigh escaped her lips.

Sucking on her teeth, she produced a small sibilant sound: tse. Her tongue discovered, flush to the enamel, a filament of tea that her right hand, with little finger deployed, now rose to dislodge. She scrutinized the morsel, flapping like seaweed against the pink rock of her cuticle, then flicked it away with her thumb. Attending to the music once again, her face was, for a long moment, quite, quite inane. She shifted and fidgeted, then brightened with sudden transport.

How wonderful, she reflected, that arid serialist precepts should beget such melody! But then was the composer not a romantic at heart, steeped in Brahms and Haydn? Ought not all art to be like this? Mosaic in its bluff single-mindedness, eschewing the dulcet ruses of Aaron? At this notion, a plump tear welled in her right eye and rollicked down her cheek, dribbling a path to one side of her mouth. Her tongue flicked out to catch the tear. How pure it tastes! Saltier than the deadest sea!

Frowning prettily, Sarah reached for a notebook that lay face-down on the blanket. She lifted her pencil, cocked her head to one side and blinked twice at the page. Words or images, images or words, which should it be? There is no time to waste. Yet time stood frozen. Tomorrow I may be dead, may I not? For ever and ever and ever. She drew a deep breath and held it. *Eine Ewigkeit.* Her pencil was poised. Just imagine.

On that particular evening, in a factory close to the centre of Grandgobier, a short stroll from the train station, Mathieu, the foreman on the night shift, was picking his way toward the din and glare of the plastics section. By his wristwatch, it had just turned nine o'clock. On either side of his path rose grey, greasy machinery, a serried herd of dormant hulks that stood in the shadows and dripped oil unobserved.

Most of the workers on the shift would not show up until minutes or even seconds before they had to clock on at 21.25, and some – Jacques and Alphonse, but possibly Bobrán too – might even arrive late, forfeiting a quarter of an hour's pay. They often did that. Mathieu wondered why, then, with a lift of his eyebrows, pushed the thought away. He quickened his pace. The foreman had to be there early: it was his job to debrief the engineers from the afternoon shift. If some of the workers sometimes came late and lost money, that was their problem. Mathieu was nobody's mother, nobody's nanny. (But Nadine? What of Nadine? I should like to dedicate the next piece to Nadine, who sadly can't be with us this evening. It's by Clifford Brown, who never grew old.)

Mathieu walked with a limp, leaning forward, yet advanced without weaving, dwarfed by the machines, tracing a clean dark line through the metals workshop. On the floor lay old wooden trays glinting with the day's angle pieces, screw-plates, cross-members. Mathieu air-trumpeted the opening bars of a tune he had been practising that afternoon: 'Brownie Speaks' by Clifford Brown. Do-bah, de-de-bah! do-bah-bah! Bah! Mathieu caressed the phrases, in homage to the dead and the dying.

An ancient yawning hold-all with a trailing broken zip, containing a paper, his midnight snack and a bottle of beer, was slung over Mathieu's left shoulder and clamped in place by a mangled left hand, leaving his right hand free to work the valves, blocking and unblocking them with deft jabs and flicks. His lips, blowing through sparse white stubble, spat out the scatted notes of a spiralling solo, as he sought communion with the jazzman's spirit: Bah! De-bah! De-de-de-de, Bah-de! 'Brownie Speaks,' and I speak back. Why did you die so young, Clifford, when you had so much to live for? (An image of Nadine, young and skinny, her hair cropped close.) Not that dying is something to eke out. (Nadine, here and now, and so thoroughly squandered.) But to die when you have a lifetime of blowing still to do. Clifford is silent as the grave, makes no reply. Dead as dead.

Memory-portraits of Mathieu's wife, snaps from a vivid past and a deathlike present, seethed through his mind and were cast aside, heaved into a shallow grave, from which they restlessly arose, returning, undead, hardening into a scar the stain that over years had formed in his mind, thickening to a canker the knowledge that he had to do something about her, and soon. (Her lovely face, through all those years, when she could laugh, lovelier still when her lines turned to furrows, her hair to silver.) Nadine couldn't be left in this state. It was an affront to her memory, a daily dereliction. It was ruining his life too – as she would have been quick to point out. Seven years already, since that first unlucky stroke, that first-last day. He had done the mourning, he had grieved and he had wept. It was time she died. (When we were young, the nape of her neck, its scent, my hands in her back, her hair rippling like runs of high notes on a piano, falling over my face like a dry spray of leaves.) Who can say what deaths we'll have to die? Mathieu thought. Maybe Clifford was lucky in his car crash. It must have been quick as a riff, as a lick. Wa-wah-wah! A climax with hi-hat, throbbing bass and cymbals. Then silence.

Now the clatter of twenty-plus injection presses came closer, and Mathieu required more volume to cut through the backing. He oiled his lip with spittle, signed off his solo with a flourish, and reprised the head, laying back against the notes, understating the tune, letting it hover like a phantom whose outline you long to see more clearly. He *speaks*, all right. Bu-Wa, Bah! Bah! It was Clifford's but now it's mine and it's free to everyone who wants a piece of it. A quick crescendo and a coda, then a dream of applause, people jumping to their feet and clapping, their hands above their heads, Nadine smiling through the smoke, somewhere in New York, proud. Mathieu pulled a wry smile. He played well, he knew he did, but nobody had ever leapt to their feet. Patted his back, maybe. Bought him a drink. Paid him a compliment.

Reaching the hanging flaps of scratched plastic that curtained the entrance to the plastics section, Mathieu slid his air-trumpet onto an imaginary stand and pushed through into the din, warmth and smells of sizzling polymers. His blue watery eyes blinked in the fumes and glare.

He screwed those faint eyes now into a slowly ratcheting focus and peered down the aisle that separated the rows of machines, spotting several workers who shook their heads at him by way of greeting. He inclined his head in minute acknowledgement. Others were too busy cleaning their machines or packing up boxes of product to note his arrival.

One of the workers, a North African, a woman whom he had sometimes encountered in the street where he lived, hurried past him with a sheet of cardboard and a sticky-tape dispenser, extending a free left arm that Mathieu grasped briefly in his right hand, squeezing it slightly: B'soir! they mouthed in near-unison. She was always a fraction friendlier than she needed to be. Mathieu appreciated that.

As every evening, the familiarity of this place, a home from home, cheered and infuriated him. A voice within him muttered: here we go again.

The nearest machine, number fourteen, was stopped, the red light on the top of its control cabinet lit up. He had better take a look. He moved toward it and clicked his tongue. (Was Nadine sleeping now or still staring at the wall-mounted TV, saliva seeping from her mouth?) The press was open and an engineer – young and lanky, with a thick moustache – was leaning into it from the other side, scratching his head with one hand, and prodding at the mould with a pair of fine pliers. Alongside him, the afternoon machine operator was taping up boxes, keeping out of the way, as though it were his vocation to go unnoticed.

Luigi, the evening-shift worker in charge of machines thirteen and fourteen, had just arrived and was lowering his old leather satchel onto the floor by the side of control cabinet fourteen. Moving closer to the engineer, he caught a glimpse of the night foreman through the halted press. Mathieu tapped at his watch, shook his head and performed a perfunctory grin: 'earlier than ever!' it seemed to say. Luigi bared his teeth, removed two packs of Nazionali and a pack of Gitanes Maïs from the pocket of his bomber jacket, and turned his attention to the control cabinet: pressures, timings, temperatures, numbers, gauges, dials.

The engineer, now aware of Mathieu's arrival, transferred his cigarette stub to his mouth so he could extend his right hand through the press. Meeting it halfway with his own right hand, Mathieu jerked his head sharply up and back and toward the control panel, in curt interrogation, his red-lidded eyes blinking. (Nadine, just lying there, her eyes closing slowly.)

Ejector pins, the engineer answered. Mathieu aimed a quizzical nod down the aisle. All okay at present, replied the engineer, who then frowned hard, staring darkly at the ground, as if searching out a pattern. Number two's on a new mould, he said at last. Need to watch it, pressure's unstable. (Nadine had been clean and dry when he had left her, but was she even now straining to shit, her vacant face contorting?)

Mathieu nodded his thanks, while the blunt ring finger of his mutilated left hand rose to the centre of his forehead where its corrugated nail probed a patch of psoriasis, dislodging some scales. What about Seventeen? he asked.

Mathieu watched as the engineer sucked hard on his dead cigarette, his cheeks coning into his mouth, then drew a lighter from the pocket of his overalls and flicked it into flame. (Nadine never smoked. Filthy habit, she always said.) Fixed it this afternoon, the engineer said, sure of himself. Mathieu felt that old smoker's pang and reached into his trouser pocket to grip the matchbox he kept there. At the same time, he raised his eyebrows at the engineer's confidence. Well, for now, the engineer conceded, with a dull grin.

Mathieu walked to the clocking-on machine, removed his card from the rack, and clocked on. Nine-oh-two. Could be a regular night. Could be easy. Which could prove difficult. Might have time to do too much thinking. About Nadine. Nadine that was. Ex-Nadine. (Nadine as he had snapped her on the boat they hired one summer in Sète, leaning on the rails, peering down at the water, her mind weakened, but still quite happy with itself.)

There were hands and arms to grab and shake on his way to the aluminium stairs that led up to the glass-fronted office. On the top step, he put down his bag, hauled a key from a trouser pocket and opened the door. From inside the office he could look out over the entire shop floor, straight down the machine aisle. All that Mathieu surveyed was his for the next eight hours. It wasn't much but it was more than he required. The only light that was on was at number fourteen. The engineer had let his cigarette go out again and was standing squinting at the dials on the control panel, his head to one side, the little finger of his left hand probing his right ear.

The workers were finishing up now, humping or trolleying their boxes of product to the pile in the raw-materials annexe, changing into street clothes, combing their hair, loosening or tightening their belts a notch. He espied one of the women adjusting her face in a compact mirror. She probably doesn't realize there is someone up here who can see her. She might not mind if she did. She doesn't need to. She's nice-looking, the way women mostly are when they keep their figures into their fifties. There was something in her lithe movements that made him feel lonely. (Nadine at that age. Never more beautiful. He wasn't going to think of that. He didn't want that image. Not now.)

Mathieu reached beneath the formica-topped desk for a Prisunic plastic bag, from which he extracted his work clothes. He changed slowly, humming 'Brownie Speaks,' but with less commitment now, and then saw Nadine again, as he had left her late that afternoon: supine, expressionless, gone. Gone? Gone where? Just gone. Extinct but still breathing. Ex-Nadine. An engineer coming down the aisle between the machines smiled up at him and Mathieu lifted his left claw in minimal salute. Who was that guy? The engineer winked at him and grinned like a fool. Mathieu stared back, biting into the matchstick in his mouth. What does he want? The woman I have loved for thirty years doesn't give me that much recognition or get much more from me nowadays: I've given up on her, I suppose. Lost faith? Lost love, more like. If my love for her has gone, it's only because she has gone. That's the truth. I have no affection to spare on engineers whose names I can't remember.

He proceeded with his changing, glancing down at his blue-veined legs, almost hairless now. The work trousers scratched as he pulled them up and he tugged tight but not too tight the length of coarse string that served as a belt, recalling the pork-belly stew and steaming choucroute he had eaten early that evening, some of which he'd attempted to spoon-feed Nadine. He felt a stirring in his gut. No, not too tight, that belt. The choucroute had been over-spiced and over-vinegary. Could cause trouble.

He put on his old work sandals and glanced at his watch. It had been a present from Nadine, how many years ago? From some time before. Before what? Before she began to stop being herself. The memory of before had become routine, shrinking to a handful of mostly still images. Curious the way a memory as it fades retraces the history of cinema in reverse: from complex, colour sequencing with wrap-around audio and visceral impact; to the gaudy hues of early Technicolor; to the jerky montage of black-and-white talkies, people's movements all wrong, either silly or strutting; thence to a handful of separate stills, immaculately posed; finally, a scuffed daguerreotype. Though Nadine was still officially extant, Mathieu had already reached the stills stage: Nadine with an umbrella on the Pont-Neuf; Nadine at Canet-Plage that other long, earlier, stormier summer, after he left the army. (She shielded her eyes from the noonday sun and smiled for the camera – a Zeiss, he recalled, that he had taken from a German.) So that was the way it was back then, and this is the way it is now. What endured was the solitary recollection of things they had enjoyed together, he and Nadine. Ex-Nadine.

Mathieu transferred his matchbox and Opinel penknife to the right-hand pocket of his trousers and rolled his shirtsleeves up to his biceps with the stern application of a man who wasn't ever going to tolerate them working loose. What oddly hairless arms I have now. Why am I losing my body hair as I age? He scanned the shop floor and pulled a face. Strange where you feel at ease. Doesn't seem right. His two favourite places: the factory at the start of a night and a jazz venue at the end of a gig. Surrounded by people and quite alone. Locked in, but free.

He reached into his pocket and brought out the matchbox. Then he struck a match, blew it out, placed the unburned end between his pursed lips and stood up carefully, pushing off from his good right knee only. His mouth and teeth worked round the match as he opened the door. Dum ching bash-bash. Into the rhythmic din of the injection presses, down the steps, on with the night shift. Dum ching bash. A place beyond Nadine: here we go, then. Me, fronting up the rhythm section; drummer sounding like he's building a six-foot fence. Into my solo, on cue. Bar one, on the downbeat. Mathieu chewed on his match and sucked all the bitterness from the cellulose pulp.

Forty kilometres away, on a hilltop road, Jacques glanced up at the rear-view mirror as he swung his lurching grey 2CV onto the main road, leaving his village behind him, passing its crossed-out name on a road sign in the grass verge.

He was going to be late again, but Philippe would be there to clock him on. Philippe only ever missed Mondays and today was a Tuesday. Jacques wanted to relax, settle into the ride, enjoy the lulling, rollicking, rolling feel of the journey.

Before it was too late to turn back, he ran a mental check: yes, he had left the back door bolted; yes, he had closed the shutters when it had got dark; no, he had not forgotten to bring his packed meal with him. In fact, he had forgotten nothing. It was all right now to submit to the gentle bouncing, rocking motion of the car.

On the seat next to him sat an old leather satchel containing his wine gourd and a plastic box into which he had packed a sharp knife, a large apple brought down by yesterday's storm, a hunk of bread, the end of a fragrant heel of smoked ham, and some of his own sheep's cheese. As well as a cushion, there was a large bag full of windfall apples on the back seat: Philippe, for a start, would want some. Jacques didn't always have ham. He would be eating well tonight. Next to the plastic box was a crisp white paper bag with the green pharmacy symbol on it. For a second, the grin that Jacques' face habitually wore vanished. Then it returned. Fret about that later, he told himself.

Somebody blinded him, switching their lights to full beam as they came up opposite. Probably the village mayor. Usually was. Nice enough man. Jacques had nothing against incomers, though this one was too keen to please: all things to all villagers. Or was it someone else who had flashed him? Was it perhaps a warning? Might there be a speed trap around the corner? Not that Jacques need worry. You couldn't speed in this crock even if you wanted to. Besides, he was in no hurry to be anywhere. Where he was headed, he had been a thousand times and more already. Five years of it now. He wasn't about to go anywhere new.

Jacques glanced at the fuel gauge, then at his watch, then he let his big body slacken and slump into the tub-like seat, his knees splaying apart. His mind voided, just holding on to the road, the familiar rattles of the car, and the surrounding mountains, already white almost halfway down. Another couple of weeks and he would be driving along gritted roads, between low walls of dirty snow and ice, the collar of his thick jacket turned up. Citroën radiators are crap, his son-in-law had once told him. Know-all prick. Jacques chuckled, then let off a slow, rippling fart, content with the relief it gave him.

Disconcerted by the after-image that the pharmacy symbol had left vagrant in his mind, Jacques glanced again at the paper bag. Still sitting there stiffly, with its hint of starched hospital sheets. Should have thrown the prescription in a drawer and forgotten about it. Bloody quack. He pulled a face. Only went to see her because Jeanne said I should. Hadn't seen the inside of a doctor's surgery in thirty years, and none the worse for it. And now a decision has to be reached, damn it.

What was it the doctor said? I had asked her was she sure it was okay to take the tablets, given I'm not in the pill-popping habit. And she looked me up and down and said that at my age I shouldn't be troubled by any side effects. She talked about disease and illness. While I waited for her to finish, I stared at that mangy stinking dog of hers stretched out on that scrap of colourless carpet with its back against the wall radiator and its hairy old chest in full view. Besides, she was saying, I'm not sure you've got much choice. You've got high blood pressure. Which has been neglected for years. Look, Monsieur, if you want to see your grandson grow up . . . You just follow my advice and take the tablets like it says on the box and come back for a check-up in a couple of months. Okay? With that be-a-good-boy-and-do-what-Mummy-says tone of voice. She wasn't asking me if it was 'okay': she was telling me. So I handed over the money and left.

Clear view tonight over the town. Can see right across it, side to side, but not down into it: can't pierce that yellow smog-cap just hanging there. Round another bend and the city's gone. And then it's back again. Now you see it, now you don't. I'm a bit old for that. Anyway, you really feel the curves in a deux-chevaux, which is exactly what I like about it. Plus it's cheap to run and easy to fix, a tent strapped to a lawnmower, who was it said that? Nothing like the pointy, flashy things they're making nowadays, all gadgetry and aerodynamics and expensive glitches.

The doctor asked a good question, though. Even if she didn't mean to. Do I want to see my grandson grow up? As it happens, not much. Not the way he's turning out. He's getting more and more like his father, the dull prick. Edith wouldn't have liked to hear me say that about little Simon. He was such a sweet child. Reminded everyone of Edith. It was as if Edith's fine features and sweet character had skipped a generation, missed Brigitte completely, and surfaced in Simon. There was nothing of me to see in him, which was fine. Edith always said we should never have let Brigitte leave home so young, but how could we stop her? It was the sixties already, right? She fell in with the wrong sort: trainee bankers and budding office execs. Big-city types with small minds. Miserable swine, grasping hypocrites kidding nobody. Jacques laughed heartily as he reminisced, shaking his head in unquenchable astonishment at the pinched misery of the rich. Why the hell couldn't Brigitte have taken up with some ordinary pot-smoking, down-and-out anarchist-artist type – like everybody else's daughter did those days? That way the grandchild would have turned out okay just as sure as the son-in-law would one day have thrown away his sandals, cut off his hair and got a regular job teaching.

When Jacques had got home from the pharmacy, he had taken his glasses from the dresser, wiped them scrupulously, drawn up a chair and sat down at the oak table in his kitchen. He had taken the packet out of its paper bag, opened it carefully at one end and extracted the notes. There was no need to rush. Stress was bad for blood pressure, right? He read the notice. Dose. Counter-indications. Directions for Use. All very doctorly. Huh, here it comes: side effects. And there it was. Right at the end of a long list: erectile dysfunction, sexual problems in men, risk of impotence. Merde, merde et merde! Impotence!

Goddamn cow of a doctor. What had she said? That I wasn't likely to be troubled by any side effects at my age? She probably had that poor miserable dog of hers neutered; chemically no doubt, since she wouldn't have either the qualification or the steadiness of eye to wield a scalpel. Poor mutt, lying there with its back against the radiator, a dead dick between its legs, glazed eyes half-open, longing for the lethal injection. That must be what made it look that way. Indigestion, halitosis, impotence and depression. It stank out her surgery. Poor wee thing. If I had had the opportunity, I could have been a vet, Jacques said to himself. I have a genuine feel for animals.

Hah! There they are, lying in wait behind that hillock, the speed cops, hiding their radar behind a thicket of bushes. Keeping us guessing. Never seen them there before. They must be under pressure to deliver some fines, earn some commission. Christmas is coming.

Jacques flashed his lights to full beam a couple of times to warn oncoming drivers to ease off the accelerator.

He glanced again at the package. Looks innocent enough, lying there on the seat. What if I take half the dosage the doctor recommended? Would that do the trick and avoid the side effects? Or would it give me a half-life plus a dick stuck at half-mast? All she knows is that Edith died a while ago. Seventeen months, almost to the day. Can't know about me and Jeanne, then. Thought everyone in the village knew. To hell with them, to hell with them all. Or maybe she does know and doesn't give a damn either way. Or disapproves even. Thinks old people shouldn't be getting any. I bet she never gets laid, the sourpuss. The mean, fuckless type. Jacques smiled benevolently.

Jeanne was good to him, they had always been friendly. But he had never expected her to want him in her bed. He liked to remember how it had happened. It made him feel warm, made his eyes feel sparkly and his lips separate slightly and tingle. He raised his forefinger to rub them gently.

They had been playing cards in her kitchen for an hour or two after supper, the way they always did on Saturdays and Sundays after Edith died, because on those evenings Jacques didn't have to go to work. At about eleven thirty, much later than usual – perhaps she had been thinking about it, perhaps that is why he kept winning – she said as she dealt the cards, I think we'll make this the last game tonight, Jacques, but you can stop here with me. Just like that. Matter-of-fact. Then, in case I hadn't got the message: 'in my bed.' She gave me this bashful grin and breathed out as if to say, I'm glad that's done with and there's not going to be any argument. I was choked. She won the next game, no mistake. I hadn't been expecting anything. It's not as if I was lonely. I missed Edith, but I could have slept on my own happily enough for the rest of my days. That would have been a shame, now I think of it.

She gathered up the cards and put them in a stack on her dresser. Then she marched to the door and shot the bolt. As if I might make a run for it. I was on my feet, shifting my weight from foot to foot, feeling stupid, not knowing how to put it. Well? she said, looking at me. So I told her how I needed the antiseptic for my dentures. And a glass. I've thought about that, she said with a bigger grin than before. I went to the pharmacist's this morning and asked what brand you use. You should have seen their faces. They made me repeat the question. For the benefit of the other customers, no doubt. It wasn't as if I had whispered it in the first place. Pathetic. Like buying something for someone's dentures was an intimate act, a scandal. The pharmacist's wife asked if you were well and I said, Never better, and then the new girl behind the counter broke into giggles, bless her.

All we did do that night was sleep and the next few times too. Didn't even cuddle. Just a goodnight peck, much like the ones we would have exchanged at the door if I had been going home. Till one night it just didn't seem right to leave it at that.

And maybe it wouldn't matter if that's what we returned to . . . if the old boy collapsed along with my blood pressure. Maybe I should ask Jeanne. Would she mind much? But what could she possibly say in reply? And what exactly would I ask? How could I put it? How would you like it if I couldn't get it up any more? It isn't something we've ever talked about. Haven't needed to. She likes making love all right, though of course she never says so. But a man can tell. Sometimes, Sunday mornings mainly, when we have made love the night before, she will get up early and potter about the bedroom singing softly, or hum a little as she opens the shutters. Maybe she just likes opening shutters. No, you can tell. Jacques grinned in the dark of his draughty 2CV. Humming: that's the giveaway.

Better concentrate on the road here. Saw one hell of an accident, when was it? While ago. It's four lanes now. In each direction. That many cars. Mustn't miss the turning. Been doing nights for how many years? Four? Five? And I still missed the turning, when was it? A few weeks ago? A few months? Ended up on a street full of burnt-out cars. This job blurs time. Sometimes time races away from you, leaving a kind of smudge; other times it just stands still. No way to remember exactly where it was either. No landmarks down here. Everywhere looks the same. Flat outskirts where the countryside sort of gives up, then a mess of high-rises, a lot of badly made roads stiffly intersecting at right angles, patches of billowing smog, billboards with gaudy adverts coming unstuck at the edges. How do people live down here in all this filth, and breathe this soupy gunk they still call air?

He thought of some of his workmates. Didn't Dos Santos have a room in a worker's hostel near here? Funny that story he told the other night, or other week, about the girls that work the hostel. Wonder if he made it up. Wouldn't put it past him. Promised I'd bring him a rabbit one evening. He'll take some of these apples, and enjoy them too. Real country boy. And then there's that guy from the Ivory Coast. He lives round here too, somewhere. In fact, maybe he lives in the same hostel. How come I never thought of that? Might explain why he and Dos Santos often come to work together. I must ask Jeanne's neighbour if he can spare me a couple of rabbits: I'm sure Jeanne would like one too. I'll do that tomorrow. Without fail. If I remember. Funny idea that, sparing a rabbit. As if you could ever have too few rabbits on a farm. Well, maybe you could, maybe you could – if it was a rabbit farm.

2. Philippe, Rémy, Danielle, Lucie, Salvatore.

Beer bubbles popping slowly, white slicks of foam slipping down the inside of a glass, recalling sea spume drying on a beach. He closed his eyes. Salt bubbles popping slowly on the hot sand, tickling the feet, recalling cold beer tingling on the tongue. Where was he? Bar or beach? He opened his eyes.

Shifting forward on his barstool, Philippe lifted the glass from the counter and prepared to take a short sip. He kept his eyes open, focusing on the frothy liquid disc as it tilted both away and toward him, stretching into an ellipse. He sighted a speck of something – an intruding imperfection – lurking there among the bubbles, adrift in the foam, at the mercy of the beer, trapped, hooked, catching on the ebb of a memory.

Any prompt (however oblique), any echo (however muted), any stray ray of sunshine on those cloud-bound November days, any surprise glimpse of whooshing, foamy liquid was enough to catapult him back to his dream come true, his fortnight alone last summer, his first ever beach holiday, his last ever escape from the clutches of a demanding wife and screaming child.

He had gone away to contemplate his life, it would take nothing less than a holiday alone: wife and child could look after themselves for a time. He was following the recommendations of friends, Jacques for one. Who would ever have imagined that Philippe, a thoroughbred Marseillais city boy, would ever be friends with a peasant farmer twice his age. The thought made him smile.

You're depressed, Jacques had told him. In Jacques' mouth, the word 'depressed' had sounded strange. As if between quotation marks. Maybe because they were eating at the time. Maybe because 'depressed' still struck Philippe as a newfangled notion, whereas Jacques was about as old-fangled as anyone you could hope to meet. Philippe had recognized the fitness of the word, however, as soon as he had heard it, and had nodded. Depressed: like a brake pedal held down. It was the right term. Besides, depression was a reason to do whatever he wanted, and especially to let the wife and kid go hang for once. So off he went. But instead of contemplating his life, as he had resolved to do, all he had contemplated for the entire two weeks were women on the sand stretched out on their backs and his tummy bobbing in front of his eyes in the water.

He had perfected the art of floating, lolling in the lazy swell of insignificant waves, his chubby arms gently paddling to maintain the perfection of his position and the delicate equilibrium of his flesh, but also to keep his mouth and nose above water as he perused his tummy, fondly surveying its surprising whiteness and roundness, the still black hairs curling wet against his motley pink skin. It was the first time he had considered his tummy since he was a child. It had changed.

Hour upon hour he had salted away this floating sensation, pickled in his memory this liquid languor, stored each bubbly day for later, for the days when routine, the factory, and the demanding child and screaming wife would reclaim him. He had kept those moments for now.

Philippe replaced his glass of beer on the counter, sensing that he was being observed.

Composing himself and sharpening his focus, he pulled himself up straighter on his barstool. His wife always told him not to slump, but then his wife wasn't there, was she? He checked the contents of his pockets laid out before him on the bare aluminium counter, as if preliminary to police interrogation: two packs of Gauloises Light, one started, the other immaculate beneath its cellophane sheath; a long thin disposable lighter; a keyring holding four keys of assorted shapes and sizes; the paperback he was reading at work; a black leather wallet bulging open, its central purse belly-up, like a bloated, bursting rabbit, yesterday's roadkill. Overshadowing all these objects, his towering beer glass. At the foot of the barstool, a blue plastic bag lay slumped against the wooden base of the bar, containing one third of a baguette, a tin of mackerel marinated in white wine and pickles, and an apple. Philippe still felt as if he was being watched but didn't look up. Where did that feeling come from? He was sure there could be no one there.

Except, that is, for Lucie, a dishevelled middle-aged woman, who sat in the gloom at the back of the bar reading the crime pages in the local paper and occasionally muttering to herself angrily, both elbows on the table, her head resting in one hand and a cigarette gripped in the other; and of course Rémy the barman who, across the counter from Philippe and at an angle, was drying the last few glasses with a cotton cloth.

Rémy did a brisk job, hanging each dry glass upside down above the counter, its stalk inserted into a wooden slot. Rémy was devoting his surplus attention to an episode of an American cops series. The sound was down low but Philippe, without straining his ears, could still make out the dialogue: *There's nothing for it. It's our only lead . . . Okay. I'll call the precinct for backup. But you'd better be right about this, Hank.* Then, as the cops drew their weapons and disappeared into a grimy doorway, there was a lot of brash music, all heavy organ work and saxophones. That's when Americans have adverts, Philippe thought, wondering how he knew that, who had told him. It's so they can get up and drink that watery swill they call coffee. And it's to make sure they buy the right detergents. Land of the free.

The phone at the back of the bar started ringing and Philippe glanced toward the barman who walked over to answer it, flicking his drying-up cloth onto his left shoulder as he went. Philippe picked up his beer and returned to his dreams of escape, solitude, freedom from care.

He had just tapped a new cigarette out of its pack and placed it against his lips when Rémy bawled out, Hey, it's for you, Phiphi! Your sister. Danielle.

I know who my sister is. Tell her I'm dead and you buried me yesterday. She said it was important. Said it couldn't wait.

Important? Shit. What the hell is ever important? And this evening was going so well.

Philippe stood in the penumbra at the rear of the bar, one hand holding the receiver loosely to his ear, the other scratching around in his groin. He stared at Lucie, the old girl hunched over her newspaper. She had started rocking back and forth, like she'd found something good. Every evening she was there, making a single cup of coffee last an hour and more. Philippe wondered whether she was some relation of the barman's, an aunt or mother or some such. Rémy did not treat anyone else with such forbearance. She looked like she had been on the game in better times, or had maybe spent a time locked away somewhere secure, for her own safety. What the hell was Danielle droning on about now?

Anyway, that's not what I'm phoning about, Philippe's sister was saying. It's that wife of yours.

Philippe's eyes narrowed, he drew a breath and moved his scratching higher up, to his gut. His sister's voice was hurting his head, filling his mind with junk that rattled like scrap metal in the back of a pick-up. He held the phone away from his ear for a bit. Yada yada, he murmured.

The fact was that his sister had always hated Odile, and was forever coming to him with mean and mischievous stories. It went right back to the playground, Philippe thought. Odile had always been a nice mover and a good-looker and Danielle had never been either. Odile and Danielle had had pre-teen crushes on the same girls and then the flutters for the same boys – except him of course. Unless maybe . . . No, all that psycho stuff was bullshit. It was everyday female jealousy: poison, plain and simple.

Philippe sighed and put the phone back to his ear.

Look, I just thought you ought to know. I'm sorry, Danielle was saying.

An apology, wow! He might actually have missed something this time. He took a deep breath, and surveyed his pack of cigarettes. One, two, three: five left. Which makes twenty-five. Should see me through the night.

Listen, Danielle, I don't know exactly what sort of trashy gossip you've come up with this time but I'm really not interested. Whatever it is, try keeping it to yourself, okay?

I don't believe you. You're a liar! Or didn't you hear a word I said? Weren't you goddamn listening?

I got distracted, Philippe admitted, observing Rémy, who had started putting chairs on tables. The bar is really busy this evening. Never seen it so packed. So I missed your drift.

Well, that *is* interesting, Danielle snapped. Tell me, are you listening now? Have I got your attention?

Uh-huh, but make it short. Whatever it is, make it short.

Fine. Your wife . . . Remember her? Odile?

Uh-huh. Odile. Philippe closed his eyes. What the hell was it about Danielle and sarcasm and subtlety? Philippe wondered. Or was it sisters generally?

What I said, Danielle said, though I didn't put it quite like this, but I could have done, and since you wanted me to make it short . . .

I did and you still aren't, Philippe said, slurring his words with exaggerated weariness. He heard Danielle draw breath.

Okay. It's like I told you already: your wife is screwing another man. Short enough? And you stopped listening because the bar is busy? She's fucking some poncey flake and you got distracted? I can't believe I heard you right. What are you, man or mouse? Or some rare sort of rock lichen? Odile is screwing some other man and you missed my drift? You're pathetic. Pathetic. What a brother! Mind you, I'm not astonished any longer, not in the least surprised in fact. How can you laugh? Tell me that!

Usually when his sister was talking, Philippe could hold the receiver away from his ear for a minute or more and miss nothing. There were a couple of good reasons for this. First, because Danielle said everything at least twice, sometimes using the very same words but varying their order a little or inverting their syntax, and sometimes using synonyms: she possessed an extensive vocabulary, albeit over a limited range of topics. Second, because she talked on a fifty- or sixty-second loop. Even now, if Philippe wanted the whole story, all he had to do was clamp the receiver to his ear and let her run on for a minute or so. But did he in fact want to hear it? That was the question. Okay. Sure. He would hear her out for once. After all, maybe Odile really was fucking someone else. And maybe that was worth knowing about.

Look, Danielle was saying, you won't get angry with me, will you? I'm only the messenger. I'm just telling you the way it is. I thought you'd want to know. Most men would want to know their wife's fucking another man. Where's the joke in that? How can you laugh? Did I say something funny? I swear I heard you chuckle. Christ! You know, maybe if she's screwing somebody else, maybe it's not surprising. Just the way things were always bound to be. I mean: anyone could see the two of you were pulling in different directions. Like: there was you, and then there was her. Her with her vulgar fake crocodile-skin stilettos. I mean *fake* probably; *vulgar* definitely. And you in those hideous down-at-heel canvas pumps, what do you call them? Sailing shoes? Christ Jesus, you have to reckon something's badly askew when a man stops caring what he puts on his feet.

At this point, Danielle left a long pause. Maybe she wanted to check that her brother was listening or maybe she wanted the astuteness of her last observation to sink in, do its work.

So it's on account of my shoes? Philippe asked slowly, staring into his beer and spacing the words out. Let me get this right: on account of my inelegant footwear, Odile was always destined to fuck somebody else? Is that it? Am I reading you right?

Oh, come on! You can laugh but your long words don't impress me. I'm your sister, don't forget. Shoes speak volumes about their owners, it's a fact, it's in all the magazines. Like pets, right? I don't get you: how can you sound so uninterested, when I've just told you your wife's screwing someone else? I mean, like . . .

Philippe could hear his sister's mind scrambling and scrabbling, its grey cells fizzing and bursting for a way to express the situation better, more succinctly, more finally. But how many ways were there to break it to your brother his wife's a cheating bitch? Philippe pulled on his cigarette and smiled. He was about to find out.

I mean, Danielle continued, choosing her words carefully now and enunciating deliberately, as if crossing an icy river on stepping stones: if Odile is screwing someone else, right?, then in that case – are you with me? – she is screwing someone who clearly – by definition, right? – is not you. There was no escaping it.

Danielle was quiet for a moment, long enough for Philippe to give her iron logic some serious thought. He frowned, lit a new cigarette from the butt of the previous one, then started into a long low guffaw. It sounded like a not quite empty oil drum rolling down a hill: there was a bit of a sloshing sound mixed in with the rumbling. Philippe could have held the receiver away from his face, like he normally did when laughing at his sister, but for once it didn't occur to him to do so. Let her hear him laugh. Danielle, however, had recovered her voice.

What a brother! How can you laugh at that? Okay, okay, laugh even louder. Be my guest. Just see where it gets you. This is serious shit! Did nobody ever tell you it's possible to be too laid-back? Odile is betraying you, cheating on you, going behind your back, and you, you with your dead-end job and your beer belly and your canvas pumps, 'scuse me! – sailing shoes. Since when did you sail anywhere? – Look at yourself in the mirror, Philippe, and then take a look at Odile. I mean: is it any wonder?

This was getting personal. This he could do without. Philippe inhaled deeply and closed his eyes, relishing the heavy dark smoke now shunting its way round his lungs, coating and re-coating his tubes with comforting tar. Then he wagged a finger at Rémy to alert him that he was ready for his coffee and said: 'salut soeurette!' and put the phone down before Danielle could say much more. The last thing he caught was, 'But if I haven't told you who it is . . .'

Philippe thought about that but just shrugged. If Odile wasn't fucking anyone then it didn't matter who she wasn't fucking. And if she was fucking someone, well, names and numbers made no difference. All in all, his mind was at peace. Besides, nobody had in fact ever told him it was possible to be too laid-back and, if they had, he certainly wouldn't have listened.

Philippe made for the toilet, where he enjoyed a slow leisurely piss. As he washed his hands, he surveyed his face in the mirror. Pudgy was the adjective that came to mind. And there was something wrong with his hair. Yeah, it needed a trim. He could ask Fernando. Fernando had done a good job on Marcel, and Marcel had a smart young girlfriend and cared what he looked like. Philippe didn't like mirrors, didn't have a lot of use for them, mostly didn't like what they showed him. He remembered what Odile had once told him, a long time ago when they'd been in love: that he had the kind of face a woman could talk to. At the time, he'd taken that as a huge compliment, but now he was no longer so sure. He looked again. Pudgy. And weary. That was all he could see.

He dried his hands and left the toilet. Lucie was still sitting there, looking like she wasn't planning on leaving yet, and Rémy was strolling toward her table with a tray in one hand and a wet rag in the other.

Philippe walked over to his barstool. A steaming coffee was standing on the counter alongside his almost empty beer. He picked up the glass and drained it in one gulp, muttering: to the messenger! He then turned to the coffee. Rémy – or Rémy's machine – made excellent coffee: dense, bitter and aromatic. This was one of the best moments in Philippe's day. He took a sugar lump from the saucer, unwrapped it carefully, folded the paper and placed it in the ashtray, then dipped a corner of the sugar lump into the coffee, watching the brown stain rise slowly through the cube. Water finds its own level, right? So how come coffee does that climbing trick? Slowly and methodically, with one eye still on the sugar cube, he filled his coat and trouser pockets with wallet, paperback, keys, cigarettes and lighter until the counter was almost clear. Osmosis, wasn't that it?

Philippe played in his head a snippet of an alternative conversation that he might have had with Danielle if only he possessed the requisite presence of mind and assuming his sister had responded as he imagined she might have done. It ran like this:

DANIELLE (syllabizing testily, for a moron): I'm tell-ing you: Oh-dile is screw-ing some oth-er man!

PHILIPPE (nonchalantly): Well, so what? Maybe I have a girlfriend, so maybe we're even. I honestly don't feel a thing, I'm not about to cry my eyes out, so what does it matter?

DANIELLE (panting like a setter): What does it matter? (Pant!) What does it matter? (Pant!) You said you don't feel a thing? I am not hearing this! (Pant!) It's one thing for you to have a girlfriend, it's quite another for . . . (Pant!) Christ, you're the man here, right? (Pant!) It's almost as if you didn't think it was a problem. (Pant-Pant!)

PHILIPPE (patiently): Well, it isn't. It won't be a problem till the day Odile tells me about it. Then it'll be a problem.

DANIELLE (screaming): She'll never tell you, you idiot. She has too much to lose. Who pays the bills? Who keeps her in stilettos? She'll never tell you.

PHILIPPE (trippingly): Then, like I said, it'll never be a problem.

DANIELLE (proudly): I know that if I ever screwed another man, Georges would flay me alive.

PHILIPPE (forensically): Yeah? Well, how would Georges ever notice? With what part of his brain would he work it out? In fact, I really don't see what's stopping you. It would be light relief. I sure as hell wouldn't tell him.

No. On mature reflection, it was a good thing the conversation had not gone that way.

Philippe sipped at his coffee and smiled, happy to have avoided any such unnecessary unpleasantness. There was absolutely no need to be nasty about Georges. One could confidently leave that to others. What was wrong with Danielle anyway? Why did she hate Odile so much? In the end, Philippe reasoned, it all came down to envy or jealousy of some sort. Danielle probably fancies the man she imagines Odile is screwing. As simple as that. And right now the fact that she never managed to tell me who she thinks it is must really be eating her up. Which means she'll phone again tomorrow, I'd lay good money on it. Maybe I'll ask Rémy to tell her I'm dead for real. Philippe chuckled briefly. If he did, she'd probably convince herself that Odile's unfaithfulness had tipped me over the edge. Sisters, eh?

With that, Philippe knocked back his coffee, smacked his lips, shook his head and grinned. Then he dumped some cash on the counter, waved and muttered 'demain!' to Rémy, eased himself down off his stool, patted his gut affectionately, picked up the blue plastic bag from the floor, and shuffled toward the door.

Hey! Rémy bawled at him. That's not like you, Phiphi. You've forgotten the papers. Are you getting absent-minded now? What're you going to do all night without the papers to read? You might actually have to do some work for a change.

Philippe laughed at that, nodding to acknowledge the justice of the jibe, and went to the till, alongside which the day's papers sat stacked.

Anything interesting? he asked Rémy, to make some conversation, as he rolled and stuffed the papers into the blue plastic bag.

Yeah. Guy found drowned in the river last night. Washed up downstream from here.

You're kidding. Anyone we know?

Doubt it. Unidentified. Wearing weird clothes which apparently included women's stockings. Probably a trannie or something. Check it out, it's a good story. You can bet there'll be more details tomorrow.

Philippe and Rémy shook hands and muttered goodnights.

As Philippe opened the glass door to the street, Salvatore was striding past, his long legs carving up the pavement, his shiny black attaché case swinging high and low, high and low, making him look like a city slicker late for a meeting. Up it went: Whee! Down it came: Whee! The long-limbed Sicilian held out his hand for Philippe to shake. Philippe pumped it dutifully and smiled his sidelong smile.

Bit of a rush, Salvatore muttered, striding on ahead, Got to meet someone before work.

There it was. A meeting.

Don't mind me, Philippe said, lighting a cigarette.

Caught by an afterthought, the Sicilian wheeled about, for a sharp second fixing Philippe in the glare of his black eyes. We must talk later.

Must we? Philippe murmured, but Salvatore had returned to his forward march, deaf to Philippe's response, and that was that.

A frown puckered Philippe's forehead. He watched the swinging attaché case as it slowly shrank into the distance ahead. He could knock someone out with that thing. Up, up, up! Whee-ush! Down, down, down! Whee-ush! The fact that Salvatore had to talk to him was bizarre but not worth dwelling on. Whee-ush! Up. There it goes again. Whee-ush! Down. Why does he let it swing free in the street but hug it against his body once he reaches the factory? A mystery. But as for this Odile business, well! What Danielle had to say, hmm! Maybe I'll think it all through when I get to work, Philippe told himself. Work is where I do my best thinking. Whee-ush! When he hugs the case close to him, it's like it's an old satchel or hold-all, the kind of thing a lot of men bring to work, the kind of thing Jacques stuffs his apples and one-a.m.

snack and wine gourd into. Can't imagine Jacques with an attaché case. I wonder when precisely that Sicilian stops swinging his case high and low and brings it into his body to hug like a hold-all. There must be a moment when he makes the switch. On approaching the main gate? Just before he steps into the factory building through the outside door? Or when he gets to the plastics section? I'd really like to know that. It can't not mean something.

A wispy cloud of irritation sailed past Philippe's mind and dispersed, casting no shadow, leaving no chill. Then he thought of that summer, the lulling waves, the shoreline, the sun, the salt water, the slicks of spume drying on the sand. And he was gone. Into the bubbly, beery, frothy brine. Bobbing like a pot-bellied dinghy on the gentlest of swells. In the foam of that other life that was always there, just within reach, waiting for him, teasing him, beckoning.

3. Fernando, Alphonse, Eric.

Turning languidly and yawning, opening one lazy eye, basking still in a dream that juggled home and happiness and Maryse, Fernando glanced at the digital alarm clock. 21.06. Twenty-one-oh-six. Puta de vida! Mas, não é verdade! He jerked his head up and round and looked again, eyes popping, Adam's apple jumping. 21.07. Mas, foda-se!

In a single sweep of jagged, jarring movements, Fernando swung his legs out of bed, shook a cigarette halfway out of a pack he angrily snatched from the bedside table, pulled on trousers and a shirt, flicked cigarette into mouth, seized a lighter from a ledge, rammed his feet into elasticated slip-ons, snapped his thumb down hard, stood up, lit up, and drew the smoke in deep. He stared at the silent TV screen on the floor in the corner. There was fucking-no way he was going to be late for work yet again. A blond cowboy dismounted, swivelled on his heels as he pulled out a gun and fired. Gypsies can be late, peasants fucking-can be late, Portuguees ain't never late: that's the rule here. Which he kept breaking, though seldom by more than a minute or two. Then another cowboy with darker skin, and eyes at least as black as Fernando's, fell to the ground, slumping. The camera moved in.

Merrde, merrde et merrde! swore Fernando with French fluency and trilling Portuguese r's. Another day. Another night in his life. He took a comb from a trouser pocket and dragged it across his head, then, with an amply licked index finger, he unstuck dust from his gluey eyelashes. What was that dream I was dreaming? And how come I nodded off anyway? That hour with Maryse really fucking-took it out of me. Wasn't just my wallet she emptied. You've got to get rid of it somehow, somewhere. Or it festers like pus, screws with your mind, causes disease. And jerking off's for kids, everyone knows that. God, the time! 21.08. Merda.

Fernando plucked his jacket from the hook on the door and checked the contents of his pockets. He switched off the TV, and left the room. No time for a shit, do that at the plant. Hope it doesn't bind me. Putting it off will do that. Better eat some dates. Pick them up from Abdul, at the Moroccan shop. Fernando pushed and pulled his belly out and back in again a few times as he reached the stairwell. Definitely a tightness there. No time to stop by the kitchenette and fix a sandwich for later. It was going to be a hungry night unless Jacques took pity. No one fucking-else would, filhos da puta. Jacques was different, a peasant stranded in the big city, just like him really. Allowing for the differences. Like Jacques at least had land of his own, something to go back to each morning. And Jacques at least had a woman to take to bed with him, to sleep not just to fuck. And Jacques at least wasn't living a thousand and a half kilometres from home. But apart from that . . . Fernando licked his lips for tar and tossed his cigarette butt at the fire bucket by the door, saw it hit the sand still smouldering. Jacques had promised to bring him a rabbit one night soon. How fucking-long was it since he'd tasted rabbit? He tried to think. The air hit cold against his face. Fucking-too long, that was how long.

The doors of the immigrants' hostel swished shut behind him. Sinking into his shuffle and tilting his head against the cold night, the bristly, taut, still young skin beneath his chin folded like a rucking carpet and scratched itself. He glanced left, saw there was no bus coming then turned right, walking fast along the pavement, almost skipping. He took a deep breath then coughed. He felt good. He was seized by a flash of Maryse's face from that afternoon, as she bit her lip and her eyebrows arched and she smiled at him properly for the first time. He had said something kind to her, he had meant it, and she had heard it. Fernando's chest puffed out. For a split second, he was happy to be alive. But it was too fleeting to register.

From an inside pocket in his jacket he extracted a packet of spearmint gum, unsheathed one of the lengths from its wrapper and laid it flat and hard and emery-like against his tongue. As he lifted his head to look down the road, his cheek stubble chafed on the leather collar. In the distance, he could see Alphonse, the guy from Ivory Coast, standing at the bus stop. Saw him at once. Funny how blacks stand out in the dark. You wouldn't think they would but they do. What the hell is the man doing? Running on the spot? I must need glasses. Yeah, he's bouncing up and down. Like he's on a pogo stick. What's that about then? Maybe he thinks he's going to keep fit. All he's going to do is get his nice clothes dirtied up, that's all that's fucking-going to happen.

Without slowing his pace, Fernando turned and looked down the road behind him. No bus in sight, not many cars either, everyone's still eating or flopped out in front of the TV, the lucky cunts. He walked more slowly now, relieved. He took out another cigarette and ran its cool papery length under his nose, tickling. He looked forward to a chat with Alphonse, funny him having such an old-fashioned French name, but he was all right, always friendly, ready for a laugh, even if he did talk a bit funny, with all those long words he knew, and that stuffy-yet-zany schoolteacher air about him.

Whatever that dream was, there had been money in it somewhere. There must have been, because he remembered feeling happy, so happy. Content. And he had woken up relaxed and with such a hard-on, if only there had been a woman there to slip it to, give her the benefit: hell, good things should be shared, no? He smiled now, luxuriating in the memory, exaggerating it a little, adding an inch, adding a mile. It was one of those lingering hard-ons that threatened – or, better, promised – never to break. Like steel, no, like tungsten, titanium, whatever. Reinforced steel, not concrete. He'd not had one like that for . . . for how long? For too long. Had Maryse been in the dream? Probably. Usually was. She was something. A real cure. A fucking cure. He'd fallen in love with her. How dumb was that? To fall in love with his 'treatment' as she called herself: with a 'prostitute' as any other cunt would call her.

His visit to the shrink reeled past him, the mortal embarrassment of it. Doctor Boulabem, a special shrink for immigrant workers, paid by the council or the union, maybe he even worked for free. Fernando didn't have to fork out a single franc. Couldn't help wondering, though, just why a doctor would want to work as a shrink for poor fuckers like him. Weren't shrinks supposed to be for rich people? Couldn't help suspecting that doctors who worked as shrinks for poor fuckers must be getting some kind of weird, sick rush out of other men's problems. Why else would they do it? Or were they too green and incompetent to get proper jobs? Not that this doctor was a kid exactly, doing this because nobody would pay him to do anything different. He had a wall full of framed diplomas and he looked like he was pushing forty, his hair greying in a hurry all round the edges.

At first Fernando hadn't wanted to talk to Dr Boulabem, maybe because of his flowery shirt and neck-beads. He looked like a fucking hippy. Couldn't be a nancy, could he? Anyway the doctor who did the surgeries near the hostel, the generalist, a friendly old French white guy who last year had treated his haemorrhoids, had recommended this Boulabem to him. So there he was then, sitting opposite this shrink, some kind of North African, staring at his fucking-flowery shirt. Right there, Fernando decided to talk about his problem, come straight out with it. Because, hell, how could you feel intimidated by a guy with beads strung round his neck?

A car hit a puddle close to him and splashed his trouser leg. Fernando swore volubly, then looked back round and slowed to a stroll. Still no bus in sight. He wouldn't have time to check how his bets had done. Philippe might know. Possibly. Just possibly. You couldn't trust the occasional gambler. Though Philippe seemed okay, basically. Doesn't give much away. Better in any case than those Gypsy convict whackoes that hang round him like flies on a baby's face.

Boulabem's waiting room had been a bit like you'd picture a brothel. A long dirty corridor with a lot of desperate-looking men – blacks, North Africans, Italians, even some Yugoslavs – to judge by their lean blond looks and the choked, spluttering sound of their language – all slouching on rickety chairs or leaning against greasy yellow walls waiting their turn, smoking and avoiding looking at one another for the miserable shame of the thing, each man pretending that all the others weren't there. But in a way it was comforting that he wasn't the only one. All those empty trousers, though. Made you think. This had to be some kind of contagion, some kind of epidemic. It made him feel something . . . How did it make him feel? He couldn't find the word. Maybe there wasn't one. His turn came round and he had taken a breath and walked in and sat down in a chair that had swallowed him up, making him feel like a midget. Dr Boulabem was a small wiry black man, with sharp Algerian features: what would he know about such problems? Everyone knew Africans were hung like horses and went at it like trains: would North Africans be any different? Fernando doubted it. Well, good for them then. The doctor's eyes were bloodshot but he was smiling. Hell, maybe he had troubles of his own, who knows? Certainly seemed friendly. The kind of guy you could definitely talk to, flowery shirt or not.

Fernando had relaxed and explained what he had come for. How he couldn't get a hard-on . . . yeah, whatever, 'érection,' sure, that was it. Hated that word. Ereção. Fernando had worked on enough building sites to know that erections were serious and fucking-dangerous things. He had bad memories from that time, not just bad dreams: erections that cost men their lives, erections that collapsed before they were properly up. Why can't people call hard-ons fucking hard-ons for Christ's sake? Still, he was in this guy's surgery, wasn't he? The doctor was entitled to call the words, wasn't that right?

Well, yes, Fernando readily granted, he did get them when he was on his own: in fact he woke up with one every afternoon. Yeah, he worked nights. So? What difference did that make? Okay, yeah, he did choke the chicken, very, very occasionally, yeah, 'master-bait,' whatever you say. He didn't enjoy doing it, he stated proudly, but sometimes you just had to, never mind what they'd told him at school that it said in the fucking-Bible, pardon me for swearing, you just had to do it, didn't you? Couldn't be jumping women at bus stops. Get arrested, thrown in gaol, and buggered blind by a fucking-whole gang of sex-starved jailbirds. And with my haemorrhoids . . . It didn't bear thinking about.

Fernando fell silent and looked at the doctor, and the doctor smiled and said, Everybody masturbates, you know.

Fernando fixed him with a sly grin, and asked, Everybody? But Boulabem just went right on smiling and said, Sure, doctors too. And when they do it, they know they're not breaking any laws, hurting anybody or ruining their eyesight.

For a moment, Fernando suspected he was being made fun of, but on taking a good look at the man, he decided he wasn't, so he laughed at the joke and then Dr Boulabem asked more questions, and Fernando said that, yes, there was another time he sometimes got an ereção, though he didn't really like to mention it, since it might seem twisted. The doctor shrugged and smiled again and, sounding exactly like the priests back home, told him, Look, Monsieur, you can say whatever you feel like here, there's no need to hide anything. Professional secrecy, you know. It won't go any further. Fucking priests!

Fernando had mentioned how at the factory, late at night or, rather, early in the morning to be precise, sometimes when leaning against the machine and polishing it hard, leaning into it so that his pants area – yeah, that's right, his *gentle* area – was hard up against the warm clinking and clanking and juddering machine so he'd get an érection, yeah, fucking-hard as steel, like a girder leaning against the metal flank of the machine. Tempered tungsten. The kind of thing you could break a plate with. The doctor smiled. Sometimes he worried he'd leave a dent in the machine. Not that he was boasting.

This doctor sure as hell could smile, Fernando was thinking. If there were prizes for smiling, he'd be fucking-unbeatable.

Well, Dr Boulabem had said, thinking things over in his own time, that's really nothing to worry about. Some people get them on motorbikes, others on the bus. It's the vibrations. The point is: when you came in just now you said you didn't get erections but we've already established that you get plenty. In fact, I'd say – to judge by what you've told me – you get more than your fair share.

Fernando wasn't used to praise in any department, and didn't know what to do with it. He smiled at first, then suddenly frowned, sensing a swindle in the making.

Yeah, well it's not when I wake up in bed alone or at fucking-four in the morning on the shop floor when there isn't a woman anywhere to be seen that I need a hard-on, is it? I need one when I'm with a lady.

So what happens?

I don't know, I don't know.

There was a long silence, while Fernando searched for the right words, felt his courage ebb like blood from his dick, felt alone. It was as if the doctor had backed into the shadows of his consulting room, withdrawing into the parchment of his swanky diplomas, though in fact he hadn't moved a muscle, was still sitting there like some fucking-Eastern holy man, waiting and staring. Fernando peered at the doctor, like it was down the wrong end of a telescope, and the doctor beamed back as if to say, What does it matter what I think anyway? So Fernando took a breath and spat it out. What happens is I get scared somehow and it just goes. That's all. I fear it's going to happen and then it happens. I'm no longer a man.

Then what?

Well, you know women. They look at it and maybe they laugh and maybe they don't and then they look at you and fucking-smile and then they look away. They make me want to hit them, but I don't. You don't hit women, however much you may want to – and, boy!, do you want to! So I run. I know you're not supposed to run either, but between hitting women and running, I reckon it's better to run. It's like I can hear their laughter in my ears, burning. Even if they don't actually laugh, I know they want to and ought to and are bound to as soon as my back is turned. And it gets so I know they'll be laughing and I'll be running, even before I touch them, even before I see them. Running from their laughter that hasn't started yet but is sure going to. It's like a habit. As soon as my pants are down and the woman's ready for it and egging me on, it's all over. Hanging there looking about as deadly as a broken bootlace.

Dr Boulabem told Fernando there was nothing wrong with him that a patient, kind woman couldn't help him cure and asked him had he ever been with a professional – that's right, with a prostitute.

Fernando shifted and fidgeted and looked up at the ceiling, then down at his knees, then blinked, a total give-away, and said, No. In his view paying for it was for losers. There was a silence.

Then the shrink said, Look, most men pay for it when they're far from home. If they have cash to spare.

Fernando had boxed himself in. He couldn't confess either to telling a lie or to considering himself a loser, or to being so dirt-poor he couldn't afford the occasional paid-for poke, so there was another silence, even more pained than the first.

How would it be if you were to look at it as a temporary measure, a sort of treatment, the shrink said, like therapy. What like physio? Fernando said, hopeful. Sure, like physio, Boulabem replied. Then he scribbled on a sheet of paper, tore it from the pad and gave it to Fernando. There was a woman's first name and an address.

You will have to pay a little more than for a street-girl, Boulabem was saying, but I think it'll help. As you can see, her name's Maryse and she specializes in men who are experiencing such difficulties. And she won't laugh. If it doesn't work, come back to see me and we'll talk again. But believe me, it will work, if you let it. Just do what she says, okay? And give it time. I don't expect I'll be seeing you again, so good luck.

And that's how he'd met Maryse. She was his fucking treatment, his fucking cure. And she had been patient and kind. And he had been compliant, obeyed instructions, done what a woman told him to do for just about the first time in his life. With her coaxing and cooing, he had become a man again. She flattered him, told him he was a tiger, said he was endowed just right so she could feel him real good without getting all bruised up inside. Told him he was tender, showed him what a woman needed, and where. Taught him how to stroke and pet and wait and listen and spin it out. Taught him to talk too. And he loved her for it. How dumb was that?

Fernando heard the bus and broke into a run, glancing round, gasping like a stuck pig, tongue hanging right out. Just another few metres! The bus passed him and stopped. From the back of the bus, Alphonse was laughing and making outlandish gestures to get him to sprint harder, like it was the world's greatest joke. Fernando's lungs felt like they were foaming, his heart like it was about to rip loose, leap out of its trap, and bound across the road like a jumping jack. Fernando made one last spurt. The doors were still open and he was almost there. Puta de vida. I used to run like lightning. As a kid, nobody could catch me. Now look at the state of me. Got there, made it. Sweet fucking-Mary. Where's my ticket?

He moved into the body of the bus toward Alphonse who clapped him too heartily on the shoulder and put out a hand in the classic European manner for Fernando to shake. Fernando preferred that. He couldn't be doing with all that fist-banging stuff that lots of blacks were into and that clumsy whites sometimes went along with, making themselves look laughable. Besides, they were in France, weren't they? Not in Africa. Alphonse was good, though. Fucking-weird, but all right. Almost a friend.

I thought you were going to miss it, Alphonse said, adding, Hey, you look like shit, doubling up in laughter like he'd told a joke, jackknifing then looking immediately mortified. Alphonse did not like to use bad language. Fernando eyed him in his smart white trousers and garish shirt, then wiped his sweaty brow, pulled an ugly face and said, So I look like shit. So what? It's not as if I'm attending my mother's wedding, is it? It's only a factory. Who am I supposed to doll myself up for? You and that bunch of ex-cons and deadbeats?

Alphonse was really an actor, that was what he'd once told Fernando. He certainly looked the part. And with that fucking-smooth way he moved, like he had a courgette stuck up his jacksie? Probably a faggot. Did you get black faggots? Never heard of one. But did you get actors who weren't faggots? Sure you did. Fucking-no way was Charles Bronson one of the sisterhood. But was he an actor, or did he just do Charles Bronson? Maybe to act is to be a fag and to be a fag is all an act. Too fucking-many questions, getting my head all raveled-up. Like a cat in Christmas fucking-wrapping paper.

Alphonse was going right on laughing, swaying, muttering, Attend your mother's wedding, that is highly entertaining, genuinely diverting, and gazing down on Fernando like he was talking to some clever salon wit. After a while, Alphonse quietened down and, as if to make polite conversation, asked Fernando, How's the gambling proceeding? Hit the jackpot yet?

What could you say to such a damn-fool question? Fernando stared down the length of the bus, which at that moment was stopped at a bus stop. Eric had just got on, looking as happy as a goat in a country downpour.

Let me put it this way, Fernando said, turning his homeless, uprooted anger on Alphonse, speaking softly, and pausing for effect. You think maybe I've won the jackpot, right? So come on, tell me, I'm interested: would that be why I'm fucking-stood here on this bus, making my way to the factory to be fucked in the arse all night by Monsieur Gérard fucking-Boucan? A flash of home in Portugal, too quick to catch, a twitch in his eye, a blur on his retina, a yearning, then gone. Fernando's spittle was growing airborne. You think maybe I've won the jackpot and you're the first jerk-off to know, right? Thirty-three million francs – that was the big win this week – and I'm fucking-standing here talking to you? FUCK you!

Alphonse laughed a nervous laugh and held up his hands at chest level, palms out, fingers splayed, an unrehearsed gesture of surrender, in fact a very fine piece of improvisation. He hadn't yet grasped the fact that gambling was a serious activity, or worked out how to deal with angry white sarcasm. It threw him onto the defensive, brought out the erudite in him. I apologize most sincerely, he said. I have to concede it was an insensitive question.

Exactly, Fernando said, pressing his lips together, nodding, still scowling, Insensível, sim.

Then Alphonse stroked his chin and wondered, What did I need to apologize for? I didn't mean the man any harm. He thought this over, then said, You must know I didn't ever intend to touch a tender point, Fernando. Speaking personally, I never gamble. In my view, it's a fool's game. Fernando chewed on that for a while, thought about getting all offended, but decided to let it go. What the hell. Where was the point in fucking-taking umbrage? Nowhere. Other than Jacques, Alphonse was the closest thing he had to a friend. It didn't do to pick a fight, did it? Of course it didn't.

Fernando and Alphonse relaxed and allowed the rocking bus to move them imperceptibly closer, then as one man they turned to look down the bus at Eric, who was sitting facing their way but didn't seem to have noticed their presence. They exchanged a glance. Where on earth is that young man's mother when he truly needs her? Alphonse asked gravely, feeling his way. Yeah, said Fernando, it has to make you wonder. Talk about green. And the English are always said to be so clever. Alphonse stood back from Fernando and looked down at him, appearing surprised. I've never heard anything about that, he said. More like cunning, sly. Perfidious, that's what they call them in this country, isn't it? Perfidious Albion?

Fernando had not heard the English called perfidious before, or Albion. Perfidos. He knew the word, knew what it meant, but had never used it, and didn't quite know how to connect to the English, perhaps because Eric was the only member of that nation he had ever met. After a while, Fernando turned to Alphonse and said, Well, in Portugal, we were always taught in school that they were clever. Historic allies, great explorers, second only to us, you know? But I have to say, this one is a total half-wit. Do you know what the little prick did the other night, Thursday? Alphonse looked blank. I took the night off, he said. Fernando's eyes went steep back and up. Sure. I forgot. Well, you'd never guess. Fernando was smiling now and Alphonse relaxed in anticipation of a good story that would illustrate the Englishman's stupidity.

Alphonse glanced down the bus at Eric who had now pulled out a copy of *Libération*, and was leaning against a side window. Who was he trying to fool? Judging by the amount of French the boy could speak, he could surely make neither head nor tail of a newspaper. Maybe he was looking for love among the small ads. Alphonse surveyed Eric with interest and a degree of distaste. The Englishman sniffed at the bright yellow flank of the middle finger of his right hand, rubbed it against his bottom lip, then raised the finger and eased it into his mouth, where he began to champ on the dead skin alongside the knuckle. He then removed the finger from his mouth, inspected the tooth marks in his flesh and commenced to ruminate on the morsel of nicotine-saturated epidermis just harvested. Alphonse swallowed hard as a wave of warm nausea flushed through him. Really! Didn't they teach them any personal hygiene in England? A fine specimen, this one! His skin, generally, was that pinky-yellow of white people who never see the sun, his hair lanky and cheaply cut, his shoulders hunched, his eyes small and evasive and of indeterminate colour, probably rodent-grey – the grey no doubt of English skies – his glasses far too large for his face, his face itself too red, as if he were forever blushing or being surprised while abusing himself. Hollow-chested, nylon-shirted, clammy-palmed, yellow-toothed and smelling like an inveterate stranger to soap and water – let alone modern deodorizers. How could a person – who was not essentially ugly and who, to be fair, owned certain features (a symmetrical face, a good-shaped head, fullish lips for a northern European, a nose neither too large nor too small) that a skilled beautician might exploit with ease – be so cavalier with his presentation? Such reckless squandering! Alphonse looked down at the hard-and-sharp creases in his own trousers, relished the discreet smell of cologne rising from his chest, while he listened absent-mindedly to Fernando.

Well, if you were away that night, Fernando was saying, you must have missed it. What happened is that he got his nose so fucking-stuck in some fat English book that he might as well have been dozing. Upshot was he completely forgot to check the product for fucking-over an hour, and when he did he discovered that for the last forty minutes or so one of his machines had been chucking out product with four defective pieces out of fucking-every twelve. The injection pressure must have dropped without warning. And it was a fucking-new mould so he should have been careful. You ought to have seen him when he found out. I thought he was going to cry. The chef yelled at him for ten seconds which must be like two minutes from anyone else. You know the chef: he's the fucking-easiest foreman I've ever known, ex-army man or not, as calm and as deep as the Atlantic, but when he does raise his voice, the windows rattle. Somebody said he plays the trumpet and that's why he doesn't smoke, but I don't see how that fucking-follows. It's not as if you'd ever have to do both things at once. He's certainly got a pair of lungs on him. And poor little Eric had to spend the rest of the night sorting out good pieces from duds, fucking-checking on his machine every two minutes to make sure the pressure was holding up. I felt sorry for him. Anyway, Philippe went over and helped him out and then, of course, Marcel and Bobrán had to join in, didn't they? So the four of them stood round the box, pulling out the no-good pieces and tossing them in the recycling bin. Fucking-whatever Philippe does, that pair of Gypsies have to do too. Have you thought about that?

Yes, said Alphonse, I did notice that, as it happens. One can only surmise that they respect him. But then, aren't they entitled to? I'm perfectly certain I respect Philippe. Don't you?

Fernando considered that for a moment, like it was a strange and inherently uninteresting notion, then slowly nodded. Yeah, well.

Eric had noticed the Portuguee and the African chatting and laughing at the back of the bus, but it hadn't occurred to him to wonder why. He had seen them look his way but had thought nothing of it: it was normal for people on buses to look in the direction of travel, wasn't it? – a kind of at-ease position for the eyes to rest in. In any case, they hadn't acknowledged him. Maybe he ought to stare in their direction, a hard cool stare, till they looked back at him, recognized his existence. Then he could mouth a real cool 'saloo!' Nah, it was hipper, probably Frencher, not even to notice they were there, Eric thought. Back to *Libération*, with a sigh. I'm definitely getting the drift of this article, third time through. Maybe if I knew something about Corsica, I'd find it easier. I'll take my dictionary to it later. Anyway I've got to concentrate on this stuff, not think about the brunette, not at all, keep her right out of my mind. Wish I had a name for her, though: 'brunette' isn't good enough any longer somehow. I need either to do something about it or drive her out of my head. Which is difficult when I see those lips every evening, that hair, those eyes, catch glimpses of that honeyed skin of hers. Above all those tits side-on. Shit. I'm going to have to give it a try, see what happens, ask her out. She's never even glanced at me yet. I bet if she did I'd come in my pants like a twelve-year-old. Christ! What's happening to me? Her tits are driving me mad. The shape. The profile. The curve. I never wanted anything, anyone, so much. Maybe it's the climate. Makes you randy. What, in November? It's been raining for two weeks straight. Sweet Jesus save me! How long's it been now? And that was with Megan. Hardly counts. This is torture. I'll go nuts. Going, Gone. Bonkers, certifiable. Wonder what loony bins are like in this country? Call them 'asiles,' don't they? Asylums: makes them sound almost harmless. I'd better read that article again. Corsica. Right. Autonomists. Okay. Grève de la soif. Thirst strike. Is that when you don't drink anything either? Or do you eat but not drink? In that case, you could order some soup and you'd be fine. The Court of Appeal in Lyon. Okay. This is goddamn useless. Her lips jump out from between the lines. Scary. Her tits. I need to refocus, redouble my efforts. Can you re-triple efforts? Don't see why not. Where's my will power gone anyway? Men are supposed to be made of sterner stuff. Three days on thirst strike. Poor bastard terrorists will croak.

Eric can see he is losing his good fight. Lust is getting the better of shyness. He's going to have to say something to the young woman in the factory, put an end to it. Or a beginning. He sets his jaw with stern resolve, calling to mind Trevor Howard grappling with his conscience in the African jungle. The bus slows down for a set of lights. He looks over the top of his *Libé*, out the window, down into the next lane. Hey, there's a beat-up old 2CV, bet it's that peasant guy, Jacques they call him. Often see him from this bus. Friendly enough bloke, but I hate the feel of his hand when we shake. Hands like sides of beef. Eric imagines inserting his hand in a king-size wrap-around rump steak, and shudders. Jacques' 2CV is cool though, really battered, must be immediately post-war. The bonnet is held down with string and there are patches on the fabric roof, like the patches you get to repair rips in tent canvas. But that car's not his, is it? No patches on the roof. Easy mistake. All look the same those cars, that identical bluey-grey. Funny the way Jacques never stops smiling. I guess he's either totally relaxed or a complete cretin. Wonder what he thinks about. If he thinks at all. He probably worries about his turnip crop, or the weather or the price of seed. He's a peasant, isn't he? Which means he must have peasant thoughts. Doesn't seem so insulting in French: 'paysan.' It's raining again now, slowly. Could almost be Croydon. This town – except for the very centre – is so ugly it makes the outskirts of London seem picturesque. Eric burps loudly and unexpectedly, no chance to cover his mouth. A young woman pulls a face and moves away. No loss, not much to look at. Nothing like the brunette. Better not burp in front of *her*. The French can be so fastidious.

Eric isn't feeling well. He's suffering the after-effects of the skinful he had that morning. Fresh out the factory, first breath of morning traffic fumes, he was just turning left into a side road to make his way home, when he heard a voice behind him. It was Philippe, cigarette on smiling lip, Marcel and Jacques standing each side of him like hired muscle, comical really, inviting him to come for a drink. Bobrán was straddling his bike and waving goodbye: he never came to the bar with them, didn't drink, he said. Eric should have said no but yes was going to be a lot easier, requiring no follow-up excuses or explanations. Besides, Philippe was giving him this huge grin. Eric's stomach churned some more and he felt another burp building. He reached into his pocket and dragged out some indigestion tablets, the kind that taste like four parts chalk to one part mint and that you're told to crunch not swallow.

It had been fun though. Philippe on a barstool, looking as comfortable as a cowboy in a saddle – John Wayne, say, or Jack Palance – like he was totally born to it. Looking vacantly ahead over his glass, like into a sunset, like there was nothing in his mind at all, but some kind of glory all the same. A faraway look. Like Camus in that newspaper photo I've stuck on my wall at the hotel. And every now and then blowing a smoke-ring and making some sardonic comment. And I discovered that with a little blanc-limé my French improves, or at least I get more words out. It helps not to be deafened by machinery.

Eric caught a reflection of himself in the glass as the bus moved off. Shit, she was going to say no, was bound to. I'm mad about her, I could get put away, in an asylum, and we've never even spoken. If only I looked like Camus, if only I was French. How can I even ask her? Those lips, that skin. I could eat her eyebrows lash by lash, as a delicacy, an hors d'oeuvre, before moving on to her substantial lips, the first course, something to bite on. Then the tits she's got on her. In three-quarter profile, hugging herself, like. Not the size or anything, just that particular angle, that tilt. Gets me right here. Something as far beyond a boner as Greta Garbo was beyond beautiful. Must be love. Never, never felt this way before. Eric snatched *Libé* open in front of him and, grinding his molars, started a new article, a full-page spread on industrial turmoil in Italy, with an interview with some guy called Sergio. Shit, I've got to ask her out, got to ask her out, got to ask her out. Out, out, out! If it's the last thing I bloody do. Like at school, swearing things in threes could sometimes work the trick. A kind of magic. Incantation for amateurs. Do it, do it, do it. And then it's done. In a trice.

Eric saw a snap of the afternoon-shift workers lining up in their street clothes at the clock-machine, waiting for the hands to show 9.25. What the blazes would he say to her with them all gawking at him like munching sheep? At least the din of the machines would drown him out. He would amble along the row shaking everyone's hand, like every other evening, then when he got to her, he'd gently yell in her ear: Êtes-vous libre samedi soir? That ought to cover it. Had to hope he could understand the answer: questions were the easy bit, you could prepare them. Imagine her face! What had he got to lose? He was going to ask her, going to ask her, going to ask her. Thrice! Hic et ubique! Where had he heard that? Swear, old mole! If he didn't ask her, it would drive him doolally. Corsican hunger-and-thirst strikes were no answer. Pissed-off workers in Turin no help. Resolve, resolve, resolve. Resolution. Not for a new year but, well, for a new life. Or at least a new girlfriend. How about that? Every day in every way, wasn't it? Fight the good fight, and all that. And shall my sword? Jesus Fuck, Eric sighed. The tilt of those tits is wedged in my mind like a hatchet in the back of my head. To be a bleeding pilgrim, eh?

4. Jean, Bobrán.

To keep his courage up, Jean was – quite literally – whistling in the dark. He had lit upon a tune he had known since the first time he had heard it, back in the fifties. It had been covered several times since then by French singers, but despite the fact that Jean knew very little English it was the original American version by Helvisse, ze King, le roi du Rock, that had stuck in his mind. Jean now switched from timorous whistling to full-throated singing: zhee rrode hup-hon-eet, RHEDURNE DE ZENDER!! HAHDRESSE HUN-NOHNE NOZUSH NOMBERRR! NOZUSH ZOHNNE!

The strange words went round and round, serving as an incantation to ward off evil spirits. In his youth, the fact that he couldn't comprehend the lyric had gnawed away at Jean's mind, but he was now reconciled to that state of affairs, accepting it to be final. Besides, his wife's sister, who knew the language of the Anglo-Saxons excessively well, had assured him that English and American rock lyrics were distinguished by all the triteness and simplicity that generally characterized that culture, so he was missing nothing. He believed her. Still, they did write good *mélodies,* you had to hand them that. Then the fear returned and Jean stopped singing.

It's a good thing the big Gypsy walks slowly, Jean was thinking, glancing behind him but seeing nothing. Marcel had lithe limbs, long young legs, the kind that can move fast if he wants them to – not that he ever does, lazy devil. He's behind me, at my back in the dark, I'm sure of it. If I turn round now he'll know I'm frightened and that could set him off. Like dogs scenting fear, their muzzles twitching. Or bullies at school, when you look away or merely blink. Not that anyone ever bullied me: I stood my ground, however much bigger and brawnier they were. Jean's private legend of playground bravery melted away as fast as it had broken surface, offering no purchase for precise recollection, no hook for proud detail. If he catches up with me . . . But why would he want to? Besides, I wouldn't let him. My legs may be short but they can still shift. I've kept myself trim.

It's so awfully dark here. They might leave a few more lights on. You could have your throat slit and slowly die behind one of these machines and nobody would find you till morning. If then. Or your cranium might be split open with a cleaver. Or you could be impaled on a rod of iron and discovered several days later by your stench. You'd be sitting there decomposing on top of a heap of metal waste, slumped behind some machine that hasn't been used since the sixties and that nobody has bothered to cart away, your body fluids pooling between your knees. You might be grinning. Or looking a little surprised, like, Hey! Was that me then? Is that all I got?

I saw him. At least, I think I saw him. I think it was him I saw. He was coming out of *Chez Hortense*. Always drinks there before clocking on. Didn't see his cousin. He's not so bad, his cousin, even if he looks much worse. Didn't see the Marseillais or the foreman either. I just bet it's the Gypsy behind me, the bigger one of the two. I can sense him loping along in the shadows with those dark lazy limbs of his. I'm buggered if I'm turning round. I couldn't walk much faster. I'm not breaking into a run in this half-light. I might stumble. He'd be on top of me before I knew it, those long lithe legs of his.

If this was an alleyway or a strip of waste ground, with that Gypsy coming up behind me, I could say my prayers. Why would he want to do that? What would he want with me? What am I talking about? Gypsies, that's what. That's what it comes down to. There's something about them. That's all it is. They despise us. You can see it in their eyes. I don't trust them. Goodness, no! But I'll be all right now, I'll be fine. Round this next, this very last dark corner, I'll be able to see the light from the plastics section shining through the curtain of scratched-transparent flaps. Another couple of steps. The noise is loud already. I'll be safe in there, in the warmth and bright lights. De-dum, De-dum-dum. RHEDURNE . . .

Jean's first lungful of scorched plastic that evening was followed by a happy sigh of relief. He could breathe better now, and his heart could beat less fast. He wiped a bead of sweat from his forehead. Ever since he had entered the factory building, he had been walking as fast as his short legs would carry him. He always hated the nightly trek through dormant metallurgy, seeing monsters squatting behind every glinting machine, coiled and poised to pounce, like the ghouls that as a feverish child he would see oozing from the patchy paint-peeling walls of his parents' bedroom.

Jean was safe now. Before him stood the clock-machine. He silently greeted a couple of afternoon-shift workers whose hands he had shaken every working night for months or maybe years and whom he could not fail now to acknowledge. He didn't meet their gaze. He didn't know their names. They were strangers. To hell with them. Then he punched his card and headed for the lift. Out of the corner of his eye, he spotted Mathieu, the night foreman, talking to an engineer and chewing on a used matchstick, the blackened tip protruding from between the man's lips. Mathieu seemed to send a glance straight through him, through his pint-sized, baggily-trousered, home-cardiganed frame, but it signalled nothing. Jean shrugged and looked away and sniffed. Mathieu the old patriot, Mathieu and the Résistance: the fellow-traveller, the red dupe.

The lift arrived, the doors clattered open, and one of the upstairs afternoon gang stepped out. Jean dutifully extended his right hand for a perfunctory shake as one corner of his mouth momentarily twisted, causing a tiny dimple to appear and disappear on his baby face, as fast and as minutely as a muscle spasm. He stepped into the large iron cage. De-dum, De-dum-dum.

The lift's double metal gates were heavy and stiff: Jean had to bring his full bantam-weight to bear. There was an empty trolley against one wall, a spray of white plastic granules on the flat wooden board. Jean pressed the up-button and waited. It hadn't registered. He pressed it again. The lift clicked into life. The five-metre journey would take a full minute. Jean leaned back against the metal wall and rehearsed the treats with which, like beads, he would string his working night. He closed his eyes. Those strange words came again unbidden to his mind: Han-deef eet gomz bag ze verrhy negzt dayee, ZEN hah'll Hunderr-stann. De-dum, de-dum-dum.

Until ten o'clock, he would have to pass the time as best he could, briefly partaking in the occupational boredom of the inchoate mass of which he was undeniably a part. But shortly after ten, Bobrán, Marcel's cousin, would bring him a polystyrene cup of dense black sugarless coffee – Jean felt for the single coin at the bottom of his left-hand trouser pocket – whereupon the two men might engage in some rudimentary conversation. From the moment Bobrán threw his empty cup at the waste bin (he had never yet missed, which impressed Jean with the force of a statistical freak), gave Jean a toothy grin and a nod, and returned to his machines, until the dot of midnight (by his Swiss *chronomètre*), Jean would methodically contemplate that day's miscellaneous events, as gleaned from the city-and-provincial paper with which his wife woke him every afternoon at two, the eight o'clock television news they viewed as they ate their evening meal, and any personal, marital, family, neighbourhood or workplace developments that had caught – or were now brought – to his attention.

From midnight to one a.m., Jean would permit his mind to ponder things beginning with the letter N, which was the letter he had reached today. Yesterday, he recalled with a twitch of his dimple, he had reminisced about:

mothers – first his own, then his wife's, and thereafter a selection of other people's; mattresses – about which he had discovered that he possessed so many precise views that he had found it useful mentally to list and classify them; mistresses – of which he had only ever had one, though the memory of her remained so important to him that he often smuggled her into this section of his night under other guises, as lover (A for *amante*), girlfriend (C for *copine*), slut (S for *salope*), ex (E for *ex*) and even sometimes remorse (R for *remords*); from mistresses, as he now remembered with a smile, he had progressed to mantises (of the religious, praying sorority); then, finally, he had thought about the sea (la *mer*) which he had only ever seen twice, both times at Nice when he was a boy, and which, frankly, he didn't care if he never saw again.

At one o'clock precisely, Jean would purge – as they said – his machine by shutting off the hopper, making the injection nozzle projectile-vomit onto a scrap of waste cardboard any molten plastic remaining in its melting chamber, and then halt the machine with its mould wide open. With the nicest attention to detail, Jean would set out his dinner on a tablecloth – freshly laundered each day – which he would spread on an upturned plastic bin. As he ate he would judge the meal his wife had prepared for him and which, following his precise orders, had to consist exclusively of items that he liked, while nonetheless presenting an element of surprise and originality, achievable either by a judicious choice of ingredients or by their juxtaposition – for example, a cheese unfamiliar yet pleasing to him, or tuna in a sauce that he had never previously encountered with any fish other than, say, mackerel. He would score his wife's efforts on a scale of one to ten, and prepare to report back to her in generous detail. While he ate his meal, he would read several pages of his current library book, always a work of military history, putting it aside at one twenty-five precisely, leaving himself sufficient time to tidy away his meal things, enjoy a quick pee and get the press working again smartly by one thirty.

For the ensuing hour and a half, Jean would think about what he had read and imagine the events and exploits portrayed, taking pleasure in picturing himself against the historical backdrop depicted. Mostly, he would settle for an important but secondary role, but sometimes he would flatter himself by assuming the role of a true hero – Pétain at Verdun, for example, or Bonaparte – or, though this worried him at times, Jeanne d'Arc, the Maid of Orléans. It was during this part of the night that he might feel rather drowsy or enjoy a fleeting erection or sometimes, and this he found quite delicious, both at once. His machine, however, the only semi-automatic press in the entire plastics section, was, most blessedly, a strict taskmaster, requiring constant attention and thereby making it quite impossible for him either to fall asleep or to repair to the toilets to attempt self-abuse. His machine, indeed, produced a new product every twenty-eight seconds and after every third or fourth product it became necessary to open the safety door at just the right moment to catch and freeze the injection-mould in its open position and, using the wooden-handled paintbrush, to apply a dab of oil to the ejector pins. Failure to perform this prophylactic task would ineluctably cause the fifth if not the fourth product to stick fast to its mould, requiring much effort to detach it, and possibly jeopardizing the quality of several subsequent products, thereby interrupting production and lowering output.

From three o'clock until four-thirty, it had long been Jean's rule to review a particular year – plucked either from within the ambling and mostly tranquil course of his own adult life or from more remote, and he imagined, grander historical times. In the last few months, however, an innovation had intruded itself upon Jean's long confirmed routine. Alphonse, a young man from the Ivory Coast who worked two of the six automatic machines on the first floor (the Portuguee Fernando and the Gypsy Bobrán managing the remaining four), had adopted the practice of reading aloud for ten minutes or so from Jean's history book. Alphonse would arrive at Jean's machine shortly after three, open the book at the bookmark, and pace up and down, gesticulating to great effect, while reading in a voice that boomed well above the machine din. Alphonse was an excellent reader and clearly enjoyed an audience. Only a week of such readings had elapsed before Bobrán and Fernando had made three o'clock at Jean's machine a nightly fixture. As soon as they saw Alphonse with book in hand, both men would pull up their chairs. Bobrán would lean back and close his eyes and smile contentedly, while Fernando would lean forward with one elbow on each knee, straining to catch each and every meaning and nuance and nodding hard from time to time, as if possessed of sufficient knowledge either to approve or disapprove of the narrative in question.

More recently still, Alphonse had begun to follow his reading with a recitation of a long speech, seemingly by a madman, from the play that he was currently learning at drama class, a play that – on the basis of the said speech – struck Jean as very modern and strange, and which Alphonse claimed had been written by an Irishman who lived in Paris and wrote in French. The first few nights, Alphonse had still needed to refer occasionally to a book, but last night he had seemed word-perfect. Jean, though he did not betray this feeling, was full of admiration for the African, whose ability each night to find an entirely new style for his recitation amazed him. One night his character would speak in short and furious bursts, another night he would sound drunk, another he might seem rather elderly and infirm, another he would have an incredibly thick African (Ivorian? Jean wondered) accent. Jean had never previously considered how much difference an actor could make. Yet the words themselves appeared to Jean to remain much the same. He would like to ask Alphonse if it was really all up to him, or was there not perhaps a right way, like with Corneille? You couldn't imagine anyone taking such liberties with *Le Cid*, could you? Jean, however, was prone to deep feelings of shame about what he took to be his extensive ignorance; indeed the more Jean read and thought and pondered, the more aware he became of the fathomless chasms of his own unknowing. So he never asked.

Alphonse's reading aloud and dramatic performances were amusing and innocuous and helped to pass the time, but Jean didn't want them to turn into some kind of carnival that might distract people from their work. Indeed, he had resolved that he would have to bring it all to an abrupt end if, for example, people from downstairs were to become interested. He would not be party to anything that might depress productivity.

Following this pleasant and still novel interlude, as soon as Alphonse and Bobrán and Fernando had returned to their machines, Jean would fall back on his year – he chose a different year each month, boning up on it at the weekend and during slow weekday afternoons. For this particular month he had elected to consider the momentous events of 1830. This would while away the time most satisfactorily until four forty, when he would once again 'purge' his machine, halt it, clean it thoroughly with a fresh damp cloth, top up the hopper, pack his bag, and prepare for home, congratulating himself, as he waited for the clock-machine hands to alight on 4.55, that he was now one whole night closer to retirement.

The lift doors opened and, with a spring thus freshly engineered into his step, Jean launched himself into the glare and noise of the upstairs plastics section. He saw at once from the light on the control cabinet that his machine was stopped. Suarez, a merry-seeming Spaniard, was finishing cleaning it. Jean walked over slowly. He waited for Suarez to notice him before glancing at the hopper level gauge to check that it had been filled. In the preceding three weeks, Suarez had forgotten on no fewer than two occasions to leave the hopper full and it had therefore become quite indispensable each evening subtly to remind the Spaniard of his occasional oversights, thereby making any recidivism significantly less probable. The two men shook hands.

Has my machine been working nice and smoothly? Jean enquired, giving the green flank of the injection press a proprietorial pat.

Impeccable, boss, chirruped the Spaniard.

Jean put his bag down at the base of the control cabinet, removed his outdoor jacket and hung it on a hook at the back of the aforesaid cabinet. He then removed his history book from his bag and placed it on a stool where he could see it. He took out his work-coat and put it on over his grey woollen cardigan, leaving only the top button undone. Jean turned round and shook hands with Suarez, who by this time had donned his raincoat and shouldered his bag.

Bon travail! Suarez said in that husky Spanish voice that to Jean's ears made their women sound lascivious and their men coarse.

Bonne nuit! Jean piped, pleased with the model brevity of their exchange.

Gingerly taking hold of the chair back, Jean spun the seat of his chair in a counter-clockwise direction until it rose on its screw to attain a height sufficient to compensate for his diminutive stature. Glaring at the seat's plastic covering, he summarily pushed the chair away from him, scorning to sit on a chair so recently vacated. He drew a plastic envelope from his bag and from this in turn extracted a sponge dampened with a lemon-scented but nonetheless powerful disinfectant with which he proceeded to wipe the seat. In defiance of weariness or backache, Jean would operate his machine from a standing position until Bobrán brought him his coffee at 22.00, after which he would work sitting down.

For Jean entertained a dark terror of warm plastic seats. Nobody, no doctor, no seeming-expert or state-funded time-server would ever convince him that they harboured no threat. Jean was immovably persuaded that germs, microbes, bacterial and parasitic life forms of whatsoever nature were capable of finding their way down and out of one man's intestinal tract, possibly on the wings of a fart, only to lie in wait upon the slick surface of a tepid seat for the arrival of the following shift; whereupon they would clamber slyly upward through howsoever many layers of clothing and unfailingly impregnate the fundament of the next sitter, viz., in this instance, himself. Moreover, although Jean kept his own anus as clean as any adept of Mohammed, with the punctilious application of disposable antiseptic tissues following each voiding of the bowels, who would dare account for the ablutionary practices of others, Spaniards, for example? Anal hygiene was not always accorded the importance it merited. Jean himself had long suffered from piles and was convinced, despite the blustering denials of his several doctors, that he had contracted them from a lukewarm seat, maybe even – and here would be a fine scandal, had he ever the means to prove it – in a doctor's waiting room.

These thoughts would now gurgle and churn in Jean's mind, finding no relief until ten o'clock when, with the arrival of Bobrán bearing aloft his coffee in its polystyrene beaker, he might turn his mind to the much happier contemplation of that day's events. It wouldn't be long now. The machine was working smoothly. Jean felt his cheek muscles relax. The book was in its place for later. He began to hum loudly, then to sing at his machine. Rhedurne De Zender, Hah-drresse Hun-nohne, be-dum be-dum-dum, Nozush Nomberrr! Nozush Zohnne!

Shaking Bobrán gently and telling him that if he didn't hurry he would be late for work *again*, his mother broke into his dreamy sleep of warmth and ease. While he rubbed his eyes, she told him of an advert in that day's regional paper: a nearby factory was recruiting day-shift workers. As the waking world sprouted ever sharper edges and sounds, Bobrán looked at the time on his wall clock, grumbled and rolled out of bed fully clothed, except for his trousers which he deftly scooped from the floor where they lay. She should have woken him sooner.

Bobrán's mother had taken a step back from the bed and was still talking and gesticulating. He glanced at her and grinned vaguely. She raised her voice, as if his grin represented some sort of defiance. She was sick and tired, she said again, of him working nights in a factory and days on building sites where anything, absolutely anything, might happen. She had only one son, she informed him severely, and where would she be if he lost an arm one night in one of those presses? She knew someone whose brother had lost a hand. Or if he tripped and fell twelve storeys? Then what?

Bobrán was nodding at his mother but not listening. He wouldn't trip, he wasn't the clumsy sort: that much he knew about himself. He loved his mother for every reason a son might love his mother – and others besides.

He must have had another nightmare earlier, or she would have woken him. It was bad luck to wake someone during a bad dream, she had once told him. So she waited till his sleep grew calm and happy, even if that made him arrive late for work. When it came to jobs, his mother meant well but didn't know what she was talking about: he had tried for day-shift jobs but nobody wanted a gold-toothed, ear-ringed, long-haired Gypsy rumoured to be in trouble with the police. In any case, he wouldn't be able to stand the bossiness of the supervisors and the snottiness of day-shift gadgé, above all their women. As for the construction jobs he did, he had not the slightest fear of heights – hadn't his father once been part of a high-wire act? That's where he got his talent from. And had his father ever taken a dive? Never in his life. And he wasn't going to either. Unlike . . . He blocked the thought. Joseph's smile. He blocked the thought harder. A loud scream then a dull thud then silence. He still thought about it many times each day.

Bobrán pulled on his shoes – he wore heavy steel-capped boots to the building site but feather-light plimsolls to the factory – and gave his mother a kiss on the cheek, while checking his jacket pockets for change and the key to the trailer door: she would be sleeping when he got back. He glanced in a mirror and tugged a comb through his thick hair. His eyes were bloodshot and he had a large pink sty on his left upper eyelid, which seemed to weigh it down, making it look as if it was drooping from exhaustion. His mother handed him a plastic box containing his night-time meal. You'll wear yourself out, she warned him. I'm fine, he replied, with a grin to prove it. Then, softly in her ear, as he kissed her cheek, Don't be nagging me.

Bobrán gently pushed the metal door shut behind him till he heard the locking click. His mother would watch TV; maybe her sister would drop round. At the factory, his cousin would expect Bobrán to be late – he was almost always late on Tuesdays – and would clock him on, so he wouldn't lose any pay.

Bobrán untethered his bike, stowed his meal box in the single rear panier, then swung one leg over the crossbar and pedalled off, his knees splaying so comically that the neighbours' kids pointed and laughed. You'd think they'd get used to it. He had tried raising the saddle, but the nuts were rusted solid. Still, he enjoyed his journeys to and from work – providing it wasn't raining – and he took them slowly. Without thinking about it, he performed a quick and spectacular wheelie for the benefit of the kids. Because he knew they expected it. Then he settled into cycling no-hands.

He loved the feeling of being on the move; it made him feel childish again, and secure, and free. He knew he could turn off at any point and go somewhere else, and if he did the world wouldn't end. He could spend all night in a bar – something he had never much enjoyed. Or go to a cinema – except that films bored him, all being the same, all working up to triumph, redemption, peace or marriage. Or try meeting someone. That's what he would do, if he wasn't going to work. He was lonely and wanted a man and had given up fighting it. He might even try phoning Moritz, his lover, a young German student, a kid with blond eyelashes, his own money, and peachy-soft skin. He didn't really want anyone else any longer. If Bobrán missed work, he wouldn't lose his job, people would cover for him. Besides, even if he did lose it, the manpower agency would find him another one. He was definitely going to work that evening but he didn't have to, he could still change his mind, and might. At any minute. He still might bump into someone he knew. Anything could still happen.

Each time he turned left or right or went straight on, Bobrán was aware of the choice he was making. Trailer to factory, factory to trailer, trailer to site, site to trailer: the journeys were among the best moments in life. He was lucky with both jobs and it was a good time of year. The factory job was cool: nobody hassled him, nobody looked particularly askance at him or if they did he didn't have to pay them any mind or pick a fight. Some nights, if everything was working well, he could even doze a little in his chair. If he ever really needed to, he could follow that old peasant's example, get someone else to look after his machines for an hour or so – the Portuguese guy would probably do it, or the African – and stretch out properly on the floor. The old peasant even brought a cushion with him for a pillow, walked straight in with it most evenings, past all the smirking afternoon workers. (Bobrán smiled, accidentally caught the eye of a woman driving a car, who smiled back, then shyly looked away. A nice-looking woman. It was funny how women smiled at him more now, maybe sensing his lack of interest, even excited or intrigued by that, or just feeling safe, who knows?) One time not long ago the Sicilian told the old peasant off about the cushion, telling him to hide it in his bag at least, saying it made us look like a bunch of work-shy bums, and Jacques – yeah, that was his name – just leaned back a little and looked at the Sicilian as if from a great distance, a long look of pity, and then he leaned back further and roared, really belting out the laughter, and told him he needed to get laid a lot more often and chew his nails a lot less. It was the funniest thing. The Sicilian standing there outraged and not knowing how to take the insult and incapable of giving one back, lacking the necessary wit, and everyone looking at the guy's nails and seeing it was true, they were chewed right down to the quick, and all the Sicilian could do was stick his hands in his pockets to hide them, the dolt. Which made everyone laugh till they had to hold their sides – even Luigi, which really pissed off the Sicilian, though of course Luigi covered his mouth with his hands. Then there was the supervisor, who was totally easy and didn't give a damn what happened as long as the work got done somehow and the right amount of product got boxed up at the end of the night. The only things that annoyed the foreman were machines left standing idle after a fault and people failing to notice when a machine was producing duds. Some of the other workers could also make Bobrán laugh: the African guy, whose machines were near his, for example, with those funny speeches at Jean's machine toward the end of the shift. This was a good time of year too. Work stopped at his site when it got dark: most evenings he was back home by five and could get four hours straight sleep – much more than in summer. And life wasn't going to be this way for ever. He was saving up. He had dreams and plans, all sorts of dreams and plans. He was feeling good now. He would go to work. He could meet Moritz some other time. Or he could go and find him now. Or he could meet someone else. He had learned over the last couple of years that there was no shortage of gentle boys with peachy-soft skins and their own money. At first this had amazed him, but now he took it almost for granted. Though he would rather stick with Moritz. He was falling in love. After years of thinking that love was not for people like him. But tonight he would go to the factory. Almost certainly. Because he wanted to.

5. Tomec, Sarah.

Tomec and Sarah could stand or sit for hours, together or apart, as they entertained their sempiternal thoughts of Art and God, the very first and the very last things, the concoction of Beauty or the scourge of Creation. But time and the workaday world, like a finely tuned old jalopy, having appeared to idle for a while, would at last slip into a low forward gear and lurch on ahead. In the dim recesses of his mind, Tomec was ever aware of the countdown of hours or minutes to the moment when he must leave his home and studio for the factory or the factory for his home and studio. Right now he had forty or maybe forty-five minutes to go. He must reach the factory by 22.00 to relieve the gate-man.

His head cast back, Tomec was tugging childlike at his sore and flaccid cock, while the water licked the film from his eyeballs. As he uncovered the glans, the corners of his mouth quivered and tightened to a wince. He soaped himself with fastidious care.

His eyes were shut fast. Would Sarah be sore too? A smile faltered and faded. He hoped not, he hoped so, he wasn't sure, he didn't know, he didn't care, it didn't matter. In that order. What had happened this morning? He drew air in through his teeth, hissing as he relished the memory.

She stopped dead still in my lap, bang in the middle of it, and with a slap across my face jerked me from my dreams of Virgil's litter gliding shoulder-high through the streets of Brundisium. My cheeks stung and I looked up to see her flushed face. She scolded me for not listening and commanded me to pay attention. In risible sepia, my primary school in Szczecin (*Stettin* it was called, in those days), complete with battle-axe schoolmistress, her dark stiff blue skirt like the flank of a steamer, reared before me and then sank back as quickly, replaced by a panic fear that my cock might shrivel to mush in Sarah's cunt. Was the vital link, the transmission broken? Was the winding gear still winding? Could I feel it? But as I locked my gaze on the pink of Sarah's babbling lips, it hardened and flexed of its own accord. She must have felt it twitch for she smiled. Resuming her rocking movement, to and fro, to and fro, as if doing a dance or, more likely, a chore, ironing maybe or grating carrots or polishing ornaments, she launched into a cackling, merry-go-rounding, raucous rant, lurching from books she has half-read to objects she has barely glimpsed to people she scarcely remembers (or has never in fact met), to plans she drops as fast as she conceives them, everything pêle-mêle and without form, the entire confection sprinkled with an explosion of near-reason and half-rhyme, all her mental debris strewn about and haphazardly signposted with looks of urgent entreaty, demanding my assent, sympathy, wonderment, outrage or dismay, with never so much as a trace of love all this while much less lust. Pah! The very thought! And then, with no warning and in mid-sentence, she froze, as if transfixed (not that she wasn't, in a very fleshly sense) and, with that squeaky, squelchy well-fucked farting sound, before I could find the words to ask her the matter, she sprang from my dick like a harrier from its perch, leaving me looking at it waving there in the draughty room like a neck with no head or a pole with no flag (that's not bad, that's even good: a flagless Pole is what I am!). Yes. Yes! Only to return after a brief perusal of the bookshelves cradling in her creamy arms a fat, brown, wide-open hard-backed book, and clamber back onto me, with her free hand perfunctorily applying cock to cunt, cool for all the world, as indifferently as she lowers a stylus onto Schoenberg. Whereupon, after commenting on two or three choice passages with an outpouring of eloquence and apposite quotation such as only amateurs can muster – now that the intellectuals have abandoned the universities (and vice versa) – she frowned, apparently in displeasure at her own discourse, threw the book to one side with more violence than accuracy and, grinning now fit to split, said 'Um, that feels good, good, wonderful . . . come on! let's fuck, I want it. Now, damn it. Fuck me!' and then made love (if I dare call it that) with a clamping and a gnashing that is making my eyes – though never better watered than at this instant – water anew at the memory. And the upshot is: my cock is red and sore. With clinical eye, Tomec performed a further examination, then shrugged. What else remains, beyond the memory? What other evidence?

She never stopped talking even when it was over and I was trying to sleep, which of course I couldn't. How could I hope to? So, while she drifted off, still murmuring about tramps – not real ones (perish the thought!) but Beckett's and Chaplin's – and then back to Moses and Aaron in the desert with their unimaginable, solitary God, pursued by a whole cloudburst of other miscellanies some of which had to do with the poet Paul Celan, like herself né Ancel, not forgetting a savage detour into the abstract ('bloodless' she fumed) art of the 1950s, I rose and sketched till the midday traffic was squawking and hissing along the street below and the tepid rays of a November sun resembling nothing so much as a strip of soiled linen slithered on its scalesome belly through the curtains. Will she be sore too, then, redder than her usual rosebud pink? Aiii! Now I've overdone the soaping. Kutas! Indeed.

While working the softening cake over his heavy haunches and into the still shallow creases of his belly, Tomec urinated to flush out the soap that in mulish defiance of Newton's famous law had insinuated its way up his urethra. Opening his eyes to the water again, he was seized by a thought that came freighted with anxiety and struck him at once as too much of a cliché for Sarah's ticklish ears (but had she then become the judge and assessor of his private thoughts?): it was that the intensity of love (but was this then love?), like imminent death, made experience more pungent and pressing, 'concentrating the mind wonderfully' – wasn't that the phrase?

Everything does seem brighter and harder-edged than previously, than yesterday, for example. The soap just now stung more than ever before as I pissed it back out. Tomec glanced round, searching for sensory corroboration. Then he blinked. The white wall tiles are dazzling my eyes more than before. And surely this shower tray is pressing harder than ever up into the balls of my feet. Have I been infected by Sarah's savage enthusiasm? At my age, I ought to be immune. He smiled that one indivisible and complacent smile that from time immemorial has graced the grizzled cheeks of older men as they rise from the bed of a disgracefully, flatteringly, younger woman. Maybe this *is* love, he thought. Though it wasn't like this last time. He pulled a face and adopted a panting, precious and girlish voice to say: 'Beauté! Excellence! Pureté! Esprit!' Then, recalling one of Sarah's favourite sayings – an inversion of Socrates's celebrated adage – Tomec, standing there beneath the shower, struck the pose of an ancient tragedian, his left foot a short pace before his right one and at right angles to it, and declaimed: 'A life unlived is not worth examining.' Tomec laughed to himself, at himself, and (lovingly? he wondered) at Sarah, and melted from the pose, deliquescing back into masculinity, middle age and world-weariness. Well, something has definitely happened: for once in my life, I know exactly how to proceed; for once in my life, work is more precious to me than sleep. There can be no further doubt: I am in love and therefore in danger.

Indeed, that morning, as Tomec fell away from Sarah, his mind sedated by a night spent in peaked cap and scratchy uniform criss-crossing the factory to ensure it was safe and secure (safe from what marauding masses? secure for what tomorrows?), and his body drained by the ear- and cock-drubbing with which Sarah had assailed him at dawn, he had left her mumbling where she lay, risen shakily, set all three easels with fresh paper, and begun to sketch scenes from Hermann Broch's novel, *Der Tod des Vergil*, which Sarah had silently pressed into his hand a week or so earlier and which, the previous night at work, he had begun to read at the factory during quiet moments between his rounds.

While Sarah thrashed and snorted in her dreams, Tomec, his mind fizzing with images of the sick poet arriving in Brundisium, had sketched with rare conviction, trusting in the potent perfection of each of his strokes, giddily certain that he had at last attained the height of his powers, where a single gesture might contain everything, all excess drained to leave only crystalline expression, the embodiment of his own new-minted economy of beauty. He had felt like a geyser spurting with ideas and images, supplied by a mind with total recall and possessed of the skill to grasp the world. This must be how Sarah felt during her ranting. If she had infected him with enthusiasm, he should show some gratitude.

Yet when he awoke alone late afternoon, he saw that it was all to do again: on examining his morning's work, he found nothing more than jotted outlines, scribbled drafts. He had received early notice of this disappointment when, as he finally dropped onto the bed a little after eleven that morning, still elated yet already aware of marauding doubts, Sarah had risen for a glass of water and, pausing to glance at his sketches on her way back, had sniffed with the eloquence of a person to whom allergies and colds are quite unknown. As she bounced back onto the bed and whispered 'sleep well,' he had detested her, and when she turned uncharacteristically to hug him, he had wanted to push her roughly away. He relented of course and so, with Sarah curled like a wife round his back, he had drifted off to sleep pondering the fact that not for the first time he felt patronized by her, this Sarah, this girl-woman, this slip of a thing, damn it! Menaced too. And why?

But the spoon-shaped freckle-backed Sarah, and even the moribund Virgil gliding supine through the mob, melted from Tomec's consciousness as his eyes fell shut and his mind pursued its time-honoured homing path to his grandmother's cramped flat in Szczecin, with its distant view of the boats that lined the shore, way back when the port was busy and the quayside bustled with livestock, gulls, and people, quadrupeds and bipeds going about their businesses with grim, Baltic alacrity.

Tomec now stood back from the shower and leaned his shoulders against the slab of white tiles. Still dreaming of Szczecin, he took his head in his broad hands and pressed hard, hoping that the application of physical pressure would clarify his thoughts: this sometimes seemed to work. Searching, he stared through the streaming water. Rarely had anything intrigued him more than Broch's description of Virgil's arrival at Brundisium, nor demanded such detailed imagining. Is it Sarah's effect or Broch's packed German prose or is Virgil speaking directly to me? (How idiotic is *that* thought?) Tomec had memorized Broch's words about Virgil and recalled them now: 'he knew of the blood that flowed within them, the spit they had to swallow . . .' Was that not the sharpness of vision to which he too aspired and sometimes, for example last night, had seemed momentarily to achieve?

But there was no blood pulsing through the figures he had sketched with feverish conviction while Sarah dreamed. He had understood that now and shook his head, scowled at the water and spat, shivering, holding back from the spray, growing cold, refusing himself the unearned reward of its tepid comfort. For if Sarah had sniffed, it was because the sketches she had seen were corpses whose stench offended her dainty nostrils. Her gaze was forensic, unfailing and relentless and, drowsy as she was and unaware that he was awake, no self-censoring kindness had been perpetrated, no feeble considerations of mitigating complexity entertained. Damn her for being right. Damn her nose, damn her nous, damn her eyes. God love her!

But how can anybody (how can I?) see the harbour and the wharves of ancient Brundisium in that dank dusk, with its grey sea and greyer houses? How do you paint murk and show the people and slums that sweat and ooze beneath it? How do you conjure a mass, yet make of it a living multitude, capturing, in an image, a vision, a moment of its history? You can't just march a dulled evening crowd into the noonday sun or throw them all into blinking relief at the switch of an arc light. Broch writes like a stenographer, giving me nothing but gaps to go on. Tomec shivered. All I have for clues is gaping holes. Fill in is what I have to do, Tomec intoned. Remember and fill in. Belief comes first. Then sight.

Yet amid the gloom there *are* shafts of light, picking out details. There is the skew-wigged white-powdered strumpet who yells invective; the boy with the dark curls who glances up at Virgil 'with amusement and reverence.' It is a start. Besides, did Virgil need to see his home village of Andes to remember its quiet idyll? Or meet Dido to describe her, or take a trip to Troy to compose the *Aeneid*? No. He rode into the midst of the flaming battle astride nothing more equine than his worthy quill.

As Tomec stepped back beneath the warm water, his limbs felt that unique tiredness that comes when love-making has been inadequately crowned by sleep. He looked down, shook his legs and arms, then rolled his heavy shoulders, like a pentathlete under starting orders. He tossed back his head again and blew his cheeks out. His wide eyes stared up into the needles shot from the shower, and he thought of nothing, a grey dull nothing, an immaculate canvas, empty and expectant.

And then it happened. With a rush and a whoosh, he saw detail upon detail, face upon face, so clear and close they seemed to tumble like clowns into a ring, with memories legible in the lines of their countenances, clusters of beliefs and desires open to imagination and inspection, articulation and elaboration. And Tomec, peering startled from one to the next, an onlooker shifting from foot to foot and jostling for a better view, committed them all to memory, storing them pencil- and brush-ready. Like dreams whose course one can tweak when half-awake, he directed the scenes before him, chose the ones he would view, re-ran those of greatest interest, impatient and at once aware that if this were sorcery then it might vanish, if a knack then he might lose it. Here is the boy with the dark curls, here the harlot, here the poet himself with his nervous eye trained on his casket of papers. Further off sways the harbour water bobbing with refuse: orange rinds, cabbage heads, broken boxes. A series of moments from the poet's progress, stations, why not?, I could do a rosary of scenes: the glance of complicity between the boy and the poet; the picture of the 'white-painted whore' and her 'gander'; the procession up 'Misery street;' the rabble of 'bipeds and quadrupeds.' How many stations between boat and deathbed, landing and calvary? Fourteen, surely. Here is a worthy pagan project indeed, a fair and timely mockery of the Jesus myth.

Recalling how the child's 'rather unbeautiful peasant's face' had excited the poet's longing for his mother and for the bucolic life he had long ago renounced, Tomec watched queasily as his vision of Virgil's boat melted from its moorings in Brundisium to reappear in jangling yet sharper focus in a quite different place, a quite different time. Uncomprehending, Tomec stood probing his left ear with the little finger of his left hand, listening to the noise of the shower and peering at the oddly familiar harbour. Then, recognizing

the Szczecin of his 1940s childhood, he erupted in laughter, clasped his broad
hams and leaned forward on his knees for support. No, Szczecin's no model,
my childhood's no help to me.

He laughed till his mind rang hollow and the pictures all vanished and
his face lengthened. He turned the shower taps smartly off and stepped from
the cubicle onto the bathroom floor, yanking a yellow towel from its nail
beside the basin.

He would have to hurry. He glanced at the travel alarm clock ('Made in
GDR'). Nine fifteen, it told him. He liked to keep it a couple of minutes fast.
His shower, a daily rite of passage from artist to factory nightwatchman, had
lasted longer than usual. Kutas! I'll have to rush to reach the factory on time
now and spend at least part of the night working on drawings for that mask
that Jan wants me to sculpt. A picture of Jan as he had appeared the previous
afternoon flickered past, as if on a black-and-white wartime newsreel. And
then there's that matter of the graffiti that has appeared in the metals section,
'Gérard Boucan, Collabo, 1942–44.' Who could have done it? Could it be
true? How much did it matter now that more than thirty years had elapsed?
And, besides, what terrible evils could even Fascist Frenchmen really have
committed, by comparison to those of my compatriots? Tomec suppressed
this last notion as fast as it formed. He would have to ask around, check
that the graffiti-agitator was not someone from the night shift, was not 'one
of ours.' Who could it possibly be? Damn it, I'm the security guard not the
bloody thought police. I won't dwell on it. Not yet, not now. Obey your rules,
Tomec! No factory thoughts till the last button on your uniform is done up
and you have slapped your peaked cap in place, the final touch, the rasher of
bacon on the back of an oven-ready chicken.

Virgil in Szczecin, what a picture! Or Gdansk, for that matter. No place
for poets, for artists, not now, not ever, probably. What was that story that
Sarah recounted when I told her where I was born? About some wretched
composer, a disciple of her beloved Schoenberg, standing at a streaming
window, staring out at freezing surf, rehearsing four-a-penny operettas
and pining for his Viennese home and his master's strictures, despairing to
compose anything against the backdrop of battleship Baltic grey.

Szczecin's no model for Brundisium, not even the way I saw it, glinting
granite and fine brick, on that last ever implausibly sun-drenched wartime
holiday with cousins Jiri and Vera, certainly not now, heaven knows, after

the bombing, the bulldozers and thirty years of architecture by committee and construction by sozzled Stakhanovites (how many of them my erstwhile schoolmates?).

In a gust of anger, Tomec pushed and pulled the towel between his legs, across his back, into the dip between his shoulder blades where drops of water must be chased down and crushed like ants. He then uncovered and lightly dabbed his salmon-pink and irritated glans, absent-mindedly now, distractedly, thinking again of Sarah. Why do I keep thinking of her? I'm not going to lose my peace of mind over a, a . . . a what exactly? A who?

His foreskin had felt sore when he had soaped it just now. It was a discomfort he had long forgotten. Would Sarah be sore too? She might be. She was tight and dry this morning. Yet it wasn't as if she hadn't been eager. Odd that, the way sometimes a woman can be wet and not excited at all and then dry but longing for it, clutching at herself. Besides, the way she climbed over me this morning in her rush to get it inside her: I was exhausted and could have gone straight to sleep. Funny that I couldn't close my eyes afterward, even though I had come like a howitzer. Sometimes it happens that way. And now when she let herself in and I was pacing up and down between my easels repeating phrases from Broch and she undressed me as I paced, then climbed onto a stool and pushed my head roughly between her legs, yanking her knickers to one side, leading me like a horse by the halter, guiding me by the scruff of the neck. And, lord, how I drank. Yes, surely she must be sore there too.

He thought of that day (a week ago already?) when, as he came to bed at dawn, treading lightly to avoid waking her, he had lifted the blanket and sheet to uncover her sex and then had stared at the light gingery hair, the moist protruding lips and had realized, frightened to identify an emotion long interred, that he loved her. Loved her, Heaven help him.

Her skin had tautened with gooseflesh, turning in hue from skimmed to full-fat milk, its tiny red bristles standing erect, and she had turned restlessly, her mouth moving, holding forth no doubt in her dreams, sounding off about poets and music, he supposed. He replaced the bedclothes, slipping into bed alongside her, calm for once, content. As he turned to embrace her, she had grunted and thrown her back at him and he had lain there watching her shoulders rise and fall, rise and fall, till his eyes had closed.

He wanted to see her vulva again soon, capture its colour and form.

Would she ever let him look at her so closely when awake? Not to make love in any way, not at all, just to see. Not even to draw, or to paint. To see for the merest sake of seeing.

Yet of course he would paint her, he must, from memory if need be. He girdled his waist with a fraying towel, stepped, urgently now, into a pair of plastic sandals and clip-clopped down the corridor, picturing her, infallibly he was certain, sleeping soundly still, breathing deep and hard, in another country, smiling as if blessed, her hectic cheeks glowing still from their recent love-making that evening. He halted on the threshold to savour the sight.

And there she was, instead, sitting bolt upright and frowning like a philosopher, her expensive school mistressy glasses (a gift from Daddy) balancing on the tip of her nose, their horn-rims ridiculously evocative of the 1940s she was lucky never to have known. From the gramophone, the same caterwauling (precisely what in the devil's name did she have against side two?), squeaking and jibbering its way to another rag-tearing crescendo, only to begin yet again. *Einziger, ewiger . . .*

Everlasting, all right. And she sits there flicking through a book, scribbling observations in the margins, hasn't registered *my* entrance, takes no notice of *me*. Stop it now Tomec. You're being childish. You're in love.

These two, Tomec and Sarah: one might suppose they had never been born like the rest of us covered in blood and primed to scream as they fisted their way through their mothers' vaginas, kicking out into cold neon glare, grasped by gloves and held out head-over-arse in the air; you would think they had never since sat on a toilet and clenched their teeth and groaned.

Just look how her white, white hand darts, how her pink, pink fingers flash! You're in love. You're being childish. You're in love. That rosy pink of the new born, that pink of her lips, her labia, her nipples, the pink of her innards, of everyone's innards. I want her eyes to look up at me, green-grey and mischievous. Up! I'm willing you! Look up! Now! Is this love, damn it? Am I smitten? Then where's the pain? Shouldn't it hurt? Smite me! Smite me!

It is as if I weren't here. How long must I wait? How long can it last?

6. Rachid, Salvatore, Philippe, Marcel.

Rachid, taking care not to scratch his drowsy daughter with his fine stubble, kissed her lightly on the cheek and handed her back into the arms of his wife, Malika, who patted the baby under her nappied behind. Starting to rock, Malika nodded at Rachid by way of 'good night and go now!' With her free hand, she passed him his jacket, in the breast pocket of which she had secreted a message. Then she smiled.

Rachid pulled on his jacket and stared back at his wife, glimpsing behind her on the wall an aerial photograph of her village, complete with distant hazy foothills. Malika was looking straight at him, swaying and, yes, still smiling. Rachid's chest tightened and he felt the pressure behind his eyes and the slight stinging at their corners that warn of tears.

Rachid faced into his wife's smile, his features impassive but his eyes full. Perhaps he was forgiven. Her smile must count for something. It was so long since he had seen it. He would tell Mehdi about it. Mehdi would be pleased for him.

The baby girl, Fatima, made a gruff gurgling sound and then appeared to laugh. A thread of spittle formed at the corners of her mouth. An imprint of the baby's cheek lingered cool and soft on Rachid's lips. His wife cocked her head to one side and murmured, You'll be late. It sounded more like an apology than a warning.

Rachid stifled the urge to kiss her: the moment had not yet come. If he tried to kiss her now she would turn her lips away at the last moment and he would see her frown slowly form. She was in control now. He could only acquiesce. He loved her. He loved his wife, his little girl, and he loved Mehdi. After all, you can love a dead person.

As he closed the front door behind him, Rachid's eyes cleared, the tension of home draining from his face, ageing it ten years in as many seconds. He descended the three steps onto the shadowy pavement, swinging to the right on hips grown stiff from routine. The Moroccan who lived upstairs was arriving home from his hospital job, glancing warily to left and right, and hauling keys on a chain from a deep trouser pocket. Rachid executed a perfunctory nod, after which his face collapsed back into its vacant street expression as he walked off grazing the house walls. Yellow buses with loud adverts swished past: washing machines, thermal underwear, a new magazine for the modern woman, low fat yoghurt – the healthy choice.

Walking past the North African grocers, Rachid spotted fresh dates and made a mental note: a possible treat for Malika, who adored dates. Tomorrow morning he would check on the price on his way to the restaurant. They might eat them in the evening before he left for the factory or in bed the following morning while Fatima slept on. Rachid looked ahead and thought of Mehdi, then whispered deep in his throat, Your mother loves dates. Did you ever know that? Mehdi wouldn't be quite five now, but I shall tell him everything, always, as if he were still here at my side.

Dim lamps strung overhead illuminated the street at irregular intervals. Rachid looked fragile in his greying suit. In the gloom between two lamps, he would fade to insignificance then, ghostly, re-emerge, regaining some brief definition as he moved into the cone of the next lamp.

He walked with a stoop, each pace the same length as the one before except where corner, kerb, litter or excrement forced him to vary his step. His feet neither dragged along nor rose much above the pavement's surface. There was no unnecessary expenditure of energy, no hint of vain athleticism. His left hand was sunk deep in his left trouser pocket, his right arm hung like an ill-fitting prosthesis by his right side, a plastic bag hooked over two bony fingers, the nails of which bore evidence of punctilious cleaning and clipping. His eyes roamed neither left nor right but fixed the shadowy terrain before him. His shoulders were tensed and curved. His walk was that of a man employed to walk, paid by the mile or paid by the hour, a sandwich-board man plying his strip or a prison guard grimly circling. When the money ran out, he would stop walking in mid-stride.

The yellow lamplight set off the parchment pallor of Rachid's cheeks and forehead and the contrasting black lustre of the thinning hair that he wore severely parted on one side. His lips were slightly ajar as if in expectation or excitement. With the shock of Malika's smile still warm in his memory, he cursed the night shift. It was the turmoil and upset of working nights that spoiled everything between them, he told himself. That, and the child's death.

At home, Malika would be getting Fatima ready for bed. Fatima's teeth would have to be brushed, stories would be read aloud, one in French, one in proper Arabic – not the patois they spoke between themselves – and blankets would be straightened, tucked and patted. On Saturday and Sunday evenings Rachid eagerly assumed these duties and then sat up late into the night reminiscing first with his wife and then on his own. If friends came round, the meal would end with the sharing of holiday photos of family and friends from back home, *au bled*. Rachid would then tune his oud and play and sing, taking care not to disturb the neighbours. Fatima's cot would be brought into the kitchen-diner so that she could fall asleep in the midst of the huddled company. That is the way it had always been, even after Mehdi's death.

Ahead of Rachid lay the factory. In the plastics section, the evening shift was ending and most of the workers would be hanging around the clock waiting for the hands to touch 9.25. A few stragglers, always the same ones, would still be at their machines, filling a hopper or taping up, coding and initialling a box of finished product.

Rachid crossed the road and turned the corner into a brighter and busier street. People hurried past him, going from bar to bar or from bar to home. Tyres screeched and gears crashed. Shutter-blinds were whooshed down, rubbish bags dumped on the pavement, goodnights were called. In the distance, a moped was revving.

Rachid began, as every night, to count. It was his secret therapy. His lips did not move: the figures stayed in his throat. He calculated the number of hours he would work that month and multiplied this figure by his hourly rate of pay. He added the night-shift bonuses, made various deductions for tax and pensions, insurance schemes and union dues, arriving at last at the amount of money he should find in his pay packet at the start of the following month. To this sum he added the more variable quantity that he could hope to make from his afternoon waitering job – mostly a matter of tips, the generosity of which he deliberately underestimated, thereby priming the probability of a pleasant surprise. Next, he subtracted rent, local taxes, utilities bills, housekeeping, cigarettes, and the small remittance he sent to family in Oran. The final figure was the amount he could put into his savings account. At this juncture Rachid usually felt relaxed and almost reconciled to the empty night that lay ahead. But today, remembering the phone call that he had received from Malika's cousin Karim, he shook his head. To hell with family, he murmured, then bit his bottom lip harder than intended and winced: Karim was doing him a favour.

Rachid had completed his accountancy therapy on time, despite the menacing and unquantifiable item 'gift to Karim?' appended to the outgoings column, just before the brick wall on his left gave way to a tall cast-iron double-leaved gate, containing a small cast-iron single-leaved door through which he stepped, to find himself, as every night, engulfed by the ill-lit factory compound.

The last sound of the outside world that Rachid was to hear that night issued unexpectedly from the little cafe opposite the gates: Hollywood gunshots. He turned and saw across the road Marcel's broad back disappearing into the cafe, the glass door closing behind him, re-muting the gunshots. All around him in the city, people lounged in their flats as they witnessed the evening western from their sofas or kitchen tables. A French-mouthing John Wayne was galloping into action, a-cussing and a-shooting. It was plain to see that the Indians possessed bloodthirsty intentions but no future. Without raising his eyes, Rachid nodded and made out the gate-man's grudging 'B'soir.'

Rachid skirted the lodge and veered left onto a strip of newly laid tarmac. Against the wall separating the factory compound from the street there stood heaps of silvery metal hoops and bulging white sacks stacked neatly on pallets. Further off were parked five apricot-coloured forklift trucks and beyond them a crooked tower of pallets as tall as Rachid. Behind him now and to the other side of the main gate was a line of single-floor buildings serving as offices, girly calendars visible in uncurtained rooms, and, beyond them, racks and sheds for a tangle of mopeds and bikes. At the back of the yard, alongside the outer wall, rose a high plinth supporting a grim statue bearing at its base the legend: André Boucan, 1834–1901. Straight before Rachid lay the workers' entrance to the main factory building: like a billiard ball shot expertly at its home pocket, he couldn't miss. A distant rumble of machinery reached him as the street noise faded.

Had Rachid tilted his head right back he might have seen the old clock at the top of the factory facade showing nine-sixteen. But Rachid, a paragon of punctuality, did not need to check the time. Besides, being a short man with a neck susceptible to stiffness, he liked to save any looking upward for occasions on which it was indispensable. Hanging his head, therefore, and eyeing the ground, Rachid pulled open the door to the factory and vanished inside.

Crossing the factory yard at his usual slope-haunched gait, Philippe heard off to his right the raised voice of Salvatore: did he mind if he walked with him? Philippe turned and saw the Sicilian striding toward him from the urinals, his attaché case already trapped like any old beat-up hold-all between left elbow and ribs. Philippe was sorry to lose these last moments of relative quiet, but it would be rude not to wait for the Sicilian. As Philippe inhaled, he clicked his tongue against his soft palate, then closed his mouth and let his cheeks balloon. He noted the acrid stench of the urinals: a balance of piss and disinfectant. He pulled hard on his cigarette and waited patiently, giving the blue plastic bag that was hanging from the middle finger of his left hand an experimental swing. A smile flickered in his face.

Catching up with Philippe, Salvatore finished reordering his clothes then extended his right arm like an unladen gantry. Philippe submitted his own soft, small hand to the Sicilian's muscular grip. All right? Philippe muttered.

Philippe pulled open the heavy iron door and pushed his way through a curtain of hanging scratched-plastic flaps that must once have been transparent. Salvatore was at his heels. As the hanging flaps fell back under their own weight, they sounded like a squall of sleet against a windowpane. The spring-closing iron door performed its dull thud.

Philippe unstuck the cigarette end dangling from his lower lip and ground it beneath the sole of his left shoe. He was working out the practicalities of a prank he had in mind to play on Jacques at some point during the night. He thought up something different most nights. As did Jacques.

The two workers proceeded at Philippe's sauntering pace through the huge metallurgy workshop. Salvatore stared at the ground while his eyebrows knitted and relaxed restlessly, like furry young caterpillars arching their backs. He was searching for a way to broach the subject. Philippe sank his free right hand deep into his trouser pocket, while his left hand rested inside the pocket opening, his blue plastic bag suspended from a finger and brushing his thigh. With his forearms he hugged his gut. It was nice that Salvatore was saying nothing: almost as good as being alone.

The smell of urinals and the sounds of the town had given way to the milder pong of industrial grease and the rising rumble of the plastics section. Around the two men slumbered a vast five-cornered workshop ill lit from roof windows and two bare lightbulbs, one at the far end, the other to the left in the direction in which they were walking. The many workbenches, arranged in rows, were cluttered with tools, papers and oily rags. Smudged calendars were pinned to bench ends next to pictures of topless girls and soccer elevens: St Etienne, Juventus, Porto, Annaba, Marseille.

It's about the strike plans, Salvatore began. I'm calling a meeting for 11.15 tonight.

Philippe looked at him blankly.

I was at the section meeting earlier, Salvatore informed him, and it seems that if they don't give us four percent, there's going to be action, probably half an hour a night, to start with. Maximum disruption for them, with presses closed down for a total of at least three hours out of every twenty-four; minimum losses for us.

Philippe looked past Salvatore and said, So? Why tell me about it? Philippe's head was hurting from the numbers. He had never had a head for numbers, the teachers had all agreed, and his parents had been disappointed. In those days, bad at maths meant stupid. Danielle was the one for numbers: she had that in common with Odile. Odile was a whiz with numbers and so managed their household accounts. Another thing Philippe was going to have to learn.

Working his caterpillar eyebrows hard, Salvatore now launched into an explanation: The day-shift steward says that the percentages, given the basic rate, differentials, inflation . . .

Philippe glanced at the luminous hands on his wristwatch and walked faster, cutting off the Sicilian in mid flow: Look, what can I tell you? What do you need to hear from me?

Then, without waiting for an answer, Philippe said, I'll strike. I've never scabbed in my life and I never would, not even now when it's about nothing more than numbers and percentages and careers in the union. But you'll have a struggle persuading the temps to down tools, and without them we'll never hurt Boucan, so anything we get will be marginal, a pittance. As things stand, you can't expect the temps to join any strike. You ought to know the score. They work for their agencies, answer to them not to the factory. They've got no kind of protection. The union will never come out for them. Why would it? The temps earn better than we do and in return they don't strike. That's the deal.

Philippe drew a cigarette from his coat pocket and paused to light it.

Salvatore smiled, showing a clean row of white teeth. Philippe was a mystery. A lot of the time he seemed like a drunk, a failure, a bum, knocking back the liquor before, after and even during work. Never saw him worse than tipsy though. Which makes him an alcoholic, doesn't it? Then, mostly you couldn't get him to say more than two words together but when you did he came right out and made a whole speech. Yet however much he said you never knew what he thought of anything or anyone. It was as though he put everything he said between inverted commas, like he was quoting somebody, perhaps somebody a bit like himself. And that smile! Sardonic, that was it. French were good at sardonic, Italians non-starters. Why was that? But if

Philippe would strike, they all would. Except the temps, of course. He was right about that.

Salvatore wanted to say thank you but that would have been out of place and anyway Philippe had turned his back and was leaning over the water fountain on the left of the curtain of plastic flaps that divided them from the plastics section. The interview was clearly over. Salvatore muttered, Well, see you later. Then he pushed through the flaps and squinted upward into the brilliant neon lighting of the plastics section.

Philippe gulped and gulped, something had made him thirsty, or did deep drafts of bubbly cold water act as an emollient or antidote to Salvatore? He raised his head and wiped his mouth. Then he straightened up and stepped through the flaps and into the din and glare. He headed for the clocking-on machine, smiling in anticipation of the prank he was preparing for Jacques and shaking the hands that various afternoon-shift workers thrust in his direction. He wondered if they grinned at everyone the way they grinned at him. Addressing them all, he said, You lucky people, on your way home to your dinners and doting spouses. He had a way of saying things that made people laugh and feel warm. They knew he was right or that, if he wasn't, he surely ought to have been.

Salvatore was standing at the control cabinet of machine number fourteen. Luigi was showing him one of the pieces machine fourteen had just produced, holding it at different angles, stammering something in his ear. The Sicilian, however, was studying Philippe at the clock-machine. The Marseillais was completely encircled, by men and women equally, young as well as old; he was busily telling them something – God knows what! – all of them leaning into his fat little face, listening and grinning like morons. Holding right-royal court. How did he do it? What did he have? Whatever it is, how come I never get to see it? How come he never shows it to me?

Philippe finished shaking hands and made his way to his machines one and two.

Marcel blinked up into the neon lights of the plastics section. His nose puckered and his lips pouted as he advanced into the group of afternoon-shift workers gathered around the clock-machine. They made way for him, falling away before the advancing wafts of aftershave he had recently applied. He was young, lissom, broad-shouldered, a little overweight but still wholesome-looking in the kindly half-light of the factory. Aware of his reputation, some of the afternoon-shift women backed away but he ignored them. Two of the younger ones, however, gamely positioned themselves slap in the path that he was bound to take after clocking on. His hair was well cut and sleekly combed and his lime-green shirt had been ironed stiff. He held his long cigarette with assurance and removed his card from the rack with a leisurely flicking gesture and punched it in the clocking-on machine. He replaced his card in the rack while glancing around to check there was no supervisor anywhere near. Then, in the full gaze of several afternoon-shift workers, he drew a second card from the rack and punched that in the machine too. He proceeded to shake hands with all the workers, giving the same quick smile to each of them in turn: to the gormless fake-blonde with the green eyes, to that Italian Gellini, who lived round the corner from his cousin, and to the faggotty northerner with his over-insistent slow moist squeeze.

On his way out of the group, Marcel shook the hands of the two young women who had placed themselves in his path. His eyes slid over them and he calibrated their appeal with the objectivity of a farmer assessing livestock. They were both decidedly fuckable, he thought. One of them was half-opening her trap and kind of jiggering about, her tongue working over those nice little white teeth of hers. Thinking she perhaps had something to say, Marcel lingered. She was short and plump and eager and he noticed that, owing to the din of the injection presses, he had to stoop right down into her pretty face to catch what she was saying. I know your sister, she repeated. Marcel straightened up and smiled and opened his eyes shock-horror wide and replied, If you know my sister, with the mouth she's got on her, then you know me. And if you're talking to me, knowing what you know about me, then obviously you're the kind of girls I should like to get to know better. He licked his lips and winked. Both the girls laughed and the taller, skinnier, hairier one who had not spoken blushed. What do you girls do at weekends? Or on your long free mornings, for that matter? Maybe we should meet up, just the three of us, eh? I like a threesome, said Marcel, moving off before they or he would have to say something more, leaving the question hanging, making it up to them to place themselves in his path again, knowing that sooner or later they would, one or both of them or maybe one of them with another friend, and then they'd all know what it meant.

Marcel walked under the office, then down the central aisle that separated the two lines of machines. He had to walk past the ends of Philippe's machines en route to his own. Philippe had just hung his coat on a peg behind the control cabinet and seemed to be looking around for something or someone. Marcel caught his attention and reached out a hand to shake and they smiled at each other a friendly everyday smile. Marcel gestured toward the girls at the clocking-on machine and said, You have to make girls like that work for it, wait for it, so they begin really to long for it, even before they know quite what 'it' will turn out to be. Otherwise, they have no respect. Besides, they have to think they're at least partly in control. That's the trick of it. Nowadays, with women steadily gaining the upper hand, you have to allow them to imagine they're taking the first fated step, but at the same time they have to know they won't be turned down. It's a delicate manoeuvre but once you've cracked it, a whole world of fresh young pussy opens up to you. And when I say 'opens up . . .'

Philippe had no idea what Marcel was talking about, imagining the entire speech was a casual comment on life in general and on women in particular. That wouldn't surprise Philippe. Hey, but aren't you getting married next month? Philippe thought to ask. Marcel walked off smiling. He had to have a couple of last flings. If he was going to settle down into a state of marital everlasting bliss, he deserved that at least.

Marcel passed down the aisle to his machines, nibbling away at his lips. They're hot those two. Hot enough to need nothing but the slightest encouragement. I'll not even notice they're there for the next couple of nights, make like I don't even see them, and then reel me in a date on Friday. It's a mathematical certainty. This time next week I'll have laid one of them at least if not both end to end, it's a blinding cinch. The shy hairy one with the long lashes first. Christ, she can't wait for it. She's got cunt written all over her. Give her a couple of years and she won't be able to find a cock big enough. That's the way they are those shy-yet-forward types. And taking her first will make the other one even keener. Whereas the other way round . . .

Marcel sat down at one of his machines and started peeling off his soft leather boots. They had cost him a night's pay and they made him feel great, hugging him like a tight young twat. Hell, feet were important, weren't they? Women always looked at your feet – often straight after your face and arse and long before glancing at your crotch. In fact, in his experience, it was mostly other men who looked at your crotch. Probably poofs but, of course, not necessarily. Things were more complicated than that: they might just be measuring up the competition. He placed his boots in a plastic bag that he extracted from his shoulder bag and at the same time removed a pair of trainers. These trainers aren't bad either, he thought: clean, white and sharp, sending a plain message that no woman could mistake.

Slowly and methodically, Marcel put on the trainers and did up the laces, pulling the first lace through his fingers caressingly, gathering the ends up, making the bow, tugging tight, tight. He half-closed his eyes and pictured the first girl, the hairy one, falling backward onto a bed, giggling as her knickers were yanked down and then coyly trying to cross her legs, suddenly pointlessly unsure, when it was far too late for second thoughts. Fuck me! Marcel whispered to himself, feeling his groin swell and that strange slight tickling somewhere up his arse that he liked so well. He turned his attention to his second shoe. He wiped his brow and smoothed down the front of his trousers, settling his dick with the heel of his hand.

7. Gérard, Claude, Cécile, Raymond, Françoise, Jorge.

Gérard Boucan, factory owner, faithless husband, and bewildered father to one wayward son, preferred to eat his evening meal at home, on his own, late. The Portuguese maid would leave him a thick pork chop with flageolet beans or a side of roast fowl with petits pois – something at once simple and substantial. And there would be no one to frown at his manners or find fault with his conversation. He didn't want people blushing on his behalf. Sometimes, however, he had no choice but to attend a dinner party – with his wife in tow. He thought of it as the tribute that he had to pay in order to live in society.

Poire Belle Hélène – Gérard's favourite dessert – was being served. How clever of you to remember, Claude remarked to Cécile, who smiled indulgently, her eyes closing gently as if feigning fatigue. Damn it, their servants probably keep a note of such matters, Claude thought. I must look a complete fool. Her chin trembled and receded and she went an unfashionable shade of pink, the pink of economy-pack raspberry yoghurt. She looked a complete fool.

The dessert was quite, quite perfect. The chocolate was piping hot, dark and bitter; the Chantilly had been used sparingly, a lofty rebuke to its customary, popular and frankly vulgar mode of deployment; as for the vanilla ice cream, it was of the classic best, free of any admixture, pure unto itself; while the pears, which had been plucked by Cook from Cécile's own orchard that very afternoon, were fresh, ripe, succulent and exquisitely aromatic. Claude sighing wistfully, There is such distinction in scent, is there not? Indeed there is, chimed Cécile.

Gérard ate like a hog, of course, as Claude knew without needing to check and as Raymond, Cécile and even young Françoise could hardly fail to observe. He larded the chocolate all around his moustachioed mouth – more a sewer than a mouth – and, with the practised precision of a pratfalling clown, landed a dollop of Chantilly and ice cream squarely on his left lapel; whereupon, he conscripted the stubby middle finger of his stubby right hand to transfer the mucky mess straight to his mouth – nay, what am I saying? – sewer.

Cécile smiled on Claude with faux-sisterly tolerance, while Claude fidgeted with her napkin. Raymond, who for dessert never partook of anything heavier than fresh fruit, looked briefly heavenward. This performance has gone on quite long enough, he thought. But Françoise, bless her sweet youthfulness, was continuing to jabber, expounding the standard revolutionary-adolescent drivel. When (on earth!) was it that children had seized power? Why (in heaven's name!) had it happened? How (for pity's sake!) had it ever caught him napping? What (for the love of France!) could be done about it? If, at Françoise's age, he had ever exhibited the presumption to express a contrary political or social opinion at his parents' dining-table – in front of their guests too! – well, he never would have dared, would he? Of course, when Raymond was sixteen, in (let me think) 1942, France was . . . – well, let's put it like this, and no stronger – the stakes were higher then. Best not to dwell; comparisons with nowadays most unhelpful; different era, thank the sweet lord. But at least we had discipline, respect, some notion of order.

In the darkly appointed dining room – all plush upholstery, onyx eggs and walnut cabinets – these five people sat around an oval oak table which, though now much depleted, still groaned with platters and dishes and sauce-boats, while the chunky ancient silver tableware, sullied now at its business ends, still sparkled. Raymond Chartier, a stoopingly tall, fine-featured man in his early fifties, was sustaining a steady all-purpose smile, while his thoughts roamed as free as a well-mounted French bourgeois on his annual African safari.

To his right sat Gérard Boucan, hereditary owner and day-to-day general manager of Établissements Boucan, a large metals and plastics factory located close to the centre of Grandgobier, and one of the region's foremost employers. He was a barrel-bellied, worried-looking man, very nearly as broad-jowled and thick of hip as his wife Claude, who sat (but where else?) at his right hand, florid-faced and shaped to match the dribbling fruit she was now devouring with such grim efficiency and circumspection. To serve Poire Belle Hélène was, she perceived, a calculated act of condescension to their irretrievably plebeian tastes and, at once, a challenge, she suspected, an accelerated audit, a spot-test of their skill, sobriety and etiquette. Gérard may have fallen flat on his face – to speak barely figuratively – but I, I, shall triumph. She picked at her dessert with dreadful resolve.

To the right of Claude, on the edge of her seat with the excitement of her own discourse, perched Françoise, the loose-limbed tousle-haired teenage daughter of Raymond and Cécile. She had keen green eyes and a fine high forehead only slightly blemished by the waves of puberty now breaking upon her. Her fingers – long and slender, as if designed to play a little afternoon Satie – dived and swooped in an orgy of Latin gesturing that her parents had always regarded with puzzlement: whose side of the family could that come from? She was holding forth intrepidly on the subject of Cambodia, critiquing a book she had been reading by one Prince Sihanouk. Her parents listened patiently, their guests with seeming politeness, though in truth Gérard's eyes were blank, mackerel-dark and glazed, his thoughts elsewhere. Claude had a cousin who had fought in Indochina and stated that Communism had to be stopped somewhere, somehow, or it might conquer the world, and then where would we be? Raymond smiled tolerantly at his daughter, shook his head or gently demurred: he had heard it all before, one must suppose. Cécile alone undertook to question and contradict her daughter, and to this Françoise responded by knitting her brow, shaking her head, and beginning again at the beginning, straining to reduce the argument to a level of simplicity that grown-ups could not fail to grasp. She pursed her lips and took a breath. As for what's happening in Laos . . .

To the right of this frisking foal (and to the left of Raymond – since we have now come full circle) sat the placid mare, her mother, Cécile, a woman whom Françoise, should she prove as lucky in her life as in her birth, might in the fullness of some thirty years come to resemble, with strong jawline and handsome cheekbones, the erect yet unforced posture of the trained dancer, a long white neck, a straight nose, a face that struck her every interlocutor as both kind and intelligent, and that was adorned with a hint of laugh lines fanning out from hazel eyes, the bright twinkling of which suggested that their owner was capable, should the mood take her, of both fun and mischief. She was attired in a lemon-coloured dress of raw silk.

Gérard regretfully relinquished his spoon alongside his empty dessert schooner, while raising the back of his left hand to screen a burp. As Françoise enlarged upon the theme of France's imperial guilt, he glanced around the dining room. Its walls were hung with musty old oil paintings not at all to Gérard's taste, which was more susceptible to the charms of modern, figurative and merry subjects, boats or horses or flowers, that sort of thing. Such dynastic moonshine was meant to impress, no doubt, but was it not most morbidly gloomy? That bewhiskered old gent, for instance, glowering over Raymond's head, has to be some kind of ancestor: the resemblance with our host is too, too striking. Then all these landscapes – snowy peaks, babbling brooks, and all that bull – and the quaint views over the city of Grandgobier, executed – one need hardly enquire – from this very hillside. Gérard pictured a man with a shaggy beard standing by an easel, backed by an interminable Alpine vista, and intoning in a sonorous bass: All this I set before thee . . . Where the blazes did that come from? Gérard shook his head, and sought restoration in his wine glass. Some classic or other. Someone dead famous in any case.

Gérard stole a glance at Raymond: he could not but admire the air of fine breeding that his host wore so complacently, the evidence of easy superiority as he tilted his head back to survey an employee, servant, or indeed guest, or to reflect from the pinnacle of his accumulated wisdom (and physical stature!) on the issue of the day. Might he not perhaps have acquired this stance at least in part by dint of local geography? Gérard was tickled by this fledgling thought and determined to run it to ground. After all, Gérard now pondered, quite apart from Raymond's height – important though that must surely be – the fact was that he had been brought up from a mewling babe in this well-to-do hillside dormitory village, had pranced and gambolled as a schoolboy on its verdant slopes, and now possessed the ancestral (or at least parental and grand-parental) mansion; furthermore, his editor's office at the premises of the newspaper that he owned and ran was situated on the very top floor of one of the shiniest and tallest skyscrapers in Grandgobier, and accordingly commanded a peerless view over the toiling, grunting and sweating ants below. Myself included. (Not that I sweat quite as profusely as those I employ.) In short, for reasons of physique, geography and architecture, Raymond has spent his entire existence hoisted far above the fray, peering down his finely chiselled nose, a god on his soaring Olympus, surveying the affairs of common mortality over the occasional goblet of ambrosia. Never saw him break a sweat. Up here, there is always a gentle zephyr stirring, while down below in Grandgobier you could be roasted alive in the summer sun, asphyxiated in the winter smog, or slowly steamed in the ambient autumn humidity. In Raymond's office, of course, all air is filtered, scrubbed, cleansed, ionized, balanced, warmed, cooled, dehumidified, rehumidified and sympathetically aromatized before it is allowed anywhere near his skin, his quivering nostrils, or his lungs.

These reflections had not prevented Gérard from observing the altercation that had been developing between Raymond and his daughter Françoise consequent to the former's intervention on some remote geopolitical matter, nor from noticing that the two ladies had fallen silent and that all table talk had been reduced to a seething and a spluttering. Coming to an abrupt end, the father-daughter exchange had left the foal looking wounded and the mare mortified. The former had then pushed her unfinished dessert to one side and, making her well-brought-up excuses, had left the table in a bona fide teenage tiff. Attractive little thing, with that school-girl moue, Gérard noted. She was going out into the drive for a breath of fresh air, she declared with a hint of defiance. Raymond and Cécile smiled at their guests.

A troublesome age, Claude observed, cooperatively.

We are all a little wild when we are young, we all make mistakes, declared Cécile, who had never made any, never been anything but tame.

Raymond nodded vigorously and looked at Gérard, as if it were his turn to say something.

But all Gérard did was assent. No doubt, no doubt, he said, preoccupied. Claude, bless her, (what man could deserve such a wife?) covered for him, developing her original intuition and enumerating the difficulties that beset the adolescents of today and opining sagely that schools were crammed with frustrated soixante-huitards, teaching disrespect and Jean-Paul Sartre: it could hardly help matters. While the politics was borrowed from her husband, the psychology was a distillate of Françoise Dolto as percolated through women's magazines, though this didn't much matter. Raymond and Cécile purred and chirruped politely, and Cécile then asked after young Paul. Françoise had mentioned bumping into him one afternoon in town as he was issuing onto the street – a point upon which Cécile had interrogated her daughter and on which Françoise had categorically insisted – from the San Francisco Bar, and had reported that he appeared to be having a great time. Cécile imparted this information warily, knowing that no parent could rejoice that their children frequented the bar in question, infamous as it was for teenage drug-taking and promiscuity of the most luridly various species; similarly, Cécile was perfectly alive to the fact that 'having a great time' was not something that children of that age should ever be allowed to do unsupervised. Not one to gloat over the tribulations of other parents, Cécile merely wished to be helpful. Claude, however, replied evasively to Cécile's expression of concern, much to the approval of Gérard who, impervious to the latest theories on child development, teenage trauma and all that hocum, listened with one ear while his mind surrendered to the imperious pull of worries more pressing than those occasioned by his troubled son.

For Gérard was indeed a worried man. First, the graffiti business at the factory – somebody, as yet unidentified, had daubed 'Gérard Boucan, Collabo' alongside the dates 1942–44 on a wall in the metallurgy section – and then Cécile's innocuous-seeming comment about the mistakes of one's youth. What the hell could she know about it? Perhaps Raymond had said something. Perhaps there was a whispering campaign already. Perhaps he would be the last to hear of it. Since the graffiti had been discovered at 6.30 that morning, in a relatively busy workshop, and everybody had denied seeing the perpetrator, suspicion had fallen – perhaps too conveniently – on the night shift. It was possible that Gérard might hear something by the morning. The nightwatchman had been briefed and had received clear instructions to investigate. It could of course have been any one of them, any one of thirteen men. Well, he could rule out Jean Herbier and Mathieu Petit straight away: Gérard's father had intervened personally to secure the former his job and the latter, well, he was the frigging supervisor. If you can't trust a supervisor . . . As for the others it was anybody's guess. As dubious a bunch of misfits, ex-cons, foreigners, jailbirds, and Gypsies as one could hope to recruit on a dark night anywhere. Couldn't trust a single one of them. Couldn't even be certain the nightwatchman was on his side. Blasted Polack. It was on their account the war had started anyway: damn it, why shouldn't Germany have Poland? France and Britain between them owned half of Africa and much of Asia. Fair's fair. But it could be any or none of them. Someone on the morning shift could have done it, any one of hundreds. It wouldn't have been hard. After all, how long can it possibly take to spray-paint 'Gérard Boucan, Collabo, 1942–44?' A minute? Thirty seconds? If it was a morning-shift worker, it would have had to be one of the ones who clocked on earliest and that could be checked, he supposed. But, hell, even that could be faked. Somebody could arrive early, 'forget' to clock on, do the deed, then double back later. Tricky but feasible, Gérard reasoned – and worth an hour's lost wages to some troublemaker.

The women had started talking about the wonders of acupuncture and homeopathy and the latest, unmissable, holiday destinations (Goa, Kenya, Reykjavik), when Raymond, smothering a yawn, interrupted Gérard's ruminations with the suggestion that the two of them retire to the drawing room for coffee, cognac, cigar and some somewhat less feminine conversation – no offence intended to your good wife or mine. Oh, but offend away, Gérard muttered just audibly. I beg your pardon? Raymond said, surprised and amused. Damned hard day, Gérard said, with a complicit smirk.

Both men chuckled at this snatch of hypocritical self-censorship and rose to their feet. Gérard glanced back at the wives and noted Raymond's superiority confirmed in his choice of life-mate. How dumpy and squat Claude appeared alongside Cécile! And what a huge nose she had! Funny he hadn't noticed that when he'd married her. Her nose had seemed quite normal then. Perhaps it had been. In which case, it must have lengthened later – presumably through lying to him. The fact is, Gérard considered, that Claude and I are of the people and the Boucans, with their thin lips, pale skin, high brows, fine bones, are of another race altogether, another *class*, (beastly word!). Their men are less hairy, their women have smaller, higher, firmer breasts. They all, regardless of sex, have strong cheekbones and pointy chins, whereas we, again regardless of sex, have ears like fire bellows and the jaws of bloodhounds. It's a matter of breeding. One fleeting glance is enough to see that *our* grandparents slogged away their entire lives in every weather on some filthy field owned by *their* grandparents. It's blinding. Formally, of course, we're all equal now, all interchangeably bourgeois. But we're only ever accepted, not loved, and we know we're intruders.

A servant had brought the two men their coffees and cognacs and they now stood on the sumptuous Persian carpet, Gérard a whole head shorter than Raymond, casting his eyes up at him and endeavouring to appear, if not his equal, then at least his courtier rather than his lackey. Raymond was extemporizing on the theme of his column, which he would compose the following day. He observed Gérard's bloodshot eyes and wondered about the man's health: he didn't look great shakes. Raymond was intending, he confided, to devote that week's piece to a commentary upon recent American statements concerning the threat that Communist Parties posed to Western Europe's stability, and in particular the danger represented by the Italian Communist Party, currently so prominent in the politics of that benighted land. Kissinger had reportedly stated that people should be discouraged from voting Communist 'with all means available.' This statement of the obvious, Raymond said, has caused such an outcry and broohaha about American interference and so on and so forth, yet I have to say that I for one sympathize with their views. Raymond then added in a stage whisper, Though don't go telling my daughter! Gérard chortled at what passed for a witticism, then nodded sagely, then sipped his cognac, then glanced up at Raymond's pensive face, then braced himself for more. You see, Gérard, Raymond said, puffing on his Corona and lowering his voice as if preparing to divulge a rare intelligence, I remember all too clearly the dark years that this country lived through not so very long ago, and I recall only too vividly the grim reality of the Communist threat. I am, as a consequence, to be perfectly candid, sick and tired of hearing praise for the glorious Resistance. Questioning it has become an absurd taboo. It is time someone stood up and pointed out that Vichy was not all bad and that the Israelites and the Communists have been exaggerating matters as usual. Sorrow and pity are all well and good, but they don't put bread on anyone's table. Don't you agree?

Concealed in Raymond's rambling eloquence, was there not a subtle snare? Had Chartier perhaps heard about the graffiti? It was not impossible. Such people had ears everywhere. He was a notoriously smooth operator. The graffiti had caused quite a stir in the factory that morning; hundreds of workers had seen it before it could be removed: one of the usual troublemakers was sure to know some smart-arsed reporter on Raymond's rag. Was Raymond, with all this crap about the Resistance, inviting him to unburden his heart? How oblique, how foxy, could the man be? Gérard decided to confine himself to truisms and generalities. He didn't want to give his side of the story until he knew more about the forces ranged against him. Besides, Raymond had made it crystal clear where his sympathies lay. Couldn't agree more, Gérard grunted at last, as if the subject was of scant interest to him, and his words the merest afterthought.

The conversation drifted into the doldrums of city council matters until a servant approached with a message on a silver platter for Gérard. On opening the slip, Gérard performed a pantomime display of irritation and surprise, and made his excuses to Raymond. I'm afraid I have been called away on urgent business. My chauffeur is waiting for me in the drive. Raymond nodded and smiled, delighting in his guest's transparent mendacity. Recalling the Poire Belle Hélène, Gérard thanked Raymond for the sumptuous dinner and entreated his host, To extend my gratitude to your dear wife and to be so kind to order in due course a taxi for my own beloved spouse. It is still quite early and I see no need to disturb the ladies who, ha ha, are no doubt very busy putting the world to rights.

Raymond bowed and followed Gérard to the door. He was relieved to be rid of the man. He wanted to retire to his study and read a little Claudel. Host and guest shook hands on the threshold, then the latter crossed the deep gravel drive to the waiting car. On reaching it and pulling the door open, he turned to see Raymond still standing framed at the entrance to his mansion, shaking his head slowly, as if puzzled. Their eyes met briefly, as vitreous and unblinking as those of parrots, then Raymond turned and the door closed.

While waiting for his employer to respond to his meticulously timed 'urgent' message and to extricate himself from Monsieur Chartier's fabled hospitality, Jorge, Gérard's driver, had been enjoying a chat with Françoise, who had been pacing up and down her father's crunch-crunching drive, smoking an illicit cigarette, when Jorge had brought Gérard's Mercedes to a pleasingly percussive standstill. Glimpsing Jorge at the wheel of the car, Raymond's daughter had recognized him instantly, having seen him address a solidarity rally for Chile one week previously. Françoise had walked over to the car and rapped on the window, tap-a-tap-tap. Jorge had glanced at her and then leaned across and opened the passenger door. With the self-assurance that her youth, looks and class fully warranted, Françoise had climbed straight in and introduced herself. She reminded Jorge of someone. No doubt it would come to him.

Jorge had been listening to Keith Jarrett's *Belonging* on the cassette player, but now turned the sound down. Françoise was flirting with him, and he liked it. It cost him no effort to appear exotic and mysterious: the young woman's imagination did all the work. To her half-childish questions, he replied in his broadly accented French that he had no idea what had happened to his elder brother or younger sister, but that his parents had separated before the coup and one was in Panama and the other in Ecuador. The manner in which Jorge divulged this information was not discourteous, but neither did it invite further questioning. Accordingly, they switched from personal matters to geopolitics: Chile and France and American imperialism. Françoise quoted Brecht at one point; Jorge countered with Neruda. His eyes smiled and he recommended a writer she had never heard of before: José de Jesus Martinez, a poet and a dramatist, a mathematician and a soldier, a Nicaraguan by birth, a Panamanian by adoption – a profile that struck Françoise as deliciously strange. Jorge quoted from memory some lines from a love poem. 'Porque tú trabajas y tienes un salario / y miras las vitrinas y te gusta la música, / debemos hacer la revolución.' To read him, of course, you would have to learn Spanish, Jorge added, for I do not believe he has been translated yet.

Seeing the great house door open and Gérard appear on the threshold, Jorge assumed a regretful expression and held out his hand, Hasta la proxima, compañera, he said in a deep whisper. Françoise savoured the moment. Compañera. She knew what it meant. It meant a band of handsome guerrilleros trekking through rainforest with rifles bouncing against their chests and brave smiles on their faces. She looked back at him as she closed the car door behind her. He winked and briefly clenched his left fist in revolutionary salute. Françoise crossed Gérard's path in a reverie of romantic and political possibility, barely noticing the bloated, beastly bourgeois waddling toward her from the scandalous opulence of her father's mansion.

Jorge clicked the cassette out of the player, turned the key in the ignition and pushed the passenger door back open for Gérard who dropped into the broad seat like an overweight labrador into its fireside basket. Get me out of here, Gérard rasped. Jorge swung the saloon down the looping drive and out onto the road. Where are we headed? he asked. Just drive, Gérard replied softly, stubbing out the half-smoked cigar that Raymond had given him and clearing his throat. He lowered his window, farted less silently than he had intended, glanced at the impassive face of his driver, loosened his belt and tie, and asked Jorge if he could spare him a cigarette.

Sure, boss, the Chilean replied, you still giving up?

What does it look like?

Yeah, me too.

There was a lull already.

So, tell me, what was the teenage Pasionaria up to? Gérard asked. Trying to terrify her family by pulling herself a Latin Marxist twice her age?

Jorge opened the window a crack, slipping nicely into his comfort role.

Actually, boss, we were discussing revolutionary tactics. How best to murder factory owners in their beds, rape their maiden aunts and sodomize their cocker spaniels, that sort of thing. The stuff we Commies get up to on a dull day.

Gérard laughed a hollow laugh and pulled hard on Jorge's cheap, untipped cigarette, savouring its dungy stench. I'm totally surrounded by your lot right now. You're every-frigging-where. In the papers, on TV and radio, at the plant, even among office-workers who you'd think would have more sense. Can't even get a driver who isn't a pinko.

Pinko? Don't insult me, boss. I'm deepest scarlet, the genuine article. Jorge fixed the road ahead with a steely gaze. But I'm a good driver. And I'm personally loyal. You know that. Jorge was cueing a call-and-response routine, and smiling in anticipation.

Right, Gérard said. I know exactly how far I can trust you . . . to the centimetre.

And I know exactly how much you pay me . . . to the centime.

Yeah, yeah, Gérard said, suddenly irritated by this piece of banter.

Jorge gazed steadily at the road ahead, which glistened with slow rain. Something was bugging his boss this evening, something out of the ordinary. Normally he could read him like a book – the kind of book that doesn't hold a lot of surprises, a guidebook to your home town, say, or a phone book containing nothing but your friends' addresses – but right now it was obvious the man was in a sulk, looking for a quarrel maybe. What the hell, bring it on, Jorge concluded. Nobody ever paid me enough to make me drop my side of an argument.

So I get the loyalty I pay for – is that it? Gérard began.

That's right. This side of the revolution, I play by the rules of your world: to each according to his cash. If you aren't happy with it, try paying me less and see the difference it makes. Or, alternatively, more.

What would I get if I paid you more? Gérard asked, sounding like he wasn't joking.

Jorge wondered what his boss had in mind. Capitalists were weird fuckers at the best of times but there was definitely something strange going on in this man's cabeza this evening. He buys my time, my driving skills. What the hell else does he imagine is for hire? He glanced at Gérard's fat insinuating face.

It depends what you're talking about, Jorge said.

Gérard shrugged and looked out of his side window. Maybe he didn't yet know what he was talking about. It was raining again and all the lights were blurred. He just felt that Jorge could be useful to him. Whatever the colour of his politics, he was a subtle man and he had contacts. He had a way of getting you to talk. Disarming, that was it.

How come you need so much loyalty all of a sudden? Jorge was now asking. Most of us make do with what we get for free from those we love. What have you been doing that's so wicked you want to rush out and buy yourself extra?

On a normal evening, with Gérard in his normal mood, this would have been enough to ease him back into his customary easy joshing behaviour, or possibly elicit a gentle 'go-screw-yourself.' Tonight, by contrast, Monsieur Boucan was engrossed in his thoughts. In a last-ditch attempt to get a reaction, Jorge started softly whistling the tune of 'Comandante Che Guevara,' but even this fell flat. Gérard did of course register the cloying earnestness – or, better, Ernesto-ness – of the dirge-cum-ditty, reminiscent of the Soviet national anthem he unfailingly heard every time he watched athletics on TV.

For the last ten minutes now, they had been winding down the hillside into the city of Grandgobier, duller and duller, flatter and flatter, more and more cars, bikes, people, mess, litter, warmth, and humanity – of the long-suffering toiling and tedious variety.

So where do you want me to drive you tonight, boss? Jorge asked at last, adding the 'boss' appellative as an afterthought, merely to remind Gérard of their relative positions, and the material nature of their relationship.

I don't know, I really don't know, Gérard replied as gloomily as if Jorge had posed him a moral dilemma. Then, without warning, turning to stare at him: Did you hear about the graffiti?

What graffiti?

So you didn't?

I guess not.

The graffiti at the plant. You sure you heard nothing?

Nope. Wasn't on the 20.00 news.

Gérard didn't laugh at that.

Fair enough, Jorge thought, it wasn't funny. Whatever it is, I'm not going to drag it out of him. If he wants to tell me what's eating him, he will. Psychotherapy costs a lot more than he's paying me.

Do you just want me to drive around?

Sure. Anywhere.

Jorge didn't mind silence, never had. In fact it was one of the things he liked about Europe. After the chaos of those last months in Chile, and his brief stay in Argentina, a period of silence was more than welcome. He wondered whether he'd ever get reaccustomed to the constant chatter, noise, and clatter back home. If, that is, he was ever able to go back. But maybe home would change too, just like he was changing. Maybe the whole country would get a taste for silence, when the screaming stopped. Maybe silence would be brought back by the exiles returning from Northern Europe, the United States, Britain, Canada, Japan: cultures where outrage or ecstasy could sometimes find sufficient expression in the raising of an eyebrow.

Silence made a nice change. Gérard was usually non-stop talk, a flow of chat about the stuff he watched on TV, the sex he had with Gisèle (his regular call girl), and the sex he no longer had with his wife but still sometimes dreamed about; the spinelessness of Giscard d'Estaing, Raymond Barre, and everybody else involved in national politics; the depressed state of the European car industry; his difficulties hiring halfway competent staff; and – when all else failed – the evils of immigration and the scourge of Communism.

Jorge had started by hating his employer, but he had never had much of a talent for hatred, really had no feel for it, hadn't been brought up to it, so the hatred had gradually turned to distaste, and the distaste to disapproval, the disapproval to indifference and finally the indifference to something close to pity. Lately, if he thought about Gérard at all, he felt sorry for the man. Fact is, he's wretched, doesn't have any fun, can't enjoy his money, has stopped fancying his wife, doesn't love his mistress, and seems worried about his son for some reason he won't go into. And now something to do with graffiti. What the hell is that about? Jorge, however, had troubles of his own. Someone had stolen his country. And Felicia, his girlfriend, was in Bolivia. Probably. He decided to forget about his boss and just drive.

It had stopped raining. People were stumbling out of cinemas, adjusting their faces to the shock of the grainy non-celluloid world, and dribbling into bars. Jorge spotted a Venezuelan friend, Antonio, with a French woman. He had seen him with her a couple of times before. She was laughing a lot and Antonio was looking pleased with himself, like he'd just told a joke, which he probably had. Antonio knew lots of jokes, he collected them especially for his girlfriends, and his French was good enough to deliver them with aplomb. He had timing. He had once told Jorge that if you could just get a girl to laugh, the other thing was a doddle.

It's my son, Gérard said with a sigh, as if Jorge had been begging him for the last few minutes to tell him what the matter was.

So what's wrong with the kid?'

I think he's bent.

Like crooked? Has he been stealing?

No, really bent. A fag. Queer, right? A shirt-lifter. A bum boy. An invert. You get what I'm saying?

The general drift. You think he's homosexual.

I'm pretty sure of it. My wife thinks so too, and she has a sense for these things, the way women do. He's sixteen, has never had a girlfriend. He acts like one, walks like a gazelle, wears flowery shirts and beads, do you know what I mean? It's probably been obvious to anyone else for years. We'll be the last to know. It's not something you expect of your own child, is it?

It wasn't a question that Jorge felt qualified to address.

Well, I've seen him a few times and it's not obvious to me. But, say he's homosexual. Is that so bad?

Bad? What are you talking about? It's fucking terrible.

Right, Jorge said. What was I thinking? Of course. But however disgusting you find it, there is not a lot you can do.

I know. I've tried.

Sorry?

I've tried.

Jorge wondered what Gérard had tried. He couldn't imagine. He didn't want to know. He certainly wasn't going to ask. It turned out he didn't need to. Gérard was going to tell him anyway.

You know my Wednesday evening routine?

Gisèle . . .

Yeah, Gisèle. Anyway, Gisèle's a nice-looking woman, don't you think?

It's a matter of taste, but . . .

Ah, come on!

Okay, sure, whatever you say, she's a knockout.

And she's still young, Gérard continued, factually.

Uh-huh, Jorge agreed, swinging the car all the way round a roundabout and heading back into town. He had spotted the first patch of dirty snow on the verges and didn't want to climb any higher. Besides, he was beginning to think he needed a drink. His boss would be happy to oblige.

Well, Gérard was saying, the way I see it, not many men in their right mind would turn Gisèle down. So, when my wife came to me and said she suspected that Paul was inverted, I thought I might try straightening him out.

With a little help from Gisèle? Jorge asked, his eyes wide open and his head shaking slowly.

Well, why not? Gérard asked.

You're right. Why not? What have you got to lose? You might drive the kid psychotic but, hell, just as long as he's no longer bent, right?

Gérard nodded as if he had been paying attention and was grateful for Jorge's understanding. In fact he'd been pursuing his own line of thought.

The thing is, he resumed, but then he just stopped dead, apparently at a loss for words. There's no delicate way to put this, he began again. The straight truth of it is that Gisèle sucks cock like nobody I've ever . . . you know. I just thought if she could get hold of Paul, suck his cock real good, then bang him like a barnhouse door, you know, give him the full-throttle geisha-on-stilts heterosexual professional work-out, it could cure him. After all, I mean, what is it that queers do but suck one another off anyway? If Paul could just see that a woman's touch is always best . . .

Shit, Jorge muttered but said nothing more. The silence continued just long enough for Jorge to decide that it was not part of his remit to broaden his boss's understanding of homosexual practices.

So what's wrong? Don't you like the idea?

I love it, I love it, Jorge replied with a shrug. It's got to be better than electric shocks. So, tell me, what happened? Did it go as wonderfully as I'm imagining?

Electric shocks? Does that work?

Oh, Christ! Jorge muttered. Forget what I said. Please?

Gérard stared at him blankly.

Tell me what happened, Jorge said.

Sadly, it seems he didn't take to her, Gérard began. She went to one of the places he hangs out, dressed cheap and teenage to look the part, got him talking, got him drinking, took him back to her own flat – quite an honour, if he only knew it – went down on him all right, she said, but couldn't really get him interested in *her*. And Gisèle – well, you've seen her for yourself – she has the kind of body on her that any red-blooded male would want to fuck from here to China, hasn't she? Even if she is starting to show her age. I'd be happy to screw her between the teats if the rest was out of my price range, know what I mean? Anyway, the point is, as far as Gisèle's concerned, Paul is a queer. She said that if I wanted a second, third or fourth opinion she could line up some of her colleagues to tackle him, but she didn't really see it would do much good. I ought to leave the poor boy alone, she said. Poor boy!

Well, Jorge said, after a moment's thought, I reckon you've done all you can reasonably do, if not more. If the kid isn't gay, then great! But if he is, you've tried your best to cure him, so you may as well let him be and get used to it.

That's all very well but I have to think about the future of the firm. People are not going to respect a boss who's bent. And they feel pity for a boss whose son is bent.

How do you know?

Have you ever heard of a boss who was a faggot? Outside the fashion industry?

Things are changing.

Since when?

You'll be surprised, I tell you. Things are changing. One day it won't be a problem.

Not a problem if a boss is bent? Neither of us will ever live to see that day. Your lot will be dancing salsa on the rotting corpse of capitalism before that day ever dawns.

Well, I can't promise the revolution will be *that* soon.

Gérard grunted.

Is that what the graffiti was about? Jorge asked after a moment's silence.

What? No. Not at all.

Right, Jorge said.

Thanks for reminding me, Gérard said, sulking again.

The two men fell into a long silence. Jorge made a couple of attempts to break it but Gérard ignored every gambit. Jorge decided to stick to driving. He inserted his Victor Jara cassette, keeping the sound just low enough to avoid pissing off his boss too badly.

8. Salvatore, Alphonse, Fernando.

Madame Yvonne Labarde, a thin woman with sparse chestnut hair, large eyes and an air of gentle strength, considered Salvatore as he strode toward her down the entire length of the machine aisle, his left elbow clamping his sleek attaché case to his side. His carriage appeared noble, his jaw manly, his cheeks rugged, his expression lofty, his stature imposing. She watched him pause at the ends of machines thirteen, eleven and ten in order to shake hands with Luigi, Marcel and Eric. His eyes seemed to smoulder, his temples were surely haughty, his gaze was certainly piercing, his neck altogether, um, bovine. Bovine? No, not bovine, bullish perhaps? No, rather, athletic, sinewy, strong. For a strong neck is as fine a feature in a gentleman as a lily-white complexion and dainty demeanour in a lady.

Yvonne Labarde stood at the end of machine number seven, a stiff flower-patterned shopping basket stationed at her feet, a winning (she hoped) smile playing upon her lips, her rippling raincoat folded over her left arm. For months, indeed, ever since the month of June when she had been transferred from morning to afternoon shift and had been placed in charge of machines six and seven, the very same that Salvatore operated at night, and accordingly had begun to see, and then with mounting curiosity to scrutinize, Salvatore striding toward her each evening, she had wondered where she could possibly have seen him previously. Everything about him was utterly familiar, utterly mysterious, from his seasonally-sensitive choice of woollen, linen, or corduroyed elegance to the unswerving symmetry of his features. Then, a week ago, as the first words and phrases of romantic hyperbole had presented themselves unbidden to her tired end-of-shift mind, she had realized to her astonishment and indignation that this 'Italian' night-shift worker – for, though sensible to the allure of his sing-song transalpine accent, Yvonne remained unaware of either his name or his specifically Sicilian provenance – appeared in all particulars (the mockery of it!) the faithful embodiment of those eminent and unreachable men about whom she had read for years but whom she had never expected to encounter: the tanned and tender princes, millionaires, sheiks, tycoons, wizards of finance and film stars who swarmed in her dreams at night and peopled the novelettes and magazines she devoured by day.

Mindful of the absurdity of her discovery that a creature fit for the pages of a pulse-quickening romance set in Umbria, Scotland, Arabia, California or Muscovy, had fetched up instead in a largish metals and plastics factory in the centre of Grandgobier, Yvonne had now begun to conceive a series of explanatory plots involving: babies exchanged at birth; mistaken, concealed or stolen identities; foundlings; fugitives from *in*justice; aristocrats with a penchant for slumming; amnesia-inducing motor accidents; and the like. It was this work of spontaneous and amused fabulation, alternating with an attention to choice of descriptive word and phrase, that accounted for the winning smile which, as Salvatore walked down the machine aisle toward her, played upon Mme Labarde's rather pale but full lips. This moment had become the high point of her day.

As the Sicilian stretched out his hand to Yvonne Labarde, her examination of his features became furtive and sidelong and her smile evanescent. She glanced at, but preferred not to dwell upon, the blemish of a small mole that stood beneath his left earlobe, rising slightly proud of the flat olive-skinned surround; she sorely lamented the recent haircut that had hacked away at his glossy black curls revealing unsuspected widow's peaks; and she frankly deprecated the ugly brown brogues that disfigured his feet. These defects, however, she told herself, were paltry, feathers in a balance mightily outweighed by the gold bullion of his multiple perfections. The two workers shook hands. What a fine specimen of manhood! she told herself, as her face cloaked this thought with a distancing pretence of sober impartiality, with each new evening's brief encounter became harder to conjure or sustain.

Since Salvatore always had several people and numerous matters on his mind, the once pretty woman whom he relieved each evening scarcely impinged. He noticed of course that she had left the hoppers full, the machines clean, the trays almost empty; to this extent she was a great improvement on her notably voluptuous but slovenly predecessor. Indeed, this woman was a paragon of regularity, a guards officer reliably at her post, awaiting his arrival, ready to insert a surprisingly soft hand into his own well-exercised and muscular one. In the fraction of a second during which he glanced upon her each night, while he mouthed 'B'soir, Madame' (which to Yvonne's ears was an unwelcome reminder more of her age than of her marital status – of which the Sicilian might be presumed to be ignorant), Salvatore conducted upon her the instant and automatic twofold check that he always found reassuring in his dealings with women: first, he confirmed that she, in common with most members of her sex ever to peer into his face, was aware of the physical beauty that he had inherited from his mother;

second, he could see that she, in common with most women at whose faces he ever chanced to glance, bore no comparison with his beloved Laure, to whom, after a long engagement, he was most blessedly to be married the following June. This twin confirmation released the balsamic smile that he now steered at Mme Labarde's dilating pupils, upon which he could see that it immediately worked its galant magic.

Having beheld Madame Yvonne Labarde every weekday evening for the last few months, Salvatore, unbeknownst to himself, now possessed in his mind and memory a well provisioned store of short-term images that, had the need arisen, for example under police questioning, he could have marshalled to create a mental picture that he could then have verbalized as follows: French in appearance, in her early thirties, rather skinny, with pleasant brown eyes, a well-hewn slightly upturned nose (in the French manner, precisely), thinning hair (what was it that caused women to go bald? He was reminded of Zia Luisa, his mother's sister, who had married badly and gone to live in a slum in Taranto, though of course Zia Luisa was fat and at least twice the age of this woman). As for his afternoon colleague's voice, Salvatore would be able to inform his interrogator that it was strong and sharp without being strident (stridency, whether of voice, bearing or opinion, being a most hateful thing in a female and a characteristic that Salvatore found to be more prevalent among French than among Italian womanhood). Finally, the woman was neither friendly nor unfriendly but rather formal and correct (possibly owing to his allure which, as he had frequent occasion to observe, affected different women in different ways, so varied were the passions of the human, and especially the feminine, heart).

Is it raining outside? Madame Labarde asked.

Where should it ever rain *but* outside? Salvatore thought pedantically. And how can I know about 'is' when I am myself now under cover? He shook his head and muttered, I don't think it *was* but I can't be sure. Dealing with the quotidian imprecision of human language was a burden that the Sicilian at times found almost too hard to bear.

With a curt declension of his shapely head, Salvatore dismissed the woman while, transferring his attaché case from its tepid berth beneath his left armpit into the sturdy grip of his right hand, he turned toward a chair situated against the back of machine number six, and onto its seat, against its backrest, he now lowered and leaned said case.

Sensing that her conversational gambit with the 'Italian' had fallen flat,

Madame Labarde lifted her incongruously floral basket and walked up the machine aisle, shaking hands with a number of night-shift workers along her way, including Philippe, who was unfailingly cordial and pleasant (even tonight when she clearly surprised him in pensive humour), and Marcel, whose hand lingered at least as long as usual and whose smile was customarily creepy. As she approached the office-end of the machine aisle and prepared to turn to the right to walk around the back of machine number fourteen and thence further round to the wall-mounted clocking-on machine near the lift, Yvonne Labarde took the opportunity to turn back discreetly and cast her eyes fondly back down the aisle toward machine number seven where she might yet catch a glimpse of the Sicilian and, to be precise, were she really to be lucky, of his posterior. For although she had never yet seen this object at anything like close enough range, it had nonetheless frequently impressed her, even though swathed according to the season in well-laundered woollen, linen, or corduroy, with its springy pertness. She could not help but think that it might possess those lateral dimples that she found so pleasing in reproductions of Greek statuary. It would not be many days or weeks before she found herself imagining, her eyes shut fast during her weekly love-making with her husband, that her thumbs, rather than being plunged into Monsieur Labarde's fair round buttocks as she sought to guide his heartfelt thrusts, were in fact paddling in the shallow depressions at the sides of Salvatore's responsive young bottom with just that trigger-happy and playful power that they had once exerted, during the years of her now distant springtime, upon the flipper buttons of her favourite pinball machine.

Alphonse didn't like to be late, didn't hold with it, felt that it showed disrespect not only toward one's opposite number on the afternoon shift (who would be obliged to linger by the otherwise unsupervised machines until the hands on the clock touched 9.25) but, worse, it suggested a degree of contempt for the job itself, for the very fact that one had a legitimate and regular source of income. And yet, despite this, Alphonse often arrived late. Something would distract his attention on the way to work or he would read too long in his room, spend too much time dressing or under the shower, or would simply miss a bus or bump into an acquaintance and become entangled in conversation. Other times, he would reach work late simply because he had run into the slow-walking, bar-hopping Fernando.

This particular evening, Fernando and Alphonse alighted from their bus at the first stop on Cours Modelon. It was spitting again. The two men walked without exchanging a word. Eric had got off at the same stop and could be seen up ahead of them, in an uncommon hurry, disappearing down the ill-lit street, almost running. While remaining abreast, Fernando and Alphonse practised quite different styles of walking. Alphonse walked like Marc Spitz swam: a minimum of powerful and smooth movements propelling him rapidly along the gleaming pavement; he was rarely seen to break into a sweat, or to dishevel his crisp clothing; more than walk he glided. Fernando, by contrast, performed with his short limbs a multitude of darting and jagged movements which found echo in the flapping and flicking of his cuffs, belt, open jacket and scarf; despite such expense of spirited energy, it was all he could do to keep up with his companion. To see the two men walking down the street side by side might put one in mind of the oddly assorted friends played by Jon Voigt and Dustin Hoffman in the American film *Macadam Cowboy*, except for a few more or less salient particulars: Alphonse did not wear a cowboy hat and was not a white Texan; and Fernando, though unshaven, syncopated of movement, and swarthy, lacked Rico Rizzo's tripping limp and up-tilted look of angry supplication.

Indeed, as the two men now approached a pari-mutuel betting bar, having passed by a closing cafe, an undertaker's premises, and a late-night grocers boasting in the window a fine display of fresh dates, Fernando did not even glance at Alphonse as he said, I just have to pop in here a second, come on in, I'll buy you a drink. Even had Alphonse had the opportunity, it would have taken him several seconds to contrive an adequately diplomatic way of refusing this invitation: he didn't want to rile Fernando again, after his 'insensitive' enquiry about the jackpot. So before Alphonse had found the words, You go ahead, I'll wait outside, and had fetched them through his mind and into his mouth, Fernando had whipped open the door and stepped inside, and was standing with his entire nervous frame bent in the direction of the bar as he held the door open behind him. Alphonse had missed his chance to hang back. The noise from the bar would force him to shout; a scene of scant dramatic interest but considerable embarrassment would have been enacted for the sole delectation of an audience whose tastes in drama were, at best, uncertain. So with a glance at his watch and a sigh, Alphonse took the door from Fernando and followed him in.

The Portuguee wriggled and elbowed his way through the melee while Alphonse remained close to the door, taking in the scene. Being neither a gambler nor a drinker, he had never been in a pmu-bar before; being no smoker, the cigarette fumes hit him hard in the chest and stung his eyes. Fernando was soon talking to a couple of men at the bar who had sporting papers open in front of them and pencils in their fists. Fernando's arms were jerking about and the men were alternately grinning, nodding sagely, or uttering monosyllables. Alphonse released his eyes from this tableau, taking in a number of similar groups equally absorbed in the discussion – Alphonse could only suppose – of the day's racing events and the prospects for the morrow. A whole universe of passion and drama about which I know nothing and feel nothing. My experience of life at times seems narrow. I ought perhaps to spend time in such places and acquaint myself a little better with this country. Who can say? I might one day need to play a gambling man. But how should I ever endure the smoke? And I'd so prefer not to gamble. It does seem an awfully foolish thing to do. And I don't drink. Even at a party I daren't take anything stronger than beer. It makes me liverish.

Yet I am curious. What do these poor men think they are doing? Having fun? It doesn't look like it: no one is laughing, no one is dancing a jig. Maybe they don't know how to sing or dance. Or worse: maybe they only sing and dance when 'their' horse wins. That laughter and dancing should depend on a win on the horses is so sad. Besides, where there are winners there are losers, isn't that the case? How could half the bar dance and sing when the other half looked downcast and wretched and was worrying about what they were going to say when they got home? No, I really can't imagine what these men think they are up to and yet it is perfectly possible that every one of them is as straightforward as Fernando, when you get to know him. Some of them will have women to go back to, some will have jobs, some will be jailbirds enjoying a leave of absence from their cells: these men are probably neither worse nor better than any on the night shift. So, really, what separates me from them are the same things that separate me from my work colleagues. Alphonse deemed himself to be set apart more by his attitude and the content of his mind and force of will than by any accidental matter of birthplace, skin colour or education. After all, Fernando too was an outsider; indeed, most of Alphonse's work colleagues were outsiders in one way or another, just as, conceivably, are most of the men here. But Alphonse felt that as a black man he belonged essentially to the vast, errant, borderless nation of the oppressed. And that could scarcely be said of Fernando, could it? Moreover, Alphonse believed that this position afforded him a privileged way of looking at everything in this country – one of the ancestral lands of the ancestral oppressor – that would always set him apart.

As Alphonse continued to meditate on the things that distinguished him from those around him, his eyes fell upon a group of three men standing right at the back, near the door to the toilets, beneath the wall-mounted television, nursing empty pastis glasses in their hands. His eyes encountered theirs for a long moment – they were staring at him and, he sensed, talking about him in hushed voices. Suddenly, Alphonse felt afraid. He glanced over at Fernando, who appeared to be settling in for the night: now he was pulling a cigarette from his pack and offering it to one of his interlocutors. Fernando seemed to have forgotten about the Ivorian's existence.

Alphonse surveyed the crowded bar, keeping his focus soft and discreet. There weren't any other black men in the room. There weren't even any North Africans, as far as he could see. And although there were a few Vietnamese or, possibly, Cambodians (for who could tell them apart?), he knew that Orientals, when it came to this kind of calculus, couldn't be relied upon. More than all that, Alphonse was the only man who did not look positively down-at-heels, the only man without a glass, the only man who wasn't smoking, the only man who was standing by himself, the only man – everyone could surely tell – who wasn't a gambler. What the hell am I doing here, they must wonder. It's a fair question. Were it not for Fernando, I would be somewhere between factory gate and clocking-on machine right now, slowing down to a stroll, taking it easy in the dark, about to arrive early, at peace with the world.

Alphonse checked the cluster of heads beneath the TV. He saw the three men, with one accord, look away from him and up at one another. He caught the sharing of a private and meaningful glance. He watched them put their glasses down on a ledge that ran round the wall at elbow height and begin slowly, lumpishly, to pick their way through the crowded room toward him. As Alphonse turned toward the door, thinking to trust to his athleticism and youth to save him from an old-fashioned Southern-US-style whupping, and feeling aggrieved that he should have to run and be made to feel the coward, he noticed that Fernando, with impeccable timing, had turned toward him and was beckoning him over and had lifted breast-high his right fist with its thumb jutting out toward his own mouth – thus repeating his previous invitation to a drink. Alphonse hesitated an instant, then, with a wry smile and a 'what the hell,' decided to take a gamble and, instead of heading back through the door into the safety of a street on which he was sure he could outrun any man in that triad of pastis-swilling decrepits, he glanced straight into the eyes of the foremost of the men heading toward him, smiled brazenly as if greeting an old chum, then made straight for Fernando. He was certain the would-be lynch mob wouldn't bother him once they saw he was with a fellow gambler-drinker-smoker-white-man. And he knew that if they did opt to push their luck, he'd be able to call not only on Fernando, whom he imagined would possess bar-fighting skills immeasurably better honed than his own, but possibly on the men with whom Fernando had just been discussing horses. The odds are good, the Ivorian teased himself.

As Alphonse reached Fernando's side, Fernando said in his ear, I'll get you that drink now. Did you know I backed a horse that came in second? Alphonse smiled in commiseration. He didn't look round. He knew the men were still staring at him, their tiny eyes stinging like buckshot at the back of his head. If he looked at them now they could only interpret his gaze as triumph or fear and any suspicion of either might still set them off, like dangling bait before hyenas: 'never let them smell your fear,' his father used to say. The barman came over and with a wink at Fernando enquired what 'the two gentlemen' would like to drink. Not whether, but what, Alphonse noted. As if we had no choice, as if we were under an obligation to consume. I won't have anything, thanks, I'm not staying, Alphonse stated. Fernando pulled a face. The barman said nothing, but his grin withered, puckering his mouth tight as an arsehole. He didn't move. Alphonse turned just far enough to place in the corner of his eye his three putative adversaries who were back at their posts near the toilets. To his relief, they had stood down: their fists melting back into hands; their chests losing their pigeon-curvature to resume their customary sunken droop; their heads, so briefly ratcheted to attention, slumping back into their raw TV-ready necks.

Fernando said, We're in a bar, what do you fucking-want to drink? Spirits? Name it, it's on me. Alphonse stared back, blankly. I don't drink. You pussy! You're kidding, right? I'll get you a Vittel.

But Alphonse repeated slowly and loudly, No-thing. The barman wasn't sure whether to scowl or to smirk so he did both at once. Maybe some chamomile tea? he asked, winking again at Fernando. Nothing, Alphonse repeated, his features frozen, as he began involuntarily to develop a reef of thoughts regarding men who wink. Fernando said, Make it two beers: I'll drink fucking-his, if I have to. You will have to, Alphonse said flatly. Fernando threw his arms out: we're working all night, can't you have a drink? Alphonse frowned and shrugged at Fernando like he didn't understand the question. The barman brought the beers, Alphonse pointed at his wristwatch, while shifting his weight from foot to foot like an amateur dramatist directed to convey impatience. Fernando downed the second beer, smacked his lips to produce some resonant swear words, and deposited a generous sum in piled coins beside the empty glasses. Alphonse looked on and shook his head. Where on earth was the sense in tipping crooks, liars, swindlers or publicans? Fernando shook the hands of the two men with whom he had been talking earlier, seized Alphonse's arm just above the elbow and marched him to the door like a recalcitrant child.

Outdoors in the fresh night air, Fernando's irritation dissipated fast. He produced a beery burp then patted his belly just below the solar plexus. Alphonse breathed twice hard in and out as if hoping to dislodge from his lungs the various distillates of tar and nicotine. Fernando started talking about his gambling loss again. Would you believe it? Fucking-just my luck. Came in second. Should have put money on it to show, but the tip seemed too good, so I wanted to make more, didn't I? Greed is what did for me. If it had come in last or broken a leg or thrown its rider, then fine, you can't argue, but, no, the fucker had to come in second, to show it could have come in first, know what I mean? It proves the tip was good though, just not good enough. Alphonse opened his eyes wide at this logic, but looked away. How much did you lose? he asked, speaking low. I'm fucking-not telling you, Fernando snapped. It's bad luck to mention your losses. I'm superstitious. I don't need any extra bad luck. Besides, it isn't how much you lose that hurts, it's how much you don't win. Luckily, I didn't have much money to spare on the bet, so things are not too bad. If the pony fucking-had come in last, I wouldn't mind so much, Fernando said, chewing it over and over. A bit more effort, a last-minute spurt. Is it too much to ask?

Alphonse turned and looked pointedly at Fernando with a performance of disbelief: eyes wide and blinking slowly, jaw lowered, eyebrows hitched high. Well, yeah, Fernando said. It was a good horse. It had legs. Alphonse laughed and enquired whether Fernando had ever, on the strength of a tip, backed a horse without legs. Fernando took offence and looked at the Ivorian with scalding eyes. Fernando's speech slowed and his diction cleared as his reasoning grew more deliberate. Look, there are people in that bar who know all kinds of stuff, study form, history, understand the whole business, know the angles. It's a good bar, damn it. What do you know about it anyway? I have friends there. They've given me good tips in the past and they will again. It's a matter of time, you'll see.

There was a silence while Alphonse shook his head some more. Then he said, We're going to be late clocking on. Yeah, sorry, Fernando said distractedly, his mind turning to the smile that Maryse would surely have given him as he presented her with some expensive gift, swanky perfume or frilly undies, say, purchased with the winnings he had only just failed to make, all because the horse had fucking-failed to put on that last spurt. Then as she tried to refuse, say, the gold-plated cigarette lighter or the alligator-skin purse, and as he pressed it into her hand, closed her fingers over, say, the pearl earrings or the diamond necklace, and insisting, No, No, I want you to have it, do me this honour, him fucking-standing there like a gentleman, in a new shirt with its shop creases still showing, and for once properly shaven with a proper cut-throat at that Portuguese barber's shop, and sweetly perfumed the way real ladies appreciate, and shrugging like it was a trifle, and proud for fucking-once in his life, standing tall in a new black pair of classic winkle-pickers.

Fernando shook his head and swore, Mer-r-r-de, Mer-r-r-r-r-de, with his trilling Portuguese r's, as he pulled from his pocket a handful of dirty coins and scraps of betting slips and blueish lint and then dutifully doled out to Alphonse two one-franc pieces and a fifty-centime bit. That covers the quarter hour, he said. It's chicken feed, anyway, Fernando added, comparing two francs fifty with the amount he should by right have won on the horse. Alphonse took the coins between thumb and forefinger, couldn't see the point in arguing, but muttered, I just don't like being late: people notice. So? Fernando retorted. Let them notice! It's only fucking-fifteen minutes, and I've made it up to you already. Alphonse thought about that then said, Suppose they need to lose someone, do you think they wouldn't check our time-keeping? No way, said Fernando. The temps would get laid off first. Are you certain? Of course they would. Or that English guy: last in, first out, right? Alphonse said nothing, reflecting that on that basis he would be the next to go after Eric.

Fernando had detected an advantage in Alphonse's silence. What's this about you not drinking? Don't you ever drink? No, I don't. Never? Well, hardly ever. Why the hell not? To me, it's the devil's own potion. What, have you fucking-got religion? No, Alphonse chuckled, but the devil exists. You're kidding, right? Is this an African fucking-thing? Alphonse laughed a healthy open-throated laugh, then, like he was talking to a child, explained, There happens not to be a single alcoholic beverage of which I enjoy the taste – I believe I have tried most of them – nor do I like the effect they have on me. Simple. Fernando remained suspicious. What's wrong with you? You don't smoke, you keep out of trouble, you don't drink, I bet you don't even fuck. What kind of black man are you anyway? I thought your lot were either soaks, shit-stirrers or stallions. Do you dance at fucking-least? Alphonse laughed out loud. Yes, I can dance, cut a country caper, do a waltz, java or samba. I can even squaredance. Fernando sensed he was being made fun of, didn't get it, didn't like it, snorted to express as much. You fucking-really can talk. So where did you learn your French? At my mother's pap, Alphonse replied. Fernando looked surprised. Alphonse thought the word had foxed him. Pap, breast, tit, teat, titty, dug, nipple, boob, bubby. Fernando shook his head slowly. What, in Africa? Obviously. Do I look Chinese?

As the two men walked through the gates of the factory, they both glanced up at the clock. The minute finger was on twenty-four, and it was a good two minutes walk through metallurgy to the plastics section. Fernando asked again, but with less conviction, almost as if it were a sincere enquiry, What kind of a black man are you anyway? Alphonse looked away and pursed his lips. Then, deciding he had an answer of sorts, he looked back at Fernando and said, I was hoping it was a rhetorical question. A what fucking-question? Fernando asked. Alphonse considered providing a thumbnail account of Rhetoric from Aristotle onward, then said, Look, this may quite plausibly surprise you but the fact remains that there are as many varieties and conditions of black people as there are of white people and that drinking, dancing, smoking, and er . . . fornicating do not define, let alone exhaust, our gamut of activities. You fucking-can talk, Fernando muttered again. Alphonse seemed not to hear him, but then, with the long tapering fingers of his left hand performing tiny rising arpeggios on Fernando's right shoulder, the Ivorian secured his attention. Without actually slowing down the pace at which the men were walking, Alphonse turned his left hand palm-up, wiggled his index finger in beckoning, and said, If you listen most attentively I will share with you a secret. Fernando looked surprised at this dramatic exordium but tendered his ear, whereupon Alphonse produced a stage whisper worthy of a Shakespearian aside, and said, In fact, there are even more varieties and conditions of black men then there are of white men. Chew on that. What? queried Fernando, as the door into the factory closed behind them. How do you figure that? All right, Alphonse said in a quiet, patient voice that he adapted to the fact that the street sounds had been blotted out and the rumble of the plastic section was still faint. Let me try this on you: it's industrialization, right? It's fucking-what? Industrialization – when a country becomes . . . I fucking-know what the word means, Fernando snapped. Alphonse clicked his teeth. In your white countries, see, with people crammed into cities and working in places like this, everyone's getting evened out, you're all getting to be the same. You eat the same food. You do the same work. You watch the same shows on TV. And when people do the same stuff for long enough, they get to be the same. That's how Europe and Europeans sometimes seem to us Africans: copies of one another, limited, regimented, conformist, tongue-tied, thwarted. Everyone here is in a hurry to fit into a ready-cut tight little box. In Africa, there's more tolerance, more difference, you are still allowed to be weird. We have real blacksmiths, tailors, cobblers, clowns, every possible kind of farm worker, peasants, every sort of rural and urban character imaginable, as well as butchers and bakers and doctors and pharmacists and bankers and brokers, even if a lot of them have been forced into factories in the towns, just like here. Except that with us that hasn't gone so far yet.

Meditating on this in silence, Fernando sighed, jerked a cigarette out of his pack and, as he brought a flame to its tip, sucked hard and swallowed. Then he said, with a degree of conviction and calm finality that was unusual for him, That fucking-is bullshit. As if he'd thought it right through. Alphonse blinked twice, then his head dipped. Yes, maybe it is, he conceded, turning his friendly eyes on Fernando. The trouble, however, Alphonse said slowly, is that you my friend are able to spot bullshit when it dribbles from my lips, but when it gushes from one of those men in that filthy bar telling you which lame sack-of-bones to bet your money on you fall for it like the last of the innocents. Fernando growled and muttered, Fuck you.

Alphonse briefly reflected that there were not many people who had told him 'fuck you' twice in the space of twenty minutes. After a moment, Alphonse glanced at his watch. If we make a dash for it, we might still make it, he said. You could have your two-fifty back. Yeah, good idea, Fernando agreed. So, shall we run? Alphonse asked. Yeah, let's run, Fernando replied. But neither man broke into a run, nor even quickened his pace. Which reminded Alphonse of something, and made him smile.

9. Eric, Philippe, Mathieu, Marcel.

Eric exhaled as he tossed the soggy remnant of his roll-up onto the floor and squinted up into the glare of the plastics section. His lungs refilled. Out of the corner of his left eye he sighted the brunette, standing just as she always stood Mondays to Fridays at this hour, tightly swathed in her street clothes, her right hip against the base of the clock-machine, and that lanky colleague and friend of hers bent over her ear, murmuring. The brunette had spotted Eric at once and looked away. He imagined he saw her mouth tighten. Now was the time, he knew. His own face felt puffed and taut. The words were prepared. Êtes-vous libre samedi . . . Ask her, ask her, ask her. Done in a trice.

The air was thick with the fumes of scorched plastic and burnt oil, the smoke from cigarettes, the reek of sweat, perfumes, stale deodorants, fresh and rotting scraps of food, aftershaves, bad breath and hair lacquers. In it met and mingled a hundred different varieties of plastic dust, talcum powders, ground insects and their desiccated waste, scuffed plaster board, body hair and bristles, shavings and clippings, plus the fluff and lint from old work clothes and boots. This soupy haze pulsed with the irregular syncopated rhythms of fourteen machines labouring on the ground floor and, muffled and distorted but echoing, a further seven machines pounding and thumping on the first floor, their glib and shiny pistons to-ing and fro-ing at different speeds, the left- and right-hand sides of their well-greased presses clamping together and wrenching apart to different sounds, their plastic products dropping with modulated whacks or percussive clatters into plastic trays stationed on the floor below. Trolleys rolled on squeaking wheels along the cement fake-stone floors, the clanking lift arrived and departed, its concertina doors opening and closing, with a shuffling of feet and a hissing of expletives. The floors, both upstairs and down, newly swept by the departing afternoon shift, were scatter-patched with stray slicks of sand-sprayed oil. Against the end of certain machines and at the foot of certain control cabinets rose tiny hillocks of drift-swept machine debris, cigarette butts, dried gobs of ejaculated plastic, neglected or malformed and discarded products, all destined for the shovel, pan and bin. The walls and ceilings were the colour of skimmed milk and where they met great cobwebs had formed that no spider had ever been observed to weave.

The machines themselves were a fresh-minted orange or a faded lime. The afternoon-shift workers moved up and down the central aisles that both upstairs and down separated the machines into two rows. In the dying moments of their shift, they shuttled to and from their machines, remembering and forgetting a miscellany of objects, seizing their coats by the scruff or hugging cardboard boxes, clutching slips of paper, umbrellas, handbags, plastic bags, industrial gloves or packs of cigarettes. Nobody wanted to clock off late: it would bespeak either a suspect over-eagerness at the job or simple-minded incompetence.

Without glancing at the brunette, Eric hand-shook his way down the line of afternoon workers, plucked his card from the rack, clocked on with limbs a-tremble and heart a-flutter, put the card back, then, with proffered hand and mouth agape, turned toward the young woman, his phrase teetering on the tip of his tongue like a child at the end of a springboard afraid to dive. Occupying the lovely hand that he had wished and expected to shake, Eric spotted an unlit cigarette. Christ, what now? The words were gone. His forehead itched. He could feel the beads of sweat burst from his skin like popcorn from the base of a hot greased pan.

The young woman looked upon him.

Du feu? she asked, her eyes pressing hard on his.

Eric fumbled in three pockets, found a plastic lighter. As he snapped it into life, she caught and steadied his quivering right wrist between the thumb and index finger of her left hand, guiding the flame toward her face until it licked the tip of her cigarette. She sucked in hard then sent the smoke straight down and stared at him. As an afterthought, she let go of his hand. Her lanky friend had taken a step back and was spectating keenly, narrowing her eyes for distance focus like a cyclist in high-speed descent.

For weeks, the brunette had observed Eric's blushing awkwardness: she would have had to be blind not to notice it. It had become an embarrassment. Her colleagues had almost stopped laughing at him and had begun instead to tease her – as if she had done anything to encourage him! She had grown impatient for something to happen, anything. Besides, she liked going out and was sure he could be no trouble. In recent weeks, she had taken to squeezing his hand harder and harder each evening when they shook, or to holding it in hers longer and longer, so that sometimes he had almost to wrench it away. And still . . . nothing. What could a girl do? You couldn't wait for ever.

Eric smiled foolishly and pushed his lighter into the first pocket he thought of. The young woman's right hand was busy with the cigarette and she was keeping her left hand in her jeans pocket. He would have to kick his heels a while. She had left him like a dishcloth on a line, just hanging there. He could hardly walk away, when they hadn't yet shaken hands, let alone spoken. If her left hand had been attainable, he might have made a grab for it and yanked that up and down, like workers sometimes did when a right hand was dirty, full or busy. His cheeks were burning, his hands dangled empty. The brunette perused him at length, then offered him one of her cigarettes, a Royale. He accepted it and began to search for his lighter. She watched as he tried various pockets.

T'es anglais, n'est-ce pas? she asked, delicately pointing just to the left of his crotch.

Eric fished the lighter out of his right-hand trouser pocket, lit his cigarette, and nodded. Then, quite unexpectedly, he discovered the words he had been rehearsing earlier lying there ready like a slice of cucumber on his tongue: 'Ett voo libra sam-dee swar?'

She made him repeat this while she thought of a satisfactory answer. Her brows knit as she blew a funnel of smoke down at the chunky buckle of his belt.

He made a gesture of apology and blurted that maybe she could teach him French. She spread her eyes wide in surprise, but waved it away with her cigarette hand.

No, thank you, she said, I won't teach you French. But we can go to the cinema, if you like. Place de la République, 8 o'clock. D'accord?

Eric didn't need to think, didn't need to speak. The brunette had switched her cigarette to her left hand and stuck out her right for him to shake. Ba-boom. Interview over. Eric congratulated himself: he had asked her out and in a trice she had said yes. Yes, yes, yes.

The lanky friend leaned back into the brunette's ear and both girls began to laugh at something, maybe at him, but Eric was moving away now. Then he turned suddenly, took a step back and asked her her name.

Fanny, she said, seriously, as if she had to think about it. And yours is Eric.

As he walked away, elated as rarely before in his short life, Eric wondered what her voice would be like away from the din: would it be harsh and shrill or, like his own, hoarse from working in those fumes and having to shout always? Voices mattered to Eric. Husky would be attractive, sexy. Shrill would be unbearable. He already liked the way she accentuated their two names, leaning back against the second syllables: Fan-*nie,* E-*rique.* How had she known his name? He could ask her on Saturday, if he could find the words. He would work out what to talk about, prepare a bunch of phrases. The brunette had screwed up her nose and dropped her half-smoked cigarette on the floor, then heeled it hard. Eric didn't dare turn round, euphoric, elated, wishing he could tell somebody about it, longing to boast of his achievement.

Be careful, Fanny's lanky friend whispered in her ear, the English can be wild and unpredictable. Fanny raised her eyebrows and laughed.

Eric was pleased he had managed not to stare straight in at her breasts. It had required self-discipline. He liked the name Fanny. You just had to forget what it meant in English. A good thing he hadn't laughed: it would have been a tricky thing to explain away, and he knew he possessed neither the language nor the wit for it. Fanny. Fanny. Or rather, Fan-*nie*. He thought of Fanny (Fan-*nie*) Ardant in that film he had seen. She was taller than his Fanny – *his* Fanny! – and her looks were more striking, her eyes larger, her nose too. But her chest was a lot flatter. She had been acting opposite Gérard Dépardieu. Eric had caught himself thinking 'his' Fanny. It was a notion he would need to consider. He didn't want to get ahead of himself.

Philippe had finished checking the hopper levels on all three of his machines. It was force of habit: Lopez, the man he was relieving, was as regular as clock-work and would never leave a hopper empty. Where had he got to though? Couldn't have gone far. Was probably just depositing his product boxes in the storage area out back. He was going to have to hurry not to clock off late.

Philippe swung his cuff up over his wrist: 21.23. He walked to the side of the control cabinet where he had hung his jacket, and rummaged in one of its pockets for the coins he would need for beer and coffee. He felt a tap on his shoulder and spun round with a ready smile, expecting it to be Jacques.

Lopez's breath hit him hard, pinned him flat against the control cabinet, there was no escape. Philippe quickly lit a cigarette to neutralize and repel the wafting halitosis, then stuck his right hand out so far and so fast that he almost hit the Spaniard in the ribs, forcing the man to step back to shake hands.

Lopez was saying something about machine number two. Words, many of them recognisably French, were pouring from him, interlarded with frequent demands for assent. Philippe looked past him toward the aisle and blew a defensive battery of smoke rings. Lopez said the engineers had changed the mould and that some products had come out malformed at first and an eye had to be kept on temperature and pressure values and product integrity and the engineers had said and then he had said and then the engineers had said.

Marcel was sauntering down the aisle. He grinned at Philippe and pinched his nose between thumb and finger. Lopez's breath was factory-famous. Lopez caught Philippe's friendly grin and moved in closer, telling him more.

At the risk of appearing rude, Philippe squeezed past Lopez and out of the man's immediate airspace. Words, words, words, and not one of them needed. Philippe could see for himself that machine number two had a new mould, and could draw his own conclusions. Things that were new took a while to settle down. That was the way with things. In the meantime, you kept checking. There was no cause for talk. Philippe turned back toward Lopez and used his broadest smile to interrupt him, saying, I would really so hate to make you late.

Lopez thanked Philippe, shook his hand, said goodbye, then, drawing on that boundless stock of jokesy commiserations employed by workers on different shifts, he said: I'll leave you to it then, you lucky devil, staying here all night. Poor me, I have to go home to a nice warm bed and fuck the wife. Lopez laughed at his wit and Philippe's smile froze while he nodded.

Most of the men might have laughed at Lopez's comment, and Marcel could probably have come up with a fittingly lewd reply and maybe even a cheeky offer to take Lopez's place; indeed, on most nights, this scrap of stale humour might have worked tolerably well even on Philippe. But tonight the idea of fucking the wife had an unusually unhappy ring. It was something he hadn't done for a long time and hadn't enjoyed for even longer and certainly didn't want to think about. Besides, if his sister was right, another man had taken to performing the task for him.

Philippe retrieved his hand and turned away. Strange bugger that Marseillais, Lopez thought. One minute he was friendly and grinning like an alley cat, kinda all-purring, then somehow he just, like, spun round and vanished somehow, or as good as. And always in a hurry to get away. What for, no one knew. And when he smiles, it seems he only smiles to himself, for himself. But the French were sometimes like that, weren't they? With them, with some of them at least, it was all self, self, self. Whereas Spaniards, as everyone knows full well, we're something else, we're more relaxed. Slowed down by the weight of these thoughts, Lopez reached the clock-machine with just seconds to spare.

In the raised office overlooking the ground-floor production area,

Mathieu, the night-shift foreman, was talking to his afternoon counterpart and a tired-looking engineer. There were no particular problems that either man could foresee for the night ahead. A couple of machines were playing up. Machine number two had a new mould. Mathieu found it hard to follow the monotones. Nadine's face appeared sleeping, slathering. He pressed his eyes hard shut to change the picture then opened them again. He thought, but couldn't be sure, that the afternoon supervisor and the engineer had exchanged a look. Then the two men nodded their heads toward Philippe who could be seen standing by the machine, scrutinizing a product that had just emerged from the press of machine number two, turning it this way and that. No problem, muttered Mathieu. If anyone knows what to do, Philippe did, he told himself. The only time Mathieu had ever been ill, the place had run smoothly without him, thanks to Philippe, who had taken over the role of foreman, without anybody really noticing. Whatever the circumstances, he knew how to act and, when he didn't, he shut the machine down and left it for the engineers to fix in the morning. No panic, no gratuitous risks, no bending over backward either. From their privileged vantage point, the two supervisors and the engineer surveyed what they could see of the rest of the shop floor.

At the far end of the floor, at machine number nine, Rachid was at the top of a stepladder, tipping an oblong bin of granules and powder into the machine's hopper. He placed the empty bin on top of the machine's control cabinet, while he plunged his arm deep into the hopper to stir the mixture. He sucked at the cigarette hanging from his lip while smoke spiralled into his eyes, one of which he screwed tight shut. Eric was standing at the foot of Rachid's stepladder with his right arm held out toward him for a handshake. Eric wanted to tell him he had got himself a date with the brunette. As Rachid descended the stepladder and his shoes touched the floor, they shook hands and Eric tried 'J'ai une date,' but that didn't seem to work. 'Avec la fille brunette,' he added, reckoning that 'brunette' simply had to be a French word. The Arab looked bemused. 'Avec Fanny,' Eric added, as if everybody was sure to know her name. Rachid, however, had heard 'datte,' the fruit, and had thought 'what, just the one?' and tapped his belly and said, 'Go ahead, you eat it, I just had my dinner.' Eric tried to say something about the cinema, but Rachid had already moved away a little, recalling the succulent dates he had spotted earlier at the Moroccan's, imagining the way Malika's face would surely look if only he took her some for breakfast. Small gifts were a way back into a woman's heart. Small gifts, kindness and patience. How come he'd only just learnt that? Why didn't bigger kids at school or elder brothers or head-patting, cheek-pinching uncles ever tell you *that*?

That Arab? asked the engineer, as Rachid smiled at Eric and extended his slender hand. The night foreman moved a matchstick round in his mouth and nodded his head. A good worker, reliable: we don't have any problems on the night shift, he said. Everyone gets on with his job. Sure, said the afternoon foreman, winking vaguely: you got no women to distract you. (Nadine looking out the car window, blinking, the last time he had been able to drive her anywhere.) Mathieu took a deep breath, looked away and hitched his trousers higher, briefly exposing a ginger-bristled belly. Sure, that's probably it, he muttered. No politics, no past, no history, no women. The less you have, the better you work, right? he said testily, turning to the engineer. The engineer looked baffled, scratched his head. Weird fucker, he thought. Been in the army, apparently. Some kind of hero, probably. Weird fucker for definite. Probably traumatized. And now he's come all over smiley and is clapping me on the shoulder with that mangled claw of his, like he's humouring me or apologizing for going off half-cocked in my face. Yeah, yeah, yeah, see you tomorrow. Have a good night's work. Weird, weird old fucker.

Marcel was standing facing his machine number twelve, his shiny-green shirt-sleeves rolled up tight to his armpits, his industrially gloved hands sunk in a sturdy, grey, oblong plastic tub. He slowly threshed a tangle of the machine's products, thereby separating the almost valueless stalks from the strangely precise and peculiarly shaped button-sized items of plastic that embodied the current purpose of machine number twelve's operation – and would go on doing so until this mould was removed and another fitted.

A light sheen of perspiration was forming on Marcel's forehead. He tried to concentrate on what he was doing, but there was no way of dismissing the usual jumble of unwelcome thoughts. Damned wedding. What if Cousin Bobrán, let alone his mother . . . Imagine if his mother turned up! You couldn't trust her not to dance a Gypsy jig. It would be just like her to embarrass me in front of Chantal's family, Chantal's thick-as-shit brothers sniggering at my back. I'll knock their rat-slime brains out if I catch them, wedding or no wedding: they need to learn some respect. But Bobrán is a liability, an embarrassment. And what was it with that sullen African showing up at my place this morning in that dark suit, waking me up and asking for Bobrán and leaving me that letter for him – which I mustn't forget. Maybe it's money, you never know. Bobrán had better come to work tonight, considering I clocked him on. Where the fuck is that letter now? It must be in my back pocket, I'll check in a minute. Where was I? That African guy arriving on my doorstep like that, not apologizing for being there, and seeming real serious about something. God alone knows what trouble my little cousin has got himself into – some damned mess I can't help him with anyway. I'm not running risks with the probation service already checking on me every time I take a piss. Not that the guy seemed the violent type, quite the reverse in fact, soft spoken, almost lady-like, with that funny French he had, sounding like he'd swallowed some ancient schoolbook. Marcel lifted a tangle of product-free stalks and dropped them lazily into a cardboard cylinder to his left, then resumed his grinding and crashing of the remaining stalks, even resorting occasionally to twisting off particularly well attached items one at a time. When the recycling cylinder was full, he'd empty it into a huge box out back, and tomorrow the stalks would be ground down and the resulting powder used again as raw material, mixed with fresh, virgin plastic granules, kind of eking them out.

Marcel's recent arousal had abated, leaving a mournful loss of tension in his limbs, the ghost of a thrill, the irritation of unfulfilled potential, the prowling of a missed climax as the curve of denim to the left of his zipper voided and his trouser-snake fell flaccid. He hauled from the grey tub the last tangle and then picked out the final few individual stray stalks and dumped them into the tall cardboard cylinder to his left. Then he lifted the grey tub and, carefully upending it to his right, poured the precious product into a cardboard box standing at the foot of the control cabinet. In the morning, that box would be half-full and he'd tape it up and take it out back. That was a safe prediction. And then it'd be checked and sold and shipped out to God knows who for God knows what possible use, but who cared? He just produced the shit.

Before replacing the empty grey tub on the upturned bin, resting against the side of machine number twelve, Marcel glanced through the gap between machine twelve's hopper and its control cabinet, catching a glimpse of the giggly girls he'd talked to earlier. They would put themselves in his way again, he was sure of it. And that would be that. He saw they were tormenting their clocking-on cards in their fidgety little fingers, and waiting their turn. Waiting their turn. And he would bide his time. It was 21.25 and they were straight-faced, concentrating on that moment of release. Their minds were turned to the outside, you could tell. They had their backs to him, and he admired the view, one arse so full and round and bite-worthy and the other all angular, just bet it had deep indentations at the sides like an athlete's, a runner's, one of those Romanian gymnasts, with names you couldn't remember or pronounce, all ovnas and vitches. He watched as they punched their cards and thrust them back in the rack and headed off through the hanging plastic flaps and out. He'd have appreciated it if they'd turned round at the last moment, their eyes languidly seeking him out. But they didn't give him a backward glance and, hell, why should they? Out they went. Out where? he wondered. Out into the night and freedom from work for a few hours, almost sixteen, the best part of a day. Home to their families, their parents maybe, or home alone. Or, who knows . . . ? To freedom and to bed in any case.

Doubt, like a dirty shadow, obscured Marcel's mind. To bed and perhaps to fuck. He thought this through. It was a Tuesday. Hardly a night out, obviously. Still, people fuck even on Tuesdays, maybe especially on Tuesdays. What else is there? Marcel snarled and frowned. His arousal was long gone now, the denim forming creases around his shrunk cock, and he had to be angry with someone, anyone, maybe himself for caring about whether those two girls fuck. Of course they fuck. Everybody fucks, except the really old, the really young, and the really ugly. The point is if they're fucked, they're fucked badly. Anyone can see that. So they're ripe for it, pears on a tree. Grandma's pear tree, for example. She had this dwarf pear tree in a big pot, took it bloody everywhere. Gave good pears too, at least some years. Ripe and juicy. Those girls are begging for it, pleading, on their knees, now there's a picture. Dirty bugger that I am. Marcel smiled like a dirty bugger. I've near-as-damn-it got a date with them. So that's okay then. Still, I don't like the idea of women I intend one day to fuck for myself fucking some other guy in the meantime. It doesn't seem right, does it? And there's two of them, which makes it twice as wrong. It's like they could both be cheating on me, the miserable bitches, cheating on me already and I've not even snapped their bras off yet, not that that tall, skinny hairy one wears a bra probably, she hardly needs to, now there's a thought, yeah, they're cheating on me and I haven't even tumbled them onto a bed or backed them against a wall, not even got a date as such, though it's a sure thing.

The women would be halfway through metallurgy by now, halfway to open air, a third of the way to the street, to bed and perhaps to get a Tuesday kind of bad fuck. What the hell.

Left floating free, Marcel's thoughts returned like a compass needle to the magnetic north of his worries. For Marcel was impatient, ambitious and a worrier. Worrying was a natural talent with him. He could worry about almost anything. Right now he was worried about being shown up at his very own wedding by the Gypsy ways of his fleck-eyed cousin and his raven-ringleted, gold-earringed, billowing-skirted picture-bloody-postcard Gypsy aunt. But if he didn't invite them, who would he invite? There had to be someone from what his bride-to-be referred to as 'his side.' He could hardly invite his father, even if he could track him down, and even if the old man happened to be out of gaol right now, which was always a possibility. If his father did turn up, he'd probably walk off with the silver or pinch some cunt's bottom. Marcel didn't want people looking at his dad, looking at him, looking back at his dad, then going 'ah-ha! right! got it!' as if they understood something. They didn't understand shit. Bobrán and his mum would have to be there, wouldn't they? And if they were there, they'd have to behave themselves, obviously. If he could just explain that idea to Bobrán, Bobrán might be able to rein in his mother. Fat hope.

Then what the hell was this business with the African? Since when did Bobrán know any Africans? Unless it was a guy from the building site. They did have the occasional black on building sites, didn't they? This one didn't look the building-site type, though. Too neat, too well spoken. His hands had felt too smooth when they'd shaken.

Marcel took his gloves off and fished in his hip pocket for the letter for his cousin that the African had entrusted to him. He looked at the neat, spidery, serious-looking, grown-up writing. Marcel felt a twinge of envy: his own handwriting was childish, clumsy. If he wanted to join the letters up, he had to concentrate on it and it took him forever. He looked at the thick white envelope. Monsieur was written out in full, and then just 'Bobrán,' like he didn't know his surname. Funny that: Monsieur Bobrán. It made Marcel think of something, but he wasn't sure what. Yeah, those old 1950s American films they showed sometimes in gaol, with those black servants kowtowing to rich white men, calling their masters' sleek-haired sons Monsieur Hank Junior or Mademoiselle Debbie-Jean. Kissing the boots of the people that kicked them. Not that Bobrán would ever kick anybody.

The word 'Urgent' was written in block capitals in the top left-hand corner of the envelope and underlined twice. What the fuck had Bobrán got himself into now? This African guy certainly wasn't muscle, and he didn't look like a fag, so what was it? If he was a criminal, he had originality and surprise on his side. Marcel racked his brains and shook his head. It was 21.26 now, the afternoon shift had gone, those girls were heading for their Tuesday-evening bad fucks, maybe, and Bobrán still hadn't arrived. Not that that was anything so out of the ordinary. He'd better turn up though, given that Marcel had clocked him on. Like Bobrán, Marcel was a temporary worker and could be fired at any moment, any day, or just let go if there was a fall-off in demand for their little bits of plastic. He had to keep his nose clean, be good and patient, keep everyone happy, especially the probation people. Some days it seemed a lot to ask of a person.

But it wasn't going to be forever. He wasn't a lifetime factory worker like that poor fuck upstairs, what was his name? Jean, that was it. A blank kind of name, for a blank kind of guy. The kind who is in such a hurry to get out of your way it's as if he'd prefer not to exist at all. But, for Marcel, this place and this job were just a temporary arrangement, a phase, a staging post. As it was for most of them. That Sicilian was a student of some sort, his wop sidekick was doing an apprenticeship, the black guy was some kind of entertainer, the British faceache was clearly just passing through, the peasant guy was here to prop up his failing farm. Who did that leave? Even the foreman was only there till his pension entitlement kicked in. So who was left? The bewildered and the lost: Philippe, the Arab – well, what the fuck was an Arab to do? It wasn't as if there was much call for them outside Arabia. Then there was the Portuguee, waiting for his big win. Fucking loser. That was about it. And me. Marcel shook his head and tut-tutted. I'll not be here long.

Marcel saw the Portuguee coming toward him. Marcel had plans. Major plans, even if they still needed some working on, some refining. Once he had the probation snoops off his back and could get some money together, he'd find something better than this: something that earned and that was risk-free, even legal if possible. No way was he ever going back to prison. He'd die first. He'd fucking kill first. And right now he was getting married, and that looked good to everybody. Settling down with a beautiful fresh young, well, young-ish, wife to come home to every morning. Things weren't so bad. He'd only been out of prison for six months, and look how well things had gone. He was on the up.

10. Luigi, Fernando, Alphonse, Jean.

The fact of the matter is that this man, Luigi, is, was, all of a slope, all a-slope, aslope, one long, sometimes meandering sometimes straight-as-a-die slope: every part of him and everything about him slopes, be it steeply or gently. This inclination may not, however, be the type of thing that an untrained eye would notice. Indeed, if you did not possess a peculiar bent to hunt down and fix in print an inventory of individual peculiarities across the aeons, it might be the kind of thing you would miss. It would be a shame because, quite uniquely, this man Luigi is, was, in fact all of a slope, a-slope, aslope, that he is! that he was, by God!

Standing up as straight as ever he did (and indeed could) – though he was still a young man in years (as his identity papers and mother could, respectively, succinctly and garrulously testify) – there was no surface upon his body that lay either precisely parallel or perfectly perpendicular to the floor beneath his boots. Was that so strange? Well, when you stand ramrod straight before your morning mirror, is not your back vertical and the top of your head horizontal? Of course they are. Spirit levels, you may object, are not much in use when it comes to engendering new members of the species. Yet conjure if you will an early-1950s human production line. When at last, presumably after much delay and dithering, Luigi's turn finally came to be manufactured, it must have been either a Monday morning or a Friday evening, each worker depressed by the numbing weight of the week to come or straining every sinew for imminent weekend furlough from wage bondage. Along came Luigi's body, hurriedly assembled from uneven parts by workers upstream, upon which, instead of placing the head (itself another botched item) squarely on the waiting neck and shoulders, the befuddled-Monday or skittish-Friday worker simply slapped or slammed it down any old how, with the result that it never quite took. Consequently, were it but possible for Luigi's head to be held in a thoroughly vertical position – by making use, say, of one of those table-mounted metal vices that so abounded in the metallurgy section – it might be demonstrated beyond disputation that his forehead sloped at the peculiar angle of fifteen degrees to the vertical, his nose at twenty-five degrees, and that the cleft of his upper lip was in fact very approximately horizontal.

Before returning to our main action – inaction, you may retort – mention must be made of Luigi's teeth, which presented a challenge to any dentist, a challenge, to judge by the physical evidence, that thus far, and universally, had been either funked or flunked, for the said teeth had remained spectacularly irregular, jutting odd-sized and ill-shaped at illicit angles and from highly unorthodox locations upon his mandibular structure. Two were particularly impressive, issuing almost horizontally (and therefore representing a rebuke to the foregoing generalizations regarding Luigi's inclination to slope or tendency to lean) from points one half-centimetre above his left and right canines. This orthodontic peculiarity led to Luigi's strict eschewal of public laughter, even smiling, as well as to his otherwise inexplicable habit of covering his mouth whenever amused and of turning away from any excessively diverting interlocutor in order to bray his laughter afar and unseen.

Here I now am, fulfilling my part, watching Luigi walk or stand, laugh or smile. I have made much use of the word 'slope,' yet there are others, a lumpish thesaurus of competing terms jiggering up and down for my attention, each suggesting (though none quite defining) some conspicuous aspect of his demeanour: slant, slide, slink, slip, slop and slouch. There is surely something about the s-and-l combination in English; it must have been intelligently-designed by the Great Phonologist in expectation of this very day and very need to describe Luigi's *slopefulness* (a shame that the Great Lexicographer furnished no better term for it). Note that even when the two letters in question are not immediately contiguous, their close propinquity still carries some charge: sidle, sally, scuttle, soil, sulk and sully are all words that recruit themselves with alacrity to any description of Luigi. It cannot be denied that there exists some affinity between Luigi's slipshod slew of a body and these two letters. Scrawled freehand in my own childish cursive, they even look the part: I can see Luigi as he leans into his machine, as he slathers over his titillating cartoon strips with their images of chisel-jawed slobs and ballooning slatterns, as indeed he slopes off down the machine aisle, heading for the coffee machine. So much for the never quite straight-up-and-down ell and the perennially serpentine ess. So much for a first impression of Luigi.

Luigi was wreathed in smoke. He favoured the slow-burning yellow cornpaper Gitanes, designed to go out almost the moment you forgot to suck. His eyes squinted, one closing tighter than the other.

Luigi possessed ivory-white skin, the skin of a man who seldom saw the sun, expanses of such skin broken only by stray eruptions of pimples and pustules, small cuts and scratches of the kind that brambles, cats and small rodents, not forgetting the jagged stalks of plastic product, may so easily impart; and two lurid tattoos.

In 1976, Luigi was twenty-four, though he could have been mistaken for thirty. His hair was beating a disorderly retreat from his brow, withdrawing, receding, retiring as if from hard fought battle, yet still luxuriant and long enough at the back, well combed and, one might surmise, much prized, though greying most treacherously in that blind spot behind the ears.

Luigi loped when walking and lurched even when notionally stationary. His posture could recall that of Monsieur Hulot on his celebrated holidays: he seemed perpetually to be leaning into or toward something most decidedly uncertain, something perhaps bathetically resembling the future, his mouth agape, bubbles of spittle forming at its corners, his lips slack, forever threatening to slobber.

If he had stood up straight and tall, Luigi might have measured little shy of one metre ninety – one can only guess. For his back was in fact bowed and his chest was sunken, as if sacrificed to the development of his biceps which were not only dumbbell-huge but on permanent display, thanks to his adherence to T-shirts, short sleeves and tank tops. On his left forearm he wore a tattoo of a former girlfriend, the depiction of whose charms had been obscured by a cheap attempt at deletion. The result was enraged and mostly crimson. On his right upper arm was pictured a heavily endowed naked dancing woman, whose form undulated as his biceps worked.

Luigi was standing at one of his machines, number fourteen, the one with the new mould, and was opening the safety gate after every third product, taking the piece into his naked hands by its fast-cooling still-scalding extremities and eyeing it suspiciously before slinging it with well calibrated nonchalance into the grey tray at his feet and reclosing the press door. Between each of these interventions, Luigi had a spare minute or so during which to meditate upon anything at all in the great wide world and to watch life as it unfolded, clattering and clunking, all about him.

Past the clocking-on-and-off machine to Luigi's right, which he glimpsed through the gap between the end of his machine and its control cabinet, the last stragglers from the afternoon shift were now trudging, shifting from foot to foot like soup-kitchen starvelings awaiting their turn, each eager not for a ladleful of charity swill but for outside air, dinner, home, telly, and his or her own private and temporary annihilation in the arms of Morphée. The most sluggish of the afternoon women plodded into view: floral trousers ping-taut over state-sponsored prolific hips, cracked patent-leather bootees, stale makeup daubed on jowls loosened by chronic dieting and obesity.

Luigi's gaze returned to his juddering, shuddering machine. Plop fell another product through the aluminium slats and into the already abundantly littered tray. The machines were fed through a hopper that funnelled granules into a melting chamber whence the plastic was hurled in molten gobs into the water-cooled metal mould which then opened to expel the hardening, steaming body. Luigi, who spent every morning as a butcher's apprentice, increasingly perceived his daytime carcasses as dead machinery and his nighttime presses as live animals: it amused him sometimes to exaggerate such parallels, and it helped the time pass less slowly.

As the press cleaved, disclosing the latest product, Luigi jerked open the safety door, reached his hand between the press sides, took hold of the product, closed the door and raised the product to his eyes while the machine resumed its cycle. Each of the twelve items had to be checked for imperfections: ill-formed promontories, low-pressure craters, scorched edges, redundant flaps. First from this angle then from that. A few weeks earlier, without a word, Mathieu had shown him how to perform this task, holding a fresh piece out in front of him, drawing with his thumb a line between his eyes and the piece, then shifting first his head and then the piece at ever newer angles, multiplying the perspectives. Luigi kept thinking about that demonstration. Anyway, this piece was perfect. Flick. Toss. Grey tray on floor. Wait for next.

There was a shuffling at the clock-machine. Luigi looked over to see Fernando and Alphonse arrive in a flurry of arms and coats, plucking their cards from the rack and punching in their presence. Why the excitement? Luigi wondered. Nobody gave out prizes for being *only* two minutes late: they deducted fifteen minutes pay just the same. You might as well take it slow and easy for those unpaid thirteen minutes.

As Luigi watched the two men, he became aware that his Gitanes-Maïs cigarette had been out for a while, so he fished a lighter from the bottom of his pocket and brought it up to the end of his now very short cigarette. He observed his left biceps with pleasure as he clicked the flame into life, then glanced back toward the clock-machine. Alphonse was disappearing toward the lift, blotted from the Italian's view by the control cabinet of machine thirteen, while Fernando shook hands with Mathieu, the foreman, who must that instant have stepped from the lift, crossing paths with Alphonse. Mathieu had probably gone upstairs to check on the untended machines, given that of the four upstairs workers only Jean had arrived and he would of course be lashed to his semi-automatic machine and wouldn't be able to do anything if one of the other machines malfunctioned. Luigi wondered for an instant why of the four men who sometimes arrived late (Fernando, Alphonse, Bobrán, and most often and spectacularly Jacques) three worked upstairs. It made no sense. It was, however, not his concern, none of his cocks, cabbages or onions, so what the hell.

Luigi didn't need to hear the exchange that was taking place between Fernando and Mathieu: he had worked chez Boucan long enough and had had enough to do with each man to grasp its drift. Luigi took a suck on his Gitanes Maïs and watched the two men from the corner of his eye. Fernando was gesturing toward the machines, informing Mathieu that he would only be a minute, he just had to say hello to everyone downstairs and would be upstairs directly, and all the while Mathieu was standing there saying nothing, just shrugging like on the one hand he didn't understand the need for greetings and on the other hand – in view of the fact that everything upstairs was humming along so nicely – Fernando could go and glad-hand whomsoever the devil he wanted, he really didn't give a shit.

Luigi stared and chuckled, pulling his upper lip down over his crazy teeth, not on this occasion to veil them from anybody's view, merely out of habit. It was a gesture that could recall Humphrey Bogart caught in a tight spot, like when at the end of *The Maltese Falcon* he tells the dame whom he thinks he loves and who he thinks just might love him that he is 'going to have to send her over.'

Luigi watched as Mathieu turned and moved away toward the raised office. Why did Fernando have to go round saying hello to everyone anyway? Luigi wondered, Was it a Portuguese thing? Some kind of politeness hang-up? Didn't anybody ever trouble to tell him he was paid to mind the machines, not to fucking socialize? Not that Luigi had ever encountered that socializing trait in the Portuguese before. Surly enough bunch normally. At any rate, that was what Lucien, the master butcher who trained Luigi, said about his Portuguese customers, once their backs were turned. Lucien's comments on people and nations were generally spot on because Lucien had seen a thing or two. Who was Luigi to doubt it?

Luigi checked another product. This way, that way, the other way. Fine. His mind echoed with emptiness like a starved stomach digesting itself in its own juices or a vagina clawing for repletion after orgasm. He stared into space, his focus relaxing, blurring. He could start checking the products every ten minutes, say, or fifteen even, now that the mould seemed to have settled. He felt nothing. He glanced at his leather satchel, propped against the base of the control cabinet, reached his long left arm slantingly down and hooked out a crisp clean copy of *Détective*. Luigi enjoyed the 'photography,' he told Salvatore. Rape, incest, murder, mutilation, swindling wives, cheating husbands, grannies with hatchets, children with supernumerary heads: it all helped to settle his mind and keep him from thinking of things that might upset him. Like how he felt obscurely and unfathomably sad as if forsaken by some god; how his girlfriend was growing ever more dull and fat; how his mother was unhappy and pined for *il bel paese*; how Lucien remained stubbornly unwilling to pay him a decent apprentice's wage; how Salvatore might be expecting him to take some particular part in the coming strike. Fuck that. Luigi had had his fill of futile militancy in Italy: it was always the men who lost time and energy, while the unions gained kudos and clout and kickbacks. He hadn't come to France for more of the same. Besides, if you're an immigrant you keep your nose clean. Punto e basta.

Some nights Fernando would edge between Luigi's control cabinet and the end of his machine and then have to squeeze past Luigi as they shook hands. Luigi always felt embarrassed by confined closeness, like when he had to go into the cold store with Lucien to fetch a carcass. There was not enough room for the two of them. He found his toes clenching and his fists balling and then came cascading images of Lucien dangling with a meat hook through his throat and Luigi's supposed loved ones dismembered and as blue as lamb shoulders. Anyway, tonight Fernando was taking the long and easy way round, back past the control cabinet of Luigi's other machine, number fourteen, toward the hanging flaps that led into the metallurgy section, then under the window of the raised office through which Mathieu could now be seen unpacking something from his bag, probably a banana – the man ate so many bananas he should have been a baboon – then down the machine aisle, and, hey!, there Fernando was again reaching an arm in toward Luigi.

Come sta? Fernando asked, with his leering smile, fancying himself a bit of a linguist, then laughing as Luigi turned toward him with his usual tight-lipped snarl. Ah, come on, allegria! we'll all fucking-be dead soon enough!

Luigi extended his long limp arm and stared sullenly at Fernando.

Merda, Fernando thought: this guy fucking-never smiles. Does he think our pay gets docked for smiling? Fernando recalled Alphonse asking him just that question one night when he was particularly glum. Angry Italians for Christsakes! – fucking-who needs them? Still, you have to say hello. Can't just miss him out like he's not here. Can't go offending people. And he always is here, isn't he? Like nailed to the spot. He's either at his machines gawping at a magazine or hanging out with the Sicilian. And that's another thing: how come the two of them stick round Luigi's machines all the time, like Luigi was afraid he'd miss something important? Fernando tried to decide if he had ever met a Sicilian not called Salvatore or alternatively Vito, but he gave up. Funny thing names.

You see the St Etienne–Montpellier match? Fernando asked, after a moment's hesitation. Fernando knew the Italian followed football but Luigi looked back at him blankly, began to crack a smile, raised his cigarette to his lips for the twinned purposes of concealing his mouth and feeding himself some more smoke, then exhaled through splayed fingers, and said, Nah, I was busy. Missed it. Good? Brilliant, said Fernando. Great goal clinched it in injury time. Yeah, I heard that, Luigi said, lowering his hand, looking past Fernando, and bringing that upper lip down over his teeth like tough old Bogey.

Fernando left Luigi to his magazine. He appeared to be reading an article about a woman who killed her mother-in-law with a pruning hook. Coming up the aisle, smoking one of those roll-ups that stank fucking-like a swamp, and with that nervous little walk was the English kid, Eric. Names again. Eric for example. Always thought Eric was a German name. Mind you: English, German, what's fucking-the difference? Rich countries where no one knows how to do a day's work – go figure! Fernando held out his hand and said, Good night, English, to which Eric responded, as always, Boa Tarde, which Fernando had taught him on their first ever encounter. Eric pronounced Boa like the snake and Tarde so it rhymed with Hardy, but Fernando rewarded him with a happy smirk. It was pretty good for an English.

Fernando's eyes fell next on Philippe, whose ready smile had never yet failed him. Not a care in the world, leaning there against the end of the machine, checking everyone and everything out. Probably just waiting for Jacques: those fucking-two were inseparable. Fernando wondered if tonight Jacques would bring that rabbit he had promised. I don't want to be reminding him. Then Fernando and Philippe shook hands and Philippe, like he'd just thought of something quite exceptional, beckoned Fernando closer and raised his voice and said, Did you bring your scissors with you? Shit, Fernando said, I forgot. I overslept and left my room fucking-in a whore's hurricane. Philippe smiled pleasantly at Fernando's word order and willing vernacular. He sometimes marvelled at the way Fernando mauled the language and it still survived: delicate fine-featured French encounters belligerent drunk with sledgehammer but French somehow comes out on top, the declared winner though the drunk too is still standing, i.e. still talking. Well, never mind, Philippe told Fernando. It's just that I saw myself in the mirror this evening. Maybe tomorrow? Sure okay, Fernando said, then stood back and surveyed Philippe like he was a picture hanging there against the wall and he had to be at just the right distance to appraise it right. Yeah, you fucking-could do with a trim. Well, that's grand. I was so hoping you'd agree, Philippe said with that ready smile of his.

Fernando crossed the aisle to where Marcel was filling the hopper of his machine number eleven, standing on the top step of his little ladder. Fernando shouted Hey!, and reached his hand up. Marcel paused, guessing that Philippe was looking his way, took off his left glove and poked his limp hand in the direction of Fernando, who pulled his hand up and down a couple of times. Fernando started saying something, but Marcel muttered, Yeah, sure, you're not wrong about that, put his glove back on and switched his full attention to the hopper he had to fill. Marcel had a terrible head for heights: three steps up a ladder and his head swam and his stomach got the flutters. Nobody needed to know.

Fernando laughed at Marcel's routine unfriendliness. 'Maybe if I fucking-wore a skirt . . . ,' he thought, as he headed further down the aisle. Between the last couple of machines on the right (six and seven), he spied Salvatore sitting, re-tying the laces of his work shoes. His smart attaché case was open beside him on the ground, revealing his hand-exerciser and a copy of Voltaire's *Lettres philosophiques*. Oh, hi, Salvatore said, with a nicely targeted business-like smile. I need to talk to you later, Fernando. There's maybe a strike on the cards and I want your view on it. Well, I ain't never yet crossed a picket line, Fernando said in a matter-of-fact way, adding, But I don't want fucking-any trouble. Salvatore nodded at that, pulled a union flyer from his case and pressed it into Fernando's hand. Fernando glanced at the small print – a swarm of ants was all he saw, squashed dead at that, motionless. We'll talk it over later, the Sicilian said. Okay? Good man!, and a pat on his shoulder. Salvatore turned his back and resumed tying his laces. Fernando pretended to read the flyer then stuffed it into his pocket and crossed the machine aisle to where Rachid was standing smoking, leaning back against the edge of the huge wooden table at the end of the section, his feet crossed, his eyes staring at the flank of machine number eight.

The Algerian appeared to be in a dream, standing with furrowed brow, the elbow of his left arm clutched and cupped by his caressing right hand, his left hand stroking his cheeks, his eyes full. His jacket was hanging off the back of a chair like something you might see on a scarecrow, while the chair's seat had been pushed under the table onto which Rachid had deposited his plastic bag. In the harsh neon, Fernando saw that Rachid's hair was sparse, his frame meagre, his skin grey.

Fernando couldn't ignore the man, having greeted everyone else. If he turned on his heels and walked back up the aisle, Rachid would look up at once and notice, and might feel snubbed or slighted. Maybe he couldn't care less. But, what if, Fernando thought, fucking-what if? Still, he couldn't interrupt him either, could he? Fernando made up his mind and advanced a little, satirically waving his left hand across Rachid's field of vision, imitating a hypnotist bringing a patient out of a trance.

Rachid shook his head as much as to say, Not today, thank you, but then took a step toward Fernando and stretched out his right hand. Both men simultaneously asked, Ça va? It was routine. They possessed an unspoken, uncontemplated sympathy for one another, though they never talked much. Maybe their varieties of French were too different: Rachid had the courteous, stilted variety learnt at school in Algeria during the fag-end of empire; Fernando had last year's idioms and swear words and a contempt for grammar: there wasn't a lot of overlap.

Something bad had happened or was happening to Rachid, you could see that. Fernando strained to think of the kind of bad things that might happen to somebody else: the illness of a person you love? false accusations of some terrible crime? true accusations of same? betrayal by a woman? disease? the death of loved ones? non-negotiable gambling debts? He looked at Rachid and asked again, You okay? and Rachid smiled again, a weary, kindly smile, and said, Thank you.

Rachid resumed his thoughtful pose while Fernando turned and walked up the aisle, wincing once or twice. His shiny new black leather shoes – which Maryse had so admired that afternoon – were pinching him, raising a blister, he realized, on the side of the little toe of his left foot. Upstairs, he would put on his comfortable old trainers.

As he walked past the end of machines one and two, on his left, he grinned at Philippe who was getting some kind of ear-battering from Marcel, and who was looking round, bored. Philippe seemed not to see him. Fernando turned right, walked back under the glass office, and round past the clocking-on machine, glancing to his right to see Luigi slumped over his copy of *Détective*, an extinguished cornpaper cigarette hanging from his lower lip. The lift was waiting for Fernando; he had only to part its heavy doors.

Inside the metal cage, Fernando relaxed against the wall and let his mind float back over the best moments from that afternoon, when his arousal had become complete and he had at last been able to penetrate Maryse, and she had looked really pleased not just for him but by him – or had she been pretending? – no, no, no, a man could tell, couldn't he? Sure he could. And Fernando had been a man again, a proper one. He had to work out how to please her reliably so that she would become his. He could stop gambling (her lip curled at every mention he made of it); he could then save money, treat her to things, get healthy, learn a proper trade – it was about time. Or return to the land: after all, that was what he knew best.

Fernando had once mentioned to Jacques that if he ever needed any help on his farm . . . But how likely was that? You may not think I'm much of a worker here, Fernando had said, and in factories maybe that's true, maybe I'm fucking-not, but that's because I wasn't born to it. But you put me in a field or a shed of animals and fucking-I can work fast and hard and long and well – your typical Portuguee that's me – never happier than when I've got my boots stuck in muck and my back bent and straining fucking-fit to snap. Jacques had chuckled at this tirade and shook his head and said, I know, I know and there's land lying fallow all around and it's a crime, but it's no use. If it was, I know you'd be the man to employ. But, think about this, Fernando: would I be here if working on my farm made ends meet? Eh? I'd work there myself, before getting someone else, don't you think? And Fernando had nodded, then both men had shrugged, embarrassed, and Fernando had walked away.

It had been so good that afternoon with Maryse, so warm, so sweet, but with every hour that passed, doubts stole into Fernando's head and he began to feel angry about her work. He knew this was pointless – after all, if it wasn't for her line of business, he would never have met her – but things seemed different to him now. He wanted to look after her; the problem was, right now he didn't even make enough money to look after himself. He knew nothing about her of course, but then what did you need to know about anybody? She was kind, and there weren't many kind people in the world. If only he could get lucky . . .

The lift stopped and Fernando slid open the heavy doors. He walked toward machine twenty-one, the huge semi-automatic beast that Jean worked, fucking-poor old sod. Jean looked up and saw him coming and Fernando gave him a raised-eyebrows greeting. Jean was standing by his chair, shifting from foot to foot. He waited till he got the machine-door shut, then whipped his right hand out of his glove and gave it to Fernando to shake. Ça va? they both asked, nodding their assent in well-practised unison.

Fernando dragged his feet over to his own machines, numbers sixteen and seventeen. He glanced up at the hoppers: both were three-quarters full. He knew he could always rely on the afternoon-shift worker, a snappily dressed young Moroccan called Tarik, to leave everything in order, the hoppers almost full, the machines clean. Reaching his machines felt each night like a reluctant homecoming, reminding him of the years he had lived and worked in Oporto: he would return every Friday evening to his village, he would round the bend – in the dark, most times of year – seeing the church loom into view, and the falling-down farm building that his family lived in. Every Friday he would wish he had a reason to stay in the city through the weekend, but he never had. In the village he would perform the grindingly predictable rituals of greeting, endure the perennial looks of reproof, the infinite demands on his time, energy and pocket.

Everything he had to do at the machines he had done a thousand times before. So it was with a grunt of grudging recognition that he bent down to the aluminium slats beneath the press doors of machine fifteen and caught the latest product as it fell through, heading for the grey plastic tray on the floor at his feet. As the press closed, Fernando held the piece up to his eye and looked at it carefully. Machine fifteen had been producing the same button-sized objects for months now, only occasionally varying the colour from blue, to white, to green, to red. Having finished his perusal, Fernando slung the piece in the grey floor tray, then lifted and emptied the tray into a tub resting on an upturned metal bin. Next he smartly replaced the grey tray on the floor in time to catch the following product to fall from the opening press and hurtle through the aluminium slats. Fernando went to machine number seventeen and repeated every action and gesture. Here, the product consisted of black, slightly chunkier objects made of a different and more lustrous type of plastic, a nylon. Again, the product was perfect. The mould had been in use for over ten days now. Fernando was comforted that there was nothing to worry about: tonight would be just the same as every other night. And he dreaded it: the echoing emptiness of his own mind, the excited dreams of winning jackpots, the thoughts of Maryse plying her trade, and the self-pity that comes with loneliness. If other men can afford women, why can't I? If other men win jackpots, why don't I? Am I not good enough? Am I not deserving? Fernando was the saddest kind of gambler: the kind that doesn't believe in chance.

At machines eighteen and nineteen, Alphonse talked, shouted and even occasionally whistled or sang out as he worked, wondering why in heaven he had to make so much noise just to hear himself. Downstairs there were many more machines and yet it was quieter. Was that because the ceiling was lower up here and the space so confined? Or was it because downstairs there were doors leading off to other sections of the factory, doors through which noise could, as it were, leak? How did that work then? Could noise leak? And if it could, would it leak like water so that there was less left behind? And would thin tinny music leak more readily than the close, dense viscous variety? He thought of violins and then of trombones, harmonicas and cathedral organs. Truly, he did not know.

Alphonse was repeating over and over in different manners and tones of voice a medley of fragments from Lucky's speech in Samuel Beckett's *En attendant Godot,* the play that his student workshop was rehearsing. Later he would recite it once again for Jean. He was determined to get it perfect. He declaimed the words he had learned, but could not refrain from interpolating elements of his own invention and then suppressing words and phrases from the original text, practically editing the masterpiece as he went through it. This had given rise to a problem with the director, who loathed his improvisations. Beckett, the young man snapped, is the writer here, not you, and Beckett is very, very precise about everything. Just look at the stage directions here! And remember that you are not a free agent in this matter. Every nuance has been stipulated. Nothing has been left to chance or to personal whim. Got it? Provisionally chastened, Alphonse strove to remember these strictures and to recite the words unchanged, but he could not help himself.

Alphonse looked up to see Marcel stepping out of the lift and glancing at his cousin Bobrán's machines, numbers fifteen and twenty. Alphonse flapped his arms to get Marcel's attention. Marcel looked at him as if to say, 'what's it to you?' But Alphonse was determined to be courteous and helpful and, besides, was wholly immune to Marcel's surliness. Your cousin's machines are fine, I just monitored them, Alphonse said. Marcel's mind snagged on 'monitored' and he pulled a face and said, Sure. He then nodded at the African and stepped over and shook his hand while glancing at Jean, who was standing by his chair at the massive old semi-automatic number twenty-one. Marcel hesitated an instant and decided not to bother with him. Looking squarely at Marcel, Alphonse felt he could read every movement of Marcel's mind. Could anybody be that scrutable?

Do you know, will your cousin be coming tonight? Alphonse asked.

Guess so. Didn't say he wasn't.

The fuckwit had better turn up, Marcel thought, I want to give him that letter. It has got me spooked. I want to get rid of it. It must be about something.

Jean stood at machine number twenty-one, wishing the time would pass more quickly. He had a rigorous yet flexible routine of items to think about from ten onward, but this first half hour was all waiting and watching. And – who could tell – maybe Bobrán wasn't coming this evening, so maybe he would not get his regular coffee at ten. That could upset him, put him off his stride, ruin his night.

Jean's legs were aching from standing up: he was growing old. A neighbour of his had developed varicose veins and Jean hoped that didn't happen to him. What a humiliating thing to have: a woman's disease. How would he ask for time off work? And then, given that it was a woman's disease, would he perhaps have to go and see a woman's doctor, a what-do-you-call-them, a gynaecologist? Stand – he would have to stand – in a room full of women with menstruating problems or fibroids. Monique had had fibroids. How would he bear the smirks on the faces of Mathieu, Philippe and those other goodfornothings downstairs? Of course it might never happen. Especially if he stopped thinking about it. Everyone knew that thinking about bad things made them more likely.

Jean eyed the seat. He would very much like to sit down upon it, take the weight off his old legs, veins and all. Probably he could sit down now without any real danger. He had sponged the seat with disinfectant on arrival and placed a clean tea towel on it. Still, he had rules. He never sat down till ten, by which time, he figured, the body heat of the afternoon worker who had preceded him should have dissipated sufficiently to render quite safe any residual airborne contamination from the man's intestines. Jean had heard of such dangers and they terrified him. At ten o'clock, or as soon after ten as Bobrán — assuming he showed up tonight — had brought him his coffee, he would sit down comfortably and begin to consider the day's events, as gleaned from newspapers, conversation and television. It was something to look forward to, since it had been a good day for events. But not yet, not yet. Discipline was essential, discipline was paramount, discipline was his talent, his vocation. He looked at his wristwatch. 21.27. Time was passing after all. Thank goodness for that. For a moment, Jean had feared that time was standing still and that he would never ever sit down again.

11. Marcel, Philippe, Salvatore, Luigi, Rachid.

Every trace of the afternoon shift had vanished and of the night-shift workers only Jacques and Bobrán were still at large; either might show up any minute: no one could ever tell for certain. The plastics section seemed spacious, tranquil despite the din, and comfortable, almost homely. Alone among men, you could loosen your belt and let your gut hang right out, what the hell, scratch that itch and roll out that fart without dissembling or fear. It was intimate.

Back downstairs at his machines numbers eleven and twelve, Marcel carefully checked the most recently ejected products, then flicked a liquid glance across the aisle at Philippe. The Marseillais was still leaning against the side of his machine, his arms folded and one foot hooked around the other. Allowing for the odd minute to check products, empty trays and so on, Philippe could while away hours adrift in contemplation, observing his workmates come and go, chewing the occasional cud. He had a bubbly little smile in his eyes and a fresh cigarette in his mouth. Okay, so maybe Danielle is screwing somebody and, as a husband, I ought to do something about that, there are rules, and I will, things'll change, but, still, life isn't half-bad.

Marcel's long ladies' eyelashes rose and fell with the rhythm of his thoughts. Why didn't Philippe get himself some new clothes, he wondered, or a new woman who would dress him better? He was going to seed, it was a pathetic sight. His bald patch was showing in the neon. Marcel lifted his left hand to a point inches above his own head, then extended his ring finger downward and with its tip poked gently at his crown. The hair he discovered there was still tolerably lush, giving no cause for immediate concern. A feeling of warmth spread through his stomach like fine chicken consommé, lapping lazily at its lining. His hand fell back and he looked again at Philippe. Maybe it was just what happened when you had a child or hit thirty-five, like grey hair and early-morning halitosis. Not my problem, though. Marcel finished what he was doing and peeled off his industrial gloves. Then he ambled across the machine aisle toward Philippe.

Philippe saw Marcel coming. He took his cigarette out of his mouth, pursing his lips and blowing the smoke down to one side, giving Marcel his all-purpose all-tolerant smile. As Marcel opened his mouth, Philippe anticipated the question, so the conversation, which should have gone: 'Shall we go get a coffee? Yeah, let's. But mine's a beer,' in fact went something like: 'Yeah, let's Shall we go But mine's get a beer a coffee?'

Philippe donned his pleased-with-myself look and Marcel laughed. Second-guessing people was one of Philippe's favourite games and he was good at it. Nobody minded: it was a harmless tease. He now uncrossed his legs and arms and sauntered out into the middle of the machine aisle from where he could see Eric bent over a bin of product at machine number ten. Remarking the tang of nicotine on his right thumb and middle finger, Philippe manufactured a piercing whistle, to which Eric, momentarily canine, lifted his snout bang on cue. Philippe performed a series of simple gestures involving his right hand holding and jiggling an imaginary coffee cup and his index finger pointing to Marcel and back at himself several times, and finally the same finger pointing up the machine aisle and jabbing in the approximate direction of the coffee- and beer-machines.

Eric's mouth hung open, a roll-up stuck to his lower lip, while his mind did a lot of code-breaking, until his face lit up as if someone had thrown a switch. No problem, he mouthed. Philippe gave him a friendly thumbs-up, as much as to say 'aren't you a clever boy?' and in the harsh factory light Eric's pimples and nose gained a proud new lustre. He would cheerfully keep an eye on Philippe's and Marcel's machines while they went off for their hard-earned coffee. A responsibility and an honour.

Philippe and Marcel glanced at one another, their heads shaking.

Talk about slow, Marcel said.

Philippe looked at Marcel like he might have a question.

As in stupid fuckwit, Marcel clarified.

It's just that everything is new to him, Philippe commented kindly. You know, I think he's all right, that kid. He'll stand sentry on our machines like a regular squaddie till we get back, won't ever unglue his eyes from our warning lights, you'll see.

Marcel looked disapprovingly at the end of his cigarette, which had burned down almost to the filter. Then he dropped it on the floor and turned the sole of his shoe on it. Come on, let's go for this drink, Philippe then said, heaving a great satirical sigh, like it was a chore and life was hard.

In the pool of light that surrounded the coffee machine, dark-eyed, smooth and stately Salvatore was talking in silken tones to Luigi, whose mind was otherwise engaged. Salvatore stood straight and tall and spoke like a news bulletin.

He was describing at length a meeting he had enjoyed earlier that evening with a handful of union representatives from other shifts and sections of the factory. The central issue, it had emerged, was the failure of management to meet union demands on improvements to wages and conditions: in a word, the negotiation of a new contract. Salvatore kept using terms and acronyms that meant little or nothing to Luigi (the works committee, the CFDT, the caucus – that kind of thing), while referring by name to individuals of whom Luigi had never heard. Meanwhile, Luigi's thoughts roamed unfettered across the story he had been reading in *Détective* until Salvatore had interrupted him to go for a coffee. How could that fat old slut in Annecy possibly have expected to get away with fucking her husband's younger brother? The wedding photo of her and her car-mechanic husband was all smiles and pouting, portending a life of measured bliss, but sooner or later, her husband was just bound to leave his workshop early, go home and discover them whooping it up on the living-room sofa, right in front of the dog, goddamnit, the husband's dog, the cheating swine. And then, having witnessed the deed, wasn't the poor miserable cuckold almost obligated to double-back to his clapped-out Renault 4 van – Luigi, who had always liked Renault 4s, savoured this detail – to fetch a large wrench? Having done which, was it any wonder that the wife and brother ended up dead and the sofa a soggy, squelchy write-off? Life's like that. You can't just grab what you want. You have to be smart. Patient. You have to work for it. Graft for it. That was what Luigi reckoned. He wondered how the story had ended, whether the husband had made an attempt to conceal the bodies, perhaps by chopping them up and burying the bits in woods – that wasn't unusual, was it? And there were so many woods around Annecy, the husband would be spoiled for choice. Luigi remembered going there once with his girlfriend, Gilberte, who liked on Sunday afternoons to go for a long drive out of town, followed by a short walk around, followed by a long drive back. Luigi hated Sunday-afternoon drives, but Gilberte always insisted they needed the relaxation. Luigi was looking forward to finishing the story when he got back to his machines. The husband would probably top himself, they usually did, though Luigi, however hard he tried, really couldn't see why. Killing your cheating wife and kid brother might be an overreaction, granted, but taking your own life was plain stupid. After all, you might get off on a technicality, like that you were bonkers at the time. And prison might be the making of you. Some people never looked back. At worst it was a doddle. Lounging around watching TV, spending time in the gym improving your biceps, maybe learning a useful trade. It had to be better than death.

Don't you agree? Salvatore enquired.

Shit, Luigi muttered. Then, playing it safe: I don't know anything about it.

Well, it seems to me that well-prepared industrial action, provided there's unanimous support, is the way forward. Clock off half an hour before the official end of every shift, that's the idea. It's been tried before and has worked. You see, the next shift would take half an hour to get the machines working again at full tilt so the company would be losing at least three hours production a day, right?, whereas each worker would only lose half an hour's pay. Then there's all the extra engineering input that would be required, given that these machines don't exactly like being turned on and off all the time.

Yeah, Luigi said, they hate it. It takes them time to settle back down. If the temperature or pressure are out by more than a fraction, there's wastage. And the company fucking hates wastage.

Absolutely. That's what we figured. So the engineers would be on expensive overtime, Salvatore continued, thinking aloud now. And if at the end of it we did secure a better deal, that would ratchet up their pay as well. I mean, you can't mess with differentials. That's the way I see it. So the engineers will not want to undermine us by keeping the machines running or anything.

Salvatore stared at Luigi, who was holding his coffee cup at an angle and tapping its side, hoping to get the moisture at its bottom to gather itself together and form a solid droplet that he could then roll down and tip into his mouth. It looked like it wasn't about to happen, at least not imminently. What moisture there was was being absorbed by the sugar sludge. Luigi was thinking about those woods near Annecy picturing the old cuckold digging away with a coal shovel – apparently, the magazine said, he'd loaned his garden shovel to a neighbour: interesting detail that, demonstrating it wasn't all just made up – and he was sweating buckets, and Luigi hadn't noticed that Salvatore had shut up and was looking at him. Luigi was too busy thinking how the killer could probably have saved himself a lot of trouble if he had ever put half as much muscle and commitment into fucking his wife as he was now forced to put into digging the hole for her and his kid brother.

Are you sure you're okay? Salvatore asked, his voice going all putty-soft, sticky, gooey.

Luigi glanced up at him, perplexed. He shrugged, but found nothing to say.

You seem like a worried man, Salvatore pronounced. Let me say something. Don't take offence. We're both foreigners here, right? We're both from Italy, right? Which makes us compatriots, okay? And you look like something's eating you. If there's anything I can do . . .

Luigi raised his eyebrows, scratched his head, and pulled his upper lip down over his teeth to cloak a nervous smile. He tried to think of something, some titbit fit for conversation at the coffee machine, but he couldn't imagine anything he could possibly want to tell Salvatore. Besides, everything was fine, wasn't it?

Luigi ran a quick check on his life. Girlfriend, Gilberte: boring as hell but no great hassle. Apprenticeship: fine if only Lucien would pay him properly. Parents: separated so no longer at each others' throats. Money: no immediate concerns. Luigi realized with wary satisfaction that he had nothing to complain about. Indeed, right now he was probably about as contented as he ever would be. In later years, he might be married, miserable, ill, plagued by screaming children or dying parents. Yeah, fuck it, this was probably a high point, he ought to celebrate, treat himself to a high-class hooker or something. Some treat to remember when he's old and sick and can't get it up no more. All in all, right now, he had a lot to be thankful for. As his grumpy old grandfather used to say when things went all right for a spell, Luigi was 'between troubles.' He smiled as he remembered the old curmudgeon and decided to give the phrase a retread.

I'm between troubles, Luigi said, turning to Salvatore.

Salvatore looked puzzled, then said, Well, you can tell me all about them, if you like. What kind of troubles are they?

I don't know. Like I said, I'm *between* them. You get it?

Salvatore screwed his eyes up like a child with a maths problem, then nodded like he understood.

What I mean is, Luigi said slowly, picking his way through the words with some care, The fact is, right now, I don't have any troubles. As such. Okay? *Between* troubles. See?

Salvatore's eyes opened very wide.

Jesus, Luigi thought, Sicilians are supposed to be smart. And this one spends his days at the university getting himself a degree. Even represents us in the union. Jesus. He couldn't even make sense of my grandad, who was so simple he was illiterate.

Forget it, Luigi said at last, mysteriously adding, you never met my grandfather.

Salvatore brightened up.

Oh, family troubles, is it? I know. Absolutely. Stuff you don't want to talk about. I'm not offended. Who am I, right? We're not close friends. But, like I said, we're both foreigners and foreigners should look out for one another, so if you wanted you could tell me anything, it wouldn't go any further. We're both Italians, right?

Luigi took out his packet of cornpaper Gitanes. Normally he only smoked at his machines, didn't feel the need otherwise. Funny how embarrassment made you want to smoke. What was Salvatore on about . . . what was he after? Was he some kind of finocchio? He didn't seem like one. Besides, he was getting married. Then what did he want? Maybe he was thinking to take up counselling and wanted to get some practice. Or maybe he wanted an ally. Yeah, that could be what he wanted, an ally for his union shenanigans. Luigi gave up trying to corner that last droplet of coffee, screwed the paper cup into a ball and slung it into the dark. Futt-chuh! it went, hitting a machine and then the floor.

Salvatore took a step back and said, I've got to have a word with Philippe.

Don't mind me, Luigi thought, looking round just as Philippe and Marcel came looming into view.

Salvatore said, Look, Luigi, we'll talk later, right?

Whatever you say, boss, Luigi muttered, but he stayed close behind the Sicilian. There was nowhere else to go and, besides, it was the only way back to his machines.

Luigi, Salvatore, Philippe and Marcel met about halfway between the coffee machine and the plastics section. They all shook hands silently, then Salvatore, turning to Philippe, said, I need to talk to you about something.

Philippe looked away into the dark.

If it's about the strike plans, Marcel and I have an urgent beer to drink.

Marcel pulled on his cigarette and grinned into Salvatore's face but Salvatore was too focused on Philippe to notice. Luigi gawped.

It's something else, something important, Salvatore said, his chest puffing out.

This beer's pretty important too, Philippe said, looking away again. So, what's it about then, the graffiti?

Salvatore's eyes narrowed. He took a half-step back and said nothing. Luigi screwed up his face in bewilderment, while Marcel said, What? There's been more graffiti?

Sure, this morning, Philippe said, keeping his eyes trained on Salvatore.

How come you know about it? the Sicilian asked.

I guess you're not the only one with spies on the day shift. Then, with an odd, tinny little laugh that surprised all four men, Or maybe I did the graffiti myself.

Salvatore nodded, as if he'd considered that possibility.

Nice idea. What did it say? Marcel asked.

A mischievous allegation regarding our esteemed employer's war record, Philippe reported.

So why did you do it? Marcel asked, eager to play straight-man to Philippe's comedian.

What else do I have to do in the middle of the night? Everyone knows I like pranks, even if it's not precisely the kind I usually pull. Too deep for everyday. Raking over old memories. Historical guilt. Apportioning blame. I usually just hide people's food or tie their shoelaces together while they're distracted. That's my level. For a joke like this you'd want some other kind of prankster: the late-situationist, radical-urban, anarchist variety, I should think.

You seem to know what you're talking about, Salvatore said.

Philippe pictured the Sicilian's attaché case swinging through the air, whee-ush, whee-ush.

Only because you don't, Philippe whispered.

There was a silence.

Look, really, I'm sorry, Philippe then said, walking round Salvatore with Marcel in his wake, but this beer won't wait, it's not just important, it's a priority. And Boucan's war crimes aren't. They're not even news.

Luigi continued to gawp, forgetting to roll his upper lip down over his crazy teeth, but nobody was looking at him anyway. Salvatore opened his mouth to make some pronouncement, but Philippe was melting into the darkness toward the beer-dispenser, Marcel behind him, repeating as his head shook, 'I'm sorry, but this beer won't wait.' Philippe had a gift, you had to hand it to him.

Rachid was at the top of a stepladder when it happened, his right arm sunk in the hopper, stirring. It had never previously caught him in the factory, but why not? It could happen anywhere, he should know that by now: once in a cinema, during a film, with Malika by his side oblivious; once at the restaurant where he worked, and he had had to go to the toilet till it passed; once in the Jewish bistrot where they served the best berbouche in town; occasionally, just walking down the street, any street; often, as he stood on the bridge, looking down at the water's rippling surface, though the bridge had now become his special place for communing with Mehdi, the place where he expected it to happen, the place he went looking for it.

Ordinarily when the fit came there was no warning or at most a teasing background melancholy, like barely audible music, merely atmospheric. But when the first shock came, it was as infallible as the tickle in your nostril that precedes a sneeze. You know there is nothing you can do. You know you will be reduced to tears. Only then will it leave you alone again for a few hours, a few days.

Standing or sitting still or waiting for sleep were worst, tantamount to inviting an attack, saying 'come and get me!' Doing things busily was best: cooking, talking to somebody, waiting on tables at the restaurant, checking product at the factory. But nothing gave you immunity.

Rachid was at the end of machine eight, standing on the third step of an aluminium stepladder, having emptied into the hopper an oblong bin containing a carefully proportioned mix of virgin raw material, colour granules and reground plastic. He had thought he was safe from thoughts of Mehdi: he still had to learn there was no time and no place beyond the reach of his grief.

His right arm was plunged deep into the hopper, stirring the mix of raw materials. Stir, stir, stir: stir the whirling patterns, shiny and dull, dull and shiny, shiny white and coloured granules and dull powder, shiny and dull like the drizzle that had fallen that day and the cars that whooshed past, dull like the pavement on which Rachid and Mehdi had stood, the child's tiny right hand held just tightly enough, anyone would have thought, in the father's large bony left. Then a rushing dizziness shrouded Rachid's vision, blurring the powder and the granules to a darkening mud colour, asphalt browns and greys. No vision as such, just an immediately familiar, intimately owned terror, as personal as the smell of one's own sex.

From that point on it was unstoppable, though Rachid had learned to delay it for seconds, even minutes, if only at the expense of making the imminent seizure more violent. Not yet the rehearsal of brute facts, the mechanics of impact, injury and death. First, like a caption, the blunt knowledge that he would not be seeing Mehdi again, that dead was dead and could not return: the empty horror of the day after the funeral, with nothing more to do. No longer to see him come and go, never again to play like a child with his child. One child had died that day, but two had been buried.

Only then, drip drip drip, the detailed recollection, the minute reliving of his child's slaughter, the precision and the banality of it, the stifled invisible screaming, the paramedics, the staring bystanders, the fuzzy bass of his own pulse thumping in his head, the moped lying on its side, an ungainly and ridiculous assassin, its long-haired, doe-eyed rider shaking himself and repeating: 'he came out of nowhere, nowhere. I wasn't going fast.'

Rachid delayed, grinding his teeth, commanding his tear ducts to clamp shut, clenching his fist on the plastic fodder and focusing on the surface of the raw material in the hopper till the colours and the individual granules and powder flakes regained some of their sharpness. He closed the hopper lid, reached for the empty oblong bin on the top of the control cabinet, and climbed down the stepladder, as if en route for the next chore. Instead, he walked to the table, pulled out the chair and dragged it to the far corner, placing it alongside the control cabinet of machine eight in a position where he would be invisible from the rest of the plastics section, sat down, as if ashamed, out of sight even from the raised glass office.

And slowly he wept. Mehdi, he whispered, seeing again in alternating frames the wide-angle street scene of death and the close-up of the boy's tousle-haired head as it slowly hit for the thousandth time the kerbstone at his feet. Rachid no longer needed to fight this off: he was ready to yield to the fit, allowing it to take charge, accepting that it had to run its course and comforted by the expectation that afterward, once the bond had been reforged, he might again speak to Mehdi, hug him close, carry him forward in his own meagre belly, a man pregnant with grief for his beautiful son.

Mehdi, Rachid whispered, Forgive me for being distant these last few days. But we can talk now. I have something good to tell you.

BOOK TWO. SETTLING.

In which Philippe and Alphonse take a look at the papers, Bobrán improvises a minor stunt, Mathieu and Tomec engage in their first ever polysyllabic conversation, Jeanne falls into a dreamy sleep, Rachid issues an abrupt warning, Lucie praises her saviour, and Moritz makes plans for the weekend. In the plastics section of Éts. Boucan, more or less everybody settles down to work, pacing their moods and moulding their minds to the night ahead. While life goes on all around them.

*

12. Men tending machines. Philippe stacks and skims.

Alphonse clattered up the five stepladder steps, his forearms scissoring like a sprinter's, his clicking fingers snapping nothing but the stagnant air. He was a flash of white and black and citrus: his orange apron was drawn tight over white T-shirt and trousers; his ankles and hands were hugged by lime socks and surgical gloves; his feet were swaddled in lemon brothel creepers, his hair was protected from staticky flakes of floating plastic by a shiny white trilby. Apart from a single blister nagging at his left heel, Alphonse felt clean and sharp and bright, a knife slicing a path through a swamp.

His feet came to an unsteady rest on the top step of the ladder. His left hand shot out to grip the left edge of the hopper lip while his right hand flicked the lid up, back and over. The sheen of his usual mood was disturbed by a flicker of revolt: the narrowly avoided barroom brawl returned to infuriate him, bristling now with imagined blows, bruises, flying chairs, bottles broken and brandished amid a bevy of uncouth epithets: a scene from a bad western.

Alphonse leaned against the hopper, his shoulders hunching, his hips curving back, his large eyes restless beneath his high forehead. This unwonted anger might be useful in my acting, he thought: the better to inhabit Pozzo, perhaps. Or Lucky? But surely Lucky has no anger in him, too abject in his abasement? Pozzo, then: Up pig! Up scum! Alphonse hurled with a nice simulacrum of fury.

He scanned the surface of the raw material. The hopper's viewing porthole, when he had checked it, had shown no light, but it was hardly to be trusted. Did not material often stick to the hopper's inside walls while a pit formed at its centre, directly above the chute? He stared down at the granular and powdery contents of the not-quite-full hopper, rejecting the urge to smooth it with his gloved hand. Better not rouse the lethal dust while his face was naked. The nose-peg he used when mixing material was stowed in his trouser pocket, hard up against his left thigh, while his face mask lay flattened in his apron pouch.

Alphonse's right hand travelled around the lip of the hopper until its middle finger could insert itself between the hopper and the hinged lid, which he now hooked and pulled up and over, catching it with his left hand to break its fall, saving his ears from a clang of metal and his throat and lungs from a puff of plastic.

Alphonse's mind idled on Pozzo and Lucky, turning over memorized phrases, cooking them like eggs on the griddle of his tongue, then sliding them out through his sizzling lips. 'Is everybody ready? Is everybody looking at me? Will you look at me, pig!' Or, less certainly: 'Hog. Will you look at me, hog! Won't you look at me, pig? Is everybody staring at me?' He scowled at the floor between his machines, just as Pozzo might scowl at Lucky. 'Pig?' 'Pig!' But why was he, Alphonse, cast as the victim in this play, the roped slave? He, a black man . . . should he take some offence? And if so, how much? Would he rather play Pozzo, the slave-driver? Well, it was a bigger part . . .

As the great semi-automatic machine number twenty-one wrenched open, Jean peeped through the gap that the cleaving press briefly afforded him and up at Alphonse: the grinning African is jabbering again, he said to himself, with a shake of his smoothly combed head – standing on a stepladder jabbering!

Downstairs, stooping beside the opening presses of machine number fourteen, his mind and sympathies still engaged by the story of the wife-murdering car mechanic from Annecy Luigi swooped low to catch the latest product piece as it fell through the clattering aluminium slats. He caught it before it hit the grey rectangular tray, then straightened up to his ordinary slouch, sweeping the object to a distance from his eyes and to a position vis-à-vis the ambient light, perfectly calibrated to permit its thorough inspection: this way, that way.

His right eye closed against a whorl of smoke careening upward from his cornpaper cigarette. He removed the stub from his mouth and lay it on a ledge to go out, while he refocused his eyes on the product, and his thoughts on the murderer. Luigi hoped the man wouldn't slit his own throat or slash his wrists or do for himself in any other way. Everyone makes mistakes. I too once considered working as a car mechanic. The moral was: if you've got a woman, keep her well fucked at all times, don't let her appetites lead her astray. Gilberte's square-featured face, smiling uncertainly, skittered through Luigi's mind.

The Italian turned the piece slowly in his large hands, multiplying perspectives, profiles, angles. To his restless eyes and revolving head, it continued, stubbornly, to appear faultless. He was looking forward to finishing the article in *Détective*, to reading its conclusion. This piece of plastic seemed perfect. He had never stared at anything so hard. No flaps, no scorching, none of those stunted, globular, bulbous bits like quick-grilled cheese fingers or napalmed limbs. The more you looked at an object, the more certain you became, but how many views were enough to know, really to know? A hundred? A million? Fuck it: if it was meat, you could get at it from the inside, rip it wide open. But with this stuff, you never knew, you only saw the outside. If that.

With a sullen but decisive snarl Luigi slung the piece down before him into the grey tray at his feet, where it came neatly to rest beneath its successor, even now dropping through the slats. Luigi took his lighter from a pocket and his cornpaper stub from the ledge, and with a thin blue flame touched the tobacco back to life. His mind was hollowed by an instant of clutching vacancy, then his eyes turned to his satchel, and his mind came to rest on the choice of reading before him: *Détective*, *L'Equipe*, and a sci-fi porno strip – intergalactic violence wreaked by hugely endowed male and female aliens. There was no need to submit to boredom.

How cool is that brunette? I can call her by her name now, can't I? How cool is Fanny, Fan-*nie*? Standing there doing nothing, yet doing so much. How cool was that?

Eric's body was still tingling with expectation. He went up onto his tiptoes to fetch down from the top of the control cabinet of machine number six the empty red oblong bin (as long as an arm, as wide and as deep as a hand). The pupils of Eric's small grey eyes shrank to dots. He had to concentrate on what he was doing, avoid mistakes, mix the right quantities of material, feed the ravenous hopper with the fodder it required. Eric shook his head, sending his mop of fair hair swaying. He carried the red oblong bin to the other end of the machine, his mind fixing on the past and future.

Fanny had just stood there, her left hand jammed tight and deep in that jeans pocket, her right hand holding a cigarette, as he held his right hand out toward her to shake hello. Eric put the tub down on the floor against a sack almost full of virgin plastic raw material, and squatted alongside. He had looked up at her, for the first time straight into her face, instead of sidelong at her breasts. He had had no choice: she had been in control. Eric opened the sack, found the scoop half buried inside, its handle pointing toward his hand. He measured and emptied three scoopfuls into the red oblong bin.

Fanny had smiled when he had looked at her. Had he smiled back? She had brought her left hand out of her pocket as if to confuse him and raised her right hand and shown him her cigarette, which she had twirled in her fingers. She had asked for a light. 'Du feu,' he seemed to remember. From that moment, everything had gone right and he had got the date.

Eric sank the scoop back into the sack and stared at the half-full bin. Had he got the date or had she got the date? Eric closed the sack of plastic and pushed it till it slumped back against the machine end.

He stood up and removed the lid from the waist-high cardboard recycled material cylinder: it was one quarter full. He would have to reach right down into it. He hesitated, twitching with memory and expectation.

The moment came again, that moment when she was just standing there, waiting for him to find his lighter, twirling her cigarette – a Royale, right? – in those long, patient, fingers. How cool was she? Had he looked a fool? Probably. Who to? To anyone looking. But to her? He might hope not.

Eric had just extinguished one cigarette but was now longing for another. He had to find somewhere better to live, somewhere decent to bring Fanny. He didn't want to take her to the slum where he lived or have to introduce her to his flatmates. But this is only a date, a first date! Calm down! Besides, my squalid little room was good enough for Megan, when she came over. But that was Megan and this is Fanny. Hell, he would have to do something about Megan. And he had to find a better room for Fanny. Wait a minute! Maybe it would be only the one date. Megan would be distraught if he chucked her. Quite naturally. He hadn't really loved her for ages. If ever. He had been meaning to tell her. But there was no need to be unnecessarily cruel. At least not until I'm sure it's over. Meanwhile, he could ask Philippe about flats. Philippe might know about flat-hunting. He had to find somewhere better to take Fanny.

Eric withdrew the scoop from the bag of new plastic material, then plunged the scoop, his arm, his entire upper body and his head deep into the recycled-material cylinder. He emerged with fluff on his stubbly cheeks, in his hair, sticking to his clothes, catching between his parted lips. Eric felt he ought to let Megan know. But what was the rush? Damn it, Megan could go to hell. What he needed was somewhere nice to bring Fanny. He would be gentle with Megan. She would be upset. To be kind, he would let her down slowly. He wouldn't ditch her till he was certain.

Eric emptied the scoopful of recycled light-yellow plastic fluff and powder into the red oblong bin, then repeated the entire operation. Three scoops of virgin to two of recycled. He didn't want to get the proportions wrong, mess things up again. He dropped the scoop back in the plastic sack, then pulled a flake of recycled plastic from his left eyelash and placed it carefully between his lips. It was warm and had rough edges. He turned to a grey oblong bin half full of canary-yellow pellets the very shape and size of the chicken-manure pellets his mother always spread around her roses. Not the same consistency, though: these were as hard as plastic could be. You couldn't even dent them between your teeth. He picked the flimsy white plastic beaker from among the yellow pellets, half-filled it, then emptied it into his hopper mix.

How cool Fanny had been! – *his* Fan-*nie* (he was sure of it momentarily). The way she took the initiative! He hadn't had to do a thing: she fixed the date, she told me which cinema, said what time. She even told me she wouldn't teach me French. She even pointed to where I'd put my lighter. I think I like a girl who takes control.

Eric plunged his right hand into the mix of materials in the red oblong bin, straight through the surface sprinkling of canary-yellow pellets, on past the warm soft powder and fluff, down to the cold velvety virgin raw material at the bottom of the oblong bin. His hand began to push and pull and blend the three ingredients till the mix seemed homogeneous, just the lunch the machine required.

Eric's mind was jumping with later and now and then and maybe. He ought to be cooler. He ought to be as cool as Fanny. He thought of his new heroes: Camus now, not Orwell; Gabin not Bogart; Brel not Lennon. How would Camus have dealt with the situation? Camus dressed for that photo, in the gabardine, with the cigarette. Camus never worked in a factory, did he? But you could picture him walking up to some left-bank intellectual in horn rim specs, say, or, no, better, a beautiful Maquisarde, right? – the very spit of Fanny, but in different clothes, wearing whatever Maquisardes wore, right? – Camus, with his arm outstretched, and Fanny the young Maquisarde, her right hand stuck in her trousers or her skirt or her dungarees – what the hell did beautiful Maquisardes wear, anyway? – and then, instead of giving him her hand, she waves an unlit cigarette at him. 'Du feu?' How would Camus have handled that?

Eric's hand stopped massaging the material. It was more than ready for the hopper: his mother's blender couldn't have got it any more even. So up the ladder with it. And down the chute. Gobble, gobble, gobble. Eric's mind went blank. Camus. Camus takes a step back, glancing down with one of those sardonic little smiles – like in the photos, right? – and he puffs on his inevitable cigarette, breathes out through his nostrils, then says, really sure of himself, cool, cocksure, Now that you've got me here, I had better ask you out, hadn't I? I had been planning to anyway. Then, before she can reply, he reaches his glowing cigarette steadily toward her so she can light hers straight from his. That blatant, that cool. Now they both know that no one is in control. It was a shame about Megan. Eric definitely felt bad about that. Though maybe not as bad as he ought to.

Moving with the slow rolling measure of a man twice his weight, twice his age, or both, Marcel bent at the knees and hip and raised from the ground a red oblong bin, which he had previously filled with a mixture of light-blue (raw) and dusty-grey (recycled) material. His back hurt and he dreaded the stepladder. As he straightened up, he lifted the bin above his head, setting it carefully on the top of the control cabinet of machine number twelve. He approached the stepladder, took hold of its left side and positioned his right foot plumb in the middle of the bottom step. He drew breath.

Marcel scaled the stepladder one deliberate step at a time. As he did so, a pack of worries fell away from him: that his cousin Bobrán would not turn up for work, leading to the discovery that he, Marcel, contrary to factory regulations, had clocked another person on; that the girls from the afternoon shift, whom he had marked out as his own, might in a matter of hours or even minutes be betraying him with their husbands or boyfriends; that the letter for Bobrán from the enigmatic African might portend some ill; that his hair loss and girth swelling (about which Chantal had lately begun to complain) might prove ineluctable; that Chantal might change her mind about marrying him and, at the last moment, call it off; that his Gypsy nature might without warning break forth to shame him; that he might either fail to find illegal work and so remain poor, or succeed in finding it only to fetch up back in prison (a turn of events that would surely kill him); and, lastly, that Bobrán and his fortune-telling mother, with their folksy Romany ways, would disgrace him at his wedding. By the time, however, that Marcel had reached the top step, all such worries, as well as others more remote, had quitted his mind, chased away by the immediacy of back pain and vertigo. For Marcel hated his feet to leave the ground and, when they did so, he could not bear to lower his eyes, let alone look upon any object or person still blessed by contact with the ground or floor, convinced that to do so would bring on a perilous fit of dizziness.

Marcel lifted the hopper lid and turned his upper body carefully to the right, his thighs hard up against the hopper. He slid the bin across the cabinet top, and eased it onto the hopper edge. His mind turned momentarily to reconsider Philippe: that man should pull himself together, drink less, smarten up. It's not my problem, but what's wrong with him? He had none of my disadvantages.

Marcel raised the far end of the red oblong bin until its contents dribbled then cascaded into the hopper. Philippe is clever, Marcel thought. He has no Gypsy or other dubious connections, no prison record, and he is respected, even liked. He could easily get promotion within the factory, or within the union. He is popular, he is trusted, yet he seems uninterested in either route. Has the man no ambition? Then there's that wife, whom he allows to stray, run amok. That's no way for a man. Marcel, for his part, was embarked upon an arduous but resolute journey away from dirt and drink and poverty and bad manners and chaos and faithless women. He was headed to a better place and a better life.

Marcel replaced the empty bin upon the control cabinet, flicked the hopper lid back over, and began to pick his way back down the stepladder one step at a time. As his shoes touched down on the floor, his mood lifted like a wish. Climbing the ladder was the only part of this job that he particularly disliked. He looked at his watch, finger-combed his hair, tucked his garish green shirt into his trousers, then sought his reflection in the glass of the safety-door to machine number twelve. He saw a square-shouldered, broad-chested, clean-cut young man. Well, almost clean-cut. Damn it, I'm not bad. He smirked side-long at his reflection.

The foreman intruded upon Marcel's field of vision, breaking into his reverie, tapping his watch, giving Marcel an interrogative cobalt stare. Marcel, in turn, rested his lazy eyes on Mathieu. He didn't trust the man. He nodded his head very slightly to one side and back again to signify, 'he'll be here, you'll see.' The foreman flicked his eyes open then shut, and murmured 'bien,' then walked off. Marcel turned and looked far away down the aisle, as though it were a landscape deserving of his softest focus.

Salvatore had changed into a neat dark-blue boiler suit, which made him look like a day-shift engineer. He had hung his clothes at the back of the control cabinet of machine number seven, having removed his keys, wallet and purse. He walked back between machines seven and six, lifted his attaché case from the chair where he had left it, turned the combination lock to 1713, the date of birth of Denis Diderot, his current Enlightenment hero, and deposited his keys and wallet in one of the sleeves of the case while dropping his purse into the trousers of his boiler suit: he would be needing one-franc and fifty-centime bits for coffees during the night. In his hip pocket, against his right buttock, he could feel the folded union leaflet in the place he had stowed it. He might adapt some of its arguments for the strike meeting later that night. He twiddled the combination lock, then placed the black case behind the chair, against the flank of machine six.

Salvatore took a step toward the opening press of machine seven, bent down as the latest product was ejected, and caught it as it fell through the clattering aluminium slats. He gave it a cursory glance. The mould hadn't been changed since October; only the colour of the products had varied. Tonight they were fake-grass green, an easy colour on which to focus. He dropped the piece back into the shallow grey tray on the floor, waited a few seconds till the next product dropped through the aluminium slats, then lifted the said tray clear off the floor, tipping all its fifty or so product pieces into the arm-deep grey tub, the bottom of which rested at shin height on an upturned square metal bucket.

Salvatore reached for his pair of factory-issue gloves, rolled up his sleeves and leaned forward to trap the near rim of the grey tub against the middle of his thighs, thereby pushing the far edge hard against the flank of machine number seven. He raised both gloved hands to his nostrils, rather as boxers do before a round, and sniffed at the ill-cured leather, wondering, as so often, whether it was cow- or pigskin, and telling himself, as so often, that he must be the first person ever in his family not to know such a thing – a genealogical freak, a brave new departure.

Salvatore had received a telegram from his brother that morning urgently requesting him to phone home, but he hadn't done so. He was aware that his mother's health was failing fast, but precisely how fast he was in little hurry to learn. He loved his mother of course. But what could he do? Could he absent himself from work for anything less than a funeral? What rights did he have?

He loved his mother, but what if he travelled all the way down there and she hung on from one day to the next, week after week, dragging it out? She was capable of that. She had always had an obstinate, inconsiderate streak to her character. What position would that place him in? He loved his mother, but he would have to ask around. Urgently. Discreetly. He was filled with doubt. He didn't want anyone on the shift to know of his troubles. He felt that to have a sick mother was a personal weakness, a character flaw. He loved his mother; but since she had to die in any case, would it not be by far the best thing if she could just do it suddenly and all in one go?

Salvatore began to thresh the product pieces, tangling them together, crashing them against the walls of the bin in order to separate the valuable button-size products from the *sprue* – that is to say, from the skeleton stalks that held them. Bent over, eyes closed, Salvatore exulted in the strength and efficiency of his body. The well-toned muscles of his back, shoulders, arms, hands and chest operated in fine harmony, while those of his legs, belly and buttocks cooperated to keep the bin firmly jammed between his thighs and the machine side. His was an efficient body: whether eating, threshing plastic products late into the factory night, climbing flights of university stairs two by two or even three by three, copulating with his girlfriend, shouldering sacks of plastic raw material, defecating, swallowing, cycling between home, university and work, ejaculating tidily into a crisp paper handkerchief from a family-size economy pack purchased for just this purpose, yawning with his pectorals tensing, sprinting with his arms akimbo – or performing any number of other more or less essential day-to-day bodily activities – Salvatore's system of bones, blood and sinews delivered excellent performance. His was the body of an athlete manqué, oiled, admirable, fully deserving the envy of men and the lustful longing of the discriminating members of both sexes.

Salvatore ceased his threshing, opened his eyes and saw that he had successfully separated most of the products from most of the sprue. He lifted a large tangle of product-free sprue and transferred it to the recycling barrel at the aisle-end of his machine. He returned to the threshing tub where he twisted the last stubbornly attached button-sized products from the remaining stalks. He dropped the last few stalks into the recycling barrel. He lifted the grey tub clear off its upturned bucket, tipped it sideways to his right and poured all the precious product pieces, two hundred or more, into a manila cardboard box standing on the floor to the right of the product tray, below the machine's hopper.

Salvatore replaced the threshing tub on the upturned bucket and glanced at the manila cardboard box. The products had piled up eight or more deep against the far side of the box, leaving the near side bare in places. Salvatore fought the temptation – which he deemed neurotic, since inessential, a bit like not stepping on the cracks between paving stones – gently to kick the box in order to scatter the products more evenly, thereby obscuring the bottom folds of the cardboard box, the sight of which he found unsettling. He might kick it later, he decided, as if in passing, almost by mistake, an afterthought. Yes, he would do it later, unconsciously.

As Salvatore sat back down on his chair, he removed the union leaflet from his hip pocket. He glanced across the aisle at Rachid, who was leaning against the edge of the huge table that filled the far end of the plastics section. Smoke from his cigarette must have got in his eyes, because the poor man was dabbing at them with a handkerchief. Filthy habit, he really ought to give it up. Salvatore briefly questioned the clarity of his own vision and considered whether or not he should clean his glasses. Normally he performed this task while talking to someone, conveying the idea that he wished to focus on them more clearly while in fact – for as long as he could spin it out (with a spit and a polish and a hunt for his special lens-cleaner) – relieving himself of the need to see them at all. While considering the pros and cons of cleaning his glasses, he stretched his left arm straight out before him, tipped his head as far back as it would go, and – with his spectacles propped like gun sights in their rightful place – stared down the length of his left arm at his left hand which he flexed and splayed to distance each finger as far as possible from its immediate neighbours, thus isolating his targets. He admired his fingernails, which were clean and sharp and recently clipped. With a satisfied nod, he completed his reconnaissance. His overview was faultless. He could have pulled the trigger there and then. He turned his sights on the union tract.

*

Philippe's small hands, like his face in the mirror earlier, were pudgy, puffy, the black hairs sleek and flat and flaccid against his pale cream skin, the Spanish summer beach-tan already faded, his nails trimmed short and neat.

Philippe had removed his industrial gloves and placed them on the flimsy and corrugated top step of the stepladder stationed below the hopper of machine two, and was now standing at the aisle-end of said machine, his hands reposing palms-down on the blue plastic grocery bag that contained that evening's trawl of papers from Rémy's bar, and which he had just laid on the lid of the waist-high cardboard cylinder that contained recycled raw material.

Philippe slowly withdrew the wad of papers, then folded the empty bag into a wedge and, leaning down, tidily inserted it into the gap offered by an ill-fastened inspection-flap on the machine's flank. He cleared his mind. The hoppers were brimming full, the products only just checked. Jacques was sure to arrive soon.

Philippe saw that the top paper on the pile was *Libération*, and that it was folded open. The lower right-hand quarter-page was occupied by an interview with Sergio, a Fiat worker in Turin. Philippe skimmed the article. His focus alighted on the words 'embourgeoisement' and 'compromis.' He smiled briefly. No doubt *Libé* had dug out someone happy to slag off the PCI. How convenient! How predictable! But fair enough. He would read it later. His eyes closed.

Against the hard warm cylinder, Philippe's belly felt warm and soft, the two contrasting convexities, respectively of rigid cardboard and of yielding flesh, met and briefly rubbed, like the noses of friendly but cautious canines, offering something more than support, something close to comfort.

Philippe noticed the dryness of his mouth. His shoulders rose, his belly was drawn in, and the meeting ground between it and the cylinder briefly shrank to a taut and vertical line. His eyes opened. He glanced at a white plastic beaker which Lopez – presumably – had left leaning against a ledge at the end of machine two. He observed that it was empty, save for a treacly dark ring at its base. Wearily, he returned his attention to the papers before him.

He worked his way through the pile, neatly checking, rearranging and refolding each paper front-page-up, then placing them in the order in which he intended to consult them, thus: *Le Dauphiné Libéré* (which Philippe noticed had the news-in-brief story that Rémy had mentioned of the drowned man), *Le Progrès*, *Le Monde*, *Libération* (of which, for once, the personal-ads section, Philippe's favourite part of the newspaper, was both gloriously intact and intriguingly ringed by a succession of previous readers), *L'Humanité*, *Lutte Ouvrière* (covered, as usual, in irregular and curvilinear doodles in green biro, as though, Philippe had once concluded, its reader had grown impatient of the revolution that the paper tirelessly announced), and lastly the Italian paper *il manifesto*. As well as the dailies, there were also that week's copies of *Marie Claire* and *Le Nouvel Observateur*. As Philippe flicked through the last-mentioned, his eyes fell on a photo of a woman whose face recalled Odile. It was seen and gone in a flash. Did he want to find it again? Take another look? Ponder the resemblance? Normally he would have taken the trouble. Not tonight.

Fluttering rather more slowly than before through Philippe's stubby white fingers, the last few pages of *Le Nouvel Observateur* came to rest at a small black-and-white advert for a product called an Electrogym. The picture showed a reclining man with a broad belt-like apparatus around his midriff and an idiotically conceited smile on his face. Philippe held the magazine open with his left hand pressing down on its spine, while he extracted his cigarette pack and lighter from his right trouser pocket. He took another look at the ad. Except for his underpants and the belt immediately above them, the man was naked. Wires led from the belt to a small oblong case by the man's side. Philippe lit his cigarette. The man was neither old nor young, neither fat nor thin. His hair was medium length. Apart from his long sideburns, he was clean-shaven. The thought occurred to Philippe that his need for a cigarette was often triggered by witnessing people taking exercise: not only was it unbearable for him to watch any form of sport on television without instantly lighting up, but the sight of a track-suited jogger or crash-hatted cyclist would also fire the same impulse; a person, however, who was merely running to catch a bus or employing a non-sports cycle as an innocuous and morally neutral means of physical transport, did not command any such stimulus.

Philippe read the first words of the advert's blurb, then began to laugh. He looked again at the black oblong case in the photograph. Mystery solved! he said to himself, inhaling. He could hardly wait to tell Jacques. He dog-eared the page. Where the hell was the old man anyway? Philippe glanced at his watch. It wasn't even twenty-five to ten yet. Jacques would be along soon enough.

Philippe stacked the two magazines at the bottom of the pile of newspapers and glanced down the aisle. People moved around, but he saw no one. His belly, relaxing against the cylinder again, had grown numb, as numb as his mind. He didn't know what to think, didn't know how to feel. Instead of betrayal, he felt . . . what was it he felt? He focused briefly on the machines and on the men coming and going, saw the foreman, the Algerian leaning against the edge of the table at the far end of the machine aisle, his feet crossed, his head down. He watched the man drop the dying end of his cigarette on the ground. Lonely, that was how Philippe felt. Had he ever felt lonely before? Bullshit, he said to himself, breathing deep into his belly to push himself back from the cylinder, opening his mouth wide to test the dryness of his tongue. Another beer is called for. Another beer. He knew the machines were fine. He shook his head and shrugged. He couldn't be bothered to ask anyone to keep an eye on them. He checked his left trouser pocket for coins. The intrusive thought that he was getting through more beer than usual and that maybe it might be advisable not to get actually pissed irritated him, as unwelcome as the farting in polite company of an ancient relative or the awakening of a conscience presumed long dead. He turned, gestured to Marcel to keep an eye on his machines, and headed up the machine aisle, past the foreman's raised glass-fronted office and out of the din and the fumes. Get that beer. Wet that whistle. Lonely? Horse shit.

13. Bobrán cycles. Jacques drives. Mathieu looks back.

Both Jacques and Bobrán had intended to arrive on time, yet both were late. For the first time in longer than he could remember, Jacques had suddenly decided to pay Pierre, his only brother, a visit and had found him at home alone: they had talked for five minutes without quarrelling. Bobrán, on a similarly imperious impulse, had gone looking for Moritz at the San Francisco, but had found Moritz's sister there instead. Among other things, Jacques was now thinking about having seen his brother; among other things, Bobrán was now thinking about *not* having seen Moritz. Both men, after their respective detours, had nearly reached the factory.

Jacques was sitting in his 2CV, waiting for the lights, ready to turn left into Cours Modelon, his right foot lightly grazing the brake pedal, his left foot holding the clutch to the floor. Bobrán, approaching the same crossroads from the opposite direction, slipped both his hands from his jacket pockets and rested one on each end of the handlebars. He then rose from the saddle and swung his bicycle into the same street. Neither man noticed the other: each was tightly enfolded in his own thoughts.

Jacques was slumped like an ancient punch-bag, his knees splayed, the round black pommel of the gear stick engulfed in his slack right hand. Bobrán was rising again from the stiff leather saddle, bracing himself between pedals and handlebars, a tingle of muscle tension sparking infinite minuscule sinewy readjustments between shoulders, arms, belly, legs and neck, suspending him in the air, about as close as he could ever come to flying, in the absence of a trapeze. Jacques' body was large and comfortable enough, one might think, to absorb without quailing any blow from any quarter. Bobrán's body, though corroded by a chronic insufficiency of sleep, was a spring coiled with residual youth and regular physical labour; indeed Bobrán still believed himself capable of any exertion, trial of endurance, or stunt.

The lights showed green and Jacques' 2CV lurched into motion, swinging round the crossroads and onto Cours Modelon. In second gear, he drove past the factory on his left, slowing down and pulling up a few yards further down as he simultaneously registered and resisted the nightly temptation to engage third gear, accelerate, then smoothly into fourth and off down the road, and still faster over the river, slipping like a thief out of town on the far side, the side he didn't know, speeding away into unknown territory, untidy outskirts, flat valley, dark night, as fast as ever any 2CV might go.

Deferring once more the thrill of the long road and the empty night, Jacques switched off the engine and placed both hands in his lap. He could have driven till morning. He had enough petrol to be in Paris by dawn. Or in Spain, maybe. What would that be like? He had never been to Paris. Boring and cold, what with this 'crap' Citroën radiator. Wrong time of year and wrong mood, Jacques thought. A yawn surprised him, snapping his mouth wide open. He yanked the clackety handbrake out almost as far as it could come, then gathered his things for the night: bag, wine gourd, apples. He saw the small white paper bag, innocent-looking and crisp, with its alternately threatening and reassuring green pharmacy symbol, blinking like a monitor in a hospital. He didn't need to take the first pill till the following morning. He could leave them in his car. Instead, he tossed the bag into his rushwork basket. It came to rest among the apples.

The corner neatly rounded, Bobrán had set his bike on a straight course, dropped his hard butt back onto the stiff saddle while he lifted his hands from the handlebars and pedalled harder, gaining not only speed but also an enhanced equilibrium as the bicycle beneath him accelerated. He savoured the theoretical risk of accident, the knowledge that some unexpected occurrence might at any moment hurl him down at the bruising tarmac or bone-cracking kerbstone. It was a danger in which he did not truly believe, assuming a family, if not a racial, immunity. Others, he knew for a fact, were not so favoured. He blocked the familiar thought. It reoccurred. He blocked it again, harder. With his hands nestling in his pockets, Bobrán's eyes restlessly scanned the shadowy road for a patch of oil sufficiently broad, an indentation sufficiently deep or a stone sufficiently large to trip his front tyre and throw the wheel out, causing him to fall. Other people fell, he was well aware of that, whether from bikes or from buildings; he did not, would not, could not fall.

Jacques glanced in his wing mirror to check the way was clear and caught sight of a bicycle as it swerved across the empty road behind him and vanished off the edge of the reflection and through the open gates of Éts. Boucan, its rider immediately identifiable as Bobrán, Marcel's Gypsy cousin: who else would arrive as late as Jacques? who else would turn corners no-hands? For an instant, the old man's mind involuntarily tracked the younger man's two-wheeled trajectory: straight past the gate-man (with no more than a nod), round to the right, past the factory entrance, toward the bike racks and urinals. At some point, the lad would have to set hand to handlebar. Or crash.

Would he leave it till the last possible moment? Of course. He was young.

Jacques opened the car door, swung his legs out onto the road and hauled himself up and out. Then he leaned back into the car, ducking down low over the driving seat, his back stiff with a warning, while his long simian arms scooped his satchel from the passenger seat and his bag of apples and cushion from the rear seat, drawing everything into his barrel-like trunk and standing back up, lightly knocking his head on the door rim, carelessly resetting his cloth cap at an incongruously jaunty angle. He closed and locked the car door and righted his cap. Then he loped off across the road, looking left and right.

As Bobrán freewheeled toward the bike rack, his feet holding the pedals horizontal and level with the right-hand pedal out in front, he leaned forward and placed his left hand on the handlebars with the index and middle fingers hooked over the brake lever, while his right hand grasped the cold metal tip of the saddle. Next, as the bicycle slowed, he lowered the left pedal until his left leg was straight and stiff and ready to bear his weight, then swung his right leg back up and over the rear wheel so that it lined up against his left leg, as his body unfolded. So doing, he ran the bike into the rack and dropped both feet neatly onto the ground, while letting go of the handlebars and saddle. A clean dismount, a perfect gymnast's landing. Clack and clatter went the bike and the rack as they negotiated and adjusted their reciprocal clasp. Bobrán yawned and stretched, tucked his shirt roughly into his trousers and removed his plastic dinner box from the bike's panier. He took his combination lock from the saddle around which it had been jangling, opened it by composing the number 171 (easy for Bobrán to remember because just two more than his height in centimetres), threaded it through the spokes of the back wheel, rescrambled the combination, and made for the door to the toilets. Marcel had shown him how such locks could be picked: he had taken fully three minutes to perform the task but had claimed that in most cases he could do it in under one. Bobrán had laughed at him. If that was his best trick . . .

Early as usual! the gate-man shouted to Jacques from his booth. Jacques acted surprised and serious. Didn't mean to be, he said. I can go back home if you like. The jovial guard glanced sideways at his TV, then back again at Jacques. What's in that bag, then, rabbits? Apples: you want one? Jacques lifted and tilted and opened the bag so the guard could take a look, then both men noticed the pharmacy package. Jacques felt like a traveller stopped at customs with contraband. And some pills for high blood pressure, Jacques declared, disclosing more than the occasion demanded. What are they, the guard asked, beta-blockers? Why do you ask? No reason: my father is on beta-blockers and he must be your age. Jacques pulled a face. The guard – bald, fat, and wearing a raggedy red moustache – was, it seemed, a generation younger than him. The guard warmed to his theme. My dad's doctor says it's the stress of his job, that he really ought to work less, quit smoking, take exercise, drink less coffee, and have longer holidays. Jacques lifted his cap, scratched his head and chuckled politely. He should spend more time in the Balearics, the guard went on, or on the ski slopes, as if everyone had doctor's pay and holidays. Jacques' chuckle shrank to a smile. The guard emitted a bitter little laugh. Or alternatively, the doctor told my dad, you can take the tablets. Uh-huh, Jacques said, picking up his bag. Then, as an afterthought, with a sly glint in his eye, But your father's had no problems? What kind of problems? the guard asked warily. Jacques looked off to his left, toward the door into the factory. He wondered how you ask a man about his father's erectile function. Any kind at all! Jacques said, stirring the air before him with his right hand, palm open and up. None that he's mentioned, the guard said. Jacques' grin widened, as if soothed by a satisfactory answer.

Bobrán stood at the urinal, supporting his dick between the thumb and forefinger of his left hand, while trapping his meal box between his right elbow and rib cage. The rushing water from the malfunctioning cistern in one of the toilet cubicles at his back drowned out the sound of his jet of near-colourless urine as it hit the wall. In the gutter at the base of the urinal floated a huddle of overlapping disinfectant rings, originally white but now yellowing unevenly, each one, like an outsize Polo mint, having a hole at its centre, the whole tableau reminiscent of some rare geological formation. Some of the rings were recent arrivals, their brand name in proud relief; others had been worn as smooth and slender as giant washers by the corrosive medium that slopped and fizzed around them. The rings were nudged in the pooling gutter by an assortment of bloated dog ends, whose tendril threads of variously brown and blonde tobacco were slowly escaping into the soup from lengthwise fissures where the paper had come unstuck. Bobrán's eyes lifted from this spectacle to the wall before him and to the crude drawings of cunts and cocks and the mysterious messages alongside them. Both the pictures and their accompanying legends blurred as his focus pressed its way through the wall, advancing as if on tiptoes to a more tranquil mid-distance.

Occasionally, when arriving late, Bobrán would bump into the nightwatchman, a Pole who didn't have to clock on until ten but who often arrived as early as Bobrán arrived late. The Pole always found something to say. Once he had asked Bobrán if he would mind his 'likeness' being taken. They were standing side by side, right there at the urinal, and the Pole was looking at him intently. Bobrán hadn't heard the expression 'likeness' before and thought the man was perhaps trying to pick him up, looking at him like that, his eyes wandering like an over-eager puppy-dog's tongue back and forth all over his face. He didn't steal a glance at his cock, though, like faggots usually do. You remind me of someone, the Pole had then said. Yet for once this didn't sound like a pick-up line. For one thing, the Pole was neither smiling nor leering. Really, Bobrán asked, who? You wouldn't know him, the Pole had replied, he died a while back. How long? More than 2000 years. People have often told me I look like Jesus, Bobrán said. Jesus died less than 2000 years ago, the Pole had said, and, besides, nobody knows what he looked like. Bobrán wondered how you could possibly know anything about anyone who had died that long ago unless it was Jesus. Poles were odd, Bobrán concluded. He had no precise picture of where Poles came from, but he knew that it was somewhere in the East and that the East was definitely where his own people, he had always been told, had originated and where terrible things had always befallen them, which was why they had eventually left: at least that was what his mother said.

Bobrán had finished urinating. He looked down, made one last push from his belly, produced a dribbly little squirt, shook his dick around a little, then flipped it up and over the elastic of his underpants, and fed it down into his trousers, where he left it nestling against his left thigh. Of course the bad things that had happened to his people in the East could have happened anywhere else – West, say, or North or South. Gadgé did bad things to his people: they couldn't help it, it was their nature. Bobrán zipped up his trousers. It wasn't as if there were good gadgé or bad gadgé, or special compass points where for whatever reason, who could tell?, something in the water maybe, or in the alignment of the planets, the gadgé were less murderous than elsewhere. Bobrán headed for the door. Gadgé were gadgé were gadgé. Gadgé families probably didn't get up in the morning and look at one another and say, Hey, sweets, how about today we go chase out / club to death / gang rape / petrol bomb some gyppoes, or perhaps, since it's raining, would you rather we stay in and terrify the kiddies with gyppo-horror stories? No. It was just the way things fell out. It all went hand-in-hand with living in houses, doing regular jobs, running companies and councils and churches and countries. Or working in factories even, say. Bobrán let the door to the toilets swing shut behind him. He frowned as he struggled to formulate a thought. Moritz was one of the gadgé, and so was his sister Heike, and yet . . .

Bobrán looked across the yard at the door to the factory which Jacques, his constant grin visible in the half-light, was holding open for him. Bobrán quickened his pace and transferred his meal-box to his left hand.

Overslept, did you? Jacques asked, as the two men shook hands. Yes, Bobrán said. And I had to call on someone. You? Much the same. My brother. Pierre. The door shut behind them, making the near-darkness of the metals workshop fade to black.

What's in the bag? Bobrán enquired. Apples the storm brought down, you want some? Jacques reflected that he ought to transfer the pharmacy package to his jacket pocket: he didn't need another conversation about his medical condition. Where we live, Bobrán replied, we're surrounded by pears and apples this time of year. Jacques slowly painted himself a picture: an orchard encampment with gaudy caravans set at odd angles; semi-naked urchins whipping tyres down a mud path; women on the river bank in robes and ringlets, broad arses in the air, as they beat bed linen in the river shallows; guitar music; hedgehogs roasting on an open fire; the clumsily-updated full-blown Mérimée-minestrone of Gypsydom.

The two men strolled in easy silence, Jacques' elbow brushing Bobrán's shoulder.

Jacques recalled an incident from years back, when he had served as mayor. A Gypsy encampment had sprung up overnight in the middle of a meadow on the edge of the village, near a bend in the river. Villagers had urged him to call in the cops to drive the Gypsies away and he had stalled. Then there had been an arson attack. No lives were lost but one little girl inhaled fumes and her lungs were damaged, no one knew how badly, the doctors were as cagey as usual. The Gypsies decamped as fast as they had arrived, but not after sending the mayor a four-strong delegation of elders to protest at his failure to protect them. The arsonist was never caught. Jacques had resigned his post. Edith, who never wasted words, least of all on those close to her, had taken his head in her work-worn hands so that his ears were covered, and had said, These villagers never deserved you anyway, Jacques, not one of them. At least that's what he thought he heard through the bone and gristle of his wife's hands. Then she had kissed him on the hairy tip of his nose. As her hands came off his ears, he told her he hadn't heard a thing.

Good, Edith had said: compliments are for children and Americans – you don't need them.

Bobrán was teasing out a thought. What was it? His frown had returned. He searched. It started with Moritz. Moritz was a gadgé. Right. As was his sister Heike. Okay. Moritz was special to him. But he had liked Heike too. Straight off. She had reminded him of Sophie, his last girlfriend, last not latest: he wouldn't want another woman. With Sophie it had been good for a while. Sophie had been his best woman ever. She was still a friend. She understood. But he was through with women. In the end it was their bodies: he didn't like their softness, their yieldingness; he didn't like the way they rubbed themselves against you when excited, like a cat mewing for its milk. A man would never do that. Bobrán distrusted cats. There was something about Heike though that pleased him. Maybe just the family resemblance with Moritz: the peachy skin, the slim boy's body, the short cropped hair, the neat small earlobes you want to suck and nibble. What Bobrán disliked most about women was their breasts; the bigger they were, the worse he felt about them. Sometimes the magazines that the Italian brought into work contained pictures of women with breasts bigger than in any nightmare of suffocation, great suety sacks the size of pillows. He was scared they might suddenly squirt milk in his face, though he knew that for technical reasons that was pretty improbable. Women's bodies were complicated. For instance, they didn't produce milk all the time like cows. Subject to the seasons and stuff like that. Anyway, he hated milk. And there was that other damned thing, about as appealing and as fragrant as a ditch in summer, all squelchy and dark. Still, Bobrán reckoned that Heike hardly had any breasts at all. That was another point in her favour. He wouldn't think about the other thing. He couldn't imagine her having one. And if she did, she'd probably keep it as clean as Moritz kept his cock. Germans were famous for cleanliness, Moritz said. Besides, even if she did have one, what was it to him? She had such a nice clean look to her. Just like a boy. As for the invitation to a concert in Germany, he would want to hear that straight from Moritz. Even to consider it. But his sister was friendly all right. Yes, he could form this thought, and hold it too: he liked Heike.

(At this hour, as at any hour, Nadine's eyes, if open, would surely be gazing in the direction of the large fading photograph affixed to the grey expanse of ceiling above her bed showing in the room's half-light a view of the beach at Fécamp.) Mathieu held himself in a classic gardener's stretch, his feet a foot's length apart, his hands pressed into the small of his back, their splayed fingers pointing downward, his shoulders square and his head pushed right back, his eyes peering up at the ceiling of the lift as it ascended slowly from ground to first floor. (If open, Nadine's eyes would be wide and void, blank and unblinking.)

The lift jerked and came to rest with a clang of metal on metal. Mathieu registered a psoriatic itch in the middle of his upper right eyelid: still staring at the ceiling of the lift, he now closed and opened his right eye twice to bathe and ease it. For months, and then years, Nadine had looked up at her unadorned ceiling until one day a new nurse, a relief worker, a girl named Rebeccah who had dark ringlets and a ready smile and was never seen again, had suggested to Mathieu that he seek out and present his wife with a familiar image since, she said, 'you never can tell.'

Mathieu had not had to think twice. He had left after work that Saturday morning and, sleeping in snatches in lay-bys, had driven day and night through rain and drizzle to the coast of Normandy, arriving on a notably sunny winter's morning at a place he had never before visited but which Nadine had mentioned with mounting frequency as her mind collapsed, and always with the lilting fondness of a bucket-and-spade 1920s-seaside memory: it had been, she had once said, her favourite place in all the world. Having neglected to bring a change of shoes or socks for the return journey, Mathieu had trod the shore barefoot while using up a 24-exposure film. He had enjoyed the tickle, scratch and prickle of sand and shells beneath his feet. Later, he had eaten a proper midday meal in a Les Routiers restaurant, slept a good sleep, rolled up in a blanket beside his car and, setting off as the cold-custard sun dropped into the sea somewhere over England, he had driven night and day through drizzle and rain back to Nadine. Later that week, when his wife had opened her eyes and gazed for the first time in the direction of the freshly-affixed half-poster-size blow-up of the beach at Fécamp, Mathieu had imagined for a moment that he caught a scintilla of recognition, a twitch in the iris of one eye, the trace perhaps of a double-take of surprise pleasure as it flitted across the brain of his beloved. Was it something or was it nothing? He remembered the young nurse's words: 'you never can tell.' And indeed he couldn't.

As Mathieu now relaxed out of his stretch and dropped his chin against his chest, his gaze slipped from the ceiling of the lift cubicle, tracked down its dirty brown wall, and came to rest on its plastic-powder-strewn floor. His moist lips pursed around his burnt-out matchstick, his sparse fair eyelashes flicked shut twice. He pulled the lift door open and stepped out, looking quickly round to assure himself that the seven warning lights, positioned one each on each of the injection-press control cabinets, were unlit.

Mathieu walked to the left-hand corner of the low-ceilinged first-floor workshop, then round the end of the huge old semi-automatic machine number twenty-one. Jean was on his feet, facing the closed press before him, waiting. Mathieu uttered a minimal greeting a fraction too loud to be ignored, held out his right hand and looked away. Jean's hand made glancing contact, while both men nodded mutely. Mathieu walked around behind the diminutive worker, wiping his right hand against the front of his shirt. Jean rubbed his hand on his trousers.

The night-shift supervisor squeezed between the end of machine twenty-one and its control cabinet then swung right and, with the stairs down to the ground-floor section to his left, he walked past the flank of Alphonse's machine eighteen. The African, bent over to thresh a full bin of finished product which his thighs were pressing against the side of machine nineteen, was concealed from Mathieu's view. Fernando, at the aisle-end of his machine seventeen, was taking pains to append a triangular Porto team flag to the shiny steel piston that moved in and out several centimetres with each opening and closing of the press. Mathieu rolled his eyes at Fernando, who shrugged one shoulder and grinned.

The hoppers of Bobrán's two machines, numbers fifteen and twenty, had recently been filled, and the grey oblong floor trays, positioned to collect each finished piece as it dropped from the cleaving press and clattered through the aluminium slats of the chute, had recently been emptied into the overflowing threshing tubs. Bobrán's absence was being covered, whether by Fernando, Alphonse, or Marcel from the ground floor. Mathieu postponed the decision whether to shut the machines down for the night or to work them himself. First he had to be sure they were not producing duds.

Mathieu went first to machine fifteen and then to machine twenty. At each machine, he had to quality-control three consecutively produced pieces: the first product that he saw fall through the aluminium slats, followed by its two immediate successors. The product-checking at the two machines would thus involve six near-identical series of actions, each series entailing bending at the hips and catching the dropping product, scanning it this way and that for imperfections, and then slinging it into the grey bin on the upturned bucket. As he took hold of each product, Mathieu's watery blue eyes scrunched up to scrutinize the plastic object in his hands while the dirt-blackened rough-edged thumb of his left hand gauged the product's softness and smoothness as though it were a unique and never-to-be-forgotten talisman. Once certain of its perfection, he tossed it, with a gesture interpretable only as contempt or disgust, into the grey threshing tub.

At each machine, the first and second of such product-checks would be followed by a wait of between twenty and thirty seconds for the, respectively, second and third products to drop. For these brief periods of unavoidable inactivity, Mathieu had over the previous months developed a routine. Since there was no time to go anywhere or do anything, he leaned on the closed door of the machine press, shut his eyes, relaxed his musculature, and strove to reach the mental place where he believed his wife Nadine now dwelt: for weeks now, and innumerable times each night, Mathieu had been perfecting the art of impromptu mind-voidance. He wanted to catch, if only fleetingly, a glimpse over the edge into mindlessness.

The exercise required effort. Every image and every thought, however minuscule, had to be chased down and crushed. At first, this was hard work, since the mental space vacated by one entity seemed immediately to be invaded by several others, leading to a hopeless jostling. With practice, matters improved. He learned to focus on one simple thought-object, the less emotionally charged the better: an old shoe, a speck of dust, the letter H, the word néant ('nothingness'). Once he had obliterated from his consciousness everything but that one last fixed idea, entity, word, image, the attempt might be made to abolish that too.

Mathieu learned, if he did not already know this, that his mental exercise was beset with problems. Firstly, although it might seem the easiest thing in the world not to think about, the fact remained that, in a matter of seconds, the press would open and a piece would drop through the aluminium slats and that, in response to that stimulus, he would instantly bend at the hips and catch the piece as it fell and then proceed to check that it was perfect. And, however momentarily empty and inactive his mind appeared to him to be, the fact that he would unfailingly respond to the stimulus of the opening press demonstrated that his mind, even when it seemed to have been successfully voided, was merely biding its time. (If there was anything that could wake Nadine now, he would like to know. But what, after all this time, could that be?)

From these reflections, it dawned on Mathieu that his hard-won and now oft-repeated experience of mental voiding still came nowhere near Nadine's permanent state of mind, which was characterized not by the absence of a particular object of thought but by the absence of any thinking subject. However successful Mathieu's mind-voidance exercise might seem to be, the stimulus sent by the opening of the press revived in him a perfect knowledge of who and where he was. Indeed, it occurred to him that the most his exercise could achieve was a kind of relaxed concentration similar to the state of blissful readiness that he enjoyed when, never more serene and oblivious to his surroundings, he would lose himself in musical improvisation.

The more he listened to the echoing of his artfully emptied mind, the more he began to discern a distant undertow and with application this began to form itself into a chord, an inverted chord, an inverted dominant chord pulsing slowly, and each note seemed to speak to him of something, someone in particular. There was the thudding root-note (Nadine, as she once was?); above this the chord's major third (Nadine, as she is now and has been for years?); then, beneath the root, he could hear the insistent flatted seventh (what to do? what to do?); and voiced more than an octave higher, an insistently irregular pseudo-syncopated flat ninth, undermining the root, making urgent though unspecific comment (eh? eh?). A fine chord on which to come back in and play a blistering, hectic solo full of altered scales and relentless searching. But, even when straining to ape and emulate Nadine's state of hopeless coma, Mathieu's mind fizzed with life irrepressible. His eyes opened, tears standing on them like droplets of rain on oily puddles, glinting. He hadn't tried hard enough.

14. Rachid warns.

Marcel was standing in the downstairs plastics workshop, halfway between Jacques' machine number three and his own machine number twelve. He was facing up the aisle, toward the raised office, and was chewing gum and eyeing all the exits and entrances while using his left hand to smooth down the belly of his shocking-green shirt. Before long Bobrán would surely arrive, pushing through the flaps from metallurgy to the right of the office, and would then, in all likelihood, head for the lift, pausing perhaps at the punch-card rack to check that Marcel had clocked him in. Or he might come round and greet everyone on the ground floor before climbing the stairs. Sometimes he did that. If Marcel spotted Bobrán arrive and make straight for the lift, he would be able to slip between Luigi's machine thirteen and his own machine twelve and intercept him. Marcel's right hand tapped his back pocket, confirming the presence of the envelope the African had given him for Bobrán. He wanted rid of it. And he wanted to know what it contained.

At his back, Marcel heard the clatter of a trolley rushing toward him up the machine aisle. Without turning round, he stepped smartly out of its path and toward the end of Philippe's machine number two. He glanced briefly at the newspapers piled on top of the recycling cylinder. Darting a glance away to his right through the gap between machines twelve and thirteen, Marcel sighted a trolley emerging from the lift, followed by Alphonse and Fernando. Steering the trolley with one hand, Alphonse was talking and walking smoothly, while Fernando jiggered up and down and scowled. Marcel stepped back into the centre of the aisle, resuming his easy gunslinger's posture. His gaze hovered over the door to the raw-materials area, situated to the left-hand side of the office and beneath the stairs to the first-floor workshop. Marcel wondered which of the converging trolleys, Rachid's or Fernando-and-Alphonse's, would reach the door first. In the absence of any other entertainment, he watched to find out. Rachid had paused to exchange a greeting with Luigi, providing Fernando and Alphonse with a chance to catch up. Marcel kept one eye on the hanging plastic flaps to the right of the office, not wishing to miss his cousin's arrival. As Marcel shunted his gaze from right to left, he noticed the night-shift supervisor picking his way carefully down the iron stairs, his left hand on the banister. Marcel checked that the warning lights on his machine control cabinets were off, noting in passing that Rachid had finished with Luigi and had now pushed his trolley through the door to the raw-materials area just ahead of Fernando and Alphonse. No surprises there. The Arab would always have been the favourite. Marcel's chewing gum had gone hard and his jaws were starting to ache. He brought his left hand up to cover a long, deep yawn, picked the gum from his lower left canine, then, with his right hand, checked the envelope in his back pocket. It hadn't budged.

The raw-materials area into which Rachid, Fernando and Alphonse had driven their trolleys, a rectangular windowless shed-like space measuring a little over fourteen by a fraction under six metres, was supplied with two openings: that just used by the afore-named three workers; another, at the opposite end, also broad enough to permit the passage of a pallet-truck. This room led in its turn into an even longer one housing all those moulds not currently in use as well as the tools needed to secure, adjust, maintain and mend them, and the crane trucks used to hoist, transport, and drop them into place. At the dark and distant end of this second storage area, to the right of a further opening through which no ordinary plastics-section worker could ever have legitimate cause to pass, glimmered side by side a beer dispenser and a coffee machine: the former proclaimed its wares in a badly scuffed pointillé, putatively photographic, image of an improbably large uncapped bottle of foaming beer; the latter by means of a stylized drawing depicting a minute cup of coffee wreathed in a steamy brown aroma.

The raw-materials room was lit by two forty-watt bulbs, one suspended just inside each of its openings. The two lights could be turned on or off together from wall-mounted ninety-second timer switches located at either end of the space, and mounted on the left-hand inside walls at shoulder height. There was nothing, after all, to show off or to hide, and ninety seconds were an ample lapse of time in which to traverse such a space or even to manoeuvre one's trolley to the relevant pallet, load it up, and exit. If the lights turned themselves off before the plastics section was regained, the glow therefrom would suffice to guide even the most weary steps of even the most bleary operative.

The raw-materials room contained two immovable, but countless movable, objects. The two immovables were: first, situated in the far left-hand corner, a perfectly L-shaped stretch of partitioning wall, into the shorter segment of which a door had been inserted, framing a smallish room for meeting and mealtime usage, which in its turn contained a single oblong wooden table and seven chairs of the stackable metal-framed and plastic-seated variety; second, a large grey-green metal-sided milling machine that served to grind into powder the plastic skeletons that constituted the residue (one might even say the chaff) of the manual threshing process, after the end-product itself had been, to prolong the trope, harvested.

The movable objects present in the raw-materials room on that particular evening of early November 1976 – as, indeed, on every evening for several years before and after this date, though with slight variations and fluctuating spatial arrangements, included (in descending order of unladen weight): one pallet-truck (stationed at the far end of the area, against the right-hand wall, straight across from the meals- and meeting-room); seven pallets (staggered in an almost regular line along the right-hand wall) bearing transparent plastic sacks full of plastic granules; twelve chest-high recycled material cylinders (standing in the immediate vicinity of the grinding machine), of which three were empty, eight were crammed with plastic stalks to be milled the following day, and one brimmed with ground plastic ready for use; two high-sided pallets (located close to the left-hand wall, beyond the aforementioned cylinders and before the door to the meals- and meeting-room), one of which corralled a higgledy-piggledy heap of differently sized taped-up cardboard boxes, each bearing the name of an afternoon-shift operative, that day's date, and the relative machine number, while the other pallet was empty and would remain so until the end of the night-shift; six knee-high shiny-lidded square-section tins (posted along the longer side of the L-shaped partition wall of the meals- and meeting room), each containing a small plastic cup identical to those supplied by the coffee-machine, nestling in a mass of shiny granular colorant, the colours being yellow, black, white, blue, red and green; lastly, just inside the door and to one's right as one entered from the downstairs plastics section, there towered three high and unstable piles of manila cardboard boxes-to-be, all still in their two-dimensional state, requiring an operative to pluck, pinch, squeeze, pinch, flick, fold, turn, tape and thereby convert them to three-dimensional utility.

Rachid had pushed his trolley to the fourth pallet on the right and was now lifting down a sack of virgin plastic granules from a neatly interleaved pile that rose to chest-height. Though a slender man, he handled the weight with ease. He turned to see Alphonse lounging on the second pallet's merely knee-high heap of raw-material sacks, with Fernando moving jerkily from foot to foot and staring down at him.

Rachid, Alphonse, Fernando. Respectively: lifting, lounging, jerking;

tight-shouldered, large-hipped, broad-jawed; slender, stout, sinewy; grey-yellow, gleaming-black, olive-brown; bending, sitting, standing; in grief, at ease, on edge; angular, undulating, ductile; a blasted birch, a sapling oak, a ragged thorn; Rachid, Alphonse, Fernando.

Rachid's scalp was dry and flaky, the skin over his forehead drawn tight and flat. As he lowered the sack onto his trolley, his chest felt constricted as if by long enforced stasis. Fernando was fizzing, shifting from foot to foot, eyes piercing the gloom, his temples sweating. Alphonse reclined on his pallet, his slim round belly relaxing, a smile gently spreading at the speed of un-harried thought as he watched the Algerian lean his ghostly frame into the laden trolley, slumping against it, gripping its push-bar in both bony hands, somehow getting it to go.

On leaving his machines and pushing his trolley up the aisle toward the raw-materials room, Rachid's thoughts had returned to the smile that Malika had given him that evening, the first proper smile since Mehdi . . . ; his mind could not entertain the words 'was killed'; the first smile since Mehdi's accident . . . ; but an accident might even be nothing, a mere spill: since the catastrophe . . . ; 'catastrophe' was the right word. Since the catastrophe, Malika had accepted only nightly hugs in the dark and then once, a couple of months ago now, in the naked late-summer heat, early one morning when she had felt him hard against her back, she had drawn him into her, simply easing him into position. They had never before made love like that – without even saying good morning, like strangers, one could imagine, but it was strong and slow, the way he knew she liked. He had found it strange not to see her face and had felt a thousand miles from her, as if one of them had been across the sea, back home maybe. Love-making by proxy. He felt that the only part of him that was touching her was the part that was inside her. It had saddened him, then given him hope. After a while, Fatima started to cry and Malika, instead of getting up at once, told him to finish, which he quickly did. He had thought that this small strange act of remote love-making might nonetheless be a start for them, a restart, but months had now elapsed with no further mark of affection until that evening's smile. It was such a warm thing.

The Algerian had hardly noticed Luigi as he let go of the trolley to shake hands with him. Rachid was going to tell Mehdi about that smile as soon as he got a chance. He didn't want anyone to see him talking to himself the way the foreman or that African upstairs sometimes did: talking to yourself in front of others was neither dignified nor polite. He would sit where he couldn't be seen, and he and Mehdi would talk. He had thought the raw-materials room would be a good place, but then the Portuguee and the African had followed him in and now there they were at the second pallet from the door, the former shifting from foot to foot and looking angry about something, the latter lounging on a sack.

Rachid always told Mehdi everything, as much or perhaps more than you would confide to a grown-up friend if you happened to have one, and in much the same terms. At first, however, just after the catastrophe, he had talked to Mehdi in the sing-song voice and light-hearted manner that he had adopted naturally when his son was alive, but that soon came to seem silly. You couldn't talk to a dead person as if they were a child, he realized. Death was enough to age and mature anyone: even a baby would grow up fast after such an experience. (The sack, as he lowered it onto the trolley, weighed more than Mehdi ever did, yet felt as light in his fingers as a dead sparrow.) Besides, at the time of the catastrophe, Mehdi was much more than a baby. (With the deferred conversation heavy on his heart, Rachid slumped forward with both hands on the laden trolley's push-bar, somehow getting the thing to go.)

The light went out as the front of Rachid's trolley drew close to the second pallet. Fernando stomped to the door to hit the timer switch, while Alphonse rose and swung his hand toward Rachid.

Fernando had been angry with both Alphonse and himself ever since stepping into the lift from the upstairs workshop. Why had he had to cave fucking-in? He had a sack of raw material propped up against the end of each machine so had no need to fetch any more. Besides, he was enjoying cleaning and shining his machines, and didn't like to leave a job fucking-half-done. Alphonse had laughed, disrespecting his work, looking with scorn (Fernando recognized that look) at the flags Fernando had attached to the end of the machine pistons, and said with that irritating laugh of his, Why do you want to deck the machines with bunting? They aren't Christmas trees. The nerve of the fucking-man! What was the matter with him anyway? Scared of going to the raw-materials room on his own? Frightened of the dark? Funny that, a black fucking-man frightened of the dark! So Fernando had stopped his spit-and-polishing of the machine's side and had taken his trousers out of his socks and removed his cook's apron (which he always donned when he wanted to clean and shine the machine), and had checked the last product piece from each press, and taken the lift downstairs with Alphonse, and had felt angry with the Ivorian. Not that Alphonse seemed to notice. And angry with himself too. I'm fucking-too forgiving, too kind. Especially after he acted that way in the bar, first not wanting to come in (Fernando had noticed that all right) and then standing at the door and gazing around at everyone like a scarecrow on a swivel, and finally refusing to take an honest drink, getting all crotchety like a bloody woman. I'm going to have to clarify things for him, not fucking-get pushed around. Who the hell does he think he fucking-is anyway?

Alphonse had never stopped talking, talking basically to himself, because Fernando wasn't listening, was he? About a play called *Godot* and characters with names like Oregano, Valdemar and Lucky – Lucky, like the gun-toting cartoon figure Lucky Luke. Fernando had always liked cartoons.

Fernando hit the timer switch, grabbed hold of the trolley he had minutes earlier sent crashing into the side of the plastic mill, and headed off for the far end of the room, fifth pallet on the right. While he was here, he might as well get a sack or two: 'le vieux Albert' (as everybody on the morning shift called the callow young man who took over Fernando's machines each morning) would doubtless be grateful. Fernando prepared a friendly smile for Rachid as he passed the second pallet on his right, but Alphonse had got up from the pallet and stuck his hand out so of course Rachid was looking the other way. That Algerian had fucking-things on his mind, anyone could see that: something bad had happened to the man. The last thing he needed was Alphonse rambling on about a play starring a cooking herb, a Polack and a cartoon fucking-horse. That African would drive you whacko if you let him.

Alphonse was one of those rare individuals who could not see another's woe without feeling sorrow too, nor without trying to do something about it, however misconceived or misdirected that thing might turn out to be. For the last minute or more, in fact ever since he had noticed the Algerian's bowed shoulders and face of grey wretchedness, the Ivorian's deeper mind (the one that does all the original and interesting work while the other handles minute-to-minute administration like how to negotiate a trolley over an uneven patch of floor, etc); Alphonse's deeper mind had made a switch from his sundry dissatisfactions with the young man tasked to direct him and his fellow would-be actors in a small-scale amateur production of *En attendant Godot* (the topic about which he nonetheless continued, much to the annoyance of Fernando, variously to drone and to babble) to the plight of the Algerian, about whom he knew next to nothing, but for whom he was experiencing an upsurge of exquisite human sympathy tinctured with a lively sense of outrage.

How dare this man, or any man for that matter, look so frightfully dry and dusty, Alphonse wondered as, from the relative comfort of his improvised throne of sacks on the second pallet on the right, he stole glances at the Algerian. And why on earth does he insist on bearing himself like someone twice his age? What can be so appalling if you're still alive and healthy enough to be appalled? If you can bear the weight of the world on your shoulders, can you not also dance? (Besides, look at the way he lifts and lowers that sack as if it were a feather: he's not half so frail as he appears.) No. If you have strength enough to lament, you have strength enough to rejoice! It's no jot harder to grin than to glower! What's the matter with the man?

As Rachid, pushing his trolley back toward the plastics workshop, drew close to the pallet on which Alphonse was sitting, and as the light went out and Fernando stomped off to hit the timer switch, the Ivorian jumped to his feet, barring Rachid's path, and executed a mock-military salute, his left arm stiff against his side and the inside edge of his flat right hand touched briefly to his forehead and then out again with a flourish as he clicked his heels together and buckled at the waist, bowing low before the Algerian in a parody of obsequiousness.

Rachid smiled a directionless smile that completely missed the Ivorian's face, let alone his eyes, coming to rest in the dark corner of the raw-materials room among the leaning stacks of cardboard boxes-to-be. He didn't notice Fernando walk past to the right of him, heading for the fifth pallet from the door. Rachid removed his right hand from his trolley's push-bar, passed it over his left hand, held it limp in midair, available for shaking. To Alphonse, Rachid's eyes appeared to express either an extreme tiredness or an unbearable indifference. He took a step toward Rachid, shot his own right hand straight out like a blade from a flick knife, clicked his heels together once again, dropped his chin onto his chest, grasped and pulled hard on Rachid's hand, and said, A votre service, mon général!

Rachid's left hand had now slipped from the trolley's push-bar, and his body had gradually rotated to the left so that the two men were standing face to face. Rachid glanced up at the Ivorian and back down at his own hand, which Alphonse was still clasping. Just trying to get a reaction, the Ivorian said, using this explanation as a preface to a rambling discourse on greetings in general and the many reasons he didn't like to ignore others or to be ignored. Rachid listened, glanced a couple of times at Alphonse's face, but thought of nothing in particular. For the time being, he could endure having his hand held by this strange person. He would be patient and forbear. It had nothing to do with him. His hand felt uncomfortable and was starting to sweat, but in all essentials Rachid was untouched.

Still clinging to the Algerian's hand, the Ivorian interrupted his flow and said, Look at me, my friend. For a second, Rachid glanced into Alphonse's inquisitive, bright and friendly eyes. Why don't we just freeze time for a second and dance? Rachid stared straight into his face. Things are not so bad, Alphonse explained. What's the use of being miserable? Can't you laugh? We could all be dead! They don't dock our pay for laughing! Rachid smiled at that. The black man from upstairs had always struck him as odd, amusing, outlandish in his clothes and extravagant in his speeches, but Rachid had nothing to say to him. Why not just dance? Alphonse resumed, heartened by Rachid's slight smile. Don't you ever dance? Speak to me. Why do you never speak? Speak!

I like to dance, Rachid said quietly, and this evening for once I have good cause and, believe me, I am less . . . miserable than I have been. But this is not the place, this is not the time and, with respect, you are not the person with whom I would wish to dance. Rachid then looked down at his hand and said, My hand, Monsieur, I should now like to have my hand back.

Alongside the fifth pallet on the right, Fernando had loaded two sacks of plastic granules onto the trolley – one for himself and one for Alphonse – and had turned to push the trolley back toward the door. As the 40-watt bulb hanging over the exit to the downstairs workshop went out again, he saw Alphonse lift Rachid's right hand into a dancing gesture, while throwing his own left arm behind the Algerian's back and grabbing the man in what looked at first like an embrace. Fernando laughed in astonishment. What the fucking-Jesus is he up to now, grabbing the man like that? Fernando wondered, peering through the half-light for witnesses to corroborate what he was seeing.

Come on, man, lay back! Alphonse was pleading, dance with me. Just a little waltz. Then, louder, Alphonse piped out the notes of the Blue Danube – Pom-pom-pom-pom-pom, Pom-pom, Pom-pom; Pom-pom-pom-pom-pom, Pom pom, Pom pom – as he led Rachid in a one-two-three one-two-three hobbling waltz free of any fancy footwork.

Initially, the long-suffering Algerian went along with this; it was tiresome but there was no need to take offence. Besides, he could see no way out of it.

The Ivorian was stronger than he was. He would have to bide his time. Rachid soon began, however, to say, No, Enough, Let Me Go; he failed, however, to make himself heard above the thudding cacophony from the plastics section and Alphonse's shrill pom-pom-pomming.

Fernando had halted his trolley alongside Rachid's and was observing the two men. The Algerian didn't seem upset. Damn it, when you thought about it, it was the fucking-funniest thing. Two men holding hands then dancing a waltz is weird enough, but Alphonse and Rachid: what-fucking-ever next? The dozy Italian turning a cartwheel up the stairs? Jean and the foreman kissing and making up? (What was it with those two anyway?) The Sicilian arriving all dishevelled and passing round a massive joint? The possibilities were endless and the night was young. As often happened, the more Fernando laughed, the more he laughed: soon he was cackling like a turkey and at the same time attempting to follow the rhythm of the dance, even though he had no partner, not even a chair to squeeze. Suddenly he got a clear view of Rachid's face and ceased laughing. The Algerian was mouthing something that looked like a protest. He still looked more weary than angry, but anyone could tell things were fucking-not right.

Alphonse was still hoping that Rachid would loosen up, get into the spirit of the dance, snap out of whatever it was. But either Alphonse hadn't registered the change in Rachid's mood or he was deliberately ignoring it, gripping the man tighter, supremely confident that his ebullience would eventually infect his recalcitrant dancing partner. The Ivorian felt such sympathy for this quiet, reserved man. He was on a mission now, a mission to do Rachid some good, to cut through his reserve, and spread a little joy. He believed he had it in his power to dispel sadness. It was a gift. An embrace, a dance: these are powerful things. In time, Rachid would respond, he would melt. But Fernando had begun to circle the pair, tapping Alphonse on the shoulder and shouting at him to let the man go. Alphonse stared at him briefly and shook his head. Fernando fell back and observed the scene, his head shaking in dismay.

Rachid, for his part, appeared to have gone limp, suspending his ineffectual protests, his eyes open but staring unfocused, permitting Alphonse to drag him this way and that in his parody of a dance but denying him the slightest cooperation. The Algerian was crouching within himself, hunkering down into his mood, coolly instructing his body inch by inch from the tips of his toes to the roots of his greying hair to relax, certain that in the fullness of time the Ivorian would let him go just as suddenly as he had seized him.

It was in this self-hypnotic state that Rachid recalled a game he had played as a child. His parents had owned an old lambskin rug on which his sister, Esmé, liked to pull him round the house in which they all lived. He would close his eyes and relax completely and become Lamby while his sister related adventures, wild travels. He hadn't thought of that game . . . for how many years? He hadn't remembered Esmé for almost as long. There had been no time to grieve for her. He had certainly not thought of her once since Mehdi . . . since the catastrophe.

Rachid felt ashamed that Mehdi must now see him like this, apparently so cowed and helpless. He told his son in a whisper, Timing is everything, timing and surprise. Rachid had regained his calm, but in a detached and distant way he was also angry, as if on somebody else's behalf. How dare the Ivorian be so domineering? What right had he to decide who dances and when? And why doesn't the Portuguee do more to rein him in? Aren't they friends?

As Rachid played dead, so Alphonse hugged him ever tighter against his own body. Inch by inch, however, like a sack of flour, Rachid began to slip downward against the Ivorian's body. Then, as the Ivorian momentarily loosened his grip (as a mere prelude to redoubling his missionary efforts), Rachid, sensing the man's guard was down, burst out of the body-lock, throwing his arms out and causing Alphonse to tumble backward in fright and amazement, landing heavily on the third pallet from the door. Rachid at once stepped forward to stand over him and, before Alphonse could rise or indeed react in any way, the Algerian stretched out his right arm and placed the tips of his index and middle fingers firmly in the inside corners of the man's eyes pressing his fingers together against the man's nose, immobilizing him. At the same time, Rachid noticed that Fernando had taken a step closer but although he was shifting his weight from side to side his arms were folded as if to declare his neutral-observer status.

Rachid had both men's attention. He ignored Fernando and spoke straight to Alphonse, looking down the barrel of his own arm and into the Ivorian's eyes, glowing now at the tips of his fingers. Don't ever do anything like that again, Rachid whispered. Then a pause. Not to me, not to anyone. Another pause. You're big, but I am fearless, because I have nothing left to fear, and I have a further advantage over you. Rachid now lowered his arm slightly so that Alphonse might, in theory, have moved, but Rachid maintained his position and his glare. I lived through civil war. I don't think either of you did. Both men remained silent. I saw things. Things were done to me. I did things to others. Pause. Don't ever test me. I am not a violent man. I have never killed a man in peacetime. I have never hurt anyone gratuitously. I never would. Then a long pause (you could count to fifteen slowly), as Rachid tried to formulate a warning that was not a threat. Let me advise you: if you ever touch me again, strike at my head, an upward blow to the jaw. Get it in quick and make it fatal. Do you understand? Alphonse nodded, and Rachid then smiled at him in a friendly way and shrugged as if to dismiss the entire event. He turned, shook himself, adjusted his jacket, took hold of his trolley and pushed it through to the downstairs plastics workshop. Did you see that Mehdi? Rachid muttered under his breath as he passed Philippe, working unhurriedly at Jacques' machine number four, doing the absent old man a favour. Did you take note? Timing is all. Timing and surprise. You ought to have known that. It could have saved you. I should have taught you that sooner.

Marcel stepped aside to let the Algerian push his trolley back up the aisle. He was keeping his eyes on the entrance from metallurgy. He wanted to intercept his cousin, find out what was going on, what the hell the kid was up to now. The letter from the African was burning a hole in his back pocket. As if he had nothing more pressing to worry about. He was going to get married, goddamnit! What could the mysterious African possibly want with his cousin? What was Bobrán playing at? Marcel slipped a new length of chewing gum into his mouth and, shaking his head from side to side, he began to chew.

15. Outside in. Claustrophobia confined . . .

Heike sat before her wine glass so prim and proper you could tell at a glance she was no Grandgobosarde, not a native of this country at all, more likely some type of Teuton: if not a Dane, at the very least a Switzer. She was the only woman in the bar who wore her hair cropped short, the only person who was reading a book; horn-rimmed spectacles completed the picture. In her right hand she held a pencil stub, occasionally twirling it between her fingers like a gerbil considering a nut, raising the blunt end to her incisors for gnawing, or lowering the point to mark a passage or scratch a comment. On the table before her, set at an oblique angle, lay a newspaper folded open and placed face-down.

Moritz walked into the San Francisco, immediately spotting his sister at the very back, sitting alone beside the door to the toilets, as far from the bar as she could be. Everything else was familiar: the smoke; the Bowie-spaceman music; the clustering and drifting customers; the lounging bar staff; Chuck, the morose Chicago-American precarious on the only occupied barstool, apparelled like Juliette Greco and smoking untipped Gauloises like it was a statement of one thing, while sipping Bourbon like it was a statement of another. Moritz said, Bonsoir Julie! to a young barmaid whose long black centre-parted hair framed an un-pretty but striking face, then hesitated a nicely calculated instant before acknowledging the American's glare: the man worked at the university as an assistant d'anglais, getting reappointed each autumn at the very last moment, when his money was all spent, his credit exhausted, and his bags packed.

Moritz paused at the bar to gaze in admiration at his sister. Heike was a picture of settled studiousness, her bright face soft and sympathetic in semi-darkness. For a moment, Moritz felt unequal to her, then fleetingly envious, finally admiring. Moritz's only sibling had always struck him as irretrievably superior to himself – but only by that same fraction by which she was also his elder – a gap that would shrink in proportion, he comforted himself, with the passage of the years and his own accumulating experience of life.

Heike had left Moritz's flat a couple of hours earlier, saying she wasn't hungry and that she wished to wander the city on her own. Instead, she had gone straight to a little restaurant she had spotted that morning on her walk from the station, which she had duly entered after a glance at the ill-typed menu posted by the door. She had ordered and consumed a simple meal.

Heike liked most people and adored her brother, yet she needed time alone, large expanses of it every few days, relayed by smaller allowances every few hours; otherwise she would grow agitated, tetchy, even tearful, for no reason that anyone could fathom. Moritz had shrugged and let her go. They had agreed to meet at the San Francisco and he had drawn a little map. After her meal, she had found her way there, identified the quietest corner and eagerly begun to read a book by the philosopher Louis Althusser, *Lénine et la philosophie,* which she had purchased that afternoon. She was hoping to impress the man who directed her Marx reading group at home in Mainz by tackling that month's set text in the original French. She was struggling but undefeated.

Moritz walked the length of the bar, sidling past his sister as if making for the toilets then, retracing his last two steps, crept up behind Heike and planted a crisp kiss on the crown of her head, the pinkish scalp gleaming in the half-light through strawberry blonde hair.

She scarcely moved, merely lifting her eyes from her book as she closed it on her pencil stub and saying, with a spangle in her green-grey eyes: a man came in and somehow recognized me and asked me where you were.

Moritz slipped onto the bench opposite his sister and laid his forearms on the table that separated them. There was only one person it could be.

What was he like?

Dishy, but a little rough-looking for my tastes. Swarthy.

Moritz smiled and nodded, relishing the plain-spoken German word, dunkelhäutig, dark-skinned. He must have seen your photo in my room, Moritz said, more to himself than to his sister. So what are you reading?

Aren't you going to tell me about him? Heike asked, as she slid her book along the table and leaned forward.

Maybe, Moritz said. He reached for the book and opened it at the pencil stub. 'Ideology and ideological state apparatuses.' Good plot?

Heike snorted.

I didn't know your French was good enough.

It isn't.

So why bother?

It's about a man.

Who? Lenin? He's dead.

No. I mean the reason I'm reading it in French.

Moritz laughed and leaned forward.

What's he like? Tell me. I'm all ears. And what happened to Jens? I rather liked him.

Heike appeared momentarily uncomfortable.

Jens and I are just friends now. You go first.

Holding a notepad aloft in her left hand and a biro in her right, Julie materialized at Moritz's side. She produced a lopsided smile and waited.

Moritz ordered a 'Pelforth brune' and a second glass of wine for his sister. Julie walked back to the bar, trailing a relaxed silence behind her. Moritz and Heike had always talked about everything. For once, Moritz didn't know where to begin.

Will he come back? Heike asked.

This evening? No. I doubt it. He'll have gone to work. He works nights.

What does he do?

Guess, Moritz said, settling back against his seat and observing Heike's mind at work, her large eyes darting, her mouth puckering up, now in a smile, now in a frown. He tasted his beer. It wasn't as cold as he liked it. He relaxed anyway. Brother and sister were back in the nursery.

Heike enjoyed games and rattled through a list of obvious night jobs – baker, security man, taxi driver, concierge, gas-station attendant, hospital porter, traffic patrol, policeman, bouncer, pimp, train driver, prison guard, office cleaner, night porter, postman, printer – while Moritz sipped at his beer and either laughed or feigned outrage at her suggestions.

I give in, Heike said at last.

Factory worker. Nights.

Heike was visibly disappointed with herself. Of course, she said. Rotating shifts?

No. Permanent nights.

Heike whistled.

Bobrán says you get used to it, it's not so bad. He says the 'three eights' is worse because your sleep never settles down, though at least you do get a long weekend once every three weeks.

His sister stared at him.

The week you switch from mornings to nights.

Heike narrowed her eyes.

Because that week you clock off Friday lunchtime and don't have to go back till Monday night, right?

Heike nodded. Okay, she said.

The problem is – he works days too. I don't know how he does it.

'Bobrán', did you say? What kind of name is that?

Zigeuner.

You're joking.

Moritz shook his head slowly.

Where does he work during the day?

It varies. On a building site at present. He says he might be able to get me a job.

On a building site? You?!

Of course not. You know my head for heights. In his factory.

You're dreaming.

Am I? What of?

I don't know. You tell me. Getting to know all his mates? Joining the ranks of the French working class? Bedding the entire shift? I'm assuming they're all men . . .

He says he doesn't have any mates there, just a dodgy cousin who hates faggots. Besides, I'm not greedy. Don't be thinking that all gays are sex maniacs.

There was a lull.

Heike shrugged.

Now tell me about yours, Moritz said.

Heike pretended she hadn't heard.

So he works nights in a factory. What else do you know about him? Do you know where he lives?

With his mother somewhere. What else do I need to know? He's fantastic. I think I'm in love. Anyway, fair's fair. Your turn.

It's complicated.

People say that when they're not getting what they want.

We haven't actually been together yet.

You mean you haven't fucked?

Do you have to be so crude?

Yes. Absolutely. On principle. Well, have you?

No.

Why not?

Heike was blushing.

I don't want you to laugh.

Okay. I promise. How did you meet him?

I joined this ML group at the university and then I heard about this Marx-reading group.

Marx-reading? What do you do? Read Marx?

Obviously. But not just Marx. Revolutionary theory in general.

Moritz glanced at the book Heike was reading. He picked it up and began to leaf through it.

Revolutionary theory, he repeated under his breath, as if frisking the concept for erotic appeal. He shook his head and put the book back down with a decisive little click.

Heike looked at him and smiled. Her baby brother out in the world, a long way from home. Drifting but still safe, still the same. She sipped at her wine.

Moritz recalled a Christmas a few years earlier, the last Christmas he had spent at their parents' house in Mainz. He and Heike had got sky-high on some Afghan black she had scored in an American bar in Wiesbaden. Then they had watched the bombing of Cambodia on TV. There was some uncensored footage of maimed toddlers. He had drunk too much Brandwein and been sick in the toilet. Later, Heike had wept inconsolably. She had stared at her brother through streaming eyes and, pointing at the spent grey TV screen, had declared, That's our war too. Either we're with the Insurgency or we're with the Imperialists. If we do nothing, we're with the Imperialists.

Then we shall slide [sic] with the Inslurgents [sic], Moritz had said.

Heike had laughed at him and jumped up and ruffled his hair, then went to make some black coffee. After that, they had talked till dawn. Their generation was going to bring about worldwide liberation from every imaginable form of oppression. That was a given. Only a fool or a square could doubt it.

Heike nodded toward the book and put her glass down. That's on our reading programme this month. This man, Horst, he teaches at Frankfurt, at the university.

Don't tell me . . . sociology?

Heike grinned, anticipating Moritz's reaction and pausing for effect. Engineering.

They both roared with laughter. Their father was an engineer.

The thing is, he's married, Heike said.

As married as an engineer . . . So what's a state-ideological apparatus?

Basically, it's what keeps people in line – short of truncheons and tear gas and prisons, I mean, open state repression – enabling the bourgeoisie to maintain the relations of production that ensure their profits and the workers who produce those profits for them are reproduced. That's it in a nutshell. Do you follow me? Things like school, church, family, law, culture, media, arts, sport. But I haven't finished reading the essay yet.

You could have fooled me, Brains, Moritz said, teasing his sister with the nickname she had earned years earlier from her schoolmates.

So this Bobrán, this Roma guy, does he drink and fight and steal and dance and live in a caravan?

None of them, Moritz replied curtly. Where do you get your stereotypes? In a job-lot special offer? Though he does live in a trailer. With his mother, in fact.

Tell me more about him. What is he like? I don't mean his taste in music. I mean in bed. I want to hear all about him.

Heike leaned toward Moritz, as if somebody might otherwise overhear her question.

I want to know how it works. Like, who takes it *in die Arsche*? You? Him? Neither of you? Both? Then pulling away again: he didn't look like a fag to me.

What do you mean 'didn't look like a fag?'

You look the part – he doesn't.

Well, thank you *very* much, Moritz said, fluttering his eyelashes and flapping a wrist.

You know what I mean. Besides, the way he looked at me was like any straight guy checking me out. He looked at my tits, damn it.

What tits?

Precisely!

He was probably being polite, trying to blend in. That's what we do. It becomes second nature. There's no way he's bi. Anyway, what of this engineering teacher, why won't he fuck you? Would you like me to beat him up next time I'm home? I could run him to ground and say, Hey you bastard, I hear you are not fucking my little sister.

I'm your big sister.

It doesn't have the same ring. Besides, I don't see how he can lead a reading-group on state-ideological apparatuses . . .

Ideological state apparatuses . . .

. . . and then not fuck because he's married. Sounds like hypocrisy to me.

He says it has nothing whatever to do with being married, it's just that his wife wouldn't like it: he'd be betraying a comrade.

Don't tell me you buy that!

Heike looked away, pulled a face, then got up to go to the toilet, as if either she didn't like the conversation or was caught short.

Moritz read a few lines of Heike's book, then pushed it aside again and reached for the newspaper that was also lying on the table, open and face-down. A small news item had been ringed in biro. The East German authorities had given the singer-songwriter Wolf Biermann a visa to travel to the West for a concert in Cologne on Saturday 13. In four days. Moritz pursed his lips and blew air out of them. Blood had filled his face, making it feel furry.

Heike was sitting back down.

Have you seen this? he asked Heike.

Who do you think ringed it?

Can you get tickets?

I think so. Horst has all kinds of contacts in the trade-unions.

Get one for me too. And Bobrán.

Bobrán? He won't understand a word.

I'll translate.

Heike appeared sceptical.

This is history, Moritz gushed. Biermann hasn't been allowed to perform in public, let alone travel, for years, over a decade. And what a decade! I want to be there. And I've never done anything with Bobrán except . . . you know.

How come you use the word fuck for everyone else but can't apply it to yourself?

I wasn't thinking about that actually. But you're right. You've got me. I'm in love. Want a confession? You got it! Let's go.

Where to? And why the rush?

Anywhere. I'm just so excited. You know Biermann's my hero. There's one artist who isn't part of any state apparatus, ideological or otherwise. Tell me how your French philosopher would figure that! We can go to another bar, where there are more straight men. Maybe you'll get lucky. I'll take you on a tour of Grandgobier by night. Or if you don't fancy that, we can go to the cinema. Come on, big sister, let's go. We're young, we're free, and we're in a foreign country.

Sure, said Heike, rolling her eyes. We're immortal too, right?

Moritz nodded.

By the way, Heike said, as though sharing an afterthought, I've already invited your boyfriend to come to Germany with us. I was sure you'd approve.

Moritz stopped in his tracks. His sister turned back to face him.

So you did like him! I knew it. What did he say?

He said he'd think about it.

Moritz laughed.

This is going to be fun, he said. I can tell.

The door to Tomec's studio-flat clicked shut. Sarah stood up. The Pole had turned on his heels and left. Don't, he had said. Don't. With a smile, and a wagging finger.

Sarah's mind was caught in the process of framing a thought, not unkind but cold and remote. Tomec had swivelled round and jerked the forefinger of his left hand in teasing but testy reproof just as she frowned at his broad back, at the blue worsted trousers packaging his hairy buttocks.

Sarah had been on the point of thinking something. Whatever it was, Tomec had put a stop to it. Would she be able to retrieve it? What had Tomec imagined she was about to think? Or say? Was there any chance he was right? What must he prevent her from thinking? He had smiled. It had seemed like a joke. But creepy too. *Don't* what?

Sarah looked round the room and began to retrace the previous twenty-five minutes, starting at the point when Tomec had walked in from his shower. She had not looked up at once and, when she had, had read disappointment in his face. She saw the familiar room anew.

The ceiling was high, its whitewash discoloured by stains, its corners hung with cobwebs. The bare walls presented a patchwork of off-whites, a crazy chequerboard of ghosts of pictures, calendars, mirrors and drawings, long since removed, perhaps on some minimalist impulse.

The room contained a grouping of three easels (in front of which Tomec had stood swaddled in his towel, still dripping from his shower), a bed (on which Sarah had sat, her breasts bare, attempting to ignore the draught that Tomec's entrance had raised). The bulb hanging from the centre of the ceiling, now motionless, had swung gently. The air, she now realized, her fine nose quivering with distaste, was heavy with oil paint, onions, spilled wine turning to vinegar, and the liquorishy smell of sex.

Against the wall stood a ramshackle bookshelf against which further books leaned in precarious knee-height piles, a box gramophone in cream and maroon plastic, a couple of kitchen stools and a free-standing, school-surplus blackboard, its ledge bearing a blue duster and assorted lengths of chalk. In a corner, then as now, stood four scuffed and bulging portfolios.

Everything had gone wrong in the minutes that had followed Tomec's arrival from his shower. On immemorial, atavistic instinct, Sarah blamed herself. If she had only dropped what she was doing and paid Tomec some attention, his departure for work would have gone better, his leave-taking might have been less teasing-peremptory, and right now she would be able to get on with her own work and thoughts. Instead of sitting puzzling about his.

Sarah didn't like to watch Tomec get ready for work, don his silly uniform. She knew he had to go, but she resented it. Sometimes she tried to prevent or at least postpone his departure, turn her sabotage into a game, inventing last-minute chores, questions, diversions, once even fishing his dick out as he pulled on those scratchy trousers. At least it had been nice and clean, all fresh from the shower. But even that time, she hadn't delayed him for long. Such discipline.

Sarah disapproved of his night job. She couldn't make it make sense. Of course he said it paid the rent and gave him the freedom to spend his days sketching and sculpting. That was all it was, he said. But she couldn't help suspecting that he derived some kind of enjoyment from it. Sometimes they argued about it, though not tonight. Maybe that explained the *Don't!* He simply wanted to avoid an argument. Why couldn't he teach at the university, say, like her father? There was dignity in teaching. She had been thinking this as she had watched him pulling on his stiff clothes and adjusting his cap: a big clumsy man with a drooping moustache and black hair going grey inexorably, one hair at a time. Were they even acquainted? And then she had begun to frame the thought that he had so effectively interdicted. Now what was it? She didn't like to have her thoughts interdicted.

The first side of Schoenberg's *Moses und Aron* was reaching a crescendo again. Sarah marched over and pulled the needle off, scratching the record. She swore, then regretted it: her father had taught her that swearing was for the inarticulate. In uncustomary silence, she stared down at the surface of the bed, seeing her notebook lying open at a sketch she had made the previous evening, an expressionistic mess of faces glimpsed on the bus home, but mainly two: that of an old man with stubbly cheeks and scarved neck; and that of a garishly painted streetwalker, a woman both childlike and ancient, young and wizened; and around these images, a mass of scribbled jottings about religion and art.

Sarah was dissatisfied with her notes. She picked up her notebook and pencil, then realized she didn't need to reread them to know that they rambled and went nowhere. She yearned to understand this music, the work of Schoenberg, the grappling of a godlike artist with God, the Unimaginable, the Invisible.

As she had sat there cross-legged and bare-breasted, rapt and fascinated in her contemplation, she had nonetheless been distracted from her note-taking by Tomec's sudden entry from the shower. He had stood there, staring at his work on the easels, while she had strained, strained, strained to make sense, at least as metaphor, of the Voice from the Burning Bush and Moses's futile attempt to resist God's summons. As if he could gain exemption by being old and wishing to tend his flocks! Then the prophet's plaintive cry, like that of any artist beset by self-doubt: 'No one will believe me!' As if one could ever draw back when possessed with knowledge! No. In matters of art, Sarah had realized, there operated a sort of *sagesse oblige*. Just as the Voice from the Bush says: You have seen horror and acknowledged the truth and therefore no longer have any choice but to bear witness.

Instead, Sarah's attention had been seized by a jagged movement, her mind wrenched from the tragic and the sublime to the banal and the trivial. Tomec had dropped his towel and was standing there in the middle of the room, not bothering to pick it up, staring at the words he had written earlier on the blackboard and then back again at his easels.

It was at this point, Sarah remembered, that she had put down her pencil and resigned herself. Cute – for a man his age, she had thought, removing her glasses and leaning back to survey him better. Tomec was scratching his head more like an oaf than an artist, a cartoon caricature from Wilhelm Busch or some such. And all the while playing with himself like a baby, pre-erotically, pulling on his zizi, absentmindedly working his finger into his foreskin, letting it close round it suckingly, and then tugging and tugging with his finger till his *truc*, his *Dingsbums*, his *whatsit*, was all stretched and funny-looking and wrinkly; and then all of a sudden it went pop! – a bit like the sound that jolly Christmas uncles make with their thumbs in their cheeks, though not so loud – pop! Sarah gazed in fascination as, with a little popping sound, Tomec's finger came out of his foreskin and his zizi sprang back to normal shape and slackness. Well, well, well! So foreskins had a purpose after all and goys could make squelchy little popping sounds. Well, well, well. Nice legs, though. Good shoulders.

That, Sarah thought, was probably the point at which I should have said something, started a conversation or got up and gone over to him. Instead of trying to refocus my thoughts on Moses and Schoenberg and God. Often it's the littlest things that trip or tip a moment, making you fight someone instead of embracing them. A microscopic misunderstanding. A rogue synapse misfiring. It happened when I saw him reach for the yellow towel in the corner and start using it to dry his feet. I threw it in the corner this morning. It was the one I slept with after we made love, using it to catch his sperm. He'll be trampling his dead seed all night, floating round his stupid factory on an invisible carpet, a fine film of his own squandered spawn. So I wanted to say something. I was outraged by the casualness. Instead, he started that stupid conversation about whether my vagina felt sore or not, because his penis was irritated and red, he said. What a question! What a topic! Unimaginable! Is that what you have to discuss when you go to bed with someone? Shall we talk about my spots next or bowel movements? My menstrual pains and his ingrowing toenails? I ask you!

Sarah was getting angry with herself for dwelling on such silliness. She would put the scene behind her and get on with her evening. With a decisive, delicate, almost avian gesture, Sarah dropped her pencil onto the bed and shut her notebook. It was time to go out. What was on this evening at the Maison de la Culture? A Fassbinder, I seem to recall, one I have already seen. But which? I could find out if Ornella is free. First, I'll have a shower, freshen myself up a bit. Maybe I won't phone Ornella. Ornella is probably with Thierry. Besides, I feel like being alone, properly alone for once: out of choice. With no one to interdict, or even influence, my thoughts.

Sarah turned the gramophone off at the knob and walked out of the room, down the corridor, and into the bathroom. She stood under the shower and soaped herself and winced childlike. She closed her eyes. She liked what she saw.

16. Marcel threatens.

There could be no doubt about it: Bobrán was in an uncommonly good mood. Shuffling to the right of Jacques' great lumbering frame, the young man counted his blessings and enjoyed the relative quiet before the approaching din. In the half-dark metallurgy section, he felt calm, breezy, untroubled, indifferent, free. He was happy he had come to work, happy he had missed Moritz at the San Francisco, and happy he had made the acquaintance of Heike. As his left shoulder brushed Jacques' right elbow, neither man said a word: they adjusted the distance between them, moving fractionally apart in the dark.

Maybe Bobrán would see Moritz tomorrow; certainly at the weekend: Heike had invited him to go to Germany with them. For a concert, she had said. He couldn't remember whether he had ever been to Germany. It was a long way to go for a concert, he had told Heike, who had just shrugged and continued staring straight at him. Besides, he had thought, he wanted to hear the invitation fresh from Moritz's own sweet lips. Possibly, Bobrán had told Heike, letting her down gently. Why wouldn't you come? she had asked. He hadn't replied. Because it would be too tiring, he had thought.

By the end of each week, Bobrán was exhausted, a rag wrung out and flung at a wall to ooze and drip from a nail. But on this Tuesday evening he felt good, taut, crisp, full of zest, full of zing. The store of sleep he had amassed the previous weekend had not yet run down. He wore super-light plimsolls that conveyed the floor's every contour. To walk in these shoes was alternately to peel and unpeel from the floor the skin of his feet, as though pacing barefoot across hot linoleum. If he trod on a 1-mm washer he would feel the size and shape of it ring up his legs and spine, speed-sketching as it travelled an outline for his brain to contemplate.

Jacques was a man of few words: in Bobrán he had met his match. The minutes of silence since their last exchange had begun to weigh on the older man. In part, this was because tonight, unusually, he was ill at ease with his thoughts. He cast around for bits of conversation. He could recall previous walks through this darkness. Some men never stopped talking, as if the dark unnerved them. Others hummed or whistled or, with no warning or prelude, clicked their tongues. Jacques recollected a thing Philippe had said on one such transit through metallurgy. It had made him smile. He would try to make it his own.

This reminds me of going to school, Jacques had just said.

Bobrán was roused from his lolling reverie.

What was the old man talking about? School, did he say? While waiting for more, the young Gypsy made a tiny sound like the first phrase of a chuckle: hfmn.

Jacques had to try again. Philippe must have prefaced the thing in some way, placed it somehow in his childhood, in Marseille, postwar, maybe he even named a neighbourhood. Bobrán was listening now. Jacques couldn't back out.

It reminds me of going to school, Jacques began again. The times I'd arrive late, and everyone else would already be there, and I'd have to walk through the empty playground and the silent hall. Jacques had invented the hall, and was pleased with it. He was imagining a big old school in Marseille somewhere, ceilings sky high. The school that Jacques had in fact attended in a nearby village had been so tiny there had been no hall to speak of, barely even a playground. It's a bit like truanting, Jacques said, trying to complete the picture and find his way to some kind of pay-off: it's a bit like being naughty and expecting a ticking-off from Miss.

It had been amusing the way Philippe had said it.

Bobrán said nothing for a little longer and then stated in an easy, thoughtful way, I didn't go to school much and when I did they were usually so surprised to see me they never told me off no matter how late I was. I think they liked it better when I stayed away.

Jacques felt foolish. He had tossed the Gypsy a fake story and received in return a scrap of something real. He felt like a swindler. He felt like the man who pays with a large-denomination counterfeit banknote for the cheapest item in the shop and pockets honest coin.

There could be no doubt about it: Jacques was in an uncommonly bad mood. Trudging along to the left of Bobrán's tensile, acrobatic frame, the old man sifted his troubles in the relative quiet before the approaching din. He didn't want to take those tablets, but perhaps his health was at stake. But what of his manhood? He had never set much store by either, but then neither had ever seemed in much danger. He wondered what had possessed him to see his brother that evening. He felt as if he had started something that would be impossible to stop and not easy to continue. What was it called? Reconciliation? He didn't like the sound the word made in his brain. It was too long and important-sounding for what it really meant, which in his experience was mainly sullen silences and compromises you regretted even before you made them.

Jacques scowled at the approaching light. He could at least look forward to talking to Philippe: that would surely be a comfort. Philippe was sensible, reliable, knowledgeable. But how could Jacques explain his worry without embarrassment? And, tomorrow, would he not also have to talk to Jeanne? That would be even worse. And then what next? Go back to that doctor? Doctors could talk rings round a man. Life was suddenly full of complications. Jacques' right elbow brushed against Bobrán's left shoulder, but neither man noticed.

Jacques and Bobrán walked into the light that splashed through the hanging plastic flaps marking the entrance to the plastics section, and then pushed through the flaps themselves and into the noise and fumes. Jacques removed his cap and scratched his head, while at his side Bobrán stared into the bright light, happy to be there, screwing one of his eyes tight shut and spreading his mouth in a grin. Jacques was thinking he should have driven straight on past the factory gate, never stopped till his head ran clear as a spring. He could have phoned Jeanne at six the next morning from Genoa, Perpignan or Paris. It would have given him time to think. Crazy idea. Think what? You could only think so much. Jacques remembered things, useless things, moments long forgotten, good and bad, very good and very very bad. There was a weary darkness in his mind, an unfamiliar dread. A mirthless, grey and foreboding smile shrouded his face and his hip joints hurt.

Still side by side the two men walked unspeaking toward the wall-mounted clock-machine, the taut short Gypsy, the large ambling peasant. Against factory regulations, in their absence both workers had been clocked on – but both needed to make quite sure. They would take it in turns to remove and check their time cards from the rack to the left of the clock, Bobrán first, then Jacques.

Their arrival had not been witnessed by either Philippe or Marcel, both of whom had been distracted from their previous vigilance: Marcel by the approach of Eric, with gaping mouth and broken French; Philippe by an attempt to dispel his dull and sombre thoughts by indulging his passion for newsprint.

Marcel was standing between the aisle-ends of his machines twelve and thirteen, his eyes glancing at and past the Englishman, who in a flurry of gesticulation appeared to be asking whether he knew of any 'free apartments.' By 'free' Marcel had to suppose the man intended 'vacant.' Marcel was temperamentally unable to focus on ugly women, ungainly men, or for that matter on sick, disabled, disfigured or misshapen animals of whatever species: his eyes would sheer off such unsavoury sights, seeking landfall elsewhere. At present he was looking variously over Eric's head, down at his cavernous chest and untidy feet, past his left ear and, in mushy mid-distance focus, clean through his diaphragm. Analogously, Marcel found it painful, indeed mentally distressing, to attend to ramshackle, halting French. Some might find foreign accents charmingly exotic but for Marcel they signified awkwardness, exclusion, prejudice, poverty, misfortune and, above all, weakness and failure. He didn't need exotic. Exotic was where he had come from.

Eric had now paused. Perhaps he had exhausted his stock of vocabulary. Or perhaps he anticipated a reply. Marcel shot a glance across the Englishman's pearling forehead, then pointed at machine twelve's hopper as though it required attention. He grinned and said, But if I hear something you'll be the first to know. He turned away, leaving Eric to shovel a thank you at his back. That went quite well, Eric said to himself, stepping back across the aisle to his machine five.

Philippe was resting his belly against the recycled-material cylinder at the aisle-end of machine two. His eyes were drifting over an article in *L'Humanité*, but his mind was distant. He felt uncommonly inert. He had drunk too much beer; and not nearly enough. His painstakingly confected chipper mood had crashed. He was worried and he was woozy. Everything had been going fine until that phone call from his sister. He was going to have to tell Rémy: no more phone calls; whoever wants me, I'm not here. Until Danielle had phoned, it was a normal evening, pleasant even. Now he was going to have to think about Odile screwing some other man. Ignorance, if not bliss, had at least been some sort of anaesthetic. He was going to have to do something, and whatever he did was sure to make matters worse.

Philippe heard a voice at his back, Ça va?, and turned slowly, giving Bobrán his right hand. Philippe was swaying slightly, his breath beery, his eyelids drooping. Bobrán stood back. Philippe stared at him. The man's eyes were ringed and dark, the left one had a creamy patch just below the iris, the shape and size of a split pea. As the hands of the Marseillais and the Gypsy pulled apart, Marcel strode over from his machines. Glancing up the aisle, Philippe saw Jacques navigate the end of machine fourteen, listing slightly to shake hands with Luigi, who began saying something to him. Jacques was smiling. Philippe's stomach warmed and his shoulders fell. Jacques was always smiling. That was the great thing about him. Laid-back, unruffled, easy. Philippe lit a cigarette. All the time in the world. Jacques had put down his bags and cushion.

Marcel and Bobrán were pinching and poking and pulling and pushing each other, continually glancing at Philippe as though it were a performance staged for his exclusive entertainment. Impervious to flattery whether overt or implicit, Philippe spectated with a relaxed and easy mien, nodding with encouragement and approval after each man's every act or attempt at wit, disbursing praise and support equitably between the contending cousins.

It's kind of you to grace us with your company this evening, Marcel told his cousin, with at least some trace of Philippe's laconic manner. Philippe cast a priceless smile in Marcel's direction.

Bobrán grinned at Philippe, punched Marcel in the left shoulder, and called him a faggot. Philippe laughed along with Bobrán, whose lush black hair fell over his eyes. Over the Gypsy's head, Philippe could see that Jacques' left ear was still captive to Luigi. Philippe raised and lowered his eyebrows twice in rapid succession, to which Jacques made a dozen or so tiny nods. Philippe inhaled deeply and his attention reverted to Marcel and Bobrán.

So why were you late tonight? Marcel was asking his cousin. Did your Mercedes break down? Marcel looked at the Marseillais for a quick appraisal of his sarcasm. The familiar image of Bobrán on his push-bike pedalling away from the factory compound each morning flickered across Philippe's mind. He smiled at Marcel, tipped his head right back and blew a succession of three perfect smoke rings, watching them rise and break up, snaking and slithering into the blueing air. Bobrán suddenly brightened with inspiration. He stopped shifting from foot to foot and moved in closer to Philippe and Marcel.

The Mercedes is fine, he quipped. But your fiancée couldn't get enough tonight. Insatiable, right? We had to take a second crack at it. Philippe grinned at Bobrán, impressed by the man's invention and cheek. Bobrán was laughing like a hyena, delighted at his discovery. Marcel attempted to cuff the side of his cousin's head but Bobrán ducked and dodged, then took off down the aisle.

We've got to talk, Marcel shouted after him. I've got something for you, something you'll want. Bobrán didn't seem to hear. What the hell could

Marcel want with him anyway? Always telling him off about something, like he was his big brother. Bobrán was tired of all that. Tired of taking it from Marcel. Marcel watched Bobrán shake hands with the Sicilian, who was engaging him in conversation. Marcel turned and, following Philippe's gaze, glanced at the opposite end of the aisle where Luigi was still talking to Jacques. Everybody's so fucking talkative this evening, aren't they? Marcel said. You'd think we were at a fucking party. Philippe wasn't in the mood to comment. He just shook his head at his feet. The two men smoked their cigarettes in silence.

You know, with a faggot like that, Marcel then said, nodding back down the machine aisle, a woman would need two cracks at it, know what I mean? Philippe nodded but neither spoke nor smiled. Marcel had missed his moment. Rejoinders are no damned good sixty seconds late and fired at the wrong person. He was not great at repartee. One man couldn't be good at everything, could he? Marcel crossed the aisle to machine number twelve, glancing to his right to see his cousin still listening to the Sicilian. Sooner or later, Bobrán would have to come back past him. There was no other route for him to take. Unless he learnt to fly. Sooner or later Bobrán would have to go upstairs and see to his machines. He couldn't rely for ever on the Portuguee and the African. Marcel could wait. Marcel had all the time in the world.

Having finished with Luigi, Jacques picked up his bags and cushion and was now heading toward Philippe and Marcel. Philippe dropped his cigarette butt and stepped on it. While following from afar the progress of Jacques' conversation with Luigi and providing encouragement alternately to Bobrán and Marcel, he had also been observing his own mood, monitoring its curve and droop. Under normal circumstances he was tolerably adept at mood management. He had had to give it a lot of attention over the years. He took pains to avoid conflict; strove to maintain stable blood-alcohol, blood-caffeine, blood-sugar, and blood-nicotine levels; masturbated dispassionately rarely less than once and never more than twice a day. More positively, he sought to capture and distil special moments of contentment or happiness, conserving them in his memory for – as it were – a rainy day when they might be 'uncorked' and decanted. Tonight, however, in no time at all, everything had gone wrong, demonstrating, were proof required, that all his efforts amounted to no more than a wicker fence raised against the tempest's blast.

Jacques coasted to a halt, put his things down on the floor and held his huge right hand out toward the Marseillais. Philippe's eyes closed as slowly as an old cat's. He could have wept.

The two men shook hands long and hard, Philippe's small puffy hand engulfed in Jacques' broad gristly paw.

I've got to talk to you, Jacques said, with a pained grin.

Funny that, me too, Philippe countered.

There was a silence. Who should go first? Suddenly they couldn't look at one another. Philippe jerked his head in the direction of Luigi's machine.

Jacques shrugged. He talks to me and the Sicilian and to Jean Herbier upstairs. I can see why he would talk to the Sicilian.

Philippe looked away to the side, as if he was interested in the wall.

It was something about a man in Annecy, a car mechanic, Jacques said. Who killed his wife and her lover. With a wrench, I think he said. Horrible. But who cares? I've never been to Annecy. Have you ever been to Annecy?

Philippe blanked that, moving his mouth around as if he was chewing on something.

Jacques took a good look at Philippe. You could see something was wrong. We'll go for a coffee then, okay?

Mine will be a beer, Philippe said, as if it were a challenge.

Huh, Jacques said beneath the din, showing the Marseillais a smiling face yet seeming somehow to withdraw. He picked up his bags and cushion and went to his machine number four. So that's what it is, he thought.

Philippe regularly achieved a state of mild inebriation by about 5.30 a.m. *chez Hortense* after work, but this was the first time Jacques had seen him getting half-pissed at work. There had to be a reason. Jacques checked the hoppers of both his machines, three and four. Both were full. So Philippe wasn't *that* drunk. Nobody else would have troubled to fill them. Jacques checked the last product pieces as they fell through the aluminium slats. At machine three, then again at machine four, he tipped the content of the grey oblong floor tray into the already almost full threshing bin to its left. He extracted from his bag his own pair of extra-large industrial gloves and pulled them on. He bent over the threshing bin and began to crash and smash the sprue together, so that the end-products fell or were ripped from the stalks.

Philippe glanced at his machines, then returned to his stack of papers at the end of machine two. His hoppers were still almost full. He'd recently checked the pieces. There weren't many products to thresh. There was nothing he needed to do. He looked down at his navy-blue canvas sailing shoes. Something about them bothered him. What had Danielle said? He put it out of his mind. He hadn't enjoyed Jacques' smiling-withdrawing trick. He could tell a real smile from a fake one. Philippe prided himself on his ability to read people. Jacques' paper-thin smile had made him feel like a child. So what if he preferred beer to coffee? So what if he had an inexplicable thirst this evening? So what if he felt like getting drunk once in a while? It was as though he had already half-confessed to something and was going to have to finish the job. Confessed! There was something paternal about Jacques. Paternal? Pastoral, even. He had never noticed that before. But maybe that was why he liked him. What an appalling thought! The father he never had, the confessor he had told to fuck off years ago. You could hear the violins. It was all horse shit. He still had a father, a perfectly good one. And he wasn't in need of any priest. So what if he and his father never met? So what if they weren't on speaking terms? That was his own choice, wasn't it? What the hell was he saying? Fuck and piss, Philippe said out loud. It was good that nobody saw Philippe talking to himself. It would have damaged his reputation.

Jacques had finished his threshing at machine three. He removed his left-hand glove and mopped his brow and temples with his cuff. He lifted the remaining tangles of empty stalks and placed them in the recycling bin that stood at the aisle-end of machine three, leaving the products at the bottom of the threshing bin. He would collect his cardboard boxes on his way back from his coffee. Walking round the end of machine three, he pulled his gloves back on. Then he settled at machine four's threshing bin. His mood hadn't quite cleared, but he could see that Philippe was in worse trouble than he was. The man had drunk too much. Jacques didn't know what to think. There were several things that crossed his mind, but many more that didn't.

It didn't occur to Jacques that Philippe's customary friendliness toward him was motivated by some sort of father-deprivation. It didn't occur to him that Philippe was suicidal and therefore pissed, nor that he was pissed and therefore suicidal. It didn't occur to Jacques that Philippe could be a latent homosexual, attracted to men twice his age who were not only past their prime but as blatantly heterosexual as any man could wish to be. It didn't occur to him that Philippe might be lonely, nor, alternatively, that he might be sick of cities, factories, busy streets, a crowded flat, his nearest and dearest, his workmates – in a word – desperate to be alone. It certainly didn't occur to Jacques that Philippe's sister might have insulted him by divulging a mortifying truth about his wife's affections – a truth which, to the conventionally minded, reflected badly upon his own status as lover, husband, man, human being. It didn't occur to Jacques that Philippe might be bored with his life or tired of working nights in a factory; that he might have read something upsetting in the paper; that he might have learnt that afternoon that he either was or was not terminally ill. It never entered Jacques' mind that Philippe's pet dog/canary/rat/cat/hamster might have died or – much worse – escaped. It didn't occur to Jacques that Philippe hadn't had sex with his wife for many months, nor with anyone else for many years; that he was bored with his life; that he was beset by feelings of dissatisfaction and had entertained fantasies about being a reporter ever since his first Superman comic, and about being a private eye ever since his first Série-Noir novel and that these fantasies were no longer pleasurable; that his daughter was a disappointment to him; that his wife was screwing another man and he wasn't at all sure he minded; that he was bored with his life. No. Jacques was not a particularly obtuse man, and he liked Philippe and paid attention to him. But all that Jacques could see right now was that Philippe had drunk too much, and that his normally ready ear was for once clamped shut.

Marcel was resting his back against the side of his machine twelve. His eyes were drifting over his cousin, who was shifting now from foot to foot, still appearing to be listening to the Sicilian. Bobrán had failed to thank Marcel for clocking him on. Like the world owed him a living. How much could it cost him to say a civil thank you? As if everyone else in the world was there to smooth his passage. He was getting slapdash, careless, verging on disrespectful. Marcel was going to have to pull him up, give him a salutary reminder. He was worried for him. The African and the journalist dipstick he had in tow had seemed serious about something. Whatever it was, Marcel didn't like it. He was eager to hand Bobrán the African's envelope, and to find out what it concealed. It was a small flimsy envelope which, held to the light, appeared to contain a single sheet. Yet it weighed and bulged in his hip pocket like a fat round flint. Sooner or later Bobrán was going to have to go upstairs, and to do that he would have to get past Marcel. Some things were inevitable.

Salvatore stopped talking. The Gypsy didn't seem to be listening to him anyway. He was just standing there. What on earth could you do with such a customer? Salvatore took a flyer from his smart black attaché case. This sets things out pretty clearly, Salvatore said. The Gypsy stuffed the paper in his trouser pocket. Sure, he said. See you at the meeting? Salvatore asked again. I'm just a temporary, Bobrán said like it was a mantra. You can come anyway, Salvatore said.

Rachid was looking at an evening paper and Bobrán was loping across the machine aisle stretching his hand out to greet him when the foreman, standing at the opposite end of the aisle, midway between machines one and fourteen, began to shout. He had come downstairs in the lift and had walked past the clock-machine on his right and then round the end of Luigi's machine fourteen. Mathieu had not been particularly impressed to see Jacques at work at machine number three, his thick arms sunk deep in the threshing bin, his broad buttocks shifting in rhythm. There wasn't much he could say about that. Jacques was at least there now, and taking charge of his machines. But Mathieu had then seen Bobrán, still in his street clothes, emerging from between Salvatore's machines six and seven and heading across the aisle toward the Algerian, holding out his hand.

Hey! Hey! Yes. You! Mathieu hollered.

Everyone stopped what they were doing and turned toward Mathieu. The foreman didn't often shout. He didn't often need to. He certainly didn't often want to. But today he felt like shouting and today he had cause.

So there stood Mathieu, at the top end of the aisle, just this side of the raised glass-fronted office, midway between machines one and fourteen, his feet set as far apart as his shoulders, his hairless forearms smeared with black oil, a large shiny wrench in his left hand, spittle spurting from around the burnt-out matchstick lodged between his teeth.

Hey! he repeated in a gathering roar, removing the matchstick from his mouth and using it to scratch at his flaking scalp. In fact, Mathieu reflected, with a flush of warm surprise, he was really pleased to see the Gypsy. He suppressed a smile. You could never tell when the man would turn up but it was always a pleasure when he did. Besides, it wouldn't now be necessary for Mathieu either to work Bobrán's machines himself or to shut them down and lose output. Meanwhile, Bobrán, his hair falling over his eyes, withdrew his proffered hand from the Algerian's reach.

Then, redeploying the arm so recently extended in the Algerian's direction and confecting, instead, an apologetic little wave while mouthing

Salut!, Bobrán spun round to face back up the aisle toward Mathieu. The little Gypsy inclined his head, reminiscent of a cur that knows it's about to receive a sound whipping, smiled at Mathieu and muttered, J'arrive. He ignored Salvatore, who at the end of his machine six stood invigilating the scene, his arms folded, but he winked at Eric who was holding a full polystyrene beaker of coffee in his hand. Bobrán liked the shape of Eric's body, the long unmanly curves, the light colouring. Reminiscent of Moritz. Shame about the face. Eric, for his part, was both repelled and intrigued by Bobrán. He couldn't have put words to it. Bobrán came far too close to him, held his hand far too long, winked and grinned far too much.

Hey! Mathieu shouted again, this time brandishing his burnt-out matchstick and stabbing it upward toward the ceiling and pointing right through it, all the way to Bobrán's scandalously unmanned machines. Bobrán accelerated and tried to dodge and weave, but was caught in a bear hug by Marcel, whose determination to intercept his cousin no circumstance could dampen.

Marcel unburdened himself to Bobrán, while Mathieu, watching from the end of the machine aisle, stamped and shouted and in his agitation broke his matchstick clean in two. Yet Mathieu remained just where he was, preferring not to intervene in what he took to be urgent Gypsy business.

I've got something for you, Marcel said as he produced a white envelope from his hip pocket and brandished it in his cousin's face like a piece of incontrovertible evidence. See this? An African in a suit and some shabby fucking long-haired journalist came looking for you and found me instead and I don't think it's funny so stop grinning you cunt and they left this for you and it stinks of trouble. I want to know what the hell it's about. You come right back down and we talk or I'll open it and fucking read it myself. Marcel paused for a second, then said, The African said it had to do with his brother.

Bobrán threw his cousin off and proceeded toward Mathieu, shambling and shrugging and grinning at Mathieu like it wasn't his fault his stupid cousin had waylaid him. Damn, damn, damn, he intoned in the deepest recesses of his mind.

The little Gypsy held out his hand to Mathieu, who took it in his and jerked it around like it was a piece of trapped machinery he was hoping to shake loose, while Bobrán squinted at the ground and thought hard. Then he froze his face, turned suddenly to look back at Marcel, and held up both hands toward his cousin, their fingers splayed. I'll be down in ten minutes, he hissed, with a show of easy confidence and a permafrost grin that wasn't fooling anyone.

Marcel was saying nothing. Gripping the edge of the still stiff envelope in the fingertips of his right hand, as if at risk of radioactive contamination, he tapped it slowly against the palm of his left hand. Bobrán's left eyelid was flickering and he blinked hard three times in rapid succession in an effort to halt it, but nobody noticed either the flickering or the struggle to stop it.

As everyone returned to their previous occupations, Bobrán headed for the long iron staircase that rose to the left side of the office. He took the stairs two at a time. He was so fit it was like flying. Besides, lifts were for cunt-fucking sissies.

17. Eric recollects.

Jean was dwarfed by the big old semi-automatic machine number twenty-one, a veritable giant among injection moulding machines. Or, alternatively: the semi-automatic machine number twenty-one was gianted by little old Jean, a veritable dwarf among machine operatives. Either way, the man and the machine made a notable and variously contrastive coupling.

The mould on machine twenty-one was never changed. All it ever produced nowadays was black plastic cable ties – the kind one might use to secure a young tree to a stake in the ground, to bind the hands of a prisoner, to throttle an uncooperative enemy or, indeed, to tie cables together under the hood of a car. Jean had once defrayed much time in the imagining of further and more fanciful uses.

On his slender left wrist, Jean wore a large watch, or chronomètre. It possessed a rather blank face, encircled by several silver dials. As well as telling the time, and the date, it could perform numerous other services. Jean's wife had given it to him several years earlier to mark his fiftieth birthday. She had asked him what he wanted and he had said without hesitation 'un beau chronomètre.' 'Un quoi?' his wife had asked. 'Un chro-no-mètre,' Jean had syllabized. His wife had taken a breath and made a mental note. Jean took pleasure in looking at it and in marvelling at its many possible uses. It was the best present he had ever received. At this moment, it imparted the news that the time was 21.42:17 . . . 18 . . . 19 . . . 20, while declaring that the date was 09.11.1976. Le neuf, novembre, Jean murmured.

Jean felt no worse and no better than usual at the start of a night's work. Both legs were aching, so that he looked forward to sitting down at ten o'clock. He eyed the tea towel he had earlier spread prophylactically over the enterologically suspect seat. Jean next registered a familiar stiffness in the small of his back, and accordingly scheduled a beneficial stretch to coincide with the coffee that Bobrán would surely bring him shortly after ten. This thought afforded him a degree of relief. His mouth was somewhat dry, but he deemed it rather soon to partake of his first spearmint drop of the night. He would let the machine produce a further ten products – no, eleven (ten was an impossibly automatic, slavish, and hackneyed numeral) – and then pop the sweet. Self-discipline should be repaid with self-conceded treats. It was a regime that he had at last perfected. Jean's mind felt relatively empty, but at this juncture of the night relative emptiness was welcome, indeed a condition essential to the little man's nightly routine.

Under his blue factory-issue coat, Jean wore a dark-grey cardigan, held tight over his pigeon chest by brown shiny fake-leather buttons, and a pair of baggy light-grey trousers too long for his stumpy legs, for it should be recalled that, although small, Jean was not perfectly formed: considering his overall dimensions, the man's trunk was disproportionately long and his legs quite comically short. His glib well-shaven puppy face, small watery eyes, schoolboy short-back-and-sides with parting and tintin quiff, all conspired with the bagginess of his clothes to give the impression that his mother still bought him outfits one size too large in the grotesque expectation that he might yet grow into them.

The great old semi-automatic machine number twenty-one kept Jean magnificently busy. As the two sides of the press separated, the worker's right hand slid open the guard, while his left seized the sprue and pulled the product from the face of the mould. His right hand then tore the cluster of cable ties from the sprue and cast them into the cardboard box stationed alongside his right foot, while his left hand dropped the empty sprue into a bin next to his left foot before quickly rising to slide the guard shut, whereupon the index finger of his right hand depressed the START button on the control panel to initiate a new cycle. The swift and smooth automatism of these movements, as finely tuned by repetition as a tennis player's backhand or a sous-chef's carrot-chopping technique, compensated for the machine's inability to function in fully automatic mode. In other words, if the machine was only *semi*-automatic, it was the operative, in this case Jean, who made up the shortfall.

This was the worst part of Jean's night: the long half hour between his arrival and the ten o'clock beaker of coffee he would take with Bobrán. Jean had to force himself to remain standing and to experience the emptiness that others – all those who lacked his discipline and resourcefulness – must endure nightly. He might elude this moment of empathetic tedium by indulging in a tantalizing foretaste of the enjoyment he would derive later that night from his reflections on the day's international-national-regional-city-neighbourhood-workplace-and-domestic events, his subsequent consideration of that night's alphabet letter (m) and that month's year in history (1830), or the dependable novelty and entertainment value of Alphonse's dramatic performance shortly after three a.m. – not to mention the reading that always preceded it. But Jean eschewed such feebleness. He had the strength to dwell in the present. This passage of time, this introit to his night, this here-and-now was a moment of rigorous and willed duress that served to remind him what life would be like without his *discipline and resourcefulness* and without the drive for self-improvement, the inquisitive mind and the active memory that he nurtured in himself. Though he might be pitied by others for his enslavement to the only semi-automatic machine in the plastics section, Jean regarded his exceptional condition with pride: was he not the only man remotely fit for the task? Indeed, it was in this first half hour of each night that Jean's superiority was rehearsed. This brief state of determined mental void was, he was sure, as close as he could ever come to knowing the minds of his fellow workers. To project this condition of indolent apathy across an entire night would be to inhabit the mental world of the Portuguee, the Gypsy, the Algerian, the Marseillais, and all the other misfits, subversives and delinquents who each night convened in this space and rotated around, and beneath, Jean and his machine.

As though in search of illustration, Jean glanced at Fernando, who (as if to order) was just then staring into the middle distance and chewing gum; then at Alphonse who was striding up and down, his mouth working to no communicative effect. Jean reasoned that part of his own unique distinction lay in his spatial fixity: while all the other men hurtle freely around this factory like peas in a rattle, or slope like drunks from machine to machine, or play like boisterous children, groups forming and breaking and reforming like so many sociable ducks upon a pond, individuals assuming every possible physical posture, some lying down when they feel sleepy, one of them even performing yoga stretches at four in the morning – what a bunch! – I alone stand (or, better, sit) solidly, soberly, immovably at my post, from evening till morn, aided and abetted by the fertility of my mind, supported by my memory, my *discipline and resourcefulness*. An individual mind is in itself an entire world. Whoever said that? It's awfully good. And I have world enough *right here*.

As Jean, fortunately unobserved, tapped the side of his head, Bobrán who had just emerged at the top of the stairs walked round the pistons at the end of machine twenty-one and extended his hand for Jean to shake. Jean dropped from his left hand the latest sprue, from which his right hand had just torn the latest bunch of cable ties then, having slid the guard shut and pressed the START button, he gave the Gypsy his left hand to shake. Coffee at ten? Bobrán enquired. That would be delightful, thank you, chirruped Jean, as astonished as every previous night by the Gypsy's exquisitely amicable offer.

As the press closed and the pistons moved and the prescribed quantity of plastic dropped into the melting chamber, Jean's hands were as idle as his mind. This blankness was the blankness of others, this boredom a foil against which the mental activity of his ordinary being shone like a gem. He felt an impulse to consult his chronomètre but resisted it. 21.42 it had read a minute ago. The press opened. Jean slid the guard door open. His left hand seized the sprue. His right hand clutched the cable ties.

> Melted or plasticized plastic material is injected or forced into a mold where it is held until removed in a solid state, duplicating the cavity of the mold. The mold may consist of a single cavity or a number of similar or dissimilar cavities, each connected to flow channels or 'runners' that direct the flow of the melted plastic to the individual cavities.
>
> D.V. Rosato, *Injection Molding Handbook*, p. 7.

There was a magic moment at nine forty-three that evening, a magic moment that nobody in the plastics section at Éts. Boucan – on either the ground or the first floor – noticed. It didn't last long. It was brought to an end by Eric when he yawned, stood up and absented himself from his machine by ambling up the machine aisle and stopping at the pile of papers and magazines that Philippe had earlier stacked on top of the recycling bin at the aisle-end of machine two. Until Eric broke the spell, not only was each and every plastics-section night-shift worker present, but each and every man was also at his designated machines. This discreet coincidence, this unwitting concordance, did not fall out every evening and unlike an eclipse of the planets could not be foretold, since it partook of human chance rather than mathematical necessity.

At nine forty-three that evening, the lift was empty, the coffee and beer machines deserted, the toilet unoccupied, and the materials room unencumbered by anybody fetching either boxes-to-be or sacks of raw material. There were no groups of operatives idly milling about, nor any single pair chewing some inconsequential cud at any particular machine; nor was anybody sitting at, standing by or lying on the broad wooden table at the far end of the machine aisle. While it is true that, in addition to Jean, only four men were actively engaged in production work (threshing sprue – Jacques; filling a hopper – Bobrán; mixing material – Rachid; checking product – Luigi), all the remainder were at least in attendance upon, and at most thoroughly alert to, the workings of industrial manufacture. Upstairs, Alphonse, his elbows on his knees, his lemon-coloured brothel creepers squarely planted on the concrete floor, was cradling in his wide splayed hands a paperback edition of *En attendant Godot*, while Fernando leaned against the flank of machine seventeen, his feet crossed, and stared at the glimmering end of his cigarette. Downstairs, Philippe, in a similarly grim defiance of tedium, peered down the throat of an empty green beer bottle, discovering no solace, while he waited for Jacques to finish with his machines and join him on the usually cheery walk to the beer- and coffee-machines. Marcel, having replaced the mysterious envelope in his hip pocket, contemplated with some pleasure the change it had wrought in his cousin, whose attention he had never seen so powerfully galvanized. Eric, his feet slightly apart, stood at ease as he rolled a cigarette, his mind lazily scrolling through the many women past and present over whom he had lusted and the select few with whom he had triumphantly breakfasted. Salvatore, bushy brows beetling over heavy and horn-rimmed spectacles, was holding a volume of Voltaire, a pencil at the ready in his right hand, his smart attaché case open at his side on the floor, but thinking about the telegram he had received that day.

Magically, then, every man was in his rightful place. Mathieu, the foreman, whose role was to troubleshoot and whose place therefore was wherever trouble might occur, was standing alongside Luigi, still unsatisfied by the performance of the new mould that the afternoon-shift engineers had that day installed on machine number fourteen.

Even the night security man, Tomec, had now arrived in the factory compound, having tethered his bicycle alongside Bobrán's in the racks near the outside urinals, and was now picking his way by the powerful light of his duty-issue torch through one dark metallurgy section after another, heading for the distant workbench at which he was wont to sit, think, sketch, draw and otherwise while away much of the night.

Every worker was in his place, either engaged in the performance of his work or ready to become so at a moment's notice – which might of course be said to amount to the same thing. For once, therefore, the factory was almost precisely as its owner Gérard Boucan liked to picture it. While the huge metallurgy section slumbered in a darkness punctured only by the peripatetic watchman's torch, the small plastics section was lit up and throbbing, its skeleton staff all present and wakeful: Monsieur Boucan might sleep (or for that matter converse, eat or whore) tranquil, serene even, in the knowledge that as he slept, ate, conversed or whored, orders were being filled, product produced, money made, output incremented, debts repaid and credit accrued. As he toured the town with his chauffeur Jorge at his side and, much later, joined his wife in their kingsize loveless bed, Monsieur Boucan might picture his family enterprise as a single gargantuan hopper feeding coin into his bulging pockets. At such moments, he rejoiced that he had created such a state of perfect peace and equilibrium in what was, after all, a messy old world. At other times, he could only pinch his chubby little flanks and smile.

It was at this magical moment, when every worker was at his post and everything was as ordained, that in the narrow street that ran parallel to Cours Modelon, skirting the rear of Éts. Boucan, so drowned by the constant din of the nearby injection moulding machines that no shutter in the apartments opposite opened, no eye peered out, a young man was being kicked halfway to death. For what reason? Because he had had sex with the little sister of one of the kickers. To be fair, the kickee was no stranger to street fights and was in a drunk and belligerent mood scarcely conducive to his own health or general well-being. On a better and a wiser day, he might (falsely) have confessed to raping and/or deflowering the wench and meekly agreed to make amends by marrying her. Instead, plunged in a despair occasioned by quite other concerns, the kickee did nothing either to avoid the beating nor, once it had commenced, to mitigate its consequences, nothing at all to pacify the kickers, nor quickly to satisfy their lust for revenge, blood and domination. Instead of displaying pain, acting cowed, aping humiliation, he heaped insults on his attackers, railed and laughed at them, sneered at them through the pain in his several fractured ribs, in effect egging them on, challenging them to do their worst. Indeed, as his dull assailants walked away from him, the kickee struggled to his knees, spat some bloody shards of broken teeth, and yelled above the factory din that if they had any more sisters that needed fucking, he was their man. The assailants paused in disbelief, uncertain what to do. He would be happy to see to their mothers too, added the kickee. That settled it. The three kickers shook their heads at one another, then retraced their steps. The smallest of them recalled that he had a switchblade concealed about his person. The kickee never saw the shaft of steel as it was thrust at him, not that he would have attempted to avoid its trajectory. All he could do was laugh at his assailants. And this he did in full-throated, joyful mockery. That was the mood he was in. He had nothing to lose but his wretched, worthless life. As it turned out, he didn't even lose that. The kickee felt the blow from the blade as a blast of cool air. Then he fell to the ground and watched as the gang staggered in alarm at the deed they had committed and beat a scuttling retreat. He smiled as he closed his eyes. About the kickers, he had always been right: they were of course pathetic, a gang of thugs that didn't know the first thing about violence, didn't know that in order to impress you have to be past caring. Later that night, the kickee was admitted to hospital, examined and treated by a team of doctors led by a surgeon from the very same district of the very same faraway city as himself. As if by magic, however, in this world of seething coincidences, it turned out that the doctor and the kickee had absolutely nothing else in common.

There are three basic operations:

1. Raising the temperature of the plastic to a point where it will flow under pressure. This involves a combined process of plasticizing (or plastication) involving both heating and masticating – this is where the reciprocating screw comes in.
2. Allowing the plastic to solidify in the mold, which the machine keeps closed. The liquid, molten plastic from the injection cylinder of the injection machine is transferred through various flow channels into the cavities of the mold, where it is finally shaped into the desired object by the confines of the mold cavity.
3. Opening the mold to eject the plastic after keeping the material confined under pressure as the heat (which was added to the material to liquefy it) is removed to solidify the plastic and freeze it permanently into the shape desired.

These three operations are also the prime determinants of the productivity of the process, since manufacturing speed will depend on how fast we can heat the plastic to the molding temperature, how fast we can inject it, and how long it takes to cool the product in the mold.
. . . / . . .
To operate the plant efficiently, people are needed.

D.V. Rosato, *Injection Molding Handbook*, p. 8.

As always occurred when any enticing female prospect stumbled upon his purview, Eric's mind began, in a headlong, dreamlike, involuntary and chaotic manner, to survey and contrast two series of females, stretched across the diachronic and synchronic axes so familiar to structural analysis, the first series figuring all those girls with whom Eric had ever shared anything partaking of the romantic – be it a shy glance across a soggy English playground or a thoroughgoing exchange of secretions with all the attendant loin-thrashing – the second series amounting to a swift scroll-though of all those girls of current interest, a flickering of images of faces (mostly) glimpsed at the factory at clock-on and -off times or at the shops he frequented, in the street, at the supermarket. This latter series also comprised those women who dwelled (at least for practical purposes) only in film-fuelled fantasies (Adjani, Ardant, Aimée, Baye, Berto, Bardot – to stick to the French and to go no further than the B's).

Fanny was exhaustively examined against every girl appearing on either axis, but above all against Megan who alone figured on both axes, who indeed represented the axes' sole point of intersection, being the one girl who was unarguably both a historical low-point in Eric's personal girl-album and, even now, an isolated peak in the current panorama, since still a definite prospect, albeit fast fading, still an eventuality, should all else fail, a fall-back, a bolt-hole against the desolation of unrelieved solitude, an intercessor in extremis to stay the flailing hand of Onan.

Eric drew one last time on the remains of his roll-up, dropped it on the floor, crushed it with his left boot, then regarded his store of cigarettes, laid out on the chair. What next? Another roll-up perhaps? Dutch this time? Samson or Drum? Or a Gauloise untipped? Mmm. He would wait a minute or two until the right choice emerged, like an idea floating free to the surface, de facto the fittest to survive, as though following rigorous brainstorming. That evening, Eric had laid before him a choice of eight possible smokes: four types of rolling tobacco; his two standard ready-mades (Gauloises untipped and Camel tipped); and two guests (Park Drive and Gitanes untipped) filling, respectively, the nostalgia and the try-something-new spots. Eric's dedication to variety in tobacco was more remarkable than might appear from the sheer quantity of cigarettes that he consumed: he was a tobacco philanderer, a nicotine epicure, a sybarite of tar.

In Eric's mind, thoughts of women, indeed, relations with women, were irrevocably associated with smoking. From his first love, the little girl next door, who, as they shared a stolen Senior Service in a thicket at the bottom of her parents' suburban garden, had offered to show him her butterfly if he would only show her his little man, to Fanny's proffering of the hitherto unmet, incongruously British sounding, Royale, sex and smoking had ever been staunch allies, boon companions. Eric took a Park Drive and lit it with a match.

The memory of his first little girlfriend stroking him to a panting hardness that day in the bushes morphed into the recollection of a Saturday afternoon film matinee in a cavernous and cold flea-pit and Cindy – a name she had adopted in preference to Philippa (since in those days everyone wanted at least to sound American). For what would be their first and last date, the two had gone to see *The Charge of the Light Brigade,* taking their places in the back row, flanked by other simmering teenagers. They had lit up as soon as the adverts had begun to roll and the lights had dimmed. Eric was on that occasion smoking a Disque Bleu, a brand he had encountered for the first time the previous week in a folk club above a pub in Dorking; Cindy's was a St Moritz, a long, slim mentholated number perfectly complementing the gold of her nail-varnish.

Sitting to his left, Cindy took frequent puffs as she fumbled for his penis and then, once she had found it and begun to suck, kept interrupting in order to renew her acquaintance with the cigarette and then to exhale smoke powerfully at his bared glans. Eric at first assumed that the smoke-blowing was an attempt to improve the taste, perhaps even to mentholate it somewhat, but a couple of weeks later when he overheard Cindy in conversation with a girlfriend referring to the oral act as a 'blow-job' (a term he had never previously heard and which he at once understood to be yet another American import), he couldn't help but wonder whether the term had in any way influenced her technique. He had never really fancied Cindy. She was short and fat, poor girl, and had a hare lip, but, as he noticed when they emerged into the fading wintry afternoon light, her skin was tanned and clear and her eyes an emerald green: he wasn't sure what the eye colour denoted, but tanned skin in February screamed class. At this sighting of her skin and eyes, Eric had developed a sudden liking for Cindy and had begun to talk enthusiastically about an American film scheduled for the following Saturday at a different cinema. He had then asked her if she would like to meet him again. Cindy had pulled a fresh cigarette from its packet and was now looking at it as if it possessed the key to an answer, which perhaps it did, if one may assume, for example, that the cigarette whose length she was now stroking prompted her to recall her very recently failed attempt to smoke meat while simultaneously beating it. Be that as it may, Cindy smiled and said, No I don't think so. She placed her cigarette between her lips and lit it. Don't take this personally, she explained, but you don't taste nice. While Eric wondered if anything could possibly be more personal, Cindy added, blushing, Besides, you did nothing for me, did you? She then said, No hard feelings, you're a nice boy. Nice boy! Poor Eric. There was no way back from that: it was all over. For a time he had wondered precisely what he had failed to do for Cindy, but then a subsequent girlfriend had told him about clitorises and drawn him several pictures.

Eric had not thought about either *The Charge of the Light Brigade* or Cindy for a long time when quite recently he had found himself on the edge of a conversation about hare lips and cleft palates. A Scottish acquaintance and now housemate in Grandgobier had been insisting that if you had the one you had to have the other. Eric, detached and silent until that point, had said, No, not true. What do yous know about it? the Scotsman had enquired. It was then that Eric had recalled the feel of Cindy's palate impeccably smooth and hard against the end of his cock. Eric had explained that he had once had a girlfriend who definitely had one of the said afflictions but not the other. The Scotsman and his friends had laughed a lot and made many noises of revulsion, presumably to express their view of harelips, cleft palates, or both. Eric was glad they didn't press him for any more precise information on the source of his knowledge. They probably assumed that he had made his medical discovery with his tongue, whereas in fact, he recalled with a start, he was sure that he and Cindy had never kissed. He wondered why. Mind you, he hadn't had much of an opportunity. She had made a grab for his flies almost as soon as the lights went down and, after that, he had found the notion unsavoury. Eric was confused. Could it possibly be that it was a kiss on the lips that Cindy had wanted from him and not the performance of cunnilingus?

Eric shook his head, then his entire upper body. He stubbed out his Park Drive and ambled up the machine aisle, stopping at the pile of newspapers and magazines that Philippe as usual had stacked on the recycled material bin at the end of machine number two. He picked out *Le Nouvel Observateur*. It always had good pictures.

18. Mathieu resolves.

Tomec was deep in thought. He was sitting on a stool beneath a bare light bulb at a workbench in the corner of an otherwise dark metallurgy department. Before him on the pitted wooden surface lay sketches and notes, and the copy of *Der Tod des Vergil* that Sarah had pressed into his hands several days previously. Fourteen stations between disembarcation and deathbed, a fine pagan notion, nicely antedating the Christian catastrophe.

Tomec lived by strict rules. He would only think about the factory and its concerns once he had buttoned up his uniform. Conversely, he allowed himself to think about what he conceived to be his *true* work, viz. his drawing, painting, sketching and sculpting, at any time at all and in any or no clothes: in his studio overalls, in his factory uniform, in bed (as we have seen) sheathed in nothing save Sarah, or naked under the shower (as we have also seen) as he covered and uncovered himself with soapy lather.

Tomec was thumbing through some loose charcoal-on-paper sketches that he had made the previous night. The one that Sarah had commented upon that afternoon now caught his eye. It was good, she had said, adding, he looks rather like me. Who is it? Tomec now looked at it again. It was a depiction of the peasant boy who, in Hermann Broch's description of Virgil's arrival in Brundisium, accosts the moribund poet and follows his litter to the room where he is to die. I wonder if the bearers stumbled at all. I might depict them stumbling. And surely somebody would have wanted to embrace the great man.

For his depiction of the peasant lad, Tomec had borrowed a number of features from the face of Bobrán, the young Gypsy who worked the night shift: the long curly hair, the wary yet innocent demeanour, the large black eyes, the youthful world-weariness. Tomec glanced at other sketches, including a botched attempt at the skew-wigged harlot. Later, Tomec would have a coffee, read further and do more sketches, perhaps draw up a list of possible 'stations.' Later. Not now. Now it was time for another tour of inspection.

Tomec's duties at the factory were hardly onerous. He had to patrol the factory, inside and out, and ensure that doors and windows were properly secured. There was nobody to check on how he actually spent his working hours, but there were six security clocks dotted throughout the factory compound, into each of which he had, at regular intervals, to insert and turn a special key. Thus was he subject to a form of remote monitoring, the discretion and impersonality of which he found positively congenial.

His night work afforded him the luxury of ignoring artistic factions and fashions and of pursuing his own aesthetic interests: he did not have to meet the demand of any public patron nor heed any market whim, for the money that the factory paid him covered his meagre needs. More than that, night work enforced a precious cooling-off period, an opportunity to stand back from his *true* work and to take stock, a time to read and broaden his mind, to make up for his lack of formal education: after all, his school had been war-ravished Poland and his university Liberation France. Tomec enjoyed the darkness and the brisk walk from key-clock to key-clock. Also, he was happy to have available, in the plastics section, a collection of people whom he might freely observe and with whom he might even converse, should the spirit move him. All in all, despite what Sarah said, this was a most suitable occupation for an artist. Were it not for this graffiti business.

Tomec stood up, glanced at his watch and picked up his torch. He switched off the desk-lamp that stood on the work bench, observing the way in which the pool of light flooding his sketches disappeared, leaving their afterimage to linger in his mind. Then he set off for the plastics section, a good brisk ten-minute walk away, passing hundreds of idle machines, through a dozen different linked workshops.

That afternoon, one of the factory owner's underlings had called at Tomec's studio-home and had apprised him of what he had termed the 'graffiti emergency.' The man had made it clear that because the 'act of vandalism' appeared to have occurred on his watch, Tomec was deemed to have failed. Tomec resented this inference, and snapped, I am paid to deter and, if the worst comes to the worst, to immobilize intruders until the police arrive; it is not my job to pursue employees who have a penchant for graffiti.

Boucan's envoy had stared at Tomec mutely, the thin lips in his flat face unmoving, prompting Tomec to save the image, to record the man's face on his retina for possible future use. The envoy had informed Tomec that senior management (which Tomec presumed meant Gérard Boucan himself) wished him to consider which member of the night shift might be the perpetrator.

And how am I supposed to do that? Tomec asked, staring at the man's long flat face.

Talk to them, sound them out, gain their confidence, confer with the supervisor, then come up with a name. Essentially, what is wanted is a name.

The envoy's face was as featureless and as broad as a shovel. If you were strong enough, Tomec reasoned, and this guy were dead enough and conveniently rigid, you could pick him up by his legs and use that face to shovel shit. Maybe that's what Boucan saw when he gave him his job.

Tomec looked straight past him. Don't you think management is overreacting? I mean: we're talking about a piece of graffiti on a wall.

The man sighed, straightened up, and his face actually hardened. Marble turning to granite.

I don't know where you come from but I would say that it isn't for either of us to judge. I would also point out that this latest graffiti message is personally offensive to our employer. So, I repeat, what we need is a name. Get us a name.

Since Tomec had had no ready reply, the man had turned and departed, with something less than a nod of his head.

Through the dark factory Tomec was now moving like a loaded tanker on a becalmed sea: slowly, steadily, silently, unstoppable. He was on his way to the plastics section to talk to the night-shift foreman, one Mathieu Petit, with whom he had never previously exchanged anything but the briefest greeting. Mathieu was not somebody to whom Tomec had ever paid any sustained attention. Presumably the man possessed a life, a past, beliefs and passions, but Tomec knew more about the flashing faces that loomed at him from out of the steam in his shower. Petit's visible skin was scaly, his eyes small and watery, his hair grey and thinning, his gait stiff and limping, his clothing dull and worn, his entire physical posture and appearance an expression of some form of obscure suffering. Ordinarily, this would all have excited Tomec's curiosity. But the foreman appeared to dwell immured in a private and incommunicable world that screamed Keep Out.

Tomec felt more and more uncomfortable the closer he came to the plastics section. The graffiti was none of his business and interrogating people was not one of his skills, nor was it something he wished to learn.

It was the third time since September that graffiti had been found. Each time the offending scrawl had been discovered shortly after 5.30 in the morning, not long after the handover from night to morning shift, and each time it had occurred not in the relatively small plastics section but in one of the many metallurgy workshops that together accounted for approximately 90% of the factory's surface area.

The first graffito had consisted merely of three numbers separated by semicolons: 28,830,000; 9.19; 4.50. Workers had milled round this graffito when it had first been noticed by a young Tunisian operative. It appeared to be an abstruse code of some sort: initially, nobody could divine any connection between the three figures, though many tried. Even the fact that the middle figure corresponded to many workers' hourly rate at first passed unobserved. It took a CGT shop-steward to identify the figure on the right as the percentage increase that the union had recently demanded of management and which had within the past week been rejected; and it was a studious, bespectacled engineer, known for the clarity of the Trotskyist slogans with which he variously entertained and irritated his fellow workers at the coffee machine or during breaks for snacks, to interpret the left-hand figure. This, he insisted, represented the annual profits in francs earned during the course of the previous financial year by the car-components manufacturing group to which Éts. Boucan belonged. How the hell do you know that, asked the CGT man, a member of the French Communist Party. He probably holds shares in it, quipped a Socialist Party member to a hail of laughter. The Trotskyist's stammered answer went unheard.

This first piece of graffito, though buried within a matter of hours beneath several coats of white paint, made a bold impression on all those who saw or heard about it, and triggered conversations and comments. Yet before many weeks had passed, everyone had begun to forget about it, and nobody had suspected that it marked the beginning of a veritable campaign.

The second graffito had come as a great surprise, and yet its content was in one sense easier to interpret than the numbers, though in another sense, much harder. It consisted of the phrase: *sous les pavés, quoi, précisément?* ('beneath the cobblestones, what exactly?') The unmistakable reference was to the 1968 slogan: *sous les pavés, la plage* ('beneath the cobblestones, the beach'). The question intrigued some of the workers for a few days, and triggered conversations, some of them nostalgic, about the strikes of 1968 and the hopes that had then been dashed even faster than they had been raised. But most just shrugged and got on with their work. On the walls of the factory's toilet cubicles, however, alongside the usual drawings of outsize genitalia, phone numbers for sex, football slogans and racist epithets targeting Jews and Arabs, began to appear a series of responses to the enigmatic question, including (rendered faithfully into English): the beach, always the beach!; repression, as ever – what did you expect?; nothing at all, dickhead!; De Gaulle, that's what!; nothing but sewers and sewer-rats!; and, with a heady mix of nostalgia and hope, 'one day, one day, we shall find out. Hasta la proxima!'

The latest graffito, which must have been daubed the previous night or that morning shortly before or after the morning shift had started work at 4.55, was indeed more personal: Gérard Boucan, Collabo, 1942–44. The workers had gathered round this in silence, tut-tutting, none venturing to do more than mutter, C'est vraisemble, l'espèce de con ('it's plausible, the swine'), and some of the younger men shrugging and whispering already, Eh, alors?

Tomec had almost reached the plastics section: another few yards and he would turn right into the passage through metallurgy workshop H, along which plastics workers themselves walked on their way to their section. He looked left toward the factory exit door that led out to the bike-sheds, pallets and forklifts, factory offices and street, but saw no one; then right toward the plastic flaps that marked the entry to the plastics section.

This graffiti thing has got nothing to do with security, Tomec was thinking, so why should I have to 'look into it'. I'm not a cop or a spy or a nark. Maybe Sarah has a point: perhaps this is a strange 'day job' for an artist. But to me it's just a job, he told himself; so I don't want to be worrying about this stuff: it's none of my business and it's a distraction from my true work. I'm no investigator. I just check doors and windows and tackle intruders. They never said anything about questioning people.

In the last few seconds before reaching the flaps, Tomec slowed and struggled to purge his mind of the graffiti business. He summoned Virgil in Brundisium and the crowd scenes that had come to his mind's eye under the shower and which he wanted to commit to paper before they faded. And then he saw Sarah, saying goodbye to him a few nights previously as he had left for work. Will I find you here in the morning? he had dared to ask, as she had drawn away from him. In reply, she had smiled a crooked smile, stepped back toward him and then placing her hand suddenly in his crotch had caught his genitals in her fist. He had gasped and his eyes had opened so wide that Sarah had laughed out loud. There was no point struggling. He was in her hands. Then, maintaining her grip, Sarah kissed him on the mouth, slightly nipping his upper lip. His eyes had watered. Do you want to find me here? Ouais, he replied, with exaggerated, comical, nonchalance. Okay, then, she had said simply, releasing her grip as suddenly and completely as one releases a screw of paper over a wastepaper basket. Then, maybe. Do you really need to know?

No, he had conceded. It's as you like: I don't mind the uncertainty. That's good of you, she said, because I don't mind the freedom. As it turned out, she *had* been there on his return the following morning. That night he had spent all his free moments sketching Sarah's crooked smile again and again from memory, and had done his patrolling at a trot, neglecting everything but the need to turn his keys in the machines at the predetermined times. Months later, when the affair was over, Tomec would look back on that evening and date his love for Sarah from the moment her fist had clasped his genitals through the coarse worsted of his work trousers.

Mathieu, who was standing by the nearest of Luigi's machines, number fourteen, looked up as Tomec pushed through the hanging transparent flaps that divided the plastics section from the rest of the factory. Tomec, instead of giving Mathieu the cursory nod that the two men generally exchanged – a sharp and unsmiling downward movement of the head signifying: hello, and, let's skip the handshake – executed a considerably less orthodox nod, an upward jerk of the head and a narrowing of the eyes signifying: we need to talk.

What does this guy want? Mathieu thought. Can't be anything much. He looks about as laid-back and unruffled as ever. I don't think anything could really bother him. But you can't tell with these security people. That look is probably part of the training. They put it on with their uniform. Now he's shaking hands with a couple of the afternoon-shift workers, as if he or they gave a damn. What is it about men like that? They're just bigger than the rest of us and take more exercise. (Nadine, he remembered, never cared for brawn – biftek, she would call it, screwing up her nose at the very smell of the idea. She said it bored her. Nadine. Her face when bored. Nadine's face now, vacant, senile. Almost the same. Boredom. Senility. People who get bored are just getting in training for senility.)

For a moment it looked as if Mathieu might ignore Tomec's greeting, for he continued to stare at the machine before him and, as the two sides of its mould parted, he bent down and placed his hand under the product shute, caught the still-hot product as it dropped through the clattering aluminium slats and, straightening up, lifted it close to his eyes to study it from a number of angles.

However, by the time Mathieu had finished this monitoring routine and with a sudden flick of his wrist had cast the product into the tray at his feet,

Tomec was standing right beside him, proffering his right hand to shake. Mathieu took and shook Tomec's hand and then, moving his burnt-out matchstick around in his mouth, asked, So, what's new?

Tomec pulled a face and shook his head and, darting his eyes toward the glass-walled office that overlooked the shop floor, asked, Up there?

Mathieu opened his eyes wide, dispelling an insurgent image of Nadine on their wedding day, putting on a little weight at last, her cheeks chubbying out. His eyes blinked and twitched while he removed the matchstick from his mouth and stared at the end he had been chewing. Tomec noted how light a blue his eyes were and how small the pupils; his lids were a baby pink, reminding him of something, something he didn't want to think about here and now. He could also see in stark relief the patches of psoriasis that decorated the night-shift foreman's forehead. As if aware of this scrutiny, Mathieu raised his left hand to his temples and, using his good little finger, scratched away at the scaly surface of one such patch. Then he glanced at Tomec slyly and said: Okay, boss. Lead the way. Tomec pulled a face but followed him. 'Boss,' again.

What the hell does this Pole want? Mathieu had been working chez Boucan six years now, six years of solid nights, six years of nights away from Nadine, and nights were when missing the way she used to be was most painful, so it was best not to see her: days, he could bear looking at her, endure her increasing vacancy. Weeknights he was in the factory, Saturday nights in some club, but Sunday nights were misery. In six years no security man had ever asked Mathieu to have a conversation in the office about anything. Security matters weren't any part of his brief. This wasn't the army. His job was to keep the machines running, to maximize night-shift output. They'd made that clear. But this Tomec Koliaich-something – the names they had! – was different, had always been different to all the others. For example, he smiled and not just every now and then either. He smiled a whole lot. Mathieu had nothing against Poles. He had had good Polish friends when friends had mattered. But, normally, security people were sullen. As if being sullen was proof of seriousness, or some low-grade kind of menace all by itself. Certainly none of the others had ever done much smiling. And this guy was the first one that wasn't French. And the first one who didn't arrive fresh from bouncing. He stopped and talked to people, made odd, unsettling, personal comments that didn't add up to anything. He is rumoured to be an artist of some sort. But he does his job. The rest is not my concern. Then why talk to me? What does he want? (Nadine's face, upturned, questioning him once. Why, Daddy, Why? Thinking he was her Daddy!)

Tomec stopped when he got to the bottom of the steps, stood aside, bowed ever so slightly, smiled that familiar smile, and let Mathieu go up first. Polish politesse or something. Might suit some Countess in Kracow but here it's ridiculous. Tomec followed Mathieu up the eight steps and into the office, then closed the doors behind him. In here you could hear another man talk and you could almost hear yourself think.

Mathieu leaned his tailbone on the edge of the table so that his back was to the glass front of the office. (Nadine eating a piece of lettuce tidily. Such a tidy eater, she had made him feel like a klutz sometimes. Probably she didn't mean to. Now she eats baby food.) Tomec remained by the door.

This must be good, Mathieu said, chewing on his matchstick and looking steadily up at Tomec. Nobody ever asked to talk to me in this office. Then, nodding back toward the machine he had just been attending: And make it quick. That machine keeps producing duds. Not that you'd know about that.

Tomec smiled at Mathieu, but got nothing back, nothing at all.

A fresh piece of graffiti was found this morning in metallurgy section D, behind one of the machines. It was found at about five thirty.

So?

You don't look surprised.

Why should I be surprised?

Had you heard about it?

How could I have heard about it? Who from? I've only just come on. Who would have told me? Besides, who, out of these guys, would know anything about it? Who, except you? What is this anyway? You think I go round writing graffiti? Are you questioning me?

Of course not. I got a call from management. They want me to talk to everyone. They think it could be someone on the night shift.

Tomec wasn't happy. This wasn't going well. He smiled. Mathieu looked down at his boots. (Nadine had bought them. When? Ten years, must be. A good purchase. She'd been in charge of his clothes too. He'd been better dressed in those days. Never a match for this guy though.) Tomec hoped that smiling might make Mathieu friendlier and buy him some leeway. But smiling didn't help, and what else was there?

It's no one on the night shift, Mathieu suddenly pronounced. Some of these guys can scarcely write and none of them would be bothered to scrawl graffiti on a wall in the middle of the night on the other side of the factory. What for? It's nonsense. Tell them it's nonsense. Anyway, what did it say this time? Another bunch of numbers or some other worn-out slogan?

Does it matter what it said?

Must do.

Without any warning, Mathieu grinned, but not at Tomec, just for himself: I'm not going to believe it was an Alain-adore-Sylvie and a heart with an arrow through it. Come on. If management is in a twitch, there must be some reason. You've got me curious. You wanted to talk about it? Talk about it.

Tomec nodded and glanced up. Mathieu's eyes were twinkling. Tomec said nothing. Mathieu had taken his old chewed-down match out of his mouth and dropped it into a green metal bin he had kicked out from under the table he was leaning up against. Tomec was puzzled by Mathieu's anger, watching his face, seeing something there he had never seen in anyone before. He would like to know what it was. Mathieu was carefully selecting a new match from the box in his pocket. He held it in his hand while he waited for an answer.

It was just a few words, Tomec started, staring straight into Mathieu's face, Gérard Boucan, Collabo, 1942–44.

Ha! Mathieu snorted. Well, well! he smirked. His mind formed the words, That sure ain't wrong, but his mouth remained zipped. Then he struck his match, blew on it, and stuck the unburned end in his mouth, like it was a new sweet. He laughed and his eyes closed and watered. Damn, he then said. I haven't wanted a cigarette this bad in a long time. (Nadine leaning right back in a rocking chair they had bought when they first moved in together, laughing fit to burst, her voice like a big church bell, nothing brittle about it, and smoking a long thin tipped cigarette.)

Seems you do know something about it, after all.

Mathieu's gaze hardened. His words now came in hard little packets, tight little pellets, accompanied by tiny jabbing hand movements.

Depends what you mean by know. Look. Whatever it is you want me to do, I'm not doing it. It's possible I told you this before: I look after the machines. That's what I do. That's all I do. Have you heard me now? (Nadine nodding and smiling, approving.)

I just need to talk to your men.

You're free to talk to anyone you like. But get this: they're not my men. That's the truth. If you doubt it, try asking them. As best I know, they're their own men.

Tomec nodded, a quick once-up-and-down nod, perfunctory, like he'd just heard a cliché.

Mathieu was looking at him slyly now, choosing his words, working up to a long sentence, by his standards a full-blown speech, scrutinizing Tomec, moving in uncomfortably close to his face. Tomec could see the scales of psoriasis buried beneath his eyebrows, glinting like baby oysters seen at low tide through a spray of seaweed.

I always figured it was your job to stop people getting in from outside, not to harass those on the inside employed to do an honest job.

My feelings precisely. I just want to keep my job.

Mathieu nodded. The cry of scoundrels down the ages. (Nadine angry now, wagging her finger at him.)

So they've got you over a barrel. They can turn you into a nark.

I'm no nark.

Mathieu's watery eyes fixed on his. Tomec moved back.

Tomec pictured himself running to his sketching bench at the other side of the factory, collecting his things, then running straight out and never coming back. I'm a good runner. I could be out there in seconds, surprise Sarah. She'd be delighted. At least at first.

Mathieu turned right round so that he could look down onto the shop floor. Luigi must have seen him move, because he looked up from his machine and nodded a reassurance.

Talk to whomsoever you please, Mathieu said. Just like you always do. It's nothing to do with me. Understood?

I've got a round to do right now, Tomec said. I'll be back in twenty minutes to talk with some of them.

I'm just the man who makes sure the machines keep running, Mathieu said.

Tomec nodded, turned round, let himself out of the glass-walled office and went down the steps. Yes, he had seen something in Mathieu's face he had never seen anywhere before and had no name for. Was it an emotion? Or an experience? A thing of some sort? A memory? No. Not a memory. A plan? Maybe. Or some sort of subjugation? But to what?

Mathieu shook his head while his eyes followed Tomec out. Now nobody was looking, he could laugh more freely. Imagine someone fingering Boucan, and on the walls of his own factory! Nice. I wonder how many people know about his war. Just a handful, I suppose. Is that why I got this job? Because he knows I know? Not that he got up to anything that special for a man of his background. It's high time it came out. Not that it will. Not yet. Thirty years is nothing. But at least there's a trickle. And trickles can turn into floods.

Mathieu walked down the aisle, right to the end, past the last pair of machines, went up to the old wooden table and hauled himself up on it. He sat there with his legs swinging, looking back up the aisle toward the glass-walled office. You could see the tops of all the control cabinets from here. Mathieu noted that all the warning lights were off. A moment's peace. As long as it didn't last too long. Work helped to keep Nadine at bay, stall her, stop her rushing back to him young, gorgeous and bright-minded.

Rachid, who had just topped up the hopper of machine number nine, descended his stepladder and, noticing the foreman sitting on the table swinging his legs – a position and an activity wholly uncharacteristic of Mathieu – approached him with his arm outstretched.

Mathieu flashed Rachid a kind of smile he gave very few people nowadays, and Rachid replied with a timid smile all of his own. They had never had a conversation, but there was a friendliness between the two men.

Rachid pulled his cigarette packet out of his pocket, opened it and shook it at Mathieu, who hesitated, then took the matchstick out of his mouth and showed it to Rachid, who nodded as though he understood. Then Rachid put one of his cigarettes in his own mouth and went back to his machine.

Mathieu stared down between his legs at the dull concrete floor while his mind returned briefly to the graffiti and then leapt back over three decades, to the last days of the Resistance, a scene he thought he had long ago erased from his mind. Nadine standing in line, young, pretty, slim and discernibly pregnant, her head shorn and her wits apparently flown, weeping like she'd lost her mother, or the next worst thing. He'd taken pity on her. Love came much, much later.

He blinked and it was gone, she was gone. He looked up.

Luigi was walking toward him down the aisle. Mathieu could see that the warning light on machine number fourteen was lit up. He eased himself down off the table and followed Luigi to the machine to see what the trouble was. His left knee was hurting again, causing him to limp.

Memories like that were dangerous: let one in and a stampede occurs.

Nadine, her face streaming, her mouth jabbering. Nadine, years later, happy and putting on weight. Nadine as she is now. Just look at her. In the space of thirty years. Nobody could ever make that make sense. Looking eighty yet barely fifty. To think of all those people I killed to order in the line of duty, people who had never done me any harm and wanted nothing but to go on living, innocuously. And now, if I put an end to Nadine's life, I could be in trouble. She would be the only person I ever killed who needed to die, who would want to die, if she could want anything, the only person I could ever kill who positively deserves to die. I'm going to have to be smart, that's all. There's no way I'm ever going to gaol. I'll do what's best and no one will ever know. It's no bastard's business anyway, just mine and Nadine's. She always took good care of me. I owe her now.

19.   . . . within strict bounds. Inside out.

Jeanne brushed her teeth, washed her face, let down her white-streaked fair hair, glanced at herself in the mirror, then checked that the window was open a crack. She picked up a book from the dresser, put it down again, turned out the light, and walked to the bed, enjoying the feel of the cold floorboards underfoot and her firm, still robust, body. She pulled back the bedclothes and climbed into bed. Lying quite still, Jeanne felt her cares lift, her wrinkles flatten, her face in the dark revert to the way it had been when she was young and – in the opinion of some at least – beautiful. Once when Jacques had switched on the lamp in the middle of the night, he had caught a glimpse of Jeanne's younger face. He had told her that for a moment she had looked nineteen. That only happens in the dark, she had said.

One summer, her niece Fabienne, then a little girl, had stayed a whole fortnight at Jeanne's house, sharing Jeanne's bed. Jeanne's sister and brother-in-law had needed some time on their own to bring their marriage to a resounding conclusion. Each evening, Fabienne had watched from the bed as Jeanne unpinned her bun, unplaited the thick hair, combed it out carefully, then gathered it all into a pony tail. On the last evening, as they snuggled up for the night, the little girl had whispered, Your hair is so beautiful, Tata Jeanne, why don't you wear it down during the day so other people can see it? Jeanne had said that grown-ups didn't want to look at old women's hair, that it frightened and upset them, so we cut it short or hide it. Then she had added, But I'm glad *you* like it, and had hugged her niece close and wished she wasn't leaving in the morning.

There was a book on the dresser that was a gift from Jacques. He had wanted to give her a present and had noticed that she read a lot. Jacques had never been much of a reader. He would say he had never had the time for it. He had asked Philippe for advice. Philippe was always bringing books into the factory. Philippe had asked a couple of questions about Jeanne and had then recommended *Les Amants d'Avignon* by Elsa Triolet. Philippe had even offered to get him a copy, sensing that Jacques would feel uncomfortable in a bookshop. Jeanne hadn't been expecting a present from Jacques, let alone a book. She asked him if he had read it and he coughed and replied, No, but I have heard it's a good book. Jeanne held it like a sparrow in her hands and said nothing. Jacques moved his weight from one foot to the other. A friend at the plant recommended it, he explained, then added: the Marseillais.

Jacques had often mentioned 'the Marseillais.' Why didn't you read it then? Jeanne asked. Because he recommended it for you, Jacques said, blushing like a child. Jeanne's eyes opened wide. He had talked about her to another man. She couldn't imagine that. She didn't talk about Jacques to anyone. Then I'll have to read it, she said. I have heard of Triolet, but never read her. She was married to Aragon, wasn't she? Jacques said he didn't know about that.

The next day, Jeanne read the first few pages. The short novel was set during the Resistance and the author wrote like she knew about it. It brought back moods, memories, some of them welcome. Perhaps it was true that time healed. Thirty years had to be good for something more than just growing old. In her mid-twenties, Jeanne had been married to a man who bored and wearied her and gave her no children. The war had come and she had joined the Resistance and had met Henri who, after a much interrupted and protracted courtship, had become her lover. In early 1944, she got pregnant but then, in her fifth month, miscarried. Henri had risked his life and the success of the mission on which he was engaged to travel to Jeanne's bedside. In the midst of so much loss on all sides, they wept together for their tiny dead child. After victory, they would have lots of children, they agreed. The whole world was going to be made anew. But Henri, like so many of their comrades, was captured, tortured and killed. After the war, Jeanne had met and quickly married Simon. He was a teacher, yet patient and gentle, quite unlike the teachers Jeanne had known as a child. She had grown fond of him. That no children had come was nobody's fault: they had tried hard. Jeanne was sure Simon would have been a good father. He and Jeanne could talk about most things. Simon told her about deportation and imprisonment in Germany. Jeanne told him about her first husband and life in the maquis, but never mentioned Henri. The war had robbed her of Henri and their child, and the peace had slowly dashed all her hopes of a better world. If there was a heaven, she would see them again there. Ordinarily, Jeanne didn't like to read or hear or watch anything about those years. But since Jacques had given her the book, and since it started well, she felt she would read on, perhaps even finish it, another night. After thirty years, it might be time to start remembering.

Jeanne breathed a sigh of satisfaction. Jacques was good for her, in ways he couldn't begin to imagine. She lay flat on her back, her feet together, her hands crossed loosely over her chest, her face relaxing in the dark, the years flaking away, her mouth curving into the gentlest of teenage smiles, her eyes open and tingling. She had plumped the pillow just right, the crisp cool sheets brushed against her chin as her breathing slowed. Her body was ready to rest, but her mind was teeming.

Jacques was good for her. She was happy with him and wanted to keep it that way. It suited her that he worked nights. She liked to sleep alone mostly and always preferred to sleep in her own bed. But she also liked to spend time with Jacques. She admired the largeness of the man, the spread, the slowness. There was nothing mean about the way he was made. Big hands, broad face, large shoulders. He was generous with his time too. Taking the trouble to please her in the little ways that matter. Doing the jobs she asked him to do. Doing them thoroughly. Doing them till they were done. Never skimping, never botching. So many people, so many men, do things in a rush, neglecting the finishing touches. Not Jacques. If he held you, you knew you were held and could relax, lean right back: you knew you wouldn't be dropped. If he looked at you, his eyes seemed to touch yours, leaving behind their light blue print. If he kissed you, his warmth slowly reverberated through your body. The smell of him too. Most men stink, especially the older ones. Why is that? What is it they stink of? It's like a mould, an ancient meaty mould. Bad meat. Something rotten deep inside. Maybe the lives they lead. But Jacques smells good. He smells of the countryside, the fields in winter, the ditches when you bend down to pick a flower, or an orchard in October, apples strewn in the rank grass. Then, for a country man, he's surprisingly fastidious. No showers or baths, but washing standing up at a sink, often just in the kitchen. Keeping himself clean. And his eating and drinking is urgent and vigorous, driven by solid appetites. He drinks, like he eats, like he does everything, long and slow and thorough, no spillage, no wastage, no drops or crumbs on the floor. And when he's done, he's done: he pushes the plate away and pulls back the chair. Jeanne had never seen him drunk. Most meals, quite suddenly, for no apparent reason, he stops drinking wine and switches to water. Just like that. He puts the cork back in the bottle and that's it. He doesn't seem to think about it. It's just how he is. City men, if you put a bottle in front of them they feel duty-bound to empty it: it's like a challenge to them. A bottle left half-empty – why, it's an indignity or a personal affront. Something comes into their eyes. Jeanne liked Jacques' silences too. She had thoughts of her own. She wouldn't want a man who talks all the time. The first evening they ever spent together without the stated intention of playing cards – about a week after they had first made love – neither of them quite knew what to do or say. They spent a lot of time looking at one another and smiling and then looking away again. The way children used to do on a first date. After a while, she had asked if he felt ill at ease. No, he said. I'm happy. You don't like to talk? she then asked. No, he said cautiously, shaking his head, I do like to talk if I've got something to say, but right now I haven't. Jeanne had smiled and had mentioned Simon, quoting a saying of his and imitating his precise, scholarly speech: If a thing's easy to understand, plain to see, then you don't much need to comment on it; and if it isn't plain to see, there's no amount of talking that will make it so. Jacques smiled and nodded at that, recognizing the style of his dead friend. He and Simon had been close – not of course as close as Edith and Jeanne – but close enough for men. Then Jacques said that neither he nor Edith had been brought up to talk very much, neither his family nor hers had ever been great speakers. After that, Jeanne and Jacques had seemed to relax and the conversation had flowed more easily.

Jeanne heard a distant car, someone leaving the village, maybe driving back into town. Then nothing. In the morning, Jacques would get home at about six, provided he didn't spend too long at the bar. Sometimes he had a drink after work with others from the night shift. He never named them, referring to them only as 'the Marseillais' or 'the Gypsy' or 'the Pole.' Odd that. Strange how men refer to one another that way. The company of men. A mystery to Jeanne. A closed book. No matter. No loss. They bring out the worst in one another. A man needs a woman to temper his inner badness. Put him with another man and the badness is doubled, multiplied. Put ten of them together and you've got a fight on your hands or an occupying army. In the morning, Jacques would be home by about six and she would get up early, open the door to his house and make some breakfast. He seemed to have accepted her refusal to move in with him. She didn't want to leave her own house. Besides, she was content with the way things were. She could do as she pleased, come and go as she liked. Jeanne wouldn't want to stay in or wait up for Jacques, or anybody else. She had done that for years for Simon, and it had been fine, but she didn't want to start again. She pulled the sheets up to her neck, comfortable, warm. She could hear something now, what was it? A faint rustling. Perhaps the plane trees across the road. A breeze must have sprung up. Jeanne looked through the dark toward the window. She could make out the sloped slats of the louvred shutters.

After Jacques had had his breakfast, he would go straight out to work in the fields or with the livestock. A morning's work. Tomorrow morning, like every Wednesday, Jeanne would look in on Kaelle, a young woman from some village near Brest, the other side of the country, about as far as you could go without leaving France. Kaelle had turned up a couple of years back with a Belgian boyfriend called Guy and a big belly. Now she had a two-year-old daughter and there was another baby on the way. They had been virtually penniless at first, living off state welfare. Guy had found a job at last and would be out when she called. So much the better. Too good-looking and sulky with it, as if nothing and nobody could ever be good enough for him. He had hit Kaelle on at least one occasion. Some women thought that if it didn't happen too often that was okay. Not Jeanne. Her first husband had once raised his hand to strike her and she'd put up her left to block it and had held his fist in the air. If you ever, *ever*, strike me, I'll be out that door and never come back. Is that clear? That had fixed it. Women who let men hit them were sad, weak, creatures. You had to pity them. Jeanne liked Kaelle and didn't want to have to pity her.

Once Jacques had had his breakfast and told her about his night – there was usually some curious anecdote – and had gone off, yawning as always, to work in the fields or with the livestock, she would cross the village on foot to the field on the other side that her cousin let her use, gather some vegetables – leeks, broccoli, onions, carrots, beetroot, courgettes – and take them with her to Kaelle. Sometimes she took toys for Janis, the little girl. Kaelle was always grateful and always offered to pay and Jeanne always said, No, just make me a nice large coffee. Then Jeanne would play with Janis, while Kaelle made some soup. Jeanne was concerned for Kaelle, and for Janis too. Janis was always dirty-faced and appeared to have a permanent cold, the floor was always filthy, the sink full of dishes. The place was cold too: the cottage faced northwest and the windows rattled in the slightest breeze. Kaelle and her child appeared happy, though – at least when Jeanne was there. Jeanne sang nursery rhymes in a strong clear voice and played games with Janis and made her laugh. Kaelle was young enough to be Jeanne's granddaughter, Janis her great-granddaughter. Jeanne reflected that if you didn't have children, grandchildren, great-grandchildren of your own, then you had better adopt others, whenever the opportunity arose. Any child would do. At first, Jeanne had felt uncomfortable with the name Janis, especially the hard foreign way that Kaelle insisted on it being pronounced, as if there was a 't' before the 'j,' and a double 's' at the end: *Tjaniss*. They had named her, it turned out, after some North-American singer who had died young. Kaelle showed Jeanne a picture of the woman, who had long unkempt hair that hid everything but her nose and chin. People looked abroad for everything nowadays. Even names. Right across the Atlantic. There were plenty of perfectly good French names you hardly ever heard nowadays. Armande or Nadège or Yvette. You only need one. When Jeanne was growing up, nothing but trouble ever came from abroad. The best thing that could happen to France was that others would leave her alone.

Jeanne closed her eyes, smiling in the dark like a teenager. After leaving Kaelle and Janis, she would go to Jacques' house and they would eat together. Afterward, they might lie down on his bed. Jacques would need to rest. Jeanne might close her eyes for a little, or read her book. By three, Jacques would be sleeping soundly, snoring a little, in a soothing, pleasant way, and Jeanne would then get up – she got all the sleep she needed at nights. She might do the dishes, if she felt so inclined, and then go home. In the evening, they would meet again for dinner before Jacques set off for work. Dinners were the best time, when he was at his happiest, quite talkative. This contentedness they shared was a funny thing. She had not expected it.

Jeanne had a brief but queasy sensation of plummeting, and then of being caught at the last moment. Jacques was gone from her mind in a swirl. She was travelling on an omnibus in Grandgobier, her father seated by her side, both of them dressed all in black. They had gone to the city on official business, something to do with Maman. Her father held her hand and talked to her softly, leaning over her, crowding her rather, his short-trimmed beard tickling the crown of her head, his breath too warm against her neck, making her want to giggle. He didn't usually hold her hand. He didn't usually lean in so close. Earlier, she had seen tears in his eyes. She didn't know if she should cry or laugh. And where was her darling Mama?

In Rémy's bar, Lucie had dropped her head on the table, laying her forehead flat upon the opened newspaper, her arms spread across the square formica top so that her hands dangled off the far edge, her right hand still holding a lit but mostly unsmoked cigarette, its long grey tube of ash drooping precariously. She could see herself from the toilets, the bar, the ceiling fan, the street door. She looked knocked-out, deadbeat, a bag lady collapsed on a table. She was happy with the way she looked. She spent a moment like this every evening. She liked regularity.

She was wide awake, staring at the newsprint blurring like fuzz on the paper. Apart from Lucie's table which he still had to wipe, and the patch of floor around it which he still had to sweep and mop, Rémy had cleaned and tidied the entire bar. He had also turned off the TV, thrown the lock on the street door, cashed up, filled the laundry bag, placed the takings in the safe, put out the rubbish, mopped the toilets and sprinkled disinfectant in the pans and, finally, left a note for Patrick who would open the place at five-thirty the next morning. All he had left to do was replenish the fridge, restock the cigarette rack, check the bottles, top up the coffee grinder: a couple of trips to the storeroom and back.

Lucie rolled her head a fraction to the left to get a glimpse of Rémy. Her saviour dropped into the focus of her squinting right eye. With his droopy moustache and straggly greying hair, he didn't look like a hero. But she knew. Just one courageous, reckless act. All it took to change her life. He was middle-aged now, medium build, a little paunchy. Except for long-term, full-time, seriously committed hippies, most men by his age had cut their hair short – but not Rémy: it was like a declaration of independence, a finger raised at fashion.

My brother could never have saved me on his own, however much he wanted to. At least he wanted to. He *was* my saviour too that night. But where is he now? Shacked up in Holland with a fat platinum airhead and three snotty-nosed snivellers, at least two of which aren't his blood. Lucie thought of the New Year's card she received every year. Family photo, matching sky-blue sweaters, fat grins and a printed message. Baloney. She reckoned the wife sent them, the cow! Lucie didn't recognize Hervé's signature. She reckoned he was a filthy pederast. As a boy, he was only ever interested in other boys. He had sure picked the right country. A country of pederasts and drug-takers. Weren't all Dutch pederasts? Strange Rémy had ever been friends with Hervé. You couldn't get straighter than Rémy. Just look at him. Nothing faggotty about him. Besides, she *knew* Rémy was straight because that night, *that* night, after she had been rescued by the two of them, they had all arrived back exhausted at Rémy's studio flat and had emptied that bottle of Chivas Regal and flopped down on her saviour's bed, Rémy had refused her brother's slobbering advances and had turned instead toward her, young though she was. So she knew, really knew. He had been sweet to her. He could have had her. She was in no state to say no. Would eagerly have said yes. If asked. Instead, he was sweet to her. The kissing was real enough. You remember everything about kissing one particular person, but not a damned thing about screwing twenty others. And Rémy was still sweet to her. Kind. She wouldn't forget. And things might still change. If there was time. Always time. Time. If she really set her mind to it, she could probably seduce him even now, steal him away from that fat old cow he went and married. Why did he do that? They didn't have children. Mind you, she wouldn't really want to seduce him. It would be unkind to everyone. Besides, she didn't want to tie herself down to any man, even a saviour. She was a free spirit. Always a free spirit, that was me, that was our Lucie. Whose Lucie? But she could fantasize. Meanwhile her forehead was on the newspaper, soaking up the ink, and she was waiting. It will be the same as every other evening. He'll come over, wake me up – or so he thinks – I'll pretend I've been asleep, he'll offer me a drink, I'll go and sit at the counter drinking it, while he cleans up the last dirty patch of the bar – where I've been sitting – and then he'll take me home – to that halfway house of screeching nutballs.

Rémy's life was a constant round of chores, unending service, unswerving petty obedience to the whims of strangers and regulars – and the regulars were no more than regular strangers. His work had infected the rest of his life. I open the door for Lucie like I'm her doorman; I cook meals for Nicole like I'm her live-in chef; I collect the papers for Phi-phi like I'm his personal newsagent, librarian or private assistant. The more you do for people, the more they take your tiny acts of kindness for granted. Is this really my nature or is it just that my day-to-day work for so many years has been to serve people, pour their drinks, prepare their coffees *just so*, placing the sugar cubes squarely in the saucers and the coffee spoons on the counter with a discrete little click, slipping the tab under the saucer, remembering their footling preferences, their brand of cigarette, their politics, their stupid hobby-horse, their football team, gawking at the dog-eared photos they drag from their wallets, go *aah!* if it's a baby and *corr!* if it's a dame? Serving people for a living corrupts and warps your every human contact. How did I get into this? Wasn't I going to be a photographer? What ever happened to that? Lucie calls me her saviour, always harking back to the first time we met; but what I am is her servant, her most devoted and most humble servant. Sometimes I have to remind myself why I 'saved' her and when I think about her life now, about the life that it turns out I saved her for, I have to wonder whether it was worth the effort, no, the risk. It didn't take much effort. Scaling a wall, smashing a window, knocking down an orderly and running for my life. Call that heroism? Still, I wouldn't do it again. What for? If someone I hardly knew, like I hardly knew Lucie's brother – some customer, say – came up to me and told me how his little sister had been carted away by shrinks and locked up in a psychiatric unit, would I lift a finger? Of course not. None of my business. I could get locked up myself. Not even if it was a favourite customer, Phi-phi, for example. I'd just have to say, No. Quietly, but firmly. I would explain. He would understand. When you're young, things are different, you don't count the cost, you don't balance the pros and cons, you just do what's right. That's the beauty of youth, isn't it?

Rémy cast a punctilious eye over the contents of the fridge he had just replenished, the coffee grinder he had topped up, the bottles he'd filled or replaced, the cigarette rack he'd restocked. He closed the fridge door and glanced at Lucie. Her head on the table. Looking wrecked. Poor old girl. Not really old, just seemed it. Younger than me. He walked over to her, put a hand on her shoulder, jogged her slightly. Almost time to go, Lucie. What would you like to drink? It's on me. Anything you fancy.

Lucie got up, rubbed her eyes more than necessary, picked up her bag and waddled with it over to the counter where she sat on a stool. Rémy followed her then went round to the other side. Pastis, she said. Unusual, he remarked, fixing her the drink. What's new? Rémy asked. Lucie had read a piece about the body of a man wearing woman's underwear found in the river, some distance downstream. I saw that too, Rémy said. Suicide, Lucie said, grinning broadly and taking a sip. Not necessarily, Rémy suggested. Maybe he was drinking, maybe he was pushed. Rubbish! Lucie barked. Then in a whisper: Suicide! Rémy didn't care to argue. It was as though the honour of self-killing was suddenly at stake and Lucie was ready to step up and defend it. If it wasn't for suicide, she said, panting with anger, I wouldn't be here now. Rémy tried to figure that out. Lucie looked at him and he looked so stupid in that moment that she wanted to yell, but she restrained herself anyway, turned her head away and then back, inhaling. Look, she whispered: if I hadn't had a shot at it, they wouldn't have questioned me about my family; if I hadn't told them what my father did to me, they wouldn't have shut me away – me they shut away, not him; and if I hadn't been shut away, you couldn't have come and saved me from them. And if you hadn't saved me, I wouldn't have been around to recognize you when I stumbled into this bar that time. I wouldn't have known you. So I wouldn't be here. Besides I'd be dead, right? Rémy nodded. You couldn't beat the logic. It wasn't worth trying.

Rémy went quiet, as if impressed by Lucie's argument. That drowned man is a suicide, Lucie pronounced finally.

Rémy filled a bucket, grabbed a mop and a sponge and headed for the one remaining space to be cleaned for the morrow. He rolled the paper that Lucie had been reading and stuck it in his back trouser pocket. He wiped the table top. He put the chair on the table. He swept. He mopped. Funny the things you find on the floor among the bottle tops, cigarette butts, spent matches, sugar-cube wrappers. He once found a used condom tied in a tidy little knot, and still sometimes wondered how it got there. A young couple had spent a lot of time at that particular table that afternoon, with the girl sitting on the boy's lap. The bar had been crowded. Maybe they'd been fucking. Only those close to them would have noticed. Someone would have said something, wouldn't they? Rémy thought about it for a bit. No, they wouldn't. Why should they? It was nobody's damn business. Some people just got off on having sex in public. A couple he once saw on a beach, in front of everyone, having it away, other people's children playing not five metres away. They didn't bat an eyelid. He remembers studying the kids' faces. They just weren't interested. The couple could have been cutting one another's toenails, or playing whist. He'd heard of people doing it on crowded metros in Paris, standing in the middle of a crush, jammed tight together. But in his own bar? Actually, he quite liked the idea. He was flattered that they might actually have picked his place. Or it could have been spontaneous. It was certainly an accolade of a sort. Regrettably, the more likely explanation was that someone had used the condom somewhere else, pocketed it, then finding it later when he or she was looking for matches or a lighter decided to dump it on his floor. *He or she*? *He*, surely! Women don't hang on to used condoms, do they? It was a long time since Rémy had had sex standing up, or even sitting on a chair for that matter. He reflected that as you get older love-making confines itself more and more to the bedroom, circling in on the bed itself, till that's where you have to do it, every damn time. When you're young, any venue is good: back of cars, down a side street against a wall, in parks, woods, fields, on a beach at 4 a.m., in cinemas, nightclub toilets. Then you get yourself a home and it's exciting to do it in the kitchen, like a celebration, against the shiny new washing-up machine, or in the bath arguing – no, not arguing, but noticing – who gets the tap-end, then halfway up the stairs taking it in turns for carpet-burn. Eventually, sadly and inevitably, you only ever do it in the bedroom, circling ever narrower, and finally only in the bed itself, and no longer off the edge of it or using the headboard for support or half-on and half-off, but right there in a pool of tepid sweat, bang in the middle, each one of you creeping broken-backed toward the centre then retreating afterward, with the sheets and blankets pulled right up, in the pitch bloody dark, nothing you much want to see, certainly nothing you want to show, and nothing left to dispute except who gets to lie in the wet patch. Just the way you imagine your parents doing it. Well, you sure can't picture them against the wall in the toilets of some night spot. Did they have nightclubs in the 1920s? Course they did! Anyway, Rémy's parents were dead now. So he couldn't ask them where they did it. Not that their being alive would make any difference. He couldn't have asked them anyway.

Rémy put his mop down and looked over at Lucie at the bar, seeing her curved shoulders, her stooped frame. She'd been pretty once, in that birdlike fragile way you could still catch sight of sometimes. If he really wanted to, he could remember just how she had looked that night. They hadn't done anything. He reckoned she'd been abused enough already. What was she then, sixteen? Younger? Jailbait. Not his thing anyway. Rémy looked at his watch. He was running late. Nicole would be home already. Maybe she'd cook tonight, surprise him. Lucie's glass stood empty on the counter. Time to go. Time to take her home. Lucie! he called. Time!

20. Bobrán performs.

Bobrán's mind, which earlier that evening had hummed like an easy, silken, single thread of wish-fulfilling dreamwork was now a frayed and raucous, buzzing cord.

For Bobrán's mind was all of a jumble, all a jumble, all a-jumble, so it was. Its braided contents looped, lashed, leapt and wound in upon themselves, knotting, slipping, coming to rest, shuttling, jerking, skipping, jagged.

To slice at that particular time through that particular soul, one might – assuming twenty-second-century mind-imaging techniques applied with the taxonomic ingenuity of a seventeenth-century anatomist – pin down, spread-eagle and strip bare five threads, here discrete, here entwined, now each as sturdy a pole as any righteous impaler might desire, now as fine a hairline crack as ever fated man to final madness. What such a confluence of talent and technique might discover we can only glimpse in imagination.

Had it been possible at that particular moment to translate Bobrán's mind into musical sound, his workmates would have been treated to a quintet performing a set of 1970s free jazz, each jigsawed strand, each instrument crashing in or dropping out uncued, no solos as such, certainly no ensemble playing, nothing but the piling-high of proliferating leads: at worst, the turn-taking solipsism of deaf soloing; at best, an exhilarating unison of disputatious anarchy teetering this side of cacophony.

The bassline of Bobrán's mind – his operation and oversight of machines fifteen and twenty, his physical movements, his liminal awareness of objects and people, his elementary actions – was unshowy and subdued, walking, nay *plodding*, furnishing barely a pulse: a bass too deep for any but a Cetacean ear. This plodding, nay *foot-dragging*, line completely eschewed the seesawing bow, nor did it scramble or scuttle out bursts of half- or quarter-notes, and consequently was more to be sensed in one's bones than heard in one's tympana. It led a subterranean, nay a *troglodytic*, existence, imposing no limits on other strands in Bobrán's mind; indeed, it was discernible only when every other instrument suddenly, shockingly, abated. Bobrán threshed, he checked, he tipped, he stood, he tapped on the shoulder of his cousin: routine acts that caused scant ripple on the surface of his consciousness. Thud-thud-thud-thud-thud went this minimal bass.

The tenor saxophone, as it scaled and paced and flourished, leonine in its cramped cage of barely two octaves end to end, mellifluously plugged all gaps, riffing on the best memories since that evening's awakening, and they were several and came tumbling. Yet this line too was restrained, driven neither to clamber into screeching high harmonics nor slump into slack-jawed growls, while Bobrán was content to savour anew the happy suckling dream from which his mother had woken him, his no-hands gliding ride to work, his barroom flirt and first encounter with his lover's sister Heike, the quiet walk through dark metallurgy with Jacques, the teasing repartee with his cousin: all from an epoch before Mathieu yelled and Marcel brandished. That letter.

Then the trumpet, smashing its snout through the throaty sax, piercing with its high notes the pelt of the larger horn, stabbing at an immediate future, an agenda of urgent to-dos: get on top of the work; reach Marcel before he rips open the letter; keep the foreman off my back; fetch Jean his promised coffee by ten; decipher what the letter is meant to reveal. Do this, do that, and now, and fast. Out front, the trumpet yelps and blasts and whinnies, its urgency bullies, shoves and shunts every other fibre, at moments, clean out of mind.

A brash electric piano plays the fourth thread, spitting and spattering notes like ash and lava, briefly interring the horns, refusing to lay back, supply fills or comp. It's a vector for anxieties that well up unbidden: Bobrán's love and fear for Moritz; the filmic memory of his workmate's death; his lancinating grief for a lost father; the Damoclean dread of police-and-gangsterland blackmail over a long-ago and frankly unregretted killing; the duties of a son and brother, when mother and sister drift and stray.

Further off, a bedraggled beat, percussion's place having been largely supplanted by each other instrument, spun a bedrock strand of flotsam memories, variously overlaid, rarely rising to a solo, barely given the space in which to build that private fence between nowhere and nothing: memories of childhood snares, working circus days, fatherly gobs of wisdom and advice, gropings with cousins in scrubby fields and vacant lots, jingle-jangle wanderings far from home, the fut-fut-fut of the bass drum, the splash of cymbals, the ch-chemp ch-chemping of the hi-hat.

Bobrán was standing in the lift on balancing tiptoes, tensed between countervailing calf muscles, his feet hip-width apart, his eyes half-closed, his arms dangled, enjoying the downward glide, like freewheeling no-hands, wishing he could take flight, sprout wings. His father had once told him you only fall when you lose the fear, it is the fear that keeps you rooted and safe. Bobrán had struggled and failed to feel fear of either height or flight, yet had never once fallen. Any second, the lift would jar and jerk and stop and Bobrán would receive from Marcel's oily hand the African's message. Then the next thing would happen. And the next. The night stretched ahead, dark and glaring. And then it would be the morning of the next day. And he would have to act.

An hour ago, in dream, his hands had kneaded the small of his lover's back, his forehead had leaned against his lover's firm and downy belly, the slim young man's cocky little spindle had lain on his lapping tongue, and he had listened to their conjoined intake of breathy pleasure. A give-and-take so fine, so fair, so far from the years of submission to the sporadic buggery of all-controlling elders. No more of that. Not ever. The lift doors opened and Bobrán stepped out. An image of Heike's face, her peach-skin down briefly refloating his dream, the tiny hairs the same hue as those on her brother's belly. If the letter was about Joseph, Bobrán must have it read. But who to trust? Later he would have to act. He would have to do. Something. He would have to say. Something.

Bobrán squeezed round the back of control cabinet twelve and sneaked up behind his cousin. He didn't want to be spotted by the foreman and shouted back upstairs again. That man was in a bad mood; normally, he never yelled; normally, you hardly knew he was in charge. As Bobrán tapped his cousin on the shoulder, his braided near-cacophony of mind resolved itself to a simple streaming melody, as if fifty years of jazz history had been flicked away and his interwoven thoughts had recollected their stripped-down measure in the places and times of King Oliver, spun into a simple motif, a dying fall, while yet again he saw his erstwhile workmate plummet, a flash of black and white, silent but for the whoosh of air throbbing in his ears and his own screaming. And the dull bass thud. Thud. Until Bobrán stepped to the edge, invisible, inquisitive and terrified. Against the side of a skip, he saw, staring straight down. THUD. Then nothing.

Marcel was standing between machines eleven and twelve, fingering alternately his pack of cigarettes and the envelope addressed to 'Monsieur Bobrán', handed to him earlier that day by the glum-looking, besuited African. Marcel's thoughts were in thrall, as so often, to a circular and pestering obsession: Bobrán was an embarrassment; Bobrán had got himself into trouble; Bobrán had grown cheeky; Bobrán needed taking down a peg; it was time Bobrán shaped up; he was going to have to take care of Bobrán. Again.

In prison, a psychotherapist, a counsellor, a Jew, had been assigned to Marcel after he had smashed his right fist so hard first into his own face and then against his cell wall that he had broken his nose and fractured three knuckles. The Jew-psychotherapist had asked lots of questions, but at first Marcel hadn't wanted to talk. So the Jew filled the silences, chatting on and on about how he was a Jew, telling Jewish jokes, anti-Jewish jokes, poking fun at himself and his Jewishness, making Marcel laugh, making himself laugh even more. Marcel didn't think he had ever met a Jew. He wondered if they were all like that. This Jew seemed to think so. But then Marcel had never before met a psychotherapist either.

One day, Marcel had told the Jew – who had earlier divulged that he was married, had a small child and hailed originally from Orléans, and who had earnestly insisted that Marcel address him with the familiar 'tu' form and even call him by his first name, Martin – that he, Martin, was quite mad and needed help. It was an obvious thing to say, but the Jew, the Orléanais, laughed like it was the funniest remark he had ever heard. Marcel almost lost interest in him, as if he had looked straight through the man. Besides, Marcel didn't like calling him 'tu,' let alone 'Martin.'

By this point, however, Martin had induced Marcel to describe the way his thoughts sometimes became stuck in 'whirlpools' (Marcel's own term), going round and round and never finding a way out, and how when sometimes things got really bad he started imagining horrors. He would see slathering pigs' heads coming out of the floor at him; perfectly ordinary sandwiches would transubstantiate to dog shit in his mouth; he would catch a reflection of himself in a pane of glass and see the wrinkled face of a grey old bat: the kind of stuff that makes you doubt your sanity. Eager not to miss a word, Martin had advanced to the edge of his seat and listened hard, while nodding a lot. Like he was having fun. He asked what it felt like to be in the whirlpool and if it seemed like it was water or some other substance. And was he afraid of drowning? Marcel rolled his eyes. It wasn't something he had given much thought. He told Martin that the whirlpool made him feel dizzy, then added, Like the time a bunch of kids hung me by my heeels from a second-floor window so I was looking straight down at the ground. But no, he hadn't been afraid of drowning, he said. It wasn't as if the whirlpool was water. It was something else, some other liquid, hot and gooey – now he thought about it – and mostly molten but with lumpy bits, like a sauce gone wrong, viscous, bubbling, coagulating, hardening into something that had no definite shape, but that didn't pull you under. He could have continued.

The Orléanais listened to this with raised eyebrows, then assured Marcel there was always a way out of thoughts that are circular and seem never-ending and make you want to scream and hit out and hurt, but that the exit can't be found unless you hunt quite desperately for it – no, not desperately, determinedly: it wasn't enough to keep your eyes open, you had to keep searching for a way out, but this was a process that could be learnt. Marcel listened hard and took it all in, and when he tried the trick out for himself back in his cell, he found that mostly it worked, and he was grateful, because it felt good to think in a straight line for once. Two days later, as it slowly dawned on Marcel that he had learnt something useful for once and could now look forward to seeing Martin again soon, he was released. Without any warning. To ease overcrowding, they said. Marcel had almost a year left to serve. He had never seen the Jew again. He would have liked to say goodbye.

But Marcel hadn't forgotten Martin's trick. For instance, a little while ago, just before Bobrán and Jacques had wandered in late for work, Marcel had been getting himself in a twitch about two afternoon-shift women whom he imagined might be betraying him already, fucking some other man, even before they had fucked him. He hated the idea. He had never been able to tolerate a woman cheating on him. It threw him into a panic. But as his rage and anger wheeled round and round, with that bit of his mind that was still free he had begun looking for a way out and then, just as he was imagining the two women arriving home that very evening and each having – maybe that very minute – a lousy useless second-Tuesday-in-November kind of routine fuck with their regular boyfriend or husband, maybe just a mile or two from where Marcel was standing, he had suddenly realized he didn't need to care, and that not caring gave him an out. Who do they think they are anyway? Throwing themselves in my way! Who ever said I had to fuck them? Do I have to do every woman who crosses my path? Of course I don't. Chantal is enough for me. We're going to be married, damn it. Marcel halted his mind in mid-course. Hold on. Let's not get carried away now. He didn't want to talk himself out of spare pussy. All I need, he told himself reasonably, is Chantal and, say, one or two, or three, other girlfriends. That's plenty, damn it. And if I do maybe fuck those afternoon-shift girls one day, Marcel thought judiciously, that's fine too, but the point is I don't need to, so I don't need to be jealous, so I don't need to get myself all sick about them fucking someone else in the meantime. The fact is – and this dawned on Marcel with the force of a revelation – you only need to get jealous over a woman once you've already fucked her, not before: getting jealous *before* is not healthy. Marcel smiled at this liberating notion and quietly thanked Martin, the Jew, the psychotherapist, the Orléanais, the father, the anecdotalist. Right now, however, Marcel's mind was stuck on Bobrán, going round and round, and it was hard to get it unstuck. After all, Bobrán was a different matter: where was the way out of that? Marcel would keep looking. It might take a while. There was a way out of every whirlpool, Martin had said. You just have to want desperately to find it. No, determinedly. That was it. Was 'determinedly' even a word? Jews had a way with words, didn't they? Martin certainly did.

In the course of what turned out to be their final meeting, just two days before Marcel was suddenly let out, Martin had asked Marcel to say who he thought he was. Marcel had gone silent and shrugged and said, Just me. Well, who's that? Martin had asked. A man. Right, okay, fine, Martin had said patiently. Anything else? A Frenchman, Marcel offered, uncertainly. Martin waited, edging forward on his seat, somehow compacting the silence. Well, more or less, Marcel then added, sheepish. Which means? Martin asked. Like you, Marcel replied. How's that? You're a Jew, I'm a Gypsy. You're a Gypsy? You know I am. But is that who you are? I don't know, said Marcel. You're a Jew, aren't you? Among other things, Martin said, with the tiniest smile. Marcel leaned forward in his chair, forcing the Orléanais to retreat, made his lips small and mean and said, Look, you're the one who keeps saying it – Jew this, Jew that, Jew the other. I wouldn't have known, would I? Well, it's true, Martin said, I am a Jew. So, that's settled then, Marcel said, leaning back again. And I am a Gypsy, okay? He said it like it was a challenge. There was a short silence, while Martin looked at Marcel. Martin then asked, How important is being a Gypsy to you? And is it good or bad? I don't know, Marcel said, appearing to take the question seriously. Okay, Martin said, with a sudden intake of breath. Let's leave it there. It's a good place to start next time we meet. Marcel had shaken his head and smiled at Martin for the first time and said, You Jews ask some funny questions. That's right, Martin said, standing up and holding out his hand. We Jews. So what about you Gypsies? How do you answer funny questions? Huh? That was how they had parted. Afterward, Marcel wondered if Martin already knew he was about to be released. It seemed too neat that Martin had left him with that question hanging. Or then again maybe not. Gypsy this, Gypsy that, Gypsy the other.

Feeling a tap on his shoulder, Marcel transferred his cigarette pack to his left hand and, spinning round, grabbed his cousin by the scruff of his neck, forcing him back against the control cabinet of machine twelve. Bobrán squirmed but didn't try to fight him off. Marcel, taller than his cousin by a head, closed in on Bobrán, bringing his own moist forehead slowly down to rest on Bobrán's lush brown hair. Marcel's mouth was inches above his cousin's ears. Tut, tut, tut, cousin, he hissed, what kind of shit have you got yourself into now? Then, before Bobrán could even consider whether the question merited an answer, Marcel drew back, releasing the scruff of Bobrán's neck and cuffing him lightly on the side of the head.

Bobrán's left hand went to his neck to knead the chafed skin and then set about rearranging his curls. His cousin was breathing a rich stench of coffee and tobacco into his face while continuing to pin his back against the control cabinet. Marcel opened the top of his cigarette pack and counted his cigarettes. Nine, ten, eleven. Huh. Then he started over. One, two, three.

Give me the letter, Bobrán said.

Not so fast. What's this about?

How do I know? Maybe I'll tell you once I've read it.

Since when can you read? If you like, I'll read it for you.

The letter's mine. You said so yourself.

Who's this African? One of your boyfriends?

Bobrán blinked.

How do I know who he is? I didn't see him. You did. You tell me who he is. Or just give me the letter.

Marcel looked down at his cigarette pack. There was a pause while he thought. Eleven, he whispered. He jerked a cigarette out of the pack and popped the end of it in his mouth. Then he fetched the envelope from his right hip pocket. Bobrán glanced at it patiently, sensing that Marcel wasn't going to let it go just yet. Marcel's thumb and finger were holding it in a tight pincer.

Marcel sucked on his unlit cigarette, then spoke around it. Like I said: it was an African in a suit, a big black guy, with a white hippy type, long hair and a beard, the kind that are always lifting stones. Poking their noses in. He said he was a journalist.

How do you know the black guy was an African?

Because he spoke. I knew this guy from Guadeloupe when I was inside. Different accent.

So was he a South African? A North African? A West African?

I don't know. West African, I guess.

So Sénégal, Cameroon? A French speaker? Ivory Coast?

Marcel stared into his cousin's face.

How the fuck would I know? And when did you eat the goddam atlas? Besides, what does it matter? He said he was the brother of Joseph. Do you know a Joseph?

Bobrán gulped. Joseph had been forever talking about Africa, different countries, different regimes. It seemed he had friends from all over. He had never mentioned a brother. Bobrán would have remembered.

Give me the letter.

Marcel ripped the envelope open and extracted a single folded sheet of paper, which he then brandished. Bobrán tore the cigarette pack from Marcel's left hand and positioned it in his own right hand so that the cigarettes lay lengthwise between his fingertips and the heel of hand. Marcel understood that his cousin was poised to crush his night's smokes. He hated to scrounge and didn't like to go without. Despite this, he still hesitated. So Bobrán made up a story, narrowing his eyes and talking in a rasp. As he spoke, he pictured Jean Gabin.

I know these people. I know the way they work. You don't want to upset them. I'm figuring they asked you to give me this letter and you said you would. Am I wrong? Marcel shook his head slowly as he eyed Bobrán's right hand.

If you don't keep your word to them, they will be unhappy. And they are sure to find out. For a start, I will tell them.

Marcel appeared still lost in thought. Bobrán attempted reason.

Look. These cigarettes are all yours, aren't they? Just like that letter is all mine. What belongs belongs. Right?

Marcel executed a rapid combined shrug-and-chuckle. Then, in a flash, the letter and the cigarette pack changed hands. Marcel opened the pack and counted the contents.

Checking that one from eleven still makes ten? Bobrán asked, placing the letter in the back pocket of his trousers.

That was too much. Marcel wasn't going to be made fun of. He rammed his cousin against the control cabinet so hard he bounced back a little. All Bobrán did, though, was display his bad dentition. Marcel's anger made him grin. He couldn't help it.

It's time you learnt respect, Marcel hissed. You're getting cheeky. You're forgetting your place. After everything I've done for you. Who got you this job?

Bobrán shook his head. He felt like a rat in a cage. He looked down at his plimsolls, waiting for Marcel to relax enough so he could scuttle round him. He raised himself onto the balls of his feet, then let himself back down. He was surrounded on three sides by solid chunks of industrial machinery and on the fourth by his cousin, who was sweating like a fat old dog – and panting too. He wanted to take a look at the letter. Maybe he could make out something. He could remember his alphabet all right: it was putting it together he had never quite mastered.

Let me past, he said.

Marcel stared at his cousin.

Let me past, Bobrán repeated, quieter and slower than before.

Marcel reached for his lighter and stood aside. Then he lit his cigarette. He wanted a coffee. His throat was dry. He cleared it, then inhaled.

Bobrán walked past his cousin, in between machines twelve and eleven, and out into the machine aisle, glancing left as he turned right, registering neither Jacques bent over threshing, nor Eric standing up smoking, nor Salvatore sitting down reading, nor Rachid leaning back staring, all of them to him in that instant at least as negligible as their pounding, spurting, wrenching, clenching machines. Bobrán would take the stairs back to the first floor and look at the letter. That didn't require a decision. His body seemed to glide feather-light yet, a little like the fabled princess, beneath his plimsolls he could feel the floor's every asperity, sensing the presence even of tiny individual spilled granules of raw material. He was making for the staircase that stretched from the far corner of the ground floor up over the foreman's glass-walled lookout to the first-floor section. Perhaps he could read the letter, get at least the gist.

Bobrán needed to think. He just needed. What did he need? Something he needed. Something. The stairs were coming closer. He slowed his pace, uncertain. To Bobrán's right, Philippe was leaning at the end of machine two and grinning, nodding a little and swaying. Maybe he had seen something. Maybe! Philippe saw everything. Seen what, exactly? What had there been to see? Luigi, now to Bobrán's left, slumped at the end of machine fourteen, was all out of focus somehow, stooped over his magazine, squinting at pictures of criminals with bars across their eyes. Like film stars in dark glasses at Cannes.

As if that made them invisible. Beyond Luigi, Mathieu was checking the latest product that machine fourteen had turned out, holding it up, this way and that, screwing his eyes down into little pits of crow's feet, chewing on his burnt-out matchstick.

Bobrán bent down to examine the soles of his shoes. There was no oil on them, no grease. He swept the flat of his right hand across each sole. It came away dry and clean both times. His mind bounced and jolted back over a debris of thought grown stale: his dream of Moritz's body, gawkier now; his mother waving a newspaper, her brows furrowed, unfamiliar; Heike's smile, like a gash, a wound too wide; Jacques by his side in the dark, droning, droning; Marcel brandishing that letter like a week-old fish. Bobrán needed to push all this stuff right out of his head and retrieve that single thread, that one fine wire, pursue it wherever it led. He reached the bottom of the stairs. He didn't know what he was doing till he did it. He needed to concentrate. He needed. Something he needed. Something. He put his right hand on the end of the metal banister. Gingerly. As if expecting a shock. With Bobrán, this was the way trouble affected him. It made him behave erratically – unpredictably. In fact, of course, if you could know everything about somebody, you could predict their actions down to the last fart, couldn't you? Well okay, it is a big *if.*

As Bobrán climbed the first three stairs, all about him blurred, fell silent, vanished: the smoke, the dust, the noise, the machines themselves, the men. He might as well have been in a big top, on his own, a child again, in the small hours, after everyone had fallen asleep in their trucks and trailers, long before anyone was going to wake up. His right hand on the banister caressed its contour, measured its angles and width, then without stooping he slid his right hand further up, leaned forward, turning at the hips, and placed his left hand on the banister just above his right. He raised and swung his right leg so that its plimsolled foot secured a purchase on the bottom extremity of the banister. And now, with both hands and his right foot already in position on the handrail, his left foot rose effortlessly, unhurriedly, to seek out its grip just above his right foot. There he crouched an instant on the inclined strip of metal, frozen as if photographed, a squirrel in a suburban garden snapped prettily on a sloping pipe. He straightened up, shifting slowly his weight to his feet and freeing his hands from the banister, his arms rising and extending like wings outstretching for flight. His plimsolled feet clung simian to the banister, his fingers sought handholds in the circus-warm air. He wanted to do this right; he had no intention of falling. No fear either. He recalled his father's advice, his supplicant tone: talent without fear is deadly, you must always have fear, never trust the partner who has no fear – on the high wire he'll get you both killed.

Bobrán was standing on the banister, his left foot forward, his hands gently stirring, his fingers splayed. Joseph was gone from his mind. Marcel was gone. Moritz, Heike, his mother, Mathieu, Philippe: all gone. A chill numbness filled every part of him from the ends of his superfine eyelashes to the innermost depths of his bowel: a mental, visceral, spiritual ravishing. His mind was back on that happy, easy, silken, single thread, humming and stretching ahead, ascending, beckoning, leading him on. He took a first step, shifting all his weight onto his left foot, raising his right foot from the banister, bringing his right leg round, easy, easy does it, settling his right foot back down on the incline, his knee bending just right, just right for him, bending before nobody but only his own need. It occurred to him that he could do this blindfold. He closed his eyes.

It wasn't long before all the men on the ground-floor plastics section – excepting Salvatore and Jacques – were standing, sitting or leaning, staring at Bobrán – or, in the case of Marcel, at least staring in his direction.

Philippe saw it all from the start, having noticed Bobrán's altercation with Marcel and seen him head for the stairs, hesitate, and then climb gracefully, as if inevitably, onto the banister, the most natural thing in the world. Philippe shook his head and indulged in a little grin. The grin felt good. He let it grow. He could do with another beer. Might settle his head. That little Gypsy has poise. Why doesn't everyone go up the stairs that way? He worked as an acrobat, didn't he? Maybe he misses it. The thrill of it. Well, there is no net here. Nothing to break his concentration. Or his fall. I hope he doesn't kill himself. This is entertainment enough. But he knows what he's doing. You can see that. He's not going to fall. Philippe lit a cigarette. When you think about it, the whole world is nothing but spectacle right now, the whole of society. Isn't that what the man said? We watch, we observe, we are entertained. We consume. Still, it's got to be better than fretting about your marriage. Philippe grimaced. His mood seemed to be lightening again. Maybe he could get on top of this Odile thing. But then again, perhaps this was only a brief reprieve. There goes the Gypsy, another small step. Lean back, enjoy the performance. It's a show, a spectacle, one great big bubble.

Bobrán was taking another careful step along his easy, humming thread, raising his backward left foot from the handrail, balancing briefly motionless on just his right foot, then bringing his left foot slowly round and placing it ever so delicately in front of his right foot, allowing it slowly to take the weight as his body shifted forward.

Luigi was the second person to notice – out of the corner of his eye as he leaned against the side of machine thirteen and turned a page. Mathieu stood to his right studying the dials on the control cabinet of machine fourteen. Crazy Gypsy! Luigi muttered, putting down his magazine, taking care not to lose his place. He's going to hurt himself if he falls. Luigi looked at Bobrán's probable trajectory, what bit of him would hit what if he fell right now. By the side of the stairs, there were odds and ends of machinery. The Gypsy would make a nasty mess. Luigi considered categories of injury: life-threatening, minor and fatal. He thought about gore oozing and intestines flopping out and jelly-like brains and whether the blood would dribble or spurt and about groaning and whimpering, lost consciousness, spiky bitty bones poking out through clothing, limbs at crazy angles. Luigi saw in a flash the bucket and mop he used at Lucien's to clean animal spillage from the marble-chip floor. Nasty mess, if the man fell. What if Luigi was called upon to describe it? As a bystander, say. He moistened his lips and relit his Gitanes Maïs. An eyewitness. Perhaps, to a journalist from the magazine he was reading? He exhaled, stood back, authoritative, practised the glance. I was just standing here, yeah, right here, minding my own business, minding my own machine. That's right, I knew him pretty well. No, we weren't exactly friends. As for that, you'd need to speak to his cousin. Yeah, I saw exactly how it happened. I was the closest. He slipped and fell and the arm of that tool went straight through his chest, pinning him there like a . . . an insect? Maybe. A butterfly? Really? Do they? I'd like to see that. Did he die quick? I'd say so. Not instantly, mind you. Well, he didn't say that much. I mean, what is there to say? You're right, now I come to think of it, there was something odd about it. Yes, mysterious even. Possibly. Do I think some kind of weird sexual practice might have been involved? Couldn't say. You never know, do you? You can't rule it out. Quote me? Sure, no problem, it's Luigi. One g. You what? Ponteggia. Two g's. Any time. My pleasure. Absolutely.

Bobrán was taking a further step along his silken, happy thread, raising his backward right foot from the banister, balancing an instant immobile on just his left foot, then bringing his right foot slowly round and placing it tentatively in front of his left foot, allowing it little by little to take the weight as his body shifted forward.

Every night, at frequent intervals, Marcel glanced over at Philippe. Just to see if anything interesting was happening. Because if it was, Philippe would surely be in on it. Marcel had just followed Philippe's lazy-eyed stare. When Marcel saw his cousin perched on the banister damn-near halfway up, his head spun. He couldn't watch. He felt giddy and sick. He stared at the space beneath Bobrán, the air through which his cousin would have to fall. If he fell. It was so far beyond his comprehension that anyone could do that, let alone that they might want to. A moment passed. The air beneath Bobrán remained unpierced, the floor uncluttered. Marcel glanced at Philippe. Philippe yawned briefly, but his stare didn't budge.

Bobrán took another step along his humming thread, lifting his backward left foot from the handrail, balancing briefly on just his right foot, then bringing his left foot round and placing it in front of his right foot, allowing it to take the weight as his body shifted forward.

As the foreman had backed away from the control cabinet of machine fourteen, checked the latest piece to drop from the opening mould, then dropped it in the threshing bin, Luigi had whistled low and long to catch his attention as he glanced up at Bobrán. Mathieu had stood back and folded his arms across his chest. Fucking Jesus! What was he going to do if the guy fell? He tried to remember where the stretcher was kept. Somewhere in metallurgy. The Polish security guy would know. He'd call him on the public-address system. Jesus, this was all he needed. What if in the meantime the man stopped breathing? His first-aid training was so long ago, he wasn't sure he'd know how to do mouth-to-mouth resuscitation. Philippe might know, maybe. Mathieu wanted to shout out, tell the man to get down at once, not to be such a damn fool. But what if his shouting caused the man to fall? Mathieu pawed the ground, grunted and chewed his matchstick to a pulp, swallowing the juiced cellulose, for once taking comfort in its bitter-sweetness.

Bobrán took a step along his thread, raising his right foot from the handrail, balancing on his left, bringing his right round and placing it in front of his left, allowing it to take the weight as his body shifted forward.

Rachid was sitting on a chair at the end of the machine aisle, his back to the huge old wooden table that occupied the far end of the ground-floor plastics section. He couldn't believe what he was seeing. Mostly, wherever he was, whether inside the factory or out, Rachid stared at the ground. Occasionally, however, almost randomly, he would glance quickly up and immediately back down again. What he had just seen on looking up had made him do a sharp double take. He had cupped the lower part of his face with his left hand, as if stroking the stubble on his chin and upper lip, in order to tell Mehdi all about it, provide a running commentary as the event unfolded. He didn't want anyone to think he talked to himself. Like an inexperienced reader unable to read without moving his lips, Rachid had not yet learned to talk to Mehdi without moving his. I wish you could see this for yourself, Mehdi, he said. Just how mad a man can be. We know – you best of all – how our lives hang by a gossamer thread. All it takes is an impulse to dart out into a road, a well-aimed moped and a kerbstone, and you're dead. You, my son. Yet there goes that Gypsy, a pleasant enough man, friendly in his own leering way, there he goes risking his life, putting himself in danger, pulling on that thread, testing it, seeing how hard a tug he needs to give it to make it snap and drop him to his death or to his maiming. And I'm sitting here watching it helpless. Like I watched your head hit that stone. Over and over. Calm. Nothing I can do. He's over there. I'm over here. If there's anything needs doing, the foreman will surely know what it is. He's craning his neck right back, now the Gypsy has almost reached the top. I guess he won't fall now. Good. But it's still a stupid thing he's doing. As if to be alive and in one piece were nothing. What he is doing is an insult to you.

Bobrán took a step, raised his left foot, balanced on just his right, then placed his left round in front so it took his weight as he shifted forward.

Eric, the last of the men to become aware of Bobrán's stunt, had noticed Rachid's uncharacteristic fixed upward stare, followed it and now stood amazed, impressed, having advanced up the aisle and taken up position just behind Philippe. His gaze kept switching from Bobrán to Philippe, to Marcel – who didn't seem to be focusing on his cousin – to the foreman who was now shifting from foot to foot like a restless cart-horse, to Luigi, who seemed to be in a dream. It was great that something was happening for once. He laughed. Brilliant. What a nutter that Gypsy is. Wonder why he doesn't work in a circus. At least he'd have a net there, wouldn't he? Instead of risking his neck. But maybe that's the idea. Eric chuckled. Must know what he's doing. His cousin doesn't seem worried, doesn't even seem to be looking. Just stands there chewing gum. What a scene! If I could paint, if I had a camera, if I could only tell Megan about it. I almost forgot. Maybe I'll try telling Fanny.

'You won't believe what goes on here at nights,' I'll start. Of course I'll have to look up the word for banister and tightrope walking. Because, basically, that's what he's doing. Jesus, what a sight! He's going to bump his head if he's not careful. Amazing. Terrific.

Bobrán had got about as high as he could go, the ceiling was within reach. He glanced down to his right at the floor far below him, spotting Mathieu's gaping mouth as it briefly ceased to champ on the remains of his burnt-out matchstick, then taking in Philippe's faraway grin, Luigi's smirk, Eric's laughing, shaking head. Not a bad crowd, under the circumstances. For a Tuesday. Mouths wide open, like he was about to dive right down their throats. Bobrán suddenly wheeled his arms round and round. Below, they all gasped. He knew they would. He felt their breath before they breathed. In his palm. On his tongue. Silken like a thread, cold as a snail's trail. Then, ever the showman, he dropped down neatly onto the stairs to his left, and disappeared safely from view.

21. Salvatore exercises. Luigi stares. Jean anticipates.

As Bobrán completed his stunt by vanishing from view, Philippe swung round, expecting to see Jacques spectating from the end of one of his machines. Throughout the performance, Philippe had imagined the old man at his back, staring and nodding contentedly, his long hairy arms swinging perhaps a little, and Philippe was ready with a grin for him, a grin that said, How did you like that then?

Philippe was disappointed. Jacques was at his bin, bent over, bovine, his great shoulders circling, his haunches moving in time, his arms deep in sprue, tugging, twisting, threshing, ripping saleable product from recyclable plastic. He was doing his job, undistracted, battling with a product made of a particularly soft and pliable plastic, some alloy, Philippe thought, mostly polyethylene, whose pieces were especially hard to detach from their stalks. Philippe's rapidly shrinking grin was caught instead by Eric, who returned it with uncomprehending, gape-mouthed interest. Beyond Eric, at the end of the machine aisle, leaning in his chair against the wooden table, Rachid was dropping his eyes back to the floor. With a weary flick of his drooping eyelids, Philippe checked the tops of control cabinets one and two: both warning lights were off. Good, he shrugged. He glanced again at Jacques. He had had a thought, hadn't he? An image. Of Jacques. He looked harder, fixing on Jacques' shifting buttocks. Bovine. That was it. Ox-like. The old peasant was threshing that sprue, putting his back into it like one of his old oxen (did he still use oxen?) ploughing a furrow, not lifting his head from his harness till he finished the job, threshing away till most at least of the products had become separated from most at least of the stalks. The clefts and creases on his scrawny neck were shaking. Philippe could see them in close-up. How was that? The folds in an old ox's neck. Philippe had seen that somewhere. An old painting. Oil? Impressionist? Maybe. On a wall or in a book? Title: *An Ox Ploughs a Field in Winter*. A bomb could go off or the sky fall in and Jacques would never notice, never falter. Or if he did, he wouldn't stop to count the casualties till he finished the field.

Salvatore was not intent on observing anyone. His brows beetled but his eyes remained unfocused. He had been reading Voltaire's *Lettres philosophiques*, which he found disappointingly frivolous and conversational. The comments in the eighteenth letter, 'On Tragedy,' had struck the Sicilian as particularly vapid. He placed the paperback volume face-down on the chair beside him, alongside a vial of lens-cleaner, a union tract he had perused earlier, his industrial gloves and a small hand-exerciser, which he now picked up and began to flex in his right hand. Salvatore was proud of his hands, which were large, long-fingered, moderately hairy along their backs, carefully manicured, lean, and above all strong. They would serve equally well a pianist or a boxer, a strangler or a surgeon. Like the man to whom they belonged, they seemed ready for anything. Having completed twenty-five clench-hold-release exercises with his right hand, Salvatore absent-mindedly transferred the device to his left hand and began again. Uno, due, tre.

He had missed Bobrán's stunt, missed the very fact that he had missed it. His thoughts returned to the telegram from Vito that had arrived for him that morning. 'Tua madre peggio. Chiama.' He could hear Vito's voice. Vito, ordinarily so careful with money and therefore, when it came to telegrams, usually so letter-pinching, writing 'tua madre' instead of 'mamma,' as though Salvatore needed to be reminded who had borne him, suckled him, wept when he'd left. This bespoke Vito's anger. Salvatore knew all about that. But Salvatore hadn't found time to phone. Tomorrow, without fail, he thought. When their grandmother had been dying, Vito had written, 'Nonna grave,' and Salvatore had known at once to leave on the next train. It was as if this time Vito was giving him a choice, but grudgingly. Or was it worse than that? Vito was the one who hadn't got away, the one who had remained in Sicily. He had always been unadventurous, timid, the stay-at-home, but he resented it. He begrudged his siblings the thrilling Northern lives he imagined they led – in Norway, France, Toronto, Belgium. Somebody had had to stay behind. It wasn't Salvatore's fault. If his mother was dying and Vito had gone to the trouble and expense of using extra letters to avoid saying so – 'peggio' (6) rather than 'grave' (5) while redundantly insisting on the filial bond (tua madre: 8) rather than the fraternal one (mamma: 5) – then maybe Vito didn't want him there right now, indeed perhaps Vito needed him to stay away so that he could pursue unimpeded some dark scheme or other; or possibly Vito simply looked forward to guilt-tripping him should the old lady die before he got there. It was also possible that his mother had told Vito to wire the family and Vito had done so reluctantly. In which case, Salvatore thought, he had better go right away. He would phone tomorrow. Probably. Almost certainly. It meant a trip across town and an hour queuing at the PTT for a booth, but Salvatore loved his mother. It went without saying. Like a son. Tonight he would think it through.

Salvatore replaced the hand-exerciser on the chair, got up and quickly checked the latest product to drop from the yawning presses of machine seven, then tipped the products in the grey floor tray into the threshing tub to its left. He repeated these actions at machine six then returned to his seat at machine seven, and resumed his reading. The nineteenth letter was titled 'On Comedy.' There ought in strictest theory to be a laugh in it, Salvatore thought. He flicked forward. He wanted to finish the book tonight. He liked to have a target. He wouldn't let the union meeting distract him too much. Nor the telegram. Nor certain thoughts he had been entertaining recently regarding his girlfriend and her university chums. He wanted to keep his mind as lean as his body, as ready as his hands.

Why is it that we are so constructed that we can look outward from ourselves to observe another object or person, even two at the same time, even more, many more, perhaps of differing types, and also that we can look inward and observe, but always with hindsight, *how* we observe, what we use in order to observe, where we observe from; and yet we cannot see and observe in the same instant both our object and our observing self? Why will our gaze only go in one direction at one time? Why should it be? What can it mean? What purpose has been served and what price would have been exacted for a finer conjunction of inward and outward eye, for, say, a simple set of simultaneously operating bi-directional foci? Not to see oneself as others see one – what good would that be? besides, one need only ask – no, to see oneself as well as one sees others and at the same time, to see the picture *and* oneself, to see oneself within the picture: that would be equipment worth having.

Luigi's machine fourteen was still causing concern, the new mould was taking time to settle in. Luigi had left his true-crime magazine open on his chair and was standing, slouching, to Mathieu's left. The way the foreman examined each piece, it was as if he wanted to dig in and burrow beneath its surface, under its skin, explore it from the inside out: he never seemed quite sure he had grasped what he was looking at, he never seemed quite satisfied. Luigi shook his head and relit his Gitanes Maïs. You had to admire the foreman's commitment. The absolute concentration. Like Lucien jointing a lamb.

Knives flashing, meat cleaving. Never cut himself. Wonder how Mathieu mashed up that left hand then. Luigi could never ask. Might be a war wound. Or something personal. Each time the press opened, Mathieu slid back the safety door, poked his left hand, his claw, into the gap and grabbed the product, sliding the door shut again and bringing the product to his watery little eyes as he straightened up. He looked down the end of it, aligning all the external sides of the products, closing one eye, turned it so that he was looking at the underneath, then at the top, then at a random selection of individual pieces, then one overall last sweep. As if disappointed, he then hurled it angrily into its tray on the floor just as the press opened. Then he slid back the safety door and seized another product: he was looking not for perfection but for faults.

Faults could be of two main types: excess pressure, revealing itself in little flaps, wings attaching to the flat surfaces of the pieces, edges that were transparent and/or diaphanous instead of hard and well-defined; or, alternatively, lack of pressure, resulting in malformed, incompletely formed, stumpy, knobbly bits, like the limbs of amputees that instead of extending into articulated hands, knuckles, fingers, stop short at a rounded stump just before or after the knee, elbow, ankle or wrist; or, better, like the rounded collapsing turrets of a sand castle when insufficient pressure has been applied with the spade or the sand is too wet or too dry and refuses to be compacted; or, better still, like the frankly ugly ends of an asparagus when the tip has rotted away, leaving a deliquescing rotundity; or imagine an intricately detailed maquette, executed in fine Gruyère cheese, of a modern-city high-rise skyline, placed for ten seconds under a hot grill; or picture the finely chiselled nose of some sharp-featured human submitted to the patient assault of leprosy. That'll do. There was a third kind of fault, much less common, but which one did occasionally encounter nonetheless: the singeing of product caused by the excessive heating of the plastic – most conspicuous, obviously, in light-coloured pieces on which one might see brown burn stains or even a kind of frilly skirt, rather like the crispy brown latticed edges of eggs fried too fast or for too long.

Luigi peered lazy-eyed at Mathieu while Mathieu scrutinized one piece after another.

It was as if seeing an object, this object, any object, was a struggle that one was simply bound to lose. However many times Mathieu turned the product piece, through however many angles, however many planes, and however many 'shots' he took, from however many sides, he could never be altogether sure he possessed in his mind a true picture of the object that he grasped in his hands. One could never see the thing itself. Not in its entirety. And before he had finished his attempt to take possession with his eyes, to own and master and encompass with his just-about-good-enough everyday-human organs of perception any single unique individual product, the press reopened and fizz! splat! clatter! crash! there was another one, brand-new, scalding-hot and in theory identical. And then another, and another. Identical? It was a theory that Mathieu was bent on testing.

Mathieu had done nothing to indicate that he registered Luigi's presence, yet he now brought his good right hand up to twist a single product off the sprue that he was presently gripping in his left and jabbed the said single product in Luigi's direction in an act of showing. Luigi stared but saw nothing of note. Mathieu now pointed to a small excrescence – present on one side only of this one piece – a tiny frill, a promontory, a protruding or abutting flourish, like some structurally irrelevant architectural afterthought on the side of a modernist building, an eruption of anachronistic ornamental stone foliage, a grinning gargoyle, a redundant corbel, a flying buttress buttressing precisely nothing. It took a while for Luigi to see it. To lower or raise the injection pressure even a jot might throw out all the other pieces. Mathieu nodded his head at the Italian and then raised the index finger of his right hand to his own right eye. Sucking on his cigarette, Luigi nodded solemnly. He would keep his eye on it. Now that he had seen it.

Mathieu slung the item into the threshing bin, then made to head into the aisle, off to check on some of the other machines and their products. As he turned, however, he noticed the magazine that Luigi had left face-up on his chair. *Medical student from Metz murders dying mother.* Before he knew it, Mathieu had taken in the student's police mugshot, the short clumsily cut hair, the heavy glasses, the weak chin in profile; and, simultaneously, alongside the murderer, in ghastly proximity, the photo of the mother smiling vacantly, embarrassed yet happy, pursing her lips to blow out candles on a cake. An image like that, unbidden, accidental, could invade your mind, blow it out as painfully as a surfeit of lentils bloats a sensitive gut. One glance and you knew the story, or thought you did. You knew just enough to want to check the details. Like: How old was the murderee? Were the candles in sharp enough focus to count? On the whole, Mathieu avoided people's pictures, didn't trust them, left their magazines, newspapers, brochures unopened, trained himself never to look at the advertising images that cluttered the city streets, disfiguring the buildings, grinning from bus-shelters, peeling from hoardings, depicting radiant huddled-for-the-camera families, couples lovingly interlaced just so, dashing-handsome men and pouting-gorgeous women. Mathieu looked up and down the machine aisle, walked over to Philippe's machine number one. The photo of the murderee was printed in bold on his retina, an unwitting intruder, blundering uninvited into his consciousness. Maybe that was the best photo they had of her. Or the only recent one. Maybe it was an old photo. She didn't look sick. But then families don't take photos of their dying, do they? So it was taken before she fell ill. Were one to turn the page, perhaps there would be other images, an entire gallery of mother-and-son snapshots, victim- and assassin-to-be – how cosy! – maybe a sibling in there somewhere too. Or a father? Where was he? Safely out of it, that's where.

Mathieu paused, appalled by his mind's vulnerability to attack. A pair of total strangers had elbowed Nadine aside, Mathieu's Nadine, dragging their entire tribe and its wretched history behind them. To hell with them. What of Nadine then? What of her birthdays? How did they go? Always the same nowadays: he opened a bottle and drank it alone. What of Nadine's photos? Stuffed in a cupboard in a shoe-box. Never mind: he held Nadine's image in his head at all times. Her images: plural. Never more than a flick away, a blink. As precious to him as his mind, as clear to him as some old blues riff, as close to him as his own breath, as vital as the spittle on his lip.

Jacques had stopped threshing and straightened his back. Another tangle of empty stalks, whose products had all fallen off during the threshing process, had worked its way to the top of the tub. Jacques dropped them in the recycling bin to his left. All that now remained in the tub was a sea of soft bottle-top-sized shiny black products and a small number of product skeletons, poking through the surface like light driftwood. Many of the skeletons had one or two or even three products still clinging to them. Jacques removed his gloves and taking in his left hand one skeleton-piece after another, he proceeded with his right to twist free each last product piece from its stalk.

Jacques didn't become aware of Philippe standing at his side until Philippe's right arm joined Jacques' left arm in the threshing tub. Philippe was standing just to Jacques' right. Jacques shifted minutely to his left. Philippe's left hip was square against Jacques' right. I'll give you a hand,

Philippe murmured, twisting a product piece from its stalk. Jacques nodded and chuckled. Philippe perceived the brief rhythmic rising and falling of Jacques' upper body, a soundless gurgling. Jacques could smell the beer on Philippe's breath. Neither man looked at the other. Neither man talked. Philippe swayed slightly. Whatever problems Jacques had, Philippe was in greater trouble of some sort. Jacques deferred to Philippe's greater need: such was his nature.

The two men stood there, patiently detaching all the product pieces that had withstood Jacques' vigorous threshing. A minute passed.

It's the worst product in the entire section, Philippe said.

It's all the same, Jacques replied.

Philippe was right. There were some products that dropped from the sprue like ripe peas from a pod, shelling themselves as they fell through the aluminium slats or hit the floor tray. Others needed a few seconds banging together in the threshing tub for the stalks to shed their load and rise to the surface; still others demanded a pounding. The mould currently on Jacques' machine number four produced the softest, most resistant, hardest-to-detach products in the entire section.

At least this mould hasn't ever gone wrong yet, Jacques said.

The two men worked in silence.

So what's your problem? Philippe asked. The sound of his own voice took him aback. Crisp. Harsh. He ought to have prefaced the subject somehow. It had come out wrong, sounding like a challenge. He had spoken too fast too. His struggle not to slur his words had overshot. You said you wanted to talk, he mumbled, overcompensating again, sounding drunker than he was.

Jacques shrugged and laughed. Philippe still couldn't hear anything, though Jacques' upper body was jigging up and down as before. Unmistakable.

I'll tell you about me later, Jacques said. You go first.

Philippe shrugged and laughed, then immediately regretted it. He had caught himself in the act of aping the other man. Philippe had an urge to make monkey sounds, ho-ho-ho hee-hee-hee, as one might to entertain a baby. His shoulders felt uneasy, bearing the memory of that borrowed shrug. He began to search for words. It was his turn to talk. You go first, Jacques had said. Philippe thought of his sister, then of his wife, but no words came. He tried to remember the exact coordinates of the problem, nail the thing down. He didn't know how to put it. His mouth was dry. He knew he should be saying something by now. What the hell did they put in beer these days? His hip seemed lodged, wedged, glued to Jacques'. He moved away fractionally, shifting his weight onto his right leg. He didn't want to be obvious. Jacques didn't move either way, probably hadn't noticed a thing.

Philippe wondered what problems a man like Jacques might have. There were a couple of things Philippe knew about Jacques, but so many more he did not. That was true the other way round of course. In fact, what each individual in that factory didn't know about each other individual could fill a book. Philippe had no idea that Jacques, who had always seemed temperamentally incapable of anxiety or tension of any kind, was worried for his manhood, angry with his doctor, mortified by a gaffe he felt he had committed with Bobrán, and simultaneously comforted by his recollection of the role he had once played as mayor vis-à-vis what his fellow villagers had termed the 'Gypsy issue.' Philippe could imagine but not quite believe that Jacques, a man twice his age, was in love like it was the first time and hadn't yet fully realized it, nor that he was upset by a spur-of-the-moment visit he had made that evening to an estranged relative (a sibling, no less). Philippe would certainly never have believed that Jacques – reliable, solid, stolid Jacques, the old peasant, old practical joker, his companion in many a fine bout of pre-dawn carousing at the bar nearest the factory gate – had that evening been tempted to drive straight past the factory and never stop till he got to Spain or Belgium.

The two men had pulled the last product stalks from Jacques' threshing tub and dumped them in the recycling barrel. The tub was almost a quarter full of soft shiny black plastic bottle-top like objects.

You need a box, Philippe said.

Shall we get that coffee? Jacques asked.

Sure, said Philippe, though mine's still a beer.

Jacques shook his head, checked the latest products to fall from the presses of machines three and four, while Philippe did the same at machines one and two. Then Philippe led the way up the machine aisle, under the stairs that led to the first floor, past the foreman's raised office, through the hanging plastic flaps, and out into the raw materials area.

The storyteller watched as they placed a bunch of people nobody had ever seen before on chairs, then set the chairs on a plinth in the middle of the room. Paper and pencils were distributed to the applicants, who were instructed either to draw or to describe what they saw. He did his usual thing. He sketched a brief description of the salient physical attributes, then noted what had to be on the bodies' minds, adopting their own voices, that is to say, assigning to each person the voice he heard in his head. He wrote of the places, people, routines, etc., familiar to each plinth-borne character, evoking also something of their pasts. This is what happened whenever the storyteller saw people. He heard their voices as they were thinking to themselves. He locked on to them like a listening device, or, better, like a ventouse gentling sucking the person's voice from the partially dilated trap of their own mind.

It must have been what the examiners were looking for. They gave him the job.

As the huge old presses of Jean's semi-automatic machine twenty-one gaped open, the little man leaned forward and, using his right hand to tug the sprue from the right side of the mould, he dabbed the paintbrush he held in his left hand at the ejector pins protruding from the mould face. Jean then leaned back, closed the guard and pressed the button to start a new injection cycle.

Though focusing diligently on his work, Jean could not help but notice through his wide-open press that Bobrán had abandoned his hopeless attempt to read from the sheet of paper that he had extracted from his hip pocket several minutes earlier. Alphonse, on his way to the lift, greeted Bobrán who, having settled at his threshing tub, extended his right hand without looking up. The African asked something, to which the Gypsy appeared to assent. Beyond them, Fernando was staring into space. The cigarette hanging from his nether lip was smouldering unsucked, as his mouth gaped.

Jean's machine was the articulated juggernaut, the trans-continental truck of the plastics section, and Jean, from his high seat at the controls, from his saddle, his throne, could look down upon drivers of every lesser vehicle, the Alan Ladd of the factory imagining himself to be its John Wayne, though clad in a home-knitted cardigan rather than a cowboy's leather waistcoat. He was glad this dead period was coming to an end and that he would shortly be free once again to devote his mind to a perusal of the day's events. His disciplined proximity to the other men, his nightly approach to their state of echoing mental emptiness, while dispiriting, represented an act of charity and generosity, betokening indeed an extension of empathy that was all the more noble for its discretion, not to say secrecy. (Besides, it did him a world, a power, of good.) The other men must never know how deeply he felt for their wretched plight. They were, quite assuredly, in their way, no whit less human than he.

Eric had watched Marcel's reaction to Bobrán's banister-climbing stunt and had bided his time, awaiting the opportunity to re-engage the man in conversation. Marcel had finished thumbing through a newspaper at the end of Philippe's machine number two and was rejoining his own machine at his customary pace.

Eric lit his roll-up and met Marcel midway between his own machine number five and Marcel's machine number eleven. Eric secured Marcel's attention by gesticulating up the machine aisle in the rough direction of the stairs. He had prepared some words.

I was frightened, not you? he enquired, squinting at Marcel through a cloud of smoke.

Marcel observed the Englishman and nodded in a way that made no answer, appearing rather to comment on the validity of the questioner's question. He considered Eric's left ear, which he noticed was large, protruding and crimson.

You needn't worry, Marcel said at last.

He falls never?

A light came into Marcel's eye. A dark light.

He used to work in a circus. You know? Circus? Elephants? Clowns?

Oh! un cirque! A circus? Un cirque! *Formidable!* But he no more in circus working, isn't it? Eric took a puff on his roll-up.

Marcel was enjoying this, though his ears and mind recoiled at the mauling the kid was giving the French language. Marcel popped a cigarette in his mouth and began to nibble at the filter. Eric appreciated the gesture, the company of a fellow smoker, the hint of complicity he thought he discerned.

Well, no, Marcel said. He narrowed his eyes. You see, one fine day he fell and broke a leg and two arms so they fired him. To evoke the fractures, Marcel had drawn the index finger of his left hand across first his left leg and then his right forearm.

How terrible! But no need worry you say? Surely . . .

None at all, Marcel said, shaking his head from side to side and registering the presence of blackheads at the end of Eric's nose.

But . . .

Somebody greased the wire, Marcel interrupted in a whisper, leaning forward. Eric's cigarette almost fell from his lips.

Quoi?

Grease, Marcel said. Like oil. Marcel used the flat of his right hand to enact a skidding movement upon the underside of his left forearm.

No . . .

Yes . . .

You are saying . . .

Eric was hopping from foot to foot, blowing smoke in all directions, as the notion sunk in. Fuck it, he had to improve his French. This was so hard to follow. And so interesting. Marcel, meanwhile, felt uncommonly powerful. He was in charge of something he could ration almost as precisely as sex to a needy woman. He was doling it out inch by inch, reeling out a rope just as long and as slow as he liked. A jolt here, a caress there. Bringing the man to an ecstasy of fascination.

Who? How? But why? For what?

Like I said, engine grease. Marcel opened his eyes wide, expressing the banality, the normality of the occurrence in question, then looked into the far distance, exhibiting his almost Roman profile. They never found out who did it, Marcel said, pursing his lips, as if to tut. Everyone hates the little runt, he then muttered to himself, momentarily carried away, momentarily believing his own yarn.

Eric looked perplexed. He was trying to figure something out. It was harder than any brain-teaser or schoolboy maths problem.

Marcel turned to go. Eric followed him, tugged at his sleeve.

Wait. A moment . . . Is it true? That which you have said . . .

Marcel laughed out loud. True? True?

Correct, Eric said. Is it veritable? Did it occur, what you said, like you said?

What's the difference? Marcel asked. Maybe it did, maybe it didn't. It might have. Why do you ask? Then he closed in on Eric, looked him in the face, stood up near to the man, breathed over him. Would you call me a liar? Would you say that I lied? To my face? No? Behind my back? No? The toes of Marcel's trainers were right up against the toes of Eric's boots and he was still nibbling on the filter of his cigarette.

Eric looked at Marcel. He thought he understood what the man was asking. No, he said. I do not say that. Jamais.

Well, if you can't tell me I'm lying, then you'd better just believe what I say is the truth, right? One story is as good as another.

Eric didn't catch that. It was too intricate a piece of reasoning. And Marcel had turned his back now and lit his cigarette, his private smoke. Eric walked back to his machine. He felt that the conversation with Marcel had gone badly wrong at some point. He wished someone could tell him where.

22. Alphonse skims and skips. Men tending machines.

At the aisle-end of Philippe's machine number two, Alphonse stood bolt upright before the waist-high cardboard cylinder containing recycled raw material, his hands gripping the far edge of the lid, in a stance reminiscent of an old-time preacher man at his lectern, staring out over the congregated faithful. Upon the lid lay a stack of papers and magazines. He recited a text that he now had almost word-perfect. A folded paperback protruded from his back pocket. He stood and held the cylinder in such a way that no part of his body – save his hands – came into contact with any part of it.

Alphonse flicked distractedly through the pile of papers that Philippe had earlier brought from Rémy's bar. With his right hand, he adjusted his white plastic trilby, then drew a wooden clothes-peg from the bottom of a trouser pocket and began to play with it while he intoned the first lines of Lucky's speech from *En attendant Godot*: 'Given the existence as uttered forth in the public works of Puncher and Wattmann of a personal God quaquaquaqua . . .'* Given that Lucky is being dragged this way and that by means of a heavy rope round his neck, should I perhaps deliver this speech in a strangled choke, Alphonse wondered? Only now noticing the clothes-peg in his right hand, Alphonse clamped it triumphantly to his nose as if inspired. He picked up his recitation: '. . . a personal God quaquaquaqua with white beard quaquaquaqua outside time without extension . . .'

Alphonse considered the nasal quality of his voice, barely audible above the machine din: it wasn't right, but wasn't any distortion better than none? It served to remind him of the rope. Alphonse brought up his right hand, grasped his throat in a single-handed choke, then continued: '. . . without extension who from the heights of divine apathia divine athambia divine aphasia loves us dearly . . .'

He interrupted his performance and glanced up and down the machine aisle, seeing nobody. How should Lucky sound? I can't believe he would speak in a meaningless drawl or a glib patter. In spite of everything, he is

* The text that Alphonse is learning, in Samuel Beckett's original French, begins: 'Etant donné l'existence telle qu'elle jaillit des récents travaux publics de Poinçon et Wattmann d'un Dieu personnel quaquaquaqua à barbe blanche quaquaquaqua hors du temps de l'étendue qui du haut de sa divine apathie sa divine athambie sa divine aphasie nous aime bien à quelques exceptions près on ne sait pourquoi mais ça viendra et souffre à l'instar de la divine Miranda avec ceux qui sont on ne sait pourquoi mais on a le temps dans le tourment dans les feux les flammes pour peu que ça dure encore un peu et qui peut en douter mettront à la fin le feu aux poutres . . .'

striving for sense, slamming phrases together in a way that is desperate but never haphazard. He is the broken husk of a once clever, once useful, once free man. I'm not playing him as an object of condescension or scorn. I don't want to incarnate a madman or a cipher. My Lucky is the wreck of an erudite, cultured, well-spoken, articulate man – a man versed in the ways of the world, far superior to his driver Pozzo, let alone to Vladimir or Estragon. Indeed, he's the very heart of the play; even if in Act Two it's a silent heart.

Alphonse pondered Lucky's speech as he ran through it, his lips softly mumbling the trickle of serious-sounding nonsense, the elipses, the non sequiturs, the stern conviction and glaring insanity heaped high in each phrase. It amounted to a mental concoction that put him in mind of a woman he had known back home, a friend to his elder sister. On first hearing her talk, you might imagine she had a brilliant mind, but the longer she talked the more confused you would become, until you found yourself wondering whether she was really in possession of some ineffable truth toward which all her talk appeared to be tending or, alternatively, whether she was not in fact delusional, and possibly paranoid. With this in mind, the aspiring actor resumed: '. . . with some exceptions for reasons unknown but time will tell and suffers like the divine Miranda . . .'

Alphonse froze. A tremor ran through his sturdy but ungainly frame, across his narrow shoulders, held so proudly square, over his broad hips and down the length of his thighs and shins, ending in a needling sensation about his ankles. His eyes, prominent and agile, blinked suddenly and his head jerked. As always, when unnerved by an unsolicited emotion, he raised his left hand and pressed its palm against his broad, high forehead, as if seeking to assess the intensity of a fever. For the first time in years, the Ivorian felt out of place. Not just in this city, he thought, or on this continent, but in this factory too, in my own skin. What's happened? What's different tonight? I always come down at about this time, take a look at the papers, usually exchange a word or two with Philippe, mostly about the news, then go and shake hands with anyone I haven't yet seen. Alphonse skimmed and skipped through the papers before him. Tonight it is as if nothing here has anything to do with me, nothing in this place, nothing in these pages. The people in the photos, the stories: nothing to me at all. Maybe it's because of that bar, those would-be thugs, who only turned back because they saw me heading toward Fernando. I know nothing of those people, their lives, their barroom thrills and gambling, but why should I want to? How would it help me play

Lucky, for example? And how I misjudged the Maghrébin, the Arab! *Is* he even an Arab? I who pride myself on my insight into my fellow man! And he is my fellow man par excellence: a fellow African even. How could I get anyone so wrong?

Alphonse picked up the clothes-peg where he had left it on the edge of the cylinder lid and applied it to the tip of the index finger of his right hand. The pressure on his cuticle was more pleasurable than painful. His finger felt longer now: the peg might serve as a gigantic fingernail, a pointer, a wand, a reprimand, something he could wag, at least at himself. He tapped and drummed with it on the papers as he sifted through them, eager to find a point of interest or at least contact. He read lines from a number of different stories on the foreign pages: in the Federal Republic of Germany, there had been a meeting of old SS officers (how dare they show their faces?); in Spain, two hundred miners were striking for pay two hundred metres underground (why did they have to stay underground, why not just withdraw their labour: was it to prevent the managers from drafting in scabs?); there was a rapprochement under way between the USSR and the Argentinian junta led by General Videla (why should this surprise anyone any more?); in Italy, US-President-elect Jimmy Carter had warned of grave repercussions should the Communists ever come to power (what business was it of theirs?); there was a report on the successes of the Cuban army in Angola (two cheers for Fidel).

Alphonse began again from the top of the pile, his peg-enhanced finger seeking out the arts pages. What was he to tell Rachid? He would have to say something, perhaps explain that he was an actor, had been playing the clown and meant no harm. He took his eyes off the paper, glanced around him, saw as through the wrong end of a telescope a number of miniature men coming and going, the foreman chewing on his eternal matchstick, the Algerian at the far end of the machine aisle leaning his chair hard against the edge of the table, his feet crossed, his head down, dropping the dying end of his cigarette on the ground.

Alphonse would attempt to explain himself without offending Rachid all over again. He would swallow his pride and apologize, slither on his belly if need be. He tried to run the conversation but no words came. Rachid would be receptive, but would look away. What if he turns his back? Alphonse was filled with admiration for Rachid: so frail-looking, sickly even, yellow-skinned, bent-backed, round-shouldered, all of which makes his strength and power uncanny, almost miraculous. And the man showed no malice. Alphonse respected strength, especially when encountered where least expected. He would talk to Rachid, make things better. Alphonse knew how to talk. Rachid would listen. Alphonse removed the clothes-peg from his index finger and placed it on his nose. It was no great help, barely a reminder. He returned it to his trouser pocket and adjusted his trilby.

Alphonse clenched his fist, pulled himself together, shook his upper body, histrionically. For an instant he had suffered a loss of nerve. Not surprising under the circumstances. From his back trouser pocket he extracted his copy of *En attendant Godot,* open at Lucky's speech, and checked the first few lines against his memory. He picked up from the place he had left off: '. . . suffers like the divine Miranda with those who for reasons unknown but time will tell are plunged in torment plunged in fire whose fire flames if that continues and who can doubt it will fire the firmament . . .'

Standing at the end of his machine fourteen, Luigi studied Alphonse. The Italian had never been to the theatre. Just watching this guy here was pretty good though. Some actor. Talking to himself, reciting stuff – some sort of poetry, to judge by the way he moves – posing and prancing and preening. He's stopped again now. Just like that! I wonder why he stops? Of course, actors are always in the news. The things they get up to. Orgies and all sorts. Drugs. Dressing up in outlandish costumes. Putting on women's clothing. Casting-couch romps. Louche associations with mobsters. Premières and red carpets. Shooting on location. Trailer romances. But that was film, wasn't it? Theatre might be different. Less glamorous. Luigi looked at Alphonse in disappointment.

The Italian took a long hard look at Alphonse, standing motionless now at the aisle-end of Philippe's machine number two, bolt upright at the recycled-raw-material cylinder, his hands gripping the far edge of the circular lid, putting you in mind of the captain of a huge ship, his hands steady on the wheel, staring out over the dark sea, into the sleeting rain. And mumbling away like that, as if to the gods above.

*

Upstairs, standing by the side of machine number fifteen, Bobrán broke off his threshing, glanced at the tops of Alphonse's control cabinets eighteen and nineteen, saw that the warning lights were off, then dropped onto his chair.

He pulled off his gloves and wiped his forehead with the back of his left hand; it came away wet with sweat.

He was annoyed with himself. Lots of other people could read. He had only managed to make out the first few words of the letter his cousin had handed him, but it was enough to discover that it had been written by a man called Albert, who claimed to be Joseph's elder brother. Joseph had never mentioned any brother, elder or otherwise. Bobrán wondered what the man might want from him. Joseph is dead, what more does he want to know? One day Bobrán was going to have to learn to read. There were times you couldn't ask someone to read for you. Writing, he now saw, could be a private place: in which case, reading had to be too. In his pocket, at this very moment, he had something confidential, intended for his eyes only, yet he couldn't find out what it was. A piece of magic enclosed in a wad of folded paper. He would have to learn the trick. You can't rely on people to remain discreet. For example, on this shift who could he trust to read his letter and not give out its contents? He could rule out Marcel, for a start.

Bobrán looked round but saw nobody. His eyes rested on the huge old semi-automatic machine number twenty-one, as its press opened. What about Jean? Bobrán shook his head slowly from side to side. Maybe. He doesn't talk much to anyone else. Except to the Italian dope downstairs, and occasionally to Alphonse. It's all so, so, so inconvenient. That's what it is. You can't always wait till someone you trust – like Moritz – is to hand. Besides, would Moritz be able to read French? He reads German, doesn't he? And he speaks French pretty good for a foreigner. But does that automatically mean he can read French? I speak French all right. But then I don't read German. Maybe if I read German I could read French. Is that how this works?

Bobrán could feel Albert's letter folded into a tight little package lodged in his right-hand trouser pocket against the top of his thigh, an unreadable object with secrets to impart, posing a threat to his life of settled routine. He repeated to himself the few words he had managed to work out: 'Monsieur, je me something: je m'appelle Albert G'somebody, le frère something de Joseph.' That was where Bobrán had given up. He had taken several minutes over 'je m'appelle.' Why did they have to write it like that anyway? To make things difficult? He was pleased with himself when at last he worked out how the letters fitted together and what they meant. Why not write it like it's spoken: 'je ma pelle?' nobody ever said 'je–mmm–appelle. How long did it take them to come up with that? Why go to all that trouble to conceal a meaning?

Maybe to keep the club exclusive, to keep out Gypsies and anyone who didn't want to spend years in their schools soaking up all the other stuff they dish out along with the alphabet. Why can't they give you one without the other?

At machine fifteen, Bobrán pulled his gloves back on, stood up, leaned in against the threshing tub and took a deep breath. He began pulling out a large tangle of sprue that had dropped all its products, then transferred it to the recycling barrel at the aisle-end of his machine. He resumed threshing the remaining product pieces, crashing them together, pounding them against the walls of the bin to separate the tiny valuable products from the skeleton stalks that held them, staring into the bin all the while, watching the stalks and the products as they fell free. Joseph's death: that's what they would want to know about. What can I say? Months have passed. I saw him slip. I didn't see him land. When I leaned over and looked down, he was next to a bright orange skip, his body twisted an odd shape. Later someone told me his back hit the side of the skip full on, must have snapped. It can't have hurt. I saw this black mess in white shorts and shirt, with red spreading. It wasn't like my friend. It was a black and white thing going red slowly. Is that what I have to tell his brother? Is that what he wants to hear? And what's the reporter for? If that's what he is. I don't want to see either of them. When I get out of here tomorrow morning, I'm going to Moritz's flat. Except that his sister will be there. I could go to Sophie's, I suppose. She'd let me sleep on her couch. I don't want Joseph's brother and some journalist finding me at the trailer. They wouldn't dare come to the construction site, would they? Or here?

Bobrán transferred some more empty stalks to the recycling barrel, then removed his gloves and twisted one by one the last few stubbornly attached coin-sized products from the remaining stalks. When there was nothing but product left in the threshing bin, he lifted the grey tub off its upturned bucket, tipped it sideways to his right, pouring all the precious product pieces, several hundred of them, into a manila cardboard box standing on the floor to the right of the product tray. He replaced the threshing tub on the bucket and walked over to machine number twenty. To his left he heard the lift arrive and its doors clang open. Alphonse was stepping out. He glanced at Bobrán, nodding a thank you. Bobrán shook his head. It was nothing, his head seemed to say.

Re-entering the downstairs plastics section from the raw-materials area, Philippe held a cigarette between the index and middle fingers of his right hand and a bottle cupped in his left, in such a way that its lip nudged and smeared the inside of his wrist. His feet dragged along the concrete floor, his face was blank, his eyes spent. Several paces behind him, Jacques loped and swung, his face relaxed into its default-position smile, his eyes twinkling.

The two men's conversation at the beer- and coffee-machines had been unusually terse. Instead of confiding their respective worries, as each had earlier intended, Jacques had simply observed that Philippe 'had drunk too much,' adding, 'whatever your problem, getting drunk at work won't help.' Philippe had met this with a grunt and an expletive, after which the two men had stood in silence while Jacques sipped at his small black coffee. Then, with one will, the two men had headed back to work, Jacques trailing in Philippe's wake.

Arriving at his machines, Philippe walked to the control cabinet of machine one. He dropped his cigarette butt and, employing much more force than necessary merely to extinguish it, ground it beneath the heel of his right foot. He looked into his beer bottle, saw nothing, took a sip, looked again, and positioned it carefully out of harm's way in the nearest corner of the grey floor tray.

At the base of the control cabinet lay an oblong red bin which Philippe had earlier filled with a mix of shiny white virgin raw material, light blue colour pellets and grey-blue fluffy-flaky recycled matter. He glanced at the hopper's viewing porthole, which showed very little material remaining. In four years of nights, Philippe had never let a machine run right out of material, nor failed to spot a product fault within minutes, nor fed the machine the wrong material, nor screwed up in any other way. It's not as if this job is hard, Philippe told himself. You concentrate on it for a few minutes or a few seconds at a time off and on throughout the night: that's all it takes.

Philippe bent down, took hold of the red oblong bin and then straightened back up. He closed his eyes a moment and sighed. He lifted the bin above his head, sliding it onto the top of the control cabinet. He took hold of the left side of the stepladder and climbed the five steps to the top. He lifted the hopper lid and turned his upper body to the right. He brushed against the hopper. He slid the bin across the cabinet top, and eased it onto the hopper edge. As he raised the far end of the red oblong bin, its contents began to dribble and then cascade into the hopper. It was then that he briefly lost control. Something within him – a dud synapse, a refractory shoulder muscle, a misfiring neurone – caused him to jolt the bin, with the result that a small portion of the cascading material missed the hopper entirely, raining down instead on the machine itself, falling either side of the melting chamber, some of it rapidly reaching the concrete floor. Philippe was quick to see what was happening, to adjust the tipping angle of the bin, and to halt the spillage. He put the empty bin on the control cabinet and with his right hand smoothed the contents of the hopper. Standing there, it seemed to him that the surface of the raw material was pulsing and fading, PULSING and FADING, coming closer to him, then receding, closer, then receding. He shook his head till his cheeks wobbled and he forced his eyes wide open in an effort to refocus. He flicked the hopper lid up and over and climbed down the ladder. He fetched a broom from behind the control cabinet and swept the spilled material into a little heap, gathered it up with a dustpan and brush and dumped it in the rubbish bin behind the control cabinet.

Philippe picked the beer bottle from the corner of the grey tray, glanced into it, rocked it gently, looked back down into the liquid sloshing from side to side, then went and placed the bottle too in the bin behind the control cabinet. He sat down heavily on his chair. He felt he ought to be angry. With his wife for fucking another man, with his sister for telling him about it, with Jacques for . . . why with Jacques? For not knowing? For needing to be told.

The extra couple of beers had done Philippe a world of good, he had needed them. But now he had had enough. He felt nothing. Which was as much as he wanted to feel. Later he could get angry. Philippe stared down at the light-blue denim covering his chubby knees. The cloth pulsed and faded, PULSED and FADED. He let it. Then he closed his eyes and the woozy pulsing waves continued in his ears, crashing, foaming, above the factory roar. After a while he got up and checked the latest products as they fell from the presses of machines one and two.

Fernando was slowly emerging from his torpor. He had a fine ereção, making him want to arch his back and yawn and stretch. In fact, he reflected happily, he had not been leaning against or even touching the machine so it had fucking-nothing to do with any vibrations. Funny how that word 'ereção' had thrust itself straight into his head. Érection. He must be getting used to it. The first time he had heard it – from the lips of that doctor Boulabem – it had sounded like a word invented just for doctors, or nurses, for medics and women in any case. Maryse used that word. Maybe one day she'd open her door to him wearing a white coat.

Fernando's right arm, which was hanging limply, his fingers almost grazing the concrete floor, felt oddly numb. He brought his hand up to his face. No cigarette. He stared at the patches of yellow skin between the knuckles of his index and middle fingers, then rubbed them together. No pain: no scorched skin. He must have let the butt slip from between his fingers before it burnt him. He leaned over. There it lay on the floor, beside a burst tube of grey ash. He had napped. He laughed shortly, happily. Maryse really fucking-took it out of him. His smile shrank. He often fell asleep for a few minutes at the start of the night shift, after a session with Maryse. She really was a cure.

Fernando's hard-on was softening now. He didn't mind that. He had nowhere to go with it. He would have his nightly Maryse-fantasy a little later, a combination of what they had done so far and what he was looking forward to the next time they met or the time after that. He wanted to try something a little special and wasn't sure she would go for it. People in her line of work are known to have strict rules about things that are too intimate, too personal. Except it's not always clear what those rules are. He wanted to kiss not just her pussy but her butt-hole. After taking a bath with her, preferably. He had never wanted to do that before to anybody. If any of his previous girlfriends had ever suggested such a thing, he would have replied, You have to fucking-be joking. But this afternoon, while they had been attempting some strange contorted position that she claimed was exciting for 'the woman' and helped 'the man' not to come too soon – the kind of thing you'd never think of doing without a manual or an instructor – he had caught sight of it, small and brown and tight and wrinkled. And suddenly he had wanted to kiss it. Like he did her pussy. Would it be off-limits? Fernando heaved a sigh and got to his feet. If only they were real lovers, there would be no limits, would there?

Fernando fetched an empty red oblong bin (as long as his arm, as wide and as deep as his hand) from the floor where it lay and pushed it up against the base of a bag full of new plastic raw material. He opened the bag, finding the scoop inside, the handle toward him. He measured out and emptied into the bin three scoopfulls of the shiny transparent millet-like beads.

Maryse was getting unpredictable. She had enjoyed their fuck that afternoon, he was sure. Possibly for the first time. What is more, she had been willing to let it show. She had been quite affectionate, giving him a kiss on the cheek before showing him the door. Okay, she can be a hard bitch, I don't doubt it. That's hardly surprising, given what she does for a living. But she is better than what she does. Like we all are. Like I am. She isn't *that* job, just like I'm not *this* job. I want her to see me as I fucking-really am. I'd do anything. She might like me.

Still holding the scoop in his right hand, Fernando removed the lid from the waist-high cardboard cylinder standing at the end of machine sixteen. He plunged his arm deep inside and brought the scoop back up heaped high with pinky-grey fluffy recycled matter, which he then unloaded into the red oblong bin. He repeated this action, then put the lid back on the bin and rested the scoop on the lid. His forearm and his rolled sleeve were covered with fluff and flakes. He turned to a small plastic box containing scarlet pellets of colorant on which a white plastic beaker lay sidelong. He half-filled the beaker then poured the pellets into the red oblong bin.

Fernando wouldn't nap again now. Alphonse had fucking-pissed him off earlier, treating the Algerian that way. Maybe he should have done something more to stop it. More? He hadn't lifted a finger. What could he have done? It wasn't so easy to deter Alphonse once he was set on something. Fernando didn't want Rachid thinking ill of him. He liked the man. Not that they talked much. There was something about him, something decent. Alphonse was out of line. You can't go behaving like that.

Fernando took the scoop from the lid of the cardboard cylinder and used it to mix the material in the red oblong bin. He enjoyed this bit of the job. Turning this mix over and over was a bit like stirring a meat stew or a great vat of pickle, getting it all even. He had worked in a restaurant in Oporto once. That seemed a long way off. This stuff was ready for the hopper now, a perfect blend. Just what it liked.

Rachid had run out of things to say to Mehdi. That happened sometimes. It really wasn't a problem. They had had a good long talk. They didn't have to be speaking all the time. Rachid had told Mehdi about Malika's smile, how she had leaned right into him, even slipping her right arm, the one that wasn't cradling Fatima, under his own, and giving him a little hug. Maybe he had embroidered a little, to make sure Mehdi grasped the significance of it.

Rachid rose from his chair, went round the end of machine eight and bent down at the aluminium slats of machine nine just as the presses opened and a product dropped through. He had almost forgotten what it looked like when Malika smiled. Well, not so much what it *looked* like: he had seen her smile at Fatima every day. What he had forgotten was what her smile *felt* like full on, directed at you. It was a beam of warmth and light: you wanted to linger in its path.

Rachid had caught the product and was looking at it carefully. During a morning shift the previous week, there had been a drop in pressure and the engineers had had to be called in. He tilted the product this way and that, before dropping it into the threshing tub. He had felt silly telling Mehdi about Malika's smile. As if it wasn't the most natural thing in the world for a woman to smile at a man. But Mehdi hadn't been around much after his death, so hadn't seen what things had been like between his parents.

Malika hadn't displayed her grief for long, quickly switching all her love to Fatima, shielding her from our storm of sorrow, yet it must have been hard for her too. She wept and raged for a week and then stopped. She never blamed him. He wished she had. It hadn't been till quite recently, when one day the rider of the moped had arrived in tears at their door begging to be forgiven and demanding to be held responsible, that Rachid had understood that nobody was to blame: the moped rider hadn't been going fast; Rachid hadn't been holding Mehdi's hand any less tightly than usual. Mehdi had wrenched his little hand free and run out into the road. He had never explained why he did that. Rachid had never asked. It was as if the child had had a death wish. Such a happy child. Could a child have a death wish? Not that it was Mehdi's fault either. You can't blame a child for dying.

Rachid lifted the grey floor tray and tipped all its products into the threshing tub. Then he went to machine eight and did the same. He sat back down on his chair. He liked his chair. There were people moving around at the top end of the machine aisle, coming and going, back and forth, but Rachid didn't pay them any mind: he preferred to look at the grey concrete floor and just think. Since Mehdi's death, Malika, Fatima and he had not been a proper family. It was as though his wife and little girl were way over there and he was stuck on his own way over here. He didn't spend any time alone with Fatima. He didn't know what to do with her. Besides, he was never really around. It was true what Malika said.

About a month ago now, Malika had come up to him while he was sitting at the little table in the kitchen and shaken him hard. He had been staring into space. Fatima was on the floor playing with a knife that must have fallen from a shelf. The knife was round-ended and so blunt that the child couldn't have done herself any harm. He had heard the toilet flush, then Malika had walked in, gently taking the knife from Fatima, as he had looked up and seen it in the child's hand. Malika had taken him by both shoulders. Where in the devil's name are you? You're growing old and grey before our eyes and we're missing you. She shook him. We haven't gone anywhere. We haven't left. When are you going to show us your face, instead of that mask, that blank grey mask? How long do you think we will wait? Rachid had looked down, then made an excuse and gone out.

What Malika didn't understand was that to come back to them, really to come back, he would have to leave Mehdi behind, and that was something he could never do. Once you have children, whatever happens to them, even if they die, they're with you for the rest of your life. That was what Rachid had thought.

In the middle of the aisle, halfway between their respective machines, Marcel and Jacques were standing laughing. Marcel had told Jacques a dirty joke. He had a great store of them. Jacques had no head for jokes, clean or dirty. But Marcel needed a solid reason to laugh, so for him jokes served a real purpose.

The warning light on the control cabinet of machine number eleven lit up. Marcel had his back to it, but Jacques saw it at once and tilted his head at it. Marcel thanked Jacques with a wink of his left eye, and went off to see what was wrong.

I guess I'd better check the hoppers, Jacques thought, turning. They must be running low.

Jacques felt so much better than earlier. Maybe it was Marcel's dirty joke, but more likely it was the threshing. He slowly climbed the stepladder at machine number three till he came to rest on the top step of the ladder. His left hand swung out to take hold of the left edge of the hopper lip while his right hand carefully pulled the lid up, back and over.

Threshing often made Jacques feel better. He had noticed this before. Tonight, on account of his late arrival and the consequent backlog of products, he had done a lot of threshing in a short time. Threshing plastic was like a lot of the jobs Jacques did on his farm: slow and repetitive and requiring all the muscles of your body to get involved, and to work in some kind of concert, while also demanding attention to detail. The other thing he enjoyed about threshing plastic was that, like threshing cereal crops, it separated what was valuable from what wasn't. He liked the way the empty skeletons floated to the surface, while the saleable product fell under its own weight to the bottom of the bin. There was a pleasing connection – wasn't there – between weight and value, density and permanence, gravity and worth.

Machine three's hopper was almost empty. He was going to have to mix up a bin-full. He closed the lid and descended the steps, then checked the hopper of machine four, with the same result.

All in all, it was a good thing he hadn't driven on. He would never have reached Spain, Paris, Italy or anywhere else. Besides, even if he had, what would he have done there but turn round and come back? Okay, maybe a coffee and some local cake might have been nice – whatever they have for breakfast in those parts. More likely he would have fallen asleep at the wheel, and ended his life upside down in a ditch. Even if he had driven for hours and hours, his mind would never have cleared as effectively as it had now. Sitting staring at the taillights of the car ahead, with only your accelerator foot and your steering hand doing any kind of work: that was no way to clear your mind. It was standing here threshing this stubborn plastic that had helped him over his fury at the doctor, and pushed all his worries to one side. He had no reason to panic. He knew that now.

Jacques was plumbing a paradox: sex with Jeanne was so good that somehow it didn't really matter. How was that? He laughed. Even if he lost his powers, his manhood – but, really, how likely was that? – it was so good just to be with her that everything seemed sure to work out just fine. If his old boy collapsed – but, really, why should it? – hell, they would always come up with something else to do at night, some other way to be close to one another and to love. If it came to it, they would just have to go right ahead and invent a whole new bag of tricks. Jacques laughed, not as before with Marcel, not nearly so loudly, but much longer.

BOOK THREE. MIXING.

In which the peasant and the Portuguee turn factory into playground, the banister-walking Gypsy gets help with his reading, the inquisitive Pole finds recruits for his tableau. On the streets of Grandgobier, conscript soldiers celebrate imminent release from military service while in the factory yoked men slacken their harnesses, unbuckle their belts, unbutton their lips. The hoppers are more or less full, the floor trays more or less empty, each man more or less universally greeted. Minds turn to murder, hands to the pump-pump, while breasts swell, bellies sag, gorges rise, and pennies slowly drop.

*

23. Colours and Textures.

Colours.   In the streets encircling Éts. Boucan, beneath the skimmed-milk light of the lamps, nothing but greys: variations of light, dark, and darkest grey, every brighter shade now drowned in a monochrome palette, gentle on the eyes, dulling the mind. The metallurgy sections, dripping with machines, showed no colour but grey – save where the night security man's torch ripped through a photo of glamorous flesh or football strip, slashed across a flag or a postcard picture of some faraway homeland. On the plastics-section shop floors, both upstairs and down-, further corrupted by the neon glare, only hues unknown to nature appeared: shiny bright pinks; gleaming dark greens; blacks like mirrors glinting; blues you will never meet in eye, sky or sea; yellows from off-custard to desiccated mustard; oranges from darkening lozenge to quick-farmed chemical-rainbow trout.

Phase Two.   Upstairs, erect before the great semi-automatic machine number twenty-one, its pint-sized enterogically preoccupied operator glanced happily at his chronomètre: twenty-two hours, no minutes, and twenty-six seconds precisely, twenty-seven, twenty-eight, twenty-nine. High time to remove the tea towel from my chair, re-sponge the seat with disinfectant, then plonk myself down, placing my buttocks in the kindly hands of the Creator. There! No sooner said than done! Ahh! That's better. But where is that little Gypsy with my coffee? On his slow and sullen way, no doubt.

Now, to consider the night ahead – and the day behind! No more dwelling on the drab lives of fellow workers! My agenda, as ever at this hour: a survey of the principal planetary, international, national, regional, city, neighbourhood, factory, domestic, and familial events to have come to my attention during the course of this day. In reverse scalar order (quite exceptionally!) in view of the unwonted salience of the domestic dimension occasioned by an event meriting immediate, albeit brief, attention: the intelligence, communicated to us by letter, that the spouse – Monique or Niquette (as I know her) – is not host, as was reasonably feared, to a lethal tumour, but rather to an innocuous cyst, now scheduled for prompt excision. A non-event perhaps, a dog that failed to bark, and yet – in the absence of any spectacular development at any other level (planetary, international, etc.) – clearly the most ponderous event for myself (the subject and centre after all of these daily contemplations) in view of both its positive and indeed negative implications, as I shall endeavour honestly to examine). From this domestic reprieve (and, to be frank, anti-climax) I shall proceed, via neighbourhood gossip, to a citywide story; thence to the latest exposure of regional administrative jiggery-pokery; only then turning my attention to national stories including the near escape of Jean-Marie Le Pen from a cowardly arson attack; finally, I shall consider the disquieting news from Argentina.

Jean leaned forward and pulled his chair a fraction closer to his machine. His feet felt good on the footrest, his back was well supported. Phase two of his shift was under way. This too would pass.

Visceral. At this moment, in a manner of speaking, there was a material link, a solid and unbroken bodily-textile-wooden-plaster-brick-mortar-and-rendering and (once again) bodily link – of a sort – stretching (by no means tenuously) from the parchment-skinned machine operative seated on his rickety chair, smoking his cigarette and staring at the grey cement floor, all the way to the other side of the wall, through the muscle, bone, gristle and skin of the said worker's hunched shoulders, via his cotton shirt, through the back of his wooden chair, his threadbare grey jacket hanging from said chair and crushed against the side of the huge old wooden table; thence across the width of that table and onward to the wall against which the table had long ago been shoved; and further on still, through the wall, piercing its plaster, bricks, mortar and external rendering, and only then entering by way of his comparatively young and substantial shoulders the body of the stab victim on the street at the back of Éts. Boucan, who, as coincidence surely had it, originally hailed from the same nation as the machine operative, and who was slumped – the stab victim – in his (unenviable but inevitable) turn, against the base of that factory's outer wall, thereby completing, in the aforesaid manner of speaking, that material and unbroken bodily-textile-etc. link – of a sort – (see above). Such links, however, are mostly silent, unacknowledged and unreported. The paramedics, for instance, attending the scene in response to an anonymous emergency call from the rundown rat-grey apartment building across the road, would have missed such a detail and, even had it been pointed out to them, would surely and rightly have paid it no heed. The victim's vital signs were more pressing, emergency-contact details more pertinent, the integrity of his internal organs more germane.

Breathing. Jacques was sat on his chair at machine three, his legs akimbo, his chin on his chest. His happy thoughts of Jeanne had slowly scattered. A delectable nothingness had taken their place in his mind. Saliva was bubbling up on his nether lip, his eyes were closed. His breathing came slowly, quiet amid all the factory hubbub. His nodding body was in equilibrium and at peace. His arms hung at his sides.

Equality. The sparkle-eyed watchman clipped his torchlight to his belt and leaving it switched on allowed it to swing freely as he walked. He had no inclination to interrogate shadows. Or people. He passed in review the men he was meant to question. He didn't know their names. He had some shorthand idea of their origins: Marseille (you could hear it in the accent); Africa (you could see it in the skin *and* hear it in the accent); Britain (you could read it from the clothes, see it in the skin *and* hear it in the accent). Some origins were less clearcut: there was a North African, anyone could see that; and an Iberian – but for all Tomec could have said at first encounter, they might have been respectively Tunisian and Catalan, Moroccan and Gallego. Mostly Tomec thought of the men in images remembered or potential: from charcoal sketch to study-in-oils to sculpture-in-the-round. There was – it couldn't be gainsaid – no egalitarianism in aspect: some people were just more interesting to look at than others.

Seven. The man was weary as hell. He walked through the plastic flaps from the raw-materials area, those great wide shoulders doing all the work, his feet dragging, his fleck-eyed face looking waxed and blind. There was white-grey dust on the tops of the thighs of his trousers and a large two-sided rip beneath his left knee, forming a little flap that hung down, winking, showing then quickly concealing a patch of brown hairy leg. He would ask his mother to sew it.

They were the same trousers as always: dirty blue with a vertical band of matt crimson, about a centimetre across, running from hip to ankle on the outside leg, both sides. Like he was some kind of fancy doorman.

He looked very serious now. He held a polystyrene cup in each hand. You could see the steam rising. Luigi stared at him, took a puff of his cigarette to keep it going. The man was on the third stair, with the face of someone trudging through mud, or walking the plank, a pirate in a foul mood. His hair in ringlets, his face unshaven, his eyes bloodshot, he certainly looked like a pirate. But were pirates Gypsies? Or Gypsies pirates? The slope-backed Italian experienced a thought.

Hey! he shouted. Bet you can't go up the stair rail without spilling a drop!

Bobrán stopped dead. He looked into the cups, each containing an espresso, two sugars, no milk. He glanced straight past Luigi, over his head, and saw Marcel watching. The cups were only half full.

How much?

Luigi's mouth opened slowly, his cigarette hung suspended. He blinked. How much what?

You said you bet.

Bobrán waited. The steam had quit rising.

Luigi shut his lips, took a puff, short and sharp and deep. He looked at the floor, noticed the masticated remnants of one of the foreman's burnt-out matchsticks. The Gypsy seemed confident. Maybe too confident? How much could I bear to lose?

Thirty francs! Luigi yelled.

Bobrán's eyes smiled blood.

That's not a bet. It's a ticket to a show in the cheapskate seats. You want me to walk that banister with two cups of coffee and not spill a drop? That's some act. I could fall. You'd better form a syndicate, have a whip round. If you're serious. Because I don't get up on that banister for less than a week's wages. Except for my own amusement. Got it?

By the time Luigi nodded, Bobrán was at the top of the stairs and his thoughts were way ahead of him.

Salad. The ambulance had arrived promptly, alerted by a family of Macedonians who, disturbed by the shouting and whooping of the aggressors, had risen from their supper of large gherkins, sausage meat and salad and hurried to their neighbours, who possessed a phone.

The stabbing victim had a strong pulse and was conscious. The paramedics lifted him onto a stretcher.

How bad am I?

You'll live. They didn't damage anything essential.

It hurt him to laugh, but he laughed. It was painful to speak, but he spoke.

I told them they were losers, he said.

Receding.   Marcel was sitting at his machine number eleven. One of the products had jammed, halting the presses. He had had to pull the guard back, detach the sprue and brush a little oil onto the mould face, before closing the guard again and initiating a new cycle. He was waiting to see if it happened again.

Marcel's other worries had all abated. He studied his reflection in the guard. Chantal sometimes teased him about his belly, saying he was four months gone, but seen like this, sitting down, no one would notice. A vivid memory made him start: Chantal, poking him in the belly that morning as she climbed off him and headed for the bathroom, pressing yesterday's panties to her cunt. Funny how some women just come and go, Marcel thought – Chantal among them: no lingering smooch, no purring endgame. Suited him fine.

Marcel jerked his head to one side to check how his hair moved. The Portuguese guy had done a good job, leaving it long at the front. Fashionable yet discreet too. That man had untapped talent. Cutting hair was no cinch: Marcel had tried it in prison and escaped a beating. He was pleased with Fernando's work. He would have to face straight into a gale for anyone to notice his receding hairline.

Marcel sometimes wondered what Chantal saw in him. She was a good catch. Sophisticated, educated, good family, and a truly great fuck. They were getting married, wasn't that enough? Maybe he had started off as her bit of rough, but he had ended up winning her heart. There was a film with that storyline. The machine press was closing and opening its great shiny jaws, closing and opening, closing and opening, smooth and regular, like a giant clam on speed.

Toilet.   Clumsily, using his behind, Philippe half-closed the door of the toilet. His left hand switched on the light, his right unzipped his trousers and extracted his cock. He sighed, blowing out his cheeks, while his bladder emptied. Rocking gently forward and back, he aimed his urine at the edge of the bowl, circling it carefully. He liked to see his jetting piss pick shit off the porcelain. A powerful and sonorous burp surprised him. His breath was foul: pastis mixed with beer mixed with coffee, the entire libation percolated through smoke.

On the floor, in the corner, to the left of the toilet, lay a small-format porn mag, open near its centre and stained with water or urine, you couldn't say which. He made out a girl pouting up at him, offering herself, breasts ballooning. The pale wall before him, beneath the cistern, showed a line-drawing in black ink of a huge phallus, perfectly vertical, reposing on two orbs. It struck Philippe as almost beautiful, something a prehistoric artist might have produced. Alongside, there was a phone number and the legend: Salope suce grosses bites. Appeler le soir de préférence.

Imagining his bladder was empty, Philippe shook his cock and put it away. As his left thigh grew damp, he realized his mistake. Okay, okay, I get it – I drank too much, he said as he left the toilet.

Stooge or Rebel?   Tomec stopped to insert his key in the security-clock. It made a decisive, ringing click, yet left a hollow echo in his ears: decisiveness was what he lacked. He should either get on with the shaming task of inter-rogation or seize the pleasure of throwing it back in Boucan's face. Or was there a middle way? Evasion? Compromise? He switched off his torch and walked through metallurgy in the dark. What if he called the men together and made it sound inoffensive, like a routine announcement: 'if anybody is in possession of any information regarding . . . ?' He imagined them closing in on him like a scrum. Do you think we'd nark on one another? He might deny he was doing the boss's bidding. They would sneer and cackle. He could say he was merely there to discuss the event. Yeah. Right. What is there to discuss? He would have no answer. So better one by one. Easy ones first. The Brit, the Italian, the Gypsy, the Portuguee, the old peasant: the dull and the ignorant. What about the African? The Algerian? Not so sure. Tomec's step had speeded up. He was perspiring. He was panting. I'll have to come up with a form of words, he grumbled.

START.   Bobrán had checked his machines fifteen and twenty, picked up a chair and taken it and the two coffees round the end of machine twenty-one. Between tearing a bunch of black cable ties from their sprue, re-closing the machine guard and pressing the START button, Jean stretched out his right arm, took hold of his coffee and brought it to his lips. He glanced at Bobrán to thank him.

As the presses closed and the melting chamber filled, Bobrán looked sideways at the semi-automatic: you might almost imagine he took an interest in the process. Jean studied his face. Inscrutable Gypsy, inscrutable like the

Chinese. You can never guess what's on their minds. Woman trouble most likely. Pretty boy like that, brown curls.

Missing your girlfriend?

Sorry?

Jean sipped at his coffee then nodded as though privy to all life's secrets.

For a young man, he pronounced, the worst thing about working nights is thinking about her tucked up alone in bed, all nice and warm while you're stuck in here.

Jean opened the guard, leaned forward, tore the product from the mould, applied a quick brushstroke of oil, closed the guard and pressed the button.

The little Gypsy was smiling . . . a shy smile, Jean thought.

I knew it, Jean said. I can always tell what people are thinking, though your lot can be somewhat inscrutable.

Inscrutable?

Hard to understand.

The presses closed.

Bobrán considered the word 'inscrutable.' Hard to understand. He thought of the letter in his pocket. He could wait till he saw Moritz, ask this little guy, or pick someone else. Someone who could be trusted or who hardly ever talked to anyone.

The letter from Joseph's brother lay compact and incomprehensible against Bobrán's thigh. He slid his hand into his pocket.

Jean watched Bobrán unfold the letter.

What have you got there?

A letter I can't read.

The presses opened and Jean pushed the guard back. It might still be woman trouble, he reasoned. A love letter. Jean separated product from sprue then, as the presses closed again, took Bobrán's letter. Quality paper, a side and a half of neat handwriting.

Pliant. Gérard Boucan had grown weary of being driven around, his chauffeur's pinko-Latino music prattling in his ears. Besides, his mind was fixed on the graffiti. Why sling such ancient history at him now? It had been a war, hadn't it? How many people came out smelling of roses? He wanted to take a peek into the factory, as if by seeing an operative or two he might get a clearer picture of his enemy. Enemy? Less than that, and more. Of course, the graffiti artist – 'artist,' pah! – didn't have to be someone from the night shift. He understood that. Still.

Gérard had instructed Jorge to drive down Cours Modelon, and take a left before the plant, then first right. There was a window high up. If his memory served, there was a ledge at knee height you could stand on to see in. He had taken advantage of it a couple of times before. He had taken his wife there late one night, just after he had met her, before she knew who he was. Twenty-five years ago? Damn-near twenty-six. Shit.

You see those men? he had enquired as she stood on tiptoes on the ledge. She wondered why she had to watch a man in a factory scratching his belly in the dead of the night.

Yes . . . ? she had said, turning back and gazing down.

They all work for me, Gérard had said, catching her scent as she put his arms round her thighs to lift her down. She was warm and pliant in his arms that night, he remembered. Her legs hadn't seemed chubby at all. But a woman changes. And then it's too late.

Anything.   Tomec had been striding fast through metallurgy, but now slowed down. He felt he was ready. He would take them one at a time, however they presented themselves: no point trying to second-guess their reactions. He pushed through the hanging plastics flaps and into the din. He turned right and walked round the foot of the raised glass-fronted office, then left down the machine aisle. Luigi was the first man he saw. Tomec stretched out his hand.

Putting down his paper, Luigi squinted up at the security guard. He smiled and placed the front half of his right hand, just the fingers, cold little sausages, in Tomec's grasp. Tomec quickly let them fall.

Heard about the new graffiti? he asked.

Um . . . Did you say graffiti?

Tomec stared at the Italian and nodded.

Luigi looked at the end of his cigarette, then flicked the ash away.

I never heard anything about anything, Luigi said, squinting.

Tomec stood back and looked past the man.

Well if you should happen to hear – as you say – 'anything about anything,' please be sure to let me know, okay?

He didn't stay for an answer.

Screw design.   Anyone who wished to understand what was going on around them in such a place as this plastics section would have needed to learn a whole new vocabulary: molten plastic flow rate, moulding cycle, shear stresses, injection pressure, screw design, parts handling, melt control, flow viscosity, compounding and colouring, plasticization. But that would only be the start of it.

Joint.   Maryse and Evelyne were sitting on a sofa in Evelyne's studio flat, sharing a joint that Evelyne had rolled. There was little demand for their business on Tuesday evenings, so they often met up, usually at a cinema.

On this particular evening, Evelyne had offered to cook a fondue. She was a dab-hand at fondue: her father had once had a Swiss girlfriend who had taught Evelyne all her best tricks. As the dope took hold, the pauses in the women's conversation grew longer, and their laughter, when it came, more random and uproarious.

Evelyne had begun to talk about her customers, a subject which Maryse, keen to keep the worlds of work and leisure separate, usually avoided. However, when her friend named the immigrants' hostel that was home to Fernando, a Porguguese customer recently sent to her by a sympathetic doctor, Maryse's ears pricked up – though her face and body (schooled in the dissembling arts) betrayed nothing.

Did I tell you I'd started working the Sonacotra hostel? Evelyne had begun.

Maryse leaned toward her, holding out the joint, and shook her head.

I met a cool guy there a couple of weeks ago. Evelyne laughed. Some of the men I already knew booked me as a birthday surprise for a fellow resident, an African. He's shy, they told me. We've never seen him with a woman, they said. 'Why not?' I thought. She shrugged her shoulder and flicked the joint.

'Why not, I thought,' Maryse parroted, bursting into laughter, then imitating Evelyne's nonchalant shrug-and-flick.

Well? Evelyne asked, also laughing.

Well? Maryse said, copying Evelyne again.

Well, one Sunday evening they led me to the guy's room, knocked on the door, told him what the deal was, then kind of bundled me inside. I had had a few drinks earlier with one of the others, so I was feeling pretty relaxed, so I tried to get this guy comfortable, even pretending to feel hurt he didn't want me, offered him the full range of options that few men can turn down. But he wasn't interested. 'Let's talk,' he said. So we talked. He was a good talker. He had a room full of books, and pictures of actors and actresses on the wall, classical stuff. After about three quarters of an hour, I said to him, 'Look, how do you want to play this?' 'What do you mean?' he said, looking cagey. 'Those guys are going to question me. Time is almost up. Shall I say we sat and chatted about the theatre or shall I tell them you were a tiger and gave this girl the time of her life? Or something in between?' His face lit up slowly with a kind of schoolboy mischief. 'Well,' he said, 'I guess your work is a kind of performance, isn't it? So why not put on a little show for them? Huh?' 'So shall we fake it together?' I said. 'I'll follow your lead,' he said, uncertainly. So I took the Jane Birkin part, without the soppy words, hamming it up, building slowly to some serious moaning – a lot more than I ever squandered on any of the guys now milling around in the corridor – and ending with a full-throated scream and a lot of post-coital-type cooing, while he joined in with some very creditable virile-bass grunting. I thought he was sweet, actually, and I was glad to see him enjoying himself. Then, as we congratulated one another in hushed voices, I undid the top of my blouse, ruffled my hair, mussed my clothing, smudged my makeup around and said goodbye. He kissed me on the cheek and said I was a great actress. I told the guys in the corridor that I was going home, calling it a day, that I was all fucked out. 'That good?' they asked, their eyes bulging. 'You have absolutely no idea,' I said. Then I walked away from them, dragging my feet, bowing my legs like I'd ridden rodeo for a week.

Vanished.   Jean had taken a pair of half-moon reading glasses from his bag. He usually wore them only at one a.m. for his meal-break, as he sat reading a book, while he digested his meal. Jean looked over his glasses, dabbed his brush in oil and passed it lightly over the knockout pins. Then he closed the guard. He picked the sheet off his knee where he had laid it. Bobrán moved his seat closer.

'Cher Monsieur,' Jean read, 'Je me présente. Je m'appelle Albert Gbenye, je suis le frère aîné de Joseph.'

Jean read well. He made it seem easy. He glanced at Bobrán, catching his look of concentration, and continued.

'Joseph nous a souvent parlé de vous dans ses lettres. Il y écrivait que vous étiez amis. C'est en vertu de cela que je me permets de vous écrire et . . .'

The presses of the great old semi-automatic machine twenty-one gaped open. Jean looked up in irritation, put the paper sheet down on his knee with his left hand and opened the guard with his right. Thank you, Bobrán said. He leaned forward and took the letter from the little guy's right knee, and then walked away. This was how he would do it. He didn't need to trust anyone. Each man could read him just two or three lines. He looked at the letter. There weren't that many lines. Exactly sixteen. Then he committed to memory the letter so far: 'I introduce myself. My name is Albert Gbenye, I am Joseph's elder brother. Joseph often talked of you in his letters. He wrote that you were friends. It is on these grounds that I permit myself to write to you and . . .' Following with his finger the rough shape of the memorized words, Bobrán found what he thought was the place Jean had reached, and folded the letter in two to mark it.

Jean closed the guard and watched as Bobrán walked out of view. Damn Gypsy. It was just getting interesting. Friends with some African. Some Joseph Gbenye, the brother of this Albert. Except that it's in the past. Maybe the guy died or vanished. People do that. Especially Africans. Well, well. Maybe he'll ask me to read some more later.

Textures.   There were no fresh petals to touch to your cheeks, no bursting-ripe fig flesh to crush between tongue and soft palate, no ivory to stroke, no pig's-liver slime, no dry-as-bone balsa wood. Yet textures there were in the factory aplenty: satiny granules, ground-glass abrasives, tungsten-hard metals, thick oozing oils, irritant fluff, slimy grease, skin-pricking dust, gravelly gunge. It was more than enough to keep touch alive.

24. Giving Way . . . Standing Ground.

Giving Way. Mathieu was on one of his rounds, limping forth from machine to machine to check product, satisfying himself that all was well.

The moment Marcel glimpsed the supervisor coming toward him, he eased back against the side of machine eleven, melted from the older man's path. He lowered his head as if fascinated by the floor, yet trained his eyes sidelong and upward on Mathieu, who stood motionless, his hand on the guard, methodically clearing his mind as he waited for the presses to open. (Nadine breathing, Nadine dead. Nadine breathing, Nadine dead. Nadine breathing . . .)

Marcel observed the loop of ragged string that sustained the supervisor's trousers. He saw the man's belly curved like a toad's, hard and muscular. He saw his mangled left hand, his hairless arms, the freshly picked red-raw psoriasis beneath his chin, the translucent scales on his forehead and face, the matchstick immobilized in the man's mouth. The presses opened.

A piece got stuck just now, Marcel shouted.

Mathieu blinked, pulled open the guard and caught the piece, thrust the guard shut again, then began to nod as he moved the product round, regarding it with distrust. Placated, he tossed it into the tray at his feet, took three short steps to the control panel, and studied the dials. Marcel's eyes tracked the old man.

Mathieu removed the matchstick from between his lips, stared at its black slimy tip, then employed it to probe his gums. As he turned and glanced past Marcel, he performed a stylized oil-brushing gesture. From the corner of his eye, he saw Marcel nod. (Nadine: what would she look like just after dying? Much the same? How different? He had loved her in every conceivable state, hadn't he? What then of death? Would he love her dead also?)

Concession. Philippe knew that Jacques had been right, but there was no need to concede the point, not in so many words.

He bent down over the peasant's grey pate and said, Keep an eye on my machines. I need some coffee. It'll clear my brains. I'll be gone a while. Like a child with a tongue twister, he delivered the words with dogged precision, determined not to slur or stumble.

Jacques grinned and opened his eyes and shifted on his chair. He looked up into Philippe's face.

Take your time.

Their eyes met at last.

We'll talk later, Philippe said.

As Jacques glanced around him, scratching his jaw, he noticed Marcel looking his way. Marcel shaped his right hand into an open fist as if to grasp a tube, raised it so that his thumb and index finger encircled his nose, then sharply rotated his hand back and forth and smiled, jerking his head in the direction of Philippe's back as it vanished through the hanging plastic flaps and into the raw-materials area.

Jacques grinned at Marcel, but his head remained motionless. He would neither confirm nor deny, barely even acknowledge the question. If Philippe was drunk, Jacques was not going to comment on it to Marcel. That made Marcel laugh.

Mute.   Gérard hadn't told Jorge why he wanted him to drive to the back of the factory. It seemed demeaning somehow, but as Jorge eased the car round the corner, Gérard told him to pull up. Under the weak light of the street lamps a man sprinkled the pavement with water from a can, then worked it around with a stiff broom.

Gérard hauled himself out of the car and shuffled along the pavement till he reached the spot. The man stopped his work to glance up at him. Gérard looked important in his crumpled but costly clothes.

There was a knifing, the man volunteered, with a glance at Gérard's car and chauffeur. Gérard took out a cigar and lit it with a match. He waited. He didn't move. The man had spoken with a thick, unfamiliar accent.

I live opposite. I saw what happened. My wife doesn't like our children to see blood on the pavement in the morning. This could be our front yard.

Gérard looked up at the factory wall and its narrow high window, smaller than he had remembered. At that moment, he might have observed Salvatore reading Voltaire's letters and Luigi in the distance with his sci-fi comic, and possibly someone scratching his belly. He looked at the ledge, then returned to the car. The Macedonian turned to watch him go. The pavement looked wet and clean.

Blood, diluted to a delicate pink, lurked in the cracks and gaps between the cobblestones, veining the gutter, imperceptible in the absence of floodlighting. By morning it would be a livid brown.

Water.   Tomec had talked to Marcel, who had winked and said he should try the Sicilian or the Marseillais. Personally, he wasn't interested in stuff like that, history, wars: not my line. Besides, where was I in those days?

Tomec looked across the machine aisle and saw Jacques on his chair, eyes closed again and dribbling, arms hanging down so low his fingernails almost scratched the floor. Tomec walked over to Eric, who put down a novel by Steinbeck. It took a while for the Pole to explain the graffiti situation. He kept glancing at the bunch of black grapes depicted on the cover of Eric's book. The Polish words *Grona Gniewu* came to him, unbidden. He had seen the film too, in Paris, not long after it was released. *Les raisins de la colère*, starring Henry Fonda. Eric looked at Tomec blankly.

Collabo? Eric asked, trying to copy Tomec's pronunciation.

Collaborationniste . . .

Oh. Qui avec?

Vichy . . .

L'eau?

Vichy . . . it's a town. You heard of Pétain?

Of course. Collabo. Okay. Vichy. Right. Eric waited.

The war. The German occupation. There were French who collaborated, right?

With the Nazis, Eric interjected.

Precisely. With the Nazis . . . You're British, right?

Yeah. But I know nothing about it, Eric said, fidgeting with his hair.

Tomec stared at Eric, then briefly closed his eyes.

No, no. I believe you. Absolutely.

How is it, Tomec wondered, that the English manage to look like they're lying, even when maybe they're not, seeming devious when merely dumb? How do they do that? And why?

Tomec had noticed that Rachid was staring at him. It was as if the man sensed something. Tomec decided to leave the North African to last: he looked like something was bugging him. Tomec turned and headed for the lift. He would try the upstairs men.

Deliverance.   . . . plastic granules are delivered to a hopper, from which they are fed through a throat onto a rotating screw. The screw moves and compresses the material through a heated chamber where the granules soften to such a degree that they become fluid and can be delivered to a section of the heating chamber known as the measuring chamber . . .

Flourish. Megan was sitting in the snug of a pub in Strathclyde, waiting for her girlfriends, Anne and Maddie, to join her for a pie. She had skipped a tutorial to write Eric a dear-john. It was long overdue. She had been patient. She had travelled all the way to Grandgobier to visit him. She had stayed a whole month last summer. When he said on the phone that he had never been so happy as in that factory in the middle of Europe working solid nights, it had been the last straw. She had kept silent. Then he had added: I belong here, I miss nothing about England. She had made an excuse and put the phone down. He wouldn't hear her tears or anger. She had gone round to Maddie's hall of residence. By England, Eric had meant Britain; by Britain, he had meant her.

Dump the wee Sassenach gobshite, Maddie told her over a game of cards.

Megan used her fountain pen and best turquoise ink, but still the letter wouldn't come right. She had a dictionary beside her, to check her spelling, and a pint of black velvet on a damp mat. She wrote carefully in a big fat hand, with many a loop and flourish. She was particularly proud of her g's and f's. Her eyes had dried now. She had almost finished her neat copy.

Murderees. Mathieu had worked his way down the left-hand row of machines, checking each product with meticulous care, seeking inner void and quiet as he leaned against each guard door waiting for presses to open, his mind assailed with images of Nadine as he tossed a product into a grey floor tray and his concentration splintered, then straining to scrape from his retina the murky film deposited by Luigi's true-crime magazine, summoning for that purpose cleansing riffs from solos by Dizzy or Bird. But Mathieu's thoughts would not stay still tonight: Nadine's imagined death mask; the face of the murderee at her birthday party; Clifford and Bird, the forever silenced, in classic photo portraits staring.

Having seen Mathieu coming, Rachid quickly completed a bout of threshing at machine eight, and headed for the toilet. The Algerian liked to take advantage of Mathieu's regular tours in order to perform his ablutions, fetch coffee or a beer. He didn't like to ask others to supervise his machines, much less leave them unattended.

Mathieu reverted to the story he had glimpsed in Luigi's magazine. He did not wonder why. He did not want to examine his curiosity. But nor could he continue to resist it. He wanted to know more about that medical student from Metz, the dementing mother and the method used.

Educational.   Salvatore was standing at his ease at the end of Philippe's machine number two, his left hand working the hand-exerciser while his right flicked through the pile of newspapers and magazines on top of the recycling bin. As Rachid, returning from the toilet, drew level, Salvatore beckoned him to his side and informed him of the strike meeting scheduled for 11.15 p.m. Rachid inclined his ear to the Sicilian but gazed back up the aisle.

Mathieu emerged from behind Rachid's machine eight and, instead of crossing the aisle to check Salvatore's machine seven, hobbled back up the aisle, his mouth working the matchstick round and round, his eyebrows contorting. Rachid hoped there wasn't a problem with his machines. Surely he wouldn't have missed something? His warning lights weren't on. Had he been careless? Ever? He needed this job.

Mathieu walked straight past the two men. Salvatore was talking about the global economic conjuncture, Raymond Barre's austerity plan, and the union's response. An avalanche of words. Rachid knew them all, backward and forward.

Look, I'll be there, he cut in.

Rachid found *Le Nouvel Observateur* in the middle of Philippe's pile of papers and walked back with it to his machines. He liked to read news stories and features. Or just turn the pages. Sometimes he read out extracts to Mehdi. It was educational, he thought. Mehdi always had funny questions, odd and original ways of seeing things, just like a kid. Rachid felt light and alert: it had done him good to urinate. He sat down, his back to the huge wooden table. The warmth from Malika's smile had not yet dissipated. He lit a cigarette and thumbed through the magazine. There was a feature on 'the family in crisis.' He would skip that.

Plot.   The storyteller despised plot. It stank out his nostrils. At the first clever contrivance, flash-forward or -back, the first rabbit out of a hat, coup de théatre or deus ex machina, he would toss the offending book at the wall and pick up the next one. The corners of his room were littered.

What did he have against plot? Perhaps if the curve of his own life had followed any discernible pattern (as some lives undoubtedly do: accusation, arrest, prison, flight, exile, struggle, vindication and redemption), it might have been easier, even natural, to cast the lives of others as stories. But most lives, he thought – good, ordinary, everyday lives – however replete with event and situation, defied story, suspense and plot, and the result of dragooning them into such moulds could only bore and irritate him. All it demonstrated, the storyteller thought, was the cleverness and prestidigitatory skills of the entertainer.

Spat.   Luigi put down his graphic novel, his head full of pneumatic aliens, shiny metal and mega-deaths. He stared at the supervisor. Back already, checking the product again so soon? Must think something is about to go wrong. All agitated. Can't keep still. Making those funny noises again. Who was it said he plays trumpet somewhere? Who would know that? Ba-ba-do-bah. Philippe? Weird. Must think he's Louis Armstrong. Louis is English for Luigi, isn't it? French too.

Salvatore strode across the machine aisle, catching his compatriot's eye.

Vieni? he asked, tipping an imaginary cup of coffee at his mouth.

Go, Mathieu said, intercepting the exchange and tilting his head sharply at Luigi's machine fourteen. I'll take care of them for five minutes.

No thanks. I'll go later, Luigi said.

Salvatore blinked, Mathieu spat. Luigi returned to his intergalactic cartoon porn.

Whole truth.   Tomec stepped out of the lift. He looked down the aisle that separated the six machines into two rows of three. Fernando was seated on a chair at machine seventeen, his head on one side, his arms and legs splayed: either deep in thought or dozing. Alphonse, by contrast, was reading from a paperback, alternately standing and crouching, gripping his own throat with his left hand and declaiming a torrent of words inaudible to Tomec in that din. At machine fifteen, Bobrán was descending a step ladder, an empty red tray in his left hand. Tomec walked over, his right hand outstretched.

B'soir. B'soir. Ça va? Ça va?

Before Tomec could ask about the graffiti, Bobrán's face lit up, his lips parted around his poor dentition, and he drew a folded sheet of paper from his hip pocket. You can read, right?

Sure.

Just two lines, Bobrán said, unfolding the letter so just the lines in question would be visible to the Pole.

Tomec's eyes travelled across the paper.

So? he asked.

Sweet Jesus! Out loud!

Oh, I see, Tomec said. Then: '. . . étiez amis. C'est pour cela . . .'

Bobrán snatched the letter back and refolded it so that the creases were both one line lower.

Just those three lines.

Tomec blew out his cheeks, but did as enjoined.

'. . . je vous prie donc de ne vous faire aucune inquiétude au sujet de ma démarche. Je suis venu en France pour connaître la vérité au sujet du décès de mon frère. Nous n'avons . . .'

Tomec stopped.

Do you want me to read further? Tomec asked.

No, thank you, Bobrán said, taking the letter back from Tomec. It's personal.

Tomec stared at Bobrán, noting the shape of his jaw, the hook of his nose, the thickness of his eyebrows, the fleck in his eye. Virgil's peasant-boy admirer? he wondered. He walked away, the little Gypsy's features fixing in his mind.

Bobrán repeated the words of the letter beneath his breath. 'I beg you not to have any worries about my initiative. I have come to France to know the truth about my brother's death. We have not . . .'

Nothing.   Not a word had passed between the two men, since Gérard had flopped back into his car seat and gestured to his chauffeur to drive. Jorge knew of only one way to shift his boss's foul mood: to goad him till he exploded. Jorge ejected his Victor Jara cassette from the car radio and inserted Boris Vian. The first number on the tape was the anti-militarist anthem, *Le Déserteur.*

Fucking switch that off, Gérard barked.

Jorge did as he was told, but with a loud snort followed by a long chuckle.

What were you doing skulking round the back of your own factory? Jorge asked, his voice a sneer. You could march straight in the front door. You looked like a thief in the night. But if you really wanted to take a peek inside, what was to stop you? I saw you eyeing that ledge. Afraid somebody would catch you doing your own snooping?

You have a lot of cheek. Nobody talks to me like that. Gérard shook his head: it was as if he wondered why. His voice was calmer already.

Fire me, Jorge said. Make me cry and beg forgiveness. Oh, Master!

Maybe I'll do just that. Give me a fucking cigarette.

Jorge gave his boss a cigarette and took one for himself, then lit both, the boss's first. Gérard breathed the smoke in hard. Jorge heard the man relax. What idiot ever said smoking was bad for you? Jorge thought.

The two men surveyed the wet suburban streets. Gérard talked of the burdens employers faced and the younger generation's disrespect for authority. Jorge listened a little, limiting his participation to grunts and ah-hahs. He recalled the conversation he had had earlier that evening with the daughter of his boss's newspaper-owning friend. Friend? Did men like Gérard have friends? It didn't seem likely. She had told him her name: Françoise. Jorge realized whom she brought to mind: he had had a cousin that age once - Carmen. Maybe she was still alive somewhere. Carmen had had the same wide-eyed look of boundless curiosity, that teenage lack of shyness bordering on insolence. Gérard had said something about respect, hadn't he? In Jorge's reasoned view, those who demanded it didn't deserve it. Carmen was Jorge's sister's eldest child. Last time Jorge saw them, they were about to leave Santiago. For Bogotá, they said. He told them he was going to France, gave them an address. Nothing: not a card, not a message.

Let's go for a drink, Gérard said, farting loudly.

Jorge wound his window down and swung the car back into town. He recalled his own belly. He took his left hand off the steering wheel and slipped it beneath his trouser belt, pressing it down on his bare skin, the tips of his fingers in his pubic hair. At the same time, he arched his back a little, feeling the stiffness in his lumbar region. He spent too much time sitting, he thought. His guts felt tight and turgid and heavy. Walking might do him good. He would contrive to park some way from the bar. The boss had fallen silent at long last.

Footwear. A tide of contentedness rippled through Alphonse's body each time he glanced – as often he did – at his lime-coloured socks vanishing into his lemon brothel creepers. He wondered if they would be right for Lucky. Probably suit Pozzo rather better.

Bobrán's plimsolls felt like a sweet second skin, leaving his feet effectively bare, pads on a cat's paw, alive to every nuance and contour when walking or standing, alert to their tingling urge to move when merely propped, suspended or dangled.

Eric was oblivious to the appearance of his scuffed and muddy Doc Marten cherry-reds, accustomed to their lazy comfort and the squelch of air under his dragged feet. Whatever they signified in England, they meant nothing here.

Beneath the din of the machines, Tomec still made out the clicking of his factory-issue boots, their steel heel and toe caps darkly announcing his arrival, departure or passage.

In his old leather sandals, the cracked tiny webs between Mathieu's toes itched, his athlete's foot immune now to every powder, unguent or cream. He flexed his toes, balling his feet, while the fingernails of his right hand poked and pushed at the cuticles of his left.

Reprieve.   Accustomed to reviewing the day's events from the largest to the smallest, from the planetary to the intimate, from the world-historical to the petty or at least local, Jean was savouring a rare procedural reversal, occasioned by the uncommon salience of a domestic development. His wife, it seemed, was neither at death's door, nor even, apparently, for the time being, in death's sights.

Jean was pleased with this news. After all, Niquette was his life's companion. She had been good to him. She put up with his foibles. She appeared to like him. Ideally, she would outlive him. And yet, having been constrained to contemplate the eventuality of her early demise, he had sought and rapidly discerned certain consolations. For although grief and loneliness might at first assail him, would he not survive? To an optimist, is not even tragedy an opportunity? Might he not, for instance, find a new wife? Might he not enjoy a period of wanton bachelorhood?

As the days of awaiting first the biopsy procedure and then the result thereof had lengthened in apparent duration while shrinking in number, Jean had begun to entertain a particular fantasy. He had always yearned to frequent prostitutes but, from an anticipated sense of shame, had never done so. He had never wished for a mistress, had never thought to betray his wife, and would never have run the risk of humiliating her or disgracing himself. But the thought of purchasing guilt-free sex, sex pure and unadulterated, sex by the hundredweight, as it were, was beguiling. He pictured lines of women parading before his wallet, his for the choosing. There would be so many different shapes and sizes, colours and hairstyles, characters and humours. Demure, raunchy, virginal, vulgar, huge-hipped (unlike Niquette), willing (unlike Niquette) to perform (for an extra fee, no doubt) such specialized services as his expanding expertise in such matters might be relied upon in timely fashion to suggest. As he waited for Niquette's fate to be declared by the professionals of health, Jean's anticipation of an impending liberation from the stuffy confines of a marriage that had long ago declined into slothful companionship prompted a remarkable and, as far as his wife was concerned, quite unsought and undreamt-of, late blossoming of passion: while her husband's imagination had run far ahead of events, the only present and available outlet for his uncustomary urges was Monique herself.

Never before had Jean's desire appeared so imperious, spontaneous and imaginative. On Sunday, in their little kitchen, as Jean had torn her cardigan from her back and yanked down her slacks, pushing coffees and brioche masterfully to one side, staring as if in scalding pursuit of some fast-receding quarry, Monique had been amazed to see that her husband, under ordinary circumstances so slow to express emotion, loved her again, almost like the first time, after all these years. She was touched indeed. No doubt it was his way of showing that he did of course love her and fear to lose her. Men were such sweet strange creatures.

Standing Ground. Sitting with the flank of machine eleven at his back and the flank of machine twelve before him, Marcel's chest felt constricted, sandwiched, his breathing flattened, his shoulders tight and hunched. He got up and stationed himself at the end of machine eleven, and tried looking up and down the machine aisle. Nothing was happening. No relief. No one to push around. No one even to talk to.

Marcel saw Rachid at the far end of the aisle, lazing on a chair, his legs straight out, flicking through a magazine, a cigarette hanging from the corner of his mouth, evidently at ease. Cool damned Arab. At his back a huge table, behind that the walls of this nightly prison, then the city beyond, wide open like a whore. Marcel lit a cigarette and sauntered down the aisle, his eyes fixing the Algerian.

He went and stood right up against Rachid. He leaned against the edge of the table, half-sitting on it. Each time he brought the cigarette to his mouth, his right hip nudged the Algerian's left shoulder. He blew smoke down at Rachid's head.

Rachid shut the magazine, got up, checked the latest products as they fell from the gaping presses of machines eight and nine, emptied the floor trays into the threshing bins, then noticed that Marcel had sat down on the chair and was, in his turn, leafing through *Le Nouvel Observateur*.

Rachid strolled to the control cabinet of machine eight and stood with his back to it. He stared blankly at Marcel. Marcel looked up, grinned at him, then stubbed out his cigarette. Rachid continued to stare, neither grinning nor scowling, scarcely focusing. Marcel seemed to read an article, then just flicked the pages.

We remain children, Rachid told his listening self and son, as he watched Marcel. Children with beer bellies, greying or thinning hair, wrinkles, aching joints.

Without looking at Rachid, Marcel closed the pages of *Le Nouvel Observateur*, and lay the magazine down on the surface of the wooden table at his back. He was breathing better now. He felt freer than before, more settled in his mood. He got up from the chair, took a deep breath, rolling his shoulders slightly. Then he toddled back up the machine aisle. He was going to have to think about his lady friends, which to keep, which to let go. He wanted to be sensible.

25. Surveying, Subtracting.

Surveying.   Salvatore had walked through the raw-materials area and entered the meals-and-meetings room, shutting the door at his back, setting the partition walls atremble like some TV-soap set. Eleven stackable plastic chairs ringed an oblong wooden table on which rested two brown-glass ashtrays, one almost full, one almost empty; between them a biro with a chewed end. By the door stood a green metal square-bottomed bin, half full of food wrappers and browning fruit peelings, mostly apple. The wall clock said 22.05, but he reckoned it was kept slow.

Salvatore took a good look at the room. Everybody would be quiet and then he'd speak. He could use a room like this where he lived. He removed his spectacles, feeling their weight in his left hand. From the pocket of his shirt he extracted a square of yellow cloth and a vial of cleaning fluid. He would need to make his points succinctly. Uncapping the vial, he placed a single drop at the centre of each lens, then worked the cloth. If he had a room like this, he would sit on a different chair each day. The Sicilian's eyes were weary. He had been living at his girlfriend's apartment since giving up his own. Why pay rent on two places? Laure had asked. One day he would have a room like this – or even larger. He would place his folders and lecture notes and books he was reading in orderly piles – like chips on a gaming table.

Reclaiming.   After Marcel had sauntered back up the machine aisle, Rachid remained at the control cabinet for well over a minute. With deliberation but no haste, he returned to the vacant chair.

Rachid brushed the seat lightly with the back of his bony hands, adjusted its position by shifting it minutely to the left. He noticed Marcel's cigarette butt on the floor, against the left rear leg of the chair. With the toe of his shoe, he shunted it under the table, out of sight.

Rachid sat back down again, his grey fingers caressing the rough edge of the seat beneath his thighs. He picked up *Le Nouvel Observateur* from the table behind him. He closed his eyes.

Sleeping.   Fatima was lying on her back, her arms outstretched behind her as though slumber had overtaken her in an effort to reach and touch the wooden bars at the head of her cot. Alongside her lay a small teddy bear, its eyes staring. The little girl's hands were relaxed and open, the fingers moving minutely, leaves caught in a draught. A dummy lay close to her left hand, a drying patch of milky saliva beside the teat. Between the child's head and the side of the cot lay an empty baby's bottle. Shards of street-light penetrated the room from the edges of ill-fitting curtains. As the chink and scrape of washed cutlery and dishes in the adjacent kitchen impinged, the child's eyes opened a fraction and her left fist briefly clenched. Her mother's face dissolved and reformed in the baby's mind, smiling again, while her father's eyes glistened and his scratchy chin closed in for the goodnight kiss. The baby felt herself fall, started, whimpered, then seemed to fall again – whoosh! – and was still. Her breathing came more slowly.

Rippling.   The Sicilian walked through the metallurgy workshop adjoining the raw-materials area, heading for the coffee machine. To left and right of him, grey machine hulks stood dormant, dripping, unobserved. Dead metal. His specs were clean and clear, allowing the glinting darkness to fall on his retina free of filmy smearing, misty clouding, or grimy haze. He liked his darkness limpid, stellar: he liked it light. His taut tall frame kept a regular pace, subduing the impulse to run, jump, leap or fall to all fours, or pace like a panther. He imagined springing leftward, rightward, sideways, up, down, through. His toned musculature was equal to demands far greater than those placed upon him by his work, study or humdrum amour; indeed it cried out for greater exertion. Yet Salvatore brushed aside all such promptings. At each step he rose on the ball of his foot; at each step he clenched his fists and tensed his thighs and belly. His skin rippled its reply. Live flesh. He proceeded smoothly, without a sound.

Renovating.   Laure had driven into the hills to eat with friends at a house that one of them, Martine, was restoring: she was three months pregnant and wanted to complete the work before the baby was born. The place was full of dust, only one of the upstairs rooms had floorboards, the stairs had no banister, and several windows were missing. A central-heating boiler had been installed and some of the rooms had radiators, but they hadn't yet been connected. The kitchen, however, had remained untouched, hideous and usable. It was there they sat sipping coffees and digestifs. Plates were piled precariously in an old stone sink. They had eaten soup, then steaks accompanied by haricots verts that Martine's father had grown and bottled that autumn. Dominique had brought along a cake she had baked after work. Laure had contributed some wine. Someone else had brought a bottle of Ricard for the apéros. A gas heater warmed the room. The curtainless window panes ran with condensation.

Laure was angry, but didn't want to make a scene. A woman she had met twice before – a new friend of Martine's – had mentioned the way Salvatore had reacted the previous Saturday evening, appearing to find it comical. Dominique had then asked, Is he some kind of puritan? Laure said he had been brought up strictly. I thought nowadays Italians were more relaxed, Martine had said, perhaps meaning to be helpful. He's Sicilian, Laure corrected. She felt she should have handled it better, defended him in some way, but she didn't see how.

The previous Saturday evening they had all met in Grandgobier at Dominique's flat, a huge place in a run-down neighbourhood. Glancing out at the fifth-floor window, someone had noticed a prostitute leading a client down the alley opposite. It was dark and there was nobody around. With the exception of Salvatore, everyone had abandoned their desserts to go to the window and watch the working girl service her customer, first on her knees, then against the brick wall, her skirt hitched up. It was dark down there, but if you looked hard you could make out what was happening. Someone turned out the light. They all laughed a lot. The frankness of the thing, probably. After a minute or so, Laure had turned to see Salvatore scowling through the dark. She shrugged and smiled, making light of it, hoping to placate him, but he beckoned her over, and demanded they leave. She tried to talk him down, saw it was hopeless, so made her excuses to Dominique. No doubt everyone now thought her fiancé was a stuck-up jerk. Which he wasn't. He just had different standards.

Martine was offering to refill her glass. No, thanks, Laure said, I've got to leave soon. I'm picking my mother up from the cinema.

People were eyeing her. The room had fallen quiet. Nobody believed her.

Skipping. Rachid sat with his left foot on his right knee, flicking through the pages of *Le Nouvel Observateur*. He had looked at most of the pictures already, from back cover to front, and was now retracing his way from front cover to back, pausing at picture captions and article intros, even reading some first paragraphs here and there, but unable to settle on anything.

It wasn't indifference. If he could find words for this state of mind, perhaps Malika could understand it. He felt both close and distant, sometimes alternately, sometimes simultaneously. He pictured a wall of cotton wool sheathing his naked body, absorbing every shock, and before his eyes a wall of mist obscuring every sight, and pillows pressed to his ears. He could tell her that, but would she understand?

Yet Rachid was noticing something as he continued to turn the pages. He completed his second sweep, turned to the contents page and closed the magazine. Children, that's what he had noticed. Children everywhere. In photos, feature articles, advertising too. Used to sell almost as much stuff as women. Fatima flashed in his mind, too fast to see in any detail, but unmistakable, trailing her name and the feelings that stuck to her: love, guilt, longing, sadness. He would swear to spend more time with her. Soon. He would rediscover how to talk to a living child.

Rachid got to his feet, rolled the magazine into a glossy-paper truncheon and, wielding it in his left fist, walked up the machine aisle, slapping it repeatedly into his right palm. When he reached the end of machine two, he unfurled the magazine and reinserted it into the pile. He returned to his own machines and began threshing at machine nine. He put his head down, pounding the bright orange sprue against the sides of the tub, beating the stubborn plastic till it dropped its product. He looked up to see Eric approaching, an unlit cigarette in his mouth, flicking the thumb of his right hand outward against his index finger. Rachid straightened up, shaking his right shoulder as if to dislodge a pain or itch, pulled his gloves off and walked to his chair. He took his cigarette lighter from the breast pocket of his jacket. The lighter was easier to reach than usual, a fact that scarcely registered. Eric lit his cigarette, gave a huge smile, and walked away. Rachid replaced the lighter in the pocket, barely noting that it didn't sink as deep as it should, that there was some resistance there, or obstruction. He returned to the threshing.

There wasn't a single item in *Le Nouvel Observateur* likely to interest Mehdi, he thought. Perhaps he should begin reading children's books. Surely that's what his son would be wanting right now, rather than magazine articles. Rachid would fill his head with childen's stories, fables, cartoons. He wouldn't have to buy them. He could get them from a library. For Fatima. Then he could share them with his son.

Savouring. Salvatore had reached the beer and coffee-machines. He pulled a soft leather purse from his pocket, checked the amount it held, then removed a single coin, which he placed in the slot. He punched the large round plastic buttons. He liked the way they receded into the face of the machine, the way the machine clicked into action, a cup dropping onto the steel grill; the way the steaming aromatic black liquid splashed the beaker. He waited till the machine clicked off and the flow decreased to a drip. He edged the beaker out and raised it to his lips. It tasted foul, it tasted good, it tasted bitter, it tasted sweet, it tasted like nothing he had ever drunk in a bar, let alone in Italy. Salvatore liked everything about this process, and especially the clarity of the transaction. He provided the coin, the machine provided the coffee: there was no middleman, no time-wasting, no chit-chat. Insert, punch, drop, squirt, take, drink, chuck, go. He threw the empty beaker at the trash can. Soon he would sense his heart quicken, his pulse race, his legs tremble, his stomach rumble, his ears ring. Coffee had an immediate effect upon him. A good effect. Coffee maddened him; it gladdened him. He looked around at the darkness. He felt lonely. It was a good feeling. It was as honest as the coffee percolating through his gut, streaking through his veins.

Nursing.   On the edge of Agrigento, in a blistering villa encircled by black railings, Giuliana de Melis, diminutive in her broad single bed, agitated a silver bell in her papery left hand. In the lounge, Vito rose from his armchair. There was a nurse, seated, knitting in a dark corner, one eye on a TV set. She hadn't looked up. I'll go, Vito said.

Giuliana heard her son approach.

Sit down, she rasped.

Vito sat where she could see him.

I want to see Totò.

I telegraphed him this morning, Vito volunteered. Perhaps he'll phone tomorrow.

Giuliana stared steadily at her youngest son. He held her gaze. His face was long and unrelieved by any hint of levity.

I want Salvatore here with me. Do you understand? I'm dying.

Your doctors don't agree.

Doctors are asses. Tell Totò I'm dying.

Vito looked into his mother's eyes, then nodded.

Giuliana seemed satisfied.

Do you want your milk now? Shall I read to you?

No. Later. You know I don't sleep.

Giuliana flicked the back of her left hand at Vito and turned her head to the wall.

Vito observed the back of his mother's head, the shiny grey hair gathered in a clasp. He noticed the little clock on the bedside table. It was late, almost ten past ten. In a while he would come back with her milk and her book, but she would be sleeping. Vito stood up.

You're a good boy, a good son, Giuliana rasped, her eyes open, fixed on the patterned wallpaper. Just get me Totò.

Soaking   Malika was in her kitchen. She had finished the dishes, swept and mopped the floor and opened the window. She had wrung out the floor-rag and stretched it over the pail to dry, and was leaning back on the fridge, enjoying a cigarette. She tried to imagine Rachid at work, discovering the note she had slipped into his jacket pocket, behind his lighter. She grinned and took another puff. How would he react? She pictured him at a machine, pistons pumping, cogs whirring, steam spewing from ill-fitting gaskets, sweat pouring off him as he pushed and pulled levers, hit buttons. He was sure to be surprised. Might he be angry? Would he think she was trying to replace Mehdi? Never that. This will be a new child, brand-new, like no other. And a brother or sister to Fatima.

Malika looked at the clean lino, drying already in patches. She grinned again. Rachid was sure to have found the note. She hadn't had the courage to tell him to his face. With her right hand she stroked her belly. For a woman who had had two babies it was remarkably flat. Of course she would have to start her exercises again now. She closed the window and stubbed out her cigarette. Then she opened a packet of chickpeas, poured them into a dish and covered them with water from the cold tap: they could stand by the sink overnight. She would cook them in the morning. Rachid loved chickpeas, and they would be good for the baby.

Hurting.   Rachid finished separating products from stalks at machine nine, straightened up and rolled his right shoulder slightly. He pulled a face and rolled it again, more slowly still.

I must have pulled something springing out of that African's bear-hug, he thought. I'm not in good shape. How could I be?

He turned his head as far as it would go, left and right.

It's as if I slept all day by an open window. Which I didn't. Wonder if anyone's got any aspirin. It'll pass. What did the guy think he was doing anyway? What was it he said? Trying to cheer me up? That's it: he wanted me to dance! Crazy man! He'll not try again.

Rachid dragged himself to his chair.

Of course, Malika says I get back pain and stiff necks and aching joints because I have bad posture. She tells me to straighten my back and not to slouch.

Rachid straightened up, leaning right back so his shoulders dug into the top edge of the chair back, then smiled, recalling the way Malika, when they first married, used to sneak up behind him and jab him in the small of his back while wrenching back his shoulders with her other hand. She, of course, was faultless: the body beautiful, the perfect posture, she walked so gracefully it looked like gliding. Which made it easy for her to creep up on him unawares. You ought to be a soldier in an insurgency, he would tease her. She would pull a face, because once upon a time – in a different life, it now seemed – she had been.

Realizing.   As Salvatore approached the hanging plastic flaps separating the raw-materials area from the plastics section, he was ambushed by a jumble of unwelcome and unruly thoughts. That was what could happen when you drank strong coffee and let your ideas go slack, he reflected. Your head filled like a storm drain, with every sort of detritus.

In no particular order: (1) he realized (with a sigh) that he needed to phone his brother, his mother. If she was really sick or dying, he would have to go. (2) He recalled (with a heavy heart) something Laure had told him that afternoon. Two couples they had often seen at her tennis club had hit the news. Salvatore and Laure had much admired the foursome for their elegance, sophistication, good-quality kit and sports cars. It turned out they had been neighbours. The fine-featured but – now that he thought about it – starey-eyed brunette had been found shot dead early on Sunday morning next to the body of the man from next door, also shot dead. It seemed she had killed him after a 5 a.m. assignation, then turned the gun on herself. Laure and Salvatore had often seen the two couples playing mixed doubles. (3) Salvatore resolved (as he passed the meals-and-meetings room on his right) not to think about the union meeting until later. He must prepare to look them in the eye. He would say what he had to say briefly, succinctly, then ask for questions, then end it. None of that aimless cud-chewing and hanging-around-drinking-beer over which Philippe had presided, merely for the purpose of using up the statutory half hour allocated for union business. (4) He thought (with a shudder) Christ! the train journey to Sicily! Almost thirty hours, most of it standing in the corridor. Maybe if he booked . . . Then what if his mother didn't die? No, he was going to have to make the journey anyway – just in case. He would find out what leave he was entitled to. Damn it, you only had one mother.

Salvatore had always envied those two couples, thought of them as perfect, though oddly assorted. The husband of the woman who had done the shooting was a short, nervous, mousy guy and the wife of the man she had killed was nice but somehow plain and dull – the kind of woman who seems dumpy, long before she is. Whereas the lovers, you could appreciate it now, both had so much life in them. What of Laure and me? Salvatore caught himself thinking. We'll be married soon. How well-assorted do we appear? I'm not mousy. She's not wild. It should be okay. I wonder if my mother is really dying. I shall call Vito tomorrow.

Salvatore pushed through the hanging plastic flaps and blinked. Everything was crystal clear and coffee bright. He was pleased he had cleaned and polished his specs.

Yearning.   Madame Labarde was sitting in the dark looking at her husband watching television from his place on the sofa. She had changed into an old dressing gown and made herself a tisane. Bernard was always there when she came in. He had just undone his flies and was scratching his testicles. The television lit up his face. He had never been handsome, and middle age, she supposed, was not being merciful with either of them. He seemed happy enough though, his wife thought, sitting there scratching his itch. Almost gleeful. He didn't need much, did he? When she had married him, she had imagined that was a plus. He was smiling. Or maybe he found the programme funny?

Before long, she knew, her husband would grunt and get up, saying: I have an early start tomorrow, or, I have had a long day today. Once he was gone, she would turn off the TV, get up and tidy the house, empty the ashtrays, open the windows. Last night, not for the first time, she had heard the neighbours noisily making love and had stood at the open window for a good ten minutes, until she had noticed a man in the block opposite leering at her. Dirty dog. He had actually nodded at her! She had slammed the window shut and drawn the curtain. She was furious. He had ruined it for her. She did so like to hear that young woman climax.

Adverts interrupted the TV programme and, as foretold, Monsieur Labarde muttered something, did up his trousers, rose wearily to his feet then, as he passed her, bent down and kissed her cheek. Unusual, certainly. But significant? Perhaps he had a lover? Or maybe he would want to screw tonight if she came to bed too early. Now he had gone, she would surely get up and do the chores.

Instead, she sat in the dark and thought of the Sicilian. He had been as remote as ever this evening. Haughty. Mysterious. Brooding. She longed for that man. The adverts ended and the programme came back on, but it had no hold on her. She saw again his noble frame, his smouldering eyes, his imperious, proud demeanour. She imagined him, as they shook hands one evening, drawing her toward him, leading her in his virile grip to the rear of the control cabinet of machine six, where they would be most unlikely to be spotted, and kissing her passionately on the neck, forcing her head back, with an irresistible gentleness. Mme Labarde's right hand sank between her legs, her left hand slipped under her blouse and stroked her breast, pulling at the nipple. She dug into her lust. She had rarely done this anywhere but in bed, alone, barely awake. For years now. Always after Bernard left for work in the morning, as soon as she heard the door shut behind him. She didn't have to get up immediately. She could make it last. Sometimes an hour would fly past. How good this felt. How sweet, how fresh the Sicilian's mouth must taste on her own! Citrus fruit and honey. Fragrances wafted on a breeze from the desert south of Libya or Egypt. She closed her eyes to envisage the most beautiful sunlit room, a chandelier hanging from a high ceiling, a modest scattering of ancien régime furniture. It was so easy. So discreet. They drank Asti Spumante purchased specially for her. And flowers. Jasmine. How had he guessed that she liked flowers? As he undressed her, he talked to her in an accent broader than she had ever before encountered. She saw coloured boats bobbing on a blue sea – the Tyrrhenian, no doubt. She pushed her lover back onto the bed, climbed astride him and undid the buttons of his shirt. He was startled by her impetuosity. His pleasure was palpable. This was going to last. Bernard would be asleep by now.

Subtracting. Rachid would recalculate his monthly income, allowing for the strike action. He would ask Salvatore how many hours they were likely to lose, then factor it in. If only he knew how much Karim needed. He couldn't not help Malika's cousin. Besides, he wanted to help him.

Lifting his eyes from the concrete floor, Rachid saw Salvatore walking down the machine aisle. Rachid got up and approached him. Salvatore glanced at the unlit warning-lights atop the control cabinets of machines five and six, then turned his attention to Rachid.

How long do you think we'll be on strike? the Algerian enquired.

It's up to you men. It's a decision for . . .

Rachid smiled as he interrupted him. He chose his words more carefully.

Is the union recommending anything more than half-hour stoppages?

Not to begin with.

I need to be able to calculate my income, make adjustments.

I understand. For the time being, if there have to be stoppages, we – he paused and repeated the pronoun with evident relish – *we* shall recommend a series of regular once-weekly half-hour end-of-shift stoppages to maximize disruption to output while minimizing loss of wages.

Rachid returned to his seat. In theory, he stood to lose no more than two hours earnings. He would assume two. He performed his accountancy therapy on the basis of the new downward-adjusted hours. As always, the mental arithmetic calmed him. Then there was the matter of Karim to consider.

Malika's cousin had asked for money to help fund the launch of a new revolutionary project among workers in the Paris area. Rachid approved. Malika approved. Rachid and Malika were not in the habit of keeping secrets. They would talk about the money. Neither of them liked loans. If they could spare the money at all, they would simply give Karim what he asked for or some sizable fraction of it. Rachid would phone him. Call it a donation, he would say. Karim would say nothing. As far as Karim could see, money was the only contribution Rachid and Malika ever made nowadays.

26. Heat and Speed.

Heat.   The air that whirled above and around the European city of Grandgobier dusted the roads that snaked through the foothills, crisped the surface of the early-fallen snow in forest and meadow, glassed every stagnant pool in the region's rivers. In the city itself, people bustled from bar to bar or from bar to home; only the drunks lingered in the cold, their words frosting as they spoke.

The core of the masonry outer walls of Éts. Boucan was a chilly five degrees celsius; the air in metallurgy was thirteen. In the downstairs plastics section, there reigned a comfortable twenty-three degrees; upstairs, a muck-sweaty twenty-nine. Coffees exited the machine at ninety-six degrees steaming, beer bottles were delivered at a pearling three. Melting chambers heated raw material to over three hundred degrees for injection into water-cooled moulds. The products that clattered through the aluminium slats and into floor trays were neither too hot nor too cold to be seized by the lukewarm hand and approached by the ice-cool eye.

Staggering.   Since entrusting his machines to Jacques, Philippe had been slouching and staggering through metallurgy. Darkness was all about him. The plastics din was far behind. His legs were weary. His belly rumbled not with particular hunger but with a warring scrimmage of beverages, alcoholic and non. His fingers, as he rubbed them, felt puffy, his hands upholstered with fatty cushions. His belt burrowed into his flesh, but if he loosened it he would be continually hiking up his trousers. He sighed and sagged and slouched some more.

He had never strayed this far through the darkened factory. What might he find in the next workshop? Or the one after that? More of the same? He would like to feel something sharp, do something hard for once, find a prick against which to kick, make certain he wasn't sleeping. It would be nice to break a machine, for example, if he had the tools to do a good job. Merely damage it and it might take some bugger's head off – or worse – an arm or leg. Destroy it altogether. The noise would clang like a tolling bell bringing the Polack running. A little violence might be sobering. What he would really like was to hit Odile. If only he could suddenly bump into her here in the dark, he could take a spanner to her head or, much better, a club-hammer. Smash her to pieces. Or leave her with her head in a stationary press, like a warning. No. No messages. No mercy. Smash her teeth. See her bending over, spitting them out. Kick her in the stomach. Christ. His head spun.

Hurt his wife? No. You bet. Why not? He could shut this thought out right here and now and no one would ever know. Or he could tag along, follow wherever it led. He looked around. A man needed a little indulgence sometimes. No one need know. Sickness swelled his throat. He wasn't in the mood. If not now, when? Had he not been provoked? He opened his cigarette packet. In Philippe's experience, a quick smoke could remedy most ills, physical, mental, humoural – but nausea? He closed the packet. He sucked his cheek in between his front teeth, bit off a piece and chomped. No discernible taste. Once, years ago now, in the small hours, he left a party in a swanky part of Paris, sports cars and limos end to end both sides of the street, lamps dazzling, his body lurching, blurring. Then, a moment's inspiration: he stepped onto a bumper, up onto a boot, a roof, then strode down the street from car to car, never slipping, never falling, a wonderful progress, boot, roof, bonnet, leap, boot, roof, bonnet, leap. Fine view of a street you get from atop a stationary Saab – when you're young and drunk and sharp and moving.

Punch her? Slap her? Kick her? Well? An image of Odile's bloodied face came to him. Yuck. Blood. Just the look of it. Without the smell even. He had created it. He had invited this image in, made it feel at home. Could he expel it now? Or could he only own it, live with it? This finally was what his marriage had given him: an impulse to uxoricide.

Philippe looked at his pudgy hands, saw the wedding ring wallowing in the trench it had gouged year by year through the flesh of his fattening finger. It would only rotate. He put the finger in his mouth, got his teeth round the ring and tugged. He worked spittle under the ring and tried again, bending and straightening the knuckle, straining angrily, then methodically, wincing, wondering if his teeth would take the strain. The ring came free. He slung it under a machine. Free! Damn it, he then muttered. Somebody was sure to find it, hock it and enjoy the proceeds. He had thrown away money. Damn.

Trance.   Alphonse ceased his pacing at the aisle-end of his machine eighteen. He had recited the whole of Lucky's speech. Should it end in a bang or just peter out? he wondered. Crescendo or fade? He had tried it both ways. It was tempting to deliver the repeated word *crâne* ('skull') as a howl – but might a dull monotone be more apt? As if Lucky were reciting in a quasi-trance a text learnt by heart but poorly understood? Beckett's stage directions were of little help. Emerging laboriously from Lucky's trance, Alphonse took in his surroundings: floor, walls, machines, bins and people.

Bobrán was standing at the aisle-end of his machine fifteen, a finger tracing handwritten words on a sheet of letter paper, his lips paddling, his forehead creasing with effort. Painful to watch. It would be so easy to help the man. Alphonse was moved to do so. He checked himself. It might be misunderstood. He had learned that help wasn't always welcome. And African ebullience could frighten people. Europeans lived in little boxes and liked it that way. The Algerian – a European of a sort, after all – had misapprehended his purpose earlier. A lucky thing Alphonse hadn't been injured, falling backward. Then the speech the Algerian had made, referring to a civil war, threatening him. They were going to have to talk.

Standing back.   Worker turns to face machine, press opens and product (plastic, red) falls from mould (steel, shiny) through slats (aluminium, dull) into tray (plastic, shallow, oblong, grey) on floor against machine base. Worker picks product (last) from others (numberless), holds it up to light and rotates it slowly. Looks at articles (identical, twelve) set along spine, six each side. Machine makes product (new). Worker drops product (plastic, red) into tray, watches press open. Product (new) falls from press. Worker bends over tray, inserts hand (right) through hand-hold (right). Grips edge of tray (left). Steps back, straightens up, raising tray from floor. Lifts end (right) of tray above end (left) of tray. Tips all products (plastic, red) into tub (plastic, grey, oblong, deep) on bucket (upturned, rectangular, iron). Puts tray (empty, grey) down on floor against machine base, beneath slats (aluminium, dull). Product (plastic, red, new) falls. Press closes. Worker (worker) stands back.

Empty.   Marcel had checked the latest products of his machines twelve and eleven and had emptied the accumulated contents of the floor trays into their respective threshing tubs. He had removed his gloves and placed them neatly on top of the control cabinet of machine twelve. For several moments he stood and experienced plain being. Without any prior planning or consideration, he had laid down all thoughts. His eyes were open and his ears could hear but Marcel remained for a time quite unaware of any motion within him or about him.

Scales.   Seated at neighbouring machine thirteen, Luigi leafed through his cartoon story of over-endowed aliens. The lush lips and dizzying cleavage of a character named Aurelia had given him the first stirrings of an erection. Luigi put his beer bottle on the floor against the foot of his chair. His freed hand dove into his pants to arrange his cock for ease of tumefaction. Mathieu's rough voice, then form, intruded.

Can I borrow that? I'll bring it back. There's something I . . .

The foreman's right hand jabbed in the direction of Luigi's copy of *Détective*. Luigi handed it to him. The foreman grunted. Luigi looked at Aurelia. The blood that was engorging his penis had cascaded into his body through his eyes. It must be Aurelia's blood.

Mathieu limped briskly to the raised glass-fronted office and climbed the steps. He was glad he had passed nobody. He felt awkward carrying a copy of *Détective*. Ordinarily, its lurid cover and assuredly lurid contents were not congenial to him. He drew a key from his trouser pocket to open the door, entered and sat down.

Mathieu glanced out over the shop floor, then round the office. There were no lights lit on any of the control cabinets. At the far end of the office, shelves were piled high with machine-operating manuals and files. He felt like an impostor. He drew up the chair, placed the magazine on the table top and turned the pages till he found the old lady, the murderee, at her birthday party. She was looking bewildered.

Mathieu scratched his forehead, detaching a shoal of scales that drifted downward onto the glossy paper. He brushed them aside with the edge of his hand. (Nadine's first birthday after her diagnosis. That same look. Or not quite. Surprised by the candles. Confused. Scared? Eating the cake with a childish grin.)

He started to read the story.

Scratched. Itch of a patch of flaky skin on eyelash or ear-shell; pang of hunger pinking in pit of stomach; hardened snot clinging in nose in spite of blowing; arthritic flash of grinding knee or hip; tickle in nostril that twitches then sneezes; blister on the heel, round, smooth and soft, bursting, dampening the sock that then sticks; food-scrap trapped in teeth, intractable to tongue; prickle of a burgeoning spot on chin or forehead; sweat running down spine and along flank; whoosh of nausea as light fails and legs crumple; liquid churn of a gut quivering to excrete; tender bruise blueing mid-shin; crackling sore throat forcing itself to swallow; ceaseless fidgeting of sleepy limbs; whip and crack of a twisting ankle; drear fuzzy pain of a bashed elbow; heaving of windpipe and larynx expelling lung mucus; whistling of the asthmatic.

The warm balm of beverage swilled in cheek then gargled; the relief of wind roundly broken; the cessation of pain upon repose; the lick of cigarette smoke on healthy gums; the comfort of a closed eye lightly rubbed; the blessing of ordinary food; the calm of a muscle relaxing; the happiness of the bowel or bladder timely voided, the itch well scratched; the throat well cleared; the leg well stretched. The promise of sleep, of quiet, of death.

Stature. Jean did not dwell on things. Nor did he harbour resentments. His wife was not about to die. She would probably bury him. She was not to blame. Besides, it was what he wanted. Wasn't it? He wouldn't much miss the crazy sex adventures he had planned for her demise. They couldn't have made him happy. Could they?

From domestic affairs, Jean had turned to condominial news. Monique and he had been notified the previous week that 'upon expert inspection it had been determined that the needful repairs to the communal roof – the cost of which was equitably defrayable among all tenants, in proportion to the size of their apartment – might safely be postponed until the spring of 1977.' Another non-event.

As for the workplace, Jean found nothing to retain his attention – though one of the drawbacks of reviewing the news from local level to planetary rather than vice versa was that he seldom heard of workplace developments before eleven, since it was mostly Luigi who brought him factory gossip, and the Marseillais who apprised him of union matters. So far this evening – and this was typical for this hour – he had seen neither man.

Next: the neighbourhood. He didn't need to scratch his head for the agenda: the proposed anti-dog-fouling measures and the plans to modernize the street-lighting. The former could not come a second too soon, while the latter – whatever his fondness for gaslights – would have to be embraced as progress, in the way of which no man (howsoever great his stature) may stand.

Stifling. Tomec stood at the aisle-end of Fernando's machine seventeen. He stifled a yawn and looked around. The air was warmer up here, he noted, the lights brighter, the oranges, creams and greens more garish. He must be casual, conversational, as if passing the time of day.

The Portuguee was seated on a chair, his eyes closed, his hands clasped on his apron, his legs straight out before him. He had removed his shoes and placed them side by side beneath his chair. His stockinged ankles rested on the floor, his splayed toes pressed against the flank of machine seventeen, whose every motion thus rattled, though with diminishing urgency, the whole length of his skeleton. At his back he heard the sounds and tremors of machine sixteen.

Fernando half-opened his left eye. A shape stood immobile in the aisle, admirably erect. It had to be the Polack: the African never stood that still; the Gypsy was shorter; ditto Jean, who, besides, would be glued to his chair; and the foreman was never quite that vertical. The night security man was the tall, immobile, erect one. The one who didn't actually work, as such, merely kept things safe for everyone else to fucking-work. Fernando's feet pushed away from machine seventeen and he sat up straighter in his chair, opening his eyes, preparing to get up.

Tomec had taken a pace toward him and held out his hand. Ça va? he asked

Fernando used Tomec's hand to pull himself up, as he muttered, Ça va. There was fucking-no way you could remain seated through a conversation with the Polack. He stood so close he'd give you a stiff neck.

So what do you think of the latest graffiti? Tomec asked with a shrug, as if the question had occurred to him on the instant.

Fernando said nothing, awaiting an explanation, unwilling to exhibit his ignorance, searching for a reply that would conceal it.

He could be Greek or Italian, Albanian or even Turkish, Tomec thought, as he observed the Portuguee. He could have been there, in ancient Brundisium, on that crowded jostling quayside, waiting for Virgil, glancing at the poet just the way he's looking at me now, furtive, curious.

I don't know what to make of it, Fernando said at last, clicking his tongue. What do you fucking-think of it?

Tomec brushed that aside. Do you like poetry? he asked.

Fernando screwed up his face, and turned his head so he could think better. He did like poetry: he liked to hear it. He liked rhymes. But not on the page. He liked Camoens even. It could rock you to sleep. But the true answer wasn't always the right one. He didn't want to admit he wasn't much of a reader. He didn't have to seem like an ignorant schmuck. And he didn't know about any graffiti.

Sure I like poetry, Fernando said, making it sound like a lie.

His head was all wrong, Tomec thought, blocks that didn't match, thrown together any-old-how, a second-rate Cubist sculpture, the kind of thing a small-town council might commission, all the wrong angles, wrong colours too. The jowls were impossibly jowly, the yellow of the skin far too yellow, the black of the eyes too black, the nose so fluted and voluted you could be tempted to stick a pair of candles in it. This man belonged in that rabble in Brundisium, shivering in the half-light, waiting for the Roman poet to arrive.

Tomec could see it now: he would have to ask every last one of these men to sit for him. Make them the crowd on the quayside, make them Virgil's welcoming committee. Why not?

Fernando sat down. He sensed he was being laughed at. Tomec resolved to bring into work his copy of Pessoa's poetry. It had the Portuguese on the left-hand page, and French on the right. He would show it to Fernando.

Tomec stared so hard you might imagine he was intending to steal your soul away, but Fernando didn't take offence. He wasn't the superstitious type.

Units.   No two men touched the machines in quite the same way. Where one man might relish their warmth and relax by their side, another would feel defiled by the very air that surrounded them and don rubber gloves prior to any contact. Each man dropped hurled tossed slung the product into trays in line with their mood, physique, state of boredom, fatigue or irritation. A chair, ladder or tub full of sprue – were they but endowed with even rudimentary sensation – could identify at once their sitter, climber or thresher, testifying to his unique working style. For the men might be variously brusque, precise, slapdash, disdainful, indifferent, impertinent, reverential, nonchalant or fatalistic. Or, alternatively, they might be gentle, approximate, punctilious, obsequious, impassioned, respectful, iconoclastic, excited or blasé. The measureless declensions and contaminations of such attitudes and humours, based as they were on influences and events largely extraneous to the shop floor, had, it must be said, scant effect upon factory output or unit productivity.

Ants. Pants.   Jean was fizzing. He jerked the machine guard open, grabbed the sprue in his left hand, used his right to tear off the cable ties. Tomec stood back and watched. At last someone appeared to have a firm opinion.

Jean dropped the cable ties into the cardboard box by his right foot and the empty sprue into the bin to his left, then slammed the guard back shut. He glanced in Tomec's general direction but didn't meet his eye. His head nodded.

Hurling round stuff like that. Troublemakers, Communists, Anarchists, Trostkyites, trash. Dragging up the past. All these years later. I'm telling you. He should face them all down. If you knew what those people did . . . the crimes they committed at the Libération. Against French patriots. I saw it. But you're too young. What would you know? Where the hell were you in forty-four?

Tomec held the man's gaze.

Poland, Tomec said. Germany.

Jean pulled the machine guard open again. His eyes were smaller than ever. He couldn't sit still on his chair. It was as if his seat was suddenly uncomfortable. As if he had ants in his pants.

Tomec walked away. He had no use for the man.

Classics.   Along Grandgobier's newly pedestrianized main shopping street, Gilles walked arm-in-arm with Margot, the wife of his friend, Jean-Pierre. Jean-Pierre walked behind the two, a restless smile on his lips. Margot had cooked an exquisite meal, which the three had washed down with two bottles of the finest Burgundy. They had raised their glasses to Jean-Pierre and Margot's splendid new flat and, as customary, to socialist internationalism. That afternoon, Gilles, wearing his army-surplus green parka, had stolen the wine from Auchan. Gilles viewed his act as a homage to a grass-roots movement in Italy known as auto-riduzione, which might be rendered as 'do-it-yourself discounting.' Gilles, however, insisted on a one-hundred-percent discount.

Gilles and Margot stopped to kiss. Jean-Pierre looked down the street and saw Moritz arm-in-arm with a girl. Margot pulled away from Gilles and beckoned Jean-Pierre to join their clinch. He declined. He knew that Gilles and Margot had fucked. He had been there, trying to get some sleep. It didn't bother him. He had dropped off in the middle of it, pondering the future of the Portuguese revolution. He didn't think Margot and Gilles were likely to fuck again.

Moritz tapped Jean-Pierre on the shoulder, and introduced his sister, Heike. The previous week, Moritz had taken over the small flat that Jean-Pierre and Margot had vacated. Heike shook hands with Jean-Pierre. Gilles and Margot broke up and greeted Moritz and his sister. Jean-Pierre introduced

Margot as his wife, grinning at Heike's confusion. Gilles, who scorned to read the Marxian classics in French translation, addressed Heike in bookish German, commenting that in her country too the collapse of bürgerlicher Ehestand (bourgeois marriage) was now in sight.

Tell Horst! Moritz said, winking at Heike.

Heike looked from Margot to Jean-Pierre to Moritz then back at Gilles.

Well, I await that with impatience, Heike said in German.

Gilles translated Heike's sentence into French.

Margot and Jean-Pierre laughed the loudest.

Let's get a beer, Gilles suggested, taking Heike's arm. Wo bist du denn her?

Pin-stripe.   Marcel stood at the end of Philippe's machine number two, sifting the papers and magazines on top of the recycled-material cylinder. He wanted to take another look at a picture he'd noticed earlier in *Le Nouvel Observateur*. Opening the magazine at random, Marcel recognized at once the shape of Concorde. He had seen reports about the plane on TV news. It was set in a stylized sky, alongside a crescent moon and twinkling stars. There was an Air France logo and the caption, Plus vite que le soleil, 'Faster than the Sun.'

Marcel liked cars and planes.

'The most ancient of man's dreams has been realized. Time no longer counts. Concorde exists. Concorde flies. And the sun, bedazzled, suspends its course while the century's most beautiful bird passes by, en route to Washington, Rio, Caracas . . .'

The following page was given over to an ad for Cafe Noir cigars, By Henry Wintermans Holland. There was a close-up of a man's hands. They were well manicured and tanned. The left hand held a cigar. The body was swathed in brown pinstripe. It had no head.

Marcel looked at his own stubby hands and pulled a face. Chantal said hands really mattered.

Odour.   The night shift was composed of smokers and non-smokers. The smokers smoked more or less frequently and entertained a greater or lesser passion for the habit. All of them had smoked for as long as they could remember.

The non-smokers fell into two categories: those who had given up and those who had never started. Mathieu and Jean belonged to the first category, Bobrán, Alphonse, Jacques and Salvatore to the second.

Jean had smoked until he had met Monique. 'I won't kiss you until you have stopped smoking,' she had said. 'I just stopped,' he said. 'Then I'll kiss you tomorrow,' she replied.

Mathieu had quit after thirty years of happy addiction, in order to manage higher and longer notes on the trumpet. He missed it.

Of the four who had never smoked, Bobrán had simply never seen the point. Alphonse hated everything about cigarettes, especially the odour. Salvatore had rejected smoking on health grounds; while Jacques, who, as a young man – mainly out of politeness – had occasionally smoked friends' cigarettes, had early resolved never to buy a packet of his own.

Free.   In the upstairs plastics section, Alphonse was again talking to himself, but nobody noticed. He wasn't declaiming, reciting, throwing his arms about; he was merely thinking aloud. Besides, Tomec had taken the lift down, Fernando had his eyes closed, Jean could see nothing from where he was sitting, and Bobrán was still fixed on his sheet of letter paper, the middle finger of his right hand poking at the top line.

Alphonse was making a speech, but it was his own, not Lucky's. Impromptu speaking was the main means by which Alphonse discovered what he thought. His mind would remain blank for a long stretch of time, then all of a sudden ideas words and emotions would clamour for expression and he would then speak his way to a standstill. From his thoughts would emerge a single word, clinging to them, marshalling them. Right now, that word was violence.

It's everywhere around me, Alphonse was saying. Yet is there any shred of it in me? I don't think so. I can't find it. I can't feel any hatred for anyone. Alphonse scratched his chin. Lucky is fictional of course, but what he suffers at Pozzo's hands is slave violence. And those men in that bookmakers' bar wanting to attack me! Their blood was up. Being passive is violence too. Vladimir and Estragon just look on as if amused, then actually make fun of Lucky: they side with the tyrant. Alphonse scratched his head. Then there's the way the Algerian reacted. I was only hugging him! I only wanted him to dance! He threatened me with . . . violence. Not in so many words, but that was the message. Lucky's mind is broken, even worse than his body, and his language has come unstitched: the body of his language is itself broken! Where is this going? Alphonse scratched his left ear.

What would have happened if they had come over and hit me? Would the Portuguee have stepped in to defend me? Would the bar have taken the aggressors' side? What could I have done? I haven't been in a fight since I was twelve. I would have covered my head with my hands and arms to shield it from the blows. Or tried to push my way though the crowd to the door, then run run ruN rUN RUN! Or I'd have curled up in a ball on the floor.

Violence. How quickly people resort to it! Always up their sleeve. Always in reserve. A thought away, an impulse. The Arab mistook my hugging for violence. Perhaps I held him too tight. Is it violence when your freedom is taken? Then what are we doing here? Can we walk out of this factory? Am I free to go? This then too is violence. Can we stop working? It is violence then that keeps us here. Congealed violence. We are free to choose, right? Either we come here each night and make stinking bits of plastic or we go hungry. There's even a man here who walks round all night, all set to spring at any intruder. To protect us? To protect the owner's assets. With violence.

It's a breath away. Maybe the Arab had no other way to react. So he threw me off. And threatened me with lethal violence, mentioned his civil war. I'll talk to him about violence. He'll understand. I'll see what he says. Maybe he'll tell me about his civil war. Feel free, I'll say. Just don't let's get violent.

Curling. Mathieu had finished the story. For the fourth or fifth time since starting to read it, he looked out of the glass front of the raised office, just to check. He saw a light on the control cabinet of machine five. He pushed his chair back, got up, opened the door, leaned out and shouted over the tops of the presses,

Hey! Britishe! Mais, tu dors?

Marcel, at the end of his machine eleven, glanced toward Mathieu and raised his left hand with index finger extended, as he moved across the aisle toward Eric's machine.

Mathieu sat back down and looked again at the pictures. He rehearsed the simple facts. The old girl was senile, bewildered. There was nobody to look after her. Her son was a medical student in Metz, in his final year. One morning he travelled to a run-down neighbourhood out east where no one would recognize him. He purchased a hypodermic needle from a chemist's dispensary. He stole from his hospital three vials of adrenaline. He injected his mother through a mole on the back of her left thigh. The old lady had a weak heart. It did the job. Simple.

Everyone was relieved. Her family, her doctor, her neighbours: they were all happy for her. Of course they were. If anybody wondered what triggered the heart attack, nobody thought to ask. It was a blessing for all concerned, everyone said. Some thanked God. That should have been the end of it. But the murderer was wracked with guilt. He felt he had killed her not as an act of mercy, but because she was in his way. Unable to keep the matter to himself, he confessed to the police. If he had had one person with whom to share the secret, he stated, he would never have given himself up.

Staring at the photo of the young man, Mathieu felt anger and disdain. To do such a thing, such a good and necessary thing, and then to regret it and confess it out of feebleness. Because he was alone. That was inexplicable. Inexcusable.

Mathieu shut the magazine and closed his eyes. (Nadine, in her prime, her lip curling in contempt at some instance of moral weakness.)

Speed. There were many different speeds within the plastics section, human and mechanical, physical and mental, synthetic and organic. The speed of injection, the speed of peristalsis, cooling speeds, falling speeds, drying speeds. The unexpected thought that was slow to dawn, the lightning realization that stabbed like sciatica, the dogged decoding of a difficult text, the itemizing calculation of expediency.

27. Collision . . . Evasion.

Collision. When walking in a crowded place – a street or a factory, for example – people mostly manage not to collide. Multiple and minute judgements and negotiations are entailed, generating a stream of tiny signs disclosing an intended trajectory and a disposition to give way or not to a fellow ambulant.

Eric had never mastered these skills. Even in England, he had been notorious in his locality for colliding not only with moving bodies, bicycles, baby buggies, but with household pets. Encountering upon his path a dog or a cat, both Eric and the animal would become confused, neither party confident of the direction in which to steer. While cats would flee spitting from such an encounter, dogs might take the misunderstanding more personally, baring their teeth or yowling.

In France, Eric's incompetence at communicating and interpreting everyday signals, compounded by the initial strangeness to him of Gallic gesturing and expression, involved him at once in a spate of collisions. The oncoming person would indicate an intention to veer left; Eric would think they were heading right and would move to *his* right. At the last possible moment, both would leap to their respective lefts. Whoops. Sorry! Er, Pardon! Further entanglement and misreading would ensue, then sometimes a second or even a third collision or near thing. To many of those bumped into in this fashion, Eric's ineptitude appeared deliberate. Women reacted with scorn, men with irritation. The more world-weary checked their wallets.

Within the factory, matters were somewhat easier. Everyone had learned to make their movements crystal-clear to the Englishman, engaging in elaborate dumbshows, and affording him a uniquely wide berth. Marcel went one step further: to the amusement of the other men, when walking anywhere near Eric, he would pipe out a rather tinny 'beep! beep!' in fair imitation of a Grandgobier municipal bus.

Intruder. Mathieu had remained seated in the glass-fronted raised office, Luigi's magazine closed on the table before him. A melody by Wayne Shorter was playing in his head. He tapped his left index finger upon his thigh. He licked and compressed his lips, as if he had his trumpet to hand. He began to scat. Da-da, da-dop, da.

The table before him stretched the breadth of the office. On it lay box files, papers and other objects. Behind Mathieu, against the wall, ran a line of dark-grey filing cabinets. Above them, affixed at their corners by brass screws, were yellow notice boards bearing charts, documents, memos, photographs and a single calendar.

It occurred to Mathieu that he had nowhere to go, certainly nowhere to rest. All the other men had 'their' machine and hence 'their' place alongside it, 'their' chair. Mathieu had this office – where he was ill at ease. He felt like a poor boy from out of town adrift in a classy neighbourhood afraid of sitting on the neat clean benches.

He got up and exited.

Tease.   It was good of Marcel to help me 'purge' the machine, Eric thought.

Eric had carelessly allowed machine five to run empty, till the press had stopped with a half-formed piece of sprue dangling from its open mould. Something had distracted him. He hoped the foreman hadn't noticed. Anyone could make a mistake. He hadn't failed to fill number six. A fifty-percent success rate wasn't *that* bad.

Marcel had shown him what to do. 'Purger': Eric couldn't think of an English word for it. You switch the machine to manual, draw back the injection nozzle and get it to eject the last remnants of molten plastic onto a piece of cardboard. Like chucking up. 'Purgative' was a word in English, wasn't it? After that, you could fill the hopper again.

Eric was now mixing a second tub full of raw material for machine five: about half new white granules, 'vierges' they called them; the other half pink-grey wispy flakes from the 'recyclage' bin. He didn't know these words even in his own language. When his hand came out of the bin it was furry with the ground-down stuff, which kept floating up and tickling his nose.

The first thing he had noticed was Marcel tapping him on his shoulder, but when he had looked up Marcel only grinned and pointed at the press. Eric had been trying to read an American novel one of his housemates had lent him but his mind was stuck on Fanny. He had noticed that his thoughts of Fanny had changed now that he had actually spoken with her. Before, all he saw was the tilt of her clothed breasts as she stood at the clock-machine, alternating with naked breasts from a girlie magazine he kept under his bed. He would have to clean up that room before Saturday, in case she came back with him. Some hope. But be prepared, he told himself. Get some johnnies.

Don't want to be fumbling for the half-empty pack I bought when Megan was last over.

More than her imagined breasts he now saw the look on her face as she withheld her right hand and asked him for a light. Her lips, her teeth. She was in control and teasing. He had never imagined that could be exciting. His picture of her kept changing.

Non-committal.   Tomec was standing by the table at the far end of the downstairs plastics section machine aisle. He had asked the parchment-skinned Algerian a question and was waiting for an answer. Rachid expected the nightwatchman to go away, but he didn't. Rachid dropped his cigarette butt to the floor and crushed it beneath his shoe. Rachid saw Alphonse standing at the office end of the machine aisle, looking through Philippe's papers. The Ivorian's lips were moving, like he was reading aloud or talking to himself.

I don't care, Rachid told Tomec at last, his eyelids drooping.

Tomec waited for more but none came.

What part of it don't you care about?

Rachid closed his eyes. Sometimes to speak the truth you have to concentrate, he told himself. If you don't want to speak the truth, you may as well shut up. But if you do speak the truth, you have sometimes to concentrate a little while you work out what it is.

Rachid gazed past Tomec and up the aisle. The African had opened *Le Monde* and seemed to be interested in something. Rachid was speaking very softly. Tomec moved in closer, not wanting to miss anything.

I don't care if the man I work for was a collaborationist, Rachid was saying. Why be surprised? It fits. You don't get to choose your employer. Mostly, I care how much he pays me. But if someone wants to write graffiti about him, that's fine by me too.

At the end of this speech, Rachid shifted his gaze so that for a moment it smacked right into the security man's face. I say: good luck to whoever did it, Rachid concluded.

Tomec said nothing.

Servile.   His powers were those of observation: ears and eyes above all, though smell and taste could often enter into it, and touch, like pain, could not be denied. His storytelling remit was to observe and report phenomena, events and thoughts, hopping like a trained flea from one surface to the next or rather, to switch simile, directed like an all-seeing, all-hearing surveillance device, by a hidden remotely-controlling, busy-bodying will. Unseen, he was ordered to see; unheard, to hear. He was unlike any preening artist, more a humble chronicler, ethnographer's informant or, if you will, some dusty archivist in the pay of a despot.

Captive.   Rachid and Tomec were still standing by the table. As Alphonse approached, Rachid looked toward his machines.

The African would be easy enough, Tomec reckoned. What would he know or feel about events that happened here over thirty years ago? Was he even born then? This was a long way from his home.

Tomec and Alphonse shook hands. Rachid glanced at Alphonse. Tomec asked his question.

You've heard about the new graffiti, right?

Alphonse slowly shook his head.

Gérard Boucan Collabo, 1942–44, Tomec recited.

Alphonse looked more interested than Tomec had imagined.

Collabo . . . Collaborationniste, Tomec started to explain.

Yes, Alphonse cut in, smiling broadly. Like Pétainiste, Vichyiste. I get it.

Tomec had never heard the word 'Vichyiste.'

So why do you want to know what I think? Alphonse demanded.

Look, Tomec said, lowering his eyes: the boss asked me to ask people what they know about it.

W-e-l-l, Alphonse said slowly. If Boucan was a collaborationist, we should hope he gets exposed and denounced. Isn't that right?

Between you and me . . . Tomec began, waving his left hand as if shooing away a fly.

The thing is, Alphonse observed: 'Between you and me' isn't good enough, is it? Why is it you are asking the boss's questions for him? Rachid was looking at Alphonse now.

Tomec searched for words. He didn't want to say I'm obeying orders.

You and I have had some good conversations, Alphonse resumed. You told me about Miłosz, remember? I had never heard of him. I went out and got the book. I read it. But that *Captive Mind* stuff isn't only for over there, is it? Because it seems to me they've got you dancing to their tune right here.

Alphonse glanced abruptly at Rachid, caught him smiling, then suddenly relaxed. He looked again at Tomec and chuckled. Maybe we all dance to other people's tunes most of the time, the African concluded. Me too, I'm no different. I'm just playing a part, doing a little ballet, keeping in shape. He performed an elegant double pirouette, coming to a halt precisely opposite Tomec.

Dishonour.   Minutes earlier, Alphonse had been reading in *Le Monde* an appeal on behalf of Michaël Stern, a Soviet doctor sentenced to eight years hard labour for resisting KGB pressure upon him to stand in the way of his two sons' desire to emigrate. The report stated that the appeal had originally been launched six months previously by Jean-Paul Sartre and Simone de Beauvoir. De Beauvoir was quoted as saying that the USSR had to make amends for this violation (racheter cet attentat) or run the risk of bringing dishonour upon itself.

Civil.   Rachid was standing by the table, looking up the machine aisle toward the office. He saw Tomec pushing his way through the hanging plastic flaps and out into the raw-materials area.

Rachid was remembering his sister and how the two of them had played Lamby all those years ago. The last time he had seen her was at a reunion of family, comrades and friends on the top of a hill south of Oran. He remembered the leave-takings, the hugging, the solemnity of the occasion. There were many people there that evening whom he had never seen again. On that lambskin rug, years before, he closed his eyes and fell into a state of near-slumber, allowing Esmé to pull and push him round the floor at will. He was Lamby, soft and weak, but it was always he who decided when they would play the game, and he who called an end to it when he had had enough. It was a game of passivity and control. His sister too had loved it. When are we going to play Lamby again? she would plead.

Standing next to the Algerian, Alphonse was trying to remember the speech he had prepared. He recalled a few of the words. Violence was one; war was another; misunderstanding was a third. Between those words had floated a fine soliloquy. He knew that if he didn't talk soon, Rachid would move away and the moment would pass. It was so much easier to deliver other people's speeches.

Look, I apologize, Alphonse said, with a shake of his head. Unreservedly.

Alphonse was standing opposite Rachid, but at a safe distance. He held his elbows in close to his body, with his forearms out toward the Algerian and his hands open, palms uppermost in supplication. He could not clown now; it was essential to play it straight. Rachid's eyes seemed to be on him, but their focus was far away.

You talked me into it, Rachid said, with the faintest of smiles. It's forgotten.

Alphonse nodded and thanked him.

Okay? Rachid asked.

What you said about the civil war in your country . . . Alphonse began.

Nothing, Rachid cut in. I said nothing about it. It gave me skills I wanted you to know about. That's all. I don't need the memories.

There was a silence.

Alphonse stuck out his hand. Are we friends then?

Rachid placed his hand in the Ivorian's.

No, he said, looking the man in his left eye and strafing him with a friendly smile. We are not friends. We work in the same factory.

Alphonse acquiesced. Okay, he said, making to go. Rachid stopped him, touching his forearm with the middle finger of his left hand. He made a sweeping gesture with his right hand, taking in the whole factory, perhaps the whole town.

This is machine time. Down time. Dead time. At best, dream time. Occasionally, dream time. Look around. We are here, that's all.

Alphonse didn't look around, but he nodded slowly. He thought about Lucky, speaking incoherently but on command, a slave to Pozzo and, to Vladimir and Estragon, entertainment. An idea came gleaming into Alphonse's mind.

Molds, Clamps.   Clamping Unit: that portion of an injection molding machine in which the mold is mounted, and which provides the motion and force to open and close the mold and to hold the mold closed with force during injection. When the mold is closed in a horizontal direction, the clamp is referred to as a horizontal clamp. When closed in a vertical direction, the clamp is referred to as a vertical clamp.

William T. Flickinger, HPM Corporation, Mt Gilead, Ohio.

Supercilious.   The factory owner and the chauffeur approached the night-joint on foot. Jorge took deep draughts of night air. He was happy to be out of the car and moving. Gérard was thinking about his son.

As Jorge held the door open, Gérard said, I've got to take a piss and phone home. Gérard liked the frank clean word 'pisser.' It made him smile. With Jorge, as with no one else, Gérard could talk as he thought. There was pleasure in that. He pulled a 20-franc note out of his wallet and handed it over.

What do you want to drink? the Chilean asked.

Whisky, Gérard replied.

Jorge went to the bar and ordered neat whiskies.

Gérard's wife Claude had just arrived home from the dinner party he himself had left so abruptly. She didn't like the way her husband had abandoned her with his friends. Cécile Chartier was so elegant, her pencil-line eyebrows so expressive of her superiority: in Cécile's company, Claude felt like a peasant.

Is Paul back yet? Gérard asked.

When does he ever come in this early? Claude said.

If you see him, tell him I want to talk.

I'm going to bed. Anyway, it'll do no good.

I'll talk to him when I get back.

Claude pulled a face. Gérard heard her silence. He pictured her face.

See you tomorrow, Gérard said.

Sure, his wife replied.

Splutter. Worker straightens up, takes four steps to right and looks at hopper over machine end. He sees material (raw) through (viewing) porthole, over (melting) chamber. He turns and walks past tray (grey) on floor, then tub (red) on bucket (metal, upturned), then past bin (small, scratched, arm-wide, hand-deep, oblong, plastic, red) on floor, half-filled with material (raw, white, shiny). Standing at aisle-end of machine, worker lifts lid (wooden) from bin (waist-high, cylindrical, cardboard) and looks inside. Mist (dusty, fine, red) rises from material (recycled) in bin (three-quarters full). Worker (worker) splutters and replaces lid on bin.

Indifferent. Lying in a bath of soapy water, Odile reminisced. On leaving the office that afternoon, she had gone straight to Yves' flat and they had fucked. Yves lived alone. She didn't love him. It was simple. Tuesdays and most Fridays. During a lull, she had decided to speak. You don't really like me, do you? she had asked. I like this, he had replied with a grin, jabbing so deep it hurt.

Odile missed Philippe. She recalled the way he used to make love to her. It was always exactly the same. He was like a tomcat or perhaps a rabbit, biting into the nape of her neck. He would lift her dress or pull down her jeans, whenever and wherever the urge took him. Mostly, he came into her from behind, sometimes bending her over a table or a chair. Always wonderful. As soon as he sank his teeth in her neck, her skin would cover with goosebumps and she would be ready for him, gaping, juicy.

Philippe had lost interest after their daughter, Olympe, was born. He had worn Odile down with neglect. For a long time he wanted only to hold her hand. They would lie in bed holding hands. Then he had given that up too. Nowadays he lay next to her like a corpse that snored. At least Yves showed some interest. At least there was a pulse.

Odile soaped herself thoroughly. She didn't like Yves' smell. Too much cologne, too clean, too . . . something. Antiseptic. He had asked her to suck his cock once. She had refused. She was sure it would taste of disinfectant. Philippe's cock had always tasted of cock.

Odile stood up and rinsed herself down. She recalled Philippe's taste.

Expert.   Mathieu's voice interrupted Salvatore in the middle of Voltaire's letter on comedy.

Tout va bien? the foreman asked.

The Sicilian nodded and leaned forward. The press opened, he eased back the guard, took the product from the mould and presented it to Mathieu.

Mathieu turned the product a number of different ways, squinting. Salvatore watched. Mathieu pulled off a couple of pieces and threw the rest into the tray at his feet. He held the pieces one by one toward the light, then grunted. He went to the control cabinet and looked at the dials, then seemed to grunt again.

As Mathieu walked back past him, Salvatore mentioned the scheduled union meeting.

Mathieu trained his light blue eyes on the man. You told me already. Yesterday, I think.

Salvatore spoke but Mathieu was walking away and couldn't make it out and didn't want to turn back.

(Imagine the murderee. Eyes open. Coronary infarct, the death certificate would say. How do you operate a hypodermic anyway? He had seen it done a hundred times but still wasn't sure. He wondered whether Nadine had a mole on the back of her leg? He could look. She had plenty of moles on her back. Did the murder victim mind being murdered? To mind, you need a mind. Where could you get adrenaline if you weren't a doctor? It would be easier to get heroin. Doesn't heroin make you throw up? He needed advice. Sound, expert advice. What expert could you consult about the best, the kindest, the safest way to murder?)

Birth   Bull-necked Jacques came to rest at the aisle-end of his machine number four, where he stood munching on an apple, a scabby red windfall, ruminating on its waxy skin and yellow pith, discarding the stiff stalk, removing his cap to scratch at his oily grey pate. He looked at his watch dial through a thicket of wrist fur. Simian, ursine, bovine: human.

Philippe had been gone ten minutes, saying he would sober up. Jacques decided to wait five minutes more then look for the man. Perhaps he would find him at the coffee machine. But if the Marseillais was wandering through metallurgy, Jacques would never find him, never even look. Metallurgy was off-limits and Jacques had a lazy respect for rules: if you didn't need to break them, why court the bother?

Then there was Pierre. Jacques was chomping on the apple pips now, enjoying the bitter-almond flavour. Now that Edith was long dead, he reasoned, why should he and his brother remain strangers? Recently, his parents had often come to him in dreams. Perhaps Pierre dreamed too. Nobody else still alive had known them that much. Pierre, two years Jacques' senior, had been around them two years longer. Mathematical. If Jacques could get Pierre to talk, what might he not learn? Jacques' parents had grown younger and brighter not just in his dreams but in his waking memory, while everyone else – even his own children, even Edith – had aged and faded. Were he to live long enough, Jacques thought, only his parents would endure; at his death they alone would gather at his cradle.

Easy.   On most nights Tomec talked to only one or two or three of the night-shift workers, but whenever Tomec did talk to anybody he watched and listened hard, observing the reactions and imagining the life of that person, second-guessing his or her opinions, anticipating their speech and gesture, busily etching in his memory the fleeting encounter just as it unfolded. On any night, one or two or three such transactions, whether earnest or jocular, friendly or cool, were sufficient. Tonight Tomec had already had to talk to the supervisor, the Italian, the Algerian, the African, the tiny guy on the huge old machine, and the bigger Gypsy. His mind hummed with faces and looks and sounds.

Although Tomec had never seen more than four of the men gathered together at any one time – he now pictured them as a group arranging themselves, as if elbowing one another for position, along the quayside in ancient Brundisium, an impromptu welcoming committee for the old and sick poet Virgil.

As Tomec ambled through metallurgy, his torch playing on the machines, he whispered, I can use these men. This is my crowd, at least its adult male members, the guys in the foreground with living faces. For the women I can use Sarah, my neighbour's wife, that angry-young-woman newsagent who cannot pronounce even 'bonjour' without a snarl, the librarian with her bleached-out complexion, and others will come as I need them: the skew-wigged harlot, for instance. As for the children, children are easy: I have only to close my eyes to see children.

Seated on the roof of one of the machines, his legs swinging, Philippe had recently finished a cigarette. He watched the progress of the security guard's bouncing torch. Tomec sniffed several times as he drew close. He ran the torch over the machine from ground level to shoulder height and walked once round it. He inspected the neighbouring machines in the same way. He shook his head and stood quite still. The air was quiet, the plastics section a distant rumble. Cigarette smoke. He walked slowly away. A hacking cough seized Philippe's throat. Tomec swivelled round, ducking for good measure, and threw his torchbeam at the source of the cough.

Philippe smiled down on Tomec; Tomec glared up at Philippe.

You're not supposed to be here, Tomec said.

I know.

Nor sit on top of machines.

I'll get down.

Tomec used the torch to pick out ledges where Philippe could place his feet.

Do you want to smoke? the Marseillais asked, shaking Tomec's hand.

Tomec looked around. I'm trying to stop, he said.

I'll not breathe a word, Philippe said.

Tomec took the cigarette, stuck it in his mouth, but waved Philippe's lighter away.

Could I borrow your torch? Philippe asked.

He explained how he had wrenched off his wedding ring and slung it under the machine. It wasn't necessary to say why. Tomec handed him the torch.

Do you need help? the Pole asked.

No.

But when Philippe crouched down and began to search among the cigarette butts and metal offcuts, dust, oil and debris, Tomec crouched alongside him. He noted the mix of beer and coffee on the man's breath. It took them a couple of minutes to find the ring. It had rolled a long way. They stood up.

It has to be worth something, Philippe said.

Tomec stared at the Marseillais, taking him in.

Do you mind if I walk with you? Philippe enquired.

You'll be going the wrong way, Tomec replied.

Wrong way? Philippe said.

I assume someone's looking after your machines, Tomec said.

I assume so too.

They walked.

I have to ask everybody about the graffiti, Tomec said.

Philippe clicked his teeth.

Tomec waited.

True or false, Philippe said, I can't see any harm in writing it.

Tomec stopped walking and when Philippe stopped too, the men found themselves standing opposite one another. Their eyes had grown accustomed to the darkness.

What are you doing here? Tomec asked.

I needed a walk. Then I tore my ring off.

I didn't mean here and now in this workshop. What are you doing here in general?

On this particular planet? Philippe asked, spacing the words for satirical effect.

Tomec waved his free hand impatiently. I think I know what I'm doing here in this factory, he said. Even if my girlfriend doesn't always agree. But you?

I really don't recall why I'm here, Philippe said. But let me help you with the graffiti: if I had done it I would deny it and if I knew who the culprit was I would cover for them. As would anybody in my position. You're wasting your time.

What would you do in *my* position?

I'd leave the men alone and then I'd lie. I'd tell the boss I'd asked around and found out nothing. Simple.

Collapse.   Luigi had reached that inevitable point in the intergalactic porn comic where the heroine Aurelia, never knowingly overdressed, had been divested of all her clothes and was being impaled at her several orifices by a series of alien stiffies, one of which appeared to be barbed. The expression in her eyes denoted agony; her nipples were pointed warheads good to go; her mouth gaped in a howl of pleasure.

The imagery had effected Luigi in calculable ways, tunnelling out his mind and tenting his trouser front. As he placed his comic face-down on the floor and considered whether this might be an opportune moment to visit the toilet, he noticed, descending the stairs, first Bobrán's plimsolls and then his red-edged trouser legs.

Luigi got up quickly, took a couple of steps to his right and checked the hopper level. Then, glimpsing Bobrán passing down the machine aisle, the Italian stepped back past the grey floor tray and the red threshing tub and removed the lid from the recycled-material bin. Peeping inside, he was met by a mist of blue plastic dust. He felt his softening dick fall southward in his pants. He spat at the floor then glanced down the aisle. The little gyppo was talking to the Arab: birds of a fucking feather.

Confidence.   Bobrán walked up to Rachid, his hand outstretched. Sorry about earlier, Bobrán said. The chef was shouting.

Rachid gave Bobrán his limp bony hand. He stared at the man.

What? Bobrán asked.

That stunt you pulled. On the staircase, the banister. Stupid.

Bobrán blinked.

Really stupid.

Maybe, Bobrán said. If taking a risk is stupid.

Rachid noticed the fleck in Bobrán's eye.

What can I say? Bobrán said. You're right.

Bobrán watched Rachid fight and lose a battle with himself. You could see he didn't like to talk about personal matters. He was twitching.

My son died, Rachid said.

Bobrán took a step back in order to see more clearly.

I'm sorry. Did he fall?

Why do you ask if he fell? I said he died. I never said he fell. Why should he fall?

I don't know.

Don't tell me Gypsies are clairvoyant.

Bobrán stared at Rachid. He wasn't sure what he was waiting for.

In a sense he *did* fall, Rachid said at last. He fell from the kerb. Into the path of a moped.

Rachid wasn't sure he had made his point but he wanted the man to go away now. Bobrán just stood there.

What do you want? Rachid asked.

Can you read?

Rachid waved toward the table, where a newspaper lay.

I can't, Bobrán said.

Too bad.

Could you read something for me? It's only a few lines. It's a letter. It's private.

Who am I going to talk to in this place?

That's what I thought, Bobrán said, pulling out the letter from his back pocket. He folded it so that only a few lines were exposed to view.

Rachid adjusted his glasses on his nose, took the paper and read out: '. . . l'intention de créer des ennnuis à personne. Mais nous sommes en colère. La vie d'un africain ne vaut pas cher ici, n'est-ce-pas? Nous aurions voulu vous offrir . . .'*

Bobrán repeated the words faultlessly.

You've got a memory, Rachid said.

You need one if you don't read.

Rachid handed back the letter.

---

* . . . the intention to create problems for anyone. But we are angry. The life of an African is not worth much here, is it? We would have liked to offer you . . .'

Bobrán tried to picture Rachid's son by imagining a miniature of Rachid: fewer wrinkles, thicker hair. What he saw looked nothing like a child.

Thanks, Bobrán said. And I'm . . .

Sure, Rachid cut in, turning his back, 'Sorry.'

Evasion.   Standing at the end of his machine fourteen, Luigi had watched the conversation between Rachid and Bobrán. He wondered at the piece of paper that passed between them. As Bobrán made his way back up the aisle, Luigi pushed his intergalactic porn mag into his back pocket and headed for the toilet. He wasn't going to give Bobrán the chance to remind him of his unwise bet, didn't want to place his money where his mouth had been. Besides, he was ready for a little relief.

28. 22.15.01.

a.

Is for Anxiety.

Aged, alone, peering into darkness, two digits pressed to wrist. Heartbeat furious. Jeanne has dreamt of Jacques and Henri meeting. Libération. Can't envisage Henri older or Jacques very young. Heart leaping but no pain. Finding something: weak, erratic but a pulse. Thought so. Alive. Tomorrow it may rain, I may die. Possibilities.

b.

Angela, Luigi's mother, x-ray-eyed, sat on a flaccid armchair before a muted TV, an unclean rug swaddling her knees, Revelations wide open on her lap. Gregory Peck and Anthony Quinn bestrode the seas, their mouths agape. Gilberte, Luigi's girlfriend, had told Angela goodnight and gone to the room she shared in sin with Luigi. 'In righteousness he doth judge and make war. And his eyes are a flame of fire . . .' Angela glanced up, quenching the vision in brine. 'And he is arrayed in a garment sprinkled with blood.' Angela thought of her slope-backed whey-blooded son with that giggling godless trollop honeying with contraceptives on Sunday afternoons, constraining Angela to turn up the TV, drowning them like kittens. Verminous. And her husband still living somewhere with that woman from Calabria, a hairy peasant, a terrone though spawned in Milan. 'And the armies which are in heaven followed him upon white horses, clothed in fine linen, white and pure. And out of his mouth proceedeth a sharp sword, that with it he should smite the nations: and he shall rule them with a rod of iron: and he treadeth the winepress of the fierceness of the wrath of Almighty God.' Amen. Amen.

c.

When you walk along the street you have to step carefully always on the cobbles, whether in Grandgobier, Warsaw or Cremona. Anywhere in Europe; anywhere beyond. Lift your eyes from the pavement? Then beware! Pan slowly. Cut. Action! Eyes primed to point the lens, hands to focus. Avoid gentle grassblades heaving through cracks in paving stones. See them drift in the dream of a cold and ordinary November evening. Newly met lovers-to-be still cautious. How to make the first move? Who to make the first move? They sense its inevitability, neither know it will mark the end of carelessness and childhood. Old couples and singletons bright-eyed yet weary this evening. See how the conscript soldiers roam the streets of Grandgobier, robbed of both song and speech: captured in a lull between rehearsing their anthem to liberation, counting down to their return to civvy street. Snapping one another in clumsy poses, they quash any foretaste of nostalgia for a camaraderie they never sought, demob happy unto death. You there in the beaten-down suede shoes and gabardine! You in the uniform! You in the wink of that child-woman's gaze! Roll through the city, frame all that is coming, and click click click!

d.
Gérard and Jorge stood outside the bar, each man with a drink and a cigarette. The soldiers had interrupted their singing and were moving off down the street, some with their arms linked.

They seem happy, Jorge murmured.

Why wouldn't they be? Gérard grumbled.

Jorge opened his mouth, then shut it again.

Jorge would never have to do military service now. In Chile, he had been a student. He had expected to be called up after graduation. He would have got to know his country properly, he told himself, maybe travelled to the south or spent time in the mountains. He would have come into contact with workers and peasants. Under Allende, it would have been all right. But Allende was dead and conscripts were now forced to fire on fellow proletarians.

What are they singing?

Zéro, Gérard said.

Zéro? It's familiar. Porque perder las esperanzas de volverse a ver . . .

They count the days. When they reach 'zéro,' they sing the word over and over. To celebrate. They're just clearing their throats. You should hear them at midnight. Gérard couldn't help smiling.

Did you sing Zéro? Jorge asked.

We were at war, Gérard snapped, going back into the bar.

e.
Albania: Hodja, addressing 7th AWP congress, scorns imperialism,

social-imperialism, and revisionism; Ankara: fighting between right-wing and leftist students – man shot dead; Argentina: General Videla announces strengthening of economic cooperation with Soviet Union; Besançon-LIP: occupied factory under workers' control holds open day – 10,000 visitors; Bucharest: Breznev to make friendly visit to Romania in late November on invitation of Nicolae Ceaușescu; Calabria (Italy): mafia demands 300 million-lire for work on aqueduct to proceed; Colombia: pro-Castro ELN, pro-Chinese EPL and pro-Soviet FARC in negotiations; Dinan (Britanny): FLB-ARB claims responsibility for tax-office bombing in struggle for free socialist Breton state; Israel: strikes protest deteriorating living conditions – Communist Party tables censure motion in Knesset; Italy: Andreotti urges austerity measures, committing his family to eat less meat; Lebanon: Syrian military units of Arab Peace Force advance toward Beirut; London: twenty-five charged after clash between National-Front supporters and East End Asian Community; Madrid: bus drivers strike ends, pay talks begin; Moscow: Ustinov, at Nov-7 parade, denounces imperialist powers for seeking to hamper world revolution; UN: China denounces Soviet disarmament proposals as fraudulent; Warsaw: Edward Gierek in Moscow for talks to secure economic aid; West Germany: minister-president of Lower Saxony advocates torture of terrorists in ticking-bomb scenario.

f.

Is for Futility –

a subjective yet calculable category, the sum of three negatives: *no* power over our day-to-day work; *no* comprehension of the purposes it may serve; *no* way up, or out.

But f. is also for the freedom to rebel, to revolt and to unite, and for a moment at least to live fully.

g.

Mathieu gazed at a smear of grease on his index finger. How much effort could it take to empty one ordinary mind? In bed once, Nadine asked him to define the good death: a bullet in the back of the head, without warning. Mathieu is trying hard now to reason, but has reached an impasse. Nadine owns nothing, neither thought nor judgement, pain nor pleasure. Mathieu, as if taking on the work of two, remembers everything. She would smile when tickled, then only when fed or defecating. Only the passion of his gaze equals the weight of her absence.

No more.

She had listened, shaken her head and said: No. Wrong. For death is the moment of fullest meaning. It is best met when ready, aware and sympathetic. At death you can summon all life before you. Mathieu imagines mind without self: thought just thinking. In combat, when is it okay to kill an unconscious enemy? Whether friend or foe, you may kill to end suffering. Even brute pleasure and pain have now deserted her. Mathieu glanced at a smear on his finger. Nadine, diminished and dying, cheated, is still no target. Killing Nadine, a terrible duty: his soul for hers.

h.
Is the hand
    that hurls into the bin the product that fingers have snatched from my mould. An elbow shoves my guard shut. Eyes stare as my presses close, a mind contemplates my needs, sinews dance attendance. Hands fill my hopper, ears catch my rhythm. Am I too hot, too cold? A hand shall provide.

i.
The little man was sitting at the huge old semi-automatic machine, still fizzing, still fuming from what Tomec had told him. A swell of indignation swept through his pigeon-chest. To smear Gérard Boucan, the man whose father had given him his first job in this factory, who employed them all, and to do so anonymously! The filthy cowards, the red swine!

'Collabo' they had called him. Yet what was collaboration? If the blockheads could only use a dictionary, they might discover that collaboration was a fine and dutiful thing. To collaborate was to cooperate, to cooperate was to work with, to assist, to abet. A fine word, a decent thing that had been twisted and bent out of meaning, dragged through the dust and rubble.

Besides, what did Boucan's accusers know of those times? Had not Pétain, so fashionably vilified, saved France twice: at Verdun and at Montoire? The collaborator was truly an unsung hero. Gérard Boucan had played his part.

Sometimes, just as you are minding your own business, considering events from your armchair, History reaches in its hand and grabs you by the throat. Whether Philippe Pétain, Gérard Boucan or little Jean Herbier, you cannot ignore her call.

j.
Is for Julie,
    eyeing Chuck lurching from the street-door.
    They're singing my song, he snarled. My folks are Chicago-Scotch. Auld Lang Syne. In November!
    At midnight it's over, Julie explained. They'll never meet again. Don't Americans get drafted?
    Chuck sprayed beer. Heard of Vietnam? What the fuck you think I'm doing here? Getting an education?

k.
' . . . and jostling like apples fed down a chute into a press.'

l.
Is for the Light
    spilling from an anglepoise lamp at Tomec's sketching bench in the distant corner of the workshop furthest from the plastics section, pooling around Philippe and Tomec as Tomec talked incessantly yet longed to be alone, while Philippe made polite noises yet wished to leave, both men pulling away yet glued fast.

m.
Every few minutes since leaving the barracks, hours ago now, one of them would break into what was finally going to be their song, for one evening only: (to the tune of Auld Lang Syne) Zéro! Zéro! Zéro! Zéro! etcetera. The others took up the tune joyfully, sometimes wistfully, always chest out and shoulders back. There was Pavel, and Robert, and Jonathan, and Émile, and . . .
    From a distance, these men might seem like trouble, meandering,

marauding. All young, all crew-cutted, some swinging half-full bottles, joshing and pushing one another, sharing cigarettes, peering unseeing at passersby, as into a fairground mirror, their own images bouncing back distorted.

Heike, Moritz and Gilles stood aside as they passed. Gilles explained the nature of the soldiers' celebration.

Did you also do this? Heike asked.

Naturally.

You didn't refuse to serve? You're not against the military?

They taught me how to use weaponry, fight battles. When the time comes, our training will prove indispensable. You can prepare the future with demonstrations, strikes and bombs, but it has to be secured with armies.

Heike looked at Gilles and laughed. Gilles watched her laugh but, seeing no joke, only nodded. Moritz glanced at his watch: 22.15.01.

n.

Is for Nadine,

for all that her eyes had seen while they still saw, her mind had thought while it still thought, her ears had heard while still hearing, her nose had smelled, her face had felt. Nadine had vacated herself like a house of bad memories, a place where nobody could bear to dwell.

o.

Philippe had found a gap in Tomec's flow, had answered a forgotten question with 'Nothing' and had turned his back and gone.

Tomec stood alone in the pool of light, his eyes closed, thinking of the tranquillity, the respite he enjoyed when snugly lodged in Sarah's cunt, when it was always her turn to talk, ideas jostling one another, feeding down a chute into his day-dreaming mind, while he lay beneath her still and quiet, poker-pricked and -faced, time seeming to stop dead, while she alone moved. Or, later maybe, lapping lazily at her sex, while she too fell speechless for once.

Her cunt was always for him a place not of inspiration but of slow garnering: the thoughts of the day, his work, his would-be art, as he took her clitoris in his lips, his teeth, pulling it this way and that, roughly then gently, absent mindedly, sucking on a sweet, rolling it like gum, alive to her flexing and clutching, all the time in the world, while she thought maybe of her Moses and Aaron and God and of what it was to create something from nothing, beauty from dust, a near-enough-permanence from the fleeting of a life.

p.

Is for Patrick

and Guillaume, standing apart from their comrades, swearing through tear-filled eyes to remain in touch. No more 3 a.m. sleepwalking patrols, forced marches, cold showers, discipline by insult, humiliation to order. But what other basis had their friendship? What else could bind a Guadeloupian shopkeeper's son to an oboe-playing architect-to-be from the Jura?

q.

The Marseillais was picking his way through dark metallurgy, stepping carefully. Tomec had shown him the sketches he made at his quiet workbench, the books he thumbed, the photographs he shuffled. The Pole had looked into his face and talked of far-off times and places, a poet and a quayside. Philippe had said nothing.

This is Sarah, Tomec had said. Philippe saw a snapshot of a shock-headed young woman with green eyes and a smirk.

And this is Virgil, Tomec had said, showing an eyeless statue.

Philippe could think of nothing, not his wife and child, not his old dreams or fears. Until nothing was a rock on his chest.

Nothing, Philippe said when Tomec finally stopped talking.

Nothing? Tomec queried.

Earlier you asked me what I was doing here. Nothing.

The Pole looked embarrassed, sharpened a pencil, shrugged as if sorry.

It was a perfectly good question, Philippe said, turning away.

Philippe saw the lights of the plastics section.

Just when you don't expect it, Philippe thought, suddenly you're free. A door slides open. My wife fucks another man and – ca-ching! – I'm free. I can leave her, live alone, move away, change my job, even fall in love. Anything.

r.

Is the random

hurling of workers, women and men, foreigners and French, Europeans and non-, old and young, crushed and jostled down a chute, molten and spat, cooled and collected, monitored, measured, boxed and dispatched, valuable at last, exchangeable, ready to circulate, primed for profit never their own, commanded to be sound, condemned to unfreedom.

s.

Jan returned triumphant, ate, tidied, lay down to rest. He surveyed in dream the entirety of his work. He must quickly pierce his hearers to the core. How to engineer the exact conditions for seamless spontaneity? To reduce an epic to a single performance spurt. Sitting in a park, Jan would ask for advice. He must seek out Tomec, have his vision sketched. He heard them behind the door, fumbling, furtive, whispering. Jan stared at the paper, listening for a voice. Narrowing to a single point, his mind sought clarity. The voice would erupt, suddenly, from nowhere, when summoned.

Yet more.

Asleep since late afternoon, Jan woke slowly, crawling from his bed. If you don't doubt your entitlement to write, you should desist. Take just one point, fill your mind, then write, dictate, declaim. Rodents among the rubble panting, outcast children in graveyards quietly playing. The passion of its presence matched the power of his gaze. He had summoned the vision and looked on its face, speechless. He silenced characters, dismissed events, ears for only the story's breathing. He paced, he prayed, he flexed his body, calmed his spirit. Words came tumbling like clowns into the ring of his mind.

t.

Is for Tide.

Instead of circling, Marcel's thoughts now ebbed and flowed, tidal, teasing at a thing the Jew, the shrink, the Orléanais, had said: Jews and Gypsies would be hated always. They would share disasters, the pogroms of old, our Shoah, your Porajmos. Like us, you will always keep a suitcase packed and waiting.

u.

If human affairs are understood to be determined by unfathomable forces beyond the reach of the individual (any individual) . . . which is to say by a conglomeration or conjugation or concatenation of universal mental struc-tures, unconscious epistemes, transcendental grammatology, operating under systems of rules that direct social behaviour without the assent of the indi-vidual (any individual) . . . then, given the unquestionable bracketing of all human agency, as well as the illusory or at least uniquely contingent quality of individuality, compounded by the burial of the subject, the redundancy of the author, and the death of man (any human) . . . then the undermining of all intention, the impossibility of mimesis or even representation, amounting to an onslaught on humanism, the dethronement of the work (any work) . . . the upending of the Enlightenment, the unseating of the lone or even collaborative thinker (any thinker) . . . the voiding of meaning, the sliding of signifiers (any signifiers) . . . cannot but lead unstoppably to the untram-melled, unbridled yet almost inconspicuous evacuation of meaning and hence the undermining of utterance (any utterance), ushering in an unalterable and unlettered because uniform, unsubtle because uninflected, ineluctable dev-astation of the uplands or indeed lowlands (any lands) of purposive human thought . . . then, if human affairs . . .

v.

The conscripts had drifted apart, as if the magnet of impending freedom had relaxed its common hold. Some viewed window displays, pointing at objects they vowed to purchase as soon as they could find jobs. Others chatted in twos or threes. Émile stood to one side, his eyes travelling between his soon-to-be-ex-comrades. One by one, he named them to himself, engraving upon his mind an image of each man. None of them noticed or approached him. They all knew that Émile liked to stand alone. They had pleaded with him to join them in this night of celebration. He had intended to spend the time reading a novel. His aloof demeanour, his confident calm, would have been missed.

Émile looked away from his comrades and across the street. His eyes met those of a crop-haired young woman standing on the edge of a group of obvious students: the men with longish hair, the women in jeans and scarves. Some familiarity induced Émile to hold the young woman's gaze. She broke into a smile, looked away then stared back. He wanted to venture across the street. He glanced at his soon-to-be ex-comrades, while the vertiginous thrill of imminent release filled his veins.

w.

When you walk through metallurgy you have to step carefully always, weaving at night between slumbering grey machines that weep oil, whether you are ordinarily stone-cold sober or wearily woozy, whether abetted by a service torch or hampered by failing eyesight. You in the shabby canvas pumps, heading back to your place in the plastics section! Step nimbly past the slicks that would rob you of your footing, the jagged metal offcuts that would snag your shoes! Amble back to your nightly nine-to-five wage-enslaved routine! Return to your unacknowledged comrades, quash any nostalgia for the instants spent in solitude or the conversation enjoyed! Alone perhaps at last? Think on your wife and child and despair! And you in the smartly buttoned uniform and comic-opera cap! Sitting in your pool of light at your sketching bench, musing on your Greeks and Romans, the dying poet, and your girlfriend's pink pink cunt, and a work so great, so vast, so littered with allusion, so resonant with living, that it might stand as a monument even to one sluggish twentieth-century backwater existence – your own! Heave aside the pointless care, the moody brooding, the self-denying self-reproach! Quash that sigh! Sketch that camera-ready vision!

x.

Betty, Eric's middle-aged mother, had written him a letter. Particular phrases dwelled in his mind. 'My dearest Eric': he was afraid a housemate might see that. As embarrassing as a mother's hug at the school gate. 'The fox came again last night. Dad put out bacon rind and stale bread soaked in milk. We watched for twenty minutes from behind the curtains, using the Japanese binoculars Dad gave me for Xmas.' Eric easily suppressed a pang of longing and indulged a sneer. The primitive wildness of suburbia, the magnanimous courtesy toward the assimilating foreigner, be he academic Indian, Chinese dental surgeon, Italian gastronome, or vulgar American with matching automobile. Or indeed that fox, with no red reek of rapine in his fur, reduced now to a residential beat, a routine sidling from garden to garden, bin to bin, lapping at the leftovers from the tables of the comfortably binoculared. 'Jilly has been promoted . . . the weather has been unseasonal again . . . Dad thinks Callaghan is done for . . . Uncle Dick is poorly . . . I have decided to take up yoga . . .' Eric had fled from just such comforts, such solicitations, and with every new letter from his mother he calibrated the chasm that divided them.

y.

Is for Youth.

Yes. Is anybody less like me than a peachy-skinned young German boy? Clean features, soft voice, smooth hands, safe family, free agent. Sitting naked on his carpet after that first fuck, peering in the mirror. 'Liberation,' he laughed. 'They call us homos. But I wouldn't want me the way I want you.'

z.

Tomorrow they'd go home, see their sweethearts or families, start growing their hair. But tonight they slapped backs and hugged for the first and last time, sad and happy they might never meet again, sad and happy they were finally friends.

They walked tall through Grandgobier, one hundred and four minutes from freedom, up and down the city streets, no wages to waste in bars, no girls on their arms, only one another and shared memories for company.

There was Pavel the prankster; Robert whose fiancée wrote twice a week; Guillaume who played oboe; Émile the bookworm; Davide who for three weeks had wept each night for his home in Aquitaine; Patrick who loved running; Ali the entrepreneur; Nicolas who wanted independence for Corsica; Jean-Marie, friends with everyone; Théophile, who insisted on being called Jimmy; Samuel, with glasses as thick as your finger and a passion for maths; and Marc who, with the right tools and materials, could build you anything, and would, for a price.

Silence had fallen, a momentary searching. One second, two, three. Ali was the first to break. They all chimed in:

ZÉRO! Zéro! Zéro! Zéro!
ZÉRO! Zéro! Zéro!
ZÉRO! Zéro! Zéro! Zéro!
ZÉ-ÉRO! Zéro! Zéro!

29. Fuzzy and Crisp.

Fuzzy.　What is it that conduces to giddiness, fuzziness, slackness of body or mind?

It is the thrill of unfreedom ending; the surge of blood-alcohol to the brain; the glimpse at a concrete floor spinning; the wrench and rush of long-postponed orgasm; plummeting blood pressure; physical exertion while fasting; getting up abruptly from a low chair; leaping from a merry-go-round; unforeseen triumph; beauty of sound or sight; a racketing horn solo with no time to breathe; last and first love; the sudden ravishment of sleep.

Furry.　The ape-armed peasant had checked his own and Philippe's plastic products at machines one two three and four and had seen that they were good. He had emptied them from their floor trays into threshing tubs resting on upturned metal buckets. He had gestured to the belly-stroking Gypsy across the machine aisle a request to keep an eye on all four machines. Lumbering now past the end of Luigi's machine fourteen, his trunk bobbing like a fat old tug across the wash of some ocean-goer, he was noticed by Mathieu the scale-faced night foreman, standing at Luigi's machine, waiting for the presses to open. Mathieu pulled his burnt-out matchstick from his mouth and jabbed it in the peasant's direction.

Eh! he cried.

Mathieu observed Jacques stop, turn and slowly dip his head.

In one man's unguarded gesture, one may glimpse the history of a family, a clan, a class, even a nation. Jacques' deference to the former army man, his officially sanctioned superior within these walls, buckled his generous frame, inclined his head, hoisted his left arm: the yanking of a forelock was narrowly averted. His eyes a-twinkle, Jacques watched the foreman open the machine guard, catch a falling product from the mould and hold it up for inspection.

Mathieu threw the piece into the nearby threshing tub and closed the machine guard. He saw Jacques' left hand rise to his ear, his thumb and index pinch and then pull at its furry lobe.

Alors? Mathieu questioned, pointing at Philippe's machines.

Parti boire quelque chose, Jacques communicated, his right thumb jerking toward his mouth.

Mathieu raised his left wrist high, his right middle finger tapping twice on his watch. Où qu'il est?

Jacques looked away to his left, his mouth opening.

Y va bien? Le marseillais . . . Pas malade? Mathieu insisted.

Si, si, Jacques replied, nodding and grinning as he fixed on a story. Maux de crâne, he said, the index finger of his right hand tracing his frowning hairline.

Mathieu agitated his left hand at the peasant, then opened the machine guard and grabbed the new product. Luigi arrived at his side from the toilet, rivulets of perspiration coursing among the blackheads on his cheeks. Mathieu felt his presence, sensed his panting, but had a matchstick to suck.

Incumbent. Fernando had pushed his chair to the end of his machine seventeen and was now sitting, his head down, his eyes open. He was observing the African who had come up the stairs like it was a dance or an exercise, two or fucking-three steps at a time, skipping hopping. Now Alphonse was standing fucking-there, right between his machines eighteen and nineteen, in his yellow and green and white. Looking like a fruit salad. He hadn't even checked the product, not even a glance. Fernando needed to tell him. So many things he needed to tell him. The African was getting himself into too many sorts of trouble and Fernando didn't want that. They were almost friends: it was incumbent. If you want people's respect, want to keep your job, don't want to be a joke, you don't dance around, you don't go hugging people who never asked for a hug, least of fucking-all moody Algerians who never say a word to anybody. First rule: keep yourself to yourself. Damn it, the Ivorian hadn't even checked his machines weren't kicking out crap twice a minute. It wasn't Fernando's way to be telling people their business. But, for Alphonse, his almost-friend, he would make an exception. The African was swaying now, his mouth gabbing away. Didn't look like singing. Didn't look like reading out loud. What was the man thinking? He had to get serious.

Approved. Automatic operation . . . is in every respect the same as that outlined for the semi-automatic method except that the 'stop' limit switch for the clamp-ram will initiate the 'clamp open' timer, which in turn will restart the cycle when the gate stays closed.

Molds that have been designed and tested for automatic operation require only intermittent observation of behavior to ensure that everything is working in an approved manner.

Timing.   Rachid had grown sick of sitting on his chair, thinking of things to say to Mehdi, thumbing his paper, wondering about Malika's smile. He told himself he had to listen more closely to her and to Fatima. They wanted him to return to them. But Rachid needed Mehdi more than any child needs a parent or any wife needs a husband.

Rachid stood up and stationed himself at the end of his machine eight. He rotated his head a little, testing the neck muscle he had strained earlier. Eric drifted into view, wanting to borrow his lighter again. Rachid gestured toward his jacket. His eyes followed the Englishman to the chair. Eric's fingers dived into the breast pocket and bounced back out with the lighter. Rachid found that odd. He had half-noticed something earlier. Rachid watched Eric drop the lighter back into the jacket pocket, and nod another 'merci.' The glinting metal top of the lighter could be seen protruding from the breast pocket. That clinched it. Rachid was as tired as always. Besides, why should he care what junk found its way into his pockets? He didn't need distraction right now. He couldn't remember a time he hadn't been tired. That particular pocket had never served any other purpose. It was his lighter pocket: end of story.

Rachid went to the chair, drew the lighter from the pocket, digging his bony fingers down. A sheet of paper, folded over several times, was wedged at the bottom. It took a while to dislodge. But then up it surfaced, like a gob of sludge from a drain. A single sheet, badly folded three times and scrunched and bent. Perhaps it had been stuffed hurriedly into the pocket. He unfolded it once. There, in Malika's hand and in the ochre-coloured ink she used, and in Arabic – a language Rachid and Malika never used together – he read his name: رشيد. His eyes sprang open. He reached for a cigarette, then looked around. Nearby, Eric and Salvatore were talking quietly, Salvatore with his usual glowering intensity, Eric on his back foot, glancing around, searching for an escape.

Rachid undid the second fold then stopped. I don't like surprises, he said, neglecting to cover his mouth. Then, beneath his breath: What is it Malika cannot tell me to my face? Is she leaving? Ridiculous. Where would she go? She could no more leave than I could.

Rachid was struck by the alien formality of his name in Arabic. The only time he and Malika had exchanged letters was during war or when family duties had separated them. He wanted time to collect himself, rehearse his reactions. He glanced at the machines. There was product that needed checking and threshing. And he could top up the hoppers. The note could wait till he had guessed the very worst. Whatever bombshell it contained, he could at least time its detonation.

Zigeuner. Gilles knew all about Wolf Biermann, had broken into a rendition of 'Die hab ich satt,' imitating Biermann's rasping anger. He was word-perfect, remembered the whole thing. Heike was impressed, called out to Moritz who had been strolling with Margot, leaving Jean-Pierre on his own to walk behind, pulling on his goatee.

Don't worry about him, his wife had said, taking Moritz's arm, he's a philosopher: he'd got a head so full of ideas, he can't ever get bored.

Moritz caught up with Heike and Gilles, joined in the chorus of Biermann's song, then the Germans clapped heartily while Gilles executed a low bow.

So are you going to come to this concert on Saturday? Moritz asked.

I hadn't heard about it. Your sister told me. I missed it in the paper. It should be something.

Well, if we can get tickets . . . Heike said, looking at her watch.

Gilles grinned an eloquent, 'Why not?'

I know a guy who may be able to help, Heike said. I need to phone.

Gilles pointed to a hotel. They'll let you use theirs.

The phone rang on Horst's side of the bed. He and Else, his wife, were tucked up in their pyjamas, reading.

Hallo? he answered. Horst heard a crackly line and a torrent of explanations.

Ja, gut, he said. Where are you? Lucky you. I'll try. How many? Four. Okay. I think so. No, I won't join you. You know what I think. Theatre for the masses. A sop. In the end, propaganda for Honecker. Or for Schmidt. It's all the same. You'll see.

Else's lips were pursed, light pink. Horst put the phone down. Else noisily turned a page.

One of the students from our ML reading group, Horst murmured, affecting a yawn. You met her, didn't you? Heike.

The one that looks like a lesbian?

Horst grunted, turned out his light.

Did you say 'four' tickets? Else asked.

Yes: Heike, her brother and both their . . . boyfriends.

Hah! said Else, quietly turning back a page.

Moritz and Gilles watched as Heike ran skipping from the hotel.

He reckons he can get them, she said. He has trade-union contacts.

I'll borrow Jean-Pierre's car for the weekend, Gilles said.

What if Bobrán doesn't want to come? Moritz wondered.

Bobrán? Gilles asked. What kind of name is that?

He's my boyfriend, Moritz said.

Gilles' head went up and slightly back, but his expression stayed fixed.

Er ist Zigeuner, Moritz announced. Then, for the benefit of Margot: un beau gitan avec un beau cul.

As Heike and Moritz discussed what to do if Bobrán couldn't make the trip, Jean-Pierre's wife took Gilles aside, nodding in Heike's direction, These Germans work fast, don't they? I like them. I like her. Don't you?

Gilles pinched Margot's cheek between his index and his middle finger. He didn't say a word.

I wonder if Jean-Pierre could fancy her, Margot murmured, one eye slowly closing.

Glutinous.　The olive-skinned Sicilian finished reading Voltaire's twentieth *Philosophical Letter* and looked at the title of the twenty-first, 'On the Count of Rochester and Mr Waller.' He wondered whether it might be worth his while to enquire of his English work-colleague what he knew of the said Count. Might he not possess some insight, hailing from the same island and having imbibed, perhaps with certain historical geographical sociological variations, the same culture?

Salvatore read the first line of the twenty-first letter: 'Everybody knows of the Count of Rochester by reputation.' That seemed encouraging, though he had reason to fear that the intervening centuries had effected a falling-off in English culture or perhaps in the Count's reputation. The previous week, Salvatore had asked the Englishman what he knew of the Quakers, the subject of the first second third and fourth of Voltaire's letters from England, only to be informed that, as best Eric knew, the Quakers were an ancient and now defunct protestant sect: the only living Quakers he had ever heard of were the ones responsible for a glutinous and rebarbative breakfast cereal, and Richard Nixon. Salvatore had struggled to square Voltaire's depiction of Quakers as plain-speaking, modest, mild-mannered and meek with the foul-mouthed Jew-baiting mass-murdering cereal-munching former president of the United States. Decidedly, the Sicilian reflected, the Quakers had suffered a falling-off as sharp as that of the entire Anglo-Saxon tribe. Or could it be that the moral fibre of the original pilgrims and fugitives had perished during the Atlantic passage?

With these thoughts in mind, Salvatore had nonetheless approached Eric, asking him what he knew of 'RRrrochesterrRR.'

Rochester? Eric said, anglicizing the pronunciation.

Salvatore dropped his head and splayed his feet a little further in an effort to sink to the Englishman's level.

Er. Une ville, petite ville. À la mer. Pas très loin de. Er. Où je vivais. Sur la Medway, er, rivière, er, la rivière Medway.

Salvatore frowned, confused: the notion that Britain, though famously an island, might possess a coast, bewildered him. He couldn't picture it.

This RRrrochesterrRR, he said, was a person, a literary figure. Not a town by the sea.

Ah, then I know the answer! Eric chirruped. This gruff man. Er. Un homme taciturne. With a beard, I think. Barbe, yes. Who loses his eyes in a fire, blind, but still marries the heroine, who is some kind of domestique. Like an au pair. He has a child, I think. 'Au pair' is French, isn't it? No? Sounds it. I saw the film. Orson Welles.

Still frowning, Salvatore brought the thumb and index finger of his right hand up to his lower lip and tugged gently. He then smiled broadly at Eric.

Oui, oui, c'est ça, c'est ça, the Sicilian said.

Trowel. Worker stands over two sacks (grey, paper, one full, one opened) propped against barrel (waist-high, cardboard) at aisle-end of machine. In open sack among granules (oval, shiny, translucent) rests trowel (metal, shiny). On ground beside two sacks stands tub (red, plastic, as long as worker's arm, as wide and as deep as worker's hands). At solar-plexus level, above sacks, barrel and tub, juts cylinder (steel, shiny). Above and along length of cylinder, second cylinder (steel, shiny) moves to and fro, as presses open and close. Aisle-half of machine shifts in and out upon base (fixed) the breadth of worker's finger (middle). Worker (worker) stoops and takes hold of trowel.

Granted. Standing by his machine fourteen, Luigi examined the product piece that the scaly-skinned foreman had handed him. With Mathieu's faint blue eyes upon him, the Italian looked at the piece as a whole, then at the products one by one, from this side and from that angle, hunting down anomalies asperities irregularities excrescences concavities discolorations, searching, knowing there was one there somewhere, searching but not finding.

Mathieu blinked.

(Nadine's face flashing, not so many years ago, at the onset, after that first stroke, searching, searching for something just beyond reach, a word, a name, an object recently mislaid, searching but not finding.)

Mathieu blinked and her face was gone again. Blink. Blank.

V'l'avez vu? he asked at last.

The slope-faced Torinese pulled an Italian 'no' grimace.

For the second time this evening, Mathieu pointed with his claw to the tiny offending flap attaching to one part of one side of one piece.

Luigi nodded.

Si ça change . . . , Mathieu said, walking away.

Entendu, Luigi replied.

Mathieu glanced across the machine aisle checking the warning lights on top of the control cabinets of Philippe's and Jacques' machines one two three four. All off. He limped across the aisle to machine one and leaned against the guard as the press closed. He voided his mind. Successfully for once. A warm empty feeling. (Nearer to Nadine. Closing in on her.) The press opened. He pulled back the guard and stared at the product.

Something wrong with Marseille? Headaches, it seems. Headaches. He never had headaches before. Something up. Not my business. Nothing wrong with this piece. Never is. Take nothing for granted.

He slung the product at the almost empty floor tray. A bin brimming with product to be threshed stood on the floor by the control cabinet and another squatted half-full on the upturned bucket. Beaune must have done that for him. Friends. Old man and younger man. Not my business. He'll have his work cut out when he gets back. Mathieu glanced round. Stray granules of raw material on the floor. Too many to count. Careless. Spilled. Unlike Marseille. Badly swept up. Unlike Marseille. Not in character. Maybe Beaune filled his hopper for him. Slapdash peasant. Not my business. Marseille doesn't spill things. Unless. Not my business. Headaches. People sick. People having coffees. Machines unmanned. I could run the entire damn floor on my own. Not my business? One day I may have to. (Nadine, eyes wide open, dead at last.)

Banging.   By the time Jacques swung slowly into view, Philippe had tipped the last drop of coffee down his throat and taken the last drag from his cigarette.

Another coffee? Jacques asked, approaching the machine.

No thanks, Philippe replied, seeming sober now.

Jacques looked at the small coin nestling at the centre of his huge right palm. He cocked his head to one side, then re-trousered it. He pulled up a wooden chair a couple of feet from his friend.

For a minute, neither man spoke. Jacques smiled into the dark, his body rocking slightly. Philippe remembered he had wanted to tell Jacques what Danielle had told him, but he couldn't find the words now to broach it. Jacques appeared to be waiting. Philippe noticed his smile.

Philippe had fragments, but no story. He liked to be laconic, pithy, offhand. People enjoyed his easy manner. Tonight, however, his material didn't lend itself. So where to begin? There was his sister, and there was Rémy, Rémy's bar, the old girl – Lucie? Yes, Lucie – and something about his shoes. Odile was banging another man. That was it. Danielle had said so. Would his sister lie? Philippe lit another cigarette. Quite possibly. Yet he believed her. Then there was the Polack at the far end of metallurgy talking about Greeks and Virgil and his girlfriend. Ringlets, big smile, smart eyes. He had seen her photo. 'Sarah.' Too young for any Polack. Before that, Philippe had lost his ring then found it again. 'My wife is banging another man.' He couldn't get the words out. They had no edge to them. Couldn't do it. Couldn't say it. Speechless. Didn't happen often.

Both men stood up. Philippe felt like a man who had pulled a girl, taken her home and then, for the first time in his life, just couldn't get it up.

I'm not in any hurry, Jacques said, clapping Philippe on the back, avuncular and forgiving. No need to worry. We've got all night. Relax.

The Marseillais laughed so hard that Jacques wondered if he had sobered up after all. He glanced at him side-on as they strolled toward the hanging flaps that separated metallurgy from the downstairs plastics section.

You had something to say too, Philippe remembered, still chuckling.

It was nothing, Jacques said.

Jilting.   Marcel counted his cigarettes. Nine. He had to pace himself. He had to have at least one left at 4.55 when he clocked off and strolled out into the morning air.

He flicked a cigarette out of his pack and lit it. He was observing the foreman who, in the Marseillais' absence, was checking the products at machine number two. Marcel wondered what would happen if he or his cousin ever dared vanish for twenty minutes at a time. Of course things were different for mere agency workers.

One of the tips that Martin, the prison shrink, the family man, the Jew, the Orléanais, had given Marcel was that he should learn to make lists, that list-making, whether with the aid of pencil and paper or simply in one's mind, was a good way of getting rid of circular thoughts, what Marcel had called 'the whirlpools.' You order your thoughts, Martin said: you don't let them order you. You might list things in different ways: by size, time, quality, and so on. It was important to dwell on that, Martin said. So you didn't forget that what you were doing when listing was listing. Something like that. Martin had said a lot of things.

Right now, Marcel was getting ready to list his current and recent girlfriends. This was long overdue. He needed to place a mental cross or tick against each one, according to whether he should keep or jilt her after his wedding. He wanted to be reasonable. Hell, he was getting married: he needed to start telling them soon. A lot of fine judgements were called for. Martin had spoken of a 'listing methodology' and of 'criteria.' That was what he needed now. For example, he could think of his women in terms of their age – but that would be imprecise, since he didn't always know or remember everyone's age. Or by height. Or by bust size. Or, damn it, by tightness of twat. (He always preferred a tight twat, always feared a slack one.) Or by the number of times he had fucked them. But such a 'methodology' would be as imprecise as age.

No. The only sure criterion was relative seniority – how long it had been since he had first fucked them. Not the first time they met. He couldn't always remember a first meeting. But he could always remember a first fuck. That then would be his criterion. That would be his 'listing methodology.' He could start with the first fucked. Which would be Germaine. Of all the women he still fucked, Germaine was definitely the one he'd fucked first. It had started when he was a kid. They hardly ever saw one another now, but when they did they always fucked. Chantal suspected nothing. Germaine would have no problems about him being married. Germaine was a good sort. But then, after Germaine came Paulette. Paulette would have to go. It was high time.

An event like a wedding can really sort out your priorities. To think he had been feeling bored earlier that evening! This would keep him thinking in straight lines all night. He had so many judgements to make. And once he had worked out who to dump, he could start thinking about how to dump. A matter of methodology again. He had warm feelings for some of them. There were others who would be tricky. One or two of them might still be dreaming he would marry them eventually. One or two might play up. The worst they could do was tell Chantal. If that happened, he could deny it all. If that didn't work, he could beg for forgiveness and tell her it had all started long before he knew her and he'd only continued with it out of kindness. Chantal knew he was no hermit monk. She knew he had fucked around. She had fucked around plenty herself. Nothing wrong with that. Before she met him. Indeed, the fact that each of them had fucked and been fucked all over town – what am I saying? – halfway round the world in Chantal's case and all over France in Marcel's – and that they had still chosen each another . . . Well, it was a kind of mutual tribute they were paying. A compliment from each to each.

Patience.   Fanny dried her face and hair on the towel, rubbing hard, admiring her body in her bedroom mirror. Her fine waist and large high breasts pleased her. She liked the way her nipples pointed upward. Her hair was short and neat, her skin still wore that summer's tan, her hips were round and strong, her entire frame compact and firm. It was a body that anyone might like to stroke and kiss. She caressed her belly, smiled down at her thighs and calves, then turned her head gently to the left and, watching herself in the mirror, delicately lifted her left shoulder, and kissed it.

The only other body Fanny had ever known at all well was that of Kosal. She had been impressed by its hardness, its elaborate musculature, the prominent veining around his neck and along all his members; but, finally, none of these aspects had pleased her. She was not going to miss his body. His physical adoration of her had been amusing for a time, but that time was now past. At least he had not been hairy.

Fanny hung the towel over a radiator and pulled on a dressing gown. She stepped into slippers.

In the adjoining room, at the kitchen table, Fanny's mother, also in a dressing gown, was playing patience beneath a strip of neon. Fanny sat on the chair opposite her. There was a bottle of wine on the table – almost full – and two glasses, one unused and upended, the other containing a puddle of wine.

Do you want something? her mother asked, placing a card. There's purée and a pork chop in the pan.

I ate at work. Where's Julie?

Someone phoned in sick. The bar asked her to stand in.

I thought she had to study.

She said she needs the money.

Fanny looked into the corners of the room, her eyes returning to rest on the wine bottle.

I'm going out, she said.

Her mother nodded and placed another card.

Pity. The long-legged Sicilian stood ramrod at the aisle-end of Philippe's machine two, flexing in his right hand his hand-exerciser, while his left hand flicked through the pages of the regional paper. He was looking for a report of the murder and suicide of his tennis-club acquaintances, but he found nothing, not a trace. As he turned toward the stairs, he noticed Luigi standing between machines fourteen and thirteen, an unlit and half-smoked Gitanes-Maïs in his mouth, his eyes trained on the pages of *Détective*.

Salvatore proceeded slowly up the stairs two by two, rising at each new step onto the ball of each foot to maximize the benefit to his calf muscles.

The moment Bobrán saw the Sicilian, he stood up and walked toward him, holding out an ill-folded, handwritten sheet of paper.

Would you read me a couple of lines? the little Gypsy asked.

As many as you like.

Bobrán handed Salvatore the sheet of paper, folded in such a way as to isolate the lines to be read.

Salvatore perused the lines once, just for himself, then read the words out in a level voice: 'quelque récompense, mais notre famille n'est pas riche. Nous sommes pour la plupart des instituteurs ou des petits fonctionnaires, mal payés et intègres. Mon voyage impose maints sacrifices à notre famille au pays . . .'

Bobrán's lips moved as he listened and continued moving after the Sicilian had stopped speaking.

Is that it? Salvatore asked.

Sure, Bobrán said, taking the sheet.

A light came into the Sicilian's eyes.

Tell me, he said, looking round and bending low, You can't read, can you?

Bobrán shook his head. I can't read words, he said.

Tell me, the Sicilian said again, are you the only guy here who can't read?

I don't know. Are you the only guy here who walks around playing with one of those things?

Salvatore glanced down at his hand-exerciser. His right hand ceased to flex, simply stopped moving. Good point, he said.

Salvatore saw Fernando, Alphonse and Jean, all at their machines. He recalled why he had come upstairs.

Like I was saying before, there's a union meeting at 11.15. About strike action, though I know you're employed through an agency.

Bobrán looked down at the letter from Albert. There were three lines left. One more reader. Unless he asked Salvatore to finish it off.

You are welcome to attend the meeting, Salvatore said. I needed to tell you that.

Bobrán was fussing over his sheet of paper, folding and refolding it.

Salvatore looked at the floor. He was experiencing a distinct feeling. He named it to himself: pitié, compassione. The things he took for granted each day – newspapers, union leaflets, philosophy books, a world of public knowledge and disseminated culture – all of it far beyond the reach of this poor benighted young man. Salvatore walked away, his breast bursting with a sense of privilege and humility, while Bobrán stood and mumbled the entire letter through to himself.*

Crisp.   What is it that conduces to crispness, grittiness, certainty of traction, tautness of sinews and sense, when the words on one's tongue and the air through one's fingers crackle and spit like flame?

It is the thrill of freedom dawning; the surge of adrenaline to the heart; the glimpse of a clear road stretching; the euphoria of success following

* Albert's letter so far, rendered into English: I introduce myself. My name is Albert Gbenye, I am Joseph's elder brother. Joseph often talked of you in his letters. He wrote that you were friends. It is on these grounds that I permit myself to write to you and I beg you not to have any worries about my initiative. I have come to France to know the truth about my brother's death. We have no intention to create problems for anyone. But we are angry. The life of an African is not worth much here, is it? We would have liked to offer you some recompense but our family is not rich. Most of us are schoolteachers or lowly functionaries, badly paid and honest. My journey is costing our family back home many sacrifices . . .

arduous effort; the wham-bang! of a quick and shallow orgasm; an unexpected reprieve from execution; bidding one's beloved an indefinite farewell; beauty of sound or sight; a solo where every note surprises and is perfect; best and worst love; the steady ravishment of life.

30. Walk . . . Stand.

Walk. One man, alternately bovine simian ursine, galumphs and shambles; a second, stroking his belly, swaggers saunters; another, leaner by far, slouches slopes; a fourth, this one scaly, limps lists; a fifth, histrionic, prances dances.

This adopted language, any language, must lack sufficient words of motion to portray with any precision, to identify, to clinch by the throat, to brandish and shake at the reader, even a mere dozen particular people, so protean and metamorphic is each and everyone. Alone the multiplication of moments thoughts actions and devices may approach an adequate rendering.

Who is it then that slinked and padded, feline, along a rail? Who now paces and strides, swinging his torch, brooding through the dark? Who, his features trapped in earnestness, advances in a workout of flexion and tension? Who moves as if hired by the hour to do so, eyes down, arms loose? Who waddles, in his canvas pumps, his head nodding?

Redolent. People rub off on places, even passing through. The space between machines three and four was now imbued with its current night-shift tenant: its mere association with the lumbering peasant, or perhaps the localized scent of his overripe apples wafting through the plastic smoke miasma, or the modest presence of his pot-bellied hold-all dumped against the base of the control cabinet.

Mathieu had checked Philippe's machines one and two as well as Jacques' machine three and had emptied all three floor trays. He rested against Jacques' machine four, waiting for the cycle to finish, the nozzle to retract, the product to cool and the presses to open. Leaning into the guard, the foreman's pale-blue eyes had crashed into the green plastic bag slumped beside the broken-zipped hold-all that the peasant brought to work every night. Mathieu had glimpsed apples, green brown yellow and spotted. Jostling apples had filled his mind. Keeping Nadine far away. Damned apples. He would like some.

He yanked open the guard, seized the product before it dropped, studied it, turning it this way and that, sighing, macerating his matchstick. Why did the murderee's damn-fool son have to confess? What did he do that was wrong? The magazine screamed murderer! No mercy for the merciful. He was a student, a child. He should have thought ahead, borne his secret to his own grave. The maths of differential pain and pleasure were outrageous. The mother had been too decrepit to suffer more than slightly; the son could vibrate to either pain or pleasure. Her slight suffering was over, his fathomless pain was beginning. The maths was were outrageous.

An alto-saxophone solo played itself into Mathieu's innermost ear as he cast the product piece into the threshing bin and bent down to raise and tip the floor tray. He sang the missing words: *Ah-preel Een Pah-reese*. Sharlie Park-her. He straightened up. To possess the means, then lack the resolve: that too was an outrage.

Mathieu glanced up at the hopper. People rubbed off. He was glad to quit Jacques' space. How would his home, *their* apartment, seem to him without Nadine? Even comatose, a person leaves a trace behind, a smear, an aura. Call it soul.

Hostess. Jorge slid the Mercedes into Boucan's garage and killed the engine. He did his belt up tight, exhaling with discomfort. The garage light was on a timer. Gérard and his chauffeur hurriedly exited the car then the garage, pushing a button for the up-and-over door to close. The two men had driven the last stretch in silence and found nothing to say now. The light went out as the door hit the ground. Gérard extended his hand, Jorge shook it, and both men turned. Gérard, heading for the front door of his mansion, glanced up and saw that his son's bedroom was dark. Jorge fetched his bike from the outside garage wall, flipped it round, dragged it onto the tarmac drive, and straddled it.

Without spending any money, Jorge could either go home or to Marta's flat. He pedalled his way out onto the road, heading for the city. He didn't have to take a decision for another three kilometres. That sweet shy-insolent kid earlier, at Chartier's house, had made him think of his cousin Carmen, his country. He needed to deal with homesick nights without resorting to Marta's. He lived in Europe; it was time he lived among Europeans. But tonight he would surely go to Marta's. He would allow himself that weakness. Her flat would be full of people he knew a little. There would be salsa, merengue, things to drink and smoke and eat, acquaintances, news from his continent country city neighbourhood, numberless Latin Americans, inquisitive young French people, including women. At the centre of it all Marta would sit stand dance officiate, beautiful, fresh, cool, infinitely accommodating. It was her passion.

In Grandgobier, every non-US American – even Canadians – quickly found their way to Marta's door. The men fell in and out of love with her, remaining her friends, observing, each with his unique smile, her subsequent liaisons; the women all liked her, deferred to her, used her, sometimes abused her – though never, never, to her face.

Excess.   Rachid was numb, then overwhelmed by feeling; empty of heart, then crammed with grief. He thought of his wife's smile that evening, felt it engraved on his retina, lingering. He imagined the tone of Malika's note: loving, pleading, perhaps contemptuous. He walked slowly up and down between his machine eight and the huge wooden table, his eyes on the ground, his arms loose. Malika's note in his left hand seemed to glow.

If I put this note back in my pocket, won't it scorch a hole? If she leaves me now, what memories of Mehdi will she take from me? If she smiled at me this evening, was it the better to betray me? If her note makes me feel anything at all, may I not drop to the ground wailing?

It will soon be time to check the pieces again, to smoke, to have a beer or a coffee, to go to the toilet: there is no escape from time or living. It is vital that I talk with Mehdi soon to impart the latest news. It might be good for me to be alone, free of wife and daughter. There is too little of anything, and too much of nothing.

Rachid tried to manage his fears and feelings, but events were beyond his control.

Wind.   The language employed here is – of course – no more his than it is yours, which is to say that it is his by adoption only. It has to pass as a catch-all for the speech of those appearing in these pages. It is a medium that gobbles up Portuguese, Arabic, Polish, Italian, Tagalog, Hebrew, Hausa, French, Romany, German, Finnish, and other no less venerable tongues with their cargo of quirks and oddities preserved to the height of his ingenuity, only to mill them, grind them, render them down, down, down into that one finally indifferent and complacent idiom that unlike any other runs no imaginable risk, either now or in the foreseeable lifetime of this tottering tribe, of appearing either quirky or odd: this now rapidly-becoming-universal linguistic dustbin; this soon-to-be-one-and-only vehicle of human and post-human thinking; this mammoth world; this pearl; this obese and ballooning beauty; this gift that goes on giving; this sullied bijou set in a world laid waste; this faithless and incontinent joy; this English.

Syndical.   Alphonse and Fernando were at their respective machines. Salvatore approached Alphonse first, interrupting him where he sat, his eyes fixed on the cover of his book, a finger holding its pages ajar, his lips babbling.

Would you come with me? I have an announcement, Salvatore said.

The grammar indicated a question but gesture tone attitude and demeanour denoted a command.

Alphonse placed his book beneath his chair, got up and followed Salvatore, who next roused the Portuguee, discovered sitting, his eyes closed, leaning right back, one comforting hand cupping his groin.

Salvatore reiterated the question-command to Fernando, who muttered in response, What fucking-now is wrong? But he rose from his chair meekly enough and went after Alphonse and the Sicilian.

When Jean looked up and saw the Sicilian, the African and the swarthy Portuguee bearing down upon him unsmiling, he appeared to take fright, as if he had strayed into a rough neighbourhood of some foreign city. Salvatore smiled to see the little man blench and his piggy-eyes dart left and right.

The Sicilian leaned over Jean, beckoning Alphonse and Fernando to draw near.

I have come with a union announcement. I'm the rep now. I have taken over from Philippe Merceau. He gestured back at Alphonse and Fernando. I don't want to repeat myself, he said.

I'm listening, Jean said, drawing back the machine guard as the presses opened. But I'll tell you straight off that this machine knows nothing of any union business.

Salvatore glanced from man to man to man. We meet later this evening at 11.15 in the meals room in the raw-materials area to discuss strike action in coordination with metallurgy, other plants within the Boucan group, and indeed other sections of industry up and down this country and far beyond . . .

Fernando covered his mouth to stifle a giggle, as he weighed the relevance of their deliberations to, say, China, or even Portugal, or even neighbouring Italy. Alphonse, meanwhile, leaned his chin on his right fist and nodded, savouring the ring of internationalism.

The planned action – Salvatore continued – is in line with CGT–CFDT–FO deliberations . . .

You can just bet it is, Jean said, slamming the guard shut and hitting the START button.

Our intent is to send the employers and their government the clear message that the working masses will not be made to pay for the bosses' economic crisis.

Jean stared at the steel press, his jaws clenching. Alphonse and Fernando nodded hard.

I trust everyone will attend. The right to meet on the employers' time is itself the fruit of past collective action undertaken within the framework of . . .

What about the machines? Fernando interrupted.

Good question! Jean piped.

You are entitled to shut them down but you may choose to keep them running. The meeting won't take more than ten minutes.

Salvatore then addressed himself specifically to Jean.

Given the semi-automatic character of your machine, should you desire to attend the meeting, you will have no choice but to suspend production. In case you consider asking one of the gyp . . . – one of the agency workers – to look after your machines . . .

I wouldn't trust them, Jean broke in. This machine is a hard taskmaster.

. . . As I was saying, Salvatore resumed, any request to agency workers to cover for your absence would breach union directives and, as your union representative, I could not, as you will doubtless understand, sanction . . .

Ripping the latest bunch of cable ties from their sprue, Jean turned to Salvatore and said, As Merceau should have informed you, I am not a member of any union and I don't strike.

Salvatore stared back. Nobody here, I am sure, is eager to forfeit wages. But there is such a thing as the greater good and the longer term.

Before Jean could reply, Salvatore raised himself to his full height and said, Thank you gentlemen, and was gone.

Love. Bernard Labarde was not snoring. A choking nightmare, rare and hideous, coupled with its probable proximate cause – a sudden shallow cough – had jerked him into wakefulness.

Bernard saw from the red digits on the face of his alarm clock that he had not slept long. By way of confirmation, he sought and failed to find his wife Yvonne lying alongside him. He might have liked to cuddle her, gently lift the hem of her nightdress, feel the touch of her legs against his; perhaps, were she but willing, should she but turn toward him as once she was wont to do, he might insinuate himself between her thighs.

The flat was still. Wondering what his wife was doing, Bernard eased his heavy legs down from the bed while raising his large trunk, till he found himself sitting on the edge of the bed. He scratched an itching ear, then stood up, retying the knot of his pyjamas cord. Careful not to make a noise, he padded from the bedroom, along the short corridor, until he stood at the threshold of the living room.

Bernard had a clear view of his wife. He saw her face first, lit by the flickering soundless television screen. Never had her features appeared to him so animated with simple pleasure. For once, she looked as joyful and as carefree as when they first met. Yvonne seemed to stare at a vision close within her carnal grasp, a vision that her hectic fingers, as Bernard now understood, had conjured and were directing.

Bernard peered at his feet. He withdrew on tiptoes. He sighed.

I have had a long day, he told himself. I have an early start tomorrow.

He returned to the conjugal bed. It wasn't long before he fell asleep, the image of his happy wife slipping slowly from his darkening mind.

Floating.   First Jacques then Philippe pushed through the plastic hanging flaps that divided metallurgy from the ground-floor plastics section. Jacques smiled broadly up into the glare, his bulk gently rolling; Philippe squinted, treading carefully behind his friend.

Luigi and Mathieu, standing at the aisle-end of the Italian's machine fourteen, saw the two men first. Mathieu forgot for a moment to chew his matchstick: Marseille looked paler and pastier than usual, he thought. For his part, alerted by the foreman's evident interest, Luigi searched Jacques' and Philippe's faces for clues, but found none.

When Philippe, just behind Jacques, turned into the machine aisle, Marcel, standing at the aisle-end of his machine eleven, began to snicker, half-expecting Philippe to trip and fall.

Salvatore, descending the stairs above the glass-fronted office, stopped still, his left hand on the rail and stared down on Jacques and Philippe but, like his compatriot, didn't know quite what he should be looking at.

From the far end of the machine aisle, both Eric and Rachid had registered not only the return of Jacques and Philippe but its petrifying impact on their colleagues.

For a moment, all eyes present – save those of Jacques – were trained on Philippe, yet he remained oblivious to his colleagues' concerns. He walked with care behind his friend, then slipped into the space between his machines one and two.

Mathieu remembered to chew his matchstick; Salvatore resumed his descent; Rachid's eyes re-homed to the cement floor; Marcel's face straightened; while every other man shrugged his singular shrug, and reverted to his previous attitude of work or respite from same.

Facing his machines, Philippe dismissed all other preoccupations; for now, nothing but work figured. He rolled up his sleeves squarely, pulled on industrial gloves. At each machine he had a product to examine, a floor tray to empty, more than a tubful of product to thresh, and a hopper to check. He calibrated his effort to the tasks at hand. For now, he could dispense with mental struggle. He devoted himself entirely to his labour. This was what he did for money. He did it as best he could. In this brief suspended state, and in spite of his heavy panting, the metallic taste along his tongue, the bloating in his stomach, the sweat that stung his eyes, Philippe was at ease.

Opinionated. Jean dropped a bunch of cable ties into the cardboard box stationed alongside his right foot, dumped the empty sprue into the bin standing to his left, closed the machine guard, and tapped the START button. He then turned his frown on Alphonse and Fernando, who hadn't moved since the Sicilian's exit. The little man's eyes threatened to bore holes in Fernando's and Alphonse's chests.

Striking is a waste of time, Jean stated. I've been here long enough to know. All we do is hurt the man who pays us a living. If he goes bust, we're out of work. What will you do then? I'll be drawing my pension.

You make me laugh, Alphonse said, laughing illustratively and leaning down over Jean. You always side with the guy in the big house, the swish car, the fancy clothes. You make him his money but where do you live? Do you even possess a car? And just look at you!

Fernando who, throughout this speech, had made a series of interjections intended to temper Alphonse's flight of rhetoric ('hey, that's fucking-not fair'; 'you don't have a car either'; 'the man's entitled to his views!'; 'fucking-easy now!') suddenly grabbed Alphonse's forearm and pulled him abruptly back, dragged him away.

You're out of line. I told you before. You don't talk to people like fucking-that. You need some advice. We're friends, right?

Alphonse was still laughing. Of course, he said, struggling to straighten his face.

Well, as a friend, you don't talk at people like that, not old men . . . and, another thing I've been meaning to say, you don't hug workmates who haven't asked to be hugged, you don't force them to dance . . . let alone moody Algerians. It's a bad thing to do. You fucking-get it? You don't take risks like that. You don't stick your neck out.

Alphonse looked into Fernando's face, noting the perspiration, then laughed, buckling up, holding his sides. Man, oh man, you are funny!

What are you laughing at now?

Here we have the demon gambler, Mr Clever who takes advice from deadbeats in a PMU bar and loses his shirt. And HE's telling ME about risk.

Fernando was momentarily speechless. He took a step back. That's different, he said. It's something else. It's not the same.

Words wouldn't come. Thoughts neither. Fernando shook his head and turned. Alphonse watched him go back to his machines. He looked at the man's back as it curved over a tub of sprue, his head bobbing up and down as though in animated conversation.

Psychology.   Fanny's mother sat at the kitchen table, uncorked her bottle, and poured some wine. She smiled at her completed game of patience, took a sip, then pushed the cards into a heap. The wall clock showed twenty past ten. She got up, went to the dresser and switched on the radio. It was Anne-Marie. Just Anne-Marie. Maybe she didn't have a surname.

Anne-Marie was saying goodbye to a sad-voiced man whom she called Arthur. She thanked him for phoning and wished him good luck. Anne-Marie's voice was patiently purring. It was the one voice you could sometimes hear all night.

Before we go to the adverts, she said, I'd like to remind our listeners that this evening we're discussing the psychological impact of infertility and, here in the studio with me is Jean-Claude Lebrun, a psychologist who specializes . . .

Fanny's mother switched off the radio. She had never been troubled by infertility. She didn't know anybody who was.

The previous evening, the topic had been, 'Children who won't communicate.' Fanny had come home late from work and caught a bit of it, while she ate her soup. They had listened to the programme in silence. Fanny's mother had wondered whether she ought to turn the programme off. Then Fanny had got up and gone to her bedroom without saying goodnight, and her mother had played another round of patience.

Western. For now, Philippe had finished with his machine number one and was threshing product at machine two, trapping the tub between his thighs and the machine flank before him, exploiting the plastic product's own weight and consistency, not fighting it, not struggling. Mathieu appeared at his side.

Ça va? the foreman asked.

Ouais, Philippe replied, surprised.

If you want to go home, I can get the nightman to open the gate. If you're ill. Sleep's good for headaches. I'll work your machines. No loss of earnings. Go home to your wife.

You talked me out of it, Philippe said.

Eh? Mathieu said, shifting his weight to his left foot then back again. I thought you had a headache.

Who said? Jacques?

Oui. Le paysan. Beaune.

He was right. I took something. I'm fine. Believe me: going home would make it worse.

Okay, Mathieu said, taking a step backward and raising both hands, like a bystander in a cowboy film ordered to 'stick 'em up.'

Trust. Bobrán processed memories ancient and modern, sifted recent impressions.

Heike was pleasant; Joseph was dead; the Algerian's son was dead too; Moritz was beautiful. Whatever he might find out later about Albert, Bobrán now knew that he wrote a good letter. The first fuck with Moritz had been a whole show: a high-wire double-act, an animal stunt, a drum roll, a brace of clowns doing slapstick; an acrobatic duo; awed silence: everything except applause.

His mother's health worried Bobrán – she didn't take care; his sister was still vulnerable; his cousin Marcel could make trouble at any time and in any way. Whatever Joseph's ghost might require, his brother would know; whatever Albert might request, at least the waiting was over. The worst thing would be if the police came back to hound him.

Bobrán stood up then sat down; he stretched out his legs, then hauled them back in. Whatever else Bobrán might do if he were able to read, he could also, he thought, write a reply to Albert. The lightest flick of his index finger was all it took to turn Albert's letter over on his lap. For some, writing was almost as easy, no?

The Algerian's son was unimaginable alive or dying; dead, he must be like any other corpse. Wherever Heike and Moritz drove him that weekend, it had to be preferable to staying in Grandgobier. The best person to read the last three lines of Albert's letter – Bobrán realized with a start – might be the chef d'équipe: when did he ever talk to anyone?

Auricular. The ears of the workers present that evening at Éts. Boucan displayed great variety. Prescinding quite from their functional capacities, sensitivities and skills – merely to judge, that is, from their outer appearances, their visible combination of gristly and fleshy appendages, even single ears – viewed, that is to say, in isolation from their trans-cerebral opposite numbers – displayed great specificity of form, size and colour. This is not to suggest that it would have been difficult to match each left ear to its right mate, were they all, for example, to have been hacked off and lobbed into a crate – like pigs' ears at Grandgobier's central market – and were subsequently, for some reason, required to be brought together again.

Take Jacques' ears, for example. These were the largest and furriest, and the fur was the whitest, rendering them, you might surmise, immediately twinnable – and yet, look again. It would not be impossible to err, for example, if the crate were to contain other notably furry ears. The lobe of the right ear, which in its entirety was larger than the left and of a deeper crimson hue, contained within its puffy midst a tiny fold, a sunken hyphen. The lobe of the left ear, by utter contrast, was small, appeared hard, carried wrinkles, indeed resembled nothing so much as a dried-out butter bean.

Next, consider Luigi's two ears. Though at first this circumstance might appear hard to pin down, were it possible to examine the ears with forensic detachment, it would clearly be found that the left was in fact hugely smaller than the right and diverged from the head at an acutely graver angle. The smallest, neatest and baldest ears both belonged to Rachid; those best concealed by hair to Eric; the dustiest and dirtiest to Philippe; the most lavishly adorned to Bobrán, whose right lobe sported a small gold ring and whose right a chunky gold stud; the best tended, scrubbed, cured and clipped to Salvatore, for which his fiancée could take much credit.

Gently. The impatience with living on in-between sensations, dwelling in compromise; the desire for gore and rapine far beyond sex and violence; the longing to possess and be possessed, to fuck and be fucked, to stab and be stabbed wholly, finally; the lust to be grasped in one's entrails, and thus to grasp another; to inhabit a person and mind and to be so inhabited; to roll and be rolled; to suck / be sucked, kiss / be kissed, fist / be fisted; fill and be filled, full, brimming, overflowing: throat, anus, vagina, belly, mind, veins and mouth. With anything to hand, any material, physical or mental: words, flesh, smoke, mercury, pictures. Only to have one's mouth stuffed with words, one's ears with sounds, one's mind popping at last, one's body twitching.

And if words, hands, vapours, and flesh should fail; if frail dicks shrink, tongues tire, and hands cramp; then why not a dagger-length of polished steel in the belly one-hundred-fold, or in the chest or head or thigh or back? Why not lumps of cold-molten lead truffling the lukewarm body like Christmas chocolates in panettone or, with the lust of Achilles, slicing the life out, dropping the liver onto the beloved's lap, plop!, wet and warm, watching it melt and gently pool, face bewildered, shoulders falling back, fingers warm and sticky, flies buzzing around their eyes, wind howling in their coats.

Differential. Eric had caught himself thinking of Megan. Why think of Megan? Everything had changed now. Maybe he would give up smoking Gauloises: Megan had first smoked them in 1974 at a John Martyn concert in Dundee. Fanny smoked Royales. If only he cared nothing at all for Megan. And did she really have to be hurt?

Eric found himself worrying about Saturday. What could he possibly say to Fanny? Something she had never heard before. But what? Maybe he ought to clean the flat he shared just in case, or at least his room and the toilet: Fanny seemed the tidy sort. Unlike Megan. If only he could be himself. But would she like that?

Eric saw himself reopening *The Grapes of Wrath*. Why read that? He needed something French now. Maybe he would look for a room alone: he had had his fill of living among Brits abroad. Megan was a Brit but not abroad – not a Brit abroad. If only he were someone else. Was it really too late?

Eric forced himself to stare at the product. Why do I care? Well, apart from the money, I like spending my nights here. Maybe it was time to write a letter home: he had kept her waiting long enough. He owed her one. Besides, things happen here. Fanny happens, for instance. If only everything were totally different. But tonight was a start, wasn't it?

Eventful.   Philippe was sitting at the aisle-end of his machine two, his left foot hoisted onto his right knee, reading an opinion piece on the front page of *Le Monde*. He had finished threshing at both his machines, had wiped his brow, and was enjoying a cigarette. From time to time he smiled and looked up, focusing on nobody and on nothing other than the smoke that he blew up and away through pursed lips.

'La fin des "grandes causes"?' was the title of the piece. Philippe supposed the question mark was 'just in case.' The byline read: Jean-Claude Guillebaud. Philippe had read this kind of article before. In the autumn of 1967, for example. Everything was over, washed up: history, politics, art, culture – you name it. Perhaps it would be true one day. Then, maybe, they'd remove the question mark.

'Would 1976,' the piece began, 'prove to be the year of great disenchantments? Of exhausted passions and broken commitment? Never in the last thirty years had the sky over Europe seemed so empty. Never, in the space of just a few months, had so many ideological "great causes" appeared to sink beneath so deep a wave of scepticism.'

The article continued on page two with a roll call of recent reversals: authoritarianism in liberated Saigon; massacres in Cambodia; leadership squabbles in Peking; countries across Africa and Latin America falling prey to military dictatorship; even Lisbon appeared to have lost its appeal: the revolutionary tourists were returning home in droves. To economic crisis and austerity.

Philippe took a deep breath, then blew out his cheeks. Bof! he murmured.

Anything happening?

It was Marcel's voice. Philippe closed and folded the paper and looked up. Marcel held out an opened beer bottle, spume dribbling from its throat. Philippe took it, nodded at Marcel, and sipped. He had sobered up enough to have one beer, damnit. He stared at the bubbles, then stood up and gave Marcel his answer.

What could possibly happen? Nothing. Nothing can happen now.

What do you mean? Marcel asked.

Philippe straightened his trousers, pushed back his shoulders and looked around. The British guy was walking toward them. So was the Algerian. From the other end of the aisle Luigi was coming his way. Mathieu was glancing down at him from the raised office. Everyone was converging. Sooner or later that happened, most nights. A scrum of people would form round him. He'd talk. They'd all talk.

Philippe took a sip from the bottle. Bobrán had just stepped out of the lift and Jacques, frowning eloquently at Philippe's bottle, was making his way toward the party. Philippe had an audience. At last he replied to Marcel's question, loud enough now for everyone to hear.

I said nothing can happen, didn't I? Well, what did I miss? Surprise me! What went on in my absence? What great human event? While I was taking a restorative walk through metallurgy? Huh? You see? While I was visiting our resident Polish artist and Boucan's hired muscle? Nothing. Right? Did I need to ask? What could have happened but didn't? You see? We're locked in here. Locked in. Locked down. What would it take for something to happen? You would first have to imagine something occurring on the outside. Nuclear attack? Possible. There might, I suppose, be a first strike on the university's famous atomic research centre. But how likely is that? It would hardly be a first choice. I mean, why hit the French? And a research lab?

It would be safer than hitting the Yanks, Jacques remarked, to a murmured chorus of agreement.

It's still not very likely, Philippe said. What about some terrorist-anarchist attack?

They'd hit the bosses, not the factory itself, Luigi said.

When did anyone ever hit the bosses? Philippe objected. I mean, outside Italy?

There could be a power cut, Marcel suggested. Knocking out all the machines, lighting, etc.

A power cut in November? It's not even particularly cold.

What about a lightning strike? Bobrán suggested.

It's dull and rainy not stormy, Jacques pronounced.

There was a silence.

Any other catastrophic scenarios, natural or man-made? Earthquake? Hurricane? Landslip? Building collapse? Bomb placed by ageing partisans still pissed with Boucan over his Vichy past?

Philippe looked from man to man and took a long drag on his cigarette.

Mathieu, who had now joined the huddle and listened carefully to the last few exchanges, nodding at the mention of Boucan and Vichy, spoke up.

Your point?

My point, Philippe declared, addressing Mathieu, is that for anything to happen it would have to come from inside, from one of us. Or the nightwatchman. Or an intruder. Or the boss.

When did Boucan ever visit the plant at night? Jacques interjected.

No, but he could. He owns it. He must have a key.

I doubt it, Jacques said, his head shaking.

Well, he could call the nightwatchman or the foreman. They'd always let him in.

Everyone stared at Mathieu, who stared back in defiance.

You bet I would, he said, moving onto the front foot. I know my job.

There was another silence.

So, Philippe said, I ask you: if, for something to happen in here, it has to involve an intruder or one of us, what might any one of us do?

Murder. Suicide. A huge punch-up. Marcel's voice trailed off.

There could be an accident, Bobrán volunteered.

Yeah, some idiot might fall from a banister, Philippe said.

Bobrán laughed. Rachid nodded hard.

Or an industrial accident, Luigi suggested. Someone could get their head stuck between the closing presses.

Someone might have a heart attack, Jacques proposed.

Okay, Philippe said, what about the kind of stuff we could do all together? Or some of us at least?

Silence.

What do you mean, all of us together? Marcel asked, his eyes narrowing.

I don't know. What about a party?

Marcel brightened up.

We could all get drunk, knock out the Polack, smuggle some girls in, take drugs. Hey, did anyone see that Yank film about a prisoner who gets transferred to a nuthouse and turns it upside down?

Vol au-dessus d'un nid de coucou, Philippe said. It starred Jack Nicholson. Everyone looked blank.

The trouble is we'd get found out, Marcel said. Shame. I know some girls who'd come along.

Everyone seemed to think about that.

There could be an intruder, Luigi suggested.

Who the hell would want to come in here at night without getting paid? Jacques said.

For a while, Philippe said nothing further. He stood back and smoked and looked away. He blew the smoke upward. His audience talked among themselves.

He has a point, le marseillais . . . Nothing can happen here . . . Short of a bomb attack or break-in . . . Nobody attacks factories in Grandgobier . . . Nobody breaks into plastics factories anywhere, do they? . . . Now if this was Italy . . . But he's right, you know . . .

Unless . . . Philippe murmured.

Sorry? they said, closing in.

Unless . . . Philippe said again . . . Unless, as Marcel said, there was a murder.

Jacques scratched his head. Eric asked Rachid to explain. Mathieu took his matchstick out of his mouth and frowned hard at it. Jacques and Bobrán and Marcel stared at Philippe. Everyone stood a little stiffer.

Anyone read crime novels? Philippe enquired.

There was some indistinct mumbling from Luigi, while Rachid whispered something in Eric's ear.

There's a genre, Philippe explained, abruptly pedagogical, where you have a collection of people stuck on an island or a train or maybe in a castle or in some village cut off by a storm. Then the murders start.

I've seen that on TV, Bobrán said.

There was a long silence.

That's not going to happen here, is it? Jacques said, looking from man to man.

Everyone laughed.

It was just an example, Philippe said.

Example of what? Marcel asked.

Well, this is a closed place, isn't it? And we could easily find a likely victim. Jean, Herbier, say. Or me. I might have some enemies. How would the deed be done? In the lift with a spanner? Or made to look like an industrial accident? But the thing is: if anything is really going to happen it's because we want it to.

We could take the Polack hostage and make him order us food, drink and pussy, Luigi suggested, eyeing Marcel.

The wop's catching on! Marcel said. He grinned at Luigi. It was like throwing a dog a bone. He even bared his teeth.

Mathieu scratched the back of his left ear with his matchstick.

Or we could smash up all the machines, Bobrán proposed.

That's a great idea, Philippe said. You go first.

No, no, Marcel said, wagging a finger at his little cousin, we would get so much less hassle from the authorities if we just killed one of our own.

There was laughter. Jacques clapped Marcel on the back. True! he said.

So, basically, Mathieu said, short of murdering one another . . . or smashing the machines . . . or kidnapping the nightwatchman . . . or being bombed . . .

Or a fire? Eric asked, looking around.

Or an occupation . . . Philippe said.

Short of all of that, nothing can happen, right? Mathieu said.

Well, Philippe said, choosing his words carefully. That's the way it looks right now. But I've noticed that when anyone says, 'It's all over. The game's up,' that's when things start happening. That's what I was thinking.

Philippe dropped his cigarette butt on the floor and turned his heel on it.

It was a sign. Away Mathieu limped. Away Luigi sloped. Away Jacques galumphed, Marcel sauntered, Eric slouched and Rachid trudged. Away.

Stand.   There are as many ways to stand as there are people. Or animals. (Animals also stand.) As many as there are activities. Or processes. Or thoughts. (Arguments stand or fall.) For the present purposes in the present place, four main types of standing may be distinguished.

There is standing alone. Close your eyes and picture Jacques, his arms swinging, his belly relaxed, his feet like ducks' feet, his head nodding, as if sagely. Now think of Salvatore, broad shoulders scrunched up, eyes likewise, mouth like a prune. Each one standing alone, in thought.

Then there is standing vis-à-vis a machine. See how Mathieu rests on the machine guard, waiting for the presses to open, his mind trying to void but Nadine stubbornly interrupting him; how Marcel stands smoking alongside his machine twelve, as if sheltering in its lee.

Then there is standing in a group, whether at one's ease or not, perhaps with attitude wagging a finger or quivering a jowl, eager to intervene; or, alternatively, leaning back, waiting for a chance to make an excuse and slip away.

Lastly, there's the standing face-off with one or more others, measuring the distance between noses, countering another's breath and words and feelings.

Many other kinds of standing are not pertinent in this place or at this time: standing on a commuter train or bus, for example; standing to survey oneself in a mirror; standing to salute in a line of soldiers or elbow to elbow in a police-suspects' lineup; standing in a lover's clinch, reliant on the other's firm foothold; or in the shower, peering down through the mist at one's feet.

31. Risking, Rehearsing.

Risking.   Acting and talking fucking-out of turn to workmates and placing money on horses are two different things. Different, that's all. One is one kind of risk, the other is the other.

Create bad feeling with a workmate and all kinds of trouble come your way. I've seen it happen. Someone can end up injured, out of work or worse. With the horses, mostly you lose money, which is bad. But if you're lucky, you get rich. I've seen that too. What is the point of messing with workmates? If you hug an angry Arab or insult a scab, say, and all goes well, what fucking-do you gain anyway?

What is so unfair is not knowing what to say. Some people always have a ready answer. Philippe, for example. But Alphonse too. Except with the Algerian just now. That was good. I'm more like Jacques. Slow and steady. Brought up on the land, you don't expect quick answers. Slow steady labour is what works. Most women don't want slow and steady. Who knows about Maryse? Tortoise wins the race, fucking-right?

Corresponding.   In a one-bedroom flat on the eleventh floor of a colourless block of flats on the edge of Wrocław, Agnes Wiewiorka sat at a small oak bureau. Before her a single sheet of letter paper and an uncapped fountain pen. On her lap a letter from Tomec. For days now, she had been thinking about her reply. She wrote without hesitation or crossings-out.

Dearest brother,

Each year your birthday comes round quicker than before and here I am once again sitting at mother's old escritoire with your last letter, thinking what news I have to give you. I would so like to embrace you. When will we meet?

Tadeusz has joined the party and Grigor has started attending church. How is it, I wonder, that Kazimierz and I, lifelong dissenters both, produced two such eager but opposite conformists? Autres temps, autres moeurs? I seldom see them now and they tell me nothing of their father.

I have three more years to work, then maybe at last I shall travel. I have always dreamed of Italy and France. Now I collect old guidebooks, in preparation. Sometimes I think you live the life that should have been mine.

Yes, I am still writing poetry, but I fear you are the only one who is interested. It seems it is too 'intimist' and too 'formal.' You can commit one of these sins and get away with it, but never both together. I persevere, of course, since it is the only way for me to make some sense of living.

I have a friend now, a man I met at a concert by the Bratislava City Orchestra during a tour. Mostly Bartók. Our ears at least could never be stopped. He is both passionate and gentle. It is good to wake up again with a man sometimes. But I do not think he loves me.

I hope I don't sound unhappy, darling Tomec. I am simply waiting now, suspended between two lives. I shall soon be free. Tell me more about your art works and your girlfriends. Send me photos of both. Does change make you happy?

I hope with all my heart that this letter finds you well. Perhaps 1977 will be the year we meet again? Your loving sister.

Economizing.   Returning from the toilet, rounding the aisle-end of machine fourteen, Eric encountered Luigi at the end of his machine thirteen, one of his yellow cigarettes suspended from his lower lip. With a flicker of his left eyelid, Luigi acknowledged Eric's existence.

Eric stopped and, formulating the question carefully, asked Luigi why his cigarettes were yellow.

Papier Maïs, the Italian retorted.

My-eese, Eric repeated. Maize. Corn. Cornpaper. Hmm.

Maïs, Luigi repeated. It's a cereal. Grows in a field.

With a sigh, Luigi removed the cigarette from his mouth and held it vertical, burning end upward. Count to twenty, Luigi ordered.

Eric started counting, then stopped, feeling stupid. Instead, he looked up and down the aisle. He saw nothing of note.

Look, Luigi said. See? It's gone out.

Luigi stuck the cigarette back in his mouth and pumped it hard, his cheeks caving. He had proved his point. He fetched up his lighter and relit the inch-long stub.

Is that an advantage? Eric asked.

Of course. It's an economy. Of time and money.

What about Royales? Eric then asked.

Royales?

The cigarettes, Eric explained. What are they like?

Luigi couldn't see the connection.

Women smoke them, the Italian said finally.

Ma copine fume Royales, Eric said.

Luigi's eyes bulged. What did he care what the guy's bitch smoked? He said nothing.

Dreaming.   Tomec sat in the creamy light of the anglepoise. On Philippe's advice, he had chased to the back of his mind the matter of the boss-offending graffiti. He had resolved what to say to Boucan's men: 'I have no reason to suspect any of the night shift' and / or 'I do security not interrogations.' That would be that.

This was going to be a quiet night. Earlier, he had heard a siren: an ambulance approaching. He would do some sketching, catch the attitudes of some of the men before they faded in memory, and graze on Broch's novel. Soon he would take his torch on another tour of the premises. He glanced at the wall telephone. 'For emergency use only,' he had been told. He opened *Der Tod des Vergil.*

The dying Roman was standing at a casement, surveying the street below, considering the mob, thinking back on his life as a poet. Tomec liked to read a page or two, light upon some suggestive phrase, bounce it round his brain a little, then shut the book.

He came to a passage on the poet Orpheus, credited with the power to divert streams from their beds, to calm wild beasts and to halt cattle in the pastures where they browsed: . . . der Traumes-wunsch alles Künstlerstums: die zum Lauschen unterworfene Welt, empfangsbereit für den Gesang und die ihm entströmende Hilfe ('the dream-wish of all artistic endeavour: the world constrained to listen attentively, made ready to receive the song and the succour that from it streams').

Tomec shut the book and his eyes.

Exercising.   Marcel, from his vantage at the aisle-end of machine eleven, stared at the back of Luigi's head. The Italian was reading one of his magazines.

What kind of exercise does a man like that take? Marcel was wondering. Such huge biceps hanging off such weedy looking shoulders: you would think they would work loose. By day he works as a butcher, right? Is that what does it? Lifting carcasses all day? Chopping meat? And the magazines he reads! Comics full of pointy-breasted blondes and sultry come-fuck-me brunettes, and those true-crime magazines with the little black bars over the nipples and eyes. You could respect a man who enjoys an honest-to-goodness porn mag stuffed with believable, gorgeous chicks, chests stuck out, legs spread, tongues lapping at lollipops. There was no harm in that. Marcel had seen plenty in prison. But what kind of a man looked at the type of magazine the Italian looked at?

Marcel liked things pure, unalloyed. Sex, for example, should not be cut with science fiction. Or with crime. Or with art. In prison, there was a guy who pored over a large-format art book full of nudes. He talked about the depiction of the nude down the ages. You wouldn't credit it. Another inmate took a popular medicine book out of the prison library; Marcel picked it up one day and it fell open at gynaecology. The diagrams of fallopian tubes were stained with sperm. Well, what else could it have been? It wasn't spit.

The other thing Marcel didn't like was ugliness. To look at Eric and Luigi was to look at two ugly but contrasting specimens. Together they were a freak show. Luigi would be tall if only he stood straight. His huge upper arms seemed to drag his puny chest inward and down. If the rest of his body were anything like his biceps he'd be a weight-lifter, instead of a weakling with popeye arms. As for the Englishman, Marcel couldn't look at him for more than a minute without feeling sorry. What a mess! What self-neglect!

Worse than their ugliness was their obvious stupidity. For example, what had the Italian been doing just now holding his maize-paper cigarette up in the air like that, getting the Englishman to watch it as it went out? Dumb and dumber! The quantity of things the Englishman doesn't know! You couldn't put a number to it. The definition of infinite, right? He has to have everything explained. You could see Luigi laying it all out. But the one thing dumber than asking a dumb question is to give that question an answer. Because then you enter into the stupidity, letting it contaminate you somehow. Contamination was another thing Marcel didn't like. It was the opposite of purity and had to be combatted. Leave the stupid to their stupidity, don't heed their questions, walk on by, look away. You don't want to be around it. Exact same thing with ugliness. But what kind of exercises would Luigi be doing anyway to get biceps like that? Working as a butcher by day. Lifting carcasses, maybe? Chopping meat?

Reminiscing.   Between them, Fernando's parents lived the overwhelming bulk of their lives in a total of just five (5) places. They both spent time in their cramped and dusty home (1), alone or together. *He* also spent evenings and Sunday afternoons at the bar (2) or in the back parlour (3) of a widow who lived one hundred and fifty metres further down the road. Weekdays he spent working in his fields (4). *She* had recently stopped working on account of pains in her back and hips and legs and neck – brittle bones, the doctor had said, too many children – and she never went either to the bar or to the widow's back parlour. She did, however, go to the church (5). She prayed there once a day. He never went to the church.

Throughout the whole expanse of Portugal, it was one hour earlier than in France: just past 21.20. Fernando will be arriving for work, thought his mother, knowing nothing of time zones, never having travelled as far as Oporto, let alone 'Europe.' She sat with her legs in a basin of water into which she had sprinkled soothing salts. She marvelled that Fernando, the child she had wanted least, and such a weakling, was now the one she missed most. He was the third child, the third boy, when she was longing for a girl. Three boys in a row was punishment. But for what? When the midwife had told her, she had wept and wouldn't look at the baby. She did her duty by him though and was rewarded, for thirteen months later came the baby girl of her dreams: perfect, sweet-tempered, with gold ringlets. Angelica. Fernando's father had taken one first sufficient look at her, blood-smeared and dark and female, then gone for a drink. And where was that child now! In Sweden, somewhere.

In the bar at the far end of the village, diagonally opposite the wall-mounted television sat Fernando's father. On the table before him, next to his glass, a paraffin lamp he had brought with him from his home. The street lamps had been cut by a late-September storm. The potholes in the street were no longer repaired, now that a road had been built to bypass their village. Only the old were left, scratching a poor living from rich alluvial soil. How had it come to this? On the TV each evening, socialists and communists in suits talked a fine talk but as far as Fernando's father could see, the revolution wasn't coming their way any time soon.

And how's the lovely wife?

Fernando's father looked up and saw the storekeeper, a man so mean he hardly ever came to the bar nowadays.

Fine, came a grumbled reply. She had been lovely once. The finest ankles and prettiest nose for miles around.

And that son of yours, still in France?

Still in France, still in France.

Where exactly?

In France, I said.

Building site?

What's the difference? He has honest work.

Fernando's father recalled through a haze of toil-befuddled years that his son had once courted the storekeeper's daughter. To her parents' unconcealed delight and to Fernando's distress, she had preferred the wheelwright's son, who had given her a brace of brats then fled one night with a whore from Aveiro. Fernando's father chuckled. The storekeeper stiffened.

Has he married?

Who?

Your son. Fernando.

No answer broke the silence.

He has lived in France long enough, the storekeeper insinuated. He hasn't become like them, has he? Soft . . .

He has girlfriends, Fernando's father exclaimed, provoked into indiscretion.

The storekeeper smiled, as if he knew something.

Fernando's father stared at the man.

A wise parent doesn't interfere, he declared.

Cheating.   Luigi closed his copy of *Détective*, dropped it to the floor, and caught a product piece as it crashed through the aluminium slats of machine fourteen. The tiny obtruding flap had neither grown, shrunk nor changed colour. He chucked the piece in the bin, pulled on his gloves, bent over the bin and began to thresh. He caught brief sight of Fernando heading down the aisle, a cloth wrapped round his middle like a skirt, like a queer. Luigi was in a sullen reflective mood. Failing to jerk off had left him enervated, morose and resentful. He had been counting on Aurelia. He scooped the magazine back up.

Luigi reconsidered the mechanic from Annecy and the tendency of

murderers to overreach, to go one murder too far. There had certainly been
no need for him to kill himself. Perhaps he had been shocked by what he
had done. Maybe the sight of blood had thrown him. He should have been
a butcher. He was probably sorry he had killed his kid brother. You never
expect to do a thing like that. But his wife, at least, had deserved what she
got. If he had stopped at killing her and, say, maiming his brother, what court
in the land would have sent him down even? She had certainly led the kid
on, jiggling her popotin at him, winking perhaps or pouting, wearing a low
decolletée while her husband was out, hard at work, fixing decent people's
cars. Perhaps she told the boy how the mechanic neglected her. Pouting at
him, winking, unable to resist a little tenderloin. You could see from the
photos she wore lipstick. Luigi imagined a large wrench hitting a face full
on. It would sound like a tenderizer on pork brisket. But it was sad about the
brother. You can't replace a kid brother. Luigi had had several women in his
life but never a kid brother. He could have loved a kid brother.

Stamping.   Sarah was definitely staying in now. She had put on Act II of
Moses und Aron, but it was hard to concentrate, even with the libretto open
on her lap. It didn't help that there was nowhere comfortable to sit in Tomec's
flat – just the bed. She would buy him a Swedish chair like the one her father
had in his study but Tomec would probably hate it: a studio is not a study,
he might say. She recalled how he had walked straight at her earlier, angry
about something, still naked, his shrunken sex jumping. He had bent down
over her and she had felt frightened and his face had neared to a blur and he
had planted a smacking stolen kiss.

     She had brought her lips up in time, not just compliant but self-
shockingly eager. Over in a second. A touch, a graze, as dry and light as
swept leaves. If he had had time, they would have made love again. And
again. With Moses and Aaron stamping round the desert for background. She
wanted Tomec all the time and he seemed to know it now, but not to care.

     Bounding to the gramophone, she had placed the stylus at the edge of
the vinyl. She could force him to listen to it now: he would pay for his stolen
kiss. She had seized Tomec's forearm, pulled him with her to the side of the
bed and pushed against his left shoulder, impossible to withstand, infinitely
gentle, until he was seated. You must! she told him, as if he might yet offer
resistance. She stared at him as the music began.

     He did seem to be listening, truly listening. But who could tell?

Sarah watched the shiny disc of revolving plastic.

As the first exchange between God's Voice from the Burning Bush and Moses got under way, Sarah had said, You see? Truly, it is not hard, it is as lyrical as Brahms. As if pressing the point, her creamy skin darkened with gooseflesh and her eyes filled. Tomec turned toward her and his lips formed a smile. He looked . . . embarrassed! How dare he!

Was he humouring me? Being patient? Ironic? Is it too emotional for him?

Look, Tomec, she had said, Of course it's intense. How could it be otherwise? It's about God, it's about Art. Then, her voice was louder and full of fear: Don't you dare tell me you don't hear the same things I hear! Don't you dare!

Tomec had put his left hand on her thigh and stroked it for a few seconds, gently, as one might a cat's back. He opened his mouth, but said nothing. She looked at his hand. Then he got up.

Melting. Fucking-moody Arabs, who needs them? I told him I was sorry for what Côte d'Ivoire pulled earlier. Some hope! I tried to apologise for not stepping in, I told him I couldn't have stopped it, that the African was carried fucking-away, just like an African. What does this Arab want anyway? Doesn't look at me. Stands there holding his piece of paper all squiggles and dots – they read backward, don't they? Why make things more difficult? Besides, how does anyone fucking-write backward? I can barely pull the trick fucking-forward. There he stands, staring and smiling, then scowling, then smiling again. So what do I do now? Do I walk away or make my point again and go?

Fernando turned as if to go, then turned back round again.

I said I'm sorry.

Rachid's eyes were full. He looked at Fernando but still didn't see him. He had heard him clearly enough this time. He put Malika's note back in his pocket. He focused on Fernando, which he didn't find easy. The Portuguee was wearing some kind of apron. It made him look like a cook.

What? Rachid said. Forget it, he said. What does it matter?

Fernando relaxed and smiled. Rachid thrust his arm out. Impulsively, you might think. The two men shook. Fernando wanted to hug the man but thought better of it and walked away.

Fucking-moody, but he's all right. It's like I told Alphonse, You have to say you're sorry when you're out of order. Arabs can be weird. Like anyone fucking-else. You have got to know that. This one's all right. Bears no grudge, does he?

Comparing. On the plastics-section night shift, Philippe was the one man who couldn't stand alone at the aisle-end of his machine and have a quiet think, a quiet muse, a quiet smoke. Somebody would invariably come up to him, crack a joke, pass the time of day, sample his wit, seek out his company and friendly smile. To think his own thoughts, to be alone in the midst of others, Philippe had to retreat the space of three metres between his machines one and two and then to stand by, lean against or sit alongside the control cabinet. Nobody would think to disturb him there.

Philippe smiled to picture the night security man sitting at his sketching bench, bathing in his pool of light. Never before had Philippe penetrated so deep into metallurgy, nor seen how the Pole passed his time. Philippe grasped just how different were their respective nights: the Pole's were spent admiring photos of his girlfriend and statues of Virgil, doing little sketches, reading a novel in German; Philippe's were a never-ending train of conversations and cigarettes and beers and coffees and bursts of work and then yet more conversations. Tomec had the better of it, clearly. But Philippe enjoyed the company of his fellow humans. He liked to be with a group, sometimes at its middle, sometimes at its edge.

Sorting. Unlike Marcel who, on the recommendation of his prison psychotherapist, was learning to make mental lists in order to break the spell of circular thinking – and even more unlike Jean, to whom listing appeared the obvious way to organize his thoughts and to parcel out an otherwise oppressive span of time – Maryse was so impervious to the practice of listing that even where to another mind a list might clearly suggest itself she was very unlikely to spot it.

For example, hash clearly came in a number of sorts. There was the sort that made you sociable, and the sort that made you withdraw; there was the sort that made you giggle, and the sort that made you sad; then there was the sort that made you hungry, and the sort that didn't: at least six sorts, without contemplating the overlaps. And she could probably have thought of more. She was also aware of the variable provenance of hash: Pakistan, Afghanistan, Morocco, Acapulco – though the latter place, in her experience, might just as well be legendary.

According to Evelyne, the hash they had smoked that evening had originated in Afghanistan. It was of a sort that first made you talk and giggle, then left you on your own, in silence, to think thoughts of abyssal profundity. Maryse was considering one of her customers, something she rarely did. Also, she was considering when and where she had last had sight of a live butterfly. That very afternoon, Fernando had asked her this question and she hadn't been able to give an answer. He had been adjusting his clothes and combing his hair when, to steer their session to a tranquil conclusion, she had enquired what he missed of his home country, and he had said, Butterflies. I fucking-miss the butterflies. When did you last see a butterfly?

I'm not sure.

Precisely. There aren't any butterflies in the city. Or not so you'd notice. If you do see one it's always the same sort. Where I live – where I come from – there's a small river close by, a river that flows into the Douro – have you ever heard of the Douro? No?

He shook his head, stopped, then shook it again. An idea had begun to shake loose.

There is a path, Fernando said, that leads along that little tributário . . . 'tributaire' . . . yes, thank you. Where nobody goes. And there's a rock that juts out into the current maybe a third or a quarter of the way and trees along the bank and you can stand on this rock and dive straight fucking-into the water, which is clear and deep. You can see the fishes as you hit the water. And alongside the river there are flood meadows and in June there are butterflies everywhere, all sizes, fucking-shapes and colours. That place, I'm telling you, is as close to paradise as we will ever come.

There had been a long pause while Fernando was bent down, doing up his laces. Then, as if trying to net the moment and bring it home, he had looked up at Maryse, into her eyes, and said.

I'd like to take you there.

Maryse had laughed and looked away. Fernando was beginning to be an awkward customer.

I like it here. I like the city.

You do? Really?

Yes.

Fernando waited for an explanation, but none came.

Oh, he said. Well, I guess it's November by now fucking-in Portugal too and all the butterflies will be dead anyway.

Hailing.   Standing at the end of his machine number fourteen, Luigi glimpsed the foreman hobbling his way back up the machine aisle toward him. The Italian stepped out almost into the man's path, but Mathieu quickly adjusted his trajectory, listing leftward to evade the Italian, upon which Luigi raised his right arm very slightly, like a man in the pouring rain hailing a taxi.

Mathieu halted, settling his weight on his better leg, and extracted the chewed-down burnt-out matchstick from his mouth. Eh? he said.

Luigi nodded back at the chair stationed at the end of his machine thirteen on which lay the copy of *Détective* that Mathieu had briefly consulted earlier.

There are a couple of good stories in there, Luigi ventured, baring his crazy teeth. Borrow it if you like.

Mathieu tossed his matchstick morsel against the base of machine thirteen.

I'm not interested in the other stories.

The one you read isn't the best.

Mathieu drew a small matchbox from his left pocket, struck a match, blew it out, and placed the unburned end between his lips. He turned to go.

Normally I don't read that magazine, he said.

Luigi shrugged. He recalled the story about the medical student. It didn't amount to much: the murderer was motivated by kindness; the killing itself was unspectacular; there was no spillage of blood, no angry relatives, no sexual angle, no sequel. What was the deal?

Getting it.   Some people just don't get it, Alphonse thought as he prepared a bin full of product, folding the colorant in slowly and carefully as if preparing cake mixture. They don't get the drama and tensions and intimacy of other people. Maybe they lack fellow feeling. Okay, I made a mistake about the Algerian earlier, I misjudged what he needed, or at least what he wanted. At least I tried. Some people never make the effort to put themselves in other people's shoes. Sometimes you really can embrace and dance a near-stranger clean out of their dejection. Fernando called it a risk. To me it was a risk worth taking. Fernando can't understand that. But why should he get so upset? The Arab has forgotten about it already. He told me so.

Fernando, bless him, just doesn't get it. His outlook is limited. My friends in Lyon would understand at once. It's not that they're cleverer or better than the people here. It's a matter of education, culture. It's what the French call la classe. Ah! Fernando, Fernando! He's a good sort, Fernando. He makes me laugh.

It struck Alphonse that there was something in that name. As he repeated it, the latest smash hit by the Swedish pop group Abba came to his mind. He had always liked Abba. Abba was big in Ivory Coast. Alphonse suddenly blared out in a heavy French accent: Zere was somesing in ze hair zat night, Ze time was right, Fernando. (How did it continue?) La-la – La-la – La-la – Laa-ah – La-la – La-laa-ah – La-la. Fernando!

No, Alphonse decided, he wasn't going to take offence at the ticking-off Fernando had given him. Maybe he'd sing Fernando the Abba song for a bit of fun. If only he could remember the words. Eef hi ad to do ze same again, I would, my friend, Fernando.

Except that Fernando, not having any English, wouldn't get it, would he?

Comforting. Beneath Angela's avian scrutiny, Gregory Peck and Anthony Quinn, the latter as swarthy as a Greek and as mischievous as any Mexican, the former the kind of man who would never trouble an honest woman, bestrode the Technicolor seas. Next door, in the room shared with Angela's son, Gilberte prepared for bed, smarting from the latest insult from Luigi's mother, preparing her complaint, Do you know what your mother said to me this evening? That she could never trust me because I was never baptized. Nothing to prevent me from lying and thieving. Luigi will shrug and make excuses for her. Like he always does. You might think he didn't care. But he does. Deep down.

Gilberte stepped out of her knickers, twisted her torso slightly to the left, and pulled in her belly. She frowned down at her small breasts, her thick hips and her lemon-peel bum: her body had a will of its own, indifferent to all the diets she had tried, the pills she had popped, the frantic exercising she had occasionally undertaken. Luigi seems not to care for me, but really he does. In unguarded moments, he can be warm. He says nice things about my eyes sometimes and never teases me about my nose. Kindness catches him unawares. It surprises him as much as it surprises me. With a mother like that, is it any wonder? He doesn't make love to me much, but then I'm not highly sexed, whatever he thinks. The best times are when he's home at night, and we sleep late into Sunday morning, and I take advantage of his early-morning erection. He doesn't mind that. Men fantasize about women doing everything, don't they? Making love to them while they sleep. Usually he keeps his eyes closed, staying there on his back while I work myself off. I don't like it so much when he climbs on top of me and grabs my buttocks and pants and sweats. His hands are so strong sometimes I think he'll split me in two perfect halves from fanny to tailbone, like I've seen him trying to do with an apple. He has nightmares in the morning and needs to be held and comforted. I don't mind that. He wants to be mothered a little. Maybe it's not a lot but it's as much as I need.

Gilberte drew on her nightdress, hugged herself, and switched out the light. In the bed, she shivered for a while.

Rehearsing. Tomec was marching again through the remote recesses of metallurgy, his torch swinging with his left hand. The thoughts of Broch's Virgil filled his mind.

In particular he was thinking about the Orphic dream of an all-powerful river-diverting history-altering artistry and considering the indolence and feebleness of art and artists in his own time. Throughout his childhood, which had begun before the Nazis came to power and had ended with their downfall, artists had mostly failed, often abjectly, even to bear witness, let alone to make or remake law. Yet only in the extreme conditions of dictatorship, it now seemed to Tomec, could they occasionally stay the hand of the mighty, effect change, speak to history; elsewhere, they were jesters at a squalid feast, babbling commonplaces, cheering each new comfortable display of hedonism, playful perhaps – but with none of the earnest purpose of a child at play.

One passage from Broch's novel bothered him: Virgil's confession that he had 'ignored the masses,' considering them 'fabulous beings,' depicting them 'as kings and heroes of fable.'

It is all too easy to upbraid oneself, Tomec reflected, but much harder to find a better way. What should Virgil have done, what could he have invented, what tradition might he have found and inflected to his purpose? Is not self-laceration itself a vanity? What person has ever met their death through Virgil's supposed artistic failure?

Tomec could imagine no answer to such a question. The authority with which Broch invoked Virgil made Tomec uncomfortable. He was embarrassed for the Roman poet. How must it feel to be depicted back into suffering with such sharp precision two millennia after penning one's last word? How must it feel to have one's feelings guessed at, one's thoughts ventriloquized, one's sins detailed, one's dying moments rehearsed? Did he live again in this German poet? Did he die again?

Tomec was aware of the rumble, crash and hum of machines as he approached the plastics section. He longed for silence. He wanted lasting peace. Virgil, transmuted by Broch's wartime consciousness, expressed scorn, fear, loathing and pity for the masses, the 'herd-beast,' yet appeared therein to identify humanity itself. Tomec would hound Virgil until his senses were exhausted and his mind exhilarated to the visionary point.

32. Read and Write.

Read.   What are they reading? A note from his wife; a newspaper article; an American novel; a letter from a dead man's brother; an advert in a magazine; a play by Beckett; strip-cartoon pornography; graffiti on a factory wall; obscenities in the toilet; a union flyer; somebody's diary; a libretto by Schoenberg; a European novel; a letter from an eighteenth-century exile; a shopping list; a political broadside; a permit to travel abroad.

No, no, no. *What* are they reading?

Words, words, words. Writing.

Precisely.

Romancing.   At machine number ten, Eric stood pounding the recalcitrant sprue, his hair flicking at his cheeks, his shoulders scrunched over, sweat on his forehead, dead breath from his lungs replaced by each quick new shallow intake.

The products at this machine were shiny, hard, green and stubbornly attached to their stalks: the bin had to contain just the right amount: too few and their crashing-together would be ineffective; too many and you couldn't get started without strewing the floor.

Physical exertion effaced Eric's thoughts, leaving a darkness into which anything – most usually fragments of rock music, impressions of acquaintances or, since his arrival in France, new words and expressions – could rush pell-mell. In this instance, the wastes of Eric's mind were gorged by love and fear and longing. He was enamoured, already indelibly, with at least the idea of Fanny: well past drooling over a conjured sketch of her breasts, he had heard her voice, witnessed the sheen and imperfections of her skin, noted the spangle in her eyes, grasped her power to change him, to throw him off every previous course. He feared that before Saturday could come she would cancel their date, or that on that evening he might fall headlong on his face. He longed for tomorrow evening, when he might see her again, teeter in the tension of her nearness, read in her eyes a confirmation of their cinema-tryst, while writing upon his own face and into his manner both boyish expectation and happy confidence.

From longing and fear and love, there soon arose in Eric's breast an unstoppable suite of fantasies: what might it be like to hold her hand and feel her palm pressed flat against his; to sit beside her in the dark hearing her gasp at a celluloid illusion; to watch her raise a glass; to see her vanish behind a door and await her return; to listen to her voice without the grind and grate of machine cacophony, perhaps even hard up against his ear upon a pillow. Oh!

Oh! but to hold her close, to take her lips between his teeth, to rub her nose to his, to feel the skin of her forearm in the small of his back! Oh!

Oh! Would he ever know that? Would he one day – maybe soon, maybe Saturday? – see her laugh, her head cast back? Would she cackle, chortle or coo? Would her molars be pristine or filled? With amalgam or gold? Would her epiglottis wiggle? Would he care? Or would she choke back her laughter, smother her mouth like the Italian often did? Never!

He yearned to see her face close up. He wanted to register the colour of her eyes, far from any neon. He wanted to savour her breath, free of plastic fumes. He had never much cared about the colour of eyes, the quality of breath, the way a person laughs, the skin on anyone's forearm. Everything was suddenly sharp. Life was edging into focus. Things mattered.

Eric saw that the floor and inside walls of the threshing bin were a lightly pitted dulled red, except high up toward the lip, where the surface, having seen less wear, was merely pearled. By contrast, the outside walls of the bin were of an even shiny red, their factory-new perfection interrupted only by the occasional adherence of wisps and flakes of recycled plastic upon a background of ambient dust. He saw Marcel like a big cat creeping up behind Bobrán, and Philippe leaning against the side of his machine number one flicking the pages of a newspaper. He saw his own face brand-new in the glass of the machine guard: the face of a man in love.

Eric lifted in his left gloved hand a mass of almost product-free sprue. He picked the last pieces from the tangle, dropped them into the threshing bin, then straightened his back, rotated ninety degrees from the hips, extended his left arm over the sprue bin and, like a dockside crane dumping trash into a river barge, released his load.

Acrobat.　　Bobrán had come from the lift, squeezed past the control cabinet of Luigi's machine fourteen and into the Italian's vital space.

So how much do you all bet? Come up with a figure yet?

Luigi's mouth fell open, his cigarette clinging to his upper lip.

Okay, Bobrán said, laughing and pushing the question away with the flat of his hand, Where's the chef?

Went that way, Luigi said, smiling and nodding toward the raw-materials area, imagining he had been let off the hook.

As he made his way toward the exit, Bobrán's upper body was violently immobilized in a bear hug from behind. Marcel squeezed his cousin's back against his own chest, and his groin into the crease of the shorter man's buttocks.

Okay! Okay! Bobrán said, as if trapped.

Marcel relaxed minutely and Bobrán spiralled to the floor, wriggling acrobatically out of his cousin's brute grip and skipping out of reach.

We've got to talk, Marcel shouted after him, his finger wagging.

Talk? Bobrán shouted back over his shoulder? You want to talk? Then, pointing at Luigi and laughing, Talk to him!

Original.   Worker grips trowel (aluminium, etc.), pushes it deeper into sack of material (raw, etc.), draws it back out, empties it into bin (red, etc.) on floor (concrete, etc.). He returns to sack for more until bin is two thirds full. He lifts lid on reground-material bin (cylindrical, etc.) and fills trowel with matter (fluffy, etc) until bin is heaped. He places trowel in sack (grey, etc.) containing material (raw, etc.). From another bin (oblong, etc.), he takes pellets (orange, etc.) and sprinkles them on top of matter (reground, etc.). He retrieves trowel from sack, mixes contents of bin (red, etc.) until virgin granules, reground, colour pellets all blend. He replaces trowel in sack (paper, etc.). Worker (worker) is ready to fill hopper.

Furtive.   Bobrán found Mathieu in the raw-materials area, sitting in the dark on a pile of plastic sacks, his hands gripping his knees, his arms and his back straight. The little Gypsy had hit the timer switch by the door. The foreman was blinking up at him.

Alors? Qu'est-ce que tu veux?

Can you read this?

If it's in French, he said. Can't you read?

Didn't you know?

I know what I need to know. Give it here.

The last couple of lines, after the fold. Please.

The light went out as Bobrán handed over the paper. Mathieu was taking his glasses from his breast pocket. Bobrán went for the switch.

Couple of lines? So you can't count either.

Please. What does it say?

'Nous avons beaucoup de questions à vous poser: comment est-il tombé
– et pourquoi? Avez-vous été témoin de sa chute? Pourquoi ne portait-il pas
de harnais de sécurité? Vous pouvez avoir confiance en notre discretion. Si
vous ne nous aidez pas dans de pareilles circonstances, sur qui pourrez-vous
vous appuyer, lorsque ce sera votre tour? Je vous supplie de bien vouloir
déposer un message à mon adresse à la poste restante, afin de me dire où et
quand il nous serait possible de nous rencontrer. Dans l'attente, je vous prie
d'accepter mes salutations cordiales . . .' *

Bobrán repeated the passage word for word, while Mathieu listened,
checking Bobrán's memory against the text. The light went out.

Is that it? Mathieu asked.

Sure.

Bobrán recalled the hours just after Joseph fell to his death. With the
rest of the day free, he had gone to Moritz's flat and the two men had made
love. He had never had sex on a bed before. He felt no shame. There was
nothing furtive. He fell asleep in his lover's arms. This ought to be normal,
he remembered thinking.

What do you want me to say? Mathieu asked.

Bobrán hardly heard him.

Did you see this man fall?

Bobrán clicked his teeth.

How did it happen?

The question caught Bobrán out.

I don't know. He just slipped. That was it. Down he went. No time to
think. Dead. No time to get ready.

No time to get ready?

Mathieu stared at the young Gypsy.

Yes. To get ready.

Do you want to help his brother?

If I can.

Mathieu spat a gob of chewed cellulose onto the floor, rummaged in his

---

* 'We have many questions to put to you: how did he fall – and why? Were you a witness to his fall?
Why wasn't he wearing a safety harness? You can have confidence in our discretion. But if you do not
help us in circumstances such as these, on whom will you be able to rely when it is your turn? I entreat
you to leave a message for me at the poste-restante, to tell me where and when it might be possible for
us to meet. In the meantime, please accept my cordial greetings. . .'

trouser pocket for his matchbox, struck a new match, examined Bobrán in the glow, blew it out and placed the unburned end in his mouth.

You don't know what's right to do?

No.

I'm the last person to ask about right or wrong.

There was a long pause.

Believe me.

Okay, Bobrán said, moving to get up.

Sit the fuck down. Thank you. Go and ask Marseille. He'll tell you what's right. But not now. This African's dead, right? You could wait till tomorrow. No hurry, is there?

No, Bobrán said, sounding uncertain.

The foreman got up to go.

I don't want to hear about it again, Mathieu said. And no more climbing banisters. This isn't a circus.

No, boss.

Get out of here!

Lecterns.   Having smoothed matters over with the Algerian, Fernando wished to recline a while in Jacques' cordial company.

The old peasant was slumped on his chair at the aisle-end of machine four, chin on chest, arms hanging loose, silver dribble bubbling from his lower lip.

He might be dead, Fernando thought. He looked round and saw machines working and men idling.

Approaching Jacques, Fernando placed his right hand on the man's left shoulder, squeezing gently. There was no response. Fernando pushed the shoulder back slightly, then let it return to its rest position. His face darkened.

Jacques screwed his eyes tighter shut than before, then opened them slowly. A sketchy image of his brother Pierre decayed before he had time to put a name to him. He smiled at the Portuguee, and hauled his right hand from his side where it hung limp. Fernando took it.

So, my friend, things okay? Like some apples? Jacques asked.

Fernando smiled and attempted to retrieve his hand, tugging.

What about the rabbit? he asked.

Maybe tomorrow.

You promised.

I promised. I never said when. Take some apples. They're good.

Fernando, his right hand still captive, suddenly moved in on Jacques, jabbing his left hand into the old peasant's guts, trying to tickle him just above the belt. Jacques squealed and let go of Fernando's right hand, then made a sudden grab at Fernando's groin, but missed. Both men laughed, Fernando doubling up, Jacques rocking.

You shouldn't have done that, Jacques said.

He got to his feet. The two men, standing now in the middle of the machine aisle, between Jacques' machine three and Marcel's machine twelve, squared up to one another, both grinning, shifting from foot to foot, keeping a couple of metres between them, their forearms out in front of them as if leaning on lecterns.

Various. By twenty-five past ten, sixty minutes after the start of their shift, much like the ingredients in a cake mix, or the variously virgin, reground and colour pellets in a well stirred tub of hopper feed, the men were thoroughly mingled. With the exception of Jean upstairs, stationary behind his huge old semi-automatic machine number twenty-one, who had so far seen only the men on his floor plus those few (Salvatore, Marcel, Tomec and Mathieu) who had had some specific reason for going upstairs, each of the thirteen workers present, excluding neither the foreman nor the nightwatchman, had at least shaken the hand of every other man present: thirteen-by-twelve-divided-by-two handshakes, thirteen-by-twelve-divided-by-two encounters of some sort. Minus five – if we wish to be precise and to take account of the absence of any contact either manual or ocular (at least by this point in what we may refer to as the narrative) between the said Jean on the one hand and Luigi, Philippe, Jacques, Eric and Rachid on the other. A total, therefore, of thirteen-by-twelve-divided-by-two – minus five – handshakes, representing, variously: the mutual bare acknowledgement of near strangers (Eric and Alphonse, say); the renewal of passing acquaintanceships (Fernando and Luigi, say); cordial greetings between workmates who had become friends (Philippe and Jacques, say); and even the confirmation of one close, albeit strained, bond of kinship stretching back into both men's childhoods (Marcel and Bobrán). Seventy-three handshakes (and counting). Seventy-three opportunities for understanding, misunderstanding, fellow feeling, hatred, love, rivalry, solidarity, envy, gratitude or resentment. A combinatory system – if one factors in the vagaries of individual mood, arousal, character, mental impairment, emotion, chemicals, illness, ageing, while further adjusting the equation to register the impact of such supra-individual forces as class, upbringing, belief, sexual proclivity, education, race, experience, associations and (however indeterminate) *influences* – capable no doubt of generating anything at all and, maybe, most often, nothing very particular, little more in fact than a flux of chaotic existence, yielding barely those patterns we all strive to seek and then discern well before we define, swinging at best from banality to extremity, and back again, ever after, world without end.

Will.   Salvatore closed his volume of Voltaire's *Lettres philosophiques.* The writer's passing comment that 'le peuple . . . en tout a besoin d'être mené par les grands . . .' (. . . the people need in everything to be led by those greater . . .) both surprised and pleased him for its simplicity and forthrightness. His lips moved imperceptibly as he memorized the phrase.

The Sicilian leaned back in his simple chair. He removed his glasses and briefly considered their lenses.

What was it, he reflected, that singled out those 'grands' whose fate – nay!, duty – it was to lead people or peoples? In Voltaire's time, birth, no doubt. But might it not now be nature's own gifts that set the leader apart? Intelligence, looks, physical stature, charisma, health, vigour, and, of course, will. A will to lead must surely be paramount.

A smile spreading across his countenance, Salvatore took a moment to consider his own case. Of lowly origins, had he not been blessed with the looks of a matinée idol? Of course he had! Was he not endowed with an uncommon ability both to learn and to speak? That he was! Did he not nurture in his heart a fine degree of noble ambition? Indeed he did! What might the future not hold for a low-born and humble immigrant such as he?

Salvatore was launched upon four different and parallel paths, any one of which might hoist him to some eminence: there was his forthcoming induction through marriage into French bourgeois society; there were his university studies, and the academic qualification to which they must eventually conduct him; there was his newly assumed trade-union role, with its earnest of political influence; lastly, there were his hesitant and covert first attempts at literature – a throw of the dice attractive to the gambler within him. In each act and plan, the essence of a man's will had a chance to work itself out.

Salvatore stood up, turned and saw what appeared to be the beginnings of a most incongruous combat, pitting the aged peasant Jacques against the ungainly Portuguese desperado from upstairs. Leadership was called for: intervention was urgent, before a blow might be struck, parried, then returned with interest; on the other hand, discretion also must have its due. Salvatore looked up and down, left and right, at ceiling and at floor, willing a sign to appear, then began to pick his way queasily up the machine aisle. It was at this juncture that he noticed, beyond Jacques and Fernando, the . . .

relaxed   figure of Philippe, leaning against the side of his machine number one, blowing smoke rings, smiling, and observing Jacques and Fernando, who were now circling as if locked at a precisely calibrated distance from one another by a mysterious magnetic force. Salvatore's steps slowed to a halt. He came to rest in the middle of the machine aisle, halfway between the aisle-ends of Eric's machines five and ten. The Sicilian sank the elbow of his right arm into the palm of his left hand, and with the thumb and fingers of his right hand began to caress his lips.

Eric, bent over the threshing tub at his machine number five, caught Salvatore's stationary left leg in the corner of his eye then, his view travelling upward, observed the thinker's pose. Turning to seek the object of Salvatore's interest, the Englishman chuckled with amusement as he tossed his gloves into the threshing bin among the tangled sprue. He took up position at the end of his machine ten, the better to observe what he presumed must soon evolve into a fight.

Rachid, from his seat against the wooden table; Marcel, returning from a visit to the toilet and stationing himself alongside Philippe; Mathieu, back from the raw-materials area, breaking through the hanging plastic flaps; Luigi, witnessing the informal constitution of the Philippe-Marcel-Mathieu group, then seeking the focus of its shared interest: all were drawn into the orbit of the slowly revolving Portuguee-and-peasant pairing – for any sport, contest, road crash, abandoned carrion, any natural or human calamity must always draw a crowd, even – nay, especially! – when its exact nature is not yet clear.

The Jacques–Fernando pairing slowed very nearly to a stop. Both men still smiled, but their eyes had narrowed, and the corners of their mouths twitched. Of a sudden, the force that had been holding the two men separate and yet together ceased its operation. Fernando broke first, darting straight at Jacques' belly, his tortoise-head appearing to retract while he made a grab for the older man's groin, hoping perhaps to grasp flesh quickly and with sufficient force to immobilize the larger man's vast arms. The peasant, laughing comfortably, pushed the Portuguee aside, throwing out an arm to dig the smaller man hard beneath the ribs. Fernando fell back, giggling like a child. Jacques' eyes sparkled as he registered this reaction. The revolving standoff resumed.

This time it was Jacques who lassoed Fernando's neck with his left arm, hauled him in, then swung his right at his opponent's testicles, after briefly baring and tickling his belly. Jacques' unabetted left arm proved insufficient, however, to the task of holding a younger and more agile man immobile: in a trice, Fernando wriggled free.

Then, allowing the peasant no time to regroup his forces, regain his breath, rearrange his limbs or ponder his next move, Fernando butted him in the belly, sending him toppling sideways onto the floor, while darting both his hands between the man's legs and seizing, through the thick country corduroys, the man's sexual . . .

apparatus.   Not unlike a wounded stag, Jacques gaped open his mouth, lolled his tongue, rolled slowly onto his back and hung his limbs in the air.

While some spectators laughed (Marcel), spat (Mathieu), gasped (Eric), looked away (Rachid), or reached nervously to pat or otherwise reassure their own genitalia (Luigi), Philippe and Salvatore, as if fired by a single trigger, moved toward the two-man scrum, the latter willing himself to intervene to ensure fair play, the former ready to intervene if only to guarantee non-intervention. Salvatore, observing that Philippe too was moving toward the combatants, appealed with arms upraised and questioning manner, to which the Marseillais, patting the air before him, intimated to the Sicilian that he could stand down.

It may well be that Jacques' spontaneous surrender had unnerved Fernando or, just possibly, that the possession in his grip of the other man's genitalia, however well sheathed in winter fabrics, had unmanned him. Be that as it may, Fernando now released his grip and sought to get up, beaming down in triumph upon the peasant. Jacques, however, his old eyes asparkle, no sooner glimpsed than seized his revenge, tripping and flooring Fernando, whom he pinned with one arm and one knee fast to the floor, while with his other arm he commenced remorselessly to exploit the Portuguee's weak point, tickling him in his belly, underarm and neck, until he squealed like a farrowing sow. Jacques pinched and tickled Fernando thoroughly and yet distractedly, as if it were a . . .

horticultural chore, a piece of hoeing or weeding, say, requiring but scant application and little effort. He recalled how Edith had loved to be tickled and how tenderly and lovingly in the early years of their marriage a tickle-fight (which he unfailingly won) would culminate.

Fernando, his strength drained by helpless giggling, any strategic thoughts of escape effectively scattered, soon entered a region of finely balanced pain and hysteria, lashing out wildly but ineffectually, feeling – because trapped and subjected – at once effeminate, impotent, vulnerable and enraged. What had seemed at first an uneven duel between a wily young polecat and a flap-eared old labrador had turned before the gaze of all onlookers – including, now, Tomec, who had just stepped through the plastic flaps from metallurgy and was surveying the scene in the attitude of a sentry – into something more like the public flaying-by-laughter of that same young polecat at the hands of an ageing but still resourceful grizzly.

The other workers approached to get a better view. Nobody spoke. Each man, as he watched Fernando flail and writhe, experienced a rare mastery over his own thoughts: Marcel pursued with the coolest resolve his inventory of lovers and his plans for a cull; Luigi, as he relit his cornpaper cigarette, enjoyed unsought inspiration from his intergalactic-porn habit, picturing in piquant detail his girlfriend Gilberte ravished at every orifice by phalluses, every one of them unmistakably his own; Eric, shocked by the brute intimacy of the scene just witnessed, grappled Fanny yet closer to his heart as lover-to-be and initiator, for it must fall to her, he realized, to walk him over the broad-spanning bridge into Frenchness and to render the sumptuously exotic deliciously familiar; Rachid, whose mind had in no wise been seduced by the mid-distance spectacle, steadied himself for the perusal of his wife's note, which he knew could no longer be postponed; Mathieu, chewing on his latest matchstick and observing Fernando's torment, quivered at the realization that he was prepared at last to place his beloved wife beyond suffering; Salvatore, one eye on the Marseillais, contemplated his own appearance, his own stance, his flexing musculature, the throbbing solicitations of duty bearing upon his own mind; lastly, Philippe, recalling his recent urge to batter his fornicant wife, laughed out loud at its patent absurdity: to think that such a podgy, amiable cove as himself could ever commit – or even imagine committing – a crime passionnel . . .

As Philippe broke into a guffaw, the more suggestible of the other onlookers (Marcel, Eric, Salvatore and Luigi) also laughed, though rather uncertainly. With so many eyes upon him, Philippe thought it best to direct his laughter at Fernando and Jacques, tapping the latter on the shoulder and, in effect, calling time-out. Tomec, meanwhile, narrowed his eyes and took note, impressed.

The combatants separated, Fernando black with comic-book rage, attempting to shrug off his humiliation. The men all returned to their machines, with the exception of Jacques who, approaching Fernando and holding out his hand, said, Eh! portugais! Tu viens boire un café? Je t'invite.

Fernando hesitated the merest instant, then followed the old peasant out of the plastics section, jabbing him just beneath the ribs with greater violence than was strictly necessary.

Ifs.   Across the road, in a fourth-floor two-bedroom flat, Goran and Iskra were drinking tea. They stared at one another across a freshly laundered white starched tablecloth. In a bedroom, a child softly cried. They had been doing their sums, arguing about what mattered most. Iskra wanted them to rent a flat in a nicer area; Goran argued they should save every centime, in case the bad times – unemployment, ill health, family calamities back home in Titov Veles – should return. Goran hated to hand over hard-earned cash to a landlord. We have to think long-term, he would say. On a good day, the argument might go Goran's way; but today, after the stabbing on the street below, with their child crying again, and Goran's brother snoring in their living room, Iskra's reasons were compelling.

This district gets dirtier and more dangerous every day. Look at the kind of people who are moving here now. You said the man stabbed was an Arab. Did we come to France to live among Arabs? Were we meaning to emigrate to North Africa? That's what this place feels like.

The people who did the stabbing were French, I think, Goran muttered. What? So?

Nothing. Perhaps you're right. But if we stay here and put money aside, and if you find work too, and if I get promotion . . . we might buy a flat of our own in a good area.

How many ifs? And in the meantime Mira cries. Just listen! She hates it here. She misses her friends. If she could bring her schoolmates home . . .

Goran's eyes were closing. He started work at five.

Iskra saw the greying skin at his temples.

Go to bed, Iskra said. And think about it.

I think of nothing else, Goran replied, rising from his chair.

Experience.   The worker feeds the machine via its hopper, the press shits out product, the worker plunges in his hand to separate the precious pieces from their fishbone sprue. To the worker, at night's end, these pieces, boxed up and ready to go, are the *end*-product, the visible fruit of his labour. The pieces say, We are the proof you did your job, worked the machine right. We are the reason you are paid. You are paid so much to produce so much. And this is all the worker needs to know. What is the product for? A car? A machine? Something electrical, perhaps? Who cares!

The boss, of course, cares. He must know. The boss will care who needs the product and how badly and what for. He employs someone to calculate the going price of every box of product that leaves his factory. To the boss, the product is not shit but food: it marks not the end but the beginning of a process. It meets a need, finds a consumer, fetches a price.

Two different cycles of meaning judder into motion, two different scales apply each time a boss and a worker look at the selfsame piece of plastic. To the worker its perfection is proof of his industry: it says something important about his recent past. To the boss, its perfection is an earnest of saleability: it promises something important for his medium-term future.

Indulgence.   Jean dropped a bunch of cable ties into the box next to his right foot, and the sprue into the bin by his left, slammed the machine guard shut, and slapped the START button with the flat of his right hand. How he hated distractions, worries! He stared at the closing press. The graffiti insult to his employer and the forthcoming strike action were the last things he wished to think about. If only Luigi would drop in on him a little earlier than usual. That man at least was a good listener. He took Jean seriously. Besides, Luigi heard things and passed them on. Jean growled and shook his head. He longed to resume his review of the day's events. He had reached neighbourhood level. The press opened, Jean noted some slight resistance as he pulled the sprue from the mould.

He decided to accord himself some treats, staggering them strategically.

This would help him keep unwelcome thoughts at bay. His back was hurting, but he would not stretch it for another six products. His mouth was dry, but he would wait until the minute hand on the wall clock had reached the half hour before fetching a spearmint from his pocket. Lastly – a very special indulgence this – at eleven o'clock or thereabouts, saving interruptions and diversions – he would remember his very first girlfriend, ask himself where she could possibly be now, and compose a credible and not unworthy account of himself, just in case he bumped into her one day, at the dentist's, say. Usually this exercise was reserved for the first Monday of each month – since to dwell any more frequently on his first love would reveal weakness, not to mention disloyalty to dear Monique. Three treats to look forward to! He sat up straighter.

Jean hit the START button rather more gently than before. Five more products till his stretch! He was back in control. Almost. Where had he been? Neighbourhood news. The butcher. Jean took up and lightly oiled his brush in readiness to lubricate the ejector pins. The press opened.

Brains.   In a town-centre brasserie, a union rep from Établissements Boucan was in discussion with his party superior. The rep had declared his optimism about the strike-readiness of the metallurgy sections.

What about plastics? Are they solid?

The night shift is an unknown quantity but, otherwise, yes.

We have Philippe Merceau in there.

He walked away.

What happened?

Who knows.

Hmm. Sometimes I think we're losing the ideological battle.

You know what he said? He said, My problem isn't Marx, Lenin or the revolution. My problem is you lot.

Sounds like a Trot.

No. I blame Solzhenitzyn. He's on every newsstand and all over the TV.

Merceau could make trouble.

I don't think so. He has existential issues.

A nut?

I said existential, not psychiatric.

Don't split hairs. Who's taking his place?

A Sicilian.

Jesus!

No, he seems okay, even if he does come on like a bleeding Socialist – smart clothes, fancy words. But he says he's with us.

A sympathizer?

I didn't think to ask. Hey, what are you looking at me like that for? It didn't seem relevant.

You're kidding, right? Don't go soft on me. We have to know what the man's thinking and whether he's affiliated and how. We're getting squeezed between the Socialists and the goddamn Trots. We need to know if the wop's sound. Maybe he thinks he's going places. For heaven's sake, wise up.

Maybe he *is* going places. He spends his days at the university.

He told you that? Well, so does my son. What's the problem? We need brains. Brains are draining away from us. Befriend him. Reel the fucker in.

Sure. I'll see.

Slender.   Think of the very worst thing that can happen, Rachid's father used to advise when one of his children was anxious about some impending event – a school exam, a job interview, or a first date. The imagined disaster was supposed to make the challenge less daunting, the fear less real. One day Rachid retorted, That's no way to live. I'm sick of comforting myself with a lesser disaster. But it was too late. It had become a reflex.

Rachid felt almost ready to read Malika's note. With an image of her parting smile fresh in his mind, he had contemplated, he was sure, the greatest horrors: she had killed both Fatima and herself; she was leaving him for another man; she wanted a divorce; she no longer loved him; she wished to return to Algeria. Had that smile been one of triumph? Of betrayal, perhaps? Of sorrow and resignation? Of quiet satisfaction? Of homicidal and suicidal preparedness?

That he might lose Malika and Fatima terrified Rachid. He could no more bear the loss of his wife than that of another child. Despite their state of relative estrangement, Malika's physical presence was as essential to him as food or sleep or air. Free of any desire, Rachid recalled the grace with which his wife always moved, her long limbs in motion, her delicate feet, her fine neck. That very morning, as so often, he had watched her wake up and stretch and rub her eyes just as he was falling asleep. He feared she might have left him and yet, at the same time, that if she remained he would never desire her again.

Labour.   Fernando and Jacques had left the plastics section arm in arm, but in the dark of metallurgy had quickly separated. They walked in silence to the coffee machine. Fernando paid for the coffees.

How's the farm? Fernando asked.

Ah, you know . . .

There was a silence.

My horse almost came in today, Fernando announced. A rank outsider. Lost by a head. A nose really. It would have been a big win.

What would you do?

With a big win? A really big win?

Jacques nodded over his coffee.

Buy some land.

Really. Where?

Back home maybe. The Douro valley. Or here somewhere, maybe the Ardèche.

Jacques shook his head and blew air out of his mouth.

I've thought about it, Fernando said. I'm going to save up.

It's tough for a man starting out on his own. You'd be swimming against the current. People are pouring off the land.

I've met a woman. I think she's the right one.

Well . . .

Fernando nodded and took a sip. He looked out into the dark.

Has she worked on the land before?

I don't think so. But she's fit and strong. And young.

She'd have to be able to put her back into hard physical labour.

She's used to that all right.

What work does she do?

Kind of a therapist. Hard to explain.

Jacques sniffed. What would you do if you ran into trouble? Would you find alternative work? Do they need therapists there?

Everywhere needs therapists.

Does she speak the language?

It's not that fucking-kind of therapy.

Jacques dropped his empty beaker into a bin. He shook his head slowly.

Well, I wish you good luck.

Write.   How do they write? They take dictation; they copy in words; they find the first and last word then string a bridge across the gap; they put down what is in their minds; they follow a train of thoughts in another language; they delete every ninth word; they select a letter, then banish any words that contain it; they fix a rhyme scheme; they eavesdrop on people speaking then transcribe verbatim; they make a mass of notes then throw almost all of them away; they check what they have then subtract, then add; they reach a judgement; they make a commitment.

No, no, no. *How* do they write?

With words, words, words. By reading.

Precisely.

33. Tears . . . Laughter.

Tears.   Earth Flesh Faeces Dust
             Blood Urine Lymph Pus
             Ashes Tears Humours Weep
             Skin Flakes Bowels Seep . . .

Face.   Mathieu hesitated at the lift door. No need to go upstairs. Machines all working well. No new moulds, their products to be checked. No men requiring supervision.

The doors opened. He peered inside the empty lift. To be encased, alone. He limped and shuffled. The doors closed on him. He leaned against the wall. The lift was still. Now came the moment of nothingness. Unannounced. Void of thought. An instant frozen. He pushed the button.

Perhaps it took energy to die, to change states, steam to water, water to ice. The lift rose slowly. Perhaps she was ready but unable, the infinitesimal effort beyond her powers. A clanking stop. In his inner ear, he heard Miles's trumpet. *In a Silent Way.* He saw Miles's face on the sleeve photo. Then the boxer on the ropes in *Tune Up.* He loved that sound: Miles's mute. He knew that face.

Stiff.   The cycle ride had loosened Jorge's gut. He had kissed Marta twice on the cheek then pushed through her partying crowd, hurriedly greeting people as he went, noting a girl he had seen the previous week: Renata, Italian, tall, green-eyed, with the blackest hair and the whitest skin. She smiled at him then glanced away.

In the toilet, with much puffing and blowing, he rid himself of two large turds, the second one so hard and glib it tickled his prostate before carving a painful exit. He opened the little window over the cistern, washed and dried his hands. He felt light and, if not quite aroused, frisky. Had he been a dog, his tail would have been wagging. Why not Renata? Why not? But how would he get her home? On his bike?

Renata was in a corner, dancing, surrounded. She looked his way. He recalled their last conversation and planned their next one.

Would you mind if we don't talk about Chile?

Is it too painful?

Let's call it that. (A pained look.) Tell me about you.

Jorge was sick of telling stories, always the same, never more than half-true; sick of watching people watching him be Jorge, the Chilean refugee. He wanted a night off.

Tick-Tock.   Tomec had watched the men disperse, first the participants then the observers. He sensed he had missed something, arrived too late. He didn't know whom to ask, or how.

You can't be everywhere, he told himself, as if making a discovery. You can't see everything. What you see is a sample, almost random.

Tomec had seen Luigi Marcel Eric return to their machines, while Rachid lowered his eyes and Philippe fell back on his papers. Mathieu had made for the lift. Salvatore had gone to talk to Luigi.

Virgil at his casement missed nothing. (Or did he?) Then he died.

Tomec stood at the end of Luigi's machine thirteen. In his brain, a clock ticked.

Licking.   Marcel was at his machine eleven, bent over the threshing tub. He was beginning to sweat. He looked at Philippe, who was reading his papers.

Marcel was thinking about his cull of lovers, and about Paulette in particular. She had grown fat, needy, weepy. She would wail. He would have to stop his ears. Or her mouth. Gently but firmly. Careful! He was not a cruel man but he had to make things simpler. He wanted to be responsible and go into his marriage like he meant it.

Paulette was never a great fuck anyway. Her only true skill was in giving head. But nobody gave better head than Chantal. With her, it wasn't a skill, it was a passion. Paulette's manner was efficient, effective, irresistible in its own way, but done to please. Afterward, you would catch yourself reaching for your wallet. Whereas Chantal didn't set out to please. She did it because it excited her. A rare and fine thing in a woman.

As Marcel stood back from the tub and looked down at the sprue and product, a pearl of perspiration in his armpit detached itself and dribbled down his flank. He shuddered and pressed his upper arm to his side, squashing the droplet into the starched fabric of his lime-green shirt. Glancing up, he saw Alphonse halfway down the stairs.

Alphonse had stopped and was peering over the heads of the workers and the tops of all the ground-floor machines. Restless, he had asked Fernando to keep an eye on his machines. Alphonse was glad he worked upstairs. If not much quieter, it was at least calmer. Some nights, however, he got bored. Fernando, Bobrán and Jean were not a lot of fun. The good thing about downstairs was that just occasionally something happened: an argument, say, or a prank.

Right now, all was still. Salvatore was talking to Luigi: the Sicilian seemed earnest, the Italian bored. Further down the machine aisle, the Englishman picked his nose, looked at his finger, then leaned forward and wiped his finger on his sock, this way then that. At the far end of the machine aisle, sitting as usual against the wooden table, the Algerian had his hands in his lap, a folded piece of paper trapped in the fingers of his left hand. At machine twelve, Bobrán's cousin looked guiltily happy about something, like a cat on a dining table picking at leftovers.

Attaché.   Philippe had glanced up from his paper to see Salvatore taking his leave of Luigi and barrelling back down the machine aisle toward his machines.

There he springs! Fresh as a tulip! Philippe muttered, closing his paper. You'd think he never ate, slept, smoked or sweated. Superman just flexes and swings. You have to wonder whether he shits or bleeds. The way he moves, he could run on casters.

Something had jogged Philippe's memory. He stepped to the cylindrical recycled-material bin at the end of his machine two, flicked through the papers and magazines till he came to *Le Nouvel Observateur.* He soon found the dog-eared page he was looking for, featuring a middle-aged man sitting naked except for a broad black belt around his abdomen, appearing to be connected by wires to a contraption advertised as an 'Electro-Gym.'

Jacques had to see this!

The old peasant had finished checking his products and was sitting on his chair, scratching his head. The Marseillais thrust the advert into his free hand.

Jacques fetched his glasses from his shirt pocket, set them carefully upon his nose, and stared at the advert. The blurb promised weight loss and improved muscle tone without recourse to diet or exercise.

Jacques looked up at his friend, perplexed.

You know, Philippe began, we're always joking about what the Sicilian keeps in his attaché case . . . Well . . . Mystery solved!

Oh, right, Jacques chuckled. Very good, very good! I thought you were going to suggest I got one . . .

Marcel had stepped across the machine aisle. He had noticed the merriment. Jacques explained the joke.

I can just picture it! Marcel said.

Philippe shrank back, retreating along the side of Jacques' machine.

Eric had approached and it was Marcel's turn to do the explaining.

Take a look at this! See that attaché case? That's the Sicilian's, right? We reckon that's how he keeps fit! What do you think?

Eric laughed uncertainly. Marcel went through it all again. Philippe returned to his own machines, his face lengthening.

Can I borrow this? Marcel asked.

Lull.   Fanny pulled open the glass door and entered the crowded bar. The air was thick with every kind of tobacco and recreational smoke. The tables were all taken. Lou Reed, backed by the Velvet Underground, supplied the mood. The prevailing colour of the furnishings and decorations was miasmal blue.

Salut cousine! Julie cried out.

Fanny stood on her tiptoes, her elbows on the bar, while Julie leaned forward to kiss her twice on both cheeks: smack, smack, smack, smack. They clasped hands across the bar.

I'll take a break in a bit and we'll have a cigarette and a talk. Do you want something? A beer?

Fanny nodded. I thought you had to study this evening.

They asked me at the last moment. Alain phoned in sick. There will be a lull soon – before the cinemas chuck out. If you want to go into the office . . . Fanny shook her head.

Julie raked the surplus foam from Fanny's beer and placed the glass on a mat advertising Pelforth.

À la tienne! Fanny said, taking a sip and turning to look round the tables. She hoped to spot a friend.

Materialist.   Observation was just one of the storyteller's powers, along with time travel, mind reading, and the polyglot rendering capability already mentioned. He was, as his friends sometimes teased, a very cunning linguist but, he would retort, no artist, mystic or seer. Such abilities as he possessed were easier to acquire than the profane allowed. In-sight, in-hearing, in-feeling, in-tuiting were not only essential to the calling, they were, in the main, sufficient. Nothing supernatural was entailed, there were no tricks, no cheap wizardry. Every day, not only did billions of people speak (some in tongues, some in wild ululations) to unseen and (mercifully) nonexistent gods, some few even claimed to obtain reply. The magic that he conjured (if any there were) was modest indeed, his claims those of a very earthbound materialist.

Rap.   Marcel had taken the lift upstairs. He cornered Bobrán at the hopper end of his machine fifteen. Bobrán smiled at his cousin as though the interview were both optional and welcome.

If you're in trouble, maybe I can protect you, Marcel said. I still have friends.

Right, Bobrán snorted: the kind who rob banks and let you sit in gaol, taking their rap. You can't even protect yourself. Friends like that . . .

And yours? Police blackmailers . . .

What are you talking about?

Just what I heard, just what I know.

You don't know shit.

Marcel stood back. His cousin was nervous. This was encouraging. Well, maybe we should talk about what shit I do know.

Bobrán wiggled the index finger of his right hand, beckoning Marcel to approach. Marcel leaned in to his cousin's face. Bobrán fixed him with a narrow stare, then jerked his eyes as wide open as they would go, and pronounced carefully: Va Te Faire FOUTRE!

Marcel was not used to being addressed this way. He said nothing. Whereupon Bobrán turned his back.

Marcel raised his fist, then let it drop. He opened his mouth, then let it close. You're on your own, he muttered.

Skin.   Even at birth, the skin that these men wore on their faces must have been of contrasting hues, a function of genetically and geographically distributed melanin: from the extreme of rosy pinkness (Eric), via some degree of nutty cream or milky olive (Salvatore) to a dark and deep brown (Alphonse). In the intervening years, sunshine had everywhere played its part, if only by its absence. Bobrán's face was sun-burnished chestnut; Philippe's a veneer of faded summer suntan; Rachid's the sallow of the lifelong sun-shy.

Quite different distinctions determined the texture of each man's facial skin: whereas Jean Rachid Philippe Jacques and Alphonse all shaved in the afternoon or evening, before coming to work, Marcel Luigi Tomec and Salvatore shaved in the mornings, before going to bed: by now, the chins of the latter group were sandpapery. The remaining men, infrequent and / or irregular shavers, had faces that were either stubbly (Mathieu), sparsely furred (Bobrán) or fuzzy (Eric); Tomec alone wore a moustache.

Health and habit played a part. Luigi's contempt for soap and water had conspired with his hatred of fresh food to propagate a complexion that was both oily and yellow except where it was red and cratered. Alphonse, thanks to a daily application of oils and unguents, had a skin that glowed and at times even shone. Jacques, accustomed to staring down all weathers, was swathed in a tough yet bluish surface-veined hide; Mathieu, the plaything of psoriasis, presented a battlefield visage upon which the proliferating forces of white desiccation waged unrelenting battle with those of slow-volcanic pink eruption.

Sticky. Gilles and Heike, their tongues and thoughts engaged in impassioned conversation, their legs accelerating as if in dynamic sympathy, had abandoned Moritz, Jean-Pierre and Margot far behind.

Up to this point, Heike had done most of the listening. She had noticed in turn: the Frenchman's breadth of social and political reference; his erudition; his vestigial accent; his acerbic humour and quasi-Leninian scorn; the occasional archaism of his vocabulary – derived from his having learnt his German, as he had credibly claimed, from the perusal of Marx and Lukács; his flouting of bourgeois morality as evidenced by his disparagement of marriage, coupledom and his enthusiastic disquisition on the Italian radical craze for 'auto-riduzione'; his rather thin upper lip, prompting Heike to posit cruelty as a character trait before chiding herself for her relapse into crass nineteenth-century physiognomism.

At first Gilles had noticed nothing but the brilliance of his own pluming discourse, but he now saw that Heike's smile had outstripped the confines of mere merriment. He ceased mid-flow, intrigued as to her humour.

What is it? he asked, halting and letting go of her arm.

I suppose you would like to sleep with me, Heike told him.

Gilles blushed like a child. We've only just met.

Heike laughed like an actual horse or a pantomime German, then took Gilles' arm.

I'm indisposed, she said.

Sorry? Gilles asked.

Indisponiert – nicht ganz auf der Höhe.

I understood the word but . . . oh, never mind.

Heike's brother and Gilles' friends were closing on them.

I suppose I could ask Margot to explain, Heike teased.

Laughing, their conversation resumed, but more slowly than before, and with less speech-making. Gilles was listening.

Place. There were towns like Grandgobier all over Europe and beyond, some even boasted factories like Établissements Boucan. In Darmstadt, twenty-seven injection presses were manned by fifteen night-shift workers, including five Yugoslavs, one Turk, and three Spaniards; in Coventry, twenty-four injection presses were worked nights by eleven men, including one Irish, one Bengali, one Greek, one Scot and one Hong-Kong Chinese; in Brescia, twenty-three machines were worked by eight assorted Puglians / Basilicatans / Calabresi, two Tunisians, a Slovene and a Sardinian; in Ljubljana, sixteen machines were (over-) manned by ten night workers, including four Montenegrin Albanians; in Katowice, fourteen machines were worked at night by Poles, one Angolan, two Ukrainians, a Cuban and a Vietnamese; on the outskirts of Göteborg, seven machines, employing two Swedes, a Ghanaian and a Finn; lastly, on the outskirts of Bilbao, an eighteen-machine factory was under construction, with Andalucian and North African manpower expected punctually to report for work.

Scythe. In Philippe's brief absence, Alphonse had been standing at the end of machine two, flicking through the cultural pages of the papers piled on top of the recycled-material cylinder. To his delight, he had discovered in the listings section of *Le Monde* that Beckett's *Oh les beaux jours* was being performed in Paris at the Theatre d'Orsay, with Madeleine Renaud as the truncated woman. Alphonse would hitch a lift to Paris straight out of work on Saturday morning and see that evening's performance, spend Sunday with his uncle in the Treizième Arrondissement, then hitch back to Grangobier on Monday. An inspired plan! His friends in Lyon would understand. Clara would understand. The birthday party in his honour could be postponed. He committed the box-office phone number to memory. He could have danced! Happy days! The play would give him insight. He hadn't been to Paris since the spring.

Alphonse lifted his eyes from the paper, euphoric, then saw Luigi. Luigi was the same as always. Alphonse folded the paper and stared.

The Italian sat at the end of his machine fourteen, his mouth ajar, his Gitanes-Maïs stub extinguished in his mouth. The African experienced a chill. He recalled the first time he had felt that chill, months ago, at about four o'clock one morning. He had shivered, then turned to find Luigi standing behind him, peering over his shoulder. The grim reaper, Alphonse had thought. Stooped and slouching and sullen and silent, exuding a petrifying blast. As a butcher, Luigi must even wield a hatchet. Not quite a scythe, but still.

Alphonse was amused by his own suggestibility. Happy days! he repeated, as he headed down the machine aisle. To his left, Marcel appeared to be suffering an access of almost comedic anger, his jaw clenched, his fists balling, his brow furrowed; Rachid, meanwhile, sat immovable upon his chair. If no one else, surely Eric or Salvatore must be sociable . . .

Parting. Upstairs, Bobrán had finished filling the machine-fifteen hopper. He examined the product. It was perfect. Just as every night for the past five weeks, ever since the engineers had fitted this mould. He made to throw it into the threshing bin, but checked himself and scrutinized it again. It was still perfect. He emptied the floor tray into the bin and rolled up his sleeves.

He now had Albert's entire letter in his head. As he threshed, he scrolled through it back and forth. Certain phrases stood out: '[Joseph] wrote that you were friends' . . . 'my journey is costing us many sacrifices' . . . 'on whom will you be able to rely, when your turn comes?' . . . ; might that last phrase be a threat?

As the letter had proceeded, Bobrán's memory of the day of Joseph's death had steadily sharpened. He now recalled his conversation that morning with Joseph; he could see the event itself with its immediate, seemingly simultaneous, aftermath; and he remembered with pinprick clarity the afternoon spent with Moritz.

Further strands were becoming entangled in the braid of Bobrán's mind. His cousin's insistent interference; Jean's itchy curiosity; Mathieu's advice, and Rachid's anger at his 'stupid' staircase 'stunt.' Then Rachid's mention of the death of his son, unnamed, who 'fell from the kerb . . . into the path of a moped.'

Bobrán failed again to picture the Algerian's son. Instead, he saw Rachid himself as a boy, his face lined and his skull balding. Or he saw a child resembling Moritz, cheeks too chubby, skin too peachy. In both cases, the child was alive.

To be hit and killed by a moped: how would that work? It was easy to see blood and brains on a kerbstone, but not the child, not its clothed body. As on a split screen, Bobrán visualized Rachid's bent back, in the grey jacket he wore to work each night, curving over his son on the sidewalk, and then the face of his lover as Moritz stretched out his arms toward him, taking his head between his hands to place that first kiss on his parting lips.

Celebration.   In the flat she shared with her husband, Monique Herbier was sipping vermouth. She did not particularly like the taste, but the effect was unfamiliar and, for the time being, not unpleasant. This conduct was unlike her, but she felt it befitted the occasion. She was on her third small glass. Not every day did you discover that you were not after all playing host to a reliably lethal disease and hence did not need sternly to set your face into a whirlwind of surgical operations, chemo- and radiotherapies, whinnying pain, desolation, the insufferable pity of bravely smiling relatives and strangers, worries for her widower-to-be – who could surely never manage on his own – and, at last, the final plunge to an agonizing death, palliated only by mind-dulling nausea-inducing drugs. She raised her glass.

What, though, did she have to look forward to? A reprise of the life she had known prior to her scare, enhanced merely – and for how much longer? – by Jean's revernalized passion, which no doubt was to be ascribed in part to his fears for her and, thus in the same measure, subject, now that those fears had been allayed, to diminishing returns at best – at worst to abrupt extinction. No. Monique had always wished to travel, while Jean had ever refused to cross any border or sea. She would start with Corsica and the DOM-TOMs, before venturing to foreign-speaking lands. She would be frugal, dispensing none but her own hard-won savings.

Monique rose unsteadily from her armchair, returning with a pencil, her diary and a notebook, in which she proceeded to register in order of priority all the tourist spots to which she now felt compelled to pay visit – this side of death.

Classificatory.   Much like noses, cocks in the main require but scant attention. While marginally distinguishable by shape, dimension, angularity, consistency (from cartilaginous to spongy), or action, few appear to be either spectacularly Roman, Snub, Fine-Chiselled, Retroussé, Winged, Straight, Cauliflower, Upturned or Mere-Smear. Yet each member of its species, each individual, may – without overstretching matters – be characterized according to its singular genius.

Accordingly, within the compass of one plastics section, no two cocks could ever, even on a cursory acquaintance, be mistaken. One specimen was exceptional for its eel-mimicking rippling muscularity; another for its conjugation of uncommon length with uncommon slenderness – as though nature had decreed that only just so much flesh were available to this class of appendage, distribute it however one might; a third, even at repose, jutted from its possessor's pubis at a jaunty angle of approximately forty-five degrees, as though buoyed up on exceptionally fore-positioned and globular testicles; a fourth tapered like a wedge or pestle, slight at its base but descending (or, very occasionally, *ascending*) to a mallet-headed culmination; a fifth was so stubby and set amid such follicular luxuriance that its head scarcely peeped from out its curls; a sixth was disfigured along its shaft by an uncontained dermatological condition; a seventh disclosed just above (or, several times daily, just *below*) its glans a geology of ageing scar tissue overlaid in more recent times by the effects of blistering, attributable to frantic self-abuse; lastly – to eschew on principle any spurious stab at exhaustiveness in this domain – two cocks there were that stood out principally for their odours, the first being frequently subject to a threefold ablutionary regime that entailed in unbending sequence: (1) thorough soaping; (2) the application of its owner's girlfriend's vaginal deodorant; (3) a prolonged sousing in eau de cologne. The second cock, by contrast, was at once reeking victim and solemn witness to its master's disregard for even the most primitive forms of hygiene, a condition, moreover, severely exacerbated by the opportunistic advances of fungal infection. Which completes the survey.

Biding. Not so long ago, Bobrán would never have dared speak like that. Instead, he would have looked away and nodded, resentful perhaps, storing up hatred (who knows?), slippery-sly but not defiant. He knew his place. A little further back and he would have submitted, dropped his head like a whipped hound, tendered his jugular like a goat, hoisted his rump like a bitch in heat. Mild and meek. As a child he would take every kind of chastisement from his slightly-elders, never rebelling or running to tell tales, filling his place in the group, even smiling, appearing to like it, or willing to pretend.

Marcel's fists threshed the sprue and products to a darkening blur, his shoulders strained, his eyes stared into the grey bin, seeing nothing, popping. The sprue and products swirled.

Little cousin thinks he's a big man now and can carve for himself, keep secrets from those who would protect him, skip bonds of family and tribe: a womanish fool, a freak, a schemer. How to deal with him? That was the question. How to teach him a lesson? And when? Timing, timing. Method and Timing.

Marcel lifted the sprue from the bin and slung it into the recycling cylinder, then roughly poured the clattering product into the cardboard box at the foot of the control cabinet. He crashed the threshing bin back onto its upturned metal bucket against the machine flank.

No, Bobrán would never have spoken like that, not to anyone. He might have looked away, grinning slyly but never openly defiant. Biding his time, perhaps. Earlier still, he would even have submitted. And liked it.

Technology.   During the process of converting a plastic raw material into a finished molded product, three basic elements in modling [sic] – time, temperature, and pressure – must be correlated in a way that will produce a part with anticipated properties.

Time involves these elements: time beginning with material entering the heating cylinder until injected into the mold (also called residence time in the cylinder); time of injection into the mold; time of maintaining pressure in the mold cavity; time of solidification or cure time; press open time; press opening and closing time; time of part ejection in relation to mold opening time.

D.V. Rosato, op. cit., p. 89

Delay.   By way of conversational gambit, Alphonse had pointed to the hand-exerciser on the floor against the side of machine six and asked the Sicilian if he might try it out. Salvatore was impressed by the ease with which the Ivorian squeezed it shut.

You're in good shape. What do you do?

I take care what I eat, sleep as much as I can, and I skip.

Skip? Like a boxer?

Half an hour a day . . . but I don't carry a backpack full of bricks.

You don't box?

I don't want to get hit.

Salvatore smiled.

Hoping to divert his thoughts from their tightening loop, Marcel had interrupted his work and was observing the conversation between Alphonse and Salvatore, but his attention was captured by Jacques, who had picked his bag of apples from the floor and plonked them down on the recycled-material cylinder at the end of machine four.

Anyone want apples? he shouted, his arms waving about.

At opposite ends of the machine aisle: Rachid stared blankly then looked away; Luigi shook his head. Marcel and Philippe stepped over to inspect the fruit. Jacques tapped Eric on the shoulder, who said, No, thanks, but got up anyway to take a look. Jacques managed to catch the eye of Alphonse, who nodded and raised a hand to signify a slight delay.

Tuesday. The best-selling novels in France and Germany this week are, *Un mari c'est un mari* by Frédérique Hébrard, and *Angst vorm Fliegen* by Erica Jong. In Athens, Tinto Brass's *Salon Kitty* is on general release. Arvo Pärt is composing 'Cantus in Memory of Benjamin Britten.' The Ballet Flamand is staging *Ulenspiegel le Gueux* in Brussels. Jan Baszkiewicz's biography of Maksymilian Robespierre has just been published in Warsaw. Newspapers in Hungary carry obituaries of the writer Szilagyi Domokos. Marco Bellochio's *Triomphmarsch* is being screened across Germany. In Madrid, Slawomir Mrozek's *Los Emigrados* is being staged at Teatro Alfil. American journalists Agee and Hosenball are being expelled from Britain. Vol. 19 of Enver Hoxha's *Gesammelte Werke* has been published by Verlag Roter Morgen. Foucault's *Histoire de la sexualité*, vol. 1, will appear on 17 November. Steve Reich's 'Trance Ensemble' is playing the Berlin Metamusik Festival. Raban Zerari's *On nous appelait Fellaghas* has been published. Sonny Rollins's trio is performing in Cascais, Portugal. In Spain, two bookshops have been attacked by far-right thugs: Libreria Rafael Alberti (Madrid) and Tres i Cautro (Valencia). Sartre has been made *doctor honoris causa* by the University of Jerusalem. Oslo's Portuguese Gastronomy Week is in full swing. Paris is hosting a 'Festival des travailleurs immigrés' until 15 November. Strindberg's *Et Drømmespil* is being staged at Copenhagen's Postusteatret. Oshima's *L'Empire des Sens* is playing in cinémas d'art et d'essai across France. The poet Reiner Kunze has been expelled from the writers' association of the GDR. Milan Huebl is on hunger strike in Czechoslovakia. Bernard Lavilliers, Georges Brassens, Rod Stewart, and Jacques Higelin are in concert, separately. Raymond Queneau is dead.

Fit.   A group of men was coalescing around the apples. Philippe stood back, smoked and watched. Marcel shifted from foot to foot, eyeing each man in turn. Philippe recognized something from nursery school: the quest for a kid to pick on. Luigi, moved by some instinct, was drifting down the machine aisle.

Eric was hunched over, his fingers clumsily manufacturing a cigarette. Alphonse had left Salvatore and now joined the huddle. Almost everyone was watching Marcel. Eric's hand shot down to his crotch, where he scratched himself through his jeans.

Now I see why you're all hunched up, Marcel said, a glint entering his eye.

Eh? Eric said. Quoi?

Look at you! You're turning into a hunchback already. And now we can see why. You spend too much time doubled up, checking it's still there.

Marcel accompanied this witticism with a nicely executed imitation of the stance that Eric had just, a little too late, abandoned and, at the same time, with an impression of a man rummaging around in desperate search of his own genitalia.

Alphonse held his sides, Luigi clapped a hand to his mouth, Jacques chuckled comfortably.

The Englishman could see he was the butt of some variety of humour. Philippe shook his head at him and winked.

Just look at him, Marcel said. Doesn't understand a fucking thing. Better off talking to the Arab.

Marcel waved a hand down the machine aisle. Everyone glanced at the Algerian, who appeared to be studying the nails of his left hand.

At least you can be sure the Arab understands you, even if the cunt never opens his mouth.

Alphonse stood back and frowned. Luigi refastened his hand to his mouth. Eric scratched first his crotch then the crown of his head. Jacques shifted uneasily and looked at Philippe, who now had the floor and knew it.

The Marseillais took a long drag on his cigarette, blew the smoke from his nostrils in a long sigh, then tilted his head to the right and aimed a weary look at Marcel's left ear.

You could take a leaf out of Rachid's book.

'Rachid' is it now?

Philippe nodded.

It was a set-up, but Marcel couldn't help falling into it.

A leaf? How do you mean?

Keeping your mouth shut is one way of not talking crap.

Jacques laughed.

Right! Alphonse said.

Luigi had relit his cigarette and moved closer to the Marseillais, who was taking his time.

In your particular case – Philippe sighed again – it may well be the only way.

Jacques slapped his thigh and nodded. Luigi stifled an ugly guffaw. Right! Right! Alphonse said.

Yeah? Marcel said, looking round at Philippe, Alphonse, Luigi and finally Jacques.

The Arab's all right, Jacques said with a shrug and a grin.

Philippe stared at the big Gypsy. For once, the Marseillais wasn't smiling.

Marcel tossed his unfinished cigarette on the floor, swore imprecisely, and returned to his machines.

Eric was left with the impression that Philippe had sprung to *his* defence. He tried to say thank you.

Forget it, Philippe said, his eyes glinting, Marcel was just dead wrong about the Arab.

His mouth wrenched open by a further fit, Luigi headed back to his machines. Meanwhile Jacques slung his great ape arm round Eric's neck, patting him kindly on the shoulder, then exclaiming, Hey! Nobody took any of my apples!

Philippe glanced down the machine aisle at Rachid then across at Marcel.

One hundred and ninety-three. The worker would study his nails for minutes on end; clap a hand to his mouth to hide a toothy laugh; stare at bubbles in a bottle; scat a trumpet solo, chorus upon chorus; pace and prance on the balls of his feet reciting text; squeeze the exerciser twenty times with his left then twenty times with his right; march through the dark with his torchlight swinging like an iron law of history; spit and polish the side of a machine till it shone; stand fish-eyed at the end of his machine and stare; lean back with his cornpaper cigarette dead in his mouth; sit rocking in his chair, his arms dangling to the floor; count each laborious piece until it was time to suck spearmint.

Hope.   Having returned upstairs to his machines sixteen and seventeen, Fernando had first scrutinized the last piece ejected from each mould, checked hopper levels, tipped floor trays into threshing tubs, then sat down and lit a cigarette. He floundered in a slough of memories remote and recent. He had overstated his hopes to the old peasant, talking up Maryse as if she could ever be more than his 'fucking cure' (though that afternoon had been sweet, hadn't it?). But for the first time, in sight of everyone, he had decisively lost the regular nut-grabbing contest with Jacques (a fucking-man twice his age!). He supposed he could smile at that. For a second, just long enough to shock and freeze, his parents and far-flung siblings flickered indistinctly and were gone. Even Alphonse had slapped him down: something to do with 'risk.' The Algerian had brushed him a-fucking-way like a gnat. He shook his head as bad thoughts piled in, but somehow they just sprang back again.

Adjusting his apron, Fernando stood up and reached for a lightly oiled rag that lay discarded beneath the jolting pistons at the end of machine seventeen. He took a deep breath and began to wipe and then to rub the orange-coloured side of machine sixteen as if it were a classic car, his pride and joy. He envisaged a 1940s Simca or Panharde. Fucking-some hope he'd ever own anything like that! He stood back and surveyed his handiwork. Fucking-not bad. He spat on the rag. He needed car polish.

Narratorial.   He could tell at a glance that an individual had, for instance, spent time in prison or in some other kind of correctional institution. It was the way they walked and held themselves. 'If I'm not immediately certain,' he boasted, 'I have only to wait till I see them enter a small room, even a lavatory will do: it's how they relate to walls. It's hard to pin down, but I've never yet been wrong. A blind man can walk you down a country lane on a pitch-dark windless night and tell you exactly where there's a big old tree or a gap in a hedge, because the air moves differently, the sounds are altered, that kind of thing. Similarly, I know things about people's past and habits from experience and observation, that's all. There's no magic. But you wouldn't want to meet me. You would feel bare, exposed to the unforgiving view of a raptor. I can even see past you, into your future. Trust me: don't ever trust me.'

Echo.   Philippe let a minute pass then replied to Marcel's angry stare with a smile. Marcel looked away. Philippe stepped across the machine aisle, pulling his cigarette pack from his pocket and shaking it so that a cigarette stuck out.

Think I'm that cheap? Marcel asked.

You misspoke and I said so. Hell, take two.

Marcel was low on cigarettes. He took two. Goddamn Philippe. You just couldn't stay mad at him.

Philippe was still holding out his pack, temptingly. As Marcel reached for a third cigarette, Philippe snapped the lid of the pack down on his workmate's fingers, tut-tutting.

Petit con! Marcel muttered to Philippe's face.

Do you want a coffee? Philippe said. I'm buying.

Mine will be a beer, Marcel replied, making it sound like a challenge.

Philippe took a step back, his face dropping, his eyes losing focus like a plane loses altitude.

What's wrong? Did you see a ghost?

I don't know. Nothing's wrong. Just an echo. A ghost, yes. It's gone. Let's go.

Rosa.   In Berlin, Wolf Biermann was sitting in his flat on Chausseestraße, a guitar on his knees, a pencil in his hand. He was waiting for some friends. With their help, he would rehearse the first part of Saturday's concert. He was thinking to open it with something to please his old fans: 'So oder So.' During the instrumental lead-in he would explain how he had come to write it – inspired by Marx's famous saying ('either socialism or barbarism'). *So oder so.* Then he'd blast out the first lines:

> *So oder so, die Erde wird rot:*
> One way or another the world will be red
> *Entweder lebenrot, oder todrot*
> Either life-red or death-red
> *Wir mischen uns, da bisschen ein*
> We're doing our meddling best . . .
> *So soll es sein . . . so* wird *es sein!*
> So should it be . . . so shall it be.

He would then interpolate a couple of new verses to make it crystal clear from the very start of proceedings, not just to the West German trade-unionists crowding the hall but to all those watching on TV, and especially to the party bosses at home in the East who had at long last granted him this visa to travel, that he was nobody's stooge and was not about to abandon his furious criticism of Stalinist bureaucracy or his stubborn campaign for communist democracy and revolutionary freedoms. He would refer, with another long aside spoken over his guitar accompaniment, to the recent publication in the GDR of Rosa Luxemburg's *Collected Works*. He would quote at length her lines on the Bolsheviks' abolition of democratic freedoms in 1917 and thus, in what he hoped would be a rhetorical master stroke, he would ram the great heavyweight mass of the GDR's diminutive political icon straight down the apparatchiks' swinish throats:

> *Die DDR braucht endlich und wie:*
> The GDR needs at long last – and how!
> *Rosas Rote Demokratie!*
> Rosa's Red Democracy!
> *Stimmt mir ihr zu? Dann stimmen wir beiden . . .*
> You agree with me? Then we all agree
> *So soll es sein, so soll es sein, so wird es sein.*
> So should it be . . . so shall it be.

That would really show them! Wouldn't it?

Wolf rubbed his hands in glee. Then came a drumming at the door.

Tingling.   Rachid folded the note and put it back in his pocket. And then he laughed. From the bottom of his lungs, the pit of his gut, the soles of his feet, a tide of rippling laughter rising surging streaming, as inexorable as lava, as random as retching. Rachid shook. His eyes stayed dry.

Malika had neither deserted him, killed herself and Fatima, fallen in love with another man, filed for divorce, nor resolved to return to Algeria. It was simpler than that and infinitely more complicated. Her smile had denoted neither triumph nor contempt, neither pity nor conspiracy, but love. Love!

Imagining the very worst, he had opened Malika's note with trembling fingers, the skin of his face as brittle as late-autumn leaf. He had cowered beside the control cabinet, out of the sight of prying Sicilian or English eyes.

He had chosen a moment when the Marseillais and the big Gypsy were out of the way. 'Mon cher Rachid! Mon amour!'

Guava.   Mon cher Rachid,

You won't be expecting this. Do you remember that morning when I told you my calves were cold – not my feet, my calves. It had been a hot night, late August. You acted surprised. I mumbled that maybe I was feverish. It was all you needed. That was when it happened. You are so predictable! I knew I was fertile and that you would want to take me if you touched or even thought of my calves. There are things a woman knows about a man and there are ways we have not just of forecasting the future but of determining its fulfilment. Three months! I shan't miscarry now! We will have a baby in April or early May. There! I didn't know how to tell you to your face. You will want to inform Mehdi. Don't ask me how I know this. Perhaps you will never let him go, but I have already done so. I loved him, but he was closer to you. This baby will be a new life for us both and I know how astonished and excited you will be – are now – as you read this. I am sorry I have refused you for so long and that on that one occasion I seemed so faraway. It was your sperm, your lifeforce, that I wanted, not you. Now I feel different again. It is you I want. Things will be as before. You must trust me. We shall be lovers. Soon you will see my belly swell, call me luscious and an overripe apricot and a guava so juicy you can't resist sinking your teeth into my side. I shall go on missing Mehdi, and you shall go on talking to him, but we shall be lovers again. Tomorrow morning, wake me when you come home, before Fatima stirs. Take me, mon amour. I am ready now. I shall be waiting for you even as I sleep. Are you ready too? I hope this night seems long to you. Come home to me. Malika.

Laughter.   Holding Sides upon a Heath
Pricking Air and Crackling Fire
Howling Mirth, Abandoned Care
Gust of Lung and Gale of Breath . . .

BOOK FOUR. MUSING.

Wherein lethargy and a drowsy self-probing overtake the ill-assorted gang: these are the slowest minutes of the night. Acquaintances have been remade, varieties of indifference displayed, enmities restated. Eyes now turn inward, homeward. A bug-eyed rabble is harangued; a moist conclusion is achieved by a forgetful runaway; a chronic mute is befriended by a person one third her age; four people settle down to write, seven to read; an industrialist retraces his steps on finding his wife asleep: so much for the main events. If you listen hard, you may hear beneath the machine thud and the city roar a scratchy burrowing sound of women and men hunkering down into themselves, their tiny hands and thoughts and feet scampering.

*

34. Flux, Forgetfulness and Attention.

The room, which even prior to Gérard's entry appeared both incomplete and unfinished – and this despite a superfluity of furniture and decorations – was approximately rectangular and by most standards spacious: its longer walls were more than four metres apart, its shorter walls more than six, making this one enclosed space larger than many of Grandgobier's finer single-bedroom apartments; the alcoves on either side of the chimney breast were deep and, since spanned by robust hardwood shelves, able with ease to sustain quantities of books, exotic objets d'art, long-playing records and framed photographs, as well as an imposing silver-finished up-to-that-minute hi-fi system of impressive bulk and discreetly West German provenance. The wall opposite the fireplace – in which the remains of several large logs still smouldered upon a cast-iron grate, and before which, supine in its basket, a greying mongrel slumbered, its eyes half-open in dream, their slack lids curling back from flickering blood-ringed orbs – was pierced, one must infer from the minute undulations of the maroon velvet curtains, by an ill-fitting and consequently draughty window, on either side of which hung a variety of oriental prints and paintings that further aggravated the mood of indo-chinoiserie that oppressed the entire room. While the colour of the curtains reverberated through the flocked wallpaper in a still more intense shade of red, inevitably recalling to the vinous-bibulous mind the tannin-rich wines of the Marcillac region, some relief at least was afforded, could one but raise one's eyes, by the lofty cream-painted ceiling from which hung suspended, seeming indeed to float on a cushion of its own opulence, a dusty yet sumptuous old chandelier, the glinting beams of which darted out across the plane but pitted surface, as if impatient to reach the coving, wherein they seemed, as distant fireworks falling upon still water, softly to drown. The floor was covered, from skirting board to skirting board and far beneath the alcove shelving, with a leavening of Persian, Mesopotamian and Turkish rugs, of which the faded and thread-bare older specimens had been overlaid by newer brighter acquisitions, creat-ing a luxuriously soft and irregular wall-to-wall platform upon which myriad small items of furniture (chairs, stools, pouffes, lampstands, display cabinets, two free-standing ashtrays, two wickerwork waste-paper baskets, a nest of coffee tables, a wooden trolley bearing glasses and bottles, a grandfather clock, and a waist-high globe) were haphazardly located as if recently set down by a late-running removals man. The room was lit in a series of overlapping cream pools emanating from wall-mounted uplighters, to which the gleams and glints of the ceiling chandelier added sporadic commentary, as if for contrapuntal emphasis. The air in this room was tepid, thanks more to the concealed double-depth central-heating radiators that lined both shorter walls, than to the perspicuously glowing embers in the hearth; the odours that wafted thereon executed an olfactory dirge, the dominant tones of which were given by: the smoke that rose and rippled from the dying wood fire, the desiccated particles of dust detaching themselves from every available exit point in the ambient dolmen of ageing paper, worn fabric, and burst uphol-stery; the radiant stench of the reposing beast; the innumerable seepages and spills, whether historical or contemporary, of pungent liqueurs, coffees, wines and eatables – in particular, those mature soft cheeses of the Brie and Camembert families most accordant with Gérard Boucan's unschooled palate, not to neglect the saliva-moistened crumbs from the accompanying bread crusts or biscuits, whose natural genius it was, having once plummeted from plate or lip, to furnish where they landed a medium ideally adapted to the cultivation of the many moulds, which, as any microscope might quickly attest, flourished in the midst of their usual complement of vanishingly tiny fauna. Thus into this stuffed yet incomplete, overworked yet unfinished space, resembling nothing in particular unless it was a Moghul's boudoir or emigré's emporium of knick-knacks, fetishes and antiquary, stepped Gérard Boucan, fresh – it might never be said – from his morning of feverish paranoia expended at the plant, his afternoon of dearly bought sensuality in the arms but most particularly the legs of his harlot, and his evening bisected (how unequally! how unjustly!) between, on the one hand, the caste-bound social-izing with Chartier père, mère and fille (not to mention Gérard's very own wife) and, on the other, his recreational chauffeur-driven vagabondage with Jorge posing as his personal Fool – Gérard Boucan, owner-manager of the factory that bore his family name, heir to a local industrial legend, husband to a bored and restive spouse, father to a wayward and distracted son, to himself an ever guiltless cipher yet now, for the nonce, a hapless victim of outrageous obloquy, was proceeding with all the elegance of an overwrought seal, his arms flapping lopsidedly and to no perceptible locomotive effect, his podgy legs briefly halting just inside the threshold, his embonpoint recruited to shove shut the door through which he had with circumspection this instant manoeuvred his preposterous frame. The sigh of relief that Gérard now heaved, a sigh that any observer might reasonably expect its heaver at once to post-face by casting himself upon a settee or armchair with perhaps an upward glance at heaven or, in this case, chandelier in lieu, terminated instead just where it started, which is to say at the door. Gérard looked around and about him, finding no obvious point at which to rest, nor pole of irresistible attraction toward which to tend. Instead of resolving where to locate himself and what action to execute, Gérard embarked upon a series of inconsequential acts which amounted to a deferral not only of action but, worse, of inaction, since the more he fussed the less he felt, the more he flapped the less he thought: he sat on one chair and then on another; stood and then turned; took three steps toward the fireplace, then loosened his belt two notches; took four steps back, untucked his shirt and vest; added one large log to the fire; scratched his scalp; poured himself a whisky from his drinks trolley; reached for a tube of charcoal pastilles on the mantelpiece; caressed the dog's back with the heel of his right shoe; set his glass down upon a shelf; swayed slightly, moving his weight from right to left foot, his buttocks splaying in order to break gentle, somehow epicene, wind; eased two charcoal tablets out of their tube and onto the flat of his tongue; recovered his glass and sipped from it while crunching the charcoal; introduced his right hand beneath his vest to massage the skin across his lower ribs, folding it sartorially between index finger and thumb; sucked the charcoal grit from his gums and teeth; cupped his left breast, clenching and releasing his hand so that his fingernails scratched at the edge of his armpit while his thumb pressed into the flesh above his nipple; swallowed his mouthful of blackened whisky then took a second rinsing sip: his delaying tactics now exhausted, he dropped onto an armchair, capitulating at last to the flow and ebb of his memories, his shuffling pack of anxieties, his gallery of that day's galling setbacks and glossary of passing guilty pleasures. He had indeed enjoyed Gisèle that afternoon though, returning from her bathroom, had caught her at repose, a vision of wretchedness, her belly distended, looking fat and forty – at thirty-two (or so she claimed). The sight had distracted him momentarily from his glum consideration of the plant audit, delivered to him that morning by his chief engineer, confirming the obsolescence of much of metallurgy and urging root-and-branch retooling. Gisèle had caught his glance. They had dressed in silence. How, in this recession, would he ever manage the financing? De-manning would be unavoidable. Competitivity must be restored. From his left breast he slid his right hand to a position just below his sternum. The strike, at least, would never amount to much: the union militants were posturing for their members.

We shall play their game, but slyly so, pretending we're upset, 'negotiating' with some display of ill grace. Arching his back, Gérard caught a whiff of himself. A brief dip in production would not in fact be inconvenient in the present conjuncture. Gérard was engaged in a bitter battle against the odours his body exuded, pitting daily showers, deodorants, flossing, colognes, mouth sprays, aftershaves, brilliantines and patent remedies for halitosis against the sickening swell of his mammalian putrescence: a single eructation or hoist of arm would overwhelm in a trice all such defensive ploys. Industrial action would not be all bad: it would give managers and supervisors new opportunities to observe the human dynamics within each section of the plant, identify emergent trouble-makers: nowadays it's all a matter of intelligence and planning. That chauffeur, for all his edgy accent and rebel music, could one day be an asset: the Spic didn't know how fortunate he was, able to do whatever he liked, floating suddenly free of family, no one to answer to, able to kick against every prick. He would realize his luck some day and then, if he's smart, he could be useful. Chilean refugee, the perfect cover: who could doubt him? Gérard took a breath, pressed out his upper belly against his hand, which he then set to work on the flesh beneath as if kneading dough. He glanced round his room, indisputably his own and no one else's, and saw how strange and foreign to him it remained: it had been his father's private den and still displayed the sophisticated print of its previous occupant. Gérard had had no idea how to reappoint the room following the patriarch's demise. The dog was different, the hi-fi new, the old man's personal letters and diaries all gone, but in essentials the room was unchanged. Gérard's eyes perused the shelves, his soft focus shimmying from the ceremonial dagger to the pair of Buddhas (one black, one red), thence to a vase and some spoons. Boucan père had once stood on this rug to tell him of trysts and transactions with sumptuous women in the winding alleys of perfumed lands, then suddenly recalling the child's age and his paternal duty to be cold, conformist, brusque and boring, had dismissed him with a sneer, sending him back to his gewgaws. Must be the music Jorge played, something in the rhythms maybe, that had brought this to mind. Or those soldiers in the streets this evening, their little hearts aflutter with the prospect of freedom, their pent-up virilities as palpable as their anthem to liberation, trembling before the waves of pill-taking women just waiting to roll over and under them. The lucky dogs don't know they're born! Had contraception existed in the fifties, how different his own life might have been! Never mind *women's* liberation! Gérard's bilious eye scoured the room. What a contrast it made with Chartier's library – which Gérard had surveyed that evening for only the second time. Everything about Raymond was so well aligned: his tanned face, athletically proportioned body, fine tailoring, mellifluous speech, tidy mind, sparkling family, every single aspect of his environment, like some shooter's perfect row of ducks. The man moved in a world intricately harmonized to his own inner workings. Screw him! Gérard saw again Claude's pained expression as she had gestured excuses for him and striven to cover his indiscretions, executing from dry social duty or embarrassment what she would once have performed out of love. Screw her too! Gérard looked with disdain down upon the burping-farting balloon of a belly that bulged before him. These days he had to lean right forward to catch the barest glimpse of his own toes: a pig's bladder of a man. How dare he be bothered by Gisèle's tummy? And yet he was. He paid her good money, damn it. That made the difference. Could she not diet, like other women? Where was her self-control? Gérard managed a small burp, a mere click. He would have to do better than that to dispel the heartburn. He emptied his glass and shook his head till his jowls slapped his neck. His thoughts turned to the graffiti, then away to the knifing, that man with his brush sweeping the pavement: it could not have happened any closer to the plant, did the victim die? Did the attackers escape? Who was it he had seen in the glinting shadows working the brush with such dexterity? It was as if the man had been born brush-in-hand to clean up after a knifing. Eastern accent. Could be a Slav or a Hungarian. Outlandish pitter-patter, mouth stuffed with more consonants than teeth. Maybe he worked in the factory. Maybe he was one of mine. He didn't address me by name. Monsieur Boucan. Was that ignorance? Impertinence? If he worked for me, he'd know what I looked like. There are enough portraits of me around the place. It was dark. I'll find him out. Perhaps it's the whisky thinking for me, but it seems the whole world teeters on the brink of madness. Or France at any rate. Which is my world. It appears my own employees are dragging up ancient history and Chartier mutters darkly of bomb-planting crazies. You never know, can never tell when people will fill the streets, burn cars, smash shops, break machinery. It's not the politics of the governing institutions you have to worry about: any opposition in that quarter was licked years ago. It is spontaneous anger, screwball violence that terrifies. I need coffee. That Portuguese slag will have gone home by now. 'You must be nicer to Concetta,' Claude keeps saying. Screw Claude! She'll be in bed now, wearing her face mask. I could make some coffee for myself.

Nothing to it. I can make coffee. Gérard heard the ticking of a clock somewhere and the dog breathing and his own guts swilling. I hate silence, he said
aloud, rising from his chair and walking to the hi-fi. He saw the tube of
charcoal tablets, but didn't reach for it. Of all the remedies – medical, traditional or fantastical – charcoal alone occasionally relieved the bloating. But
not tonight. He inserted a cassette of Sidney Bechet numbers and pressed
PLAY. How come he always thought of Grandfather, when his dyspepsia
flared up? One of the things they now had in common. He too liked dogs.
His grandfather had told him once, as they stood outside, looking at the night
sky, 'you have broad shoulders on you, and you will need them, it will fall to
you to build this company back up – once your father has run it into the
ground, as he surely will. He's a dreamer, but you are like me. Businesslike.
Dull, maybe. Do they call you dull? They do? Take it as a compliment. Settle
for dull, son. Dull will see you through.' Grandfather. He died not long after
that. He was never dull. And now the graffiti. Who am I dealing with exactly?
Do I need to know? Just what do they think they have on me? What hard
evidence? Everybody betrayed somebody some time. That's the nature of
occupation. Screw occupation: it's the nature of life! Gérard knelt down by
the dog and stroked his head. He enjoyed the feel of the pelt as it shunted
forward and back against the skull beneath. He noticed the music, the clean
tremolo of Bechet's saxophone. He had bought the right hi-fi. You could
always count on the Bosh. There was pleasure in this music, a pleasure he was
still able to appreciate: night clubs at three a.m. in faraway countries, lovely
ladies, smoke, tolerant laughter. Gérard fell back upon his armchair, slumped
and farted and burped all at once. Such relief! His chest felt so much better.
It was at least as good as shooting his wad into Gisèle. The charcoal was working. Maybe. He had an odd feeling. His mood had lifted like dew. It was this
music. He felt alone. Not lonely. Never that. But alone. His thoughts stopped
right there. For a moment, the flux was stemmed. Alone. That was the word.
The one word. The only word.

↔↔↔↔↔

As Heike and Gilles turned a corner, rejoining the main pedestrian thorough-
fare, they encountered a group of carousing draftees, several with arms linked,
some holding bottles of beer, accompanied by a couple of stonier-faced and
more observant outriders. Gilles broke from Heike, thrusting his left fist aloft.

'A bas toutes les armées! Vivent les bidasses! Vive le prolétariat international!'

Some of the soldiers appeared perplexed, but one (Ali) detached himself from the throng, stepped toward Gilles and countered, 'Vive la France!' To which Gilles, with no eyelid batted nor heartbeat skipped, replied, 'Vive la France révolutionnaire!' Ali approved with a nod, stepped forward and shook Gilles' proffered hand.

Gilles waded into the midst of the soldiers, who closed around him like ice on a pond. 'Alors,' he said, glancing from man to man, 'c'est ce soir la fin?' 'Beh, évidemment,' Émile replied, looking round and finding the crop-haired girl watching him. Gilles was soon holding forth, questioning the men about their service experiences, relating his own, setting them on a roar.

Moritz had caught up with Heike and had taken her arm. Jean-Pierre and Margot lounged, conjugally speechless, against a wall, smoking and watching Gilles. 'Er gefällt dir, gell?' Moritz asked his sister. Heike laughed and blushed. 'Dir auch?' she teased.

Moritz took a long hard look at Gilles, pondering the question. 'I don't doubt he'd be interested,' Moritz declared. 'He's the polymorphous type. But I happen to be in love with my gorgeous Gypsy, remember? Besides, I'm not keen on body hair.'

Heike appeared to give this last point some consideration and then said, 'Look, do they have all-night pharmacies in France?' Moritz's eyebrows leapt in surprise. 'That *was* fast work, Schwesterchen. There are machines in the gents of most bars. I can get you a pack. But what about your engineer in Frankfurt?'

Heike cackled. 'My period's early, stupid! Anyway, I've always got my coil. It's just a sticky little trickle for now, but I need some tampons fast. Before the dam breaks. Lillets, preferably. You know, the type you . . .' 'Please! Spare me! There should be an all-nighter on Boulevard Jaurès. It's a couple of minutes walk, over that way.'

Heike hesitated, glancing at Gilles. 'It's okay, sis,' Moritz said. 'I know where the man drinks. We'll see him later.' 'It's just that he's such a good talker,' Heike said, following Moritz. 'Right. Of course,' said Moritz, crossing the street. 'So what was he saying then?'

Heike frowned. 'He was talking about armies and the need to capture them if you want to defeat late capitalism. He says culture isn't enough, Gramsci is bullshit, and violence is inevitable. And cleansing. That's what he said.' 'He referred to "Late Capitalism"?' 'Jawohl. Spätkapitalismus.' 'The man's optimism carries right through to his choice of erudite jargon,' Moritz remarked.

'Spätkapitalismus is a perfectly everyday sort of expression,' Heike said. Moritz took his sister's arm. 'If you say so, mein Schatz. In which case, I'll try it out on Bobrán. He's a perfectly everyday sort of guy.' 'And universal font of wisdom, by the sound of it,' Heike observed. 'Oh, ouch!' Moritz said.

↔↔↔↔↔

Luigi did not so much entertain conscious thought as act toward it in the guise of a nervous and precautionary gate-keeper, ever keen, when in doubt, simply to shut it out. Only in nightmares and dreams – to which he was morbidly subject – might his defences be o'erleapt. At waking moments, all unsolicited notions and impulses were swatted away as effectively as a cow with its tail chases flies from its clap-caked rump: the flies keep on coming of course, but cannot settle.

Luigi's fastness was under assault from several quarters. He was particularly afflicted by cinematically vivid memories, recent and distant, impersonal and intimate. It took, for example, the mere shadow of the idea of his father or, indeed, the hint of an echo of the circumstances that had attended his and his mother's forced departure seven years earlier from their place at the centre of Italy's suddenly insurgent industrial triangle, to cause the aforesaid cow's switch to flick and flail.

Regretful yearnings might be met with greater equanimity, according to how well-breathed they appeared. That his mother had failed to give Luigi a brother (or even a sibling), for instance, had by this point supplied Luigi with an inexhaustible source of self-complacent sorrow, an explanation and an excuse for his every disadvantage, false start or setback: a reliable decoy and diversion. Similarly, his unfulfilled craving to love and be loved, instead of spurring him tirelessly to seek a person eager to bestow and worthy to accept the romantic passion of which he dreamed, persuaded him only to salvage the salvageable, cut his cloth, trim his sails and play it safe. He had, he thought, made his peace with youth's amorous follies: the best thing about Gilberte, he considered, was that she was there and her being there sufficed to deaden the impulse to seek any truer love. After years of solitary pining, he was attached to somebody. His need for a woman – a tangible not a fantasy one – had indisputably been met. That was that. He must look no further.

The visions of horror that troubled Luigi's sleep each day possessed their counterparts in sudden waking urges to inflict upon random or convenient others or to submit his own person to violent degradations. Insusceptible to eradication as he supposed such monsters to be, Luigi had evolved, he hoped, a means of domesticating them, or at least of keeping them sturdily encaged. He had succeeded so far in constraining within a respectable trade and a venerable craft his desire to flay and to gut bodies, to dismember carcasses, to joint limbs, to strip out sinew, gristle and cartilage, and finally to slice and dice red and other meats. He had similarly managed to corral his inclinations toward rape and torture within the confines of a paper-thin tribe of graphic-novel aliens, whose yelping and screeching, whether in humiliation or in eye-swivelling cruelty, might, all venom drawn, instantly be shut away again, recommitted to latency, silenced, and stowed in pocket or bag.

In the years since 1969, Luigi had trained himself never to look back: to him, the past was no foreign country – to which he might, were he so inclined, pay a visit – but rather a jungle of terrors he had deliberately abandoned. His sights were trained not even on the present but on the future perfect and, indeed, on the perfect future: the present was no more than a compulsory staging-post; it had to be borne, endured, gone through; it was to be viewed from the plateau or promontory of an imaginary and much better dispensation, wherein he *would have* become comfortable, *would have* amassed some wealth, *would live* in perfect futurity.

But the distinctive and original spirit, the unique set and peculiar working of Luigi's mind, in a word its genius, was that, once amnesia had been imposed upon recollection, and a cap of steely self-censorship lowered upon the less tractable of his cravings; when, that is to say, his mind's inner promptings had been stilled and his appetites at least fed, if not quite sated, then at last was he free to look outward with detachment and to indulge his sensuous perception of the innocuous objects and phenomena that encircled him at every step of his way, achieving in their midst a sensation of contented stasis that permitted him indeed to look upon everyday things and to contemplate them truly as they flitted before him and paused, froze, as it were, an instant, before vanishing into the ditch of all that was past and gone.

↔↔↔↔↔↔

Marcel and Philippe stood silently at ease in semi-dark metallurgy close to the coffee- and beer-dispensing machines. On their walk-through from the plastics section, Philippe had asked Marcel when the happy day was to be, but Marcel had answered distractedly that they hadn't named it yet. Then Marcel, as an opener for a comment he had carefully prepared, had said, 'So nothing can happen here, right?'; Philippe, however, immediately blocked his workmate's conversational setup by blowing out his cheeks and announcing, 'That was talk. Just talk.' These gambits essayed and aborted, each man had been glad to return to his own beverage, cigarette and thoughts, tolerably comfortable in the other's company.

A little later, Philippe emptied his polystyrene cup, contemplated briefly the brown foam ringing its midriff, then in a single smooth movement scrunched it and tossed it into a convenient green metal bin. Marcel similarly jettisoned his empty bottle. 'All right?' Philippe then enquired, taking the lead. 'Sure,' Marcel responded. As so often, walking appeared to set tongues free. 'Look, would you come to my wedding?' Marcel asked abruptly. 'I hate weddings,' Philippe parried. 'Besides, why me? I wouldn't know anyone there. Do you need to make up the number?' 'Something like that. I've got nobody. Chantal has family, you know, friends, the whole thing, even girls from work who'll turn up to gawk. I suppose I could pay you.' 'You don't know how much I charge for attending weddings.' Marcel tried another tack. 'Chantal has a younger sister, a looker. Not my type, anyway. Not that I would. Though I might. If she seemed interested. Anyway, I could put in a good word, talk you up a bit. You could borrow some of my clothes.' Philippe pictured himself in a purple satin shirt and kipper tie and shook his head. 'Surely you've got some family,' Philippe said. 'What about your cousin upstairs? And don't you have a father?' 'My father's inside, last I heard. And can you imagine Bobrán at a wedding? I wouldn't trust him not to turn cartwheels up the aisle.' 'You're getting married in front of a priest?' 'You know what I mean.'

Philippe was wondering if he was off the hook. 'Well, will you do it?' Marcel asked. 'Oh, I don't know. You said you haven't even fixed a date yet.' 'So when we do . . . ?' 'I'm not promising. Ask me in a couple of months. Just leave the sister out of it. If I'm going to get into trouble, I don't need any help from you.' Marcel pulled a face, caught hold of Philippe's arm and stopped walking, turning toward the man so they were facing one another. 'How does free pussy get to be trouble?' Philippe blew so much air out of his mouth that it lifted his fringe in a quiff. 'Is this a point of philosophy?'

Marcel ignored that and began to free-associate. 'You're married, aren't you? I mean, I've been thinking about this. Nobody can fuck the same woman for years on end without any time out, can they?' Philippe neither demurred nor acquiesced. 'Though, personally,' Marcel said, growing thoughtful, 'I've decided to slow down a little. Lose a few of my girlfriends. There are one or two, I can tell you, who are definitely surplus. Fair's fair. Out of respect for my fiancée. On the other hand, there's no need to become a raging monk, is there?' Philippe stared. Marcel hadn't finished. 'Because, the way I see it, if you don't look out, marriage and children can cut your balls clean off. If you overdo the abstinence. You don't want to be turned into a eunuch, sitting there holding a baby's bottle. What's the matter? Seen another ghost? Is it something I said?' 'Yeah. I'm haunted tonight.'

They started walking again and soon reached the hanging flaps. Philippe pushed through them first, bending his steps toward his machines. Marcel followed him through. 'That man ought to talk to somebody,' Marcel thought. 'He's not well. A man who ate, slept and fucked properly would never look the way he looks tonight. Poor old Marseille.' Marcel patted his paunch and straightened his hair. He experienced a sudden contentment.

↔↔↔↔↔

Seven gazes. It was 22.32 on the shop floor chez Boucan. Seven men gazed.

At his machine nineteen upstairs, Alphonse had put down his copy of *Godot* and, having checked the latest products to issue from his machines, had enjoyed a long slow stretch and yawn and then settled back on his chair to watch Fernando who was polishing the flank of his machine seventeen. Alphonse marvelled at the application and industry invested in what seemed to him a pointless task, noting the muscle rippling around Fernando's neck, the sweat extruded at his temples, the strained focus of his eyes, but above all the man's stance, the shape that Fernando enforced upon his body in order to perform his elected task. Leaning briefly against the side of his own machine nineteen, Alphonse imitated the Portuguese man's demeanour, hoping to imprint it on his own muscles and store it in his private compendium of dramatic attitude.

Sitting at his huge old semi-automatic machine twenty-one, Jean was able, in his turn, at each opening of its massive press, to gaze upon Alphonse – should he so desire – and to observe the man's actions; Jean, however, saw nothing in the Ivorian's characteristically eccentric behaviour to detain his attention, which consequently remained engaged upon an orderly review of the day's events – domestic, neighbourhood, national and planetary.

Fernando's eyes, confined to the orange-painted surface of his machine, restlessly observed and assessed the sheen achieved by his busy rag, while avidly prospecting for duller neighbouring patches in need of a thorough polish.

Downstairs, Marcel had resumed his favoured position, standing at the aisle-end of his machine twelve where, after checking his cigarette count, he allowed his public gaze to wander freely, attracted by this man's movement and that machine's warning light, while his thoughts loitered in a similarly circumscribed fashion.

Eric had just finished rolling himself a cigarette in which he had mixed Samson and Golden Virginia tobaccos in roughly equal proportions. His attitude, as he glanced around, was that of an extra-terrestrial peering in through a cosmic chink at the lives of entities in an unknown galaxy: everything he could see was incomprehensible to him and, to that extent, fascinating and mysterious. He knew he had everything to learn but no earthly idea where to begin.

Philippe was standing at the aisle-end of his machine two, his gut relaxed against the side of the recycled-material cylinder, his fingers turning the pages of the newspapers and magazines he had brought from Rémy's bar. His eyes played like a lazy water-boatman on the surface of the print, drifting briefly with the current of one article before scudding across to the next. His interest might be hooked by any small matter: a peculiarity, a freak event, a paradox, a metamorphosis, a misprint, anything humorous or rich or strange.

Tomec, on his torch-lit march through metallurgy, licensed to seek intruders in the dark and, should the need arise, to immobilize them, now turned his inspection inward. He longed to fall upon and arrest in the stark glare of his imagination the vision of a world bodied forth in its people, far from either the foreboding of his childhood years or the horrors of his adolescence, but remote too from the current state of stagnant slumber in which the various lands of his birth, childhood and adoption seemed so helplessly to flounder. His dream was of a world of poetry and potentiality, neither ancient nor modern, and of people neither oblivious nor yet fully conscious of their own powers of becoming.

35. Decisions, Friendship and Product.

Me standing here, standing here like I'm on sentry duty. Nine cigarettes left. Same old thoughts. Standing here at the end of my machine. Looking left. Standing here. Looking right. Belly in! Give it a little stroke. Then stretch that aching back! Standing here, damn it. No one coming. Observe! the man said. So what do I see? The Arab sits smoking, eyes crafty, eyes Arab, eyes closed now. Marseille yawning, reading some paper. He's standing too. Doesn't look up. I'm standing here. Out of this! Old peasant snoozing. Sicilian's nose in his book. English sucking at cigarette. Me standing here. Out of here! It's like standing in my cell. Looking at the right wall. Standing there. Looking at the left. Standing and staring. Here, no one ever stares back. Or not for long. In prison they stare at you through the peephole. You never know quite when. Screws staring at you. Screws screwing you. Here, I'm the one who stares. Some people look at me all wrong. People I wouldn't trust. The little man upstairs, his eyes darting like greased rats, prison rats, grey and small and slimy. Cousin Bobrán's eyes, big and brown, showing no respect. The foreman and the Polack security goon aren't ever to be trusted: they have to be what they serve. You don't always see things even when you're staring straight at them, the shrink used to say. Call me Martin, he said. Don't mind if I do – now I'm out. So – *Martin* told me it was good to sit and stare, not just to watch the world go by, but to count it all out, count it back in, make a list of all you see. Sounded cranky at first. Still does. But it's beginning to make sense. Because otherwise you miss things. Like I missed those afternoon-shift girls. I must have looked at them before tonight but I swear I never saw them. The hairy one had a spotty face, I think, so maybe I never lingered. Now the spots are gone I can see she has long skinny legs on her and tits that are both hard and soft in all the right ways and places. And her friend, or whatever the hell she is, too small and stout and giggly to notice ordinarily but, once you've seen her, so obviously game. Jesus the way she arranges that curl on her forehead, must take real trouble over it in front of a mirror: come and fuck me, it says, I'm wide open. Chantal . . . What made me think of Chantal? We're not even married, haven't even named the day – like Marseille said – and I'm sure I'll be through with these afternoon-shift chicks long before. Besides, I'm limiting the others, pulling in my horns, trying to be reasonable here. A man has to have fun before he gets married. Sow some wild. I've come to a decision about Paulette. And maybe Gina too. No rush. Nothing hasty. I'll get round to it. I'll go down the list. One by one. In the appropriate order. But brand-new pussy? Short-term pussy? Why pass that up? Within reason, fucking other women is good for Chantal. She gets to benefit too. Other fucks keep me on form. It's a muscle like any other, someone said. A little extra exercise will make me a better lover, a better man. For Chantal. Plus it can take some pressure off her. There are times she doesn't want any. That's normal, right? Women don't have our appetites. Even Chantal. If I maintain other outlets, I won't be getting ratty with her. Then there are things Chantal doesn't like doing and it isn't fair to ask. I'm reining myself in, working down the list, having a little clear-out. Paulette, for a start. Gina too. Gone. Have to figure out how. But you don't refuse brand-new pussy when it's thrust in your face. It'll never hurt Chantal. She is the one I love. Really love. Besides, she's the only one who wants me and not just my dick. Which makes her special. Chantal . . . The Arab ambling past the end of my machine. I'm thinking of pussy. Marseille looks up from his paper, misses my eye. I'm still thinking of pussy. The Italian lopes down the aisle. Blank. Nothing. Total grey area. No pussy thoughts possible. He makes me queasy. He hurts my eyes. He's heading for the Sicilian. There. Pussy. Definite pussy. The peasant is drooling now. Pussy. You're kidding! Oh, Jesus! Pussy! Get out of here! The peasant's jolting now, waking up, wiping the drool on his cuff. Pussy of sorts. Martin – it's true: there are things to see even here, if you just stand back and look. Though the changes are slow and tiny. Martin recommended looking at others as a way of distracting my mind. He said he'd read about it in a magazine. He said I could trick my mind out of 'circularity.' 'Circularity': his word for the eddies, the whirlpools. I miss that man. I miss listening to him talk. When he talked, I'd think of things I'd never imagined before. There's plenty to see even here if you want to look. But I don't. I keep thinking about Chantal, wondering what she does on those weekends in Nice. Not that she goes all that often. Sends me cards. I check the postmarks. Stays with an old aunt, she says, a 'great' aunt. Remote family. Father's father's sister, she said. If my father's father or mother's mother ever had brothers or sisters, which they probably did, they'll be in Slovenia, Slovakia, Slavonia, Slavekia . . . where the hell, probably in some mass grave, dead, shoulder to shoulder, knee to nose, arse to elbow most likely, with Martin's father's father's brothers and sisters. Or ash in the wind. Maybe she does stay with her great-aunt. Those weekends would be so long if I had no girlfriends that I'd be a fool to cramp myself too much. I don't want to end up one weekend with her in Nice and me in the stalls beating my meat to some flea-pit skin flick. I've got a lot of decisions to take. For example: which of the afternoon-shift girls should I tackle first? I don't know their names. Which is awkward. I'll ask next time I see them. Not tomorrow, though. I'll leave them to simmer a little. See them wiggle their arses, stick out their tits and pout. I'll think of them as Hairy and . . . Curly. I'll do Curly first. Someone is fucking her, you can tell. Just not doing it right. You want so much more, don't you? And I can give it to you, believe me. (Damn it, I'm dribbling.) I'll go to hers straight from work or mid-morning before she comes here. Best to go straight from work. She'll start making the coffee, I'll slip it to her from behind, she'll have nothing much on, then I'll drink up and go – unless she fancies a second crack at it. Hairy will need a lot of talking to; I may have to sip raspberry-scented tea and pet her cat or talk to the canary, pretend to give a damn. She may want to sit on my lap. She may coo. But it'll be the better fuck. She's dying for it. It could even be her first. And there'll be no hubby or boyfriend on her case. Of course she might grow soppy. You can't tell. And all that hair! I swear she shaves her upper lip! I bet she has a rug running from her navel right down to the tops of her thighs. I'll roll around in it like it's long lush grass, grab fistfuls of it in my teeth. Hair traps all the juices too, holds in the odours. I hope she doesn't bite. I'll have her under the shower, in the bath, rivulets running through the fuzz on her cunt. Hope she doesn't trim it. Bald pussy is about as alluring a prospect on a woman as a shaved head. If she's shaved it, I'll make her swear to leave it alone for a month and I'll be back. She can wait if I can. Man, oh man! Chantal, now, she isn't at all hairy, for example, and I wouldn't want her to be. She's perfect just the way she is. Chantal doesn't need to be hairy. There's Hairy for that. Just like Chantal doesn't need bigger tits. Gina has the tits. But Gina's definitely on the list, simply has to be. Chantal is the one woman I love. Other women are a distraction, but distraction is good, isn't it? Keeps you from getting obsessed. Martin would agree, though he'd put it differently. Saves you from 'circularity.' Some writer he told me about wrote in a magazine about sitting outside a bar watching the buses go past, and the pedestrians too. Martin kept talking about it. Really impressed. Some guy, sitting with his pastis, timing and counting and logging the street and pavement traffic all day long. I'd never heard of pavement traffic before. He couldn't shut up about it. Said I ought to try it, adapt the technique, make a note of my thoughts while doing observations. I could try it here except most of the time there isn't a lot going on. And when something does happen, there's no time to notice any details. Everything's either too slow or too fast, too little or too much. Blink and it's gone. Like in my head. Maybe that's the point. There's either nothing at all or a churning whirling mass. I'm still just standing here. Standing here. Marseille has lit a cigarette. I've got nine to go. English dipshit has put out his dog-end. I'm thinking about Hairy. Pussy. Sicilian is talking to Italian, both looking bored. Sicilian sitting. Italian stooping. Total eye-ache. Hairy and her twat! That twinge in my back again. Stretch! That's better. Chantal . . . I need options. I suppose pussy isn't everything. No? Since when? But, hell, I need work options. Not this stupid sucker's job. I've been here months. Standing here like in my cell. Here I could move if I wanted to. The peasant's head is lolling. Maybe he'll fall off his chair soon. That would be something. Me standing here! Shit. I need to take some decisions, work through the list, see which women to dump, figure out what's best. Marriage is serious. You have to take responsibility. Be sensible. But you don't turn down fresh pussy. Like you don't refuse new business if you're a businessman. It'll only go elsewhere and there could come a time, a lean time, lean years maybe, when you regret all the jobs, all the pussy you declined. It could come back in dreams to haunt you. And in the meantime, right now, Curly, and even Hairy too, may be getting fucked by someone else. Though probably not Hairy. I don't mind women fucking other men once I'm through. Jealousy is not my thing. Gina would be easy to stop seeing. She is putting on weight and those fine tits of hers are beginning to drop. Besides, her attacks of guilt really piss me off. I don't want to hear any more about how she really truly loves her boyfriend, but he just doesn't know how to take her, is too serious and solemn, too tame and tidy, puts her feet to sleep, blah! blah! No girl wants a solemn fuck, Gina says, and I believe her. But she talks too much. I could do without Gina. You don't want to hear about their boyfriends when you're climbing over a woman. So that's Gina and Paulette gone. Definitely. I need to lose some others though. I'm noticing I've been growing tired of Florence lately, it's been creeping up on me, but I'll miss the food, the meals she cooks. We always fuck on a full stomach, which is different but fine. She could turn her hand to anything, I dare say, but her seafood and sweets are what I'd miss most. I really don't mind her tying me up either, if that's what gets her horny. I'm just sick of having to lick her out, even if my mouth by that point is all full of sweet and seafood tastes anyway. Just seems there's only the one way Florence can ever come: with my thumb up her twat and my middle finger jammed in her arse up to the second knuckle, sucking on her clit like my life depends on it, easing my finger and thumb together in a gentle pincer. It was sort of novel the first few times, but it's getting to be like lifting a ten-pin bowling ball when you've absolutely nowhere to pitch it. I mean: anything to please! But in the end it's humiliating. Even if she keeps herself as clean as a whistle, inside and out. Women like that are basically dykes, even when they don't know it yet. And the jaw-ache! Another woman could do that for her about as well as I can. Or nearly. I could definitely do without Florence, despite the cooking. So that's three down. I wonder if she'd cook for me if I wasn't fucking her afterward? No hope. She's a hard bitch, at bottom. Whereas Paulette is too soft for her own good. It almost seems a shame. Paulette is sure to cry but Gina and Florence will be fine. They're the proud type. They won't shed a tear till I'm well out of sight. Maybe not even then. The question is: dump first or fuck first? Sometimes, if you break the news first, you get a terrific goodbye-fuck, the fuck of the year. Come to think of it, last fucks are often better than first fucks. It's probably the added emotion. First fucks always promise more than they deliver. That Spanish girl, just before I got nabbed, was a tremendous last fuck. Kept me warm in prison just thinking about it. Dolores somebody. Dolores. I heard she went back home after that. I wonder if Chantal's great-aunt in Nice is real. I've seen the photo: she must be real. But the whole weekend? How likely is that? The last time Chantal came back from a weekend in Nice she fucked me very nearly to a standstill. It made me suspicious. It was like she was trying to wipe the other man off her body, pushing him back down out of her cunt, sweating him off her skin. Would a woman think like that? Would Chantal? You never know how someone else would think. Martin said people do things without knowing why. Because of what he called the subconscious. A level of thinking we're not even aware of but which is actually in control, gurgling along underneath all our thoughts like a sewer. Creepy idea. If I've got it right. Anyway, I'll have a complete list clear in my mind by the morning. I'll know what to do. With Paulette, the smartest thing would be a phone call. Cowardly, but quick.

↔↔↔↔↔

Marie closed the book. For over half an hour, the two young women had been sitting in Mathieu Petit's living room quizzing one another across a small dining table, a textbook shuttling between them. This was useless, Marie thought.

Stéphanie didn't remember a thing. They were supposed to be revising for an examination on basic nursing procedures. 'Okay, so I'll resit,' Stéphanie muttered, eyeing the closed doors. 'That's fine for you,' Marie said, 'but I don't have that luxury.' 'I need to qualify and find work fast.' Marie always had to remind everyone how poor her family was. Didn't she realize how *passé* it was – and vulgar – to harp on about one's class origins?

Earlier that day, in the university canteen, Marie had mentioned to Stéphanie that she had found casual work, looking after an old woman three nights a week while the woman's husband worked. Her classmate had offered to keep her company, but Marie had hesitated. Monsieur Petit had made her promise not to let anyone else into the apartment. He probably feared she would invite a boyfriend along for the night, or throw a party. Marie had talked to Stéphanie only a couple of times, but had wanted to trust her. 'If you like, I'll help you revise,' Stéphanie had suggested. That had clinched it.

'Does she drool?' Stéphanie suddenly asked. 'Does who drool?' 'The old lady, of course.' 'Why do you ask?' 'I'm bored. Well? Does she drool?' 'No. She doesn't drool. Not exactly. If you must know. Look, we're supposed to be revising.' 'Which room is she in?' 'That one,' Marie said, pointing to a door. There was a silence.

'Is she fat? I kind of imagine her fat.' Marie drew herself in. 'No,' Marie said carefully, 'she is *not* fat.' Stéphanie was sweating profusely. 'What's the matter with you?' 'Nothing. I'm trying to get a picture,' Stéphanie replied. 'Do you change her nappies? Well?'

Marie barely heard the question. That afternoon, revising with Stéphanie had seemed like a good idea. It was an oral examination: you had to be quick and confident. Marie continued to scrutinize Stéphanie. The young woman kept removing a cigarette from her pack, then putting it back in again. She had probably resented being told she couldn't smoke.

The first thing Mathieu had asked Marie was whether or not she smoked. Stéphanie was now picking at her scalp with her fingernails and pursing her lips like it hurt. Her hair was shiny and flatter in some places than in others, like cheap carpet held down by badly positioned tacks.

Stéphanie stood up and strode to the door that Marie had indicated. She was taller than Marie, thinner too. Marie was alongside her in a flash. Stéphanie tried the door. 'It's locked,' she whispered, glancing down at Marie.

Marie took her by the right arm, just above the elbow. 'It's time you left,' she said. Stéphanie seemed surprised. 'You tricked me, didn't you?

She's through the other door, isn't she? I only wanted to look at her.' Marie tightened her grip. 'You're hurting me,' Stéphanie said. 'It's time . . .' Marie began. Stéphanie nodded.

After Stéphanie had gone, Marie went to check the old lady was all right.

Nadine was lying, as always, on her back. She wasn't drooling. She rarely drooled. Her eyes were open, but there was little life in them. Her face struck Marie as beautiful and melancholy. Her lashes were long and fine, her ears small, her skin still perfect. Wondering how long the old lady had been cooped up there, Marie walked around the end of the bed, imagining that Nadine's eyes were following her.

There was a tube of water-based lubricant on the bedside table. Marie removed the cap and squeezed a little of the jelly onto a piece of gauze, then applied it gently to the woman's mouth. Her lips glistening, Nadine appeared to be smiling. Marie wanted to push the corners of the mouth further apart but checked herself. 'I can't call you Madame Petit any longer,' she said. 'I think I shall call you Nadine. I hope you won't mind. I don't want to be over-familiar. My name is Marie. We could have been friends, you know.'

↔↔↔↔↔↔

Just as Jacques' default expression was a grin, though his feelings might be flecked with annoyance, anger, boredom or discomfort, so his mood was set fast to blithe cheeriness, even when his thoughts were troubled by passing worry, setback or sadness. If the vessel of his mood was as a pot-bellied vat, its contents were a tepid porridgy medium in which no great agitation or anxiety could survive. Any cares, concerns or resentments that chanced to land upon the surface of this gently corrosive gruel would slowly sink, dissolving away to nothingness, and leave not a trace behind.

This temperament had, however, been placed this evening under severer strain than usual. Jacques' visit to the doctor had not gone well, and his perusal of the small print of her prescription had filled him with indignation. Driving to work, he had taken a wrong turn and, guided – he would surmise – by a personal daemon, he had fetched up at his estranged brother's flat, where a fraternal meeting of minds had not been consummated; his walk through metallurgy in the company of the younger Gypsy had ended in a minor misunderstanding; his desire to broach with Philippe certain intimate fears had been frustrated – he knew not quite how; he had been rudely awakened from an early snooze by Fernando's urge for ragamuffin manual-testicular combat; lastly, dwarfing all such wrinkles upon the surface of his mood, much as a rift-canyon amid gentle valleys, there would surely have run in any man endowed with a meaner fund of equanimity a fathomless gash of sadness and disappointment at Jeanne's recent refusal – howsoever gentle – to reside any more permanently beneath his roof.

Jacques' particular temperament was quickly able to engulf, neutralize, digest and absorb all such matter. He had no need to summon the balsamic memory of any pleasurable and reliably renewable sensation, nor to give himself a talking to or ticking off, nor to cozen his wits with some prattling self-reassurance, nor to recite like a rosary his reasons to be happy, nor yet to clasp a brittle courage to his heart, while whistling through clenched teeth.

Nor did it ever occur to Jacques to consider the solidity of his humour. He took his prevailing mood for granted – not because he was incapable of stepping outside himself for the purposes of self-contemplation, but rather because he was temperamentally disinclined to do so: that is, he was never of a mood to examine his mood. At most, when afflicted by an unwelcome thought or sentiment, Jacques might mutter reflexively, 'fretting gets you nowhere,' and the very voicing of this wisdom would bring the bootless fretting to a halt. In the unlikely event that anyone were ever to quiz Jacques regarding the basis of his all-weather cheeriness, he might have replied that his conscience was clear and his sleep untroubled by regrets, unsated appetites or any particular dread.

The resilience of Jacques' mood reposed in fact upon a set of beliefs of which he was himself unaware. For Jacques supposed himself to be blessed by fortune and so powerfully protected by a personal yet discreet providence that it was safe for him to forgo any calculation of self-interest, placing his trust in the kindness, or at least the indifference, of others, while following the dull promptings of chance. In day-to-day practice, this induced in Jacques a certain passivity, even a complacency: he was content for people and things to come to him and, while he would seldom seek friendship or initiate conversation, he was disposed to greet the advances and overtures of others with a steady grin, a twinkling eye and a nod of measured approbation.

↔↔↔↔↔

Eight pieces. It was 22.34 at Établissements Boucan. Eight single product pieces, each different, each denoting a specific mould, sat huddled in the confines of a postcard-sized self-sealing polyethylene envelope which, in its turn, lay trapped in one of the inner pouches of Salvatore's attaché case. Viewed together, these items might one day recall to Salvatore's mind the memory of a succession of largely undifferentiated work shifts.

Each of the eight items had been produced by a specific combination of machine and mould invigilated by the Sicilian at the moment of its production. Three of the eight recalled for Salvatore his first week at Éts. Boucan, when he had been trained on the morning shift and had operated machines eight and nine: there had been a mould change at machine nine on the final day of his training. On joining the night shift, Salvatore had been assigned to machines six and seven and it was at machine six – which had seen three changes of mould – that four of these five items had been produced; the fifth aforesaid item was still being manufactured at machine seven, which, as must now be clear, had undergone no change of mould since Salvatore had started working nights.

To any outside observer, each of the Sicilian's eight bagged product pieces would be immediately distinguishable not only from its seven jostling neighbours but from the scores of other products produced by the plastics-section machines during the course of any year. Such distinctiveness was achieved neither by any notion of the items' possible end-uses – since such end-uses could rarely be guessed by mere tactile and visual examination – nor by any possibility of neatly describing, let alone naming, the said items. For although several product pieces approximately resembled bottle tops or caps or buttons or stalks or clips, most resembled nothing in particular at all, calling to mind, at most, some form of intricate and petrified insect or plant life. Since the vast majority of product pieces were destined for use in the hidden recesses of machinery seldom encountered in everyday life, a worker on quitting his employment at Éts. Boucan might live out a long, varied and interesting existence without ever again coming face to face with any of the items whose production he had overseen.

What made each item so easy to tell apart from all of its co-manufactured fellows – even for an observer who had never had sight of any such items before – was a play of several directly observable physical properties: colour, degree of shine and/or translucency, shape, angularity, the presence of protruding elements (like pins or antennae), weight, density, hardness, smoothness. To the workers producing them, however, a secondary series of characteristics, relating to and indelibly recalling the experience of the individual items' manufacture, would come into play: some items left their moulds stubbornly attached to their sprue, with the result that vigorous threshing was required; some, when separated from their sprue, emitted a pungent and displeasingly sweet or acrid smell; some items were abrasive to the touch, others silky, sleek and soft; some products clattered or made dull thuds against the side of threshing bins, others appeared to hum or whirr as they were tipped from tub into cardboard box. After working with the output of particular moulds, a worker's forearms might display some surface scratching or possibly a mild chemical burn or his hairs might carry a fine powder, whether dry or sticky, or they might stand upright and on end as if electrified.

↔↔↔↔↔

Feels like I'm running up- and fucking-downstairs all night trying to dissociate myself from that loud-mouth fucking-African. Why offend people? Why do that? Don't we have to get on with one another? First he picks on the Algerian and then on this poor little old git, this luckless sad slave to that semi-automatic monster. I don't get it. Besides, little Jean is mostly so nice to Côte d'Ivoire, letting him recite those weird-arse speeches, downright encouraging the man. Jean can see we're kind of friends. So how can I make it clear that I don't always share Côte d'Ivoire's opinions? Jean was watching Fernando approach. He smiled, though not directly at Fernando. Fernando didn't know if he should feel emboldened or expect some cutting remark. The little guy had quite a tongue on him sometimes. If you're such a titch, you must need one. Jean had smiled because he generally approved of the proud Portuguese race, and found this man comical and pitiable in equal degrees. Jean wondered if Fernando still lived in a foreign-workers' hostel, surrounded by criminal-and-immigrant scum. Portuguees were hard workers and kept their noses clean – everyone knew that – and they hailed from an ancient historic nation that possessed much in common with France. This Portuguee couldn't be blamed for all that Communist claptrap sweeping his country of origin. Fernando came to rest about a metre from his colleague's right elbow. As Jean heaved the machine guard open to extract a piece, Fernando said, 'Not much time off with that machine, is there?' Jean looked Fernando between the eyes, 'Well, we're paid to work, aren't we?' Fernando wondered, glancing away and seeing Bobrán sitting at his machine, his eyes closed and his lips mumbling, and then at Alphonse who was pacing again, learning lines from his play. Maybe the little git reckoned he was the only one who did any work here. Fucking-no! the man meant no harm.

Fernando decided to stay put. Both men were relaxed. It occurred to Jean that he might be able to do Fernando a favour. Monique and he had a room in their flat they never much used. A modest rent would come in handy and Monique could stop nagging him about those odd jobs she always said needed doing. Jean had never heard of a Portuguee who wasn't a dab-hand at DIY. Of course, Jean would need to clear it with Monique first. Jean narrowed his eyes as he glanced at Fernando: 'Are you still living in that hostel?' he enquired. 'Yeah,' Fernando replied, scowling. Did he fucking-need reminding? Where else was he likely to live? And how could he ever invite Maryse 'back to his place' when 'his place' was a hostel? So how could they ever be boyfriend and girlfriend instead of fucking-cure and patient? If he could stop being a loser for once in his life. But if he did anything dishonest, Maryse would sense it at once. It was an odd fact that Maryse was the most honest person he had ever met. Go figure! Maybe he didn't know her yet. He had tried to pay her once after his 'therapy,' though he had already left the money on her table on arrival. A simple mistake, resulting from confusion and embarrassment. She had noticed at once and had handed it back. Any shopkeeper fucking-would have pocketed it. Maryse was the first woman he had ever lusted after whom he would also want as a friend. It would be second-best, but still pretty good.

Fernando remembered why he was standing next to Jean and what he had wanted to say. 'I could see what you were getting at earlier,' Fernando offered. Jean looked perplexed and impatient. 'When you were talking to the new union rep – the Sicilian, you know – when the African bit your head off . . .' Fernando watched the little man's eyes and waited. Jean brightened up and launched into a tirade on the evils of union militancy. Fernando was rescued by Alphonse shouting, 'Ta machine!' Fernando's machine sixteen had come to a halt, its mould wide open, sprue dangling from its knockout pins.

36. Courtship, Rebellion and Religion.

Jorge pedalled hard: the early-winter air streaming against his face caused his eyes to water, smearing his view of the road ahead, forcing him to blink clear the film. On the crossbar of his bike, and therefore, geographically at least, between his arms, perched Renata, as spare and crisp as any well-wrapped item of freight.

Renata kept her glance oblique and her eyes half-closed against the cold, while reading from the careering parade of bars and shops and clubs and offices the circuitous route that Jorge was weaving through the town.

The tops of Jorge's thighs were registering an uncustomary strain as his legs drove and surged alternately down and up; his shoulders grew stiff as he steered his bicycle, his arms bent out as if to hold up a globe, each describing a semicircle that terminated in a gripping fist at one end of the handlebar. Jutting out on either side of the bike, commanded to avoid all contact with Renata's legs, Jorge's knees rose and fell in such a way that, if observed from behind, the image of a terrified frog paddling for the dappled undergrowth might come to mind.

The effort expended on conveying his cargo through the clean hard air pleased Jorge, presenting a nice contrast with the hours beguiled that day in his boss's car, half listening to slack and slurring talk from his own and other throats, inhaling tobacco smoke while sampling other odours both chemical and animal that rose from a bed of traffic fumes.

Amid the city night's tinnier noises and subtler aromas, Jorge felt at peace and alone. Released from constipation, his trunk felt free and light enough perhaps even to dance. Renata, in contrast, was hunched and tense, shivering in expectation, the crossbar of the Chilean's bike digging into her flesh, jarring at every jolt against her tailbone. She remained untouched, however, though girdled by the arching arms and pistoning legs of this still strange man whom she had desired for weeks, and into whose orbit she had resolutely propelled herself. Their bodies moved like blocks upon a loom or celestial bodies in some cosmological model, forever near yet fixed in their separation.

As the bike approached 'Les 4 Arts,' Jorge stopped pedalling. 'Would you want a drink?' 'No,' she replied. 'But if you desire.' As Jorge hesitated, a man he recognized from meetings in support of Chile called out: 'Salud, compañero.' Jorge grinned askance and checked his distance from the kerb.

He didn't need conversation. He pulled up and dismounted, holding the bike steady for Renata to clamber off. She stood and stretched while he bent to chain bike to railing.

Renata had never taken a good look at Jorge outside of a political meeting or Marta's flat. On little more than a hunch and a hormone, she was placing herself in his power. When he straightened up and looked in her direction he didn't smile. It was unusual for her to be reckless with little-known men.

The bar was crowded and understaffed; people queued for drinks. Jorge and Renata stared from the door speechless. The sound system was titanic. Jorge recalled why he hated Led Zeppelin. Renata took control. He couldn't bring himself to shout for drinks. 'Do you have beer at your place?' she yelled. Jorge beckoned her close. 'Wine,' he said. His lips brushed her ear. With a vigorous nod toward the street, she disguised a shiver.

Back on the bike, Renata and Jorge had only been moving for a minute when a draftee soldier, somehow shaken loose from his fellows, lurched into their path. Jorge swerved, fetching up against the side of a grey corrugated 2CV van. The impact thundered like a crashed dustbin lid. Jorge's right knee and shoulder would be bruised, but Renata was unscathed. The soldier, jerked into a semblance of sobriety, returned to his chanting companions.

In the commotion, Renata had grasped her pilot's left arm and she was now slow to let go. 'What is it they sing?' she asked. '_Zéro_. They've counted down the days. At midnight they turn back into civilians.' 'It's like Cenerentola,' Renata muttered. 'Cendrillon. Pumpkins . . . Horses back into white mice. At midnight.' Jorge smiled. Cenicienta, yes. Renata's shoulder blades relaxed against Jorge's breastbone. His chin chafed her left shoulder. His knees, rising and falling, knocked and rubbed against her legs. For several minutes, she rode in his arms.

Arriving at his edge-of-town high-rise, Jorge halted to let Renata dismount, then tethered the bike with one combination- and one key-operated lock-and-chain, lacing them through the frame and the spokes of front and back wheels. He pointed the way to his block.

They walked in silence, without touching. It was misty. Without warning, Renata heaved a sigh and hopped onto a low wall, raising herself above Jorge like a hedge-priest leaping onto a soapbox to address the crowd. Jorge stopped and turned his face toward her, smiling. Renata bit her lips and looked away. He realized he wanted to sleep with her. Renata fetched another sigh, deeper than the last. 'Ecoute-moi!' she enjoined. 'Je t'aime. Bon. Voilà. C'est dit.'

Jorge's smile withered. 'Tu te fous de moi . . .' 'Pas du tout . . .' 'You don't know me.' 'Yes I do.' 'How can you?' 'I've been watching you. We've talked. It's very simple.' Jorge laughed then stopped abruptly. 'I am not going to argue,' he said. 'Will you get down from that wall?' Renata saw no reason to get down. Things had not gone as intended.

Jorge was holding out a hand. Renata took it, stepped down, let it go. Again, Jorge pointed the way. It was as if nothing had happened. She frowned. 'Shall we go up?' he asked. She seemed to hesitate. Jorge wanted her. Before, he hadn't cared. 'You are perhaps completely insane,' he said, fidgeting with a hand at her hair. 'But I like you and it's cold. Can that be enough for now?' She could see he was embarrassed. She hadn't guessed he was shy. She let him take her hand. Jorge shook his head and stole sidelong glances. Renata stared straight ahead.

↔↔↔↔↔↔

Mehdi was not listening.

Rachid's eyes were growing used to the dark. Malika's note had stunned his senses. The first shock of delight had quickly passed: it was as if his feelings could not be reconfigured to entertain joy for any length of time. He could not whoop, could not blub. All around him, machines and men carried on working as before. The sheet of paper in his right hand, so recently feared as a potent threat, had grown limp from perspiration. He had asked the Englishman to look after his machines and then had hesitated between coffee and beer. He did not usually drink at work. He chose beer. He wanted to tell Mehdi the news. Malika had been right to foresee that. Mehdi ought to be happy to welcome a new brother or sister. Rachid would promise Mehdi he'd tell the new child all about him. Could he hear Mehdi's voice now? Faintly? Congratulating him? No? The beer was cold and hard on his tongue. He threw his head back and gargled. The words to summon Mehdi would not come. Rachid remembered how his son, three years old, would concentrate so hard on a toy or a picture book that his father had to plead with him to put them down and pay attention. 'What is it now, Daddy?' the child would say with a patient sigh. Sometimes if Rachid spoke to him too earnestly, Mehdi might turn and say, 'Go on then, papa, I'm listening now.' Rachid walked up and down, the bottle in his right hand: ten paces this way, ten paces that. He looked around him, comforted by the blurred nighttime shapes of machines whose outlines would be sharp and jagged in the light. He welcomed the absence of any gazes that could challenge the freedom of his own. Mehdi might not be listening, but Rachid would talk anyway. As if to himself. 'This is how things stand. Maman has not left me and never will. Nor will she ever return to Algeria, commit suicide, kill Fatima, betray me with another man or file for divorce. The night terrors are over. Even while she sleeps, she is waiting for me. That is what she wrote. With a new life inside her, growing into a baby.' Rachid spoke but, for the first time since the catastrophe, he sensed that Mehdi could not hear him or, if he could, had nothing to say. He clenched his teeth. The facts are these. Malika is pregnant, three months pregnant. It must be true, though I never saw her nauseous. Malika once said it is girls who bring on sickness. Can that be true? With Fatima, she threw up every morning for weeks on end. Not with Mehdi. Perhaps, then, it will be a boy. The one time we made love – I can remember each second of it – she conceived. Yes, what is now is pregnancy and what is past is conception. What is to come is birth, a gurgling baby, colic, teething, smiling, and very soon a toddler beginning to walk and talk and adore us back. That time we made love, I thought of nothing until it was over, hurled about in a storm of abject gratitude. Afterward, I imagined she had been overtaken by sudden, urgent, irrefutable desire – as when we were young: I have been waiting for it to happen again. Perhaps, though, she calculated everything coldly, chose the perfect day, who knows? – fed me herbs to enhance my fertility. I might feel manipulated. Shall I? Cheated somehow? Shall I feel cheated? Tricked into an extra bout of fatherhood? Rachid recalled how Malika once joked that they were both so fertile all he had to do was look at her in a certain way for her to get pregnant. What he ought to feel right now was elation, surprise, delight. Pregnancy is cause for celebration. But who can celebrate alone? Here, the only person he could tell was Mehdi, but might not Mehdi feel he was being shoved aside to make way for the living and the not-yet-even-born? Rachid returned to the pool of light surrounding the drinks machines, put down his bottle and reread Malika's note, imagining her voice of calm. As he reached the last lines, his throat seemed to thicken, his chest to constrict. He would be gentle. And slow. And long. Afterward, life would begin again as before, never so innocent, but better: 'lovers,' as she had written. This was safely in his future. For he and his wife not to make love in a few hours' time, he would have to die, be knocked down like his son in the street, or fall prey to a mad assassin, a stroke, some freak industrial accident or nuclear strike. What Philippe had said now made him smile: 'Nothing can happen here, nothing that we don't ourselves enact.' Maybe. But nor can anything prevent Malika and me from being lovers again. In a very small matter of hours. Had he ever loved his wife as much as at this moment? He replaced the note in his lighter pocket. This shift would be long indeed, but he would have Mehdi for company, wouldn't he? Their conversation was urgent, if he could only find the words. He sipped at his beer and recalled that night, that early morning in August. After they stopped talking, Malika had said in a dull flat tone that her calves felt cold. Your calves are cold? he had repeated. I just said so, she replied shortly. 'I could make you a hot-water bottle,' he had suggested. Silence. 'Or I could rub them.' 'Whichever's easier,' she had replied. Rachid had turned right round in the bed so that his head was close to her ankles, his own feet tucked beneath his pillow. She lay on her side, facing away from him, her slender back seeming broad and high for once. He took her lower foot, her right one, into his left hand and with his right hand cupped her left knee. He rested his forehead against her ankles, his lips against the sweet cleft cushion of flesh where her calves touched. He rolled his face slightly, rubbing his rough cheeks against her. After several minutes, when he thought she might be sleeping, he'd turned back round so that he was lying behind her, then she yawned and reached for his sex, felt its hardness in her fingers, and said, as if half-asleep, 'Don't fuss, Rachid, just do it. Take me. Please.' Is this what it is to be manipulated? Well, good then! He was no fetishist. He didn't love *women's* calves, he loved his wife's calves. He had never understood those rich and powerful men back home with their several wives or those men here in France with strings of girlfriends. What was the point? Could you love them all? He had slept once with a woman he hadn't loved: it was a thing never to repeat. It's so easy to picture sex with a woman you don't love, don't even know, and you can imagine every detail. But to do it, to find yourself in a bed with a woman you merely like or find enticing, is the height of misery. Making love, when there is no love, is a parody, a mimicry, a conversation with someone who is not there. Mehdi, or my dream of Mehdi, the way we talk together, is more real than that. Yet here too there is a falling-off. To have Mehdi *really* standing here, *really* listening or even not listening, not paying attention, perhaps *really* talking back: that would be something else. He would not be as he seems to be. I conjure Mehdi into existence every day and I could not stop doing so even I wished to: after all, he often appears to me quite unbidden, as he did just now while I was checking the hopper; and as he does at other times, at the bridge, for instance, when I go there after work to watch the river. Mehdi, still alive, full of questions. 'What are you watching for? Why, Daddy, why?' Like Fatima now. Not long before the catastrophe – his death: call it that! – Mehdi had wanted to know what happened when people died. We told him, as we have now told Fatima, that when someone you love dies you hold them in your mind and memory, you close your eyes and see them, their voices sound in your ears, you feel their breath on your face. If you hold on to someone, they continue to exist somewhere. Isn't it only when you stop talking to them that they die? This is the situation then, Rachid told himself, heading back toward the plastics section. I am alone with Fatima and Malika, and I love them. There will be a new baby. I shall talk to Mehdi and explain what happens next. That is all. He will understand. I was always expecting to grow up a second time with Mehdi, to grasp at a childhood I missed the first time round. He would be almost five now. I do not have to let him go. He lives within me. Malika understands this better than I thought. After all, the world would be an atrocious place were it inhabited only by the living. I was going to begin teaching him about our history, describing how I grew up, the hopes we had, our reasons for coming to live here. I wanted to justify our ways to our child. I had been looking forward to that. Perhaps it can still happen. If only I can get Medhi to listen.

↔↔↔↔↔

Nine friends. It was 22.37 in 'Berlin, *Hauptstadt der DDR.*' In the spacious main room of Wolf Biermann's apartment in the Chausseestraße, Franz, Jörg, Doris, Hans, Hartmut, Gertie, Petra, Jurek and Bettina had gathered to wish their friend well on his brief concert trip *nach drüben.* For the last twelve years he had sung and declaimed his poetry from this room alone, though tapes of these packed sessions had fanned out across the country, reaching deep into homes, works canteens, university dorms, barracks. The prospect of appearing before thousands of Western trade-unionists and of the concert then being broadcast to an audience of millions, East and West, had him fizzing with excitement.

Tonight Wolf wished to consult his friends and comrades, get their reactions to his concert plan, and test out the additional verses he had written for 'So soll es sein,' as well as the first few tentative lines of his latest – unwittingly prophetic – song, 'Preußischer Ikarus,' which he hoped to finish in time for Köln.

Everybody had brought something. There was GDR and Czech beer (purchased respectively by Hartmut and Bettina); a bottle of vodka and some Russian caviar (from Petra's recent trip to the USSR), rye bread (baked by Hans), herrings (caught by Jörg near Rostock, then marinated in his flat), French cheese (brought by Doris, whose grandmother had a sister in Stuttgart), Leipzig sausages (bought by Gertie on a trip home), a pot of Blaubeermarmalade (from Jurek's dacha near Chorin); and two bottles of Romanian wine (which Hans, a government employee, had been given in return for accelerating a building application).

Wolf stood near the piano, his left foot on the stool, a guitar loose in his arms as he picked at tunes and accompanied the talk – his own and that of this friends – with little flourishes, melodic quotes, ironic trills, or bombastic percussion. His friends sat and stood around him, fully partaking of his excitement, in awe of his talent yet fearful for him too. Wolf appeared to have no qualms at all. 'It'll be just like singing to you. We've had our disagreements, haven't we? I'll make mistakes, start again, forget lines, throw in stories and jokes, get angry with hecklers. What do they expect from me after twelve years stuck in this room – the spit-and-polish performance of some old *Konzertsgangster*? I'll tell them at the outset that I'll take any question, meet any challenge. I won't have it said that I ever ducked an argument. If Greens, liberals, SPD-ers, DKP-ers, KPD-ers, Maoists and anarchists want to take me on, fine! I've been practising for twelve years. I've grown rusty practising.'

Wolf reached for his wine and took a long draught. For a moment, his eyes had ceased scouring the room for reaction, demurral, or a challenge. His friends looked at one another, some raising eyebrows, others shaking heads. Wolf might be walking into trap. Wolf didn't know the West. What if Wolf were provoked by some Stasi-planted heckler into an un-nuanced attack on the GDR? Under pressure, would he be able to walk the anti-capitalist anti-Stalinist tightrope as well in the Western spotlight as he does here in the Eastern shadows?

'Ach! Don't look so scared, comrades!' Wolf laughed, putting the glass down. 'Well, what exactly are you thinking of performing?' Bettina asked. 'New songs, mostly,' Wolf replied. 'But also "Ermütigung," "Der Hugenottenfriedhof."And I want to open with "So soll es sein." I've been working up some new verses and a preamble to them, reclaiming Rosa from the SED. Hands off her, damn it! She's ours! I'm going to stuff her call for democratic freedoms right down the party's gullet. But mostly I'm going to do unrecorded stuff, bring it right up to date.' Jurek blew out his cheeks, while Gertie performed the feat of simultaneously rolling her eyes and shaking her head. 'You've got to sing more old songs,' Doris objected. 'I agree,' said Hans. 'At least half of the material has to be familiar.' 'I don't see why,' Wolf said, briefly thoughtful. 'You don't want to piss off your old friends,' Fritz said. 'Why ever not?' Wolf said, his face a portrait of impish glee. 'I piss you off, don't I? And we're still friends, aren't we?' Hartmut said, 'Man, everyone's going to be w-w-watching this, if it's t-televised.' 'Everyone?' Wolf joked. 'Nixon? Brezhnev?' 'Well, wh-who knows? The l-l-latter, maybe,' Hartmut replied, glancing around for support. 'Honecker won't want to miss it,' Petra said.

Wolf leaned his guitar against the side of the piano, sat down on the stool and put his right elbow on his right knee. He stared from face to face. 'Well, I'm fine with Honecker watching it, but I tell you who I really hope will see it. Ordinary proletarians. Students. Kids. Pensioners. Not just the party bonzos, but our people. I want Cottbus and Dresden to turn into ghost towns for one evening, everyone heading for friends in Leipzig or Berlin, anywhere there's a decent West-TV signal. And I'm hoping tapes will circulate and reach Prague, Budapest, Warsaw, Sofia, even Havana. Even Moscow. It's a rare chance to fan the flames of revolutionary revival.' 'They'll be watching in the West too,' remarked Jörg, who had friends in the Netherlands and family in Denmark. 'There are plenty of Left-Communists in Italy, France, a few even in Britain. Madrid too. Lisbon.' Wolf smiled then broke into cackling laughter, wagging his finger at Jörg. 'I've said this before. The West doesn't matter. You don't get it, do you? The old owl of history has fallen asleep over there, *drüben*, frozen on the wing: unemployment, austerity, overproduction, narcissistic consumption, economic paralysis. Change will come here first. In the East. It always does. From the bottom up. From the workers, who won't take it any longer. From the coalmines, shipyards and factories. Universities too. You'll see. Look at Poland. Forever stirring. If I matter at all it's only because I am too good not to ban. I provide a little mood music, bring people together, get them talking, piss off the big shots. Enough talk already! I'm just the singer!' Wolf snatched his guitar from the ground. Here's how I'm going to do 'So soll es sein.' Tell me what you think. Honecker had better be watching.'

↔↔↔↔↔↔↔

Three traits there were that sustained Alphonse's attitude toward people and his outlook on the world, and these were: credulity, empathy and curiosity.

The young man's credulity took the form of an unchecked drive to suspend disbelief in almost any play, film or story, and likewise in almost any person with howsoever approximate a flair for self-presentation or talent for deceit. His immediate response to the fictional arts was unconstrained by questions of aesthetic quality, proportional merely to the power of the emotional stimulus: he would drench as many tissues while watching *Love Story* as he would during a production of *Roméo et Juliette*. The pitch of suffering portrayed in film, play or novel elicited from him a mathematically commensurate reaction as he resolved and dissolved himself into each character in turn, experiencing the scorn and anger of first Capulet and then Montague – to pursue just one example – and then thrilling with the infatuation and thereafter the amorous despair of each star-struck lover, the sorrow of the nurse, the remorse of the reconciling parents, the gloom of friar and prince.

Related to this first trait was the empathy that Alphonse felt for the persons he encountered: not merely would he take upon trust almost any story related to him by someone met in blood and sinew, he would soon become convinced that he partook fully of that individual's mind, mood, thoughts and feelings. His sense of empathy was so powerful, imaginative, trusting and imperious that on occasions he believed his grasp of a subject's experience to be superior to any account that the person in question might themselves furnish. Only grudgingly would he ever acknowledge that what he viewed as a gift of clairvoyant insight could at times be fallible or imprecise, indeed – on occasion – utterly mistaken.

In completion of this triad of sustaining and distinguishing traits there was an impulsive curiosity. Alphonse was hungry as much for fictitious – whether celluloid, stage-lit or paper-printed – as for real, potentially palpable, people. The work that novelists, playwrights and filmmakers accomplished in manufacturing figures in whom he could believe had a parallel in the work he himself undertook through the obsessional and more or less intrusive observation and mimicry – both mental and physical – of all those he met.

These three traits – credulity, empathy and curiosity – worked together like guy ropes to sustain the triangular tent of the Ivorian's outlook and attitude, ensuring that he examine only other people, essentially strangers, while himself remaining frozen in the role of student, imitator, character and actor: his task, he was sure, was to portray the said strangers from the inside out, making them clear first to himself, then to any interested third-party spectator, and lastly – should it so fall out – even to themselves.

Should, however, one of these traits or habits of mind be challenged and fail, the edifice of Alphonse's outlook upon the world would collapse as completely as any tent cut free from one its guy ropes. His curiosity might be rebuffed by an uncommunicative or aggressive person; his billowing imaginative empathy might be harpooned by an astonishing revelation; his suspension of disbelief might collapse under the weight of some blatant absurdity in plot or protagonist: whereupon his attention would fold in upon himself – as would the credulity, empathy and curiosity that ordinarily he so assiduously and unthinkingly directed at others.

In these circumstances, however, Alphonse would appear to himself as any other stranger or human object of enquiry: he would experience his own mind, feelings and moods at one remove. Alphonse's own self was, in other words, permanently displaced, forever off-centre: it could never appear as the frank motor of his actions. Thus it was that Alphonse was incapable of conscious self-indulgence, egotism, self-pity or true narcissism: for since he was incapable of being at once the subject and the object of his own interest, he was by that token incapable of solipsism. The peculiarity of this psychological complexion might be traceable in theory to some precise set of determining relationships or experiences, whether remote or recent; any such speculation, however, remains beyond the bounds of this novel, and must await the greater scope and knowledge of a subsequent narrator.

↔↔↔↔↔

Returning to his machines eight and nine, Rachid had nodded a thank you to the Englishman, while positioning on the huge old wooden table his half-empty bottle of beer and that day's *L'Humanité*, borrowed on his way past Philippe's collection of magazines and newspapers stacked on the top of a recycled-material cylinder at the end of machine two. After scrutinizing the latest pieces, Rachid had emptied both floor trays into their respective threshing tubs. He looked around, lit a cigarette, and sipped at his beer.

Rachid saw Salvatore interrupt what he was saying to Luigi in order to free a piece of sprue that had stuck to the mould of machine seven. The Italian glanced in Rachid's direction. Rachid looked away. Luigi placed his right boot on the vacated chair and relit his cornpaper stub, swallowing a cloud of smoke. His elbow rested on his right knee, his right hand cantilevered the stub out into the air, swinging it slightly, as if interested to watch it go out again. The Englishman had come to stand at his left shoulder but hadn't been noticed.

Luigi was considering Salvatore, wondering why the man didn't make more of himself. Tall, handsome, a winning smile, a talker, a dresser: in Salvatore's place, he could have had women eating out of his hands. Hands? Out of his goddamn trousers! Luigi enjoyed a lewd smirk away to his left. What was that Arab staring at now? Rachid looked away again. He was drinking a beer. Luigi found that remarkable.

Luigi surveyed Salvatore's back again, noted the tightness of the man's buttocks as he leaned into the mould to brush a little oil onto the knockout pins. If I had his looks I'd be screwing half the morning shift. He doesn't even notice they're all in a lather over him. Me they don't even see. At five a.m. when they come in, filing past us standing there all broken and bent like donkeys queuing for the knackers, I'm nothing to them but the ugly dumb sidekick. I make him look even straighter, taller, cleaner, eleganter, sophisticated-er. God, there are so many crumbs, so much gravy at that table, going begging! If only he'd stop and dine a little, I might get a spoonful or two myself! I could at least screw the disappointed or the not-so-pretty or just anyone who wants to get a little closer to him. I'm not proud. I could bear that.

Luigi felt his sap rising, his cock thickening. He was going to have to get some relief, stop his thoughts drifting any further that way. He'd give it another try, and soon. He didn't often fail to bring himself off. Some damned thing had intruded itself earlier between cock and comic, some niggling fucking doubt worming its way in, sabotaging proceedings, leaving him standing there pounding away as it grew limper by the second. Maybe he'd seen those pictures too many times. That was the thing about dirty pictures: you have to keep seeing new ones, because once the shine is off them, they no longer do the job they're supposed to – and you can hardly take them back.

Salvatore closed the mould, checked the first piece then turned back to Luigi, acknowledging with a nod of his head the Englishman's presence. Luigi, taking his boot off Salvatore's chair, backed right into the man, who apologized excessively and confusedly. Luigi saw that Salvatore had that look on him that threatened philosophy or union politics or reflections on life.

Luigi gestured over to the Arab. 'The man's got a beer. I thought they didn't drink.' 'Well, *good* Muslims aren't supposed to,' Salvatore pronounced. Eric looked from Salvatore to Luigi to Rachid, to Rachid's bottle, then his eyes widened, and he nodded. He tried to form a sentence but the Italian looked away and Salvatore asked out loud, 'But are all Arabs Muslim, I wonder?' Luigi just roared, 'Are Italians Catholic?' 'My point, precisely,' Salvatore said patiently. 'There are indeed Italian protestants, Italian Jews.' Luigi shook his head and bared his teeth.

'Do you have Jews in England?' Salvatore asked Eric, sounding as if he really cared. Eric made him repeat the question, then burbled, 'In my class at school, there were three . . .' 'Three?' 'Three,' Eric confirmed. Luigi and Salvatore stared at the Englishman, shrugged, then glanced at one another, then away. 'How did you know they were Jews?' Salvatore asked. 'They didn't say Christian prayers or sing Christian songs, you know, les "hymns.:"' 'What, you pray at school in England?' Salvatore asked, feeling the mantle of Voltaire caress his shoulder. 'We have to,' Eric stated.

Luigi didn't seem to be listening. He was looking in Salvatore's direction but his eyes were unfocused. He seemed to be playing with himself. Or maybe scratching. Salvatore moved closer to Eric. 'I read somewhere that people no longer go to church in England . . .' 'That's right, they don't.' 'And yet – let me get this right – you pray in school.' 'We have to.' 'So nobody believes in it?' 'I don't think so. I never met anyone who did. But it isn't the kind of thing you talk about. It isn't polite.' 'Polite?' Salvatore shook his head and smiled. 'Che ipocrisia! Les anglais sont vraiment bizarres . . .' 'Yes,' Eric said, nodding like a dog on the rear shelf of a car lurching between speed bumps, appreciating for the first time one of the peculiarities of the land and culture of his birth. 'Yes. I suppose it is *bizarre*.'

Luigi looked from man to man, then said: 'My mother always says it was Jews that killed Christ. She prays for their conversion. I've heard her. Nobody forces *her* to pray. Nobody has to. And nobody could.' Salvatore then said, like he'd only found this out: 'Christ was a Jew, you know.' Luigi spat a filament of tobacco onto the floor and grinned. 'Yeah? Are you sure? Well, that's completely fucked up. Whatever you do, don't tell my mother.' Then to Eric: 'Do Jews drink?' Salvatore got to the answer first: 'In England, everyone drinks. Right?' 'Pretty much,' Eric confirmed. Luigi frowned suspiciously, 'So even Arabs in England drink? Even Muslims?' 'I never heard of Muslims much before I came to France,' Eric said. Luigi looked surprised then glanced up the aisle and saw the chef standing at his machine fourteen. He nodded to the others and walked away, taking his hands from his pockets as he did so.

37. Fear, Freedom and Trumpeting.

Fear shaped and fed Jean's every moment: he must surely either have been born timorous – if such a thing is to be imagined – a babe entering a harsh new world quailing in anticipation of hunger, pain, sorrow, loss, defeat and humiliation, weary of existence before the initiating slap were administered, the first stale breath drawn; or he must have secreted and accumulated cowardice patiently, like a squirrel burying nuts, every slight and hurt duly cherished and interred, to be dug up industriously during some winter of the soul in order not to stiffen a spirit of defiance but further to trammel and thwart a naturally fawning and trembling disposition.

To manage his fear, Jean had devised a singular line in courage: he was emboldened to direct and discipline his puny body and compendious mind, to shore up his faltering resolve with a streaming patter of self-praise, to cultivate potential flatterers with titbits of reward, to subjugate dependants with threats of chastisement or favours withdrawn. For what else is courage, he considered, but a disregard for the suffering of one privileged person: oneself? What is it but self-cruelty?

Jean's nerves were bad that night, yes, bad. He had tics, loathed the dark, could not grin without rictus spasm, could not look closely at any man without the dread of sphincter dysfunction. He feared dark places and eyes, faces, faeces, quick movements, sudden quarrels, embarrassments, conundrums, stuttering incomprehension, nudity in man, woman, child or cherry-arsed ape, the ribaldry of women, the mockery of children. He dreaded now, as much as at five, six or seven years of age, to be discovered sitting alone in a wide hall on a wooden bench amid a tepid pooling, with grownup fingers quivering and pointing at his face and children snickering.

Fear might be adduced to explain the majority of Jean's vices: his envy, avarice, rage, and his assorted bigotries – against homosexuals, Jews, Arabs, blacks, women, Chinese, Gypsies, Commies, hippies, Americans, Indo-Chinese, Protestants, the poor, the rich and above all the middling. His few allegeable virtues arose also from obvious fears: his disinclination openly to thieve; his kindness toward animals neither small nor defenceless; his willingness to give money to beggars of sturdy aspect; his attendance, however infrequent, at the hellfire church of his parish.

Jean believed that his diminutive stature had held him back in life. What might he not have achieved, he often wondered, had he been born to plains-reared giants rather than to stunted mountain folk. Who ever noticed the small man? Who admires, let alone obeys, a man little more than a midget?

And yet who was it who worked the largest machine on the floor, the severest taskmaster? Proudly Jean pictured himself at the wheel of the hugest artic ever built, steaming down the highway, honking his horn, flashing his hazards, scattering lesser lorries to the hard shoulder, terrifying all with the hissing of his air brakes, looming over the small fry like a conductor on his plinth, a general glorying at his chart, a cowboy athwart his towering stallion.

↔↔↔↔↔

In a grand hotel sunk in the forested hills just east of Grandgobier, Chantal had been dining with her fuck-friend, Bruno, a Belgian man of business whom she had encountered on a boat in a storm in April 1973 while holidaying in Greece. They met several times a year, always in a hotel, usually in Lyon, and for one night only. They would eat copiously, talk of their lives and loves, then retire to their room and screw like starved athletes, with no more words exchanged than those to denote approval, indicate a mistake, provide encouragement, log a request. Exhausted, they would say goodnight, turn their backs on one another, and sleep like sloths.

In the last year, since Chantal had got to know Marcel, these encounters had undergone a slow and subtle change. It was as if they were waiting for the end, Bruno especially. Once, after listening to an account of Marcel's prowess, Bruno had asked Chantal why she still agreed to see him. She had looked surprised. 'Because with you it's different. Besides, I knew you first. *This* has nothing to do with Marcel.'

This evening, over the aperitifs, Chantal had told the Belgian of her happy engagement. 'Congratulations!' he had said raising a glass. And then, a twinkling of sadness in his eyes: 'So is this our last night?' 'Well, maybe not quite the last . . .' Chantal had replied, catching her lower lip between her teeth. 'After all, Marcel and I haven't quite fixed a date. Let's not rush into . . . or out of . . . *things.*'

Chantal had asked after Bruno's wife. Bruno had waved a hand. 'No change.' Lowering his voice, he had confided, 'But I have met someone . . .' 'Really?' 'I'm not sure it'll amount to anything . . .' Chantal had leaned forward. 'Tell me all about it. Who is she?' 'She's African. From Zaire.' 'How exciting!' Bruno had blushed like a girl. 'Is she very beautiful?' 'Exquisite.' 'And like a tigress in bed?' Bruno had pursed his lips and looked away. 'No. Just like a woman. Unique.' Chantal relaxed back in her chair, cradling her glass. 'Ah . . .' she said.

A little later, as they tucked into dessert, Bruno asked Chantal about her work. 'They want to promote me,' she said, frowning. 'So? What's the problem?' 'I'd be in charge of sales, scouting for new haulage contracts. I'd miss talking to the truckers and joking with the other girls in the pool.' Bruno laughed. 'I remember you saying you liked it when they radio in and talk dirty.' 'Did I say I liked it? Well, I suppose we all do. It isn't threatening. We never meet them.'

'Does their talk excite you?' Bruno asked. Chantal sucked the last slop of mousse from her spoon and pushed back the plate with deliberation. 'It all depends on the voice,' she declared. 'Provided they don't sound in any way creepy and their idea of sex sounds like fun, I store it up and see if Marcel will oblige . . . or you, of course.'

There was a moment's embarrassment, which Bruno dispelled with a shrug.

'There was this guy yesterday,' Chantal resumed, 'Georges. A real chatterbox. He likes to tell me about the prostitutes he meets at different stopovers. Yesterday, he said I should come ride with him some day. I thought for a minute he was really going to proposition me, name a time and a place, you know.' 'Would you have gone to meet him?' 'Hell, no,' Chantal replied. 'What did he say?' 'He said, "You sound young. I bet you're nicely built. The road makes us horny." Then he said, "Do you know what I'm doing right this minute as we speak? Can you guess what I've got in my hand? Staring straight up at me? Maybe it's the vibrations, or the hours we work, or the boredom. If you were here, we could pull over. Tell me what you are wearing. There's plenty of room in these cabs. I can do it again and again. Tell me about your tits," he said. He demanded to know what shape they were and how big. He asked me about my nipples. "What colour are they?" he asked. "Right now, are they hard or soft? Are you wearing a bra?"' Chantal laughed. Her face was red. Bruno saw her glass was empty again. He didn't move to fill it up. 'You can't get too angry with them,' Chantal said, more reflective now. 'I told him he should keep his eye on the road or stop and jerk off.'

Bruno and Chantal had moved to a small round table in the bar and were drinking digestifs. The lights were low and there was a tape of contemporary crooners: Dean Martin, Aznavour, Sinatra, Sacha Distel – even Demis Roussos. When they heard Roussos's voice, Bruno and Chantal smiled, sharing a memory.

Bruno was always a little slow to suggest they go to their room, as if boyishly uncertain. Chantal liked that about him. There was no rushing. He looked good tonight – in that clean-cut Belgian way. Not stuffy at all. Suave.

There was a moment's silence. Chantal slipped her right foot out of its shoe and gently caressed Bruno's left ankle. He didn't look up. 'What are you thinking?' Chantal asked. Bruno, who was thinking about his wife, murmured, 'Nothing much.' Chantal experienced a passing sadness. Bruno sensed it. 'Shall we go up?' he said.

↔↔↔↔↔

Philippe glanced down at his newspaper. Why was it so hard to concentrate? He kept going over the same paragraph twice, thrice. By this time of night, he should be halfway through Rémy's stack of papers, harvesting it methodically, scythed columns folding before him like rows of silvery rye, each page a bristling bright new field. Philippe wondered whether 'his' news could ever trump 'the' news. Ridiculous! And am I not eerily calm? Too calm? Less than two hours have passed since I spoke to Danielle on the phone. Odile is fucking another man. Do I doubt it? Well, no. It has the indelible ring of truth: you recognize it when you hear it. Though it's strange to think of her caring enough about sex to find a lover. Maybe *he* had found *her*. She was easily seduced. A prey to easy flattery. I ought to be a little shocked at least. Why am I not? Why am I not angry? He recalled his momentary lapse into frantic uxoricidal fantasy, the alcohol-propelled atavistic impulse immediately ludicrous, comical, unseemly. If I ever did anything like that – which I never could – it would have to be in a place without mirrors. If ever I caught a glimpse of myself raising my hand in anger I'd burst out laughing and that would be that. Too ridiculous. One look at the pasty podgy face growling and baring its teeth and I'd collapse giggling on the floor, giving the wife her chance to take the carving knife and disembowel me on the spot, then plead self-defence. The neighbours would swear before the judge they heard me shouting at her. They never liked me. So am I incapable of anger, violence? What kind of a male mammal does that make me? How would a walrus behave? Or a dolphin? The males are probably carefree cuckolds, if not raving queens. No, dolphins wouldn't give a damn: they'd go back to blowing their bubbles. Maybe I'm a dolphin. I was probably born in the year of the dolphin. I must check with the Chinese. It would explain a lot. I lack the requisite primate rage. I might try to synthesize it, talk myself into it, work myself up to it, cast myself as indignant victim, wronged innocent, and so forth, beat my flabby breast, cry ape tears. Why is all that stuff not for me? What kind of a man am I then? Philippe was perfectly familiar with stories of proud husbands and perfect family men who, always 'inexplicably,' killed their philandering wives the moment they surprised them in two-backed flagrante with their hapless fouteurs, then butchered the pretty progeny before, as the saying most commonly went, turning the gun upon themselves or, by way of embellishing variant, leaping from grimy bridge or unassuming balcony. *Détective*, which Luigi read so avidly, was crammed with such stuff. 'True Stories,' it was claimed. No doubt. Up to a point. No, Philippe would not be supplying these publications with any such appetizing copy. Never mind the sight – the mere thought of blood made him sick. What kind of weakness was that? And what did it mean in practical terms? Well, it meant that for technical reasons he would only ever be able to murder – if at all – with the use of an instrument so blunt it will never draw blood. Severely limiting, you might think. Hard to do that much clubbing when you don't like to break a sweat. Or was it just that he couldn't feel any hatred for Odile? Yet he had loved her. Passionately. It took an effort to remember that now. Years ago. Deeply. He had known what that meant. Philippe's thoughts and feelings were rearranging themselves inexorably, transforming the past and the future, bloating the present with unfamiliar feelings and busy calculation. Odile was fucking another man. Odile fucking another man. Another man. Fucking Odile. Another man fucking Odile. Another man was fucking Odile. Fucking Odile! Philippe sensed no personal affront. Indeed, upon sane and approximately sober reflection, it didn't seem to him that it was a personal matter. Danielle wouldn't understand that. He could hear her risposte: 'some man's screwing your wife and it's not personal? What could be more personal!' Splutter, choke, roar. He was a mouse, she had said on the phone, hadn't she? Not a dolphin at all, then. A rodent. Still a mammal. For his part, he was getting used to the notion. Cuckolded? Hum. Sure. He was a cuckold. It made perfect sense. He ran the soft tip of his right index finger around his temples. Not the slightest bump. Perhaps they took time to swell. Definitely a cuckold though. It was as clear as day. Yet between the information given and the recognition of its givenness, which is to say its truth, there had fallen a flash of time, an instant, perhaps an hour. Even self-evidence takes a while to declare itself. Odile has betrayed me, Philippe whispered. Betrayed: so much less, yet so much more. No hurt, if none is felt. Betrayed. The thought, little sooner stated than tediously obvious, was wreathed already in a haze of stultifying banality: no proof, corroboration, evidence circumstantial or forensic were now required. His attention had been lacking, which, now supplied, peremptorily registered the occurrence, confirmed the fact, recorded the deed, with all the fuss and emotion of an automated franking machine descending upon a postage stamp. This then is how truths are known, Philippe reflected: it is through the mental seizure of self-evidence. There! Of the knowledge in question, however, Philippe had been a most unwilling recipient. With no whit of mercy or forbearing gentleness, his sister Danielle – for purposes known (if at all) only to herself – had forced the obvious upon him – damn and bless her! – and he could not now un-know it. Philippe stood at his machine, his stubby fingers thumbing the pagers of *L'Humanité*, his mind elsewhere, absorbing nothing. Philippe's understanding of the raw fact of Odile's adultery – a gross term for an act so fleeting and merely skin- or at most cunt-deep, scarcely visceral – consummated a revolution in his perception of past and future. My marriage to Odile is over. Just like that. It was over before perhaps, a walking cadaver, no longer fully sentient, though not yet certifiably dead. Nostalgic sentimental feelings for our early days of shy courtship and frantic rutting may now be expected to incubate. All in good time. No need to rush things. Since he had found and identified 'the end,' he could now see that his love for and marriage to Odile possessed a discernible middle and a crystal-clear beginning. Like a revelatory philtre cast upon the surface of a murky water world, the mist had cleared and the creatures, the rocks, the weed, the very grains of sand stood magically delineated, sharp and neat. Also metamorphosing in his mind was his future. Instead of an endless tunnel of miserable weariness, I see before me now a dark wall, a collision, a crash of separation with all the recriminations and guilt apportionment and tiresome sorrow, infinitely indispensable and boring, but surely not *too* bitterly awful, since he and Odile had always been friends first and last, as well as everything else, hadn't they? And after that the unknown: white light, a distant scenery where anything might be constructed, an empty house, full of promise. In a word, freedom in matters of the heart and, in time, perhaps new arrangements for living and even working? And their child? Ah, Olympe had somehow slipped away from him. Nowadays, she barely said hello. A grunt was a treasured acknowledgement. But, separated from Odile, he could perhaps win her back, become her friend. Danielle, poor inept malevolent sister, had done him such a favour. How she would kick herself when she saw him wriggle free of his marriage, a happier man than before. The exhilaration of impending liberation! A fine prospect. Anything was possible now. Even, in time, a stronger friendship with Odile. Who could say? Philippe closed his paper and got up. He placed it at the bottom of the pile, then went to the control cabinet. He gazed at the numbers, the dials with their clock-like hands ever trembling. His mind was nicely empty, his body pleasantly numb. He felt settled. The nervous tingling in his limbs had gone. He knew exactly where he was and he didn't mind at all. He didn't need to close his eyes and summon up beaches, topless bathing beauties, bubbly sea-spume. He hadn't felt this good for months. He was at the factory, he reminded himself. This was where he earned his living, chatted with his workmates, read the newspapers, had a laugh, and in the small hours even cultivated his love of crime fiction. He was not in the habit of taking his job home – as the saying goes – nor of bringing his domestic troubles to work. He turned back from the control cabinet, glanced at the opening presses, then stooped over the floor tray to catch the hot product as it clattered through the aluminium slats. He straightened up. Checked the piece carefully. Heard the presses open again. Chucked the examined piece back in the floor tray. Repeated the process. Stoop. Catch. Check. Chuck. Then he bent and raised the tray high into the air, tipping its contents into the threshing tub and, smartly repositioning tray on floor, barely in time to collect the next clattering piece. Then the other machine: Stoop. Catch. Check. Chuck. Stoop. Catch. Check. Chuck. Bend. Raise. Tip. Smartly Reposition. He might do this or something like it for the next thirty years. Or – and this was a brand-new thought – he might take a risk, live dangerously, either invent for himself a new way of earning a living or wind up destitute, without fixed abode, a bummed cigarette in one hand and a plastic bag of possessions in the other. There had been moments in the last few years when he'd dreamt of such a state. He was a free agent now! It was that simple! It can't be! Of course it is! I can't wait to tell my friends. Jacques will be the first to know. Everyone will urge caution on me like a douse of rain. Except perhaps Rémy. Not that he's a friend as such. More an acquaintance. But, damn it, I'm going to be free. I can't wait to tell Odile. Oh. Hmnn. Well.

↔→↔→↔→↔→↔

Ten eyes. It was 22.40 in the metallurgy and plastics factory of Éts. Boucan, in the West European town of Grandgobier. Of the twenty-six eyes present in the plastics section – not forgetting, as indeed one never must, those of the roving Polish night security man – just ten merited particular note, these being arranged, as is universally customary, in five pairs, although in the cases of the first and second pairs, separate and specific mention has to be made of each individual eye, since the differences between them far outstrip the elementary matter of left-right positioning which, taken on its own, signifies only that in order to enjoy bifocal clarity it is no lesser handicap to possess two left eyes that it would be to possess two left feet when hoping to cut a figure on a dance floor.

Bobrán's eyes differed slightly in outward aspect. Whereas for those happy people provided with two indistinguishably identical eyes, it is unusual and, it has to be said, both disconcerting and creepy to find one's interlocutor constantly displacing his attention from one's left to one's right eye and then back again, this had long been Bobrán's typical experience when conversing with others, convincing him that people in general were shifty and untrustworthy since unwilling to meet his gaze head-on. As far as Bobrán himself was concerned, however, both of his eyes were more than ordinarily serviceable. He saw everything he wanted to see and then some, whether at a distance or at close range. He suffered neither eye-itch nor eye-ache, only eye-tremor, but only Moritz had ever noticed that. Nor was he troubled by overactive lacrimal glands, sagging lids or allergy to dust, cats or pollen. Yet to an indifferent onlooker, neither eye appeared at all healthy, though the irises themselves were of a passably pleasant light brown colour. Both eyes were in fact bloodshot, though the left one was, at least on the night in question, much more bloodshot than the right. Also, both eyes had yellowish-to-rust-coloured flecks extending from beneath the lids and covering much of the corneas, albeit with irregular gaps. Again, these flecks were of unequal size and shape, those in the left eye being larger, perhaps thicker. Whether there was any connection between the blood-shooting of the eyes and the flecking will have to remain here a matter for mere speculation, lying as it does far beyond our present competence.

The eyes of Mathieu Petit, the night-shift foreman, also necessitate separate discussion. Rather small, both were a washed-out-denim blue glistening from a constant bathing in tear water, though droplets only ever formed, separated and descended his cheeks on the occasions – infrequent enough at the best of times, but of an exceptional rarity at work – when he indulged in or was overtaken by conspicuous mirth or hilarity. What differentiated Mathieu's eyes was, first, the view of the world they afforded their owner and, second, the state of their immediate setting. The left eye was moderately astigmatic, making it useless for the close inspection of products or for the perusal of ordinarily sized print: he would screw it shut to accomplish the former task and don glasses to perform the second. The right eye, on the other hand, though it provided its possessor with an infallibly clear and sharp picture of matters both proximate and remote, possessed in a far-flung corner of its retina a minuscule imperfection, an interruption in the tissue, a minute mole that over many years had neither grown nor shrunk, and which, when for whatever reason he raised his gaze rightward to the sky, caused him to perceive either a tiny flash of indeterminate colour and duration or a short-lived image of a floating furry stick. As for the environment of Mathieu Petit's eyes, whereas both upper and lower lids were chronically afflicted by psoriasis, with the result that his eyes often appeared to be ringed in girl-baby pink, there was a disfiguring patch of the same dermatological eruption extending from his upper-right eyelid and intruding into his sparse right eyebrow and which had no equivalent on the left side of his face.

The six notable eyes remaining fell in time-honoured fashion into three pairs of near-identical individuals. Those owned by Eric were indifferently and uncertainly coloured, sometimes appearing green, sometimes grey, sometimes bluish, according to the surroundings, play of light, and so on. The almond shape of his eyes, on the other hand, and the fact that they possessed unusually pronounced epicanthic folds might have imparted to him, had his hair colour only deigned to collude in this deception, some hint of Inuit or Eskimo ascendants.

Rachid's eyes, at a first encounter, appeared unexceptional. They were a dark brown, neither protruding nor sunk, neither large nor small. Moreover, they performed their office with diligence and efficiency, never failing to furnish a reasonable copy of the world through which their owner moved, rarely clouding, never faltering, satisfactorily effective on the darkest of nights. What would detain any acquaintance or interlocutor was the deep scoring and scouring of the skin circumscribing the orbs themselves. For a man of his years, Rachid possessed an Alpine topography of criss-crossing channels, valleys, lines, striation and fluting which, denoting suffering and sadness or at least a heavy toll of life's grim experience, could not fail to arrest and intrigue all but the most incurious or flint-hearted of his fellow humans.

Lastly, Fernando's eyes were exceptional in their absolution from the general rule of ordinary, moderate, everyday plainness that governed the remainder of the man's face, his nose being too big, his skin too sallow, his hair too wiry, his lips too unevenly fleshed, his brow too narrow, his ears too crinkly, his entire head far too small, his neck too short, his jowls already too ponderous. On account of their immediate environs, Fernando's eyes, like a flower that blooms atop a dunghill or amid some blistering vacant lot, tended to remain unremarked and therefore unappreciated. Fernando himself was quite unaware of his best feature and failed therefore ever to conscript it to any purpose, even when consciously attempting charm or seductiveness. Maryse, however, who, congruous with her current occupation, set little store by men's faces or bodies, was in fact an eyes-woman – in the same sense that others are 'buttocks-women' or 'lips-women' or that some men, perhaps a majority, may be said to be 'breast-men' – and Maryse had noticed Fernando's eyes, had peered into them more than once already, uncovering there, to her surprise and bewilderment, such pools of deep longing and such wells of untapped tenderness that could not but vex and disturb her imagination.

↔↔↔↔↔↔

Having reseated himself against the side of his machine number one, in close proximity to the machine aisle, and without any reading matter in his hands, it was as though Philippe had broadcast an open invitation to forgather; hearing the call, they had swiftly formed a standing semicircle around him: Marcel, Eric and Jacques. Tomec, arriving from metallurgy, had quickly joined the grouping.

Philippe smoked and listened to Marcel entertaining the others with an account of what he had heard in the toilet. 'I was sitting there on the can when someone came in and started going boo-beh-boo-boo. I couldn't figure out who it was at first. Then the baby noises stopped and I heard sighing and cussing – I thought it was someone who had caught a dose and it was burning: that happened to me once – then I heard him say "putain de prostate de merde!" and I recognized the foreman's voice. After that his piss began to flow and he started up again: boo-boo-beh-boo-boo. Maybe he was happy he could piss at last. The old man's fucking cracked.'

As Alphonse, who had just come down from upstairs, approached the group, Jacques and Eric moved apart to accommodate him. Philippe looked at the end of his cigarette, and said, 'That's called scatting.' Everyone looked down at him. 'Those sounds he makes are called scatting. It's a jazz thing. He plays jazz. Scatting is what jazz singers do when they run out of words. Do-be-do-be-do.'

There was a moment's silence. 'You're shitting me,' Marcel said. 'Absolutely not. He plays jazz . . . on a trumpet. But he keeps quiet about it. It's personal, right? Not everyone brings their personal stuff into work.' Marcel gave Philippe a sharp look, but kept his mouth shut.

'Are you talking about the foreman?' Alphonse asked. 'Who the fuck else?' Marcel said. Alphonse sniffed and started jiggering around a lot, but that was pretty normal for him: he never stood still for long. Jacques and Eric moved back to give him the space he seemed to require. 'So what kind of jazz does he play . . . le swing?' Jacques asked, imparting an old-fashioned square-dance movement to his arms and thus to his question. Philippe smiled up at his friend. 'It's probably a bit more modern than that.' Philippe looked again at the tip of his cigarette and opened his eyes as wide as they would go.

Alphonse took a decision. He aimed his voice at Philippe but spoke loud enough for everyone there. 'You've heard of Charlie Parker, Thelonious Monk, John Coltrane? No? That's the kind of stuff he plays. Bebop-type jazz.' Tomec nodded like he recognized the names. 'Be-bop?' Marcel said. 'That's the sound he kept making in the toilet: be-bop, be-bop. Well, more or less.'

'How do you know that's what he plays?' Philippe asked Alphonse, abruptly forensic. 'I heard him once. I saw him,' Alphonse declared. Philippe swung his head downward, as if the better to absorb such startling new information. Everyone watched Alphonse, backing away from him, waiting for more, placing him centre-stage. 'I was in Lyon a few months ago,' the Ivorian began slowly. 'I often go there for the weekend. I have friends there.'

'So the fuck what?' Marcel snapped.

Alphonse squinted at Marcel, then resumed. 'We went out to this cool bar. There he was, the chef d'équipe, standing up there on the stage, wearing a clean shirt and trousers without string to hold them up.' Marcel, Tomec and Jacques glanced over as Mathieu walked up the machine aisle and stopped at Luigi's machine thirteen to check its product. They all shook their heads and turned back to Alphonse. 'Was he any good?' Jacques asked. 'Well, I'm no jazz aficionado. It's hard to tell. But he seemed pretty good to me. He swings. You know. There were people in the audience tapping their feet. Like they do.'

'Did he see you?' Tomec asked.

'It was a small place and there weren't many people there, so maybe he should have done, but he mostly kept his eyes closed while he was playing and looked at the ground between numbers. He didn't seem that interested in the audience. It was like he was on his own. I don't think he saw me. It was the bass player who talked to the audience, not that he had much to say either.' Philippe was chuckling, happy about something, as if he were a kid and had just received a present. 'So the man's good, the man's good,' he murmured.

Marcel broke up the group around Philippe's chair by strolling over to machine number thirteen, where Mathieu was holding up a piece of product, his left eye screwed shut. Jacques, Eric and Alphonse drifted across in Marcel's wake, while Tomec headed for the stairs. 'So . . .' Marcel said to the old man, as the product he had been examining hit the floor tray, 'I hear you're a jazzer, a – what is it? – a scatter? A trumpeter? Right?' Mathieu stared back, his eyes blinking. 'What?' he said. 'Our African friend here saw you playing in Lyon.' Marcel glanced at Alphonse then back at Mathieu.

'Saw me in Lyon?'

'That's what the guy said,' the big Gypsy replied. Alphonse nodded and looked apologetic, as if he had betrayed a secret.

'So?' Mathieu asked, his feet starting to stamp. He removed the burnt-out matchstick from his mouth and picked at the crown of his head. He stared in turn at Jacques, Eric and Alphonse, his faint blue eyes leaping from man to man. They were grinning like effigies.

'What do you want?' Mathieu asked, suddenly impatient. He noticed Philippe, who hadn't moved from his chair, 'What's wrong with them tonight?' Philippe shrugged and tapped the side of his head. But Marcel wouldn't let go. 'You're a musician, right?' he said. 'So are you going to play us some Mozart over our dinner later? We could light some candles. We'd appreciate that.' Jacques scratched his head and began to back away. Eric looked from man to man, clueless. Alphonse stood back and studied Mathieu in silence, his lips moving like he was learning a part.

The foreman suddenly stamped hard, clapped his left hand to his left temple so hard you might think it would hurt. 'Bande d'abrutis!' he yelled, staring at them one by one. Jacques was slinking away. Marcel was laughing.

Eric looked bewildered. Alphonse was calmly observing the scene. Mathieu replaced the matchstick between his teeth, elbowed the men aside and walked away, spluttering yet grinning, 'Bande de petits connards! Bande d'abrutis!'

38. Success, Persons and Attachment.

Eleven centimetres. Luigi had measured it so many times: eleven. Maybe a smidgeon more. Depending how hard he dug the end of the ruler into his flesh. Not a lot to boast about but enough to work with. To date, he had had no complaints. It isn't always the broadest shovel that shifts the most shit. He stood in the toilet cubicle, his back against the door. In his left hand he held his intergalactic porn comic open at the page where Aurelia is fucked by an alien while contemplating open-mouthed the menacing approach of a superbly mounted and splendidly erect farm animal. There must be a mathematical formula accounting for the design and measurement of all the elements on display here. The proportions were infallible: the fullness of the cartoon character's lips to the size of their gape; the roundness of her breasts to the waspishness of her waist; the pallid smoothness of her skin to the dusky ruggedness of the animal's hide; the sweetness of her pained expression to the hideous snarl of the alien. The scene might inspire pathos or horror, could imaginably move some persons to reflections on power relations between the genders or on species-specific endowments of multifarious kinds, but to Luigi, and to the many men who either did or might exploit such material, its most powerful effect was physiological, firing and tweaking, as the pages turned, just those transmitters that had evolved to determine priapic engorgement in the adult male of the tribe. In his right hand, Luigi gripped his eleven centimetres, his fleshly shaft of innocent delight, squeezing it between strokes, petting it, pampering it like a much loved hamster. For all response, it twitched. He turned the page to see the line-drawn animal's phallus half-engulfed by Aurelia's jaws. This was where Luigi's previous self-pleasuring attempt earlier that evening had faltered, where stiffness had failed and detumescence, like a hurtling ebb tide, had set in. In that instant, his masculine identification with the beast of burden, the donkey, *il sommaro*, had without warning struck him as questionable. This niggling nexus of erectile failure and existential doubt had coagulated at a level of consciousness that it was impossible for Luigi – as indeed it would be for any man – instantly to access. The crescendo of arousal that this page, this particular depiction of dual violation, oral and vaginal, had accomplished for Luigi on several past occasions depended, he now intuited, on his momentary sense of kinship with the hugely-hung donkey, a natural-enough fantasy for a man of Luigi's centimetric insecurity. Given the voluminous attractions of the reassuringly paper-thin Aurelia, any man might be forgiven for wishing to take the donkey's place and for supposing that Aurelia would be flatteringly grateful for such a metamorphosis in her assailant, indeed might cooperate with all the more alacrity in heft of haunch. Yet if Luigi had experienced earlier that evening a failure at precisely this page, a page that had brought him to a successful judder-and-spurt on five previous occasions, it was the dawning and yet unarticulated sense that to be placed, by anyone at all, let alone by some anonymous sneering graphic-artist type, in the position of an ass, was demeaning. Luigi had never much liked animals of any variety. Donkeys were, in his view, filthy and stupid creatures that he associated with his louse-infested cousins in Puglia. Viewing this page now, with its mixed charge of memories, Luigi took evasive action. He restricted his focus to Aurelia's mouth, blanking out every part of the donkey save one and, as his hand quickened and he felt the crowning moment approach, he closed his eyes and pictured Gilberte attaining an ecstasy similar to his own while he laboured, tilled and ploughed her with his mighty and asinine prong. As Luigi's semen slapped and spilled against the porcelain, his left hand closed the adult comic. Sensing that the book's utility was now spent, and moved by a spasm of generosity toward the Universal Onanist, Luigi slung the comic into the far left-hand corner of the cubicle, where it came to rest upon its spine, its pages fanning gently between partition wall and long-handled brush.

↔↔↔↔↔

On the eve of Eric's departure for France, his father had knocked on his bedroom door, entered and said, 'I fear you are something of a butterfly, Eric: a person blown about on any passing gust or fancy.' Eric had heard this in astonishment. His father had smiled askance and muttered, 'Good night then,' and had withdrawn, a ghost fusing with the shadows of the darkening landing. Never before had his father, a man of few words and fewer demonstrable affections, ever spoken to him, however briefly, in such a personal vein. Yet it was not until several months had passed that Eric, finding himself alone, cold, hungry and penniless in a dingy hostel in Thionville, had pondered the matter rather than the manner of his father's declaration, concluding that his assessment was right and fair and to be taken as a compliment, butterflies being often beautiful and seldom harmful.

A better figure of analogy for Eric's approach to living, though one not likely to occur to his father, was that of the restless hitchhiker. Rather than plan out his life's journey in detail, selecting with care his destination, stopovers, means of conveyance and expected times of departure and arrival, Eric preferred, when he sensed that it was time again to sally forth, to place himself, as it were, at a busy turnpike and to entrust his future to a combination of chance and the caprice of people as yet unencountered, in the blithe expectation that such risk would bring its own rewards and that the process of travel would be the more exhilarating.

This relinquishment of responsibility for his own fortunes sprang from an alliance of two factors: on the one hand, the distrust – at times congealing into contempt – which he harboured for the principal determinations of his life and character thus far, *viz.* family, class, religion, history, friendships, language, nation, culture, schooling, fashion; on the other hand, the dawning comprehension that precisely because his character and life appeared thus determined any choice that he could call his own would ineluctably and from its inception be ill-motivated and ill-conceived, to the point of illegitimacy. What mattered to him was not that he was in Grandgobier, but that he was no longer in England: Lyon, Bordeaux, Germany, Sweden, Macchu Picchu or Idaho might have done just as well. He felt he had escaped from a crushing future of mediocre duties, routines and pastimes, though into quite what company, life and occupation remained a mystery of barely embryonic interest. The main task – to cast himself adrift upon the world, yielding to the mercy of elemental humanity – had to some degree been accomplished.

If, as some maintain, the illusion of selfhood depends either on a recognition by the particular self of its own accumulated content, amassed from a flow of experience, or on its conscious projection into a future, Eric's case was hopeless and he appeared condemned to a life of inauthenticity. Yet his choosing not to choose; his wilful submission to randomness, whim and risk; his surrender of responsibility and freedom; his counter-evolutionary impulse, as if possessed not of a selfish but of a self-destruct gene; his brazen disregard for his own reason; his flouting of elementary personal interests; his eager capitulation to each and every assault and assailant – without the rewards and pleasures promised by a more coherent and resolute masochism: these traits nonetheless constituted – the paradox has to be allowed – a specific and resolute mode of living, an existential self-positioning from which, having in part suspended the operation of some of the aforesaid determinations (class, schooling, family and religion, say) and having thoroughly jettisoned others (fashion, friendships and nation, say) he might embark upon a dismantling of his character, which in its turn and in the fullness of time might allow for the transformation, recovery and refoundation of yet other determinations (language, culture and history, perhaps). Only of course with the wisdom of a distant hindsight might Eric ever hope to interpret in this or in any other way the wellsprings of his current custom of resignation, indiscriminate deference, and withdrawal of the will. In the meantime, the day-to-day conduct of his life, never quite instinctual, was certainly pre-conscious.

↔↔↔↔↔

Tomec stepped from the lift. They were all here: the Gypsy, the Portuguee, the African and the little guy. Bobrán was sitting at his machine number twenty, staring and yawning and rubbing his left cheek with his left fist. He hadn't turned when the lift doors clanked open. Alphonse had come tripping up the stairs and was now at his machines checking product. Fernando, standing to the rear of his machine sixteen, a rag dangling from his right hand, glanced at Tomec, then resumed his polishing of the machine side. Jean was hidden by the huge semi-automatic, but could be glimpsed as its press opened: his face seemed to Tomec to be frozen in a scowl.

Tomec wandered round the floor, checked a window he knew to be screwed shut, leaned against the wall at the top of the stairs, watched the clock over the lift door, its second hand doing little jerks. Fernando walked up to him, stood opposite him. Again Tomec pictured Fernando in ancient Brundisium, at the quayside. The Portuguee had a face like one of Pasolini's film extras, not pretty but compelling scrutiny and evoking worlds of unaccountable experience. Tomec had wanted to ask Fernando to sit: yes, that was it. Now the Portuguee was clicking his fingers in front of Tomec's face. 'Fucking-where are you, man? On fucking-which planet? You don't look ready to tackle intruders!' Tomec took in the man's jowls, his lips, his light stubble. 'I was having a bit of a dream,' he conceded. Fernando nodded and shook his head. Tomec wondered why the man had come to stand opposite him. 'Can I do something for you?' Tomec asked. 'Fucking-can you!' Fernando answered.

'You asked me if I like poetry,' Fernando said. 'Last time you came up.' 'So I did,' Tomec said. 'I can't remember why.' Fernando made to move away, but Tomec stopped him. He gestured at the rag Fernando was holding in his left hand. 'I'm polishing my machines,' Fernando said. Tomec nodded.

'I think I was wondering whether you liked Pessoa,' Tomec said. 'Who?'
'Fernando Pessoa, the poet.' 'Sure,' Fernando replied. Then, as if inspired,
'How fucking-do you get to be a security man? What do they pay you?'
Tomec looked surprised. 'It's not much better and you have to learn martial
arts.' 'What's the point then?' 'Working nights has advantages. You can be
alone for hours. I like to be alone. So you read poetry, do you? Do you read
Pessoa?' 'No. I just heard of him. Isn't he dead?' 'Forty years now.' 'Oh.' 'You
should read him.' 'Why?' 'His poetry's beautiful.' 'Beautiful,' Fernando said,
pressing the word flat between tongue and palate. 'Women like poetry, right?'
'Some do,' Tomec confirmed. Fernando flicked his rag at his knee. 'Thing is:
I want to give a lady friend a present. Something personal. Something she
could keep. And like.' Tomec caught the drift. 'Sounds a great idea. Assuming
the lady likes poetry. Pessoa was Portuguese. You could read the poems in the
original.' 'She doesn't know any Portuguese.' 'Well, she could read them in
French, while you read them in Portuguese. They sound better in Portuguese.'
'How do you know?' 'You're right. How can I possibly know?'

Maryse had told Fernando she had once been enrolled at the university
to study *Lettres*. She had joked about the fact that lots of women students
do a little prostitution on the side to balance their budgets, but that not a
lot of working girls do any studying. Fernando couldn't see what was funny
about that. It was a kind of talk he didn't like. He had grinned a bit anyway
to oblige.

Tomec had made his mind up now. He was going to ask the Portuguee
to sit. His face was perfect. He was a man in the crowd. Just as much as
Bobrán was the peasant boy. Both were perfect. This place is a quarry, a face-
mine. 'I'll bring you in my copy of Pessoa,' he said. 'It has Portuguese on
one page and French on the other.' 'Did this Pessoa write love poetry?' 'Kind
of,' Tomec said, racking his brains. 'Let me think. Wait.' Fernando flicked
his rag again. 'There's a poem to Lydia,' Tomec said. 'I don't remember the
title. It's about a river. It goes like this. It's probably better in Portuguese:
"Come and sit down with me, Lydia, on the bank of the river. / Quietly let
us watch it flowing and learn / That life is passing, and we are not holding
hands. / (Let us hold hands.)" Tomec watched while Fernando repeated the
words. 'Is that it?' he asked. 'No. That's just the beginning. I can't remember
the second verse.' 'I like it all right,' Fernando said. 'Which river is he talking
about?' 'I don't know. I don't remember. I'm not sure he says.' 'If it's the
Douro, I'll give her that poem. The Douro is personal.' Tomec thought a

little, then said. 'It probably *is* the Douro. Almost definitely. I'll bring you in my copy of the book. My girlfriend gave it to me.' Fernando looked up. 'She did?' 'Uh-huh.' 'So it's really a good present for a woman who likes poetry?' 'Absolutely. Pessoa was a great poet. You must read it too.' 'Why me? I'm not much of a reader.' 'She may expect it. She'll probably want to talk about it. That's normal. You could tell her about the river.' Fernando's face lit up at this suggestion, then darkened just as rapidly. 'What do you know about the Douro?' 'Nothing, I just . . .' Fernando had turned away. 'Look,' Tomec said, 'I'll bring you in my copy.' 'Oh, fucking-sure.' Fernando said, over his shoulder. Tomec called out his name. 'Look, Dos Santos, if I was Portuguese, I would be proud of Pessoa. He was a man to boast of. I rather wish he'd been Polish.' Fernando turned back toward Tomec. 'Fucking-how could he have been Polish with a name like that?' 'Well, Pessoa means person, doesn't it?' Tomec said, on a hunch. 'In Polish, he might have been called "Osoba." "Osoba" is our word for person.' Fernando had lost interest.

↔↔↔↔↔↔

Bobrán had ceased rubbing his cheek with his fist and had risen, stretching, to check the latest pieces as they issued from machine moulds fifteen and twenty. At each machine he emptied the floor tray into its respective threshing tub. He saw that the hoppers were more than half full and sat back down. He hunched his shoulders and flexed his toes, observing the ends of his plimsolls as they curled and creased. His eyes remained unclosed, his lips unmumbling. For a moment he had almost fallen asleep. He was not tempted to drop his guard again. As so often, in that brief twilight consciousness Bobrán had espied himself watching in horror through a casement the man he had killed – now mysteriously resuscitated – renew his attack on his sister Yitoune, ripping her dress from her shoulders, while an unseen force hauled him back from the window, his flailing fists meeting not brittle panes but empty air, the assault on his sister proceeding unwitnessed but sufficiently imagined, Bobrán's delicate eye spared any glimpse of sisterly breast. Hungry for the reassurance of banal reality, Bobrán assessed his cramped and neon-lit world: Alphonse was reading; Jean could be glimpsed each time his machine mould opened; the Polack security man was stepping into the lift, his right foot frozen mid-air as Bobrán looked away: dead men do not return to rape again. Not on this earth. Dead men stay dead. Bobrán would have to talk to Joseph's brother. Albert. He was real. Marcel had mentioned someone else – a friend of Albert perhaps, or a reporter. What can I say to Joseph's brother? 'How did Joseph fall – and why?' he asks in his letter. 'Did you see him slip?' Albert wants to know. It's hard to talk of such things to a man whose face you've never seen. What do I owe him? He must have a face something like that of his brother. A bit older or younger, otherwise much the same. The nose bigger or smaller, the cheeks broader or flatter, the eyes larger or closer together. That kind of difference. He says he's angry. An angry face, a face a bit like Joseph's but angry. I never once saw Joseph angry, even when he had cause. Maybe if Joseph had angered a little easier . . . but what good are maybes? Listen, I'll say: since you ask how he fell, I'll tell you, though I didn't see him slip. The truth is I heard him go. The sound of his boot on the plank, a little squeak, then an 'oh' of surprise. Just surprise. He slipped. Simple as that. Five storeys. It takes a second or two. To me it seemed longer. He screamed his lungs out all the way down. You would too. I know I would. Then a thwack. Then more screaming, but pain this time, not terror. I was looking straight down at him now. His body was twisted up and jerking, his feet kicked once or twice, his voice had gone. Bobrán felt a stiffness in his own neck. They want the truth? He circled his head slowly, trying to loosen up. He rolled his shoulders, one at a time. It was only Tuesday and he was exhausted and some stranger asked for truth. He had to be at least this exhausted if he was ever to sleep. Either sleep seized him by the throat unawares or it didn't come at all. If there was a mattress here in the corner to throw himself on, he would sleep there right now. He needed to get away, leave this place, shrug off this mood. A weekend with Moritz and his sister Heike. In Germany at some concert. A distraction. A holiday of all things! Then come back and talk to Joseph's brother. Some fun before the shit flies. If shit has to fly. Falling asleep exhausted in a car or a van, in Moritz's arms, the sound of other vehicles racing past and the car's own engine. Thinking and dreaming this thing right through. I don't want to see Joseph's brother cry. A face something like Joseph's crumpling as a hand rises to wipe an eye. I don't want to see his grief. And I don't want to look away. Joseph is in heaven, and his brother had better not weep. I haven't wept since that morning. It's disrespectful to weep. I can see you're upset, Moritz had said. Why aren't you crying? Your friend's dead. You should cry. And I told him, Because he's in heaven now. Moritz laughed. I could have slapped him. Instead I stared. He's in goddamn heaven, I repeated. Moritz could see I meant it. People pretend they don't believe in such things, heaven and hell, but at bottom everyone does. Of course they do. You believe in whatever's obvious. For instance: it's raining outside. That's obvious. We know exactly what it's like. We don't have to go out in it and get wet. It's no less obvious that there's a heaven. Everybody knows what it's like. Everyone has the thought of a reward some day. Or at least a rest. We know what has to come after this life. Nobody has to tell us. That's what I'll say to Joseph's brother. He has no reason in the world to cry. And as for 'why did he fall?' What's the truth of that? He fell because he was tired, clumsy, unlucky. I'll tell you the truth, I'll say, just don't ask me to testify. Any trouble with the police and I have to leave the city. Fast. Except that I can't leave my mother. She needs me. She has got more used to living in only one place than anyone – least of all a Gypsy – ever should. She feels safe and comfortable in her trailer here. I can't leave her and don't want to uproot her. You don't have to understand. As long as I live here – which is as long as my mother lives here – the police own me. You don't need to know why. I'd like to help you. Joseph was a friend. But there's nothing to be done. Besides, your brother didn't die on account of some boss's negligence. He was clumsy and that day he was tired. It had rained. I should have stayed closer to him. He was always slip-ping and stumbling. I had caught him more than once. Over the coming weekend – in the car, on the back seat with Heike or Moritz – Bobrán would think what to say, which words to use. Who would be driving? Did Moritz drive? Bobrán had to figure out what to say to Albert. Faced with Joseph's brother, he might become tongue-tied and stuttery. Then the thoughts would press in from all sides tempting him to do something crazy or dangerous or painful – to make them go quiet. First he needed to know what to say and then he needed to think how to say it. If Moritz drove, he could think and sleep next to Heike. How long could it take to get to Cologne? He'd felt a buzz with Heike earlier, like she fancied him but was surprised. He liked that. He was through with women, but the idea that his lover's sister fancied him, or might do, gave him a tingly feeling. She had been more than friendly. She reminded him of Sophie. Tall and fair. Not pretty exactly, too heavy in the jaw, too serious. Sophie was much prettier. Heike was the kind of woman who looks like a dyke but probably isn't. He remembered Sophie telling him when they first met that he was that most attractive kind of man: strong but obviously intent on seeming less strong than he was, sensitive, the kind who appears gay but then isn't. He had wondered how wrong she could be. At that time, he still thought he was bi. Later he had decided to specialize, to

concentrate on what worked best for him, surrendering to his true preferences. Except it was triumph not surrender he felt. A trip to Germany to see
a concert – some man who hasn't played in public for years. Go along for the
ride. Why not? The music will be German of course, brash and loud. Never
mind. I don't want to talk to Albert until I'm good and ready. I'll know what
to say before I see him. You want to know the truth about how and why your
brother fell? You think maybe he was pushed? Maybe someone greased the
plank? That kind of thing can happen. But I was the only person up there
with him. If anyone tells you I would do a thing like that, they're lying. Who
wanted him dead? No one. Who particularly wanted him alive? Again, no
one. Except me. And you. And, frankly, we didn't count much, did we? Not
when it mattered. I was a friend and close at hand. You were family, but far
away. What's the difference? Neither of us could save him. The contractors
couldn't have cared less. Of course they couldn't. Why would they? There's
no shortage of blacks and Arabs and gyppoes and Portuguees – not to mention out-of-work français de souche – eager to fill the boots of anyone unlucky
enough to slip and crack his head open. Negligence? You can call it that. No
one was wearing a harness. No one ever does. Except if the boss gets wind of
an inspection. I don't wear a harness. I wouldn't want to. It gets in the way.
It slows you up. Don't look at me like that. Listen. There are two sorts of
people who should never work up high: those prone to giddy spells and those
who are clumsy. Joseph was both. Joseph used to trip over himself walking
down the street on a day it hadn't even rained. Didn't even have to leave his
laces undone. I never stopped telling him. Bobrán laughed. He imagined
Albert, faceless Albert, grinning wryly in recognition. He could see the grin,
a big grin, a grin full of sorrow and longing, but he couldn't see the face it
lived in. Bobrán shook his head and looked around. He was talking to himself. Didn't everybody? The Ivorian certainly did. The Portuguee too. Not so
sure about the old man at machine twenty-one. He probably didn't have much
to say to himself, for all the books he read. It would be nice sometimes to
slow down, do nothing, not to have to go away merely to rest. Empty time.
Home time. Bobrán had never had much empty time. If he had empty time
enough perhaps he could wriggle free of his terrors. The memory of killing
the man who raped Yitoune never bothered him. He could remember any
single detail, however tiny, but chose not to. What came to him in nightmares
was the terror that the man had not died, or that he could return to life, which

– if you thought long enough about it – was probably the same thing. If only he had a few weeks or months of empty time, free of work, to get healthy again, to sleep each night in Moritz's arms – he never had nightmares there. Think of sleeping like that for weeks on end, not just Saturdays and Sundays. Knowing it was going to last and last. He could find other peachy skinned boys. But he didn't want anyone else. What could he tell Albert? Everything was so different with Moritz. It had used to seem wrong to do it more than once with the same person. Before that it had seemed crazy and daring to do it with anyone who wasn't close family. Odd there are so many rules and laws against doing it in the family. You can't talk about it, can't be blatant, otherwise the authorities, social people want to move in, trample all over you. Then when people have sex with the same person all the time, what do they do? They go and get married! So they become family! It's creepy! Then of course they yearn for an outsider again, to make them feel less weird. Moritz would never be family. He was far too good for that. 'Go home!' is what I'll tell Joseph's brother. Go home, there's nothing for you to find out. Your brother worked without safety gear. So what? We all do. Anyone who is a stickler for safety wastes all our time, makes himself unpopular. We get bonuses in our pocket at the end of the month if we get ahead of schedule. I liked Joseph, we got on well enough, he was a good worker, but he was clumsy. He knew he wasn't safe. Everybody knew it. He told me he was looking for a ground-job. He wasn't looking hard enough. Go home now. And remember: he's in heaven. Do Africans believe in heaven? Of course they do. I'll tell them he didn't suffer. I'll say it was over in a flash. He just fell. I heard him say 'oh,' like someone slipping on a pavement. I looked down and there he was. Quiet. Kind of peaceful. They'll believe that. Go home now. The truth! I rushed down the ladders to be by his side, jumped the last four or five metres, landing badly, hurting my knee, but got to him before he went. He muttered something I couldn't make out. Then the supervisor was all over me, hissing in my face and I talked so quietly he had to shut up and listen. He gave me the day off and I went to Moritz's, caught him just as he was leaving. So we went to bed. The first time in a bed. After that we had breakfast. We ate liver sausage. Moritz made German coffee, long and weak. Then we made love again, like never before, morsel by morsel, like time didn't matter. I wanted all of him, greedy as a pup, lapping him up. I drank his seed and licked my lips. I wanted more. He had more to give. I've never had such a thirst for anyone. The next day the supervisor called me into the site-trailer and said, No one saw what happened. You and Gbenye were alone up there. If I say I saw you help him on his way, who's going to doubt my word? Everyone knows Gypsies hate blacks. So if anyone talks to you, you know what to say. Till this thing blows over, everyone wears safety gear. Yeah, even you. That lasted ten days. There was no investigation. That's the truth. Some of it. But it isn't for Albert's ears. No, I'll say. I can't help you. And when my turn comes, as you say in your letter, who will I be able rely on? It's a fair question. Maybe nobody. But I still can't help you.

↔↔↔↔↔

When the phone rang, Sarah leapt out of the shower, dashed and snatched up the receiver. She wished she hadn't. It was her elder sister, Simone. Sarah was thinking her father might call.

Simone was complaining about her boyfriend. Sarah had heard it too often. About once a fortnight for years. She'd been eleven when Simone and Fabrice had started going out. She couldn't see why Simone went on suffering. Such weakness made her sad. It was so undignified. He was humiliating her. She should just leave him.

'Fabrice is just cold,' Simone was saying. 'That's all there is to it. It isn't his fault. But if I was ill, I don't think he'd visit me: he'd wait till I was better. If I died, I don't think he'd bring flowers to my grave.'

Sitting cross-legged on the bed, Sarah shook her hair free. It was well rinsed but there were still some suds on her shoulder. She patted them with her towel. 'What are you waiting for to leave him?' Sarah asked. 'But it's been so long,' Simone replied. 'I've wanted him so much. I've been so patient. I don't want to give up now. Just some spark of affection. I don't expect much. He isn't a bad person. He's just mean. And not only with money. With himself. With his time. And in bed. You know. I don't expect him to say he loves me. He never has.'

Sarah held the receiver trapped between left ear and shoulder, rubbing her hair dry with the towel. She hated what she was hearing. She wasn't sure yet how to react this evening. She never calculated it. She just let it happen. Sometimes she listened politely, stupefied or bored. Sometimes she got angry, 'Just kick him away! He's no good.' Sometimes she'd be plaintive, 'How can you be so weak! Show yourself some respect!' Or she'd feed her sister counsellor-type questions: 'So how does that make *you* feel?' Tonight she wanted to weep.

Before she hung up, Simone would always dutifully ask Sarah how *she* was and usually Sarah, not wanting to oppress her sister with her permanently happy excitement about life – including her man of the moment or her (always brief) man-free state of carefree non-attachment – would invent some complaint or misgiving, blow up some fault or grievance. But when she finally put the phone down, Sarah would find she was thinking about the invented, or at least inflated, fault and that talking about it to humour her sister had made it real enough to bother her.

Sarah had decided for once to say exactly what she felt about her life. Maybe Simone ought to hear that it is possible to be happy with a man, at least provisionally.

'So what about you and . . . what's his name . . . ?' Simone asked her, on cue. 'His name's Tomec.' 'Papa said he's an artist and middle-aged.' Simone was trying to prompt something critical. Sarah smiled. Her father never liked any of her men. She didn't introduce them to him any longer. But she could talk about them over the phone. Discussing her men with her father was all right. Sarah never felt any pressure to make them seem better, worse or different. Besides, her father's judgements belonged to some other realm of feeling. Parallel. Interesting but not pertinent.

'Tomec is fine,' Sarah told Simone. 'Odd. Unusual. It's visceral with us.' 'Visceral? Physical? That sounds good, I suppose. Fabrice . . .' 'No. Not just physical. Mental too. Viscerally mental. He thrills me. For now. It could be over tomorrow. I don't want to talk about it. I won't mind if it ends. He makes love to me – to me, looking me in the eye, seeing me not himself – as if nothing else mattered and then, when I've fallen asleep, gets up and works as though that's all he cares about. When he eats, you'd think he loves nothing but food. He eats like a farmer. Great slurping sounds.' 'I wouldn't put up with that,' Simone remarked, as if to show she had some standards. 'No. It's all right,' Sarah said. 'Don't you see?' Simone didn't see and didn't know what to say. How could table manners be so lightly dismissed?

'When does he sleep then?' Simone asked. 'Sorry?' Sarah said. 'If, as you say, he works while you sleep . . .' 'Oh, heck, I don't know. I'm not sure he *does* sleep,' Sarah replied, irritated. 'Does he snore? Fabrice snores . . .' 'Snore? For pity's sake! I'm not sure he even breathes. I must remember to check.' Sarah felt that she had been tricked into saying too much. It wasn't

Simone's fault. It was just her way. Any conversation with Simone, as soon as it touched on men, seemed to act as a kind of pollutant. She was going to have to face that fact. Sarah made an excuse and put the phone down. Poor Simone. Poor little big sister.

39. Science, Intermittence and Voice.

Twelve workers. Of the thirteen people employed that night at Établissements Boucan, only one was immune to feelings of enmity, revulsion, or workaday shock and antipathy toward his fellow humans, alive or dead, close or distant, there or gone.

Contemplating the remaining twelve men in order to chart them on a scale from most to least shockable – to adopt shock as the common denominator for the various sentiments under review and to register as the key quantifier the number of his fellows to whom each worker had already that particular evening responded with some degree of qualifying shock– it may be observed that the subjects fall into four broad categories:

> **high** shockability (experiencing shock in relation to six or more workmates
> – ESR > or = 6);
> **mean** shockability (experiencing shock in relation to four or five workmates
> – ESR = 4 or 5);
> **low** shockability (experiencing shock in relation to two or three workmates
> – ESR = 2 or 3);
> **sole** shockability (experiencing shock in relation to just one workmate
> – ESR = 1).

With a pleasing neatness never to be taken for granted in any field of human-scientific research, each of the four shockability categories (high, medium, low and sole) have been shown to accommodate precisely three of our subjects, i.e. 25% of our working sample.

To enter into specifics, taking the high-shockability coefficient (ESR > or = 6), it may be observed that Jean, Marcel and Salvatore scored respectively 9, 7 and 6. In the case of Jean, reactions of shock, outrage, fear, anger, scorn or at least annoyance were elicited readily in respect of any of his workmates, but so far this evening had been triggered by Alphonse, Tomec, Marcel, Salvatore, Mathieu, Rachid, Jacques and Philippe. In the last three instances, any actual encounter with the 'Arab,' the 'clodhopper' and the 'Marseillais former-union-rep Commie screwball' [*sic*: Jean's terms, see appendix 3] had been unnecessary, since mere sight and passing reference in the intercepted conversation of others had proved sufficient to fire the responses.

Marcel was also susceptible to animosity, though in his case this most frequently assumed a racial or aesthetic form: while he experienced a low-level skin-revulsion toward the black African, the parchment-grey Algerian and the epidermically white Pole, not to mention his naturally swarthy and occupationally sun-burnished cousin, his inability to meet the eyes of the Englishman and the Italian was occasioned predominantly by what he perceived to be their respectively native inelegance and personal ugliness. Interestingly, Marcel's inevitable displeasure at Salvatore's olive skin was in some measure offset by the man's masculine bearing and feminine comeliness. Be that as it may, Marcel cultivated his scorn for the Sicilian in terms that were cultural rather than aesthetic or racial: Marcel could not help but distrust the Sicilian's see-through eagerness to please bosses, unions, and plausibly influential fellow workers, while disparaging his self-projection as bourgeois-to-be (attaché case, university accoutrements, abstemiousness in regard of tobacco, alcohol and even, Marcel dimly sensed, in matters of pussy – Salvatore's very hand-exerciser spoke to Marcel of some scrabbling resolve to waste no minute, loosen no belt, risk no indiscipline, throw off no fetter, sip at no rising sap of guiltless pleasure).

Salvatore himself, the subject who scored the third-highest ESR-coefficient, harboured many a feeling of contempt vis-à-vis his coworkers, yet such feelings had all been, as it were, pre-purged of the grosser forms of prejudice. The Sicilian would talk down to Jean, Jacques and Mathieu, deeming them all to be of scant *long-term* consequence; likewise, Salvatore would disregard the social and political views of Alphonse and Rachid, assuming these to be uninformed by any true understanding of European historical and industrial realities; in analogous fashion, Salvatore perceived the Portuguee as conforming to a national type (over-diligent to the point of self-sacrifice, concomitantly putting other workers to shame, etc.) and the Brit as a maverick departure from any obvious behavioural norm or perhaps, mutatis mutandis, a confirmation of his nation's notoriously ambiguous eccentricity. Although the Sicilian believed himself, on the basis of his will and resolve and ambition, to be infallibly superior to his fellows, and indeed had nightmares in which he was much abased by the discovery that he too bore the stamp of their lowly origins, his feelings of animosity or shock had been focused so far this evening on just six of his fellows: the Portuguee and the old peasant, on account of their display of puerile, self-indulgent and possibly crypto-sexual horseplay; Jean, for his simultaneously arrogant and insolent reaction when informed of the forthcoming union meeting; Philippe, for his superciliously polite insistence on the prior claims of his beer belly over Salvatore's own more cerebral solicitation; Marcel, for finding therein an occasion for merriment; and, finally, Luigi, for having spurned his invitation to accompany him to the coffee-machine.

Owing to constraints of space, our comments in respect of the medium-, low- and sole-shockability-coefficient categories will be confined to a small number of contrastive features. For greater elucidation of the points made here, the reader is referred to the seven hundred pages of initial findings herewith appended: through an assiduous redeployment of the methodology exemplified here, the attentive reader will be able reliably to reach identical conclusions. Fresh studies of longitudinal detail and comparative length, on both this and further sample-groups, are under preparation, though methodological continuity, given the present economic weather – not to mention the vagaries of scientific caprice – cannot be guaranteed.

To complete, as promised, this partial review of early findings, the subsequent may be stated. Within the medium-shockability target range (ESR = 4–5), the revulsions of the three respondents observed (Eric, Luigi and Bobrán), though each ordinarily prostrate to sentimentalities of disgust or even distaste, etc., possessed character foibles that countered said impulses, respectively: an ebulliently optimistic albeit exoticizing curiosity in his newfound national home and acquaintance; a hard-learnt attitude of personal isolation from industrial events and people; an unexplained tolerance of other people, a quality not to be mistaken for indifference.

In the low-shockability category (ESR = 2–3), the three personages implicated (Alphonse, Fernando and Tomec) might well prove in any imaginable social setting to be poorly reactive to stimuli of human discordance: stated less technically, they were variously ill-equipped for negative emotions more acidulous than mild disapproval; or, to reposition the same datum more colloquially, each of the three tended, for whatever reasons, actually rather to like people.

Finally, the sole-shockability group (ESR = 1), comprising Jacques, Rachid and Philippe, necessitates further characterization. Jacques (as has been exhaustingly noted in Chapter 35, section 3, of appended report) was temperamentally unaware of anyone who did not stubbornly resolve to befriend or otherwise to impinge upon him. Accordingly, he really noticed only Philippe and Fernando; moreover, so far this evening, only Philippe had occasioned any kind of ripple in Jacques' mood and this on account of the Marseillais' state of untimely near-inebriation. As for Rachid, the depth of his bereavement, very lately compounded with an intensity of post-impregnative joy, ensured that almost anything experienced and anyone encountered at work must fail to engage his frayed emotions; so far this evening the only exception to this had been Bobrán, whose death- (or at least injury-) defying banister ascent had outraged the Algerian's resurgent attachment to life. In Philippe's instance, ordinary intemperance was trammelled by a sickly unwillingness to condemn others, an obsessive capacity for sympathy (and, when that failed, for tolerance) and an extremist-hippy conviction that to understand is to forgive and that 'there but for fortune, etc.'; however, under provocation, any such forbearance and magnanimity could occasionally be suspended and this evening had in fact been waived once already with respect to one particular person – himself. For the Marseillais' fleeting urge to hurt and to harm his allegedly and, on cursory reflection, credibly deceiving spouse had shocked him, appalling his reason and affronting his sense of decorum. Mercifully, thanks again to the clemency of his nature, this shock was now receding just as steadily as his awareness of the liberating benefits promised by undisputed cuckoldom advanced.

The thirteenth man – Mathieu – in spite of his frequent operational recourse to yelling, and regardless of the shop-floor belief that he was as capable of anger, outrage, shock and indignation as any other man, was in intimate fact a stranger to all such feelings, dwelling, as it were, in a realm beyond the reach of what he considered to be irrelevant others. His experience of living, and in particular of military discipline on the one hand and of a solitary all-consuming romantic love on the other, had coalesced one day to deliver to him all sealed and certain the astonishing and irreversible determination to bracket from his sensibilities the run of ordinary humanity, to treasure for the remainder of his allotted span just two things on this earth: the priceless love that was being stolen from him inexorably and far too soon and the musical passion that he had stumbled upon carelessly and far too late. All else was dross with which it would often be necessary to deal but that could never be permitted to hurt or distract.

↔↔↔↔↔

In the raw-materials room, Jacques and Philippe were reclining on adjacent pallets, each man half-sitting half-lying atop a pile of firm but gradually yielding sacks of plastic granules. Twice Philippe had risen and walked over to press the light-switch timer, but on the third occasion, to Jacques' shrugged acquiescence, he had given this up. The light that filtered through the scratched plastic flaps hanging in the opening between this huge room and the plastics shop floor was sufficient for the two men to make out each other's gesture and expression.

So far Jacques had done most of the talking, his left hand occasionally slapping his left knee for emphasis, his right hand gripping one of the apples he had brought in to work. As Philippe listened to Jacques' disjointed account of his doctor's appointment, he smoked or, between cigarettes, played with his packet or lighter. He was interested in Jacques' story, laughed as he pictured the doctor's mangy old dog, but wondered what point was being made. Also he was awaiting his turn to speak. He kept revising what he would say. It had to be light, easy, throwaway. He wanted to balance his surprise at Odile's betrayal with his sudden excitement at the possibility of a future without her.

Jacques was laying out his reasons for not liking to take pills. He had never taken pills, he said. He didn't like putting strange chemicals in his body, he said. Philippe told of a neighbour who was half-paralysed after a stroke: he hadn't wanted to take pills either. Jacques was quiet. 'You don't seem persuaded,' Philippe remarked. 'When I got home from the chemist's I read the small print,' Jacques said. 'Side effects: impotence.' Philippe lit a cigarette. 'Side effects don't happen to everyone. But they have to be mentioned. There are legal reasons. Besides, if you're dead or paralysed . . .' 'No. You're right,' Jacques said. There was a silence, which Philippe broke. 'If I was you I'd tell your lady. She'll tell you what matters most to her.' Jacques said nothing.

Mathieu came through the flaps and hit the light switch. Seeing the two men on the pallets, he flicked his right hand at them and said, 'You're all right' and returned to the plastics section. Philippe took a long puff on his cigarette, pushing the smoke slowly back out through his nostrils. 'You're not going to take those tablets,' Philippe stated. Jacques shook his head slowly. 'Go see another doctor then. Go see a man. A man will understand. Maybe there's a different kind of drug. Some other approach.' Jacques nodded. 'All I can see is that dog,' he then said. 'I don't want to wind up like that dog. Do you like dogs?' 'I'd rather keep a pig than a dog. Pigs are cleaner.' 'You never kept a pig.' 'I had a dog once,' Philippe said.

Jacques took a bite out of his apple. Philippe flicked his cigarette away onto the cement floor. They got up and ambled toward the plastics shop floor. Philippe wondered if this was the moment. Why not? It ought to take Jacques' mind off those tablets. And maybe make him feel he's lucky he's in love. Philippe halted in the pool of light before the hanging plastic flaps. 'Guess what happened to me today,' he said. Jacques interrupted his munching. He hoisted his eyebrows. He was no damn good at guessing games. Philippe smiled and said, 'Ah! I'll save you the trouble: I learnt my wife's got herself a fancy man. My sister told me. How about that?' Philippe brushed through the flaps and into the plastics section. Jacques removed his cap and scratched his scalp with the middle finger of the hand that was holding the apple, then he followed Philippe through. Jacques watched Philippe return to his machines; Jacques returned to his. 'He'll say more, when he's feeling right,' Jacques told himself. He glanced over at Philippe. Marseille was looking somehow relieved, no, downright pleased with himself.

↔↔↔↔↔

Back then, Salvatore was fired by a vigorous yet ill-directed ambition. He would like to have money, but money was not his goal; he could imagine the rewards of power or influence, but did not yearn for either: what he craved was respectability, social ease, personal success. He could picture it so well. He would in the fullness of time be elegant, fit, tanned, his hair pepper-and-salt. He would work at something in an office with a broad mahogany desk, well appointed shelving, a well polished parquet floor, photos of his family on discreet display. There would be a landscape painting, an original, on one of the walls. It would be French and local and dependably uplifting. He would have a personal secretary or assistant, neighbours who saluted him in the morning. His children would go to the best schools. His wife would in every likelihood possess an Afghan hound. His opinion and expertise would be sought and heeded. Above all, he would be taken seriously, renowned as a man to be reckoned with.

Yet this ambition, this projection of present fantasy onto a conceivable future, operated only intermittently, since Salvatore's ordinarily lucid vision was liable to sudden misting and his usually solid confidence might at any moment fall prey to the termites of doubt. For there were occasions, sometimes mere instants, sometimes entire days, when Salvatore felt unsettled, uncertain, unequal to any role or responsibility, present or future, imminent or imaginable. The flaw in Salvatore's otherwise promising ambition was its imprecision. While the mahogany desk was imagined in sharp detail – down to the number of its drawers and the motifs of its marquetry – he had not the slightest notion what he should be doing there. With no vocation, bent or ruling passion, the Sicilian had no clear highway to follow in pursuit of his fabled future; instead, he multiplied plausible pathways, scattering his attentions and energies like an angler casting ground bait, hoping against hope that something might eventually bite. In the process, he glimpsed many possibilities. Could he not succeed so well at university as to become an academic or schoolteacher? Might he not rise through the union to become a permanent officer? Might his connection to Laure, and to her family of lawyers and business people, not lead to some serendipitous opening? Perhaps his penning of quasi-philosophical mini-allegories could lead to some coinable celebrity, if not quite fame? Perhaps – and here all purchase on reality was relinquished – his sheer good looks, charm and crystal Italianate diction might see him snatched by some TV or cinema casting director lost on his way to Nice or Grasse, say, and reduced to roaming the side streets of Grandgobier? Salvatore liked to interpret his failure to identify for himself any single calling as evidence of the most politic sagacity, repeating to himself the proverbial warnings about eggs and baskets, and fortunes wagered on a single playing card. Unpossessed of anything so mean and cramped as a calling, he could rely on effort, cunning, resolve and vigilance. He boasted to himself (and frequently to Laure) that he could work harder and at more things simultaneously than anyone he had ever met, and that he owned the cunning of the fox, the will of the mule, and the patience of the puma: indeed, these zoological cornerstones of his self-belief never faltered.

Salvatore wasted no time with people who could not, in any imaginable set of circumstances, promote his personal cause. At university, this ruled out everyone either junior to himself or engaged in a parallel and unconnected field of study. From his social life, it barred those of modest background or stunted aspiration. In his factory and union dealings, he simply overlooked the unpopular and the isolated, the maverick and the clownish. Although courteous, attentive, even solicitous toward professors at university, Laure's family and wealthier friends, union officials and even, among his fellow workers, Philippe, Tomec and Mathieu, toward lesser people he would appear distracted and absorbed, as if anatomizing some great, pressing and intricate truth.

The Sicilian's soaring social ambition, the intermittence of his self-confidence and his feeble focus on practical avenues of self-advancement might all be traced – as we shall perhaps see in later books – to his formative environment and interrupted education on his island of origin. Like drink to lechery, this background was an equivocator: it had both made him and marred him; it had set him up and taken him off; it had first persuaded and then disheartened him.

↔↔↔↔↔

At the San Francisco, Fanny had been sitting for a full fifteen minutes waiting for Julie to join her. The novel she was reading irritated her. Her glass was empty. She didn't want another cigarette. Either Julie could take a break now or she couldn't. No big deal.

Fanny got up, thrust her book in her bag, and went out onto the street. There were lots of people standing around, but there was no one to talk to. Julie had seen her leave. Fanny would hang around for only a minute or two. Julie placed a glass of frothing 1666 on a mat, took the 20-franc bill from a clutch of bony fingers, and shouted to the manager at the till that she was taking her break. He pulled a face but she wasn't looking. As the fingers returned reconfigured as a cup, Julie dumped the change. She heard a thank you and threw a smile. She was too useful to fire. Who else would have stood in at two hours' notice?

'So much for the lull,' Fanny said, as her cousin came toward her. Julie shrugged. 'Look, sorry. Some evenings are like that. The back office is warmer.' 'I've got to go soon.' 'Then let's walk. It's freezing out here.' Fanny took Julie's arm and they walked off down the street.

'So did you speak to Kosal today?' Julie enquired. Fanny heaved a sigh. 'He has taken to writing letters. He's waiting for me to come round.' 'What's wrong with him?' 'He wants me to have his baby. He's told his family. It's a matter of pride now.' 'Well, if you go out with a Cambodian . . .' 'You think Europeans are different?' 'He could be dangerous.' 'I don't think so.' 'You don't want to think so.'

Fanny opened her bag. 'Want one?' 'Sure,' Julie replied. Fanny took out her pack of Royales and her BIC lighter. She placed two cigarettes in her mouth, and bent down. Julie moved in close. The flame sputtered, but the cigarettes lit all right. Fanny handed Julie hers. The young women walked a little way.

'If you had a new boyfriend . . .' Julie said.

'Well, there maybe is somebody . . .'

'You're joking! Since when? You amaze me. You have no one at all for a couple of years, then the same one for months on end, then all of a sudden two at a time.' 'I've finished with Kosal.' 'You've been saying that for months.' 'Well, I mean it.' 'Because he wants a baby.' 'No. But that would be reason enough, don't you think?' 'Why? Wouldn't you like a yellow baby?'

Fanny pulled away from her cousin and halted in the middle of the pavement. 'Come on. You know I'm not like that. If I wanted a goddamn baby, the colour wouldn't matter.'

'So who is this guy?' 'He's nobody. I know nothing about him. He works at the factory.' 'A loser.' 'Nights.' 'Convenient. You won't have to see him much.' Fanny burst out laughing. 'Either I'm transparent or you have insight to burn.' Julie smiled at the compliment. 'What is he this time, a Morroccan? a Spaniard? a Black? What have you got against French men?' 'He's English.' 'English? Jesus! Did you ever go out with a French man?' Fanny said nothing. 'I didn't think so. And since when does Boucan employ English?' 'Boucan employs anyone who'll do the work.'

Fanny took a breath. 'Look, this English guy . . . it's nothing. He kept eyeing me. The guys on the shift were starting to make jokes. So I asked him out.' 'You asked him out?' 'Well, it ought to make things clearer for Kosal. When he sees I'm with someone so completely different, he'll know it's truly over. This guy could not be less like Kosal.' 'Kosal could kill him.' 'Sure. With his little finger. But he won't. Kosal isn't stupid. Where do refugees run?' 'I see you've given it some thought.' 'Sure.'

'Look, I've got to get back to the bar,' Julie said. Fanny nodded and turned.

↔↔↔↔↔

He missed his wife's face most when looking straight into it. At Eric's machine ten, Mathieu slid the safety door back. He seized the product from the mould, shut his bad eye, brought the piece close, lined it up. Twelve pieces to check for irregularities, anomalies, this way, that way. Shutting the press door, head shaking to chase away stray thoughts, Pole with graffiti. Who cares? Gypsy with letter. It's high time all hell broke loose over Boucan's war. Presses clanged shut. Smudged cigarette butt lying on floor, red lipstick: afternoon woman. Damn thoughts. Empty mind! Into that smudge: as good a hook as any speck of dust. He had to ransack every seeming-identical product for hints of difference, unconformity. Till no one could tell the products apart. No detail, no angle, no feature. Chase down particularity, however minute. This way, that. His job and his alone was to patrol the product for identity, compliance. Once, in the early days, with nowhere to go, he had sat with Nadine under blankets in a car. They had undressed only one another's faces: hers beautiful, pained, relaxing beneath his tribute of kisses, shy at first; his rough and lined, never pretty yet hard and gentle too, insistent first but submitting as she grew bold. Now he would sit and stare into that face that was once a crowded stage of rushing thoughts and feelings, stray ideas, odd memories, but had finally grown identical to itself. No detail, angle, feature changed any more. His responsibility, his alone, for the fate of an unchangeable face. Only death could bring alteration now. Nadine who had loathed the static, despising nothing more than the boring, the tedious: if her face could speak, she would say what to do. He missed her face and what it would say. She would be impatient. For a change. Back then, entire nights were spent kissing. Till their tongues ached and their lips swelled and their skin shone from rubbing. For Mathieu, kissing could have sufficed. Her face had become his world. As she healed, her voice returned: moral, even, reasoning, deep, sure but not proud, argumentative, indignant sometimes. And with her voice came desire. At machine nine, Rachid holding product out, pointing to a defect. Mathieu took the piece, turned it, finding the tiny protrusion. He checked the dials. Nothing. Good man, he murmured. Beckoning, he raised finger to eye. Will do, Rachid replied. Mathieu nodded. The Algerian had offered him a cigarette earlier. After all these years he was still tempted. He'd told the new nurse no smoking near Nadine. Her name was Marie. Seemed a good girl. Void thoughts! I who still have thoughts, have only these! Marie mentioned family, responsibilities. Fix on the protrusion. Empty! But there was no approaching Nadine's mindless state. People pursuing mind abatement should see her. I seek only the suspense of brain noise. Hope she is not locked in, thoughts hurtling. Can't be. I've watched it from the start, the chipping away, tiny stroke by stroke. A thousand cuts, with a few to go? Enough waiting! In a lucid rage years before, she had punched him, grabbed his chin in her fist, wrenched his head aside. First you SAVE me then you ENSLAVE me! Speak! What does this face HIDE? what does this lip MEAN? She yanked his lower lip. He lashed out in pain, instinctive. The shrink said, 'we could sedate her.' No. She had got better slowly, and he had learned to speak to her. The Algerian sat, paper on lap, while Mathieu checked machine eight. No faults, nothing. Mathieu waited, eyes closed. Mind like a sink, plug pulled, thoughts draining, gurgling. Whoosh! The image held. Empty. An instant's success. Then across the machine aisle. Gypsy staring down here. Silly tease earlier. Mozart! Had to yell to stay in character. He arrived with African's letter. Waved it at his cousin. None of my business. Damned thoughts. Italian recommending stories, trying to be helpful. The Gypsy often did help. With Britishe, for instance, keeping an eye on his machines, covering for the sap. That student in Metz was pointing the way. Nadine needed to die. Decisions happen while you're asleep, playing music, or doing nothing. Mathematicians wake with the solution, musicians dream their missing riff, poets the rhythmic image. What to do with a beloved wife who has died before your eyes but still breathes? Sleep yields no answer. The safety guard left a slight bounce in the foreman's fingers, his focus blurring, his eyelid itched, his hip ached: the force of the clamping press and the thrill and shudder of injection trembled through his claw. Nothingness, no warning. Jolts and jarring announced the mould's imminent opening. Mathieu relaxed, his senses bristling, improvising. At Salvatore's machine seven, Mathieu pulled back the guard as the presses opened. He took the gleaming product. The Sicilian stood and studied him. Mathieu reviewed every detail, then threw it in the bin. He waited for the next. From unexpected nothingness leapt a record-sleeve image of Miles on the ropes in a ring. Then, a beat or two later, the theme of 'When Lights Are Low.' The beauty of face, the slump of body, the bird-nose. Nadine, he thought. He had never seen that before. Nadine's face in Miles's. Not just her look. Mathieu had been a soldier far too long to think of killing without recalling combat training. You kill one of theirs to protect one of yours, or just because you can. You kill your own if fatally impaired or suffering. But this was no combat. Whose rules apply here? You have to have rules. Nadine said the best death was when you were alert and in sympathy. Sympathy! Death must be stared down, she said, 'like a faltering foe.' She had seen it often, she said, but she didn't say when or where or who, and he wouldn't ask. If you could arrive at that moment, your life crammed into your mind, splayed and still pulsing, eternity would be just an instant of supreme consciousness, at one with being, necessity, chance and history: your own, but that of humanity too. She could believe that. But instead of dying clear-sighted and conscious, it was her clear sight and consciousness that had died. Instead of a unique instant of eternity at death, she has an eternity of identical instants that make a mockery of life. You could almost believe there was a God: sardonic, cruel and vindictive. Even pain and pleasure had been taken from her now. As her mind had shrunk, his love of music had grown. He would drive out to the motorway, stop on some slip-road, slam on his hazards, and blast away at scales, jazz heads, popular song, lullabies: intuitive blowing, impetuous. The notion to kill her came one such afternoon, returned in dream, then dull hypothesis, horror, resolve. At machine six, he slid the door open. He shut his bad eye, brought the product close, lined it up. Sixteen pieces. Side view. Lengthwise. Salvatore stood behind him. Mathieu's mind emptied easier now. Seconds at a time. Echoing slightly. Stupid boy-student confessing to mother-murder! Matricide: sounds so much worse, earns you a longer sentence. While the little Gypsy's African friend is dead for what? Harnessed, huh, not funny, to some construction company's profits. And Boucan's war record all unknown: captain of industry, respected employer! And and and! Nadine. Damned thoughts. I've a task before me. No, several. Mathieu recalled each stage of her memory loss. He played her songs sung by Fernandel but got no reaction. Or, as when they had shared a bed, he pressed the heel of his hand to the ball of her foot, closing his fingers round the knuckles of her toes: nothing, not even a prehensile arching. Sometimes he found he had retreated from her, accusing himself of not caring. He had promised her: no institutions, no imprisonment. But is a person whose face never changes and whose voice never speaks still a person? Are you bound to respect them and honour a promise? Is it murder to kill the breathing dead? Standing at machine six, Mathieu smelt sickly-sweet English tobacco and saw the cover of Eric's book. He caught the product. Examined it head-on. Extra careful. Nadine had loved the Americans: Dreiser, Sinclair, Dos Passos, Steinbeck. He nodded at Britishe. Thoughts. Dross. Watching the Portuguee and the peasant play-fight, he had remembered squaddies in Indochina on his watch, letting off steam, suddenly serious, one pulling out a knuckleduster. Half a lifetime ago now. Hemingway too. *Pour qui sonne le glas* was the first film we saw together. Afterward, I called her my 'Ingrid-rabbit.' Till her hair grew. He knew how Nadine's voice had been – strong vowelled, rather low, a little breathy, yet somehow clipped – but he couldn't hear it. At times he thought he dreamt her voice, but on waking found it had died on his lips. He tried musical comparisons. Coltrane's playing on 'Naima.' Not right. Not quite. Tenor saxophones were not after all entirely human. Part of what he liked about the trumpet was that it never tried to trick you into thinking it was anything other than a musical instrument. Two or three times now Mathieu had experienced a sensation of empty-mindedness, leaning on a safety door, time frozen. Once, the Ivorian had gently nudged him, 'Chef . . . You've stood there for two minutes, four pieces . . .' Mathieu had jerked into motion. But Nadine, ready and primed to die, lacked sufficient energy for that change of state. He missed her voice most when he listened to her breathing.

40. Loyalties, Writers and Recantation.

Pierre examined his face in the mirror above the washbasin. He had been struck by Jacques' relaxed and ruddy appearance earlier that evening: his brother seemed hardly to have aged. Pierre's face was grey. From the corners of his eyes radiated spider-leg wrinkles not of laughter but of worry and the tedium of forced retirement.

On the narrow glass shelf at the base of the bathroom unit stood a tumbler of whisky. Pierre kept the whisky hidden for emergencies. He hadn't seen Jacques since Edith was buried. Before that, the years stretched away. They never had much in common – except Edith.

Pierre heard the apartment door shut. He hadn't expected Fernande back so soon. She appeared behind him, framed in the doorway. He looked at her face alongside his in the mirror. Her eyes blinked down at the whisky then back up. There was a change in the way she stood.

'I thought you were spending the evening with your friend,' Pierre remarked. 'It's almost eleven,' came the reply. Pierre lifted the tumbler from the glass ledge and took a casual sip of whisky. Fernande said nothing. 'What's wrong?' she then asked.

Pierre replaced the tumbler on the shelf. 'Jacques came past.' 'Your brother?' 'Do we know another Jacques?' 'What did he want?' 'He said he had lost his way.'

They both laughed shortly. 'It surprised me he remembered where we lived,' Pierre said, turning about and leaning back against the basin. Fernande moved aside, freeing Pierre's path, should he care to leave the bathroom. 'Oughtn't he to be in bed with the livestock by now?' she asked. Pierre produced a weak smile. 'He's taken a night job at Boucan's.' 'Things must be desperate. He should sell up and take it easy.' 'What, like me?' 'Well, he'll have no pension, will he?' 'I don't know.' 'How did he look?' 'He looked all right. He'd probably say it's the fresh country air. You'd think he hadn't a care in the world.' Fernande caught the direction of her husband's thoughts. 'Well, you worry too much.' She turned and exited the bathroom.

Pierre took his whisky and followed her into the lounge. 'I can't understand him,' Pierre said. His wife went into the bedroom, where she started to get undressed. Fernande might be thinking about something else now, or perhaps nothing at all. He could never hold her attention for very long.

Pierre stood at the door and watched the clothes fall from her. 'He said he would come back. He said he wanted to talk about the "old days."' Pierre assessed his wife's body. 'I'm going to bed,' she announced. He wasn't listening. 'I said to him, "what old days?" but he just chuckled and said, "when we were kids." So maybe he wants to rake over our childhood.' Fernande brushed against him on her way to the bathroom. She seemed to float. How did she do that?

Pierre never thought back to his childhood. Whenever he did think about the past, it was the same events that came to mind: an odd mix of squalid routine and low drama. His memories had hardened like beans stored too long. For years, Pierre had been a cop, a detective. At first he had been moved around a lot. He had even done a stint in Paris – long enough to make a single fateful mistake. Then he had been returned to Grandgobier. He had spent his life among fellow officers, informants, small-time crooks, pimps, fraudsters, and prostitutes. He had formed some strong loyalties and known betrayal too. He missed the urgencies and emergencies of people living on a knife-edge.

The whisky had calmed Pierre down. It didn't always work. He wondered if he would pay for it later. He could put the cap back on the bottle right now or he could stay up and empty it. There was nothing he had to do tomorrow. He patted his stomach. It didn't seem to be complaining. 'Are you coming to bed?' Fernande called. He thought about her body. 'Sure,' he answered, pouring himself one last shot.

↔↔↔↔↔↔

Tomec dwelt in a state of such detachment that neither his purchase on the physical traffic and mental uproar of the era through which he was nonetheless moving toward some sort of maturity, nor his understanding of the experiences and feelings of the men and women whose actions, conversations and bodies accompanied him upon this journey, were ever better than tenuous. This detachment was occasioned, in part, by the conviction that life itself was somewhere else and that beauty belonged unalterably to another time and to cultures partaking of none of the ambient banality and gossamer consumerism of mid-1970s Grandgobier, to whose precise horrors, however, Tomec remained largely unaware since temperamentally insensible. He dwelt, in short, in a far-flung fantasy.

Tomec's art and imagination were propelled and impeded by a fluctuating dread of plagiarism or repetition – whether of others or of himself – which in its acute phase could be bodied forth in sudden pains or aching, fevers or nausea, rendering every brushstroke or tap of chisel or twist of clay an agonizing act preceded by trembling uncertainty and followed by a fit of sometimes frantic sometimes sullen despair. He was persuaded that it was only by creating something utterly new and original – by which he intended the hitherto unimagined – that he might redeem his life by furnishing – late but not too late – a justification for his arbitrary survival into adulthood, with its unavoidable trousseau of new nation, language, and epoch of relative peace and comfort, while so many of his schoolfellows, friends, not to mention every single cousin and sibling except one, had failed so to survive. He was propelled, in short, by an original guilt.

Increasingly, Tomec had arranged his life around such promptings: first, by seeking and finding work that insulated and consequently (he supposed) *freed* him from encounters with other artists; second, by immuring himself against any supposable contemporary influence – the very possibility of which he could construe only as interference if not contamination – while he sustained himself on a diet of mere classics; third, by adopting a procedural attitude toward his own work that compounded reflex deferral with a neurotic search for proliferating complexities, ensuring that his projects remained unfinished, the dilemmas with which they presented him unresolved, the essential and even elementary operations preparatory to their accomplishment unexpedited, and all lacunae unfilled; fourth, by pursuing obscurity and an aesthetic of personal hermeticism, which escalated periodically into a terror of revealing his hand and of being found wanting – indeed, of being found *out*. In short, the clarity that Tomec sought was unavailable to the naked eye.

It was Tomec's purpose to raise the fallen figures of the present times by employing them in the construction of something more adequate to their historical and social experience. What Tomec saw in his circle of acquaintance, the chance meetings that befell him, the neighbours, occasional lovers, men at his workplace and his gallery of laboriously recollected dead, appeared to him in the guise of a crowd of auditioning actors to which he turned as grist to be milled, odds and ends to be whittled and shaped, then as beasts to be driven into a single tableau or suite of portrayals capable of transfiguring them all, hoisting them – poor unconscious forked creatures – from oblivion into a realm of transcendent meaning. The actual life of any such human ingredient, the mind behind and within any usable face, the visceral history of any salient body, the archaeology of any special posture: all such matters lay beyond his attention and beneath his purview. At a time of triumphant absurdism, flaunted minimalism, voguish pop-art, serial abstraction, and generalized contempt for art, Tomec longed for the universal and resounding statement that might explain, at least to himself, the context of the times into which he, the undeserving survivor, and all those who had been lost both to themselves and to him, had been hurled at birth. Tomec wished, in short, to construct from the fallen dust and driven filth of encircling postwar humanity, through the diminutive descendants of unknown ancients, a tolerably realistic panorama of momentous events, whether grandiose or intimate: the death of a poet, say, or the rise of a people, the birth of a false prophet, the torture and killing of hope. In shorter still, the past had – for now at least – blinded Tomec to the present.

↔↔↔↔↔↔↔

Four writers. At 22.47 that autumn evening in the European city of Grandgobier, four people already mentioned in the pages of this compendium were engaged in the act of writing, without availing themselves, it is fair to observe, of any typewriter, dictaphone, assistant, secretary, or other human or mechanical amanuensis; each instead grasped in their professional, cheery, eager or punitive fist a pencil or pen with which they scratched out their meaning in the time-honoured and venerable manner.

*

Sotiris Petrakis, a freelance journalist, was at this moment perched on the edge of a wobbly bidet in a seedy town-centre hotel, classic wire-spined reporter's notebook resting on his bedenimed thigh, ballpoint pen unravelling a tidy and professional longhand. On the other side of the bathroom door, in the bed nearest the window, Albert Gbenye, a man whom Sotiris had met for the first time that morning in Lyon, lay flat on his back in the half-light, his hands touching palm to palm beneath his chin, his eyelids lowered but not closed, his attitude and placid expression that of some presumptively holy subject commemorated (if not quite conserved) in funerary sculpture. Albert, by contrast, was breathing.

Sotiris had been the right man to contact. 'Who gave you my phone number?' he had asked at once. Albert had named the only paper to accord his brother's death more than five lines in a sidebar. Sotiris nodded and said, 'Entendu.' He had written the article himself, researching it on his day off, and had had to fight to get it in the paper: Grandgobier was outside the Lyon paper's normal geographic range.

Half an hour later when they met, Albert eyed Sotiris with suspicion. 'What's your interest? You must know I can't pay you.' 'I make no kind of assumptions and I do my own fact-checking. Can you pay my expenses?' 'No.' 'Right. Then this is how we stand. I can spare today and tomorrow. I'll go to Grandgobier with you and help you out for forty-eight hours, but Thursday morning sees me back here. That's what I do for you. What you do for me is the following: anything we find out – but, *anything* – I write up exactly as I see fit. You get no editorial control.' 'What can be worse than that he's dead?' Gbenye shrugged. Sotiris waited, wondering if he should answer that. 'The truth holds no fear for us now,' Albert then pronounced. 'All right,' Sotiris said, 'I think we have a deal.' Albert took the reporter's hand and shook it. 'What's in it for you?' he asked. Sotiris cracked the tiniest smile. 'I'm researching a book on immigrant workers' conditions in this country. I've got a small national publisher interested. It'll include a section on accidents at work. You're looking at me like you don't get it. I'm a nosy Greek. My parents were just immigrants. They always will be. That pisses me off.'

The two men had gone back to Sotiris's apartment, eaten, then left by train for Grandgobier. They had a compartment to themselves. Albert watched the suburbs trickle past then started talking about his brother, growing up together, and why Joseph had left. Albert opened his bag and handed Sotiris some letters his brother had written home. After glancing through them, Sotiris asked for and obtained permission to xerox them the following day. Then he handed them into Albert's safe keeping.

The edge of the bidet having grown uncomfortable, Sotiris lowered the lid of the toilet and moved over. With no shorthand, Sotiris's notes were skeletal, impressions really, keywords to jog his memory. If he went to bed now, by the morning they'd be useless: he would have forgotten the detail. He wasn't sleepy and, besides, they had an early start the next day. First off, they had to find and talk to Joseph's Gypsy friend.

*

Before going to bed, Monique Herbier sat down at her dining-room table and opened her page-a-day diary. Tuesday 9 November. Flicking back a month or so, she saw that her recent entries had failed to fill the allotted spaces, though her handwriting had grown gigantic in the attempt. Well, what is there to say when your life hangs suspended on some doctor's diagnosis? She uncapped her fountain pen and got ready to write small and cramped. Her mind was brimming.

Today the hospital phoned. Their initial 'probabilistic' diagnosis has been overturned. The test result has come back 'negative.' And this time it's 'conclusive.' It took a moment to sink in. I feel so excited. I had been steeling myself for chemo, radio, maybe even surgery – if 'indicated': now there is an expression I never want to hear again – and once I had lost my hair and vomited out my guts and my hips had wasted away and my breasts were empty pouches and flesh hung in flaps from my arms and legs – after all that suffering the most I could expect would be a lousy 'prognosis' anyway. Damn it, I kept thinking, I'm only sixty-two! Now I feel excited. I'm repeating myself. Exhilarated, then. It's more than a reprieve. Elated. Now I'm thinking: there's no time like the present, you have only one life, seize the day! I've spent the last month mourning the life unlived, the fun not had, the places not visited. It has been a memento mori. Nowadays, people live into their seventies, even longer. I'm fit. In fact that's today's main news. The only item that matters to me. How could it be otherwise? I half-expected to see it on the 20.00 téléjournal. Jean was glued, as always. I just kept thinking: Raymond Barre, austerity, Lebanon, go hang! But Jean has been sweet, patient and kind – and loving – ever since he thought he was about to lose me. Poor lamb. Whatever would he do on his own? I shall repay him by making the very best of myself. I can still be an attractive woman. But I now know that it's my life to lose and therefore my life to live.

Monique lifted her pen from the page and reread what she had written. Something else was on her mind. She had a quarter of the page left. She would have to write even smaller and perhaps creep up the margins. Spilling onto the next page was against the rules.

The thing I've not touched on here for years – for years there was nothing to say and recently I have held back out of embarrassment and because I feared this diary might soon fall into someone else's hands – is love, sex. Jean has been very attentive, even 'biting me' (as he puts it) – a flourish he hadn't troubled with for so many years. And to think I once discouraged him – from a sense of shame! There have been some absolute innovations too – which I would blush to describe – but which reveal in him an imagination I had never guessed at. At least I hope that's where they come from. He hasn't asked me to do anything repugnant, and I don't think he will.

Monique looked at what she had written. Now it was done, it didn't seem so very important after all. She had just three lines left.

However, this is not so very important now that my life expectancy has jumped back up from years (if lucky) to decades (likewise). What I really want is to see a bit of the world, e.g. the pyramids and Niagara. I can budget – why not? I worked all those years and I have my pension.

Monique sighed: she was going to have to use the margin. She turned the diary on its edge.

I've understood something very simple: I'm going to be the one to die when it's time for me to die, so let me live my life the way I want to!

*

Françoise needed an introductory paragraph. She had been commissioned by one of the guys from *Carnets Rouges* – well, more asked than formally commissioned, really – to come up with an article on Argentina. When she said she was still at school, he had shrugged and said, 'Anyone who can talk can write, and you seem to know a lot about Argentina.'

In the city library, she had read everything relevant from *Le Monde*, *Libération* and *Rouge*, going back months. She had taken notes and drawn up a plan. And now she was looking at the latest edition of *Carnets*. For her article to make an impact, she knew she had to avoid splattering the readers with facts and dates and numbers and names, which would quickly grow both harrowing and boring and are hard to interpret correctly. She had to situate the events in their historical-materialist context. So far she had the following.

> *1ˢᵗ paragraph*: Although our era is indelibly / profoundly marked by the betrayal of revolution, ours is not fundamentally a time of defeat. If no truly unalienated society may yet be said to exist – except as the great dream of humanity, which is to say, the great dream of alienated humanity . . . for of what dreams would humanity once freed of the fetters of capitalist alienation not be capable? . . . this dream appears more and more / increasingly to be of a premonitory type (i.e. destined to come true). For what is the real / true / concrete meaning and content of bourgeois Equality and Fraternity? This content is (quint-) essentially economic, enforcing / imposing a situation / state of (social) relations designed to aid and abet the / a? relentless process of capitalist accumulation. This content and meaning represents the daily activity of social (because *socialized*) individuals: it is the firm, the state, art, our very education, even time itself.
>
> 2ⁿᵈ paragraph: Yet in Argentina today, revolutionary forces have faced more than a defeat, they have suffered a disastrous reversal that has brought about the installation of a regime that, etc . . .'

It was a bit rough, but Françoise felt she had the bones of it right. She liked 'social (because *socialized*)' and 'concrete' was always, well, concrete. On the other hand, her second sentence was a mess and she ought perhaps to remove any reference to destiny, a bourgeois-romantic notion if ever there was one.

The Kraftwerk cassette in the background came to an end with a loud click. Françoise glanced at the chart above her bed. Wednesday was all hard sciences. She decided to change the music. The choice was between Léo Ferré, *Ferrat chante Aragon* and Patti Smith's *Horses*: words she could follow or words she could not. Was she feeling in more of an anarchist-playful or communist-wistful mood tonight? Or perhaps a touch decadent-rebellious? She closed her eyes and stretched out her left hand. She laughed at the childishness of this act of divination. She was glad the young men and women who produced *Carnets Rouges* could not see her now. Her fingers alighted on a cassette case and she opened her eyes. Ferré. Damn, she thought. She reached for *Horses*. There was something about the starched white shirt and long, yes, equine, face. Something she couldn't name. She inserted the cassette and reached for her nightdress and yawned. Patti started to snarl – and to whinny.

*

'Chère Maman et Papa,' Danielle had begun her letter, 'I do wish you would have a telephone installed.'

Curled up on the sofa, with her husband's bugle-then-whistle snoring intruding from their bedroom, Danielle had picked up her pen and pad in a punitive frame of mind. Earlier that evening, Philippe had dismissed her yet again in that offhand manner of his that never failed to infuriate – when really he should have thanked her for being a true and loyal messenger. Was it her fault her tidings were unwelcome? Her parents asked for news of Philippe in every letter they sent. After the way he had treated them! They still thought the world of him. Not that he would ever realize that, the jerk. Why couldn't he bury the hatchet, sheathe the sword, mend the bridges, swallow his pride, pour oil on . . . what is it? Next time she phoned him, she would tell him just that. He would chuckle and call her 'soeurette' – which sounded friendly – but would he listen? Of course not! So now Danielle was angry and felt impelled to exact righteous revenge on her feckless brother: and what could be better than to hint to his still adoring *maman et papa* that their wayward favourite was in fact a contemptible *cocu*. Of course it wasn't something you could come straight out with: it had to be worked in, folded gradually like almonds – or arsenic – into a cake mix.

'Phoning is so much easier than writing a letter. So much more direct,' Danielle resumed, warming to her theme. 'You always tell me that in an emergency I can phone M. et Mme Lanaudie next door but the whole point is that telephones are not only for emergencies! Telephones bring people together! It is *fun* to talk! It's true!' Here she paused, and gathered her thoughts. If she botched this, she would have to start the letter all over again. She couldn't post something covered in crossings-out. George's snoring had grown less regular. More of a grunt than a snore. Maybe the dolt was dreaming. Where was she? Phones brought people together.

'I had Philippe on the phone earlier – though of course he *never* answers the one that Odile had installed in their flat, so I caught him at the bar where he drinks before work. He sounded fine but – I don't know how to put this delicately – I have heard that Odile and Philippe are not getting on so well.'

Danielle wasn't sure that that was sufficiently explicit, but she didn't want to be vulgar. She sucked on the end of her pen. Her eyes glinted. 'It could be just a malicious rumour. After all, he seems fine, just the same as always, and certainly gives nothing away. But I have a woman's instinct in these matters.' Danielle leaned back, hesitated, held her breath, 'Sometimes I wonder if he would notice if his wife was missing from his bed one morning. Still, you really mustn't worry about Philippe: I am quite sure he'll get back in touch when he's good and ready.'

Danielle smiled. She had hit the right note. Her parents could draw their own conclusions. They weren't entirely stupid. She searched for a way to close.

'I must end now. It's rather late. Almost midnight and George is *begging* me to come to bed. So I'll sign off. Your loving daughter.'

Danielle possessed two kinds of envelopes: one for special people or occasions, light blue, heavy, stiff and delicately perfumed; the other white, flimsy, with dotted yellow lines for the name and address and a row of five little yellow boxes for the postcode. Danielle reached for one of the flimsy white variety. She could picture her father fingering one of her blue envelopes, raising it to his nose and sniffing. She didn't want him or her mother to think she lived the life of some pampered duchess.

↔↔↔↔↔

Fernando spat twice, once into each of his palms, then slowly rubbed his hands together, wringing them in the manner of an ancient mourner, while his face expressed bland satisfaction. The bodywork of his machine seventeen now glinted like a car in a showroom, and his PORTO team flag fluttered at its end on a tepid draught that ascended the stairs from the ground floor. Fernando dropped his rag into a rubbish bin and sat down, rewarding himself with a cigarette. As well as buffing machine bodies, over the previous hour he had filled both hoppers; in the previous *half* hour he had emptied both floor bins and threshed all accumulated sprue; in the previous five *minutes*, he had quality-checked both products. Fernando sat like a man always ready to rise, the line where his buttocks met the backs of his legs hingeing precariously on the sharp plywood edge of his metal-framed chair, his feet planted half a metre apart, his knees splayed wide, his right elbow pressed upon his right knee with the forearm vertical, the middle- and index fingers of his hand shuttling cigarette to and from mouth. In this position, squinting to his right where the stairs made landing, Fernando was alert to any eventuality: if the rhythm of the machine should break, he could spring to his feet. At his back was a wall and his hands could make fists at a moment's notice. It was the attitude of a man at midnight athwart a suitcase in the dimmer recesses of a poorly policed coach station. When the cigarette ended, what then? The factory was bright-lit and implacable, minutes and seconds to be measured in machine clang and product fall. The first moments of boredom and emptiness were the hardest – by midnight the numbing would be complete and thereby bearable. Besides, there would be relief: the union meeting at eleven-fifteen; the meal-break at one; Côte d'Ivoire's reading and performance after three. Complementing such regular or predictable fixtures, there would be numerous small movable rewards: trips downstairs to chat with Marseille or Jacques or to talk football with Luigi; visits to the beer- and coffee-machines or to the toilet, moments flicking through magazines downstairs, and his nightly erection exercises. Fixtures and movable rewards: visible sunlit peaks of distraction and release. Fernando recalled something Marcel had said the previous week: 'Yeah, and this here isn't really a plastic cup of coffee, it's a carafe of Chateau Lafitte.' Jacques had laughed and Philippe had blown a smoke ring wriggling up at the ceiling. They had been digesting in the meals room and joking about where each of them belonged and Fernando had just declared, 'Well, what you see of me fucking-here – a worker in a factory, an immigrant – was never meant to be. I'm a small farmer, back in Portugal. A mistake was made. I'm going to wake up one day. This life isn't real.' Fernando hadn't been offended by Marcel's sarcastic riposte, he had even laughed along, but then he had come back: 'I'll tell you exactly where I belong: in a field or a stable, my arm up a cow's rear, tying a rope to the hoof of some calf. I know everything about animals, birds, crops. I can spot the first signs of blight, mildew, animal diseases too. By the time I left home, I knew more than a barnful of agronomy fucking-students. I carry round with me all this knowhow so that it hangs off me useless, like fucking-slack skin, like a . . . like a fucking-lizard. You picture a lizard? That's fucking-me!' This was all true, but it left Fernando with a dilemma: Maryse. What could he give her? What did he have? He kept thinking that maybe he had nothing because he was nothing. If he wasn't what he was meant to be, then what was he? To make Maryse something other than his 'fucking cure,' he had to be something other than her needy customer. Fernando dropped his cigarette on the floor between his feet, then used his left shoe to rub it into the floor. It couldn't be about giving her the stuff women are supposed to want – scarves or broaches or even music or poetry, nor about being cleverer or more handsome or more elegant. It wasn't going to be about money either. Or not only. He had to have the right work, the right money, the right attitude: he had to be the right person for her – or for any other woman. Only then would she see him as something other than a suitable case for treatment. He hadn't ever been 'right' since he'd arrived in this country. Fernando shook his head and sniffed. He saw Eric crest the stairs. Probably going to talk to the little guy. What could they possibly discuss? The English fucking-wouldn't understand a word. Sit there like the grinning cat in *Alice no País das Maravilhas* which Granny read aloud to him – till she died one day. Years ago now. But how to get the right work, place to live too – he could never bring Maryse, or any other woman, to the hostel. How to make money? That was the trick. He'd do anything. Even crime. Providing nobody got hurt. Robbing the rich wouldn't bother him a jot, but nowadays that's not such an easy thing to do. They've got bodyguards, armour-plated doors, bars on their windows, burglar alarms, paranoia, firepower, the law, the police and the state. And what have I got? I can't even tell a lie. Fernando scowled, took his cigarette pack from his breast pocket, flicked open the top and contemplated the contents. The first time he'd met Maryse, she had asked him when last he'd had 'sexual relations' with a woman. He had wondered for a moment just what counted but hadn't been brought up to demand the definition of terms and never really caught up with that kind of thing since, so he mumbled, 'well, it's been more than a week.' Maryse had looked at him so hard it felt as if she had somehow crawled right into the lines on his forehead, swelling his skin up all tight and heavy. 'I don't think you've done it for months, maybe years. Am I right?' 'Okay,' he had said, 'not doing it's not a sin.' After that she had put him at his ease and, for a first time, it had gone okay. She had told him so. Fernando took out a cigarette, tapped the filter end on his knee. If I could just have a farm, he thought, even manage someone else's. If I could win the jackpot, I could buy myself one. One good win, then I'd stop. Because in the long run, you always lose – they have formulae to make damn sure. And serious crime is out. I couldn't do prison. Not with my haemorrhoids. Though maybe something low-level, low-risk, low-pay. A courier, a bag man. Or a lookout. Or a driver. I could learn to drive. That Gypsy downstairs could probably recommend some avenue. But how do you ask an ex-con for crime-career advice? Maybe I could slip it into the conversation casually. No. I need to change, get solid. It's the only way to win Maryse or any woman. Gifts wouldn't do it. The first time he had wanted to show her his affection and gratitude, he had taken her flowers and chocolates. It had been a bad idea. She had shaken her head and chucked them into her metal bin. One of the tulip stems had hit the neck of the bin and snapped just below the flower. 'You really don't have a clue, do you?' she had said. He had turned and was going to leave without a word, but she got to the door first. 'Look, it's nice that you like me. I like you too. That makes it all a lot easier.' He had hung his head. If he could just stop being a loser. He could be anything if he had a woman like Maryse alongside him. A man needs a woman. To be a man. He could be a new person, stronger, more sensible, smarter, get the right work, earn the right money, screw like every old lady's wet dream. He pictured himself clean-shaven, nicely turned out, suave, supple as an eel. But there was a catch: you had to be like that already to get the right woman, and without one, how could he make the necessary changes? If she could only see what he could be. Men need women and women need insight. That's it. She could love him for what he could become and then, damn it, he'd become it. If she just had a little faith. It ought to be so easy. Why do women have so little faith? Why couldn't she see in him what he could see in himself? What Fernando saw was a picture that never changed. It was his future and it would come to him as surely as death, but it would come a lot sooner. He would have a wife – maybe even Maryse – and children. He would have a piece of land, a smallholding, maybe his own, maybe rented. From the window he'd look down into a valley. There would be animals and hard, hard toil. That didn't scare him. He would make a living from the earth, the way his people always had. Who was to say that wasn't his future? Before she had died, his granny had held his hand and told him, 'You are going to be all right.' He only had to close his eyes to see her saying it and to feel the silky skin on her bony old hand. It had cheered him up so often. At different times, it had meant, 'you'll find a way to go abroad,' 'you'll find work here in France,' 'you'll find a place to live.' And now it meant, 'you'll find a way back home.' His time that afternoon with Maryse had been good. They had hardly talked. He had behaved like a lamb, did just what she'd trained him to do, all the preliminary fiddly boring stuff. He'd been a man right from the start, almost as soon as he had touched her. Then once they'd started fucking properly, he'd been so strong, so hard. He had lasted more than four minutes. She had a wall-clock which he glanced at before he stuck it in her and after he took it out. She didn't seem to mind that. He could have lasted longer, but she started moaning and carrying on and he knew it was just to make him come, which it did. And she knew he knew. That was probably the point. She had told him he wasn't going to need her services much longer, and he had wondered if he knew enough now to fake a relapse into flailing flaccidity. Fernando leaned back on his chair and yawned. He would have to do his erection exercises later. See how long he could hold it. Without touching or stroking or anything. Just flexing it, keeping it up like a hammer. Building muscle. Building control. Last Friday he'd achieved a personal record: nine minutes. He could try beating that. Fernando closed his eyes, took a deep breath. Maybe next time with Maryse would be even better than this afternoon. Or if not next time, the time after. Some time. One day. The moaning wouldn't be fake. She would ride him, taking her pleasure from him, no longer the therapist, the real woman now, fucking him for herself. Later as he slipped out of her, she would tell him he'd been a tiger. She might even make a little purring sound, the way women did in films. She might stroke or pat his chest. 'I've never come with a customer before,' she could tell him, still out of breath. Fernando had a nice languid erection now. A freebie. Quite unexpected. It was the kind of boner you wake up with, if you're lucky. Fernando pursued his mix of memory and hope. One day Maryse would say as she drummed her fingers slowly on his biceps and sighed, 'I know our time is up but the next fuck is on me. If you're feeling up to it. Ah-ha, I see you are.' Fernando chuckled happily. He would be up to it. He got the girl. He was going to be all right. Granny said so.

↔↔↔↔↔

Eric had wandered upstairs, after asking Marcel to watch his machines. Jean signalled to him to pull up a chair. Jean always had something to say and mostly didn't expect Eric to say much in return. Also, he spoke slowly and clearly and repeated himself a lot, as if he thought he was talking to a dimwit. Eric reckoned it was good for his French.

Besides, he found Jean amusing to look at, though he was careful not to show it. Stan Laurel always came to mind: the baggy trousers, the glass-smooth face – sometimes Jean's hair even had a cow's lick. Tonight the little man seemed angry. Something about unions ('syndicats') and 'pourriture' – didn't that mean rottenness? Then Jean mentioned Joan of Arc, Jeanne d'Arc, repeating the name till Eric got it. What did Eric know about her? Eric opened his eyes as wide as they'd go. Alphonse had come over and was standing next to Eric's chair, but he wasn't saying anything.

Jean closed the machine guard and stared at Eric, waiting for something. He seemed angry. Eric felt obliged to say something. It was odd to feel threatened by a pint-sized comic turn. Then the press opened and Jean grabbed the cable ties, ripping them from the sprue. Eric mentioned a play, a 'pièce de théatre' he had been made to read at school. George Bernard Shaw. Jean knew the name, turned it straight into French, pronouncing it slowly so Eric could get it right next time. Alphonse grunted, but said nothing.

'The Maid – la Pucelle – was hauled before three judges – a pig, a sheep and a donkey,' Jean said, 'did you know that?' Eric had recognized two of the animal-words: 'cochon' and 'mouton.' 'Arne?' Eric asked, unsure, looking to Jean for elucidation. 'Ee-aw!' the little man said, rolling his eyes as he brayed. Eric had once faced a magistrates court. Best forgotten. He pictured the animals resting their hooves and trotters on the old oak bench. 'But the Maid saved us from the English,' Jean said. Eric grinned, taking the tease in good part. The plot of the play was coming back to him now. Joan had confessed under torture and then recanted and been burned. That was the story of the play, he attempted to tell Jean. Jean didn't seem to understand 'recanter.' Eric tried 're-chanter.' Then Alphonse usefully corrected Eric's French: 'retracter,' the word is 'retracter': to retract.

Alphonse launched, uninvited, into a disquisition – wholly incomprehensible to Eric – about confession-recantation plots, of which he cited several. Jean listened attentively as he worked his machine. Alphonse said he had met a lady on a train once, a Swiss lady who spoke French with a Spanish accent, who told him about a man named Edmond Peluso, a self-styled 'citizen of the world' who had fled in the 1920s from fascist Italy to a Communist's exile in the USSR, only to be arrested in the Great Purges, tortured, forced falsely to confess to being a fascist traitor. At his trial he had retracted the entire thing, demolishing one by one every detail of his painstakingly fabricated confession. Alphonse was unstoppable. Eric had moved the chair aside to let Alphonse get closer. By the end of it, Jean was shaking his head so hard it was beginning to affect production. He was losing time getting the guard shut, forgetting to apply oil when products began to stick.

'How can you compare la Pucelle to some Italian coco?' he hissed as soon as he could break the Ivorian's flow. 'You people understand nothing of France, of her destiny, of our history . . .' Alphonse appeared to be taken aback. He even appeared to apologize. Why was he drawing such hostility this evening? He had only meant to say that the confession-recantation plot didn't have to be Christian, French or the principles of the protagonist even necessarily laudable. It was the thing itself that mattered, the story. That seemed to shut Jean up. He just stared. Maybe he was thinking. Eric would have liked to hear the whole argument again and preferably at half the speed.

As Alphonse shrugged and moved back to his machines, Jean, having put down his oily paintbrush and slid the safety guard shut, beckoned Eric to lean in close. 'Ces gens-là,' he stage-whispered, 'ils causent, ils causent, mais qu'est-ce qu'ils comprennent, hein?' Eric didn't like Jean's eyes. Little piggy eyes. Traces of blood trickled in the guttering. Eric hadn't looked at them closely before. 'Ces gens-là . . .' People like that. What did the little man mean? Eric didn't want any kind of quarrel. He hadn't come to this country for a fight. More to get away from one. His French wasn't up to it, was it? Besides, what did he know? Jean was staring him down now, waiting for some reaction. 'Vous avez raison. Sans doute,' Eric mumbled. Jean smiled. It was enough. I wonder how he sees me? Eric suddenly wondered. What kind of animal am I? Cochon? Âne? No, no. Mouton. He sees a sheep.

41. Butchery, Contentment and Solidity.

In his dimly lit bedroom, Lucien Martinet, master butcher, mentor to Luigi, thriving entrepreneur and happy husband, reclined Pompeian where slumber had seized him open-mouthed, a business magazine inverted upon the coverlet alongside a delicate and lean right hand.

In the day area of their apartment, Mme Marthe Martinet was putting away the last few dishes and cooking utensils. She hung her apron on a hook and examined her palms, surveying the results in erosion and escarpment of six half-days spent each week in a cold butcher's shop dabbling in grubby coins, compounded by connubial sink-duty most evenings.

For dinner that day Lucien had cooked calves' sweetbreads with shallots, nutmeg, armagnac and cream: he appeared to have employed every kitchen implement at least once while never finding the opportunity to wash any item or to wipe any surface, leaving the floor slippery with sauce, the cooker crisply caked, each greasy cloth, slimy sponge, rag, brush and scourer requiring overnight immersion in the most powerful astringents. The meal, to be fair, had been exquisite. Lucien took pride in his ability to regale his customers with original recipes and precise recommendations, claiming truthfully that at home he cooked meat five evenings a week and never served the same dish twice.

Marthe kneaded Apulian olive oil into the flesh of her hands as she reviewed the kitchen: she had returned everything clean and glinting to its appointed place; a bin bag lay plump at the door, ready for the early-morning descent to its rainbow-greasy patch of pavement.

Over dinner, her husband had expounded his latest business thinking. He talked of the power of music to build complicité between customer and artisan: he cited an article, relayed a percentage. Was it not time they turfed out the tinny radio tuned limpet-fast to Radio Monte Carlo and bowed to the latest in stereophonic twin-cassette hi-fi?

Marthe had listened attentively. It was up to her to provide dialectical tension, urge caution, carp a little. Moreover, she loathed offal and was glad of an excuse to lay down her fork. 'A butcher's shop is no supermarket or trendy boutique,' she had prefaced. Lucien smiled. 'Of course. But the point is to make our customers comfortable, calm them even, not to entice them in to hear our music.' 'What would we play?' 'Rock music and chanson française. The kind of material we might listen to ourselves. Eddie Mitchell,

Johnny, Serge Lama, Clo-Clo, Barbara, Gainsbourg. French music. Strictly hexagonale: Breton harps, yes; Corsican wailing, no.' 'But not everyone likes Eddie Mitchell. We might put people off.' 'How many customers would we possibly offend enough to make them go elsewhere for their cutlets? Besides, we would try things out. Luigi might have some ideas.'

Marthe tried to picture Luigi with ideas, then shook her head. Lucien transfixed his final sweetbread. 'Luigi is younger than we are. He'll know what people listen to.' 'If you say so.' 'He's a good worker and he's never going to be competition. You're too hard on him. He's nothing but a butcher's boy. He couldn't run a crêpe stall.'

Marthe admired her husband's entrepreneurial drive. He never rested. His effort to improve his business, expand his clientele, grow turnover, increase margins, diversify supply and offer original products knew few bounds. He would wake in the middle of the night and whisper, Marthe, tu dors pas? And she – ever a light sleeper – would always manage to answer, Non, mon amour. Dis-moi tout. He would then divulge his latest thoughts and dreams, talking her through the numbers, there in the dark. His biggest dream was to move to larger premises or to open a second shop. Marthe would listen, ask questions, caress and sustain him with gentle praise. Sometimes while he talked she would stroke his back and sometimes, absentmindedly, her hand might steal its way around his haunches and creep through the slit in his pyjama trousers. His talk would slow or slur momentarily but would quickly recover and soon without fail he would grow excited and cease talking about gadgetry and profits and refurbishment and meat and instead, however briefly, pay a tribute to her caresses.

Marthe pinched her skin to test its revived sheen and elasticity. By now Lucien would be asleep, his magazine on the floor. He earned his rest. Butchering was hard physical work and then there was the constant banter with customers to sustain. Back home, further energy was expended on his chaotic evening culinary performances and (at least) twice-weekly quickfire goatish coupling. Whenever Marthe sought to convey her estimation of his prowess in any of these domains – sometimes upon prompting, more often spontaneously – Lucien would take the compliment as his due, relating it to his possession of exceptional couilles: for it was these, he insisted, that gave him the edge, the oomph. 'If I had had the opportunity to study anatomy I would be a doctor not a butcher, but I know enough to say that oomph, physical, mental or bestial, is related to adrénaline, and that adrénaline, in the ultimate analysis, flows from one's couilles – of which, as you well know, I own an uncommonly good set.' At this point M. Martinet might also mention testostérone which, as he understood it, acted as intermediary elixir, catalyst or accelerant between testicules and adrénaline. Lucien lacked the requisite Latin but, during a coffee and cigarette break, his apprentice Luigi – an Italian after all – had been happy to expatiate for his mentor's edification upon the etymology of testostérone, relating it to the Latin testes (testicles) and to the Italian tosto (tough, strong or hard).

Upon relaying to his wife the gist of Luigi's philological extemporization, it had struck Lucien that Marthe was more than ordinarily pensive. 'Cheer up, ma chérie,' he had urged. 'You have no call for testostérone. I place mine at your disposal. You have your looks and your feminine guiles. We are complementary. Made to fit. Like plug and socket. Bulls and cows. It's a law of nature. I'm the plug.'

In that case, Marthe now reasoned aloud, surprising herself not only with the lightning rigour of her logic but with the androgynous force and volume of her voice in the echoing kitchen, it is I, 'the socket,' who supply the current that makes him function.

↔↔↔↔↔↔

Five stations. Five of fourteen. Enough to be juggling with.

It was 22.50 on that Tuesday evening in November. The Polish night-security man marched between the machines of dark metallurgy, while images – of ancient Brundisium, its buildings and streets and foam of people, Virgil on his litter, the Andean boy in attendance, the manuscript chest pregnant with the *Aeneid* – jostled like cells in the conduits of his imagination, congealing into five spawning clusters, suggesting five evolving stations. Of course more would come later, as Tomec passed out of the first section of Broch's novel ('Water') and journeyed onward through sections titled 'Fire,' 'Earth' and 'Air.' The last station of all would represent a moment just prior to the poet's final breath.

At a level quite separate from the crowding imagery, a host of organizational principles, compositional criteria, associative strands, circles and ellipses, lists and boxes roughly pushed themselves forward like so many wharfside stevedores battling for day-hire. The moment he reached his bench, he would rip a single sheet of paper from his sketchpad, apply ruler and HB pencil to draw a sharp lengthwise line, bisecting the sheet into two equal areas. He would then trace at right angles six further equidistant lines, thus creating fourteen squares, one for each station. Here he would begin to plot, clockwise from top left corner to bottom left corner, his fourteen scenes, encounters, moments, events, marking the course of Virgil's calvary. His marching pace quickened, his head shook, his torch swung. No, no! He should instead grasp that single sheet and with jagged pencil strokes divide its finite space into five unequal and uniquely proportioned zones, each to represent just one of Virgil's first five stations. 'Stations of the Book.' That was it. In each zone, he would note some or all of the following: the physical space occupied by the poet (centre / periphery / absent but implied by others' gaze / demeanour . . .), the poet's attitude (lying / standing / leaning . . .), his physical portion (body / bust / head . . .), other persons depicted (salience / inter-relation . . .), presiding sense, mood, atmosphere, colours, prominent objects . . . the elements proliferated. No, no: no set of uniform criteria, no standard approach! A separate sheet for each station, each station discrete in its very conception, because *sui generis*, each station unique from its very first contingent of preparatory notes.

Washing dialectically back from matters of creative handling to the substance promoted by Broch's text and pullulating in darkening imagery, Tomec considered the station scenes as they arose in turn, haphazardly, higgledy-piggledy. A vision of the poet alone in the crowd, borne upon his litter, glancing toward his manuscript casket. Then the glance exchanged with the Mantuan boy, picked out and, as it were, illuminated from on high. Then the mob in the throes of ribaldry, mocking Virgil. Next the boy's urgent command hurled at his fellow citizenry, 'Make way for your poet!' Lastly, the look of understanding passing between poet and boy and the boy's tribute encapsulated in the words, 'Speech turns to song in your mouth.'

Indeed, should not these stations possess captions or legends, carved (or at least printed) at their base? And might not these be lifted verbatim from Broch's text? One caption might be, 'Exposed to every sort of laughter.' Another: 'the wish to remain alone and unobserved became imperative.' Another: 'he had knowledge of the blood that pulsed in their veins.' Or another, indeed, 'Make way for Virgil!'

Tomec arrived at his sketching bench, tore a sheet from his pad, adjusted the anglepoise, raised his pencil, and considered where and how to let it fall.

↔↔↔↔↔↔

As his chin hit his chest, Jacques' eyes opened. An uncomfortable contraction in groin and belly caused his knees to jerk closer and his shoulders to push from the chair, while Jeanne's countenance faded from his consciousness. His trunk hinged forward, his arms rose and his palms found and clasped the tops of his thighs. He had never liked the smell of lavender. Until now. Especially not on a woman. He remembered saying once to Edith, 'Why do you think your friend wears lavender?' Edith had looked surprised. 'Jeanne?' she asked. Jacques had nodded. 'She was harvesting it today. Picking it.' 'But she wears that scent all year round.' 'Really?' Jacques now stood up slowly. With his left hand he pushed his cap right back, so that its peak pointed straight up from his nape. His right hand pulled and then patted at strands of his sparse silvery hair. Irritated by the adherence to his buttocks of the seat of his trousers he wiggled his hips. He wondered if Jeanne was reading the book he had given her. She had seemed pleased. What would her husband think, could he but see them together? What would Edith think? Sometimes Jacques imagined they might be watching. It made him nervous. The dead must at least be curious. Otherwise, they are unseeing, unconscious: extinct. Jacques chased that fear away, and looked around. He eased his cap back down. This wasn't a job for a grown man. More like babysitting. Except that machines don't need lulling. They do the lulling. There, the Italian has nodded off. Grown men! Like the Portuguee. What he says is right: he could grow food. Instead of this. It's all nonsense. Just be glad it's not your entire life, Edith would say. She's right. I've been lucky. And not just in love. Sure, I love Jeanne now. I'm not ashamed. I wonder if she loves me. Neither of us breathes the word. Why should we? Jacques chuckled. And this job tides me over, till farm prices rise again, as they someday surely will. The Algerian is checking his product. Bottle-top-like things, all shiny black. Made to fit on the end of some other piece of plastic. Seems only yesterday that bottles were glass and bottle-tops metal. And soon there will be something else or they won't exist at all. This factory, this work will be gone. Superseded. Us too. Forgotten. But my land won't go, the animals won't go, the need to eat, to produce crops. That will remain. So? What of Pierre? Our childhood together? Is it time for reconciliation? Reluctant to perform any needful routine task, Jacques stepped over to machine four, bent and caught the product as it fell through the aluminium slats. He scrutinized it, dropped it into the floor tray, which he then lifted and emptied into the threshing tub. He glanced at the raw-material level displayed in the hopper glass. Turning, he saw someone bent over a newspaper. Then someone else, eyes half-closed, smoking for dear life, pulling at the weed like it mattered. Another, tormenting a scrap of paper. Two men speaking, their eyes fixed away from one other, knuckles clenching, fingers grey. His breathing coming, going, steady. In here. He thumped his chest. Jeanne's refusal to live with him properly continued to surprise Jacques. How beautiful it was to lie in bed with her! How unimportant their love-making seemed! How well she sang, on waking the next morning! How soft her touch! How different from Edith's! Which had been loving always, but never lingering; gentle certainly, but never caressing. Moving up the machine aisle, his arms swinging low, his joints well oiled, Jacques' retinas recorded not only the machines ranked before him on each side, the haze of greys and colours and the blur of jagged movements, but also three men: Marcel (that grin again!); Luigi (don't let him corner me!); Philippe (distracted by newsprint!). Some things just happen, Jacques reflected. Like taking a wrong turn and ending up at your brother's apartment block. Standing in an orange aluminium-cellulite-walled lift. Pierre at the door-phone. You alone? Who's asking? Maybe Pierre didn't recognize my voice. Then he said, Jacques Who? That clinched it. I can go away if you like, I said. From the glass-fronted office, Mathieu could see Jacques. He could watch all the men, the warning lights and machines: the men were temporarily idle; the machines busy. Knocking out plastic. Not for him. Jacques hadn't needed to see his brother. He could have driven straight past the factory too, and on all night. That temptation had always been there. He had never once run. Never woken up in a strange town or bed, never risked his farm or marriage on a hunch or a simper. Too old now to be alone. Jacques was frightened to be away from home for long. In the city, he feared he'd die and never get home again to breathe his farm air. Each return was a daunting climb. Back home, he never thought of home. But at this machine, his eyes open, he could see every clod. Turning into the space between Philippe's machine two and his own machine three, Jacques glanced back down the aisle, catching sight of Rachid, Eric and Salvatore standing close together though at odd angles, appearing to be silent, each one perhaps in his own world of feeling or thought. Jacques failed to marvel at this notion. Pierre: Not tucked up with your livestock? Jacques, spreading his arms: Working. Pierre: Nights? Jacques' arms going out again: Chez Boucan.

Pierre whistling. City got you! Is no one safe? Jacques shuffling. Pierre inter-
cepting his brother's glance. There are more insects here than in St Auguste.
It's the garbage chutes. Bringing neighbours closer together. Microbiologically.
No point fretting about people, Jacques thought. Pity the doctor's dog! Or
some jailbird, with no hope, no chance to act. But Pierre? Or Marseille? Or
Fernando (as he makes me call him)? Up the ladder! Lift the lid! Take a look!
Check the piece! Leave till later! They can act. They're free. Down the ladder!
Jacques stepped to machine three's opening presses, caught, checked and
dropped the product. Having lifted and emptied the floor tray, he replaced
it, correcting its position with his right toe. He walked to the hopper, ascended
the stepladder, and lifted the hopper lid. He carefully picked raw material
from the inner face of the porthole. This job isn't for grown men. I'm sad for
the others. What led him to Pierre's flat that evening? Not worth worrying
about. Seeing that doctor? Contemplating impotence? Closest thing to death!
Every turn you take, right or wrong, means something. I'll come by again,
Jacques had said, leaving. You know where we live, came the reply. Pierre
didn't seem to care, but then he had never smiled much. Would Jacques have
known if Pierre had died? Certainly. Pierre's woman would have phoned.
Pierre had had the harder life. He'd even taken a bullet once in the line of
duty. Perhaps Jacques had visited him to distract himself, to shift his ideas
about a bit. Or maybe he had hoped, now that Edith was long gone, that the
rift between them might be healed. Who knew why anyone did anything?
Even oneself? Or what made a difference to people, even brothers? Edith's
death might take them back to the time they were little boys, to the time
before Edith. She had been the prettiest, boldest, most brazen and most fero-
ciously courted girl in the whole village and Pierre, the elder brother, the
better-looking and the cleverer one, had been rejected in favour of Jacques,
the quiet kid, the slow coach. Jacques clicked his tongue, cleared his throat.
He swung his arms. He took a breath, released it slowly. Arms crossed, his
hands palpated both biceps. He jiggled up and down on his knees, as if testing. He raised his eyebrows unevenly. He sidled to his chair, patting his thighs.
Like some strange workout before sleeping. Then, pinching the cloth of both
trouser-legs just above the knees in order to ease the material up his thighs,
Jacques hinged from the waist and seated himself heavily. He adjusted his
cap, lowering the peak over his eyes. His arms dropped to his sides, his fingers
trailed just above the concrete surface of the floor. He pictured Jeanne in bed,
sleeping or reading the book he had given her. He would wish he was with

her. One night, she had turned on the lamp while they made love. Almost put him off his stroke. She had laughed, seeming contented. He saw well in the dark. They caressed each other's faces. A pleasing looseness in Jacques' groin and belly now allowed his legs to splay, his knees to fall apart. His scrotum relaxing, he felt his testicles drop down, as if lowered on a loosening line, slipping gently to rest above his anus. His eyes closed, his chin fell to his chest. An image of Edith, lithe and young, emerging from a mist.

↔↔↔↔↔↔

Marcel was bored. This happened most nights, sooner or later. It wasn't that he didn't have things to think about. He needed to consider his wedding plans and to decide which women to cut loose. He needed to ponder his future. There were plenty of topics. However, right now, these matters wearied him.

Standing at ease at the aisle-end of his machine, he glanced to left and right. He discarded the notion of going upstairs. He didn't yet know what to do about being told to fuck off by cousin Bobrán. Effective retaliation took time to finesse.

Marcel surveyed the shop floor: Philippe was reading; Jacques sat with his hands clasped over his cardigan and his eyes closed; Luigi's cigarette was about to burn his lower lip; Eric appeared to be checking his product. Who did that leave? An Algerian staring up at the ceiling and, up there in his glass-walled lookout, the foreman, jazz-man, 'scatter'-man, chewing on his matchstick. What a lineup! And the Sicilian, Monsieur Electro-Gym himself. Marcel counted his cigarettes, then stuck one in his mouth. He'd light it later.

Marcel wandered down the machine aisle until he came to rest at the end of Salvatore's machine six. Salvatore glanced up from his chair, quickly stowed in his attaché case the book he had been reading, then spun the combination rings. Marcel grinned and lit his cigarette, blowing smoke down at the Sicilian. 'Combination locks are the easiest damn things to pick,' he observed. Salvatore showed interest. Movies sprang to mind, featuring bank vaults, robbers with stethoscopes and swag bags. 'Don't you need to hear the clicks?' 'You can feel them, sense which numbers are right, so they fall into place. Child's play.' Salvatore grinned. 'Well, if it's child's play, be my guest: play!' Marcel made a fractional move toward the attaché case, then halted, glowering. What the Sicilian had meant was, 'Given that you're a child . . .' Marcel had been standing too close already. Now he towered over Salvatore.

The Sicilian attempted humour. 'Of course, if anything goes missing, I'll know . . .' 'You'll know what? That it was the thieving Gypsy?' 'I didn't mean that . . .' Marcel watched Salvatore squirm. 'I'm no thief. I wasn't locked up for thieving, but I met any number of Italians who were.' Salvatore's neck hurt from craning. He stood up slowly and stepped back. 'I didn't mean to imply anything . . .' Marcel fell back a step and confected the smile the Sicilian had longed for. 'You're all right,' Marcel assured him.

As press number seven opened, Salvatore wrenched back the safety guard and grabbed the latest piece from the mould. He seemed to check it, then dropped it in the floor tray at his feet. Marcel picked it up and examined it at length, then tossed it back. Salvatore spoke first. 'I hear you're getting married. So am I.' Marcel didn't know what to make of this gambit. 'Happens all the time,' he said at last.

Salvatore began to discourse on marriage, the need to settle, the yearning for stability and permanence, the urge to make your love official. Marcel let the words wash over him. He didn't know a man could talk like that. He stood and smoked, nodding and smirking. He sized the Sicilian up: good muscle tone, good posture, no belly, no slump, but somehow uncommitted. Who would come off worse in a fight? Marcel knew he couldn't stand a chance against Tomec – he had seen the man in action once – but he would probably take any of the others and most of them with one hand tied. The foreman might be a challenge for despite his age and injuries he would fight dirty and take pain like a sponge. But Salvatore? Marcel couldn't be sure. It would be interesting to see. A contest between Eastern experience and Southern strength, prison-yard cunning and wholesome stamina. Salvatore was flexing his hand-exerciser again, but still talking love and flowers and bullshit. Marcel felt impelled to advance a different viewpoint.

'The thing about marriage is that it gives you absolutely guaranteed pussy on tap round the clock – so that anything more is a bonus, a second helping.' Marcel hadn't asked a question, yet he was clearly waiting for an answer. While Salvatore racked his brains, Marcel said, 'I'm wondering what your fiancée looks like. I'm picturing the intellectual type. Heavy glasses. But hot. Am I right? Is she a ball-breaker?' In the place of Laure, an image of his mother burst unbidden into Salvatore's mind. Even a trained mind can let you down, he thought.

Marcel patted Salvatore on the shoulder and laughed. Both men relaxed a little. Marcel pointed down at the hand-exerciser, limp in Salvatore's left hand. 'There was this one guy in prison who spent all his time in the gym hauling weights, but one day he got taken apart by a wiry little Dijonais, half his size. It didn't seem right to interfere.' Salvatore nodded, instantly in charge of himself again, shutting both his mother and Laure back in their boxes. 'I know what you're saying. You never know if a man can take care of himself until you test him.' Marcel looked at the Sicilian's hands. His left one was working the exerciser again. Across its hairy back, venous hosing stood out, blue ridges overhanging snaking yellow valleys. Marcel gave a nod and returned to his machines.

One of the many drawbacks of being tall, strikingly handsome, and exceptionally fit, Salvatore reflected, was that you inevitably attracted men like Marcel, spoiling for a fight. He was probably a homosexual, but didn't know it. The sex talk was a cover. So disrespectful. Behind the times too. Salvatore looked at his watch. The waste of conversational and nervous effort was exasperating! What he needed to know was what Marcel, a temporary-agency worker and therefore non-unionized, planned to do if there was a strike. That was what mattered. However, Laure's glasses were in fact on the heavy side. Funny the things you don't notice. He might mention it to her. She'd listen. She knew he had an eye for things like that. Also, it was essential he phoned his mother. Tomorrow. At the very latest. She might actually be dying at long last. Oh God, he didn't mean that. He loved her. He would miss her. But then there would be Laure. He wouldn't be an orphan. Salvatore switched the exerciser to his right hand and flexed harder.

↔↔↔↔↔↔

Any attempt to extrapolate from superficial physique to matters of mental disposition or temperament – always a foolhardy procedure, whether in the adventurous realms of descriptive writing or in the experimental calculations of material power – might never be met with a more resounding rebuff than in the person of Rachid Boulabel, with regard to whom any attempt at a simple-minded read-across between these two domains would deliver to the hapless experimenter in politics or to the fearless adventurer in writing an object lesson in the vagaries of human constitution.

For Rachid, whose body appeared as frail as any late-autumn foliage – his cheeks hollow, his shoulders curved, his skin sallow, his limbs rickety, the crown of his head progressing from sparse to lunar – possessed a solidity of psyche to inspire envy in many who could boast far superior endowments of the physical variety.

The darts of outrageous sorrow and grief that disease, war and, most recently, casual catastrophe had visited upon Rachid, with torture of self and loved ones, massacre of comrades and family, capped by the hideous absurdity of peacetime death-by-moped of his first-born son: none of these had penetrated Boulabel's mental carapace, disrupted his understanding of the world, or measurably shaken his reason or wit, since these faculties subsisted at some remove from his emotions. He had wept but carried on. He had eaten, gone to work, looked after Fatima, conversed with Malika, read the newspapers, never once in all his wretchedness fearing for his own sanity. And wept again. Melancholia was endured, even at times embraced, but madness was confuted and repelled.

One of Rachid's unreflecting mental habits was to imagine the immediate future. This was an attention-shifting topic-changing move: rather than attend at any moment to his present pain, current anguish, instantly accessible woe, he would imagine in detail an event – however routine – looming in his immediate future. Weekends might have to be carefully planned, rendered predictable through the imposition of ritualized practices, but weekdays and nights lent themselves to this stratagem. As he fell asleep, he would cast his mind forward to waking, considering what he would wear, how he would breakfast; upon waking and dressing, he would anticipate collecting Fatima from the nursery and greeting Malika upon her return from work; over his evening meal, he would imagine his imminent walk to the factory; and at night, he would contemplate arrival home, construing and re-construing his entry into the sleeping apartment, his shedding of clothes, his thoughtful prostration beside his silent spouse.

By keeping his thoughts deflected from the present and interdicted from the past, Rachid honed an unusual armoury of mental muscle. He came to believe that he might now survive any shock, merely by puckering his focus to a vanishing point, while slashing away at all earlier dreams and aspirations. Though once inspired by a vision of socialist revolution sweeping the country of his birth and its neighbours from the pit into which nationalism had hurled it, in the wake of all the depredations and debaucheries of European colonial rule, latterly his ambitions for universal justice, economic equity, social liberation had shrunk to the dimension of mere family domesticity, as if it might be plausible in the climate of 1970s political reflux to place one's trust in 'socialism in one family.' However, though becalmed by historical reverse and intimate tragedy, the ambitions that as young man and boy he had cherished had not been wholly extinguished. Whenever induced to think or talk of such matters – for example, in occasional late-night conversations with Malika's indefatigably militant cousin Karim – Rachid would defend his outlook and attitude on the grounds of necessity and survival. He was living to fight another day, he would claim as he looked past his cousin. There would be time. Present time. In the future.

42. Donkeys, Sensation and Waddling.

Fernando loping down the machine aisle snagged the corner of Philippe's eye. 'Hey, we need to talk,' Philippe said, folding the newspaper on his lap, 'that nag you tipped lost me money.' His smile seemed to conceal menace. 'Well, it came in second,' Fernando said. 'I put money on it to win,' Philippe snapped, remaining seated. Fernando fidgeted. 'How much did you lose?' 'A week's wages.' 'Shit,' Fernando muttered. 'You?' Philippe asked. 'Forty francs.' Philippe shook his head, then hissed, 'I trusted you! You said you were doing me a favour! You didn't believe in your own tip.' Fernando darkened, his left eye blinked. 'Sure I did! It was solid.' 'Forty-francs solid.' 'I had it on authority. I didn't have fucking-any cash. If I had had . . .'

Fernando looked away. Philippe rolled his paper into a baton. Fernando took a step back. 'It nearly won,' he said. Philippe thwacked his calf with the baton and said, 'Nearly won!' Then he appeared to choke, grinned and burst out laughing. Fernando scratched an eyebrow and glanced up. Philippe's laughter started bitter but quickly lost its edge. 'Oh hell, I can't keep this up any longer,' Philippe blurted. 'What's fucking-so funny?' Fernando asked. 'Your face!' Philippe said. 'It's like a tombstone. Do I look like my wits are flown? I didn't put a centime on that donkey. I'm surprised it finished. In a month's time it'll be cat food. That bookies-bar is notorious. There are scams they're working you haven't even dreamt of. One day it'll be busted wide open, the small-time guys will go to gaol, then the guns will come out.'

Fernando looked puzzled. 'What are you talking about? How do fucking-you know?' Philippe looked away from Fernando, sighed, then stared back into him. 'I listen. I look. I ask questions. I talk to people. I read things. I take an interest.' 'Okay, okay,' Fernando said. Philippe interlaced his fingers and actually started twiddling his thumbs.

'Look,' Fernando said, his face brightening, 'I suppose I could do you that haircut for free.' Philippe burst out laughing again. 'But if I told you I didn't lose a centime! Besides, what do you want me to do with a few spare francs, except spend them on pastis? I'm a drunk, damn it! No, forget I said that. I'll take the haircut.' Philippe glanced over at Marcel standing at the aisle-end of his machine. 'You did a decent enough job on him. He keeps checking his reflection and patting his hair. How much did you take?' 'Six francs.' 'Not bad.' 'It's a skill. It takes a long time to learn. I had to buy scissors and stuff.' 'How come you didn't offer me a free haircut when you thought I was down a week's pay?' 'I figured you'd hit me.' Philippe grinned, while Fernando cocked his head this way and that, assessing the task. 'What kind of cut do you want?' 'Just a trim, a tidy-up.' Fernando sensed it was his turn to mock. 'Your hair's a mess, do you know that?' 'I'm hurt.' 'Who's been doing it up to now? I'm betting your wife.' 'Not any more,' Philippe said, 'the job's yours.' Then, avuncular, 'But do me a favour: stay away from those crooks. I don't want my personal barber mown down at dawn.'

Fernando nodded and walked away. He felt he had had a close escape. And that Philippe had saved him from something.

↔↔↔↔↔↔↔

Upstairs, seated at the huge old semi-automatic machine, the little man was experiencing a perfect instant of dull vacancy. To be savoured in retrospect. For the time being, Jean was what he did. No more no less. He pressed START. The mould closed. He waited. The mould opened. He slid back the guard. He tore the cable ties from the sprue. He dropped the cable ties in the box, the sprue in the bin. He slid the guard to. He pressed START. He waited. Into Jean's bladder, as he leaned to the right to slap the button, his kidneys delivered the critical drop of urine that lit up the 'Bladder Full!' light in his cortex, wrenching him from mental torpor as the thought fired, 'I need to go. Where is the foreman?' It was a long-standing arrangement that Mathieu operated Jean's machine for one brief bladder-break at around 22.45 and for another at 03.15. Jean glanced at his chronomètre. Gift from Niquette. 22.52 and 46 seconds. 47. 48. Dear Niquette. Heavens alive! So glad she wasn't dying. She would probably outlive him. He wouldn't grieve at his missed brothel visits. Not a lot could rock Jean Herbier's boat! He ploughed his furrow, knew his place! Mould open! He could still fantasize. Besides, sex with whores might be better imagined than real. And Monique still might die. You can't rely on anything. Reprieves aren't always final. He should know. The damned foreman was running late. Through the open mould Jean glimpsed the African. Dwell on him? Black man, prancing around, mouthing stuff. Good reader though. Offensive about the Maid just now. Can't expect him to understand. And earlier, siding with the union. Never know what is good for them, do they? What do you think? But the Italian wasn't there to ask. The Italian would nod and smirk. He usually came upstairs by this time. His machine was still malfunctioning maybe. Time to brush mould? Not quite.

Sticking only slightly. One more product and then. Slide the guard to. Press START. Funny all the people who end up here. Not just in this factory. In France. East Europeans. Fugitives from Communism. Like the Polish night security man, I had always assumed. Still, all those Czechs, Hungarians, Yugoslavs: dissidents flooding in. So why don't our Commies go and live over there? Cohn-Bendit, Marchais, Krivine, Mitterand, and the rest of them. When it comes down to it, they don't like it up 'em, that's why! The other side wouldn't give them much of a welcome: they're born troublemakers; indeed half of them are Jews. Jean glanced sideways, sorry his interlocutor's space was still empty. The Italian was a good listener. When in the mood for intelligent conversation. Press START. Wait. An instant of dullness again. Which the other workers experience all night long. I could proceed with my news review, though the Italian or the foreman are sure to turn up at once if I do. Besides, the Italian may know something about the graffiti or the strike plans. Then on to regional, national, international and planetary develop-ments. But first my pee. Just time to dwell a little more on the domestic. Dab the brush in oil. Not too much. Lightly over the ejector pins. Slide guard. Press START. Because now our crisis is past, I must talk to Monique. Sit her down. Give her a chance to express gratitude for my kindnesses and indul-gence. Then gently pull back from trips abroad. Now you're not dying, what's the hurry? Let's wait till I stop working. Or you could go alone! I can look after myself for a week or two. Watch her face! Then look away as she looks up. Monique was good to him, though it didn't come as naturally as it ought, in a wife. He would set her new tasks, be distant for a bit. Find her new chal-lenges. Keep her in trim. Suggest new pursuits, courses of study even. She was always busy improving herself. Perhaps a new diet. A special anti-cancer one. He'd heard of some. It's best to control a woman's intakes, including the mental ones. After all, the mind is an orifice too. Obviously. Waxing and waning like some kind of giant. Letting things in, pushing them back out. Giant what? Mollusc, let's just say. The measure of a man is in his relations with women. Who said that? The Bible probably. Though not in so many words. Men understand it at once. Measure, indeed. If only I had been larger, taller, what could I not have achieved? Mustn't think that. Always thinking that. Rip the cable ties from the sprue. Dump ties in box and sprue in bin. It's absolutely true though. The world could have been my mollusc. Turned down for military service on account of my size. Nobody ever made a uniform that small, some dickhead had joked. I remember balling a fist then thinking how much bigger he was than me. A man who hasn't been to war always wonders how he would have shaped up. Coward or hero? I always knew which side I was on, but never had the chance to show true commitment. Let alone draw blood. Might now be the time? Perhaps Boucan could use a man on the shop floor, a man who kept his ear to the ground, and could be discreet. I wouldn't mind a confidential role. I could still be useful in a strike. Meticulous. Patient. Dogged. Prudent. I have qualities. Press START. Now that Monique's health was fine, wouldn't it be funny if he was the one about to croak? Not funny exactly. His heart had never been right. The doctors couldn't find anything of course. He probably oughtn't to be working. He recalled the night he had had palpitations. A Sunday morning. Woke at 04.00. Had only just fallen asleep. He had felt his pulse. Crazy. All over the place. Boom-rata-ping-boom. Then nothing for ages, then bu-boom. Monique had put her ear to his chest. He told her to tap out the rhythm on his forearm. She kept yawning. Doctor said to come back if it ever happened twice in the same month. What the hell do they know? They don't feel what I feel. Or I could join the FN. You have to stand up for your own. Voting isn't enough. I could sell the paper. Or put up posters at elections. On my way home from work. There's no one on the streets at 5 a.m. No point getting beaten up. Caution, not cowardice. Jean glimpsed the little Gypsy as the mould opened. Worth a thought? Seems to be sleeping, slouched on that chair. I could teach him to read. In our meal breaks. Five minutes a night. The African might help. Probably couldn't be bothered. Either of them. I have nothing against these people, in their own countries. But if I did drop down dead, if my heart did give out, or if I fell into the jaws of this machine, would they follow my casket? Would they bring flowers to my grave? Would they hell. It's memory they lack, French memory. They have no memory of this country, only of their own, which doesn't count. It's like a missing link. You can never truly belong where you weren't born. For their children, it'll be different. Provided there aren't too many of them. Whereas I remember everything. What like? Well, I recall when the roads were one-lane and empty. They have no idea. I remember when young people were respectful. I remember when women were graceful. 'Graceful.' Say that word now and people cackle. Young people have no memory and therefore no nostalgia. And where is a society without nostalgia? Nostalgia is a brake on the revolutionary impulse. Without it, chaos. The Italian – Luigi, funny name that . . . – will come up soon. I'll see if he knows anything. Not about nostalgia or the past, of course. He's allergic to history talk. The past is bunk, he says. Makes you suspicious. Not even original. The foreman had better come soon. I can't hold it for ever. Monique bought me my favourite beer. Belgian. Proof that every nation is good for something. Or their monks are. Goes straight through you. And now my back's beginning to hurt. Press START. I'll move the chair in closer. I don't want to damage my spine like I did two years ago. Or was it four? Agony and belts and straps. For months. Painkillers to knock out a rhino. Never took a day off. Never complained. Only Monique knew how I suffered. I have worked this machine with a bad back, fever, flu, bronchitis, a urinary infection – that was a tough one: pissing into a bottle behind the machine that time the foreman spotted me. Tried to explain but he wasn't interested. I didn't care if the other men saw. They understood. Everybody owns a bladder, don't they? The product's sticking a bit now. The Portuguee hadn't started here yet. Maybe it needs oil again already. It was that old Tunisian who worked the Portuguee's machines. Not that they were ever exactly his machines. I know what I mean. One night the Tunisian didn't come in. Then someone – the Marseillais downstairs probably – announced he was dead. Everyone was shocked. We stopped for a drink. The foreman found a packet of biscuits and passed it round. Biscuits with currants in. I never liked currants. Then the foreman said some words. No, the Portuguee could definitely be useful. Useful to Monique. Do some DIY. They all know DIY. Keep her off my back. Pay some rent too. Nothing extortionate. We're not Jews, are we? He could have the little room. Portuguese are Europeans. Christians. A mix of Latin and Celt. Like us, give or take. Nothing wrong with that. With an extra bit of Arab thrown in. That's history for you. Invasion. Rape and Pillage. Not their fault. Portugal is south of Poitiers. Brush oil now or next time? Next time. Press START.

↔↔↔↔↔

In the kitchen he shared with Eric, Callum, a square-featured man from Aberdeen, was drinking, smoking and munching a baguette smeared with pâté de campagne and Daddies' sauce. Meanwhile a further housemate, Chris, swaddled in a greatcoat on a vast and fetid armchair, his knees up to his chin, gripped a bottle of beer in his left hand, a roll-up in his right, while a half-consumed novel by John Wyndham languished between left knee and chair arm. Equidistant between these men stood a paraffin stove with yellow guttering flame.

Callum was waxing homesick, alleging his heart beat only in the Highlands, and longing loudly to be in Scotland 'for the lambing.' Chris waited for a chance to return to the Chrysalids. 'I can think of only six places to drink in this town,' Callum said, pausing for dramatic effect. Chris sighed and waited. 'And one of them is right here.'

There was no need for Chris to request a review of local hostelries: Callum was going to supply it anyway. He had lived for a time in Glasgow and liked nothing better than to recount famous lock-ins with singers, fighters and poets – 'true Clydesmen all.' Chris wondered how Callum had induced himself to abandon such an idyll. It was a long way to come to drive a deliveries van.

Chris worked in a dairy. It was a steady job. People weren't about to stop using milk. He came from a village in County Durham. He kept himself to himself.

'Ach! it's the tastes you miss the most,' Callum was moved to reflect. 'The smells tae. Heather in the gloaming and such. But mainly the tastes. Six years I've been away. I'd kill for a fish supper, man! Or black pudding. Or snakebite with Tennents. There's nae replacing the tastes you knew as a bairn. Six years. Think on that number!'

Chris looked at all the fingers of his right hand. Plus one, he told himself. Not wishing to inject any life into the conversation, he said nothing.

Callum started to croon, 'I'm not in love' by 10cc. Chris cradled his book, set his face to a frown, and read.

*

At a filling-station six kilometres south of Le Puy, Jules Romanès, Marcel's father, plunged a coin into his cash-pouch, the skinny pads of his fingers chafing against the rough leather as they floated back up and out.

The Saab was taking off down the road, accelerating hard. Romanès returned to his booth, pulling the door tight shut by its cold slick knob. There was nothing to this job. Nights were quiet midweek. The pay was honest and sometimes – when you did someone's windscreen – you might get a tip. You hoped for muddy weather or national holidays to make people generous.

The Saab driver had handed him a key to unlock the cap. The tank had taken for ever to fill. Romanès had stood there in the drizzle. Soon it would be hard to find a car the kids could siphon without taking a screwdriver to the fuel-tank cap.

Jules Romanès thought how his son would admire that Saab, how Marcel loved cars in general. He wished he could visit him, make it all up. He hoped his son wasn't back inside. He probably wouldn't want to see me, Romanès thought. I might go down anyway, catch a glimpse of him. See him going about his business. Or with a woman. Maybe a child too. Best of all if I could tell it was his. Like any fool can tell Marcel is mine. Same shape of head. Same skin.

Jules shivered. He had plugged in a fan heater. Against all regulations. The booth didn't get any warmer.

*

Rémy sat on the sofa with his half of the TV-dinner. Nicole had kissed him, promised to cook him something tomorrow, then gone to bed. She hadn't showered all day. He liked the way she smelt. If she had lingered, he would have kissed her forearms, working himself up, holding her hands in his.

He pushed the tray away and lifted his glass of cut-price Burgundy, hearing already the click it would make on the pine table as he set it down. It was then he had a hunch. Rémy felt that the old girl, Lucie, was in danger. The sensation was as imperious and as unequivocal as a wave of nausea: it was like knowledge. He rose, took his coat from a hook, let himself out. He'd be back soon. No need to trouble Nicole.

He stopped on the landing. 'C'est complètement idiot,' he whispered. He stood in the dark. He leaned back on the door. What could happen to Lucie in her safe house? Could she be attacked? Could the place burn down? If I turn up and there's nothing, she'll think I'm as crazy as she is. If I hesitate and I'm too late, I'll never have to worry about her again. If I arrive in the nick of time, I'll be her lifelong slave. If I'm not already. She prompted the only big and generous action I ever accomplished, didn't she? I'm forever in her debt.

Rémy let himself back in. Walking on tiptoes. Spooked. He sat down and finished the wine. How will I fall asleep tonight? If only Nicole wanted a piece of me. That always works. I could try her, I suppose. It's been a while. She used to like being woken that way. She might still come through. Rémy watched his empty glass as if it had the answer.

*

In Malmo, Angelica was standing by the phone in the entrance that she and her boyfriend shared with neighbours. She lifted the receiver at the first 'ping.' It was her Spanish friend Rosa. They waited tables together at a town-centre cafeteria. Angelica spoke softly, cupping a hand round the mouthpiece.

'Tenías razon. Me voy . . . France, I've made my mind up . . . I told you already I have a brother there . . . No, Ricky didn't hit me again. He can't apologize enough . . . Because if I stay I'll always be looking out . . . Tonight, as soon as I've packed . . . He's sleeping . . . Yeah, he's on earlies tomorrow . . . I'll leave him a note . . . You don't understand . . . But I'll miss you too . . . I've had it in this country. It's not only Rick . . . We talked about it already, didn't we? You can visit me . . . Maybe . . . Well, I do . . . I'll write you . . . Listen, Listen! Could you pick up what Carlo owes me? It's nine full days and one half . . . Yeah . . . No . . . Are you sure? That'd be great. Look . . . Er . . . Have you, by any chance, got it on you? . . . That's such a help to me. I didn't want to land penniless on my brother's doorstep . . . I'll come round . . . I wanted to say a proper goodbye anyway . . . Half an hour, twenty minutes . . . No, but thanks . . . With a truck driver . . . Midnight from his depot. He'll drop me at Charleroi . . . Somewhere in Belgium . . . I'll hitch . . . Don't worry about me. Soy portuguesa! Indestrutível.'

Angelica put the phone down and went back into the flat. She listened carefully. Light snoring came from the bedroom. Ricky got such colds! He needed to eat more fruit. She was always telling him. Or vitamin C. Angelica took out a large hold-all from a cupboard.

*

Paul Boucan sat on Antoine's pallet-bed, waiting for his student friend to bring him a cup of lime-blossom tea. Antoine's flatmate, Marielle, came into the room. 'Ah! c'est toi!' she said, with a thick nasal lisp, unsurprised.

Marielle plonked herself down on a chair, the legs of which were painted light blue, while the seat was deep orange and the back a livid green. She began to construct a joint, arranging the needful materials on a Captain Beefheart album sleeve chosen from Antoine's collection.

On the wall behind Marielle, a giant jeans trouser-zipper was depicted halfway down, in the same colours as the chair. Paul noted the sharpness of the zipper's teeth.

'Do you like it?' Marielle asked. Paul nodded. 'I'm actually studying biology,' Marielle said. 'But if you've got a spare wall, I could do you something. I don't charge. Moi, j'adore le pop art.'

The first time Paul had come to Antoine's flat, he had met a rat coming down the stairs, just as he was going up. It had teetered mid-flight on a nosing, eyeing him, its left forepaw clenched in the air, its head jerking this way and that like a boxer drilling to dodge blows. On an impulse it had turned, dropped its head, and beat it back upstairs.

Antoine entered the room with a tray bearing a saucepan, three cups and six biscuits. On top of the pan a plate did service as a lid. Marielle lit the joint and took a mighty puff, holding the smoke down hard. She took another, without letting the first one out. Antoine sat at the end of his bed, while the tisane infused. Paul picked a copy of *Carnets Rouges* from the floor. It came open at an unsigned article beside a black-on-white image of Ulrike Meinhof. Head and shoulders. Some kind of linocut, he reckoned. The lady's eyes were missing.

'I'll have to go soon,' Paul said. Antoine passed him the joint. Paul's Solex was downstairs, inside a street door that didn't shut properly. He needed it to ride home on. Marielle exhaled her smoke in giggles. Paul took a careful drag and glanced again at the picture of the German. He felt unbearably young.

*

Bobrán's mother was panting and pacing. She had thrown open all the windows in her trailer. The stench the intruder had left behind was dispersing too slowly. Why do certain women douse themselves in costly perfumes? Whores trying to hide their rottenness. Don't they know we'll always sniff out their commerce somehow? The bitch arrived at my door, rubbing her hands already over my threshold, pushing herself in here where she's not wanted, warning me of malicious tongues! acting the part of my friend! but

in fact speaking for the rumour-mongers, sullying my son with her innuen-
does, Bobrán who never hurts a soul, whose every secret is open, who lives
like a shroud in the clear light of day. He does not need to tell me what he
is. I am his mother! How dare that raven talk of God and man and sin! She
should look to her own household, I told her. That shut her beak. If that's
your attitude, she said with a sneer. I picked up the frying pan. Only to see
her cower. I wouldn't demean myself. Bobrán never cowers. What god should
he dread? What wrong does he do? He saved his sister. Saved her honour,
her body, kept her whole. Yitoune and I know who Bobrán is. Only we. The
things men do together are unclean, the reeking bitch said. Sticking things
in where things are only ever supposed to come out, she said, wrinkling her
superfine nose. He's my son, and if he did wrong I'd know it. Besides, even
killing is not always murder. No lion ever murdered, did he? Nor can it be
wrong to love. What god condemns it? Nobody could be a better brother.
Does any woman have a better son? That crow has no son at all. Her God
gave her nothing but girl-childs. At night she howls with envy. I could pity
her. Whatever God wrote in the Bible is not for me to know. It was long
ago. He would be easier on us now. The God I believe in would love Bobrán,
would have respect for him. He is a mild God who searches out the good in
people. How dare she come here, upsetting my thoughts, corrupting the air
I breathe, menacing my son, then slinking away into the dark like a serpent.
I'll keep this to myself. Bobrán won't need to know. He who works so hard
always! That such forked and evil tongues should exist! The she-snake won't
return. Now I'll close these windows.

↔↔↔↔↔

Prison had marked a watershed in Marcel's life. Until the day of his incarceration, childish allegiances still swelled his breast and quickened his pulse,
even ancient loyalties retained some hold. His cell's four walls, however, had
quickly stripped him of any sense he was a Gypsy, a proletarian, a Christian,
a citizen of France, or even a native of Grandgobier, just as they had vapor-
ized every feeling for former associates, and scoured his affective tissue of
significant adhesions to social or family relations. In later years, it seemed to
Marcel that the prison staff had impounded all such trappings along with his
watch, wallet and ear studs: I shan't be wanting those back, he would recollect
saying, as he deposited them on the guard's metal tray.

Marcel's imprisonment, while placing his body under lock and key, had disclosed a freedom that was tantalizing and ticklish, starting at his now studless ears but quickly taking possession of the interjacent matter: a freedom from human solidarities. After all, in the weeks between his arrest and his sentencing, everyone and everything to which he had previously cleaved had proven either indifferent to his plight or impotent to mitigate it.

Embracing silence, Marcel had at first refused food, company, conversation and cooperation – not in protest at his conditions of detention but rather in order to contemplate without distraction the arguments for and against self-slaughter. Then, partly in response to the gentle promptings of a prison psychotherapist, he had started to consider what might be made of his life, how he might control his less serviceable impulses, and even acquire some influence over the whirlpools of thought that frequently tormented his mind. At night, his eyes fixed on the ceiling, his toes aligned like those of a corpse filed in the steel drawer of a city morgue, Marcel had begun to imagine his future.

On release from prison in the winter of 1975, Marcel had observed the world through the agreeably hard-focus and wide-angled lens provided by the streets he frequented, the bars he used, the rooms he slept in, the strangers he encountered, and then increasingly through the films, television, publicity hoardings and magazines that flickered before him. Marcel's outlook became imitative and acquisitive as he embarked upon the creation for himself of a singular face with which not only to meet the faces that he met, but even, when necessary, to face those faces down.

Alive as never before to the delicate and spectacular gradations apparent in the human features, behaviours and attitudes ranged before him as upon a supermarket display shelf, eroding his previous and simpler understanding of people as workers, students, old, young, foreigners, French, male, female, friends or foes, Marcel discerned communities of consumption that he might aspire eventually to join: that of Alfa Romeo drivers; that of Lacoste-shirt wearers; that of moderate Glenfiddich drinkers, and so on. Just as this work of persona accretion proceeded, Marcel's life goals emerged as from beneath a fairytale mist both clearer and more modest: he desired a settled home, one special woman, a modicum of respect, a reliable vehicle, a means of securing comfort without risking re-incarceration.

The slow evolution of his long-term aims and the piecing-together of a world-worthy and storm-proof personality might sometimes coincide.

Recently, sensing that Chantal was the main woman for him, Marcel had happened to see a film starring Lino Ventura as a tough-talking plain-dealing cop. On the ring finger of the actor's left hand, Marcel, who had always appreciated jewellery, had spotted a chunky gold wedding band, which he had immediately coveted. On leaving the cinema, Marcel's thoughts had turned tenderly to Chantal, and within days he had engineered circumstances likely to prove auspicious to a marriage proposal. His ring finger would never look right until sheathed with that gold.

↔↔↔↔↔↔↔

Laurent, Alphonse's mother's brother, was strolling along Boulevard Vincent Auriol in Paris's 13th arrondissement, accompanying Juliette, his girlfriend, to the street door of her chambre de bonne, which lay across the river in the Douzième. They had been together for months now yet he still couldn't get her to sleep a whole night through in his apartment, nor to explain her reluctance. Even at one or two a.m., she would get up and leave. 'I like to wake up at home' was the most she would say.

Accordingly, they spent many evenings, not a few afternoons, and even the occasional morning at Laurent's apartment. But to share a night it seemed he had to take her away for a weekend.

They had met in mid-July at a Fête de l'Humanité fringe meeting about African liberation struggles. Juliette, a historian researching her doctorate, had spoken of the Ivorian landed bourgeoisie and its long-term collaboration with the now 'former' colonial power, France. Laurent had been impressed. They had discussed her thesis. A liaison had easily and naturally ensued. With August fast approaching, it had proved too late for Laurent to wriggle out of any part of his Breton summer-seaside commitments with his estranged wife and children. Besides, Juliette appeared quite content to spend the month, as usual, with her parents' and siblings' families in the Lubéron. In September, Laurent and Juliette endured a dull weekend in Strasbourg, followed in October by a much worse one in London.

The couple walked arm in arm in silence. Laurent, who taught maths at a lycée outside Paris, devoted most of his energies to community matters. He was a born organizer, completely wasted – his friends often teased – on teaching. He had long run a successful Ivorian club, but now set his sights rather higher. He wanted to found a cultural association that would bring together West Africans of every nationality and background. A forum was needed in which Senegalese, Togans, Camerounians, Nigerians, Ivorians, Ghanaians, Liberians, Mauritanians, Sierra Leonians and others could meet, socialize, agitate, party and debate their histories and current conditions in their countries and regions. Juliette thought it was a good idea. Laurent had innumerable contacts and the charm and cheek to pull strings and, when necessary, to bluster. He got things done. As she pointed out to him, 'there is a critical mass of Africans in Paris now. If anybody can bring this off, you can.' Laurent was grateful for her support.

Stopping now at the street-door of her tiny top-floor flat, Juliette said, 'You're miles away, aren't you?' 'You said you liked walking at night in silence,' Laurent replied. 'Do you want to come up?' 'Do you want me to?' 'What are we going to do if you come up? You can't stay.' He grinned. She didn't. 'You're not getting tired of me?' Laurent asked. 'No,' Juliette said, 'but I am tired. Besides, you know I like to be alone sometimes.' Laurent nodded. They kissed goodnight.

She took the key from her pocket and watched him go. He was too old for her. That was a fact. Whenever they met anywhere, he always pulled his gut in as he walked toward her. Not that he had much of a gut. It was the self-consciousness of the older man. Yet again, she had fallen for a man too old for her. She couldn't say she hadn't seen it coming. She had seen *him* coming. She thought it would be a short fling. Juliette was incapable of short flings. She took people seriously. And the longer she knew someone, the more serious she became. She began asking questions, making demands. Usually, that finished it. With this particular man, however, the more questions she asked, the more answers she received. The more demands she made, the more this man, this Laurent, seemed determined to satisfy her. And never in quite the ways she expected. He was at the end of the street now. She could see he was about to turn left, vanish from view. He had relaxed and was positively waddling. He probably assumed she had let herself in by now and would not still be watching him. Laurent kept her interested like it was an art form. But at least they didn't wake up together. That would be the end of it. She'd start missing him and grow possessive. She knew herself a little by now. Next thing, she'd be moving in with him. Which might be fine for a while. But, damn it, he was too old for her. Too old. Looked at another way, perhaps moving in together was the way to end it. He had turned the corner now and was gone from view. The street looked fantastically empty. As if Laurent had never been there. Waddling. Right there. Where she now made out a Laurent-shaped hole, his absence a silhouette. She turned the key in the lock.

43. Psyching, *Speculans* and Skimming.

Standing here like this at my machine feeling so sharp so alive knowing that everything changed in an instant that instant I saw that the brunette no! Fanny no! Fan-*nie*'s right hand was holding a cigarette so I couldn't shake it and she looked at me and said Du feu like it was clearly a command not a question and everything changed everything. I really mustn't mess up now I need to focus on these pieces but they all look just the same it's like doing a kiddies' spot-the-difference puzzle counting the little lines in one picture counting the little lines in the other except here it's the sticky-out bits but all I see and think and hear is Fanny and the way she pronounced her name Fan-*nie* leaning back on the second syllable and her voice husky and soft beneath the din then E-rique though how did she know my name? And even if she stands me up on Saturday night dumping me with my wilting flowers or gift-wrapped box of chocolates like an idiot outside the cinema in the rain and on Monday evening laughs in my face with those lips spread wide that she pursed to say Du Feu and her head thrown back and her tits tilting for ever away from me even so there will always be a before and an after that instant at the clock-machine because everything that happened before is now more distant and strange than ever it was and all the plans I need to make now for Saturday night are making me think of different futures and all of them imaginable and possible because although I mustn't take anything for granted I do have a date a date a date a date! with the brunette with Fanny maybe my Fan-*nie* so I'll go straight home from work tomorrow morning no blanc-limé with Philippe and the big Gypsy and the peasant chez Hortense no! but home and start cleaning the place the kitchen the toilet my bedroom in case Fanny comes back and I'll buy some fancy drinks and eats and change the bedclothes and buy new sheets (if Chris or Callum will lend me the dough though they're bound to moan and fuss the tight gits) but I can't be explaining how Megan once came on early or be switching the light off so Fanny doesn't spot the brown stain in the centre of the sheet but how come blood goes brown anyway? I hope that Scottish smoothie isn't around on Saturday night or I could bribe him to stay out late because women go for that sort and he's got the lingo and all the patter! I bet he can lick ladies' boots to a sheen in three languages. Still I mustn't get ahead of myself or *expect* Fanny to come back or seem like I've counted my chickens but just be cool cool cool however much effort that takes and practice too and preparation so everything is just right and anyway maybe she'll take control like she did at the clock-machine which is thrilling more thrilling than even her tits could ever be though the wondrous shape of her whole – well – person is all I have had to go on for weeks now till I heard her voice and saw her close up and felt her cool cool way and mischievous glance and firm command which is all I can see now blotting these pieces right out but I'm sure they're fine and I simply can't stare at them any longer so maybe I should sit down and try reading again but Steinbeck is suddenly boring English seems dull even American writing seems tedious and to think I loved it and studied it for three long years at Sheffield and now all I want is French – I should have studied that – but now I've got to learn it and I'm living in the right country aren't I? It's as if that instant with Fanny has turned me on a sixpence and now I really know that I'm here to stay and that what I said in my letter to Mum about this factory being the centre of my world is truer than I knew when I wrote it even if it shocked her and besides if it isn't Fanny it'll be someone else though I don't mean to be disloyal in my thoughts already but it's true and I'm not going back to England now and it's over with Megan it just has to be unless of course she wants to come here at Christmas and if, say, I'm alone otherwise because, say, it hasn't worked out with Fanny but even then no! Imagine instead a Christmas with Fanny – what would that be like? No-oh-ell, No-oh-ell, All the angels did sing, Something something, Born is the Ki-hing of Ih-his-ray-ell. Except in French, obviously. So I have to plan things right and then trust to chance to mood to Fanny to circumstances and let things just happen – like load the goddamned dice so I don't have to play them – and I'll have a shave and a good shower at the all-day hotel at the station and scrub my nails and clean out my ears and soap my privates because you never know it did happen once on a first date though Fanny is French but what's the difference? What's the difference? Am I kidding myself? Everything is the difference! Whatever happens with Fanny even if it's noth-ing at all I now know I need a new place to live because I can't be sharing any longer with ex-pats a Scotsman who listens to Genesis and some Durham miner's son whose evening excitement is to hurl a cricket ball ricocheting round the flat like it's a squash court no! I need to live with French or at least non-English. Why wasn't that clear to me two hours ago? And I need French – the language but not *just* the language – maybe I haven't been trying hard enough but I need it now to think straight and it's as urgent as my need of food to live and of a woman a *French* woman to feel right in myself and my need to stay here in this town in this factory till I grow into the place and it grows into me. I'm tired of everyone I've been, the books I've read, the words I dream, the clothes I wear, I don't know, even the way I eat pickle with everything. What else? Everything, that's all. But it's the feeling of lugging this fat corpse of English words and ideas and ballast of upbringing and Val Doonican on TV and *The Archers* and everything so familiar and known and everybody predictable and boring in England the moment you meet them and they open their mouths and my tongue bound up in doughy knots and prevented by English from speaking the single language I now need which is French and which is so much better livelier freer not so buttoned up and battened down and it's all so obvious now that it's embarrassing once you've grasped it and how come I've only just realized that you have to forget what you know before you can learn what you need? Embarrassment . . . My parents embarrass me my friends the country I come from the school I went to the books I read my clumsiness my background my body my smell but my thoughts are the worst it's the inside of my head . . . Every time I shuffle inside a bookshop here the very first table I see blows my mind with stuff from every country in the world and all epochs and disciplines and viewpoints jostling like apples down a chute heading into the great French Mind and all utterly promiscuous and available somehow in a way that nothing ever is in England where you have to apologize endlessly if ever you stray outside your allotted zone and jump through hoops to feel entitled to look at anything you haven't already been schooled exactly how to see but the people here on the buses read Michel Butor and Merleau-Ponty as if they were Harold Robbins and Dale Carnegie and if they read anything English of course it's American and it's Gregory Corso but in French! Malcolm Lowry in French! or Kerouac's *Sur la route*! Borroughs's *Le Festin nu* . . . I am being born anew and getting a fresh chance, a French chance, 'cause I was never going to make it as an English suburbanite though my parents maybe like to think this is all a late-teenage diversion an aberration and still hope I'll grow out of it and come home and get a job and put on a suit and turn into Hendrix's white-collar conservative or Dylan's Mr Jones. No! I've seen the light my *light* and it's French or if not exclusively French then it's European. England's dying and I don't care. I'm out of England now and now I want England out of me, root and branch, out out out! I know that at best I'm a fucking cipher here to everyone – to the big Gypsy I'm the butt of some joke I don't understand, while those Italians blast the English for 'hypocrisie' and I know they're right of course they're right though I don't yet know quite how and even Stan Laurel in his cardigan upstairs thinks I'm a sheep and the African makes me feel lumpish and uncouth and what the hell does the brunette see anyway? why is Fanny (Fan-nie!) willing to meet me for the cinema? Surely going to the cinema with someone you hardly know means the same here as it does back home. 'Home' did I say? Home? But could she find me attractive? Why not? Opposites attract, right? Maybe the pasty-faced, narrow-shouldered, cave-chested, spotty, prolonged-adolescent type is exotic here. I'm kidding myself now. Hell, I'm not that bad. I have my points. Long hair's still cool in France, right? I can look okay in a dark cinema. So what am I going to say to her? I'll spend from here till Saturday evening learning phrases but I just hope she's not one of those women who have to discuss the film as they amble out the cinema because the French take film so damn seriously and they're right of course they're right and I will take it seriously too as soon as I can read *Cahiers du cinéma* and understand more than two words together. It's so weird to be here and to feel this stupid and unschooled and at the same time childishly excited as a new language opens up before me, even if it's happening too slowly. Damn it, I'll prise it open like a fucking oyster if it kills me. Everything in England from parents school family friends exam results university always told me I was clever or if not clever at least not hopelessly stupid provided of course I worked twice as hard at everything as everybody else so I had to come here to learn the truth which is that I am stupid, clumsy, slow, boring and can never be anything else until I've sloughed off everything I've known up to now and it is this dumb factory and Fanny or someone like her that is going to strip me down like with paint-remover so I come out the other end smooth and shiny and naked as a worm but with a brand-new language and an embryonic mind and a life ahead of me and the chance to stand aside and see things straight and yes! I've been waiting without knowing it all my short life for this sensation and it was that moment at the clock-machine when I saw her hand wasn't empty but held a cigarette in it and that instead of shaking it and then maybe chickening out all over again I was going to have to find my cigarette lighter and psych myself up and pop the question. She could have got a light from any one of her shift-mates who of course just stood there grinning. She *made* me then and she's going to make me on Saturday. Do what? I can't know quite what it'll be but it'll be good it'll be new. Du Feu? You bet.

↔↔↔↔↔

Luc never ceased to blame himself. Not for anything he had done or omitted to do but for having served as the instrument of something that seemed like fate. The brakes of his moped had been tested and the tyres changed shortly before the accident; his reactions had not been blunted by tiredness or drink nor his nerves jangled by any narcotic; nor was he of a reckless or absent-minded disposition. He had tried to swerve and miss Mehdi – to Luc, the child was always 'Mehdi' – but had still been the material cause of the child's death.

Luc had picked himself up from the tarmac, kneading a shoulder and then picking grit from his left hand, expecting the child to do much the same, but Mehdi's head had struck kerbstone. The autopsy made Luc's criminal innocence plain, but his guilt was beyond matters of intention or will.

Luc was sitting alone at a bar, drinking beer slowly. Beside him sat a stranger who spoke French with an American accent. Luc had worked late, then eaten at a restaurant with his boss, a Swiss named Richard Müller. After the accident, Müller had been patient, allowing Luc time off, overlooking some lacklustre work. Now he was issuing a gentle warning. 'Are you going to allow one tragic accident to ruin your life? You are a talented young architect. The work you did on Villeneuve was brilliant. But recently . . . Talent has to be tended, cultivated, if you want a career. It's eighteen months, isn't it? Besides, it would help you to focus on work. Times are hard. We can't carry anybody.'

Luc nodded and said, 'I understand. You must do what is best for the firm.' Müller pushed his chair back and exclaimed, 'React, Luc! Wake up! What good does all this grieving do anyone? The living need buildings in which to play and work and grow and you can design them and do the job well. Réagis!' Luc had thanked his boss and promised to try. The two men looked one another briefly in the eye. Müller shook his head and picked up the bill.

Luc's beer stood before him on the counter. Soon the barmaid would take it away and he'd decide whether he wanted another. Earlier he had had the queasy feeling that the barmaid was flirting with him. Women seemed to find him more interesting than before. Perhaps it was his quietness, his brooding. Could they smell his anguish? He distrusted anyone who would flirt with him in this state.

The previous month, one evening after work, Luc had found his way to Rachid and Malika's home. Surprised to see a woman with a child in her arms open the door, Luc had not known what to say. He had stared at Fatima, who had clung to her mother. Rachid appeared behind them, recognizing the visitor, and signalled to Malika to withdraw.

Rachid had looked squarely at Luc and said, 'What can I do for you?' 'I never stop thinking about your son. Can I call him Mehdi?' 'I can't stop you.' 'I wish there was something . . .' Luc started. Rachid felt his teeth clench. Then Luc surprised himself: 'I could almost wish it were my own son I had killed.' Rachid's fingers quivered. He looked at them. 'Then you never had a son.' 'No.' 'So you cannot know what you are saying, though you may mean well.' Luc was shaking his head. 'Look, young man,' Rachid said softly, 'it wasn't your fault. It could have been a truck or a car. Or some other young man on a moped. There is nothing I can do for you and, trust me, there is nothing you can do for us.' Then, with a downward nod of his head, Rachid had shut the door.

↔↔↔↔↔

Fernando Dos Santos's unique constellation of work ethic, rural orientation, and current environment made his life course almost algorithmically certain. Indeed, given the advances achieved across the human sciences during the preceding hundred years, it ought to have been feasible by the fourth quarter of the twentieth century to employ their findings and categories to the fore-casting of his individual destiny.

Some such life-prognosis discipline (LPD) might have proceeded, for instance, by assessing a subject's vital force and propulsive temperament ('character-energy'); thereupon charting (through a method that might entail questionnaires and interviews) the subject's skills and attentional propensities ('aptitude-outlook'); thirdly by analysing the ethnographic environment, peer and non-peer stimuli and opportunities (aspiration-setting); deriving, finally, a range of graded narratives corresponding to the person's likely futures ('outcome-speculans'). Such a model would require fine-tuning to capture contingent issues and events*: accidents; illnesses; windfall fortunes, the outcropping of unimagined abilities; the eclosion of pychoses; the emergence

---

*N.B., LPD predictive methodology does not yet claim to be fullproof. In the case of Dos Santos, for example, a life-changing decision cannot be ruled out, since some low-grade evidence of impetuosity does exist. Moreover, the subject's mix of honesty, generosity, curiosity and yearning for a fast-retreating past might yet attract the sympathies or attentions of individuals in a position to assist him. As he has put it himself, 'If I only had someone by me, I could be somebody else . . .'

of social and other conflicts; the eruption of unimagined appetites and proclivities; – or indeed the impact of any such variables on the loved ones, relations, friends or associates of the subject.

Were such a discipline to be invoked in the interesting case of Fernando Dos Santos, salient passages from the concluding report might well read as follows:

(a) character-energy: (i) the subject excels at the performance of repetitive tasks, oblivious to physical discomfort and mental tedium, maintaining a job-sufficient level of awareness while, as he expresses it, 'going somewhere fxxxxxx-else with my head, like dreaming . . .'; (ii) the subject takes pride in his aptitude for labour, aligning this with elements of national, gender and class identity – 'it's what we [Portuguese] are known for', 'women have no use for men unable to harrow five-acre fields . . . ', 'if you're a worker, you can be either a good worker or a bad worker: simple!'.

(b) aptitude-outlook: the subject possesses a fund of rural knowledge, including an unscientific but detailed understanding of plants, animals, geology, agronomy, meteorology relating overwhelmingly to pre-1960s conditions within a geographically discrete part of the Minho (region of Portugal); the subject's other skills and interests are few and, as in the case of sports-related gaming, offer little basis for personal fulfilment or financial security. The subject is inclined to entrust his future to chance, averring, for example, that 'anybody can get lucky, why not me?'

c) aspiration-setting: the subject inhabits the most backward sector of a modern sciences-oriented city. Moreover, his social life plays out within the shifting immigrant communities that overlap at the hostel where he resides. The subject appears to lack insight into his own socio-economic and occupational prospects. Deficient in city-relevant social know-how and with low milieu-specific self-esteem, the subject is attracted into the orbit of any man possessing the qualities he most signally lacks: verbal wit, ease with the opposite sex, elegance of manner, charm, story-telling verve, the ability to act without scruple. In male company especially, the subject presents himself as naturally subordinate yet tends to take sudden offence, to sulk or to express resentment for minor and even imaginary slights. With women, the subject is unable to grasp his interlocutor's vantage point and is by turns awkward, grateful, or bitter, sensing betrayal. About women, the subject has commented, 'I love the bitches, but I've yet to find one who'll do me for free.'

(d) outcome speculans. While the subject's character-energy and aptitude-outlook might in other (geographical and / or historical) settings point toward fulfilling employment, community respect, financial independence, conjugal contentment and family responsibilities, in the circumstances in which he in fact finds himself and from which no obvious escape route beckons, LPD suggests that the subject's future is bleak. It is his stubborn attachment to his childhood aptitude-outlook, compounded by his refusal to adapt his aspiration-setting that condemn him – and this despite positive elements within his character-energy – to a future of lost bets, transactional relationships, factory-level employment, precarious accommodation solutions, deepening isolation, deteriorating nutrition, alcohol and nicotine abuse, disregard for own health, escalating crankiness, etc. Life expectancy: 49–57 years. Likely cause of death: cardio-vascular disease. Legacy: none.

↔↔↔↔↔↔

Gérard Boucan was feeling much improved: the whisky had cleared his head, the charcoal had eased his bloated gut, Sidney Bechet's treacly tremolo had lightened his mood. Noting these disparate changes with satisfaction and congratulating himself on the robustness and resilience of his constitution, Boucan stood to remove his shoes and socks, then paddled hither and thither upon the thick and overlapping carpets adorning the floor of his study, halting at the fireplace to dabble the toes of first one foot and then the other in the thickly furred rills of fat that upholstered his mongrel's shoulders. The dog did not so much as raise a greying eyebrow.

Gérard waited for his son to come home, hoping to tackle him on two delicate topics: girls and drugs, with speeches prepared on the pleasures of the former and the perils of the latter. With some force it now struck him that he would prefer to discuss these and almost any other matters with his driver, Jorge. His mind skipped to that evening's impulse drive to the rear of the factory and to the recollection – prompted by the sight of the familiar old window ledge – of his first meeting with Claude at which he had disclosed to her through that rear window the empire of operatives and machines he was one day to inherit. He recalled again how game she had been that night. A smile of ghostly affection bared his charcoaled teeth as Gérard felt the boyish urge to pay his wife a visit, to convey to her the emotion he had recollected twice this evening in such tranquillity.

Gérard Boucan shambled toward the door of his study, fastening his belt and doing up the shirt buttons he had freed earlier when troubled by heartburn. He exited the room and climbed the stairs steadily, the balls of his bare feet squeaking on the polished wood of the stairs. In his momentary fervour, he entertained the image of his wife, just married, or – better – ten or fifteen years later, still turning toward him as he breezed into the bedroom, her arms gaping, the bedclothes cascading from her swelling bosom, a book falling to one side.

The bedroom door was ajar, the light was out. Gérard slalomed his frame through the gap. Standing in the dark, he heard steady breathing. Claude had always been good at simulation, making the noises her husband wished to hear: to pretend to be asleep when he wanted her to be awake was no challenge. Gérard hesitated. In the early days of their union, Claude would have been happy to be awoken by him, perhaps with some news, or merely to take him in her arms, or to listen as he expounded some industrial or financial concern.

Standing on the threshold now, Gérard could find no sufficient pretext upon which to rouse his wife. They had lost the habit of conversation, of sex, of sharing a silent embrace. They had slowly moved from collaborative to parallel living, like toddlers regressing in their patterns of play. Noiselessly, Gérard withdrew.

Claude sat up in bed and listened for the distant click of her husband's study door. Satisfied, she plumped her pillow, switched her bedside lamp back on, and resumed her book.

↔↔↔↔↔

22.57. Seven readers. On the ground-floor plastics section, every single operative had now found something to read.

*

Flicking through his copy of *Détective*, Luigi was brought up short by the pictures of the medic from Metz and his mother. He forgot to suck on his cigarette. Presented with so much variety – kidnappings, rapes, troilism, bestiality, sado-masochism, incest, blackmail, bondage, serial killings, paedophilia, and so much more – how odd that the chef d'équipe should find a story of merciful matricide uniquely interesting! Luigi's eyes trawled the words and pictures for clues to the conundrum. He took the dead cigarette from his mouth and examined it. The chef had not so much as glanced at another story. Luigi lit his cigarette butt and half-closed his eyes, savouring this gestural correlative of enlightenment. He looked at the raised office front and spotted Mathieu peering out. Luigi pointed interrogatively toward the stairs. Mathieu touched his right eyebrow and nodded permissively. That's it! Luigi said to himself: the man's from Alsace, right? Metz is practically next door. He probably knows the family. Everyone knows everyone else in Alsace, right?

*

Rachid turned to the TV listings in *L'Humanité*. Antenne 2 was showing *Les enfants de la guerre*, a feature film set in Ireland. There followed a talk with: Mme Bethy Williams, Catholic, from 'Movement of Women for Peace'; Mme Florence McCormick, Protestant, from the same organization; Mr Franck Card of Sinn Fein, the Catholic autonomist movement; Andrew Gowdy of the UDA, a Protestant extremist movement; John Sucher [*sic*], an English journalist; and two unnamed French journalists. Rachid had once taken a close interest in Ireland. He wondered if Malika would be watching. Rachid detected within himself a murmuring flow of reviving interest in the affairs of this world. Mehdi's death had blotted out sun, moon and stars: perhaps Malika's pregnancy would end the eclipse.

*

Jacques leaned against the recycled-material cylinder at the aisle-end of Philippe's machine number two, swaying slightly as he perused the front page of *Le Figaro*. Raymond Barre had granted an interview: Mon objectif, une France prospère et respectée ran the headline. Jacques grinned. If the prime-minister had said his goal was a wretched and despised France, that would have been news. Barre even vowed to defend the franc. Surely not!

Jacques liked to present Jeanne with some snippet of news on his return home. Something to chew on over breakfast. Occasionally the night shift itself provided, but she wouldn't find the young Gypsy's acrobatic antics amusing and, as for the graffiti business, Jeanne's view of Boucan was low enough already.

Jacques skipped a page or two, then shut the paper. For once, he would arrive empty-handed. He chuckled in anticipation. No news at all? Jeanne would ask. He would turn his hands palms-up. At first, she might suspect some trick, but then would surely declare: 'That's the best, Jacques!'

*

In *Libération*, Philippe skimmed a two-page spread on the Italian communist party's 'historic compromise.' It was wearily familiar, starting with commentary evoking the 'hot autumn' of 1969 when factories had briefly filled with students and universities with workers, and everything seemed possible. The slogan of that distant epoch (Vogliamo Tutto! 'We want it all!') had given way, now that the PCI was backing the Right's austerity measures, to the bleated exhortation to workers to Sacrifice! Sacrifice! Gianni Agnelli, Fiat's boss, had praised the party for its 'sense of national responsibility.' Philippe, who had been in Turin that autumn seven years ago, curled his lip and turned to the interview with one Sergio Luca, 42, a worker at Fiat Ferriere.

Luca, though no card-carrier, had cast his vote in the Communist electoral landslide five months previously. Considering the party's attested popularity, Luca found its eagerness to shore up the power of Christian Democracy bewildering, and the authoritarianism of its grass-roots cadres alarming. Luca – who in the heady days of 1969 had been employed at the Mirafiori plant in Turin – lamented, 'And where have all those intellectuals gone, those students?' As for the union reps, Luca said they abused their power, looking for support not to their fellow workers but to their party bosses. He concluded, 'In the end, to bring this system down, there'll be nothing left but the gun. In '45 we had our chance, but we didn't take it.' Philippe grunted at that, muttering briefly, 'That's it all right: we never miss an opportunity to miss an opportunity.'

*

Across the machine aisle, Marcel was gazing at a full-page ad on page 17 of *Le Nouvel Observateur*. The picture showed an apartment with high ceiling, parquet floor, a wicker armchair, a potted plant and nothing else. A man and a woman could be made out at the door bearing boxes. The copy beneath read: 'History will record that the 1970s saw our civilization accomplish a great leap forward with the appearance of a new type of man for whom the cultural dimension of existence at last became the very basis of his quality of life. Such men are effecting a clean break with the archaic behaviours of preceding generations. For example, when they move into a new apartment, often their very first investment is a new hi-fi system. And very often that hi-fi system is a K******.'

Marcel read the text twice, then stared at the photo. He didn't give a damn about hi-fi, but the apartment was a dream. There was a huge empty space in the middle of the parquet floor. He and Chantal would fit that space to a tee.

*

Eric was reading *The Grapes of Wrath,* engrossed in the description of a land turtle. He liked the way it was placed centre-stage. The piece ended with: 'His yellow toe-nails slipped a fraction in the dust.' Eric murmured 'perfect,' putting the book down to check that neither machine had stopped. Steinbeck's words and phrasing were familiar to him, intimate and exact: 'the hind feet kicked his shell along . . . the armoured tail clamped in sideways . . . the old humorous frowning eyes . . . a light truck . . . flipped the turtle like a tiddly-wink . . . its legs waved in the air . . . the horny beak opened a little . . .' To Eric, this text was close and warm and snug. But suddenly sticky and stifling too. It wasn't Steinbeck's fault: Eric was to blame. The embrace of a language that offered itself for such instant delectation was repugnant to him now. He wanted words, unknown words, that would run and hide and cheat – even fight back a little.

*

Salvatore opened his attaché case and extracted a union flyer. He glanced at his watch: the meeting was in eighteen minutes. He familiarized himself with the main points. He didn't want to rely on notes. First, he must set out what the CGT factory branch had so far gleaned from its survey of in-factory wage-rates, following management's refusal to divulge the full picture. Then there was the intimidation issue involving – what was his name? Letour, Jean. Damned fool, but that was not the issue. Then he ought to say something about the rise in unemployment locally. Lastly, the main point of the meeting: to apprise the men of plans for a rolling series of half-hour end-of-shift shut-downs as part of the nationwide campaign against Barre's austerity plan. That was it. Short and sweet. The main thing was to keep it simple. He didn't want to be talking over the men's heads. He drummed his fingers on the flyer. There was a slight ache there. Was he overdoing the exerciser? He committed some numbers to memory: in the greater Grandgobier area, 12,750 unemployed workers, of whom 9100 registered at the city employment agency, of whom just 2680 were in receipt of benefits amounting to between 30% and 90% of their previous salaries, leaving 10,020 with no income whatever. No, he could refer to the flyer for the numbers: no one could expect him to reel off statistics from memory. Salvatore put the tracts away and drew out the hand-exerciser. Then he put the exerciser away and shut the case.

44. Uncommunicative, Single-Minded and Antic.

As he reached the top of the stairs, Luigi saw Alphonse, Bobrán and Fernando each sitting meditative at the end of their respective machines, eyes half-open but unfocused, conjuring in the Italian's mind a trio of prayerful churchgoers scattered upon pews in the nave of a vast and sombre cathedral. In his hand the Gypsy caressed like a rosary the note from Joseph's brother; the African's copy of *En attendant Godot* lay face-down beneath his chair like a fedora; Fernando's hands palpated and stroked like a supernumerary digit the shaft of an unlit cigarette.

Skirting the great old semi-automatic machine number twenty-one, Luigi checked that his own cornpaper cigarette had indeed extinguished itself. Respectful of Jean's loathing of tobacco, he had not sucked at it since receiving the foreman's nod. Luigi now lodged the stub behind his right ear and drew up a chair close to the little man who, as he began to speak, extended his right hand to be shaken.

Jean was having some kind of bad night: Luigi had arrived in the middle of a long rant that could only now properly be vocalized. The theme was respect – for one's boss, family, nation, religion, but above all for work itself. Luigi let Jean run his mouth, and grinned at such conviction.

'Sooner or later, everyone realizes they have to serve somebody. Or something. It might as well be Monsieur Gérard Boucan and his machines. We make bits for cars. What's wrong with that? Without cars, the world would go nowhere, the roads would be deserted, and motorway stopovers would all go broke. We are part of something much bigger than ourselves. Our work has dignity.'

Luigi was relieved he didn't have to talk. He was tired, hollowed out in body and mind. Like drunken party guests, characters from his intergalactic porn mag and from *Détective* mingled with people from his own life: Aurelia, snarling in wild pleasure, gave way to Gilberte, while the medical student from Metz injected Luigi's own mother, who had morphed for the occasion from crafty bigot to doddering Alzheimic, while the foreman looked on, spittle swinging from his matchstick pacifier.

Jean was ranging far and wide, from strikes to immigration, from unemployment to stagflation, from the machinations of 'cosmopolitan plutocrats' to the misdeeds of the marauding A-rab: no one could escape unscathed. Luigi registered the voices ancient and modern that sounded

through the little man, naming them briefly, but letting them go. He took
no view on politics or on people: politics belonged to a past he was trying
to forget and to a place he had fled, while people now appealed only to his
entrepreneurial aspirations in the guise of potential customers.

Luigi was being more than usually uncommunicative. 'Maybe you
think I lay it on a bit thick?' Jean ventured. Luigi shrugged. Jean tried again:
'Well, okay then, have you got any stories for me? Anything to take my mind
off my bladder . . .'

Luigi placed his left hand on his inflated right bicep. He was aware of
Jean's arrangement with the foreman and knew better than to offer to operate
Jean's machine himself. Some nights he would relay a story from *Détective*
or some analogous source. Jean would listen hard for a political, military
or historical angle. Indeed, it pleased Luigi that any such considerations
were rarely pertinent: you were not told how a serial rapist cast his vote, or
for which party a murdered prostitute occasionally canvassed. Even in cases
of town-hall bribery and corruption, the political colours of the deputy or
councilman seldom figured. Which was as it should be.

No, that night Luigi had no stories for Jean. The Italian was still shaking
his head when Mathieu hobbled into view.

↔→↔→↔→↔

The mind of Gérard Boucan closely resembled the room in which he sat most
evenings. Cluttered, cramped, in need of an energetic dusting, it supported
a mass of uncongenial matter either directly inherited or lazily accumulated,
with the result that its proprietor experienced no sense of ownership – let
alone pride – in its contents or workings. Although, just like his room, his
mind felt foreign and wrong, he did not know, and could not begin to trace
in memory, how it had got this way.

With increasing frequency, Gérard Boucan experienced alarming
surges of affection for strangers, wishing softly to whisper to or to embrace
women – and even men! – whose names he did not know, including never-
previously-noticed employees encountered during shop-floor inspections or
among his floridly obsequious clerical staff. His mistress, Gisèle – with whom
he maintained an intimate and entirely elective relationship, nourished and
replenished by standing order – pleased him less and less; as for his wife, it
was only in a fit of puerile nostalgia that he could imagine addressing fond

words to her. To reconsider the old teaser, were he to be compelled to save just one person, his wife or his mistress, from a conveniently burning building, he would probably, he thought, abandon both to the flames.

Gérard Boucan reluctantly accepted the fact that unknown children and even patently semi-feral teenagers glimpsed from the safety of his chauffer-driven car appealed to him more than did his son, for whom, in happier times, he would have been happy to lay down his life. At best, Gérard sometimes told himself, he had lazily sired one more person fated, if lucky, uneventfully to grow old and die.

At times M. Boucan caught himself longing to believe in an entity 'higher' than himself and fellow creatures. He would then recall the strictures of his unlamented mother who, on learning from his own lips of his loss of all faith, commented: 'I'm afraid, Gérard, this does not surprise me. If you cannot believe in a God who loves you as his own creation, it is because you lack the necessary imagination. God creates some people too dull ever to believe in Him: to the believer, this is one of His mysteries.'

In moments of drunken lucidity, Gérard repeatedly reaffirmed his chosen course of action: suicide, but in slow motion. All he had to do was live tomorrow as he had lived today, remaining firmly on the rails, accomplishing his business and family duties, taking the decisions that his plant managers indicated, going through the motions required of him by national law and local custom, suppressing the few weak dreams and urges that still came to him unbidden. Since his unhappiness was itself undramatic and supremely mediocre, he deemed the gradualism of his suicide most fitting: after all, what was the rush? Everyone dies.

Once in the early 1970s, during a brief stay in Paris, Gérard had paid anonymously for a therapy session with an exorbitantly expensive middle-aged psychoanalyst whom Gérard subsequently discovered to be of the Maoist persuasion. The diagnosis had stuck in his mind. 'You are, I have no doubt,' the blue-smocked cultural revolutionist had pronounced, as he stowed Gérard's cheque in the middle drawer of his writing desk, 'a textbook study in absentee-father bourgeois self-laceration: pathetic, infinitely solipsistic, even slightly pitiable. Short of social revolution and the liberation-through-expropriation of your entire class, your best hope is to follow an extended course of therapy with myself.'

'I don't live in Paris.' 'Don't live in Paris? Then your case is truly beyond help.'

↔↔↔↔↔↔

Laure had left Martine's house in the hills in plenty of time to pick up her mother from Cinéma Charlot.

Waiting in silence at traffic lights, Laure's mother tried to find words to express her reaction to Oshima's *Empire des sens,* which her daughter that very morning had so enthusiastically recommended. The castration scene had upset her. 'Maybe I was expecting something like a Kurosawa,' she began. 'Oh, mother!' Laure exclaimed, 'that's like expecting Godard to turn out a Lelouche.' 'Hardly.' 'You know what I mean.' 'What did Salvatore make of it?' 'Are you joking? I went with a friend.' 'Ah-ha.' 'What does "Ah-ha" mean?' 'Nothing. Darling.'

As the lights switched from red to green, a gaggle of swaying, chanting soldiers crossed in front of the cream Citroën DS. Cars either side of them hooted. Laure's mother waved her left hand at the digital clock which showed 22.58 in Martian green. 'Zéro, zéro . . .' sang the draftees.

As the car moved off, Laure said, 'I just danced with one of them.' 'Really?' 'I left Martine's early so I stopped for a coffee.' 'I see.' 'No, you don't.'

The streets were dark now, the interior of the car likewise. All they had was their voices. 'He was small and thick-set, not my type at all, but he came straight up and asked me to dance. I said yes. They all seemed so full of life.' 'Once you're married . . .' 'Precisely. It won't seem right, will it?' 'No. Men can be stupid.' 'Yes, maman, *you* should know.'

They drove through the outskirts. 'You're not getting cold feet, are you?' 'What do you mean?' 'About the wedding. It's not uncommon during long engagements.' Laure looked at the road. 'Listen, Laure. You can tell me to mind my own business, but I worry, you know.' 'Well, you needn't.' 'Does Salvatore really, you know, excite you?' '*Maman!*' Afraid of being interrupted, Laure's mother spoke fast. 'I don't mean, "Is he good in bed?" though that's pretty important, believe me, when things go wrong – as they always do – because if you can still go to bed and, well, catch your foot in your hand, that makes up for a lot. But, no, I mean intellectually, emotionally. Does he make your heart race? Do you miss him when he's not there?'

Laure heaved an immense sigh and took a bend too fast for the DS, the tyres screeching. 'Do you want me to drive?' her mother asked. 'No. I'm fine,' Laure snapped, shifting down. 'Look, *Maman,* if you're asking me whether I love my fiancé: of course I do. He's perfect in every way. Why wouldn't I? It's just that sometimes I feel I haven't lived much yet. And Salvatore approaches everything as a deadly serious project. He's so single-minded. And always in a hurry. There's nothing wrong in that, is there?'

'Well, I married your father at twenty. In those days, unless you were Simone de Beauvoir, that's generally what you did if you loved a man. I had no choice.'

Laure pulled the car up: they had reached her parents' villa. 'Oh, choices,' she said, 'I have nothing but choices.'

↔↔↔↔↔

Eight moods. Plus one. Despite all reports, the storyteller could not do Homer, could not even do Balzac. For gods and heroes, derring-do, stirring stories or merely the solid depiction of people caught in the social flow of universal history, a greater narrator must be invoked, for this one was almost played out, his grasp of moment-to-moment eructation, motility and synaptic misfire grown weak and shallow, his tricks almost exhausted. Besides, Grandgobier was no Ancient Ilium and before him flitted neither Achilles, Odysseus, Helen nor Penelope – barely a Goriot or a Cousine Bette.

Hunkering down, therefore, in his own turn, into his own mind, seeking that stillness from which all dreams and monsters arise to press their claims, the men and women of Grandgobier traipsed again before him, alone together now, their eyes sunk in their sockets, their turtle heads retracted, their minds precipitated out in fine clarity for a late bout of meditative musing.

*

Tadpole-letters held writhing in Bobrán's hand, words known by heart: 'I have come . . . to know the truth . . .' Was any request more natural? Is not each man my fellow? To say what I know might place me in trouble with the powers of policing and justice. To say nothing would shrivel my soul, making me each day more cowardly, more selfish, a louse who dare not help his friend's brother and who knows there is a corner of Africa where the Gypsies of Europe are reputed to care only for their own sort. I shall speak with Philippe.

At Jean's machine, Mathieu leaned against the guard, while inside the mould plastic cooled and hardened to cable ties. If Nadine could speak to him in such a moment . . . but to speak you need a mind. In a dream then? He knew what she would say. If not her voice, he could catch her tone and drift. 'Stop dithering, *chéri*. Now that you have found a means to do it with little risk of discovery, it should be done. And suddenly.' The presses gaped. Mathieu opened his eyes, slid the guard back and pulled the product from the mould.

Referring back to Broch's first scene, Tomec had gathered to consciousness all the vital GRIST of detail and now, his mind confronted as by a slow-trundling carousel laden with overmuch imagery, he stood suspended at his sketching bench, impatiently seeking a CURVE, a first line with which to pierce the virgin paper. He longed to lie down in the cool, oily dark, submit to the passage of time and await the knowledge he needed. Instead, he laid down his pencil, took up his torch, and headed for the plastics section. Surely all humanity was there?

Rachid had folded the world away in his newspaper, his feelings returning to a fine balance of fear and hope, the new and the old, grief receding and joy defiant, expecting an imminent and necessary conversation with Mehdi, while also anticipating an overdue homecoming to Malika's arms. How he would embrace her belly, aiming kisses through its wall at the new child's cheeks, willing them to dimple! And to think that Mehdi had grown so old!

Handling like a prewar cement truck, Philippe's mind was steered by its reluctant owner back to Odile and cuckoldom. All sense of liberation had vanished, yet he was free of anger. What remained was sullen anticlimax and a desire somehow to sleep off his domestic woes as he would a hangover. His marriage, hopes of revolution, and youthful ambitions were sliding from him. He watched them go and shrugged.

Glummer still than Philippe but less hopeless, Fernando emerged from the common dream-state into self-pity, but with his anger still intact: why fucking-not me? he wondered. I could be strong, I could be loyal, I could be loving! What chance did any woman ever give me? Are they not all whores and bitches? Even – God forbid! – Maryse?

Opening his eyes, Jacques was happy with what he saw. Amid the machinery, all was easy: Marseille lighting a cigarette, the foreman descending the stairs, the Italians gabbling. 'It did me good to see my wretched brother: I realize how prodigiously I've been blessed.'

Alphonse emerged from contemplation fizzing with frustration, irritation, humiliation: his fingers flexed, his scalp itched, his griddle-tongue spat words back into his mind. He would speak. But what, how, where and to whom?

↔↔↔↔↔

He sprang from his chair. Today he had taken it and taken it. Enough now, quite enough. He jogged Fernando's shoulder, 'Hey, smoke it, don't stroke it! Want to see a show?' The Portuguee spread his eyes wide, put his cigarette back in its pack and got up, a sideways glance at his machines. Alphonse went to whisper to Bobrán, who nodded, matter-of-fact. Then the African strode back over to Fernando, noting his friend's look of sullen desperation. He wanted to help. 'Zere was somezing in ze air zat night, ze time was right, [bellowing] FUR-NAN-DOH!' What the Portuguee heard was a tune he recognized and his own name comically mangled at the end of a string of jarring Anglo-phonetic weirdness. 'Viens,' the Ivorian then ordered, serious again, heading for the stairs with his workmate in his wake: 'It's okay, the little Gypsy is on our machines.' Halfway down, gripping the banister in his left hand, Alphonse stopped to peer out over the ground floor. 'Just look at them!' he said to Fernando: 'Did you ever see such a bug-eyed rabble?' For an instant, Rachid, seated at the far end of the machine aisle, his chair against the old wooden table, staring through the cloud of smoke he had just exhaled, appeared to hold Alphonse in check. Marcel and Salvatore had also seen the two men on the stairs: Marcel spat at the ground as he looked away, while Salvatore's attention was seized by Marcel's gesture. Fernando glanced up at his workmate, 'You're not planning something, are you?' 'Me? Plan something? Never!' Alphonse replied, resuming his descent, tripping lightly. I've no script, no part to play, he told himself. Not even a walk-on. It's going to be ad lib. Stand-up. But tragi-comedy, no? He touched down on the ground floor, turning left toward the head of the machine aisle. How am I going to do this? Not that I have to do anything. But I do, I do. I could walk right down to where the Algerian is sitting, leap onto that table and harangue the multitude. But they'd have to come close and crane their necks because if they stood at a comfortable distance my voice would never reach them through the din. Or I could grab a threshing tub, upturn it, mount it like a soapbox – till some clever dick shoves me off it from behind. No. I'll just . . . Philippe had noticed the African and the Portuguee hovering at the end of his machine number two. He darted them a sly smile and gestured toward his pile of papers. Alphonse waved it away like a diversionary ploy. To know what he wanted to say, he was going to have to start speaking. As for the soapbox, he need only imagine it. He stepped back into the middle of the aisle and began to address Philippe and Fernando, making large arm movements, and glancing up and down the aisle at nobody in particular, but somehow inviting everyone to gather. He talked in vague terms about how he had something on his mind. He felt it was best to say nothing precise till everyone was there. He ran a riff about getting things off your chest and how his drama teacher was always telling him 'to externalize.' Philippe and Fernando looked fittingly bored. It was all fine. Meanwhile, the big Gypsy was taking off his gloves and sauntering over; the Englishman, the peasant, the Italian were all shuffling near; the Algerian had got up from his chair, as had the Sicilian. Once everyone is within earshot, Alphonse told himself, I can curtail this preface, get onto the main business. I'll throw them onto the defensive, right from the start. But keep it entertaining. Play the madcap actor a bit, even the crazy nigger, but turn it on and off like a tap so they make no mistake I'm serious. Everyone's here now. I'll just think out loud, speak my thoughts loud and clear. Or pretend to. Once you can fake sincerity, acting is a cinch. Who said that? Okay, onto the main meal. 'Hey, I'm just thinking aloud here, guys. If you prefer, I could sing or dance or play-act. I'm not really used to speaking out like this but I've been having a bad day and I want to, uh, share it with you.' He pronounced 'share' like they were all part of some psychotherapy circle. It raised a smile. They were looking sympathetic now. Pregnant pause. Nice. Fernando was pulling at Alphonse's arm. 'What is it? I'm just warming up . . .' 'You're not going to be hugging anyone, are you? Because if you do, I swear I'll smack you in the mouth.' Alphonse swung round and attempted to hug Fernando, who threw an easily ducked punch. 'That's just our private joke,' Alphonse told his audience, with a wink for the stone-faced Algerian. 'Where was I? Yes, I've had a bad day. I won't hand you any bullshit. I'm no speaker, not one for rhetoric. Did I say I've had a bad day? I've had a normal day. I'll draw you a picture. I'll make you a list.' I've got them now, they're leaning in. If I just drop my voice, I'll be able to reel them in close. It was the picture that did it, the promise of a picture and a list. People love pictures and lists are easy to understand. 'So this bad day, this bad-normal day started at the hostel this afternoon when I woke and went to make myself a coffee.

A Vietnamese guy I'd never spoken to felt he just had to tell me the stories he'd heard of me screwing one of the prostitutes who works the hostels at weekends. It all started as a joke. She was sent into my room as some kind of present. I did the groaning, she did the keening. It was like Birkin and Gainsbourg recording 'Je t'aime' in separate recording booths: I never even touched the lady. But my fellow inmates' fantasies about the black man ran riot and now I'm reputed to be as horny as a jack-rabbit and to possess a third leg. Pathetic. I said to the Vietnamese guy, 'Don't believe it,' and he smirked and told me I was a pretty cool customer. I mean, do I look like a cool customer? Okay, don't say. Then I went to do my shopping and the checkout assistant talked to me in pidgin: 'Monsieur, Vouloir poche en plastique?' Alphonse paused, looked round, paced himself. Rachid was smiling faintly. The same thing happened to him, you could tell. Most of the others at least knew what he was talking about. He noticed that pairs had formed: Salvatore had drifted further up the aisle to stand alongside Luigi; Eric had homed in on Rachid; Marcel had edged closer to Jacques; Fernando had fallen back to stand alongside Philippe; Tomec had arrived from metallurgy and stationed himself next to Mathieu. Alphonse encompassed his audience at a glance, speaking again now, but slower than before, as though spinning out a bedtime story for a four-year-old. 'Later, on my way to work, in a PMU betting-bar I was almost set upon by a group of right-thinking thugs – our Portuguese comrade standing here probably saved my skin, after getting me into the scrape in the first place. Then, since arriving at work, I've been insulted, snubbed, rebuked, patronized and ignored. About the only thing that hasn't upset me this evening was being thrown to the floor and threatened with grievous bodily harm – at least I think that was the gist of it – after getting too friendly with one of our number.' Alphonse measured a moment's silence, while he stared at his lemon-yellow shoes. 'Like I said, this has been a normal day. So far. In the meantime, here I am busy learning lines for a play where I'm booked to be the slave – the only black man in the production and I get to be slave? Believe me, I'd rather be the slave-driver. Or typecast, say, as Caliban in Césaire's *Tempest,* where at least I'd get to rail at the white man Prospero: "I know that one day my naked fist, my naked fist alone will be enough to smash your world!" Hey, don't be frightened, don't cower! I'm not in fact particularly quick to take offence. And, except when I'm acting, I don't pretend to be anyone else. I just play a little mad sometimes, assume an antic disposition. It frees people to think whatever they like. Because in fact *they* know nothing about me, even if they try real hard, whereas, without arrogance, I can truly claim to know everything about them. Isn't that just part of the imbalance, the inequity that comes with being an immigrant?' Alphonse looked around him carefully. 'Most of us are immigrants, aren't we? In one way or another. Okay, don't answer that! Give it time to settle! The fact is: we know more about the mighty of this country and continent than they could ever know about us. We can understand their Corneille, if we choose to, or their Proust. Consider this: whereas they can't find my country on a map of Africa, scarcely even know which 'side' it's on, I can name the last prime-minister of the fourth republic, the departmental capital of the Lozère, the date Eugène Sue's *Mystères de Paris* was published just as easily as I can read that Englishman's Shakespeare. You'd be astonished how big Brecht and Strindberg were in Côte d'Ivoire in the 1960s. The thing is: we can *be* the mighty of the earth, not just act them or ape them. We contain them already. So of course I could play the slave-driver: I contain him too. We're so much bigger than they are. That's the privilege of the man who's been colonized, exploited. You have this great big hole inside you, the hole that's left when your original culture has been ripped away. It's massive, because our culture was massive. They hollow you out, create this space in which our voices, if we're lucky and clever and work hard, can rise and swell . . .' Alphonse, like it was a practised party trick, mimicked Armstrong singing 'What a Wonderful World' before sharply segueing into Robeson singing 'Joe Hill,' his sound rising sepulchral, dank and dark, towering over the machines. He caught his breath for a provisional peroration. 'With this great hollow void, this cavern inside of you the size of your stolen culture and history, you have all the space you need to eat them up, consume their history and culture whole, gobble it down for breakfast, play at being them, then return and make your own self and build your own human destiny anew. Or, alternatively, you can stay hungry, stay hollow, burrow right down into yourself like a tick for warmth, and go mad.' Alphonse ceased suddenly, brutally, as if winching each man back down into an icy pool. He noticed how dry his mouth had become, looked around, wishing for water. The men were whispering, looking at him strangely; only Rachid and Philippe nodded and smiled; the others seemed bewildered or, in the case of Tomec, entranced. Alphonse wondered if he should rush to reassure. It's just talk, it don't mean a thing, he might say. I can still be your funny smiling boy, whoop and make the ladies squeal, he might say. He said nothing of the sort: he reckoned he'd said enough. Eric had turned to Rachid for a summary: 'Il parle du colonialisme,' the Algerian supplied. Tomec had raised his eyebrows at Mathieu, whose face remained impassive, his eyes restlessly checking the control-cabinet warning lights. 'Ci capisci qualcosa?' Luigi asked Salvatore; 'Fa la vittima,' Salvatore replied. Marcel turned to Jacques, 'What's he on about?'; 'Search me!' replied the peasant, raising a flat palm over his head. That at least was unambiguous. That at least was open to no misconstrual. Alphonse turned squarely toward Jacques and Marcel. 'You're wrong. You know you're wrong. Don't insult yourselves. Or me. You know precisely what I'm talking about. You're immigrants too, one way or another: you too have been colonized. Nothing I said goes over your head. Nothing escapes you that you don't want to let go.' To Marcel, Alphonse was sounding like a schoolteacher. He took a step toward him. 'If this country is as wicked as you say, if Europe is so bad, what are you doing here? Nobody invited you. There has to be something you like: our food, our women, our cars, hi-fis, our – you know – civilization.' Alphonse smirked. 'Our *civilisation*? Are you talking to me now as a Frenchman?' 'What the hell else?' Alphonse sensed danger and avoided a straight answer. 'Okay. Then I'll answer you as a foreigner to a Frenchman: we're here because you're there. Simple as that. No other reason. Of course there are things we like here. But the sun shines brighter in Africa, believe me! And the food is fresher, the people mostly kinder, the women more beautiful – since you seem to be so interested in that. We never came of our own free will to "your" countries till you had pretty much finished pillaging and raping ours.' No one said a word. Alphonse laughed, trying to break the tension. 'I guess I've said my piece. I'm feeling better now. Thanks for listening.' The men started to ebb away to their own machines. Alphonse headed for the stairs, Fernando trailing behind him. Halfway up, they looked out over the ground floor. Everyone was back at work, emptying floor trays, threshing product, filling hoppers, checking pieces, mixing material – generating value. 'You sure-fucking woke them up, boss,' Fernando said. Hmm, Alphonse murmured, 'Was I good? Did I not weaken a little toward the end?'

BOOK FIVE. STIRRING.

In which the plastics-section night-shift workers come barrelling back, meddling, stirring, dishing dirt, talking turkey: Salvatore speaks to the unionized and Philippe makes an announcement; Bobrán asks a favour of Alphonse and Mathieu addresses a request to Tomec. Beyond the factory, Jorge and Renata consummate their nascent passion, Jeanne is awoken by dreams of another era and Angelica makes an escape. As the hourglass of this chronicle runs down, each worker is caught one last time, frozen in his particular smile or snarl. Abandonment, deferral, interruption, redemption, and mere suspension are all assayed: an end is in sight.

*

45. Never was a killing.

Never was a killing better blessed or more richly deserved: had I had to sack a city to prevent or avenge such an outrage to myself my sister my mother, I must have done it. And can police officers really own me? What dread should I fear? What wrong did I do?

Bobrán's eyes itched: a mild formication over the cornea, a tiredness compressing the eyeballs, a sty that tingled but would hurt if squeezed, a flickering in eyelids too long held open. His toes flexed also.

'I have nothing to tell you' sounded hollow now – weak. He blinked. He remembered the letter by its folded stiffness against his buttock, rehearsed some words: 'schoolteachers or lowly functionaries, badly paid and honest,' Joseph's brother had written. What was meant? Who wasn't being honest?

Bobrán had looked after the Ivorian's and the Portuguee's machines. He had emptied their floor trays, checked and threshed his own product. He had sat back down at the end of his machine and closed his eyes.

Honest. Honest? Now his toes needed scratching. The man he had killed would have raped Yitoune, and killed him, then raped again. There was only ever one chance.

He would love to run and hide. Or just run and keep running. He had been a good runner. He accused himself of cowardice. He wanted a pause in life, not a stop. He imagined Heike naked, standing alongside Moritz: same skin, hair; different sexes. He could look only at Moritz's sex. Brother and sister holding hands. He felt them drawing him toward them. He wanted to back away.

In Germany and in the car, if he travelled with them to the concert, he would hear German. Not unpleasing to his ears, though his mother said it was ugly. The war, she muttered. The camps. She never said more. Not to her son. The words in Albert's letter squirmed against his skin, slithering from the page, spermatozoa sprinting.

The itching subsided, his eyes closed. There was a shuffling noise drowned in the din. He glimpsed the Ivorian mouthing thanks. He could feel nothing now for Joseph. The man would be in some African heaven. At times the little Gypsy felt too much, at times too little. For a while his banister stunt had scrubbed his thoughts clean.

Why the fear? It angered him. Fear that angered. Why be owned for something you did right? It was a sickness gnawing at him. He could talk to the foreman, talk to Philippe, but only someone who loved him could advise. His mother mustn't know and Moritz . . . Yitoune loved him and knew. Yitoune he needed. Yitoune.

With the exception of Bobrán, all the operatives were busy, bent over threshing bins, examining product, preparing tubs of machine feed, one even standing on a stepladder to tip his mix of pristine granules, recycled matter and colorant into an open hopper. There was a straining of muscle, a thrashing of gloved hands, a retinal labour of scrutiny and a mental effort to recall, contrast and evaluate minuscule details. The disciplined action of human sinew upon clashing machinery, labour upon fixed capital, was further transforming the fruits of previous petrochemical processing. The output, in virtue of its potential for combination with other components in automobiles or miscellaneous domestic appliances, might at last be put to final use, having been apportioned a value and exchanged for coin. Supplementary to the operatives' manufacturing engagement, in the interstices of their beings, a restless traffic of observation, thought, imagery, feeling, and reasoning proceeded, generating a low but sustained rumbling, sombre as distant thunder, thrilling as the first strains of song.

I've talked to almost everyone and there's an end to it, Tomec told Mathieu.

Almost everyone? Mathieu said, his tongue working around his burnt-out matchstick.

It wasn't one of our lot, Tomec stated.

Our lot.

Nobody sneaks off in the middle of the night to daub graffiti, Tomec asserted, observing the foreman's left hand, marvelling at its perfect acquired deformity.

Mathieu's face slowly morphed to sad, as if its owner had been let down.

Besides, even if it was one of ours . . . Tomec began, drawling the 'ours,' giving it the full two syllables: noh-tres.

Yes, Mathieu said, spitting his matchstick straight out at the wall so it sprang back, Even if it was.

So that's what I'll tell them, Tomec ended.

You tell them that.

Tomec gazed out over the shop floor. The nightwatchman liked to see things laid out before him, loved the open plan. Mathieu preferred a cluttered stage, blinded by a deluge of light, the auditorium black and silent, invisible before him.

At his machine seventeen, Fernando was threshing recalcitrant yellow products from their sprue, crashing the skeleton pieces against the walls of the tub: sometimes there was nothing for it but to twist the last pieces off one by one. His body felt good. His thigh-muscles tensed against the lip of the tub, his shoulders swelled, his midriff stiffened and hardened like a tube or a corset or a cock: a full-body cock.

The Ivorian could really talk a storm, it had been like watching a film, but where did all that come from, all that talk? If I could ever talk like that, I could talk myself into a genuine job or at least a fucking-whole pile of money. Everything comes back to money. Money, and how to get at it. Whatever was legal but still lucrative.

Fernando had talked to the downstairs Gypsy, when was it, a week previously? Sounded him out about some edge-of-legality schemes and scams. Marcel had expounded the concept of 'attitude to risk,' testing his views on (a) the eventuality of incarceration and (b) the need occasionally to hurt people who got in the way. Fernando had flunked it. Never, he had said. And then, NEVER.

I could drive a truck, he thought, if I could fucking-drive. I wouldn't nod off. I'm too old already for an apprenticeship. I could run a stall, if I had some wares to start with and could afford the pitch. Crime is out, I've thought that possibility right through. I need one big win, just enough for a plot in the Minho. Or in the Ardèche: I guess I'd miss France if I went home now.

He picked some tangled skeletons from the tub and dumped them in a cylinder for grinding down, then tipped the shiny product into a cardboard box he'd made up earlier. He stretched. His body felt tired but good and tight.

Wiry. He would sit down to his exercises soon. He had gone nine minutes the previous Friday. He would like to improve on that. After the meeting maybe.

He recalled Maryse's instructions. 'You need to get one twice a day and hold it as long as you can. If you don't wake up hard, stroke it. If it needs some help, get a magazine.' Fernando didn't like pictures, it wasn't nice for the girls, he had no business seeing them naked: what if I recognized someone? Maryse said, 'Once you've got one, flex it. It'll get stronger.'

Mostly, for his exercises Fernando thought about Maryse, the things they'd done the last time or the very first time, after he had embarrassed himself as he had known he would. She had said it was just fine, they had talked a lot, then she had invited him to take a shower with her. He had never washed with a woman before. Thinking of that shower made him hard again.

A prostitute had once called him 'Monsieur Mou,' cackling and shaking his prick between thumb and middle finger like a cat with a dead mouse between its jaws. The look in her eyes! She got her money, didn't she? If Maryse judged him cured, that's what he'd return to: prostitutes with bad attitudes. I never dreamt I'd need to fake impotence to hold onto a woman.

On the streets of Grandgobier, and from those hostelries whose doors were still open, a hodgepodge of drinkers, lovers, Tuesday-night stragglers, miscellaneous groups of friends and acquaintances, and even tipsy draftees contemplating the start of a final furlough – lifelong this time – trickled slowly, bound for apartment blocks where others prepared themselves for the night ahead or slept already. As the humans vanished, cats crept from alleys and backyards to hunt rats emerging from street drains and gutters.

Philippe was a natural contrarian. He found fault not only with the speech and actions of others but most frequently with his own reflections and impulses. Any hackneyed thought or unexamined belief or kneejerk impulse caused his lip to curl and, whenever discovered in himself or friend, triggered evasive if not corrective action, generally in the form of a witticism. This made him an interesting but not always an easy friend and acquaintance.

Philippe's urge to contradict was born of no desire to overwhelm or even to persuade but rather of a love of argument, dialectic and precision. It had first emerged in the form of a naive literalism: once, at the age of three, to his father's delight, on hearing his mother remark that his shoes were growing too small for him, little Philippe had rejoined: No, Mummy, it is my feet that are growing bigger.

No sooner had Philippe's father identified this precociousness than he set about to encourage his son to approach each daily task in an original, experimental, even 'mistaken' way: seeing that Philippe was right-handed, his father challenged him to draw left-handed; hearing him recite the alphabet in time-honoured order, he bade him learn it backward also. It was but a short step to attacking soup with a fork, riding a bicycle on one wheel only, and taking both sides in every dispute.

During adolescence, Philippe's critical habit of mind had spread to the emotions, leaving him unable to anger when needled, to sob at tear-jerker movies, to feel his breast swell during the Marseillaise or to flourish a fist for *l'Internationale*. Within his extended family of devout Soviet-line Communists, Philippe came to seem a most suspect sort of outsider: impatient of doctrinal orthodoxy, bored by fun-for-all party-staged jamborees, attracted to the affectations of one lefter-than-thou dissenting *groupuscule* after another, and apparently quite incapable of emoting appropriately . . .

Salvatore liked to employ in all his acts a healthful vigour and efficiency. At his machines six and seven, in under two minutes he had threshed the small amounts of product outstanding, separating sprue from pieces, casting the former into cylinders for grinding down and the latter into cardboard boxes. He had also checked the raw-material levels in both hoppers, and the integrity of a recent sample of each machine's output. Uncharacteristically, he had broken a sweat.

Running a forefinger across his brow, it was with some irritation that Salvatore imputed the moisture collected to an attack of nerves prior to public speaking rather than to the expenditure of energy. He recalled his agitation when first invited by Laure to meet her family; when called upon at university to speak to a packed assembly, he had positively panicked; here, however, before a collection of illiterates and semi-crazies, any lack of self-confidence appeared, at best, incongruous – certainly a country mile beneath his dignity.

Yet a droplet of perspiration rolled down each cheek from hairline to jaw. He sank his left hand into his trouser pocket but it came up empty. While he bent over his attaché case, flicking the combination rings, he noted a further dampness, gathering in the hollow of his chest. From a light-blue cellophane packet he extracted a paisley-patterned pink and yellow paper handkerchief.

His right hand closed to conceal the tissue, as he glanced up and down the machine aisle. Taking two paces toward the control-cabinet, he dabbed at his skin, while appearing to interrogate the dials. He pressed the tissue into a ball and made to hurl it into a corner, but changed his mind at the last moment. His closed fist remained briefly at full arm-stretch. He retraced his steps to the attaché case, opened it, and stowed the screw of tissue safely inside. He sat down.

To catch Salvatore at thought was to witness mental absorption of Olympian athleticism: his eyebrows bristled, his eyes all but closed, a frown shrouded his face, and a fist clenched beneath his chin. Beneath this onslaught, one could only surmise that any thought paler than bold black on bare white was doomed to retract, retreat and very soon surrender.

The object of the Sicilian's flagrant ratiocination was in fact Alphonse. Salvatore had found the Ivorian's harangue unbearably assured. He distrusted the man's preening arrogance. Though Salvatore was loath to agree with anything the big Gypsy said, the man did happen to be right: if Africa was so wonderful, wouldn't they have stayed put? If I didn't have to be diplomatic I'd gladly tell the Ivorian what I really think. But I represent the union now, which is a responsibility. Still. They come over here and some of them are fine, know their place, can even be turned into good union men; but others, like this Ivorian, or whatever he is, loves just to lord it, pretending to know more about us than we know ourselves, calling us immigrants, putting us all in the same boat as him, and why? Because he wants to be in the same boat as us! But what does a Sicilian, just for example, truly have in common with a sub-Saharan African? As for the radical posturing: petty-bourgeois individualism. Without robust organization, without disciplined party cadres to play the historically leading role, a revolutionary stance is nothing but a dirty habit, 'une sale manie,' as Laure's favourite singer puts it somewhere. Though he may have been singing about something else. Be that as it may, 'une sale manie' is what it is.

Salvatore smiled briefly, no more than was necessary. His fist had unclenched, his eyebrows had regained their sleekness. Alphonse had upset him for a moment, but Salvatore had dealt with his doubts now. He stood up tall. It was then that he noticed an irksome dryness in his mouth. He remembered Jacques' apples. He headed up the machine aisle.

At machine one, Philippe smoothed the surface of the raw material and lowered the hopper lid faster than he had intended, raising a puff of dust. As he descended the stepladder he noticed how much steadier he felt. His throat tickled and he coughed.

He dropped his gloves on the chair and went to stand at his pile of newspapers. Sweaty, and out of breath, he shook a cigarette from his pack of Gauloises Light. Marcel, who had finished his threshing, came over. The two men stood side by side. Philippe turned the pages of *Libération*, checking he hadn't missed anything; Marcel looked at the photos in *Marie-Claire*.

Philippe had turned to a regular column titled 'Taulards' (Jailbirds) giving news from or about prisoners. Philippe coughed some more, then swore.

What's that? Marcel said.

Just something that pisses me off.

Yeah? Why?

In fact it might interest you . . .

Yeah? How?

Didn't you do time in Loos-les-Lille?

How come you know that?

You must have told me.

Why would I have told you?

I don't know. But how else would I know?

I don't know. You tell me!

What do you mean 'you tell me?'

Philippe and Marcel had stood back from the cylinder and were staring at one another. Philippe kept coughing and clearing his throat.

How come you knew I did time in Loos-les-Lille, if I never told you?

There's no other way I could know.

Well, if you're sure.

Of course I'm sure. Sometimes you say stuff – after a drink or two.

About places you've been, things you've done. What am I supposed to do, forget it?

Well, I forget everything you say.

Philippe coughed. Marcel stood back, afraid he'd catch something.

So what is it? Marcel said.

What's what?

What pissed you off?

A guy died, took his life. In Loos-les-Lille.

Happens. Let me see.

Hanged himself. It's right here. Philippe put a finger under the snippet.

Marcel took time reading it.

Philippe inhaled some smoke, stood aside, then leaned right back to blow a perfect smoke ring almost vertically upward, ruining it at the last moment by coughing. Squinting back down to his left, he saw Marcel suck on his front teeth, his tongue pushing up ahead of them and sticking out for a moment between his lips.

You knew him, right? Philippe said.

Yeah, I knew him a little, on the inside. Marcel chuckled and repeated the expression 'on the inside.' I met him right here in Grandgobier, not in Loos. Prisoners get moved around a lot. 'Inter-prison transfer,' they call it. It keeps prisons churning, stops the inmates settling and making trouble.

Sure.

Marcel looked at Philippe, his pupils shrinking to dots and his whole face darkening again.

I didn't really know the guy. So screw him, right?

(Coughing) Screw him? If you say so.

He had only a year to go, Marcel muttered.

There was a silence.

Anyway, I thought you'd like to know, Philippe said. He might have been a friend.

He was. That cough's fucking unhygienic.

I thought you said . . .

I know what I said. I didn't really know him. But he *was* a friend. A prison friend. Screw the system, right?

Sure. Screw the system.

Their conversation at an end, both men gazed down the machine aisle.

What they saw was Salvatore standing at the end of Jacques' machine four, his feet planted a hip's width apart on the cement floor, one of the peasant's windfalls in his left hand. Jacques, labouring like an old mule, was threshing his obstinate sprue, but you could see from the tilt of his grey head he had one eye on the Sicilian.

Salvatore rubbed the apple briskly on the breast of his overalls. Then, with the absorption of a Karate artiste about to split a brick, he positioned the apple between his two hands with one palm gripping one hemisphere and the other the other, while his surgeon-manqué fingers crowded round the stalk and his thumbs nuzzled at the fruit's puckered brown anus. Taking a deep breath and holding it down, Salvatore snapped the apple clean in two.

Jacques' head lost its tilt, while Philippe and Marcel turned to look the other way along the machine aisle, toward the raised office. It appeared that Luigi had also witnessed Salvatore's trick and that he found it so amusing he had to cover his teeth.

By the time Philippe had attained adulthood, his outlook on life had become thoroughly sceptical, one might say almost scientific: he recoiled from anything that smacked of faith, took nothing on trust, shunned every teleology whether utopian dystopian or visionary, sought not final answers but better questions, distrusting all censorship and claiming 'individual freedom' as a proletarian right and duty. Charged by his self-proclaiming Leninist family with an 'infantile disorder,' Philippe sought instruction and comradeship beyond the confines of his immediate home and neighbourhood.

While his family, keeping themselves strictly to themselves, attended international solidarity meetings and raised funds for faceless fighters in distant struggles, Philippe sought out and made friends among Marseille's vast inter-meshed diasporas of Algerians, Italians, Romanies, Armenians, Arabs, Iberians, Africans, Turks, Moroccans, Slavs, Greeks, Jews and Corsicans: he enjoyed their food and drink, observed their family relationships, absorbed their histories, imperceptibly adopting non-French modes of behaviour, dress and language several decades before it became *de rigueur* for young whites so to do.

After Philippe left home, travelled, married and had a child, settling at last in Grandgobier and involving himself in workplace and labour conflicts, his contrarian habits mellowed. Once the revolutionary moment had passed, his record of employment and political engagement began to strike him as evidence of a dated and now forlorn entryism. He appeared trapped: separated from family, ideologically adrift, unhappily wed, largely unbefriended. Faced with wifely infidelity, Philippe could discover within himself no jealousy, wounded pride, or masculine scorn: any powerful feeling, liable to register in frozen spasm upon his face, conjured to his mind a self-image that was always already inauthentic, fundamentally secondhand, essentially fraudulent.

Yet as the ringing truth of his sister's news sank in, Philippe began to experience an elation for which he could not yet account. It was as if a stopper upon his personal ambitions and desires had been removed, a stopper that he could never have drawn by his own strength alone. His contrarianism itself would be free to unravel slowly. There would no longer be any need for it. Beyond family, faith, teleology, soon beyond wedlock, he was condemned to be a free man.

Renata and Jorge were in Jorge's bedroom. Renata sat on the edge of a large table, made from a pallet that Jorge had taken one night from a building site; Jorge stood between her legs, looking at her closely, trying not to think of Felicia somewhere in Bolivia, maybe. They talked unhurriedly, took sips of wine, kissed each other's faces, and puffed on cigarettes. Earlier, clumsily, Jorge had tried to plant a kiss on Renata's lips, but she had turned away so that it had crashed in her hair. Please, there's no rush, she had said.

The flat door had opened to the sound of women's laughing voices.

Your co-tenants? Renata had asked.

My landladies. Frédérique and Babette. Sisters. They sublet me this room.

Will you introduce me?

If you like. But it's unnecessary.

Then I'm in no hurry.

Renata giggled and pushed her glass away, as if the wine were to blame for something. She lifted her lips. They kissed, then Jorge pushed his wine away too. He didn't want either of them to do any more drinking. He eased his hands gently under Renata's buttocks, lifting her from the table. He was surprised by how light she was. Felicia had been . . . Felicia *was* . . .

They aren't lovers of yours, are they? Renata asked, linking her legs very slowly and gracefully behind Jorge's back.

No. What do you think I am?

Un hombre, Renata growled, attempting to sound South American.

Well, Jorge said, I don't fuck women I just happen to live with, unless . . .

Jorge didn't like either the conversation or his part in it.

Unless you happen to live with the women you fuck . . . ?

Jorge nodded and felt himself blush. He was glad of the dim lighting. He wanted to say, 'Your tongue isn't good just for kissing,' but caught himself in time.

Jorge held Renata in his arms until, in the adjacent bathroom, one of Jorge's flatmates pulled the chain. They found themselves laughing abruptly into each other's mouths. Jorge slid his arms up to Renata's shoulders, pulling her upper body toward him as her legs floated down to the floor.

Are we going to do this . . . ? Renata asked.

How much do you want to?

Hah! Well. A lot.

Then so do I.

Jorge stood back and stared at Renata. Was he waiting for something more? she wondered. He lit a cigarette. No, he thought, this time Felicia has gone. Completely gone.

Shall we get undressed? Renata murmured.

Wait, Jorge said, stepping back toward her. He held a hand out. Allow me . . .

You're trembling, Renata said, catching Jorge's hand in one of hers.

Well, it isn't the drink, he said.

They began to undress one another, in a hurry now, getting in each other's way, pushing and pulling. There were no more words.

Yitoune wasn't there. Philippe was there. Downstairs. Bobrán always knew how to find Yitoune, but she didn't live in this or any other factory. He could make do.

Bobrán nodded to the Ivorian to look after his machines. He didn't wait for an answer. He went halfway down the stairs.

Luigi was turning round, his hand coming off his mouth, grinning still. Philippe was looking in his direction too, but he didn't seem to focus. Marcel pulled a face and began looking at a magazine on Philippe's pile of papers.

As far as Bobrán could make out, Philippe was not busy with anything. He kept coughing but otherwise looked as bored as he ever did. The chef d'équipe had advised Bobrán to leave Philippe for a bit. But advice doesn't have to be followed, does it?

Any luck getting a syndicate together? the little Gypsy asked Luigi.

I'm working on it, Luigi said, one eye closing.

Good, because this gyppo doesn't risk his back for less than a week's wages. Unless he happens to be in the mood. And then he'll do it for free and without an audience and there's no one to stop him.

Bragging again? Luigi said, lighting a Gitanes-Maïs and seeking a pose.

And you can fuck off too, Bobrán said.

46. Talking softly.

Arriving from metallurgy, marching as from the factory gates or the wide world beyond, Tomec saw the lights of the plastic section dappled through plastic flaps and a man who was pushing through them – either the Marseillais or the big Gypsy.

As the Marseillais leaned over the water fountain, he noticed Tomec's distant swinging torch. While Philippe's right hand cupped his cigarette, shielding it from any splashes, his left hand gripped the metal surround.

Just as Philippe had walked past the bottom of the stairs, Bobrán, on his way down, had hailed him. Philippe had tapped at his chest and spluttered, Hopper dust. I need water. Bobrán had hesitated, then resumed his descent.

Philippe drank long and deep, interspersing his draughts with a little gentle gargling, then he straightened up and took a puff from his cigarette.

Tomec was alongside him now. You could tell the man had walked fast. He was panting to get somewhere. Light through the flaps revealed a sheen of sweat on Tomec's face. Philippe wondered if this was what Poles did – a kind of national characteristic, no worse than any other: they stand around maybe and stare a lot and then occasionally, when you least expect it, they sweat.

Philippe's cough had eased. Funny how water always worked. Picks up the dust and flushes it away somewhere. He grinned up at Tomec but Tomec only stared at the back of his own left hand and frowned. Maybe Poles frown when they sweat.

I took your advice, Tomec said.

Advice?

About the graffiti.

Philippe raised his eyebrows.

A complete blank. You have to help me.

Tomec wiped his forehead.

You said I should leave the men alone and lie to the boss.

Philippe chuckled as he took out his cigarette pack.

Do you take nothing seriously? Tomec asked.

Not when I don't have to.

Philippe wondered if sweating went with being earnest.

Tomec peered through the scratched flaps. He took a decision.

He set his feet further apart as if commanded to stand at ease. Tell me something: what do you see when you see one of your workmates?

Philippe took out a cigarette and began tapping it on the side of the pack.

It depends what he's doing.

Say he's breaking up products in a bin.

We don't break things up. We separate the product, which is saleable, from the sprue, which gets reground and reused.

All right.

So, first of all, I see what is there before me.

And nothing else? Just a man separating product from sprue . . .

Philippe positioned a cigarette between his lips and pulled his lighter from his trouser pocket. It lay in the flat of his palm: silver, square and cold.

It depends who he is.

You're making this difficult.

Then you make it easy! Tell me what you see.

Philippe's cigarette had leapt up and down as he talked.

I see the person, whoever he is, stripped right down, striving for something. The location switches, the time and season change. He could be loading a mule, mining for clay, scratching figures on a wall. I see humanity, strength, nobility. Something timeless.

Timeless. Is that it?

Well?

Philippe clicked his cigarette into life, took a puff as deep as a yawn. As he nodded and fixed the night security man, he dealt two perfect plumes of smoke from his nostrils.

You see broad brush strokes, no details, no specific person or event. You see what you want to see. Like you read what you want to read. Virgil. Or something about Virgil. What's the difference? Maybe you see the things you never see in the mirror but would like to.

Don't be clever. What do you see?

In the mirror or here?

I don't care for mirrors.

Philippe blew a smoke ring off to one side.

I see everything I know about the place and the situation and the person. Which isn't much. Then I see everything I can't know but can't stop myself imagining. Which is damn near infinite. The man's story, his connections, all the stuff that is unique to him and all the stuff he shares with others by living alongside them. His history. The history of his history.

Okay, Tomec said, making to go.

To hell with that! Philippe said. Is that what Poles do?

What?

Ask a question then walk away when they get an answer?

You call that an answer?

Anyone can frown, Philippe said. It takes character to smile.

Okay, Tomec said, pushing through the flaps.

Philippe leaned back over the fountain. The water was cold and clean. Philippe reckoned he liked Poles. They were different.

In Mathieu Petit's flat, Marie was talking softly to Nadine.

I feel as if you're listening. Or that if you were, you would understand and say something interesting. Monsieur Petit said I could talk to you, that it could do no harm. I asked him what I could talk about and he said, Anything you like. My wife is unshockable. Then he did a little laugh and said, Always was. Anyway, I hope you didn't mind hearing about my family and my boyfriend. My aunt never listens. She talks a lot but doesn't hear anything other people say. She's not deaf though. She must think she's interesting. Yak yak yak. Oh, well. I think I'm running out of things to say. I could go next door and do some revision. Shall I leave you alone? I'm just thinking aloud now. Monsieur Petit's nice, isn't he? Dumb question, right? You married him. He said you liked singing and especially 'Le Temps des cerises.' He said he imagined I could sing, because I have a good talking voice. He called it 'melodious.' He sings, he said. To give his lips a rest, he said. In public. Like a lot of trumpet players. I can't picture it. With me he's friendly but, you know, very correct. He doesn't talk much, does he? Anyway, you have absolutely nothing to worry about. He's really not my type. Though maybe he was good-looking in his youth. I think I should just shut up. I'm not as silly as I may be sounding right now. I'm really not. I'm the serious sort. I feel relaxed with you. Please don't think it's because you don't talk back. It goes deeper. I keep looking at that photo over there. You were really beautiful. In M. Petit's eyes, you still are. Do you know that? Of course you do. If you know anything. You know what? I think you're beautiful too. Don't imagine it's pity that's talking. I'm not sentimental. If I didn't like you, I'd let you know. I see a lot of people worse off than you. People who never leave their toilet, not even to eat, but can't stop thinking and remembering. You had love and you weren't always poor, were you? My mother was dirt-poor till she was in her forties. She was beginning to remake her life with my stepfather, a decent enough man, then she died. He died too. A broken heart. Sweet, really. I don't think you're to be pitied. In the least. I know all the words to 'Le Temps des cerises.' My grandfather used to sing it to me when I was tiny. 'Quand nous chanterons . . .' I need to clear my voice. But I'm not in the mood now. Maybe later?

Luigi was sitting at the end of his machine thirteen, a product piece in his hand, his eyes closing. A cornpaper cigarette hung half-smoked from his upper lip; a knot of chewing gum lay hard by his lower left canine; in his right shoe, a rucked sock gnawed at his heel; his pelvic area registered a post-orgasmic listlessness. Nobody ever sat down with a product piece in their lap, but Luigi had. Twenty-five seconds attention was the most any piece demanded, but Luigi kept turning this one over and over. Till his eyes lost their focus and his grip relaxed. At this machine, the mould hadn't been changed for weeks. With a new mould, at first you compare each product with an engineer-approved model left for you by the man from the previous shift. Then, once you've checked a few dozen, the pattern is ensconced in your brain, to be buffed and burnished by each subsequent piece you examine, till the one true and perfect comparator is right there in your head, glowing sharper than a memory. Luigi worked his pelvic musculature to retract his testicles so that his cock, briefly glued to his underpants by a gout of dry-ing ejaculate, tugged itself unstuck. Luigi considered what it took to bring him off these days and how different his climaxes were inside a woman and out – well, in practice, inside Gilberte or out into thin air: stronger inside fellow flesh but so much harder to arrange; longer-lasting and with greater spinal spasm but requiring more intricate negotiation and tedious displays of humanity. You get what you fucking pay for. One way or another. Luigi felt the hard scratchy sprue in his hand, opened his eyes a crack to glimpse the product piece, then let them close again. You never lavish so much attention on anything else. Not even meat. You cut it up, get your blade down into it, know it from the inside out, but you don't stand and stare at it. You'd get fired, arrested, or carted off to the funny farm. The world could well be chockfull of ill-formed objects. You would never notice. I should go home one time and pick up every knife, chair, cup and picture frame just to see if it really is sharp, stable, unchipped, true. For anything to be perfect, it must always be the result of applying just the right pressure at just the right temperature to just the right material in just the right circumstances. Or some similar set of parameters. Parameters. That's a word the Sicilian uses. That's where I heard it. I'm getting educated in this dump. For instance: for a butcher, such a working parameter might be sharpness of knife. Try slicing meat with a blunt knife. I'll think of another example in a second. With a topic-changing yawn, Luigi recalled the Sicilian talking earlier that evening and himself thinking he might be at a high point in his life – for lack of bad things happening. Fuck that for a notion. This couldn't be as good as it gets. He wanted what Lucien had: a pliant wife, still game and not too fat; a successful business; respect in his neighbourhood; some trainee sucker to do the donkey work, the carting and the mincing and the sausage-making. Then straight ahead, no left turns, all the way to the cemetery. Lucien was twice his age, but his woman was better than Gilberte. He wondered if he'd ever want to take Gilberte in a walk-in cold store. Why not? She's no fusspot. She'd go. But by the time Gilberte got to Mme Martinet's age, would he really want to fuck her in a deep freeze? Or anywhere else for that matter?

Bobrán could have gone back upstairs but to intercept Philippe it was best to be around: the Marseillais did nothing all night long but he was never less than occupied.

So what was that letter? Marcel asked.

It's not something to talk about here, Bobrán replied, glancing vaguely round at Luigi, Jacques, and Eric, and tapping his nose. I'll tell you later. Alone.

Bobrán was wondering who he could pass the time with. The Algerian looked like he didn't need company. Jacques had his cap pulled down over his eyes. The Englishman was reading some damn book. The Sicilian was eating an apple like it was a test of his virility – not that he and Bobrán would have anything to talk about.

Marcel stared at his cousin and smoked. Bobrán stood back and put a hand in his lush brown curls. Marcel looked away.

I told you about the wedding, right?

Sure.

Just don't come as a fucking Gypsy.

What is it – fancy-dress?

Dress like a Frenchman. Okay? And tell your mum the same.

I'll get her some trousers and a beret.

Don't be funny with me.

A trouser suit.

It's a gadgé wedding and don't forget it. You're all the family I've got.
Don't wreck it for me.

I'll leave my tambourine in the caravan.

Ha ha.

Upstairs, Alphonse had caught up with his threshing and topped up his
hopper. He sat at the end of his machine nineteen, staring at the old semi-
automatic machine twenty-one: every time its press wrenched open, he saw
Jean reach his left hand in to take the product, then lean a little to the right
to press the START button before the press clamped shut again. Alphonse
wished Jean could have been downstairs to hear his performance. If he could
remember what he had said, he might reprise it for him later. He struggled
to bring it back to mind. He had riffed on how much we know about *them*
and how little they know about *us*: the relative inequality of basic ignorance.
And he had touched on the fact that all working people, all wage slaves, are
essentially immigrants, constrained to live like foreigners in a country they
create anew each day for the benefit and enjoyment of their oppressors. Jean
needed to hear that.

Returning from the water fountain, Philippe tilted his head at the foreman,
who halted on his way up the machine aisle. Mathieu removed the burnt-out
matchstick from his mouth and leaned his weight on his better leg.

You know about the strike? Philippe asked.

Sure, there's a meeting in ten minutes. I thought you'd stepped back.

I have. The Sicilian took over. I've been thinking.

Tell me, Mathieu said.

The temps may be expected to work straight through.

So?

For half an hour, they could be made to keep the entire section running, all twenty automatic machines. Unless everyone leaves their hoppers empty and their threshing bins full – which could be construed as negligence.

So?

It wouldn't be much of a strike, would it? They wouldn't make a lot of friends, would they? Both of them gitans . . .

Get to the point.

You'll be striking, won't you?

You think I'm a blackleg?

Then couldn't there be a safety issue? Poorly-trained temps working unsupervised?

Mathieu stuck the matchstick back in his mouth and grinned briefly.

I like it, he said. It's bullshit but it's neat. I'll think it over.

You'd be sticking your neck out.

I know what I'd be doing.

Mathieu walked to the lift. Philippe returned to his machine.

Surprised by the notion of making love to Gilberte some distant summer's day in a butcher's walk-in refrigerator, Luigi had chucked into the floor tray the product piece he had been caressing, yanked up his irritant sock, gathered his gum-cud from his left canine and deposited it on the rear panel of Marcel's machine twelve, pressing it onto a convenient ledge. He had risen quickly to his feet and crossed the aisle to stand at Philippe's papers. As he began to sift the pile, he lickingly detached then relit his Gitanes stub, taking care not to break the skin of his upper lip. Amidst all the blah-blah-blah of politics and commentary and adverts, there were at least some brief stories to feed Luigi's imagination. Yet these were so stripped of detail, background and character and were told in such a telegraphic manner as to appear banal: you would not have thought it possible that rape, prostitution, gang violence, paedophilia, incest, corruption and murder could be so purged of all passion and humanity. Yet so it was. Shuffling the papers, the Italian glanced about him. Jacques had stood up and was now skilfully employing a large Opinel to cut slithers from an apple, which he then spiked and proffered to the Englishman standing alongside him. Salvatore was stationed at the end of the aisle, leaning back against the wooden table, eating the apple that Luigi had earlier glimpsed him split into two hemispheres with his bare hands, a nice trick that brought to mind a film Luigi had seen with Gilberte, *Le Jour du Chakal*, in which a hired assassin, an Englishman about as cold as a North-Sea haddock, gently snaps the neck of a woman he has picked up the night before in a hotel bar. Serving her right of course. Luigi experienced an access of affection for Gilberte, not so much as a wave, but rather more than a rill. He found himself enumerating her virtues: she was no slattern; her voice was not harsh or shrill and she knew when to shut up; she had as yet shown no disloyalty; she was not unkind to either animals or children; she was not a bad cook; decisively, it had been Gilberte's lumpish image rather than that of the voluptuous Aurelia that in the end had made him shoot his wad. That was not nothing. He could show some appreciation. There was nowhere these thoughts could take him. Luigi, with the deliberation of a man lifting a fragile vase from a table and lowering it onto a mantelpiece, hoisted his attention from his absent girlfriend and deposited it on his machines. He would check the pieces, sit down and close his eyes. He would give in and drowse a short minute or two. Stooping and trudging like a soldier in a dugout, Luigi re-crossed the machine aisle.

Pierre was in bed with his wife, talking softly. He pressed his left fist into his belly, hoping to shift or soothe the pain.

My stomach's bad now, he told Fernande.

His wife said nothing.

You think it's the whisky.

She yawned.

You're probably right.

Pierre got up and went to the dresser, returning with two large white tablets.

You're upset about your brother, she said. That hurts as bad as whisky.

He thinks he can come back and ask me questions now Edith is dead.

His wife said nothing.

I know, Pierre said. She's been dead a while. But Jacques thinks he can just come round. Everyone likes to imagine they're better than a cop. Especially a bent cop, a cop who went bad. People love to sneer at us. Because once we're disgraced or retired, we don't frighten them. We're the lowest of the low. Do you realize that? Well, do you? Fernande? Fernande!

Pierre raised himself on one elbow, looked at his wife's face in the half-dark. He thought about kissing her but decided not to.

He settled on his back, his hands joined over his stomach. The tablets seemed to be working. He heard a police siren. 'I wonder who those bastards are harassing tonight,' he thought. Then he grinned and closed his eyes. 'Glad it's not me.'

Alphonse had wandered round the end of machine twenty-one and had come to stand alongside Jean.

All right? Alphonse asked.

Sure, Jean replied, not looking up.

Coming to the strike meeting?

Nope. I don't abandon my post.

Alphonse stared at him.

So you don't strike?

You've not been here long.

Alphonse's face fell.

So what does the union say?

I never asked them. I'm not a member. I'm not paid to go on strike.

Alphonse said nothing. Jean broke the silence.

What are you going to recite tonight? Something different?

Same play, different speech. I'm trying to get it word perfect. I tend to add in things of my own. I'm trying to stop doing that.

Till later then.

Yes.

Alphonse sat for a moment longer, then got up.

Back in his library, Gérard had found and refilled his tumbler. Pushing the door closed behind him, he distinctly imagined the distant click of Claude's bedside lamp. Since it seemed plausible she might so deceive him, was she not capable of deceit on a grander scale? He had long taken it for granted that nobody would ever wish to bed his wife out of anything but love and that, equally, nobody but himself could ever be so stupid as to love her: he had never needed to think any further. Recently, however, he had stumbled upon an article in a business magazine about rich and powerful women who paid for sex: it seemed there were brothels nowadays to cater for this market. He wondered if he should have her followed, but quickly dismissed the notion,

figuring to himself the sordid humiliation of having to listen to some winking gabardined lush answering the indelicate question with either a 'no' or a
'yes.' As these thoughts dissipated, Gérard's blood-alcohol reached the precise
level at which a personal discursive switch was always thrown: he began to
address himself in the second person. As always, the first thought couched
in this mode, the thought which indeed confirmed that such a threshold
had been attained was, 'Gérard, you'd better leave off the sauce. You've had
enough.' At which point, he would grimace, as he did now, and pour himself another shot, but a small one, a finger. 'You have options, you know,'
he reassured himself. 'You can go to bed. You can wait up for Paul. You can
have that coffee. You can open a book. You could even call Raymond. You
could certainly call your chauffeur.' He looked at the clock and took a sip.
'You could ask Raymond point-blank whether he has heard about the graffiti.
Not a good idea. What do you have to worry about? You only ever did one
really bad thing and – apart from one dead man – who could possibly know
of it? If the graffiti writer knew, he would have daubed a word much worse
than 'collabo.' They know nothing. Take it easy. Or you could phone Jorge.
For a chat. He won't be asleep yet. In fact, he won't even be home yet. He'll
be out revelling with other Latinos. All that bunch know how to do is dance
and screw, dance and screw.

Bobrán found Philippe alone at machine number one. He handed him
Albert's letter.

What, aloud?

I know it by heart already.

Then why?

Just . . . Please.

Philippe read the first line, then began to make his slow way over to
the far corner of the shop floor. Bobrán trailed behind him.

Philippe finished reading and handed the letter back. He lit a cigarette.

So what can I do?

The chef said I should talk to you. But not tonight.

Philippe blew smoke to one side.

So?

I saw this guy's brother take a dive, Bobrán said.

A dive?

You know I work building sites during the day.

Yeah. And to think there are peckerheads who say you people are work-shy.

Bobrán grinned and nodded.

How come you don't use safety gear?

You know.

I do?

Harnesses slow you down and most of us have no need of them. I have no need of them. This guy's brother, Joseph – we worked together. We were like that. (Bobrán lay his index fingers together). He was clumsy but he was smart. He read books. Sometimes he spoke like one. He should never have been there. He was a bit like you.

A bit?

Definitely.

So you'd better tell his brother whatever he wants to know, right?

Bobrán said nothing.

Merde, Philippe said.

Bobrán looked up.

You can't, can you? You're frightened. Right?

Well, it wouldn't be easy, Bobrán said.

Philippe took a deep drag on his cigarette.

So you have problems with the cops, right? Which you don't want to make any worse?

Bobrán's lips pursed and he swallowed. Philippe blew a smoke ring.

I'm not telling you what to do. If you walk away, be sure you can live with yourself. And if you don't, make sure your back is covered. Because your friend's brother – once he's uncovered his precious nugget of truth – he's going to go straight back to where he came from, and leave you right here in the shit. He'll be sorry about it maybe, but that's what he'll do.

How do I do that?

How do you do what?

Cover my back.

Philippe hesitated.

I don't suppose your cousin could help in any way.

You're right. He couldn't.

Then do you know any lawyers?

Do I look like I know lawyers?

Don't joke about this stuff.

You're right.

Philippe took his time finishing his cigarette.

I know a couple of lawyers who might take an interest, Philippe then said.

I don't have any . . .

They're the sort who'd work for free.

I don't want to create trouble for anybody.

Now you're sounding like that fucking letter. I'll talk to them. I'll see what they say.

It hadn't taken Angelica long to pack a hold-all. She was surprised how little it weighed. The keyring was too chunky to fit under the door so she removed the keys. She recalled a fairground one summer in Aveiro where she had won a doll playing a version of shove-ha'penny, after her brother had vanished to France. The keys scudded away from her nicely. They'd be lying there on the lino. Ricky would find them all right. She stood up. There was no way she could feel ashamed to be sneaking away like this. He had hit her once and might have again. Then he had drunk too much and got down on his knees and begged for forgiveness. She couldn't say it. That was when she knew. She had half-expected him to cry, but he didn't. She closed the street door. She could walk to Rosa's apartment in a quarter of an hour. The air would do her good. The keyring she'd keep. There were other front doors.

Luigi sat back down and closed his eyes. He just couldn't fathom the old-timers: the little guy upstairs, with his hard work, his punctuality and his snotty rage; then that sleepy damned peasant over there, offering slivers of some half-rotten windfall to a man clearly eager to wolf down the whole thing. Living in the country made you a moron: everyone knows that. Luigi recalled the time his car broke down on a rain-swept hillside. He had walked for over an hour before he'd found a couple of surly old decrepits in a freezing shack, huddled in rags, feeding a lamb from a dirty bottle. Jacques probably lived somewhere similar. Bet he takes his animals to bed with him. What would that be like? A sheep would be nice and tight, wouldn't it? It might give you a better spend than a woman. Certainly less trading required. And you wouldn't get cold with a sheep. Luigi opened his eyes a crack and bared his teeth to laugh. Peasants! Luigi noticed Mathieu checking the product at machine fourteen. The foreman was all right. Knew what he was doing. Never missed a fault. That's army training for you. There he goes again, turning it over and over. I've learned that from him now. Funny the way you never see the same product twice or even in the same way. You never see the whole thing. If you did, you'd only need to look once. It's the same with people. You only get a single shot. And then another single shot. You see from only one side, only one angle at a time. You have to guess at the bits you don't see and piece together a picture. Stacking the shots one on top of another. And another thing: every good product is effectively identical. Not actually identical, just sufficiently identical. Whereas every dud is misshapen in a unique way. I wish I could ask the foreman how his hand got that way, but I never could. Questions you just can't ask. Luigi yawned and the yawn seemed to correspond to a moment of emptiness. Into the void was sucked the image of Aurelia and a shadow-memory in his testicles of his recent orgasm. It was right that some whoring woman should whimper and bleed and cower and beg for yet more pain and humiliation and, hell, if they're going to do that anyway, if that's written into their eternal nature, why wouldn't you want to be the one to give them true cause? Even if you have to be a donkey. Not that he'd ever want to hurt a real woman – Gilberte, say – however vast his contempt, no, his hatred. He could shift his feelings elsewhere, like shifting his attention from piece to piece, from article in a newspaper to advert in same. It was better than going to confession. It kept you healthy, made sure you didn't do any real harm. It had to be preferable to relying on some sodomite priest, some little-boy fellater, little-girl finger-fucker, bastards all. I'd take the cleaver to the lot of them. I'd do it myself. May they burn in the hell they make others believe in. It must be packed with their sort by now. The foreman winked at him. That's good. Machine fourteen has been okay for almost an hour now. I could catnap. I'm not thinking about Aurelia any more. It was Gilberte who brought me off. To hell with Aurelia. Gilberte deserves me, bless her. Besides, in the heat of it I threw that mag at the toilet wall, didn't I? Maybe I was a little hasty there. It could still have helped me get it up.

The little Gypsy and the Marseillais had wandered back to machine number two, where Philippe had just checked the latest product to drop from the press. From across the machine aisle, Mathieu, having spotted Bobrán, removed the burnt-out matchstick from his mouth and jerked it up at the ceiling.

As Bobrán headed for the stairs, Mathieu yelled, Plus de cirque, s'il te plaît!

Bobrán instantly assumed Mathieu's gait, hobbling and limping up one stair at a time, rubbing an arthritic hip and clamping his spittle-spray teeth round an imaginary matchstick. Mathieu looked up and down the machine aisle. Even the Englishman seemed to get the joke. The foreman glanced up at Bobrán. His old eyes were sparkling. The little Gypsy disappeared from view, head and shoulders first.

Mathieu called Philippe over.

Oui, chef?

You're right about the agency workers. It wouldn't be safe for them to work unsupervised. Not during a strike.

Philippe smiled. He was pleased with himself.

Can you tell the Sicilian? the foreman asked.

It would be better coming from you. Once you've explained it to the cousins.

Mathieu sighed and nodded.

Do you think the little one's in trouble? he asked.

Not yet. It's up to him. He wants to help the dead guy's brother.

Natural enough. I don't know what I'd do.

Philippe looked at Mathieu, expecting something more. But the foreman turned away.

After leaving a letter for Fanny, Kosal walked to the San Francisco. Julie saw him come in and look around. She read his sadness. She beckoned him over. He leaned across the bar, shoulder-to-shoulder with the American.

You just missed her, Julie told him.

She won't answer my letters.

She says it's over.

Kosal pulled a face and made to go.

Wait.

Kosal leaned back over. Chuck was trying to listen in now. He couldn't keep his eyes off Julie's breasts.

She has a new boyfriend, Julie whispered. She didn't ask me to tell you.

Kosal looked Julie in the eye.

I'll kill him.

It's not his fault.

Kosal seemed surprised.

Then I'll kill myself, he whispered.

Chuck giggled. Julie looked from man to man, then hastily down the bar.

Did you say what I think you said? Chuck asked.

Kosal watched Julie gesture at the manager. She looked agitated.

Look, pal – Chuck was saying – don't go killing yourself over some tramp. Whoever she is, she's not worth it. Have a drink on me and calm down.

I don't drink, Kosal said.

I take it all back. Kill yourself.

Julie put a firm hand on Kosal's right arm. He stared down at it.

Go home, Chuck, Julie said, without looking at the American. You're stinking drunk. You'll get yourself hurt.

Kosal stood up abruptly and shook his head at Julie.

Who do you think I am? he asked. I wouldn't touch the prick.

Then he turned and left, leaving Julie open-mouthed. Chuck was laughing and relating the story to a stranger who had come to sit beside him.

47. Keeping moving.

Rachid sat on his usual chair, his mouth screened by his fingers, enjoining his dead son to listen and to respond. His voice declined to a drowsy mumbling then fell silent. I am sick of getting no reply. Should I give up trying? Is that what you need? As he yawned, his eyelids quivered and the index finger of his left hand came to rest on the bridge of his nose.

In a whining parody of his father's voice, Mehdi proclaimed, I am here, I have been listening. You say I must be happy for you. Why? The tautness across Rachid's forehead gave way to a tingling. His lips hesitated, uncertain whether to voice his son's erupting words or declare his own shock. His son prevailed.

I have nothing to do with this baby, Mehdi said. We will never occupy the same space. It will not know me. Until it too dies. There is no passage between our worlds. Only a crank could believe there could be shared speech. You wanted a reply. There. Did you imagine I was alone? The world of the dead is crammed: new arrivals every day. You cling to me as if I could alter your history for you by being both dead and alive.

There was more to come. Rachid raised his right hand to rub his forehead. He would play the patient father. Then, instead of Mehdi, he saw Malika and Fatima sleeping in the dark, either side of a flimsy partition wall. He floated high above them. This is the longest night, he told himself.

Having noticed Luigi's slumped frame, Tomec, with the fingertip precision of a child playing Spillikins, retrieved from beneath his chair the discarded copy of *Détective*. Glancing at Luigi's lolling head, Tomec took a step smartly backward and opened the magazine. Marcel, who was studying the security man's manoeuvrings, materialized at his shoulder, cigarette in mouth and right hand scratching belly.

Acknowledging the Gypsy's presence with a minuscule modification in stance, Tomec proceeded to turn pages, paying special attention to the illustrations. He paused at a photograph showing an under-attired young woman seated at a bar beside a standard specimen of balding manhood. While she pouted and teased, Mister – owing to an excess of leering – was in danger of toppling from his stool. The caption explained that the lady was employed by an agency to entrap husbands suspected of philandering and that she had a wire 'concealed in her vertiginous cleavage.'

Tomec lowered the paper and turned fractionally toward Marcel.

Could you exhale in some other direction?

I wouldn't have thought you'd go for that stuff, Marcel remarked, as he blew a volley of smoke down at the sleeping Italian.

You don't know me.

I'd never fall for a trick like that. That kind of woman is never free.

Tomec read the article. Marcel counted his cigarettes.

It's an act, Tomec observed, a piece of vaudeville. Once the job's done and she's no longer 'that kind of woman,' maybe she is . . . free.

What do you know about it?

I've worked in bars.

What's on the next page?

With a flick of the wrist, Tomec passed Marcel the paper.

Sarah's friend Ornella had rung to suggest they see Fassbinder's *Angst essen Seele auf* at the Maison de la Culture on Thursday. I'd love to, Sarah had said at once, deciding then and there to share with Ornella her latest conversation with Simone.

I'm so terrified of hurting her I never say what I want to say. I could write a book and title it, *Things I Never Told My Sister*. As usual, Simone was complaining about her boyfriend, and then she tricked me into talking about Tomec. She said my daddy referred to him as a middle-aged artist. Doesn't that sound bad? If I listened to him, I'd end up with some dynamic young Israeli.

What's wrong with that?

It would be hate at first sight.

What do you have against Israel?

Are you joking?

No. Really. To me, Israel is necessary . . . perhaps a necessary evil.

An evil? Wait a minute . . .

Well, not an evil, just necessary. Maybe the day the smoke and the ashes are sucked back down the chimneys and the Arabs from Morocco to Iraq and the Slavs from Poland to Vladivostok welcome back with open arms the Jews they chased out in the forties and fifties and sixties, and if – ojalá! – Spain and Portugal and Salonica and Turkey take back all the Sephardi . . . Then, maybe, Israel will not need to exist as a home of last resort for Jews. That's what I think.

There speaks a Gentile.

That's unfair. Anyway, what's wrong with 'some dynamic young Israeli?'

It's just the way they are. You know.

No, I don't.

Intent on being as dull and as earnest as any square-jawed Jew-baiter. They want to take our Talmudic experts and our artists and filmmakers, forge a new man, a new Jew, with tattoos up his arms, who can fix the drains and build motorways and fight wars. The hitch is: it's the most lamentable waste of Jewishness. We're a diasporic people, a philosophic people. We've fallen for a gentile fantasy we can't afford.

So, instead of an Israeli, you take up with a Pole.

He's a French Pole. With Jewish ancestry. On his mother's side, the side that matters. Besides, he's an atheist. Like me.

You are? But you're always talking about God.

All the best Jews are atheists. Some say we have a gene for it. It doesn't put a stop to God-talk. As a Catholic, you've got to know that.

I'm lapsed.

Oh, Jesus! Everybody's lapsed.

Philippe had ambled down the machine aisle and was standing just to Rachid's left, leaning against the huge old table. The Algerian's eyes flicked open and shut. He shifted back in his wooden chair so the seat edge worked at an itch behind his knee. His left hand remained across his face, his right hand cupped and squeezed his left elbow. He kept hearing Mehdi's question, Did you think I was alone? Philippe was looking at the Sicilian. He nudged the Algerian.

Look at him, the Marseillais said.

Rachid looked at the Sicilian.

Like a mime warming up, Salvatore was performing a series of contortional facial exercises taking him through every age, emotion and experience known to humanity: from the bewildered discomfort of the colicky babe to the depths and shallows of geriatric despondency and glee.

He must think he's alone, Philippe said.

Rachid guffawed. Not even the dead are alone, Rachid muttered.

Philippe stared at him.

It's nothing, Rachid said. I need a coffee.

They walked together through the raw-materials area. They purchased their own coffees.

I could see you enjoyed the African's speech, Philippe said.

I'd forgotten about it, Rachid said. It was entertaining.

He's an actor.

You can tell.

I should leave you to your thoughts.

You're all right.

Philippe remained another minute, finishing his coffee and looking into the shadows, then left Rachid standing there.

Jean peeped through the opening mould as he leaned in to grab the product. All three of his upstairs colleagues were where they were paid to be. How often did that happen? He tore the cable ties from the sprue. That African had no business to mention an Italian commie in the same breath as la Vierge d'Orléans. Or to act all outraged when I said I wasn't attending any damned union meeting. START. I guess Blacks are drawn to Reds, I've noticed that before. They think it's about equality. If it comes to a stoppage, he'll probably call me scab, blackleg, jaune. Maybe they all will. I've got a thick hide. Just look at that! I knew it couldn't last. Now the Portuguee's at the African's machine – they're like a pair of girls the way they chat. At least the Portuguee said sorry for the African earlier. I pretended I hadn't noticed. Didn't want him imagining things. Damned foreman couldn't apologize for being late to relieve me, could he? I was bursting. I'll just dab some oil on the pins. Not too much. START. There. At least when I come back the seat is never warm. I'm sure he never sits down. Good thing too. In fact, he never sits anywhere, does he? I've only just realized that. The African is doing all the talking. The product came away real nice. Just the right amount of lubricant. I wonder if the Portuguee could use our spare room? He might be handy. We'd charge him something. Nothing exorbitant. I could see what he says. START. The sprue bin is filling up. Boredom now. Odd about the foreman never sitting down. Things you don't see till you do. Now the Portuguee's vanished! I'm betting he's gone to the toilet. If I'm wrong I'll see him coming back up the stairs.

Albert Gbenye, flat on his back, crisp sheets gathered like a ruff round his neck, was waiting for sleep. His nose registered two smells: that of the blanket, an acrid mix of soap powder and something unpleasantly more organically human, overlaid by the smoke from Sotiris's cigarettes, wafting into the room via the gaps and cracks around the bathroom door. Albert could not picture his brother in this harsh country, among these ugly people with their dry music and their flat voices, shivering and concocting plans for escape in a room not unlike this one. Albert had always imagined Joseph in a place that was clean, tidy, cool rather than cold, either light or dark but never sombre. Albert had certainly never thought of Joseph falling asleep like this beneath a flickering neon sign, with the sound of a fading moped and a shout. The bathroom door opened. Albert remained quite still. The Greek kicked the foot of his bed and swore. Excuse-moi si je te réveille, he said. Je ne dormais pas, Albert replied. Bonne nuit. À demain.

The tide of elation that had broken over the Englishman on getting a date with the afternoon-shift brunette was receding.

For a start there was the small matter of how to behave at the clock machine Wednesday, Thursday and Friday evenings. For tomorrow a big smile might do, nothing complicit or flirtatious. Thursday he might lean over and say 'I'm looking forward to our date' – if he could find the words and deliver them through the din. What would that leave for Friday? Another smile, fractionally smaller than the Wednesday one, and a 'see you tomorrow?' Maybe. How the fuck do you say 'look forward to?' Callum would know, the unbearable smoothie. But if he asked him, he'd laugh and tell Chris. One for the dictionary then. He could use a week to prepare. Then what about kissing her? Oh, boy, how he wanted to! He could try it during the film, provided she gave him some sign, like snuggling up. Should he hold her hand? Put an arm round her? If they kissed, she'd have to lean toward him, wouldn't she? In which case her tits would travel his way, press up against him. Holy Cow. If he kissed her there and then in the dark, what should he do with his arms? He could try pushing one in between her neck and the chair back and somehow squeeze her far shoulder with the other one? What if she wanted to watch the film? You never can tell with the French. If Megan were here to practise on, he could see how the bits would fit. Everything was always straightforward with Megan: she was as gauche as he was. Fumbling around in the nude once, she'd blurted out impatiently, Not there! You're knocking at the wrong damn door! And with no more ado she had grabbed it in her fist and led it straight to the stable. Fond memories! Still, things had to be different with Fanny. No use thinking of Megan. Besides which, he was getting way ahead of himself. He would have to learn some finesse – a French word, naturally. He'd need some spontaneity too. How about after the film? At the bus stop? And who should pay for the bus? She might insist on going dutch, modern woman and all. I could arrive early and buy both cinema tickets if I knew which film we were seeing. Not that I could give a toss. Of course if it's horror, that would provide an excuse. She would take refuge in my manly arms. If only I could trust myself to read the signs and do the cool and natural thing. Natural! What's natural? Saunter up to her, Hey! how nice to see you, *je suis* absolutely *enchanté de vous voir*. Or *de te voir*. God! he didn't know which. If she wanted a kiss, she'd make it clear as day. It was her country. But mightn't she like him to take the initiative, be the man? French women are sometimes funny that way, aren't they?

As he let the last strummed chord of 'Enfant Perdu' fade away, Wolf Biermann looked up through the smoke and alcohol haze.

Well, my friends, I can't leave that out, can I? Doris?

Why condemn those who, like Flori Havemann, have chosen freedom?

Freedom? For whom? For himself? Look, I'm no politburo-judge: I don't convict or condemn anyone but, from my viewpoint, he made a mistake and I'm entitled to say so. 'Enfant Perdu' is just a song, about a single event, the loss of my friend's child to the West, but, okay, the song claims that what we're building here is socialism, and that Stalinism can be overcome. Most days I still believe. Besides, the only freedom worthy of the name is freedom for *all* and that, my friends, requires liberation from both capitalism and Stalinism. The smaller Germany is still the better of the two. And just look at Flori now! As I state in the song, the West has turned him into a clown. In the DDR you have only to whisper to be heard – and hounded – whereas *drüben* you're free to scream at the top of your lungs but nobody's listening. So where do we make our stand, we democratic Communists? Here. Right here.

Wolf's r-right, Hartmut said, pounding his fist on his knee. He has to walk a f-f-f-fine line. This is the s-song of a s-socialist, a true b-believer. There have to be some es-s-ssentially pro-GDR songs, as well as ones that pour sc-sc-scorn on the regime. Or else . . .

Or else what? Biermann interjected. I'm free to do whatever I want. You think this room has been a gaol to me? I'll say it again. I'm free. *Trotz alledem*. Well, Hans? I see you scowling.

I think this trip is a test and a trap, Hans said, staring straight at Biermann. A trap set for you by the regime. You're an artist so you're naturally arrogant. But party bigshots can be creative too. You're walking right into it.

Wolf shrugged, leaving the field open for Gertie and Petra to take issue with Hans while Jurek started arguing with Bettina. Wolf picked up his guitar and, after a moment's noodling, began carefully to pick out the melody of 'Preußischer Ikarus.' Nobody was listening.

Tomec was at the end of the machine aisle, button-holing Salvatore.

So what has the fac de philo got you reading this week?

Lettres philosophiques.

Voltaire.

You read it?

Probably. I forget everything I read as soon as I read it. But I never had much time for Voltaire's anglophilia. I prefer his later work, his onslaught on superstition, 'Écrasez l'Infâme!' And his pamphlet on the Chevalier de la Barre . . .

Who?

Le Chevalier de la Barre. A harmless seventeen-year-old tortured to death in 1766 for refusing to salute a procession. They began by driving iron pins through his shinbones. Funny what you remember. He wouldn't apologize to the priests.

I haven't seen . . .

It's largely forgotten. But if you ever visit Abbeville, you'll discover a monument 'erected by the proletariat to the emancipation of the human mind,' depicting the scene most vividly. You can see the executioner with his hammer raised, the judge, a clerk, and a cowled prelate observing that everything is done just right.

I'll look out for it. Now, if you don't mind . . .

They say it was the Lisbon earthquake that steeled him.

Earthquake?

In 1755, first of November. 30,000 people died. The churches, crammed with the pious, were razed, but the bawdy houses on the other side of the city were all left standing, their fornicating clients unscathed. Isn't that delicious? Voltaire took it as evidence that God thinks plate tectonics are beneath him. Voltaire wrote a poem about it.

Tomec was grinning. Salvatore scratched his chin.

I've got a meeting to prepare.

But of course.

From his earliest years, Mathieu Petit had been animated by two impulses:

to discipline himself through repetitive drilling, and to feel and demonstrate loyalty to some entity larger than himself, be it team, nation, ideal or idea. Each of these impulses, like a mighty wave, produced within its dying collapse a weaker yet still powerful, countervailing current: his habit of self-disciplining was countered by a well patrolled attraction to chaos, mayhem, cacophony and the disorder of unstructured living; analogously, his urge to cleave faithfully to some larger corps or cause was opposed by the insistent claims of an ego given to outbursts of radical insubordination.

This original structure of underlying drives had led Mathieu to three partly successive and partly overlapping commitments: to the military; to his beloved wife Nadine; finally, to the music of contemporary jazz. When young, the army had supplied a means of escape from a claustrophobic family and regional culture into what at first appeared to him in the guise of an agent for the defence of progressive, anti-bourgeois and civic values. Following the humiliations and triumphs of, respectively, the Occupation and the Resistance, Mathieu found himself mired in increasingly vicious colonial conflicts, while all his allegiance and powers of assiduous attention shifted inexorably toward his wife, whose image he began to discern in each war casualty, each captured insurgent.

Later still, with his service years at last behind him, and his wife's mind contracting and her will fracturing, his passion for the constraints and freedoms of jazz moved in to fill the gap. Accepting her husband's need for consolation, Nadine had referred to his trumpet as his new woman: I like your new woman – she would say to him – she has my blessing. The first time Nadine teased him in this way, Mathieu left the instrument in its case for several days until she complained. 'Where's that new woman of yours? Take her out! Play with her! I like to hear the two of you arguing . . .'

Jean beckoned Fernando over.

What's your position on the strike?

Fernando looked blank. Jean pressed START and sat back. It sounded like a trick question. Position . . .

Are you attending the meeting?

Sure, Fernando replied. I don't want any trouble. With anyone.

Jean's bullet eyes were so close together he could have got by with a monocle.

I might have a room for you. If my wife agrees. In our apartment.

Fernando looked up but said nothing.

It's a small room. We wouldn't ask for much rent. You could help us with some DIY. Any good at DIY?

I can turn my hand to most things. I've done tiling, plumbing, plastering, painting, basic joinery, locks. I'm not good with electrics. But I have a girlfriend. She's shy.

If it's just one, not a whole string of them, and a regular girl . . .

She's regular. You could set your clock by her.

Jean looked puzzled. Fernando was brightening up.

Your wife wouldn't mind?

My wife is thoroughly modern. Besides, there's a rear entrance you could use.

A rear entrance?

To the apartment. It's discreet.

The rent?

I'd have to talk to my wife.

Fernando walked away. It had to be better than the hostel. Provided there was a place to cook. He tried to imagine Jean's place. In France he hadn't seen the inside of many flats. He would make it homey, nice for Maryse.

Jean felt the first flush of impending landlordship tingle in his veins. He could act generous, make nice with his tenant, while getting DIY work done at a knockdown rate and trousering a modest rent. All for an empty room. This must be how an employer felt: proud to help out and thrilled with the proceeds. What of Monique? Monique would jump at it. She was the mothering type. He'd get her a gift.

Back down the machine aisle to his machines eight and nine, Rachid felt again the itch behind his right knee. He sat down and wriggled his left hand up his trouser-leg, finding a small tight pimple. Malika would tell him he ought to eat more fruit. He squeezed it but it wouldn't burst. Malika would tell him to leave it alone. He let his trouser-leg down. The Englishman was watching.

It was good to think of things and people other than Mehdi. He had been neglecting the living. Sometimes you are all I ever think about, he whispered. Do you know that? Mehdi was there now, Rachid was sure, but was saying nothing.

Rachid placed the middle finger of each hand at his temples and rotated the tips gently against his skin, through the hairline and out again. He stared at Eric till Eric looked away. He felt the familiar pang of Mehdi's death, the longing for a past embrace, the warmth of the child's body against his or held like a sandwich filling between his body and Malika's. Against this feeling there now leaned the knowledge of Malika's news, and an image of new life swelling into the shape of a child.

We dead can look after ourselves, came Mehdi's voice. We don't need your condescension.

For the second time this evening, for the second time ever, Rachid felt indelibly junior to his late son, infinitely less experienced in the ways of life and death. He needn't fear after all that he would one day have to leave Mehdi. Why? Because Mehdi was leaving him.

Martin, the wandering Orléanais, the family man, the prison shrink, was sitting on his living-room sofa, a newspaper open at his side. *Weasels Ripped My Flesh* – a Frank Zappa album – was playing on the stereo. Armande, Martin's wife, returning from their child's bedroom, lowered the volume a notch, then joined him on the sofa, her legs curling beneath her. She picked up her book. Zappa's guitar run soared.

You aren't reading, she said.

It's nothing. Work. Did Rachel do a nappy?

No. A nightmare. I turned the light on. She soon calmed down. What does a three-year-old have nightmares about?

Martin sighed. His wife noticed he hadn't folded the newspaper away. She laid her book on the floor.

Come on, she said.

Work, I told you.

Tell me more.

I don't like to bring this stuff home.

Well, it's here, isn't it?

Sometimes it intrudes when your guard is down. You open the newspaper and . . .

Martin handed his wife the paper, his finger on a five-line story in a sidebar. She read the piece twice.

You've never worked in Loos-les-Lille.

He was transferred.

Ah.

He was starting to talk to me. He had been raped.

In prison?

At home first. As a kid. Over and over. He was imploding. I knew . . .

You couldn't have done any more. You can't stop people hanging themselves.

I can't help wondering.

Well, *could* you have done more?

Maybe. If I'd been prepared to piss off the governor, put my job on the line by opposing the transfer.

Would they have listened?

Probably not. They'd have said there are plenty of shrinks in Loos-les-Lille.

Martin flapped a hand.

I feel I'm nothing but a band-aid, he said.

Sounds like self-pity.

Martin looked at his wife.

I'm okay, he said. Read your book.

Armande did as she was told. Martin read the spine. *La vie est ailleurs.* Life is Elsewhere. The hell it is, Martin thought.

Salvatore was at his machine, looking into the distance, his lips moving, rehearsing what he wanted to say to the meeting. 'As you are all aware . . .'

I can do this, he thought. I know how to talk. The hind leg off a donkey, Laure says.

He walked up the machine aisle. He wanted to see if Luigi had woken from his nap. The Italian was sitting on his chair, a product piece in his hand, turning it over and over.

Salvatore leaned against Luigi's machine fourteen, glancing round. He noticed Jacques. Everyone was nodding off tonight. They'd better not fall asleep during the meeting. The man was actually dribbling! He must think he's on his farm. He'll be getting up soon to do the milking. Someone should tell him these machines aren't cows that go on producing milk however you treat them. Presses have to be fed regularly, cajoled and monitored. You don't just put them out to pasture.

What do you see here? the Italian said.

Luigi was holding a product piece out before him. Salvatore glanced at it.

I see what's there.

But we never see the whole thing, Luigi said.

What? Is something wrong with it?

If it was meat, I'd know it inside out by now. You really get acquainted with something when you take a knife to it. Here we only ever see one side at a time, a single shot. So how do we tell good from bad?

Salvatore decided Luigi was being perfectly serious. Luigi wasn't making fun of him. He wouldn't know how. He had to find him an answer.

We compare it to an ideal model. That's what we do.

Luigi looked up at Salvatore.

How's that?

These pieces are just imitations really. The only real product piece doesn't actually exist as such. It's in our minds. If you like.

The only one that's real doesn't actually exist?

Luigi shook his head.

In philosophy, that's known as a paradox, the Sicilian said.

'In the butcher's trade, that's known as bull . . .' began the rejoinder that formed in Luigi's mind. But he didn't want to offend. So he got to his feet and caught the latest product as it fell through the aluminium slats. Seems real enough to me, he muttered.

Jean was glad he had offered the Portuguee the room. Monique and he needed a distraction now she wasn't dying. He'd put it to her in the morning, or maybe later, when he woke up. Doing a workmate a favour. Needn't mention the DIY till after he's moved in. Assuming she goes for it. Oh, she'll go for it. She'll like him. She likes people. I don't have to tell her about the rent. That'll make it more natural when he starts doing the DIY work. Quid pro quo. She'll tell him he doesn't have to. He'll say he enjoys it.

With the memory of a goldfish, and irascible as a snake, the storyteller could still pick nits with the best of them. Pedantic? Precise. That's what he'd say. What kind of hand was he dealt? He had done his best. It was like being hauled about by the scruff of his neck. Marched round an aquarium, his face slammed against the glass of a thousand fish tanks, instructed to report on the thoughts of the finny tribe, the gurglings he overheard, the little fishy actions he witnessed. Or like having his head clamped in a vice, while the fish were swum past in formation. 'Tell us what you see, damn it!'

Why? Because he could read their minds, render them into this consommé of English, a watery breuvage, which was all that was demanded. He would have preferred reptiles, or big-game cats. Did he get to choose? Can you find fault? Then fuck you too.

Philippe noticed he was feeling better. Another coffee and he'd be fine. He leaned a little forward in his seat and squeezed his thighs, then nodded and relaxed back. His mind tripped to the conversation with his sister earlier that evening. It was almost time to think about it. He did all his best thinking at work.

After her excited allegation regarding Odile – endowed with the ring of truth that pertains to a fact you can only fail to see as long as you refuse to pay it any attention – Danielle had proceeded to disparage his manhood. That had been a mean blow. Then hadn't he said something disobliging about Georges? He'd certainly thought it. His sister had just said, 'If Georges ever caught me cheating . . .' when Philippe had interrupted to enquire: 'How would the jerk ever notice?' Nicely put.

As for the rest of the conversation, hadn't Danielle disrespected his sailing shoes? True, he hadn't done a lot of sailing in the last fifteen years or so, but that could change. Is everyone who wears basketball boots obliged to play basketball?

Leaving the bar, Rémy had had to remind him to pick up the papers. That was how badly his sister's news had unsettled his thoughts. Then Rémy had mentioned a story about a man found drowned in women's leggings. In the local paper.

Philippe got up, shoved the front of his shirt under his belt, and moved to his pile of papers.

Right then Marcel was imagining a hanged man. Swinging this way and that from a ceiling. They had shared a cell. Talked all night a few times. Marcel supposed the cells at Loos-les-Lille must be pretty standard. He wondered how the guy had managed it. He didn't want to recall the man's name. Robert. There. You can't choose to un-know something. He was going to think of him as 'the hanged man.' The Hanged Man. No Gypsy tarot-bullshit now, fit for Bobrán's mother! Fact is: you can never tell who'll do a crazy thing like that. Same with women: you can never tell who'll turn you down or freeze you out. Always unpredictable. Except those afternoon-shift girls. Proving the rule. Hairy and Curly were his names for them. Times you recall a name and don't want to; other times you have to make one up. Robert Castel. Poor bastard. Didn't know I knew his surname. I never hurt him. I suppose I saw his surname in the paper just now.

Fuck this. I'm going upstairs. Find out what's in that African's letter. Get my mind off the hanged man. He's dead. That's what the Orléanais would advise: distract yourself, break the circle, observe others, keep moving. See what cousin Bobrán has to say.

Alphonse sat on his chair against the control cabinet of machine eighteen, his arms crossed, his chin on his chest. Was a trip to Paris this weekend to see *Oh les beaux jours* at the Théâtre d'Orsay a practical prospect? His uncle in Paris didn't have a phone in his apartment. He might try leaving him a message at the school in Créteil where he worked. Or he could send a telegram – Peux-tu m'héberger ce weekend? Ton neveu. – after which Laurent might leave him a phone message at his hostel. I could always turn up unannounced. But what if Laurent – and what-was-her-name? Julie? Juliette! Shakespearean . . . – were away for the weekend? Where would I sleep? A park bench in November? I can't afford a hotel. The irony of it! To be a tramp for one night in the hope of gaining insight into Beckett! I suppose I could hitch straight back down again. Who's going to give a black man a lift in the middle of the night? Only takes one. Or I could forget about Paris and go to Lyon as usual. It's a good routine. Comfortable. In Lyon I'm a different person. It's good to switch lives: Grandgobier during the week; Lyon at the weekend. Every Saturday morning straight out of work and onto the 9.35 train. 105 minutes straight dozing, usually in a corridor, then bus number 74, hello-hello-kiss-kiss and a leisurely bath at his friends' place, lunch, rest, evening out. On Sunday a long sleep-in with Clara arriving early and joining him in bed if the mood takes her. The rest of the day spent with friends and Monday back to Grandgobier. And this weekend they were throwing a birthday party for him. If he phoned to tell them he was going to Paris, they'd be disappointed, but he couldn't not phone. He'd miss the routine, the warmth. Sunday morning in bed with Clara? She was the one person who never made him feel exotic. In Lyon, he was part of a gang; in Grandgobier he surrendered to radical anomie: hostel, factory, drama workshop, reading his books, talking to himself, clowning, nearly getting beaten up in a bar. I could be more careful. No, no. It's Paris then. Madeleine Renaud in *Oh les beaux jours*. I've talked myself into it.

Philippe had found and read the piece on the drowned man. Five lines. Fifty-five words exactly. He counted them twice. A man's obituary. So he wore stockings and liked river swimming . . . at night . . . in November. Luigi was coming over, his mouth hanging open already, words about to spill out. Philippe wasn't in the mood to talk or joke. He wanted to be anywhere else. He wanted to yell out. He was tired. TIRED.

Did you see that piece in *Libération*? Philippe asked.

Luigi looked past him. Philippe extracted *Libé* from the stack, pulled it open at the spread on Turin.

There's an interview with a Fiat Ferriere worker called Sergio Luca. You worked there, didn't you?

Luigi shook his head and scowled. He had known several Sergios back then. He pretended to look at the article. Jacques and Eric were approaching. I'm in no mood for this, Philippe thought. From the other direction, skirting the raised office like a ship docking, the grinning security man loomed. In a matter of seconds the three newcomers were jabbering away, while Philippe and Luigi stood there mute. Luigi had worked at Fiat Ferriere, Philippe was sure of it. Jacques was sounding like someone Philippe didn't know. He seemed to be addressing the Pole. Philippe closed his eyes. He imagined a beach, dissolving.

Why would we be surprised if the Boucan family were collaborators? Most workers were for the Resistance and most bosses were for Vichy. It stands to reason.

Everyone stared at Jacques. And then at Philippe, who coughed briefly. The man's not wrong, he muttered, walking away.

Mathieu had taken to jazz and to improvisation almost as soon as he picked up his first trumpet. The music matched his spirit as perfectly as the instrument fitted his face and hands. Within days he was picking out melodies, embellishing them, losing his place, starting over, having the time of his life. He didn't do it for self-expression – there was nothing of the romantic about him: no, with Mathieu, it was a fact-finding mission, a cognitive act full of surprises and discoveries, a form of thought, even sometimes a substitute for thought or a short cut. His mind was always clearer after a night's playing; even at the end of a short solo he knew better what he had to do. Often a problem or a puzzle that seemed intractable before playing would unravel as he played.

Mathieu experienced something close to magic when improvising with other musicians. He didn't care who he played with, just as long as they had good ears, some skill, and could make room for others. Making jazz – especially with strangers – was the opposite of the family singing in unison he had grown up with as a child, and an antidote to the years of marching to the drumbeat of the military band. After a couple of hours in some club, Mathieu would shake hands, give his name to anyone who asked for it, get in his car and drive home in silence – the only time there would be no music of any kind issuing from the speakers. In the hour or so that followed the end of a gig, memories of events long forgotten or repressed would come to him unsought and stripped of any power to sadden or humiliate; practical decisions would be taken that, however grave, he knew at once required no further examination.

48. Chain-reacting.

At the water fountain just inside metallurgy, Philippe was wiping his mouth as Jacques swung through the plastic flaps.

I'm going for a coffee, the old peasant said.

Philippe followed Jacques back into the plastics section, round the raised office and out again into the raw materials area.

I had one with the Arab, Philippe said, as the two men reached the drinks machines.

The middle finger of Jacques' right hand shoved coins around in the hollow palm of his left. He glanced up at the Marseillais.

Are you going to tell me any more? he asked.

Did you ever feel so humiliated and weary you're afraid you could just drop dead or start howling any minute?

If I ever felt that way I'd lie down and sleep it off.

I knew you'd have the answer.

What if your sister's wrong?

She can't be.

But if you didn't suspect a thing . . .

It explains too much to be wrong: absences, whispering at the phone, new clothes, things you don't want to know about. She's happier than before and it can't be anything I did. Still, I'm busy dreaming of freedom now, alone again. I could fall in love. You know how good that is, right?

You're positively elated. It won't last.

That's what friends do, Philippe thought. They bring you down to earth.

So why don't you want to take the damned pills? he then asked.

Side effects. One in particular. I told you.

Philippe laughed and shook his head, as if urging his friend to be reasonable.

Besides, Jacques said, I never take pills.

You take Doliprane, don't you? For headaches.

Nope.

Antibiotics when you're ill?

Not in thirty-five years.

Philippe had run out of arguments. A smile played across Jacques' face.

If you were really free, he asked, what's the one thing you'd do?

Philippe was baffled.

Go on. Say it. What would you go to with a spring in your step every morning, like I go to feed my pigs?

Philippe pictured Jacques lugging a pail of swill.

I don't know.

I think you do.

Philippe didn't want to seem like a dreamer. He hardened his voice.

I'd like to find things out. Crimes, for instance. I'd like to investigate. Not as a cop or a private investigator. I don't want to be showing sad old gits photos of their wives with other men. Corruption in high places. Where organized crime meets politics. I have connections. I'd know where to start.

What are you waiting for? You'd never regret it, would you?

Philippe looked down at his canvas shoes and grimaced.

Claude put her book face-down on the coverlet. Gérard's attempt to pay her a visit had torpedoed her concentration. What had he come for? What did he expect? 'Come to me, darling?' He still liked to talk sometimes. Provided she didn't question his account of himself. Such vanity. She knew him like the back of her hand. She glanced at her left wrist. The liver spots were getting worse. She reached for her ear plugs and her mask, re-plumped her pillow. She switched off the bedside lamp. She was tired enough, quite ready for sleep. If it chose to take her.

Bobrán glanced at the clock above the lift. Past eleven already. Moritz and Heike would have met up by now. He wondered where they were. They had probably gone on to some other bar. If he went to Germany with them, he'd see them at the weekend.

Marcel stepped out of the lift, looking angry. Bobrán yawned.

You seem happy, the younger cousin said.

A guy I knew killed himself.

Killed himself . . .

Hanged himself.

How come?

In prison. We shared a cell.

What did you do to him?

Nothing. It was over a year ago. It has nothing to do with me.

Both men looked away.

'You fucked him, didn't you?' Bobrán thought.

So how did you find out? Bobrán asked.

It's in the paper. Marseille showed me. What did that African write you?

I didn't want to talk about it downstairs. People jabber.

They do.

He's looking for his brother. Says I can help.

What's it to you?

I worked with his brother on the site. He went missing.

So?

So this guy's come from Africa to trace him.

People don't vanish.

I couldn't agree more.

Is that it?

That's it.

I suppose you've no reason to lie.

Don't mention it to anyone.

Why not?

Maybe he was in trouble. I've troubles of my own. I don't want my name tied to his. People jabber.

You said.

With much proud exercise of mental discipline, Jean had hauled his attention back to bear upon the day's developments, abandoning at last the domestic, parochial and regional spheres to dwell upon the item of national news he found most compelling: the cowardly arson attack perpetrated under cover of darkness upon the apartment of the National Front leader. Jean was not to be distracted from this outrage by the glimpse that his gaping press afforded of the Gypsy cousins in conversation, Alphonse's back in the foreground and Fernando's face in the background. Ripping cable ties from sprue, Jean cursed the leftist vermin who could accomplish such infamy. He smacked the START button then plunged his hand into his left trouser-pocket to fetch up a palliative spearmint drop. Jews and Arabs, possibly in concert, had surely woven the plot – the former driven by millennial loathing of the Gentile, the latter by fantasies of revenge upon Europe's superior civilization. Praise be that no soul was injured: neither Pierette, the leader's loyal and most fragrant consort, nor their sweet-tempered and retiring child Marine, nor Jean-Marie himself, a paragon among politicians, a byword for stalwart integrity and patriotic pride. Jean pulled back the guard and reached his right hand into the press to seize the product. He stretched his back, considered a further spearmint treat, and planned his meditation on his first ever girlfriend. His thoughts appeared unusually disordered, and his rage at the assault on Le Pen was overshadowed by more proximate affronts relating to the Vierge d'Orléans, to the graffiti allegations against his employer, and to the strike action afoot: somehow he couldn't assemble quite the vinegar that elementary Frontist solidarity seemed to require. Instead, he experienced a flush of crabbed malevolence laced with an unaccountable self-contempt.

Looking up, Alphonse saw Tomec approach the Gypsy cousins. Bobrán seemed relaxed, Marcel sullen. The nightwatchman hovered behind Bobrán, while Marcel eyed him. The Pole's jerky movements recalled to Alphonse's mind a dance, surely Mediterranean, possibly Greek. Marcel was waving Tomec into their space now, signalling to Bobrán to step aside. The Pole crossed his arms and, leaning back, asked whether either man was attending the strike meeting. Bobrán shook his head. Marcel asked, Why? Tomec said he was supposed to know where people were. Alphonse walked over to Fernando.

What is it about him? Alphonse asked.

Nothing. He's nosy. He talks about poets, Portuguese dead poets. A love poem to Lydia, Fernando muttered to himself. He's an artist by day. I heard he's dangerous if crossed. Professionally. Otherwise harmless.

Alphonse nodded, provisionally impressed. Then he walked over and joined Tomec and the two Gypsies. Marcel was explaining that nothing could happen inside a closed factory that someone inside didn't start. Alphonse objected, talked of freak weather and break-ins, while Tomec listened. I've heard this before, Bobrán said. Marcel laughed as if he found his own remarks amusing.

At Evelyne's apartment, Maryse and her friend's conversation had died from the narcotic effects of hash, alcohol and a mishmash of music from Alain Stivel to the Soft Machine. Both women were well past stoned and when they did say anything it tended to be at cross purposes.

After a long silence, Evelyne resumed her account of the African Sonacotra resident who, having been offered her services as a gift from the other men, had preferred to talk.

I forgot to mention that I asked if we could meet again, Evelyne said.

Maryse yawned, then seemed to come round.

You did what?

I asked him if he liked to dance. He gave me this arch look. All Africans dance – is that what you think? he said. I didn't say that, I said. Do *you* dance? Not much and not well. Nor do I, I said, but I like it. So do I, I suppose, he admitted. What about it, then? I do have a life outside this work, I said. Then, after staring at me for a bit, he smiled and apologized. Obviously it wouldn't be for sex, he said. Obviously, I replied. Okay, sure, he said. Leave me a message. I'll phone you. Do you think he will?

Will what?

Phone me if I leave him a message?

I don't know. I'd never see a client outside work, not even if I liked him.

How can you like a client? This guy isn't a client. He turned me down.

In the main, the whole thing's idiotic, pitiable, sad. But no one gets hurt.

And you can like people like that?

I've got to go. Is there any hash left?

Outside this factory, real things can happen, Marcel told himself. Outside, there's no lockdown. As the lift glided downward, he leaned against the wall. Chantal will be waiting, he thought, glad to be woken, hot hot hot. After which I'll sleep. Late afternoon, I'll go and deal with Paulette, let her down, let her go. Maybe a farewell fuck. It'll relax me. I've always hated Wednesdays. It'll improve my mood. I hope she doesn't weep and wail. I can't bear to see a woman cry.

The lift arrived on the ground floor with a bump, but Marcel didn't move at once. A woman crying pisses me right off, he thought. He noticed his balling fists. You almost want to hurt them to give them a reason. Bobrán used to whine. Things best not remembered. If Paulette does start carrying on, I could push her head south, really gently. She'll know what I want. You can't blub with your mouth full. Then I'll go. I wonder if she'll swallow. My final image of her, a parting shot. Whether she spat or swallowed the last time would tell a lot about her. Normally she swallowed. He reckoned she'd spit.

Marcel walked round Luigi's machines, noticing the Italian then the Brit. It wasn't that the Brit was ugly exactly, it was the details that were so fucked: chewed nails, untreated spots, hippy-freak hair, plastic trousers. Did he piss himself? Even in September he was wearing plastic trousers. He must have sweat streaming through his groin. But the wop was worse. You wanted to clamp him in a vice or nail the dim fuck to a wall: anything to make him stand straight.

Marcel checked the product at his machine twelve. Boredom threatened. What was it about boredom? Mind like a flywheel spinning. Eddying. What of Bobrán's missing-person African? Marcel reckoned his old associates might help if asked nicely. When Marcel had left prison, he'd gone to his boss to say he wanted out and that he wasn't a liability. The boss had given him some money and turned serious: we're better at locating people than Interpol. Marcel hadn't asked him what he meant. Shame Bobrán was too proud to ask for help. Conceited prick.

Rachid marvelled anew at his wife's manipulation of him. Her letter was unapologetic: she had no idea he might be angry or resentful. She had wanted his sperm not him. That's what she had written. How was that okay? She had taken him for granted. He shook his head. He wanted to laugh. If in September – when their sudden coupling had occurred and conception resulted – she had asked him if he wanted another child, at best he'd have snapped 'NO!' thinking 'how dare you try to replace Mehdi?' At worst, he might have said something tasteless about virgin births, blaming her for the sorry state of their conjugal relations. She would not have been slow to hit back. It was much better this way. How did she know I'd be delighted? After Mehdi died, I hardly saw her, let alone Fatima. They were shadows, black on white. Grey. All I saw was you, Mehdi. Do you hear me now?

Philippe's wife Odile was talking to Josiane, a work colleague who'd become a friend. They were drinking thé à la menthe at Odile's home. Josiane had told her about an affair with a younger man. Odile didn't want to tell her about Yves. 'I understand, I do really,' she was saying. 'It's not much better with Philippe at present. You know how it is. I can predict every move he's going to make a second before he makes it. It didn't use to be like that. I wish that just once when we're sitting on the sofa in front of the TV, me with my crossword and him with his beer, he'd turn the set off, drop to his knees on the carpet, yank my knickers down and take me there and then. Don't laugh, Josiane! Don't tell me you never have such thoughts. I'd drop my pencil that fast! We're supposed to dream of black men, Belmondo, horses, three-in-a-bed, whips and chains, but, hell, hubby on the carpet panting like a walrus would do me fine. It's not funny. Sometimes I lie awake in the morning long-ing for it, with him beside me stinking of factory and booze. That's how my days start.' Josiane looked at her friend tenderly, 'Have an affair. It won't hurt him.' Odile looked back and smiled. 'Maybe I should,' she said.

Jacques checked his hopper levels and products, then stood back. He swayed forward and back, his arms at his sides.

For the second time that evening he thought of his parents, sensing them standing together, not touching. Maybe it was from seeing Pierre after so long – the only other person who could remember them well, assuming he chose to. How severe they looked in photographs! Jeanne had never known them – not to speak to. Why should she? A funny thing, the rift between brothers or, for that matter, between a brother and a sister. His rift with Pierre had been all about Edith. Easy to understand. But why was Philippe so angry with his sister? Bitter. I was never bitter with Pierre. Just distant. But I had Edith. Why be bitter?

Tomec had come downstairs and positioned himself at the end of the machine aisle. He was watching the men preparing their presses to be left untended throughout the union meeting. Tugging at his moustache, a jumble of half-formed thoughts paraded through his mind. He was eager to return to his sketching bench on the other side of the factory, plan his Virgilian sta-tions, and read further into Broch's novel. But he'd promised Jan he'd start sketching the mask he wanted. Jan wanted to look like no one at all. But he already did. How do you design a mask for a man who lives his entire life in one? Just follow his instructions: finer nose, smaller mouth, higher brow. Mechanics, essentially. Don't go upsetting him. Artistic temperament. Hooey. Toward morning he'd start work on Jan's mask. In a few hours. No more time-wasting with the graffiti nonsense. Enough already! Tomec felt a rare urge to talk to his sister. She owed him a letter. He heard her voice. He wouldn't have minded talking to Jan either – but Jan had no phone. Sometimes Jan called him from a payphone. They talked better when they weren't face to face. With Sarah it was the other way round: they talked best face to face in the dark or half-light of early morning. He wouldn't know what to say if he phoned her. It would be like eating together. Long pauses. Politeness. He had never phoned anyone from work. Emergencies only, it said. When he phoned Agnes, they always laughed. She said his Polish had grown old and quaint from never hearing it spoken and reading too much Mickiewicz. He could tell her anything. He might even talk about Sarah. What could he say? That she might not be beautiful but he found her so. That she maddened him and gave his mind no pause. That he could never tire of making love to her. He could tell his sister that much. But he wouldn't say how soft Sarah's lips were, nor how she seemed to love having sex with him but couldn't say so. He wouldn't describe how she had looked that evening, naked from bed, squatting on the floor, her creamy shoulders arching over the gramophone, how her nipples swelled and filled as her breasts fell forward and her hair swished across her face as though she were suddenly bashful. Really listen, Sarah had told him. You've got it bad, mój brat, Agnes would say. Then he'd enquire about her love life and she'd do a hollow little chuckle and deny she ever felt lonely, though he had not asked that. Sarah had infuriated him the previous evening, making fun of his uniform. Do you know what you look like? A security guard, he'd said. So? They pay for a security guard, they get a security guard. No, she had said, you look like a policeman in a comic opera. It's obscene! You could teach!

Alphonse had left his products checked and threshed, his hoppers full, and had asked Bobrán to keep an eye on everything. Downstairs, he went straight to Jacques' hold-all and chose the reddest apple he could find. He saw Jacques smiling.

Do you grow these?

I prune the trees. They grow themselves.

Alphonse bit into the apple then nodded.

I have cousins who work on the land.

Where?

Home.

Jacques couldn't picture an African field. Only desert or jungle.

What grows there?

Fruit, vegetables. Millet. Corn.

Millet? We don't eat a lot of millet.

Jacques had to be the same age as Beckett's tramps, but how different! Vladimir and Estragon never smiled – not the way Jacques smiled. And Jacques was never funny – not the way Vladimir and Estragon were funny.

Jacques thought about farmland in Africa. 'Fruit' would mean bananas and dates, possibly oranges. Not apples. Was Alphonse eating his apple like it was an exotic fruit? What did it mean to be so far from something you know so well and that no one around you can imagine? If Jacques had gone on driving earlier, he could have reached Africa eventually.

Do you know you're funny? Alphonse asked, finishing his apple.

With a shriek of tyres and a slammed door, Jeanne's young friend Kaelle, having fallen asleep reading an Astérix comic, was woken by Guy, Janis's father. He had promised not to go to the bar. The door-slamming signified 'you won't tie me down, I'm still wild at heart.' He stamped into the bedroom, talking about a perfect job some barfly had told him about – on the other side of France. Kaelle suggested they talk about it in the morning. Guy accused her of never backing him up. Kaelle asked him to lower his voice but Janis had woken already and was coming into the bedroom. As Kaelle got out of bed, Guy stared at her belly. She pretended not to notice. Then he winked at her and grabbed at his crotch. Kaelle prayed that by the time Janis was settled Guy would be sleeping. Tomorrow she could try talking to him about his drinking. Anyway, he hadn't hit her for ages. Jeanne would drop by later and Guy would go out with barely a word. He said Jeanne was an interfering old crow. But Janis loved the old lady and would play with her happily while Kaelle made soup and set the table.

Like Alphonse, Fernando had entrusted his machines to Bobrán and gone downstairs early for the union meeting. He ambled to the aisle-end of Philippe's machine two where he leaned against the recycled-material cylinder and flicked through Philippe's magazines. Memories of his first ever long-afternoon session with Maryse clung to his mind. He thumbed *Le Nouvel Observateur* in search of distraction, pausing at fields, mountains, grass, water. That first time, when he'd come so fast, Maryse had said, that's fine, now we can talk. Talk? What about? Anything: what do you usually talk about? I don't talk a lot, he had said. A luscious ad for Club Med yawned before him: sand, sea, flesh, heads thrown back, guitars, a yellow bikini, mile-wide smiles. The women had shoulders broader, breasts larger, skin clearer than Maryse's. The men had to be models. Maryse had talked that first afternoon, she was good at talking, then she'd suggested a shower. He'd even talked too. He didn't want this recollection right now. He had felt shy. He would always feel shy. His body had never been that of a male model, his jaw had never jutted. Soaping her, he'd become a man again. He flicked further, arriving at green pasture, an ad for whisky, then one for menswear set amid granite and white water: Germany, Ireland or Scandinavia or Scotland. More like home than Grandgobier. He seemed to recall seeing a butterfly beneath a parasol, a beautiful butterfly. He flicked back, urgent suddenly, as if it could fly the page. He found the Club Med advert, searched the scene. They'd talked about butterflies that afternoon: what he missed from home. The scene showed a tambourine he hadn't noticed earlier, pectorals, sea shells, spume, men's manicured fingernails. Fucking-no butterfly.

Marcel was at Fernando's elbow. Fernando felt the Gypsy breathing on him and looked up, then round. Those guys probably prefer one another, Marcel said, a finger stabbing at the ad. He saw the security guard at the far end of the machine aisle leaning against the table, the Algerian sitting alongside him. With pussy like that to hand, what a man needs is magnetism, Marcel said, his voice dropping as he gazed down on the Portuguee. Not much of an audience. He had stuff to say that mattered to a man. Philippe was slumped on his chair, gazing into space, pallid, paunchy, looking like he'd died somehow this evening. What a bunch! That lanky wop at machine fourteen was scrunching up his eyes to follow the foreman's spastic jerky gestures. The peasant was talking – probably about his rotting apples – to the African, who was grinning up at him as he munched. What no-hopes! He caught the peasant's eye and with a narrowing glare drew him over, the African tagging along. Three people, three listeners. Hey, he started, I worked out what the Sicilian, your big fucking union rep, uses his hand-exerciser for. Ah bon? said the peasant, witless. 'The hand-exerciser,' Fernando murmured, puzzled. Marcel stared at Alphonse, who said nothing, seeming content to wait. Marcel watched the black man as he moved this way and that, never stopping flexing, stretching, keeping himself lissom and supple. The big Gypsy's face spread, bisected in a grin, priming their attention. It was a mystery, he stage-whispered, but I think I've solved it. Is he learning the piano? Fernando wondered. Is it for strength and technique? Alphonse asked. Marcel winked, leaning back a little and, glancing round to see if the huddle he had created had captured Marseille's attention. In a manner of speaking, he replied. Then, as Marseille – sure enough – glanced up, Marcel executed a quick and unmistakable up-and-down pumping movement in the air with his right hand shaped to grip a bottle. It's for stamina, Marcel declared. Jacques pulled on a hairy earlobe and laughed obligingly, while Fernando cackled and looked round. Alphonse, for his part, smiled and stared at Marcel, whose lips merely pursed.

Mathieu fingered the flap running along one edge of a single piece on the sprue from machine fourteen. Borderline. (The term – 'limite'– that the very first doctor used. Ah, Nadine! No longer borderline.) Lower the pressure and other pieces will be malformed, raise it and there'll be excrescences all over the place. He pointed out the problem to Luigi again, said he'd keep an eye on it during the meeting, then hobbled off. The way he leaned right forward, limping, you'd think he'd fall. Gilberte had taken Luigi to a film she raved about. Laughed the whole way through. This guy who walked like that, but was taller, didn't limp at all, and went on a holiday, never spoke or hardly. Had this weird way of playing tennis and then sank in a folding canoe, the fucking highpoint. Then his holiday ended. The foreman didn't really walk like him, and yet. The Portuguee was laughing. Luigi caught Marcel's gesture. How could he know he'd jerked off earlier? He couldn't. Wasn't about him then. Looking at a magazine. Probably talking about some famous wanker, yeah. Luigi glanced around. Marseille was stirring. Maybe he would join the others around the papers.

Paul Boucan had left Antoine and Marielle's apartment. Antoine was lounging on his pallet-mattress; Marielle put Soft Machine on the turntable. He's young, that kid, she said. Still living with his parents, Antoine confirmed. Marielle nodded, crumbling some hash. He fancies me, Antoine murmured. *Fancies* you? You heard me. But you're not you-know, are you? No way! Why encourage him then? Well, he's interested in history, including family history, the resistance. So? His father's Gérard Boucan. Boucan? You mean, Éts. Boucan? Sure. You devious bastard. Gilles said I should cultivate him. Marielle's fingers froze over the joint, her face darkened. Gilles told you to use him somehow? What's the problem? He's just a kid! His father . . . It's not his fault who his father is! Marielle's tongue travelled along the paper, then she rolled it shut. Sometimes people get used, Antoine said, leaning forward to take the joint. If Paul, despite his class and his daddy, ends up on the right side of history, we'll have done him a favour, right? Marielle was waiting for Antoine to pass the joint back. She looked at the zip mural. The teeth had taken forever, she thought.

Marcel and Fernando moved apart as Philippe joined them at the papers pile. Marcel reprised his solution to the hand-exerciser mystery. Marseille cracked the tiniest smile. Alphonse shuddered, turning to see Luigi coming alongside. Chilly, isn't it? he said. Luigi glanced down the machine aisle. Salvatore was at his machine seven, filling the hopper. Nope, it's never less than warm here, the Italian said. Marcel was pointing at the magazine still open at the Club Med ad. Look at those babes, guys, Marcel said. Everyone at least glanced at the photo, including Eric who had just squeezed between Jacques and Alphonse. Well? Marcel asked. As I was saying to our friend here (nodding at Fernando), nobody's going to convince me that those men are balling those women. And the women, their hair so perfect, their eyes like ice: you can see they haven't been done for a week. The men have no magnetism. Money, maybe. As Philippe took a deep breath and dropped his cigarette to the floor, Marcel noticed his left hand was missing its wedding ring. The man looked pitiful. Been drinking too. Magnetism is what you need, Marcel said again. Look at me. I get more than my share. Why? I'm not that much better-looking than the average horny young stick-insect, right? It's just because I want it and women can see I want it. I'm not proud and I'm not ashamed. Men don't need to chase women, they only need to show constant interest: the bitches can smell it on us, so let them do the legwork! Throughout Marcel's talk, Luigi and Fernando had grinned and nodded but Alphonse had backed away from the papers pile and begun to mimic Marcel's stance and movements, pushing his belly out, stroking it, thumping himself on the chest, using the heel of his hand to push down into his groin, as if to rearrange rampant genitalia: this impersonation was peculiarly accurate and might have been amusing, but nobody was paying attention. Marcel's speech was directed at Marseille: he just hated to see his workmate looking so sad. Yeah, yeah, I'll bet you're a real stud, Philippe said with a sour grin. With a nod, Marcel appeared to confirm this assessment. You see: I don't mind the odd rejection – it takes a lot to make me cry. Well, excuse me, Philippe said, but I need to talk to our union man. As Marseille turned away down the aisle, Marcel wiggled his eyebrows at Jacques who, regarding him sternly, said, Leave him alone, will you? Yeah? replied Marcel, who then pointed at the peasant's left hand and said, You still have your ring.

Teach? Why would he want to teach? What could he possibly teach? Draftsmanship, he supposed. He'd rather die. Besides, what was wrong with appearing in a comic opera? Sounds good to me. If I could play a kind of Good Nightwatchman Schweik . . . Sarah thinks artists should subsist on their immortal genius and a diet of air but what I crave is pork sausage, black bread, dark wines and rich cheeses. How does that add up? Every evening I have to remind myself at least once what I'm doing here: it's the regular wage, this routine that shapes my days and nights and weeks, the balance of solitude as I patrol the darkness or sit at my bench and read or sketch and the neon-lit near-anonymous company of this plastics section. The fact is: when this place shuts for August, I get no work done. At Christmas, same thing. Here is where my painting and sculpting is thought out and planned and my studio is where they get done. What could be more perfect? If I had to teach, the first thing I'd say is: structure your days and nights, secure an income that is just sufficient, spend plenty of time among people who are neither family nor friends: in fact – get yourselves night jobs in a 24-hour factory. Sarah can't see it. Obscene, she says. Comic. I shouldn't have minded. I only minded because she wanted me to. I was hurt that she wanted me hurt. Stupid. Besides, it *is* comical. What am I for? Who would want to break into this dump? To do what? Steal a box of metal clips, maybe . . . or a tub of grease? Make somebody an original birthday present. Or – who knows? – creep in at dead of night, start up one of the machines in metallurgy and do a little manufacturing on the sly – just to keep their hand in? I'm proof the boss cares, that's all. I'm a roving deterrent for those gangs of nineteenth-century machine-breakers that still loom so large in the nightmares of twentieth-century industrialists. If that's it, that's okay by me. I don't care.

Philippe loitered at the aisle-end of machine seven until Salvatore dropped the product he was checking and looked round. The Sicilian appeared to take his presence there for granted, beckoning him closer with the earnest look of a man hurrying to fulfil a vocation. Before Salvatore could open his mouth, Philippe said, I've apprised the foreman of our concerns about the agency workers in the case of any strike action. He said he would think about it. The Sicilian corrugated his brow. What does that mean? he asked. Muttering that the foreman would explain in his own time, Philippe shook his head and looked down. His eyes fell on Salvatore's open attaché case. He glimpsed the hand-exerciser, a tube of boiled sweets, two hardcover books bearing the stamp of Grandgobier University Library, the paperback of Voltaire's letters from England and, amid a mess of poorly printed union flyers, the framed portrait of a smart young woman; also, a used paper handkerchief twisted into a ball. For an instant the Marseillais regretted his decision to resign his union position. It would be a pleasant distraction to have to address a meeting. He would be sensing a slight excitement, would have some jokes prepared, might even feel useful: he wouldn't be thinking of Odile. Do you have any tips? Salvatore enquired. Philippe looked up at his face. Tips? he repeated. Advice for your successor, he mumbled. Ah, that! Philippe snorted. Be your own man, he said, as he walked away.

As Philippe had struck out down the aisle to talk to the Sicilian, the men hanging around at the end of his machine two had stepped back from one another as if the ties that held them had snapped. Luigi and Alphonse had picked up and opened papers, the former feasting his prurience on a gory domestic incident in Clermont; the latter attracted by a snippet on an immigrants' theatre in Clichy. Eric, turning over Marcel's mockery of Salvatore-with-hand-exerciser, battled to unburden himself of the notion that the Sicilian's attaché case gave him the appearance of an homme d'affaires, an expression encountered and committed to memory that very day and now delivered with a confident flourish. Jacques rewarded the Englishman with a pat and the words, Très juste, très juste. Fernando, standing between Eric and Jacques, turned to see Rachid rise from his chair rotating his right shoulder and rubbing his neck with his left hand. The anticlimactic numbness affecting the Algerian's senses as the shock of his wife's message wore off was offset by the muscle sprain sustained earlier while freeing himself from the Ivorian's faux-balletic clasp. Fernando, noticing that Philippe was heading slowly back up the machine aisle, weighed the judiciousness of again broaching the matter of the free haircut. Obscurely, he felt he would like the others to know that he had a tentative hair-cutting arrangement with the Marseillais.

Madame Yvonne Labarde, having climaxed, cleaned her teeth, showered and donned the nightie with the mickey-mouse motif, laid herself down beside her snoring husband. She wasn't the teeniest bit sleepy. She ticked herself off for her Sicilian night-shift fantasy, but who did it hurt? She deserved some fun, was still attractive; women praised her figure, and men ogled – and not only Gypsies either. What she wanted was love. Didn't women do night shifts elsewhere? Maybe in the north, at Citroën or Renault, say? No woman had ever worked nights chez Boucan, but why not? Nurses do nights! Female cops do nights! What if she applied for a transfer? Yvonne imagined the look on her workmates' faces. Suspicion, envy, innuendo – and that would just be the women. What would it be like? As her eyes closed, she pictured a group of men leaning and lounging at the wooden table beyond her machine seven, drinking and smoking, enjoying a little banter, passing round newspapers and maybe pornography. That would all stop if there was a woman there. It seemed they played cards, even the foreman with the gammy leg joined in. Alright for some. Daytime foremen were forever on everyone's back, sucking up to management, dreaming up new regulations. Two pee-breaks per shift was all they were allowed now: a tough one if you've got cystitis! What do men know . . . If she did nights, she'd probably be stuck upstairs and never see him anyway. Besides, as the only woman on the shift, everybody would be watching her. She might be the target of jokes, lewdness of all kinds. The morning and afternoon workers would assume she was carrying on, eventually someone would joke about an old burst mattress abandoned in some deserted part of metallurgy, then it'd become 'common knowledge' she was the factory bike, after which nobody would speak to her. Even if unions and management let me work nights, I'd have to find at least one other woman to make the switch with me. Actually, with or without the Sicilian as lover – what a joke! – nights would be more convenient. I'd be home in time to wake Bernard and make him his breakfast, after which I'd sleep. I'd have the whole afternoon to myself. All I have now are mornings and what use are mornings? By the time I've eaten and dressed and done the chores, it's time to head for the plant. If I did nights I could read. It seems they all read. If they ever caught us with a book on afternoons or mornings, they'd fire us on the spot . . .

Fernando waited till Philippe was back at his papers surrounded by his workmates then said so everybody could hear, When do you want me to give you that fucking-free trim, tomorrow, yeah? Philippe flashed a thin smile at everyone standing there. Let me get used to the idea. I have to check my wife won't leave me if I arrive home as bald as a prick . . . or, worse, looking like Jacques here. Jacques nodded and smiled, adjusting his combover in comic compliance. Rachid, Tomec and Salvatore were all on their way up the machine aisle. Alphonse noted how Luigi, on spotting his compatriot, fell away from the group like some reptile retracting its head, inching imperceptibly back toward his machine fourteen, to which Mathieu had returned again, one hand on the machine guard waiting, the other picking at his neck.

Philippe observed Tomec, sunk in thought: funny kind of artist with a mind like a clipboard bristling with questions. Rachid glided more than he walked, like a camel over hot shimmering sand. Marcel kept opening his mouth but Philippe didn't want to hear any more homespun sexual philosophy so grabbed the local paper and shot a question at his listeners, Anyone see the story about the man who washed up a couple of kilometres downstream? I think it was Sunday. Wearing women's clothing? I'm not reading it out: take a look. And he handed the paper back to Luigi just as Salvatore arrived at the Italian's side. Meanwhile Rachid had come up behind Eric, while Tomec had stationed himself behind Jacques and was eyeing each man in turn. Luigi and Salvatore read the snippet and handed the paper to Fernando who shrugged and passed it to Marcel. Philippe was noticing how Tomec watched every-body. What the hell did the man see? It's as though we exist on the other side of a pane of glass, insects wriggling, pinned. Alphonse had taken the paper from Marcel, read it and handed it to Rachid who frowned, read it twice, then muttered, I think I saw that, then louder to Jacques: I think I saw that happen. Jacques beckoned to Philippe, who leaned in. Jacques asked the Algerian to speak up. Rachid knew that all eyes were on him now: Philippe's attention had enlisted everybody else's. I went to the bridge on Friday morn-ing, Rachid said. I sometimes go there after work. You know. I saw this arm in the distance, raising itself from the water. I think I saw the man go down. In the middle of the river. Nothing I could do. I forgot about it till just now. Marcel looked from Rachid to the others. Are you kidding? Did you tell anyone? Like who? Rachid asked. In any case, Fernando said, maybe it was someone else. What do you mean? Marcel asked, screwing up his eyes as if to grasp the point better. Well, not the guy in the paper, Fernando explained. Philippe looked at the end of his cigarette and said in a tone of deep seri-ousness, Fernando's right, there could be lots of people taking a dip in that sewer at five-thirty on a Friday morning in November. Jacques stood back, swinging slightly, watching the point sink in and Philippe smile at its success. This was good. Philippe was master of ceremonies again. Such resilience was a pleasure to behold.

Standing tall in his starched uniform, Tomec glanced from man to man, not following the conversation but recording instead the way the bodies before him swirled together and apart, together and apart, like rippling detritus washed back and forth against the quayside in Brundisium. All eyes were on the Marseillais, arms legs ears heads feet all directed toward him too, though the Marseillais himself cast his eyes repeatedly upon Tomec. This has to be the model of my multitude, Tomec told himself, these the forms and faces that press round Virgil as he is borne on that litter from the boat. True, there is nothing more banal than people just as they come: raw, wholesale and unalloyed, submitted to your senses in such kaleidoscopic close-up you could stretch out a hand to touch them, were it not that everything is broken and has to be reassembled shard by shard, transfigured, and only then sucked back through the centuries and millennia, deep into Homeric or at least Virgilian times. Yet between ancient times and the vulgarity of nowadays, between Coliseum and Consumerdom, there swarmed in Tomec's mind and memory the alternately enraged and enraptured mobs of a prewar childhood, the marching cannon-fodder divisions and smoking city-sized hecatombs into which those mobs were so efficiently milled, with the lines of half-dead / half-alive surviving starvelings who then wandered, their paths crisscrossing, picking through Europe's rubble, as Tomec too had fled. Upon these masses and their lives and fates – the immovable and dead centre of Tomec's own small history – he could not yet dwell, an appointment he could only defer while superimposing earlier crowds of carnival revellers, prison wreckers, insurgent workers, medieval marches, or indeed the glut of men, women and children that stood to welcome – as if to his place of birth not death – Virgil the poet, *their* poet, in an era when a people might still elect some ownership in an artist.

Wresting the men's attention back from Philippe, Marcel opened *Le Nouvel Observateur* at the advert for Concorde. Plus vite que le soleil! he intoned. Isn't that something? Isn't that beautiful? Wouldn't you like to fly that? He thrust the picture under the nose of each man in turn and each man acquiesced – even Philippe did a concessionary shrug – until it came to the nightwatchman. What I see is a flying penis, Tomec stated. At which Alphonse snorted and said, A supersonic dick! That's why he likes it. Marcel shook his head in disbelief while several men chuckled. He took a fresh look at the image of Concorde and shrugged. Doesn't look anything like a cock, he muttered. Salvatore, discomfited by the conversation, had offered Luigi a coffee so the two Italians headed off for the drinks machines in metallurgy. Alphonse waited till Salvatore and Luigi were out of sight then followed them. I wanted to ask you something! Tomec called after the Ivorian, who didn't seem to hear.

While Rachid checked his watch – 23.12 – and lit a cigarette, Tomec set off in pursuit of the African and Jacques easily fended off an attempt by Fernando to make a grab at his crotch. Jostling and joking, Jacques and Fernando then also headed for metallurgy, with Eric tagging along at what he hoped was a safe distance. Rachid found himself standing between Marcel and Philippe but he lingered, as if he had something to say, yet he said nothing. Then Marcel waved a hand at the man's cigarette pack and demanded, Are you going to give me one of those? Rachid reached for his pack, then changed his mind. He hadn't liked the man's tone. It was as though he was being asked to pay for something he hadn't bought. No, he said, matter-of-fact. Marcel bit his tongue and looked to Philippe, then away down the aisle. You could never trust Marseille to take your side. Then Philippe and Rachid moved off, the former to the right of the raised office, presumably for another drink at the water fountain, and the latter, shambling, ghost-like, floating, toward metallurgy and the meetings room.

Other than Bobrán and Jean upstairs and Marcel and Mathieu downstairs, the plastics section was empty of people. Marcel looked up and down the machine aisle. He liked it like this, he thought. If the machines were switched off, he thought, you could hear a pin drop. He walked down to the huge old wooden table, repositioned Rachid's chair and sat on it. He liked the view from here. Why didn't he have machines eight and nine? How come some lousy Arab had them? Huh?

49. Paralysed force.

Eric pushed through the hanging flaps, behind Jacques and Fernando, who walked like intimates, shoulders rubbing and elbows knocking, dawdling in the gloom of the raw-materials area. In the distance, past the stored moulds and glimmering drinks dispensers, Tomec's torch twinkled among the turret lathes and machine punches. Jacques turned back expecting to see Philippe, but saw Rachid, feet dragging, eyes downcast, hands in jacket pockets. While the others lingered near the pallets, Eric opened the door to the meetings room and looked inside, observing a wooden table bearing two empty ashtrays and a biro, surrounded by seven chairs, which he counted twice. Making himself useful, he went to report his findings to Fernando and Jacques. Jacques counted men out on his fingers – Marseille, the African, you, me, him, our Algerian friend here, er, the Italians: eight. Fernando returned to the plastics section for the extra chair, leaving the Englishman, the Algerian and the peasant looking like a pile of bricks with no mortar. Jacques turned to Rachid.

You saw him die?

Who die?

The man in the river. The transvestite.

Oh. Probably.

Noticing Eric's look of incomprehension, Jacques ruffled the hair that hung like a lampshade around the Englishman's neck.

The Ivorian skipped, walked and, where the light sufficed, ran through the raw-materials area, past the idle moulds, the drinks machines where yawning Italian bent before silky Sicilian, on into metallurgy, glad to be alone, away from the din, smoke and glare. Here he paced, memorizing lines from Lucky's speech, yet distracted by the look he recalled on Rachid's face as he had turned to the Englishman to provide elucidation. Earlier, the Algerian had nodded. Had Alphonse been attempting to please the Algerian – wrest forgiveness via admiration, or at least approval? Alphonse lost his place in Lucky's speech, then began again. It went better: '. . . par l'Acacacacadémie d'Anthropopopométrie . . .' The thought of witnessing Madeleine Renaud utter Beckett's words enticed him closer to a decision: if he could just get a ticket, he would skip his party in Lyon, upset Clara, go to Paris, hitchhiking back if his uncle were away. Fearless? Desperate? At the betting bar, with those men approaching, eyes bloodshot, fists balling, he'd been fearless. Would the

Portuguee have raised a finger? Thugs reminiscent of the big Gypsy, deserving to be mimicked and mocked but on their own grounds dangerous enough. I'm a clown, he should tell Rachid.

Mathieu relaxed his hard belly against the guard of Luigi's machine fourteen, jolted by the shuddering as the injection nozzle retracted, waiting for the press to open. (Nadine, I'm coming now. Nadine, wait for me!) The press opened. Mathieu slid back the guard. Ever the trained soldier, he missed nothing: the big Gypsy had gone to the end of the machine aisle and was sitting against the huge wooden table; the Portuguee, back from raw-materials, was taking a chair from Philippe's machine one, while nodding in Mathieu's direction. Oh, sure! Ba-dum-dum. Dum-blah! Lost inside the trance of Nadine's lost mind, Brownie's lost Bounce, lost to Clifford's music, lost. Clifford would be middle-aged. Lose your life, lose your mind . . . Nadine had her wits till she was nearing sixty. A single huge stroke could have been a mercy – still would be. Clifford dead at . . . ? Da-dum. There sloped the Marseillais, bearing a beaker of water from the fountain: cough still bad then. This piece is not right, still has that proud little flap. What if it worsens? (Nadine, let me save you. From life, living death.) I'll shut it down. Let the morning engineers fix it. I'll decide round about midnight. 'For Nadine: "Naima."'

October 1949, Grandgobier. Jean's first day chez Boucan – no plastics back then. His uncle had pulled strings with Georges Boucan, whom he had known during the war. Jean started in the office: he wrote good French, even typed. Besides, wasn't he too short and weak to work machines? Disliked at once, he was ordered to deliver an urgent crate of steel coils to far-off metallurgy workshop four. Someone followed him to see if he put the crate down anywhere. Never did. Passed the test. And failed. Next day, no warning, they pressed into his hands a set of clean overalls and a note for a workshop foreman. You can take off that tie! they said. The overalls swamped him. An old-timer made him do up all his buttons, roll up his sleeves and trouser-legs, tuck everything in: 'you don't want to get caught in the works.' Jean proved punctilious, docile, tolerant of even the worst machines. The men froze him out, called him a stoolie, which he wasn't: no attempt was ever made to recruit him. He had one friend – a Hungarian anarchist, who joined the factory in 1953, and loathed Communists yet more fervently and with better cause.

Fernando bore the chair aloft, past the men at the raw-materials pallets, and into the meetings room. There, like a waiter after the diners have left, he flicked the eight chairs into alignment around the table. He had worked in a restaurant once, a good one. He'd love to take Maryse to places like that. As his girlfriend. Or to his apartment. If he had one. How different it would be! Light and airy. No maroons or purple. No clutter. No funny lighting. Would she like his taste in decoration? He knew nothing about her. That afternoon she had touched his arse – brushed it – maybe by mistake. No. Why did you touch me there? he had asked. Trust me, she replied. Then she pushed him over on his back and straddled him. At first, it didn't seem right. But then, he had to admit, it had been sweet, fucking-so sweet. He didn't know how old she was. Soon he'd do his exercises. Try beating nine minutes. Without even touching it. Just recalling things. Like that look she sometimes used. As good as placing a jack under a car and cranking. Of course it'll lift. He didn't even know her birthday.

Salvatore was standing in the glow of the drinks machines, feet apart, shoulders back, beaker of coffee between thumb and ring finger, little finger adrift: Salvatore talked and Luigi, head wreathed in smoke, stooping, listening. Man to man. Thus did Salvatore calm his nerves. Luigi made him feel better. Salvatore smiled down at him.

. . . 'by the Acacacacademy of Anthropopopometry of Essy-in-Possy of Testew and Cunard . . .' Alphonse stood in dim metallurgy reciting a stretch of Lucky's speech, his head twisted at an improbable angle, his back and legs bowed by habitual burdens, his eyes darting, his skin tormented by Pozzo's rope. Tomec had followed Alphonse to this place and now approached, his torch extinguished, catlike, patient, till Alphonse came to rest, which he did on the words 'but not so fast for reasons unknown . . .' [n'anticipons pas on ne sait pourquoi . . .]. Tomec coughed.

Is that from Césaire's *Tempest?*
No.
I liked your speech. You mentioned Césaire.
It's Beckett. *Godot.* Lucky. I have to learn it.
I should have recognized it.
Why?
I saw it once. Years ago, in Paris. Aren't you late for your meeting?

I'll be there before it starts.

Well, don't mind me. I'll be the audience.

Alphonse began again at 'for reasons unknown.' Tomec wondered how to use Alphonse and whether to ask him to sit. If these men are truly my multitude . . . or part of it . . . But the man's physique is wrong – he's too tall, too handsome. Really quite heroic-looking. Everybody else bears some mark of living. But this man, who turns into an orator one minute and Lucky the next, brings nothing but earnestness. Maybe it's enough. He could stare after Virgil like a man obsessed. Maybe his attitude is as good as another man's broken teeth, potbelly, bald head or mangled limb. Alphonse stopped again.

So what did you like about my 'speech?'

The delivery. The passion.

Alphonse's eyes narrowed. Tomec imagined he could read the Ivorian's thoughts.

The earnestness, Alphonse pronounced, reading his.

Upstairs, Bobrán rose to check the latest products dropping from Alphonse's and Fernando's machines. His eyes strained to focus, discovering no defects, then he hurled each product into the furthest corner of its floor tray, grinning as it ricocheted around or crashed into a tangle, the sprue shedding pieces as it settled. As he sat back down, worries descended like a summer haze of midges, goading him, when all he craved was stillness. Why did Yitoune not come to see him? Busy with her lover-woman? After Moritz, he longed for his sister most in the whole wide world. (How then must the Algerian miss his son . . . ?) Soon I shall have to see lawyers. At dead of some night, Marseille will seek me out with a name or a number to call. Meanwhile, who cares about Marcel's hanged man? And what if Joseph had jumped . . . ? I could nod off and sleep for a year. Bobrán hadn't seen Moritz since Sunday. Right now Heike might be walking with him on her arm: two peach-skinned German seeming-boys in Grandgobier's drizzle. What was the difference anyway? Just a question of cock and cunt. He had enough cock for two, if it came to *that*.

Philippe took a sip of water. His throat tickled but the cough didn't come. Jacques was saying something, but Philippe wasn't listening. The old peasant liked sometimes to talk about farm affairs, crops, animals. You only had to listen. Philippe noted Luigi lumbering toward them, and the Pole stood in the distance, lit by the drinks machines, talking to the Sicilian. Philippe grinned in Jacques' face, Is that really so? he said. Jacques looked puzzled, then slapped him on the shoulder: he wasn't going to take offence. Philippe closed his eyes and blew a smoke ring high into the air, not checking how or when it broke up, leaving that to others. He was there and he wasn't there. His sister's phone call had changed things. He didn't wish to talk, take his place in the midst of the men, be looked up to. He needed a rest from that. He felt altered. He wanted to stand on the edge and observe – himself too. He was angry with Danielle – not for knowing or telling, but for sounding gleeful. For Odile he felt sad. He clicked his teeth. This isn't good, he thought. He opened his eyes and saw Eric, Rachid and Fernando.

April 1983, Grandgobier. It had required determination, a legacy from his mother, and a bank loan, but there Luigi stood, teeth straightened and whitened, flanked by his pregnant wife, celebrating the relaunch under new ownership of a recently failing boucherie-charcuterie. Lucien and Marthe distributed slivers of pâté-en-croûte and raised mini-goblets of wine. À la jeunesse!!!

Gérard spoke to his empty tumbler, Who's in charge here anyway? Then, smacking it down on the mantlepiece, he swivelled so sharply his foot caught on the carpet, almost flooring him. He pulled himself up. You're in charge, Gérard. It's your house, your library. You can wait for your faggot-son, phone your lady-whore or your pinko driver, or go upstairs and lie down – here he squeezed the words out in a maudlin whine – beside your beloved wife. Ha! You can phone someone. Said that already? Make a damn fool of yourself slurring your words probably. Look around! (His arms swinging, he thought of old people he'd seen exercising once in a park in Peking.) All this is yours! he declaimed, diabolically biblical. What do you really want? His eyes closed. He imagined marching to the kitchen, tearing a long stretch of bin bags from the roll, then returning to his library to dispose methodically of most of its contents, certainly everything passed down from father, grandfather, great-grandfather, great-great . . . Do it! he blurted. He hesitated. Wait to see how things look in the morning? Dawn brings on cowardice. So do it! Gérard sat down. Another finger of whisky might ease a decision . . .

In the ill lit raw-materials area, the plastics-section night shift – excepting the agency workers (Marcel and Bobrán), the non-unionized security guard

(Tomec), the lifelong anti-syndicalist (Jean), and the foreman (Mathieu) – lolled, leaned or lounged around the pallets, awaiting a signal from someone – presumably from Salvatore who had just joined the throng – that it was time for the meeting to start. Until then, cigarettes could be smoked, glances cast, jokes told, and news items recounted.

Rachid stood to one side, frowning and paying no heed to the others. Eric's attention jiggered from one man to the next, his ear bending to each snatch of semi-comprehensible conversation. Jacques maintained a fond eye on Philippe, noting the integrity of the smoke rings he blew, and storing up words and soothing notions with which to console his friend, the moment the opportunity arose.

Luigi had broached with Fernando the topic of sleepless Saturday and Sunday nights. Salvatore recommended an early-morning radio phone-in show.

I know the one! Fernando exclaimed. It's hosted by 'Camille.' She has a throaty, sexy voice.

Luigi shook his head slowly.

I suppose, Salvatore said, raising his eyebrows as if to assert that sexiness of voice were beneath his dignity.

I'm so exhausted on Monday mornings, Luigi observed, I worry one day I'll chop my hand off.

Eric leaned in, his face an etching of perplexity.

Luigi est apprenti-boucher, Salvatore explained, smiling.

Since Eric only blinked, Fernando supplied a scene enactment complete with gestures, credible expletives and mock howls of pain. As Eric opened wide his mouth to say Ahhh!, Salvatore exposed his own pristine left wrist for all the men to see the ticking time.

After turning his back on Salvatore, Tomec marched through deepest metallurgy, neglecting to poke his torch-beam under machinery or into corners in pursuit of Boucan's foes. Intolerant of distraction, impatient of shadows, he hurried toward his sketching bench. It had occurred to him that he could depict humans only from life and that every figure at his crowded Brundisium quayside and ensuing street-scene 'stations' must be found among the multitude encountered in these days and in this life, each cajoled, induced, corrupted (if need be) into cooperation. This realization, which had first seemed a boon, bringing the humdrum round of his night job into the orbit of his daytime artistic endeavours, filled him with despondency. If each ancient character were so opaque that its model must be identified in living flesh and blood, the work itself would have to be of mechanical precision. He halted, grunting. Everything must be transmuted. The faces and bodies I see each night and day are only grist, to be digested like food, broken down to release their nourishment: building blocks for something new. Mimesis is senseless: no pattern can be traced. Mechanical regularities must be detected and asserted. Placed within a scheme of transfiguration. Exalted.

Rachid had never liked crowded airless rooms: nothing good could happen in a space that could serve as a cell. As the other men made their short trek from the pallets, he hung back, looking around and listening to insistent promptings within him, noting the balance of moods and concert of small voices. Mehdi was there now, latent; Malika, Fatima, Karim, a breath away. Further off, his parents, mislaid comrades, and, incongruous in that company, suing for acknowledgement if not celebration, the foetus growing in his wife's belly. Held fast by teasing bands of expectation and memory, Rachid, his arms and legs pressed into his retracting body as though to prevent it from flailing, advanced his thoughts with tiny sideways steps. The people and objects available to Rachid's senses appeared intrusive and impertinent. He looked through the Sicilian, finding no substance on which to fasten. He met Philippe's eyes only: otherwise his gaze fell short, fetching up on noses, chins, cheeks or ears. As for Alphonse's inquisitive eyes, Rachid frankly avoided them. Eric alone precipitated him into some simulacrum of communication. Why me? Rachid wondered. What blind-dumb instinct made the Englishman seek my help in interpreting his brave new world?

Filing into the soon-to-be smoke-filled meetings room – behind Jacques, Philippe and Alphonse, but ahead of Rachid – Eric's heart fluttered. If Megan could see me now! He recalled how on the phone she had jeered that time, claiming to be terrified that on some future visit she would find him in a beret, speaking English like Maurice bleeding-Chevalier and chewing on raw garlic. To be truly scathing, her accent always broadened tha' wee bit – as if her occasional scorn for him were part of the glorious eternal campaign against the Sassenachs and all their works. But this was true life: gritty unions, strike action, politics. Besides, surely it was Greeks or Turks who chewed garlic. Or onions. Funny how Megan seemed younger than him, but wasn't. Fanny, who probably *was* younger, seemed older. Certainly older in love, teasing, and joking. In spontaneous cool, in her language . . . French, in her being . . . French. Eric slipped into a fantasy of instruction by a younger-older woman: a Fanny-tasy. His Englishness might yield to French seduction, never to Scottish abrasion. Like a snake's skin, he would slough it off. Simple. He stood at the threshold . . . of the meetings room. He need never go back. No more shivering on platforms that stank of disinfectant and coal, waiting for trains reeking of greasy chips and beer. This Saturday he'd see Fanny. Take her to the pictures. He'd bone up on expressions like 'limited action,' 'all-out' and 'wildcat.' He longed to see Fanny's face outside the factory. Oh lord! please may she not be spotty! Perhaps she wore slap to work . . . Spotty girls made him think of England. Spotty girls with smelly knickers. Never again!

Looking past the heads and bodies before him, Jacques glimpsed the table, all places still untaken, and wondered where to sit. He wanted to stay close to Marseille, alongside or opposite. Alongside, they could chat easily; opposite, they could exchange glances. Jacques wanted to put Marseille right about something, but this wasn't the time. The Italians stopped just inside the meetings-room, backs against the wall, letting others past. Fernando edged down the left-hand side and sat on the end chair. Philippe drew in his paunch and shuffled down the right-hand side, pulling Jacques behind him by the sleeve. Marseille had shrugged earlier, when Jacques told him about the drug's side effects. He reckons that at sixty-something it can't matter. I should set him straight. Virility still matters to a man. And to his woman. If it doesn't get hard, what have you got to work with? What have you got to share? It's like a hinge, right? You're joined. Something to swing on, like a kid on a door. If it doesn't get hard, what have you got to hang the door on? I don't want some doctor un-hingeing us. Philippe let go of Jacques' sleeve. Both men sat down.

February 1971, Grandgobier prison. Marcel sat on a plastic chair. Behind him, a wall. Across the table, two interrogators took turns to circulate, smoke, speak, look out the window: Bonnet Blanc et Blanc Bonnet. A uniformed woman did shorthand. The cops leaned forward, good teeth and foul breath. They either yelled or wheedled. He glanced at the woman's legs. She crossed them. He was offered a deal to name names. He played it long, seeing how high they would go. He would need money to get to the other end of the earth, switching identities ten times. They didn't come close. He was small fry. They had caught the monkey, missed the organ-grinder. He had stood lookout in the street, raised the alarm. They had no idea how many robberies he'd been involved in. He had no previous convictions and was discovered without a weapon. His associates – including Jimmy, the boss's younger brother – had escaped with almost the entire haul. Nobody had been hurt. It didn't take much to do the maths. He could rat out the organization, Jimmy first, test the boast that they could trace anyone to anywhere. Or be the model prisoner, get out early, go straight.

Alphonse turned to look back at Rachid. I'm going to have to explain myself, he thought. I'll be self-deprecating, disarming. I'm a clown, I'll say. I know something's eating the man. Does nobody else see it? Actors cultivate empathy. What should we do? Keep it locked in the theatre, away from life? No, use it!

Alphonse slipped into the seat next to Jacques, while first Eric and then Rachid sat down opposite them. With Salvatore and Luigi hovering at the door, Philippe, Fernando, Eric and Rachid all produced cigarette packs and lighters, laying them out smartly on the tabletop. Luigi dropped his cigarette butt on the floor and stood on it. Everyone continued as before, chattering or silent, attentive or oblivious to their surroundings.

I liked the show, Jacques murmured, his left elbow nudging Alphonse.

Good. What's that you smell of? I never sat near you before.

The farmyard, Fernando said. Better than fucking-poncey aftershaves.

Eric glanced up at Luigi who was just then laying a length of chewing gum along his tongue. Luigi removed the gum, tore it in two and offered Eric the drier half, shrugging when the Englishman declined.

Salvatore coughed, then coughed again. Slowly, the men fell silent.

It's almost 11.15, the Sicilian began.

Still standing but gesturing to Luigi to take a seat, Salvatore said he would briefly outline the economic and political context.

Hey, it's school time, Fernando said.

Everybody except Salvatore and Rachid – who seemed to be paying no attention whatsoever – laughed a little, which broke the ice.

Bobrán felt he needed to concentrate. Things were slipping away from him. He had checked the machines and tipped Fernando's and Alphonse's sprue into their threshing tubs. He took a deep breath, then crouched down on the floor in the middle of the machine aisle, placed his palms carefully on the concrete and raised his body and legs smoothly and slowly into a handstand. Then he strolled. Like a man at ease, glancing this way and that, wondering why life wouldn't leave him alone. He could be happy with nothing more to worry about than where to meet up with Moritz and how they would make love. But Joseph's death, and now Albert's letter, were calling him out, and soon he would have to meet lawyers. It was more like being lived than living. The killing too had never seemed like a choice . . . he could not have *not* defended Yitoune, though he had had no quarrel with the man he killed. Trouble came knocking at his door. Bobrán thought how different people fared! Joseph was clumsy so he slipped and died. Predictable. Almost a yawn. Meanwhile, Cousin Marcel did something very wrong to a cellmate but nobody found out and the other guy hanged himself. What happens to people bears little relation to what they intend and none whatsoever to what they deserve. What happens to me feels like fate. Trouble doesn't scare me and when I see it I know it's mine. It's better just to own it. Meet it head-on. With a smile and a shrug. Bobrán halted and, with perfect poise, lowered his legs to the ground and stood up, rubbing his hands.

Fucking-way this guy talks – socio-economic and politico-industrial – they never talked that way in school, though people laughed when I said that, even Marseille. The Ivorian had no business commenting on the old timer's smell, talking out of turn, what's wrong with him? He's looking to get slapped down, nearly caught it with the Arab. Now it's crisis, austerity, and Monsieur Raymond Barre and what do Italians fucking-know about crises anyway? Land of economic miracles and industrial triangles! There are more Portuguese my age in France right now than fucking-in Portugal – and he's telling me about crises. You wouldn't have dared call a meeting like this in Portugal during the dictatorship. No use telling them that. Look at us all! It really is like a classroom here: Jacques' eyelids drooping; African on the fucking-edge of his seat, top of the form; me daydreaming in the back row; Englishman struggling to follow, poor dunce; Luigi looking like the teacher's bag-carrying pet; the Arab, jesus!, god knows where he's at! So I said much truer than I knew. Funny thing strikes me now about Maryse: she's not really my type. I've always preferred the large-breasted luscious-thighed woman. Could I ever be her type?

Mathieu bent down at the end of Jacques' machine four and chose an apple. Crossing the aisle, he polished it on his trousers. Marcel looked up.

If there's strike action, it won't be safe to work on.

Not safe?

No supervision.

Marcel grinned sideways. He knew it!

I'll tell my cousin . . .

No, I will.

Glimpsed through his opening press, Bobrán struck Jean as uncommonly flushed – for such a sallow creature. Probably been playing with himself, the little man reasoned. After all, someone must have a use for that dirty magazine in the toilet. You couldn't help but see it, discarded in the corner, those fluttering women leering up at you as you're unzipping. He punched START. The press closed. Before being distracted by the little Gypsy's flushed cheeks, Jean had been contemplating national news, the prime-minister's austerity plan, the arson attack on Le Pen's apartment; but this evening several things had knocked him off course, disrupting his routine. Strike meetings always upset him, though he knew where his loyalties lay, and what he had unswervingly to do. He began to whistle a wartime ballad. He pulled back the guard just as the press opened. He had never joined a strike, never prevaricated. They had called him scab, ostracized him before and might again. He ripped the cable ties from the sprue. The meeting would be getting under way. He could just picture the men, hanging like fools on the words of propaganda from the new union rep, the Sicilian, talking of rights, demands, never of duties.

Salvatore could see he was losing them. Nobody seemed able to keep up. Was it too late at night for political economy, the oil crisis, global contraction and international competition? He stretched his left arm out before him, stared down its length, splayed his left hand and examined his fingernails. Satisfied, he decided to wrap up his introduction, adapting a slogan from the CGT flyer in his attaché case: 'Enough lies about the need for austerity to secure economic growth!' 'Bravo!' Philippe muttered. Salvatore pressed on. 'No more talk of sacrifices from workers, while the bosses just get richer!' Jacques snorted, coming round. 'Our working and living conditions are deteriorating, squeezed in a vice of rising prices, creeping unemployment and attacks on workplace rights!' Fernando nodded hard. The Sicilian decided to risk it. 'I'll just say a few words now on each of these points in turn, and share some statistics with you.' As Salvatore shuffled a sheaf of roneographed charts the union had supplied, he saw Luigi's eyes glaze and Jacques start to drool. If he could only hold on to the Ivorian, the Marseillais, the Portuguee, the Arab and the Brit. That would make a sort of quorum.

May 1978, Grandgobier. Mathieu looked round the apartment one last time: kitchen, toilet, second bedroom. He mustn't forget anything. He lingered in the main bedroom, where Nadine had spent her last years and where she had died. When they had first moved in, they had been happy there. It took an effort to remember that. In the living room, he leaned against the wall. Something was missing. His eyes opened wide. He descended the three flights of stairs, walked briskly to the car and took out his trumpet. He climbed back to the apartment, sat on the floor, his back to the wall, his knees apart, opened the case and fitted the mouthpiece. While he caught his breath, he considered which piece to play. The neighbours were sure to complain within minutes. He wanted something short, self-contained, no soloing required. He placed a mute in the bell of the trumpet, then changed his mind. The sound had to be soft, deep, but not muted, never muted. He counted himself in and played Monk's 'Crepuscule with Nellie.' He had never known how good the apartment's acoustics were, nor loved the sound of his old horn better, nor felt more at peace.

Settling to the mood of the meeting, Luigi fixed his focus on a middle distance far beyond the flimsy partition walls of the meetings room. While it might be imagined that his mind was far away, floating in some private dreamland or, alternatively, that he were labouring diligently to absorb Salvatore's regional and provincial unemployment statistics, both were simultaneously true. He listened carefully to the numbers, shocked by the recent increases, dismayed to hear of local layoffs and partial closures at nearby factories where acquaintances of his mother were – or until recently had been – employed, while at one and the same time entertaining anew his fantasy of a conjoined half-alien half-terrestrial Aurelia-cum-Gilberte, severally penetrated by volumetrically enhanced replicas of his own very personal phallus so that the composite's tongue lolled and wagged, its eyes rolled like a fruit machine hitting the jackpot, while the nineteenth stage of multiple orgasm – that grail of modern womanhood, tracked and plotted in innumerable glossy-magazine how-tos and ten-point plans – claimed its latest celebrant. 'The struggle for improved pay and conditions cannot be divorced from the defence of jobs and security of employment!' Salvatore was saying, as if reading aloud. Luigi nodded, enjoying renewed tumescence.

Gérard stood in the kitchen, spooning ground coffee into an American percolator. He leaned back against the drainer. He was sobering up in time to talk to his son. Not that Paul always slept at home. Turning, Gérard caught his reflection in a saucepan, his forehead sinking into wrinkles like a Camembert. What a family! he thought. Frigid wife, faggot son, fart-filled father. And no privacy! He felt he lived under surveillance. Even his past was investigated. By subversives. Claude might even be having him followed. She had to wonder. Even if she knew, she might never say a word, storing it up till it served her turn. How do people see me: the private-eye – if he exists; the scribblers interested in my war; Claude herself; Paul; my workers; Gisèle? Adulterer, collaborationist lackey, husband, father, capitalist pig, regular john, what else? If I were parachuted onto some island, I wouldn't know who to be. To that foreigner sweeping blood from the pavement, I was a nobody, some lush stumbling out of a chauffeur-driven car. Jorge might be home. He always finds something to say. He calls me names and doesn't care. If he's with someone, he says so. Lucky prick.

Salvatore concluded his opening remarks and sat down. Luigi shook his pack of Nazionali at the table. Eric turned to Rachid, eager.

Sum that up! Philippe challenged.

Rachid frowned, then spoke.

Capitalism is in crisis again. It's not our fault. The unions know just what to do. Thanks, I'll smoke mine.

That's it! Philippe said.

August 1967. Young Pioneers International Camp, Prague. In bright moonlight, Philippe swam toward the lake shore. Night bathing was prohibited but he was angry. Besides, what were they going to do? Inform the cadres in Marseille? That morning he'd skipped the factory visit and caught a bus to Terezín–Teresienstadt. He wondered why so little was being made of the place. At supper, the camp-organizer enquired where he'd been. Philippe told him. 'Why the interest? Are you a Jew?' he asked. Philippe surveyed the crowd seated round the trestle table. 'Asked in that tone of voice, certainly I am. I'm sure we all are.' A Greek comrade sitting opposite, said 'I am.' Nobody else said a word. As he waded out of the water, Philippe was surprised by a girl's voice and hurriedly covered himself. Gala, a Bulgarian, was sitting on a log. 'That was a good thing you did,' she said. 'Then why didn't you speak out?' 'Because – unlike you, *visibly* – I am Jewish. Things are never so simple.' Philippe dressed, feeling ridiculous. Gala told him of her parents – a doctor and a laboratory technician – who spent the war in Canada, then returned 'to build socialism.' 'What of the rest of the family?' Philippe asked. 'We don't know. Gone. Cattle trucks, probably.' 'Cattle trucks?' 'That's how we say it.' They talked till late in Gala's tent. They shared their hopes that capitalism would collapse and that the socialist countries would democratize. They talked of workers' movements sweeping Europe and of a youth awakening. Finally, Philippe took Gala's sleepy face in his hands and said she was beautiful. 'It's just summer camp,' Gala laughed.

Eric congratulated himself on being, for once in his sorry life, in the right place: 'I have arrived at the moment when the entire world is shifting perceptibly on its axis.' As Eric sat back and rolled himself a cigarette, he glanced around the table, scrutinizing his fellows with quiet satisfaction. 'Here we are,' he thought, 'preparing for strike action in coordination with other parts of this fine factory, following a mature examination of all circumstances socio-economic, geo-political, politico-industrial, industrial-economical, etcetera.' Eric's only regret was his humiliating dependence on interpreting and simplifying summary in order to comprehend proceedings. He resolved to seize the nettle. He would undertake at the first opportunity an intensive plan of study that would enable him eventually to master the French language to a point not merely of competence or fluency but to a pitch of innermost assimilation at which the mighty genius of the culture – already dimly perceived – would assuredly act upon any residual Englishness as an irresistible solvent. It shall be my aim, he swore as he lit up, to banish this awkward Eric-impostor, to shed altogether my past and background, to pass for, nay to be, a Frenchman, that is – a European!

Tomec had reached his sketching bench and perused again the description of the quayside crowd in Broch's *Der Tod des Vergil*. It was this crowd he wished to portray repeatedly and in all its guises, indeed through fourteen stations, as it swirled around Rome's immortal poet, raising him from the ship and bearing him head-high through the streets of Brundisium to the room where, after visits and visions, he was to breathe his last. But were not all crowds one? Tomec asked himself, jumping up again. Take a thousand people at random: could they not with equal conviction bear Virgil on a litter, march Christ to Calvary cheering, storm the Bastille or the Winter Palace, rampage through the streets on Kristallnacht, or as I saw them in '45 – millions not thousands – stream this way and that through the rubble-lands of Europe, a burst tide driven still by deadly dreams and ancient hatreds but more forcefully by the human lust for at least physical survival? *That* is the crowd that meets me in dreams, that has pursued me to this spot, but it is a multitude I cannot bear to look upon without shielding my eyes . . . unless, perhaps, one by one.

50. Grasping the gist.

At 11.15 that November evening, in a flimsily walled room used by the plastics section workers of Établissements Boucan for meetings and meals, and situated to one side of the raw-materials area, itself located midway between plastics and metallurgy, Salvatore, newly appointed union representative, was seated at the head of the table, with Luigi, his compatriot, by his side. Glancing along the table, the Sicilian saw on his left the Algerian, the Englishman and finally, at the end of the table, his shoulder to the wall, the Portuguee; along the right-hand side, he saw the Ivorian, the peasant and the Marseillais. Salvatore considered his mental bullet points: wider context, disclaimer, grievances, strike rationale, questions. He had covered the context already and – thanks to the Arab's succinct interpreting – even the Englishman had grasped the gist. The disclaimer now appeared redundant, but since he had prepared it he decided to deliver it. He cleared his throat but instead of looking deferentially toward him, as might have been anticipated, every man faced across the tabletop at the workmate seated opposite: Philippe glanced at Fernando (who grinned), Jacques at Eric (who appeared ecstatic), Alphonse at Rachid (who closed his eyes as slowly as a cat). Luigi, in the meantime, craned his neck to look down the bare centre of the table but perceived nobody.

As it happens, Salvatore announced, I'm neither a communist nor a Marxist. Indeed, I'm moved by no particular ideology. The fact is that our grievances need to be addressed and that industrial action is the best way to get the bosses' attention. I'll come to the specifics in a moment, and to your questions later.

Marcel sat on the old wooden table at the end of the machine aisle. He counted his cigarettes, then closed the pack. He could chew some gum. Anyway, he didn't need a cigarette right now. From here you could see the tops of every control cabinet on the floor. He swung his legs together in and out. If a light came on, you could be straight there, yanking back the guard, extracting the piece, scratching your head, then shouting for the chef d'équipe. The foreman was upstairs checking the machines and telling cousin Bobrán about the safety issue and how the machines would have to be shut down if there was a strike. You can't work on unsupervised, can you? Maybe there really was some such bullshit rule. This way the two of us won't be lining up for the shift change at five a.m. under the hostile gaze of the morning workers clocking on, perhaps even refusing to shake our hands, not knowing that as agency workers we have no say, thinking we're scabs, Gypsy scabs. Fuck them. Now it won't happen. Marseille is clever, thinking that up. 'All for one, one for all.' Amazing that the foreman fell for it.

The tabletop was clean and cool beneath Jacques' forearms. When Salvatore said he wasn't a communist, Marseille snorted and Jacques looked at Fernando who didn't seem to be listening and Jacques remembered he had promised him a rabbit. Back home he never thought about this place, as though it didn't really exist. But the drowning man the Arab had seen must be real, and Marseille's wife's lover. If Marseille cared for her, he should be patient, wait it out. If he didn't . . . what was the problem? Jacques reckoned Edith had strayed once, though you could never be sure. Salvatore was saying the strike wasn't 'ideological.' When was it men started bleating like sheep? Who needed to be persuaded anyway? Strike action was worth a try: end of story. Besides, how come Salvatore had taken over the union role from Marseille? It was good to see a glint in Marseille's eye again, looking sober now. Wonder if the African can really smell me through this smoke? He's right though: we're all immigrants, one way or another. I saw that last spring when Brigitte brought little Simon, complaining about flies and 'animal stench': to think my own daughter could produce such a town-bred sissy . . .

Bobrán examined the latest piece from Alphonse's machine nineteen. He jumped when he sensed Mathieu standing at his shoulder.
    If there's a strike, you can clock off with the others.
    Okay.
    That way's safer.
    Okay.
    Bobrán stared at the piece. Mathieu felt there was more to say.
    Okay? he asked.
    Okay! Bobrán said, eyes wide.

April 1974, Grandgobier. At the end of a warm spring day three weeks before Mehdi died, Rachid, on a whim, stripped and joined his son in their short deep bathtub. Son and father splashed one another, then Mehdi seized from a shelf a battered metal jug and a pair of wooden bowls, proceeding very carefully to pour water to and fro between recipients. Taking advantage of Mehdi's absorption in this task, Rachid soaped his son's neck and back, while Malika, entering the room with a clean towel over her arm, stood already humming a French lullaby. Moments later, as Malika patted Mehdi dry, Rachid relaxed back into the water at ease at last but with one eye still on his son. It was a moment of absolute happiness. The naked beauty of the child enchanted him. He had not imagined parental love would be physical also. Mehdi began pulling on his zizi, stretching it like a band so that it flicked back at his belly – a new trick with a favoured toy. Malika fussed that he might hurt himself but Rachid exclaimed: 'we're stronger than you women imagine. We don't break easily, do we?' 'We don't break easily!' Mehdi piped.

Talk, talk, talk. Italians fucking-talk, can't they? If everyone in metallurgy and on day shift strikes, of course we'll come out too. Strength in numbers, don't stick your neck out: fucking-what is there to discuss, droning like a priest? No, but gifts will never work with Maryse, she'd pull a face and hand it back and say something bitter. If she could fucking-just glimpse what I could be, imagine me something else, not a client or fucking-patient anyway. If it's like the Polack said (didn't he?), women like poetry, doesn't Maryse have shelf-fucking-fulls of books at her apartment? Well she does, so she must like poetry. I like it myself, don't I? If I told the Polack I did, then I do. Do I tell lies? Okay. So I could learn lines about some Lydia by Pessoa Fernando, wasn't it? Even shares my name. Because Maryse won't take a gift-book, but I can fucking-spout the words, can't I? If Alphonse stands and recites, how hard can it be? 'Lydia, come and sit by me on the banks of the river something-something hold my hand.' In French. She'll see me as somebody else, somebody she can't fully imagine, a mystery.

Alphonse sat alert, glancing round, but mostly at Salvatore and Luigi. It wasn't every day there was a meeting to consider taking industrial action. It broke the routine, making this night stand out from the others. Salvatore was talking like a man laying down the law, and Luigi kept nodding up at him, encouraging him, maybe because nobody else did. Rachid, seated opposite Alphonse, was staring like he'd seen Banquo's ghost, while Philippe smiled at nothing and nobody in particular. The others didn't seem to be listening at all. It was hardly the height of democratic participation. To Alphonse, everything came back to Beckett right now: *Godot* at the bus stop, *Godot* in his dreams, *Godot* for breakfast. Estragon and Vladimir make the same gestures, say the same things, as if nothing changed – except that Pozzo is sighted one day, blind the next, like that's a detail! Still, compared to switching from slave to master or master to slave, perhaps it is. This meeting would be effectively identical whatever the business. Unless Luigi ran it instead of Salvatore. Or the Algerian or Portuguee or Englishman or peasant. Or me! For that to happen, of course, everything would have to change.

The coffee, strong and sweet, worked. Gérard was feeling increasingly reasonable. He would not trash his library now, just do some tidying. Clutter he didn't need. He took a roll of plastic bags from a shelf, then refilled his cup. Clarity was returning. Sharpness. He stood taller, slimmer. He heard the front door open. Paul.

December 1976, Province of Agrigento. Meeting Salvatore from the train, Vito told him he had arrived just in time. But on being led in to see his mother, Salvatore felt he had got there too late. Giuliana failed to recognize him, waving him away, telling the nurse not to allow strange men into their villa. The following morning, however, she demanded 'Totò' be fetched immediately. He spent the best part of four days at or near her bedside, hearing stories from her childhood and suffering passionate declarations of maternal love. Each evening, as her mind became clouded from exhaustion and drugs, Salvatore withdrew to eat with Vito, who spoke bitterly, She wants only you but I'm the one who stayed behind. Sometimes she thinks I'm staff. I sit with the nurse and grow fat watching cowboy series on TV. Salvatore invited Vito to come to France 'once this is over' but Vito retorted, I don't speak French and don't want to learn. On the Sunday, Salvatore began the twenty-seven-hour journey home. He purchased panini and beer through the train window at Reggio and Rome. At Paola, an old man came into the compartment carrying a cardboard suitcase and two live hens, strung together by their ankles. Salvatore put down his volume of Diderot and stared at them, hanging calmly upside down between the man's legs, their eyes bright. Salvatore's last conversation with Vito, as they had stood on the platform at Agrigento, rang in his ears: You came too soon. If she dies now, will you return tomorrow? No. Then you'll never see her again alive. No. You'd better not miss your train. Grazie. Di che?

Bobrán rubbed and kneaded the palms of his hands. They were dry from the building lime he worked with most days and chafed red from pounding the concrete floor. Yet he felt good. Acrobatics – even walking on his hands – thickened his thoughts and purified his feelings, making what mattered matter more. He noted the burn in his shoulder and arm muscles, the weight of his back against the chair, the rise and fall of his chest as he breathed in and out, while the familiar ache of hunger in his stomach and idleness in his legs imparted an urge to spring and leap. From the corner of his eye, Bobrán saw Mathieu drop a product from Fernando's machine sixteen and hobble toward the lift. Since the chef had now checked every machine, Bobrán could relax, close his eyes, surrender to his dreams and longings. He recalled a clearing in a forest he had loved as a child. Yitoune was there, to one side, with her lover; Moritz and Heike strolled arm in arm, staring; his mother, at the fire, held a ladle; at the clearing's edge, Joseph surveyed the scene from beneath a tree. But where was he? Invisible. Floating.

Mathieu hit the emergency stop, suspending the lift between floors. Nobody will need it, he thought. (Nadine's eyes open, following him, alert again, beady.) As from some distant tenement, he heard 'Brownie Speaks,' played by Clifford himself. When jamming with strangers, Mathieu often called this tune. Yet what did it come down to? Thirty-two bars of notation. A bunch of dots on a page and some chord symbols as pointers. Plus tradition and an ear. Dead and dry till you breathed life into it. And then? Freedom. At the war's end, when both were as good as dead, he and Nadine had breathed life into one another. They had pulled each other up when either alone would have died. People said he had saved her, but they both knew she had saved him back. What is that love that you breathe into an almost total stranger just to save yourself? Da-da-da bum-da. Mathieu pressed the down button gently. 'Brownie speaks and I speak back,' he muttered. Once I soloed for so long, the sax player and guitarist left me on stage with a drummer and a bass player and went and bought beers. I didn't notice. They told me later.

Gérard listened to his son padding across the hall. He opened the kitchen door and called out,

Paul!

Paul turned. It seemed to Gérard that his son's look was free of affect: neither hate, love, interest, scorn, pity nor expectation. Paul came toward him in the guise of a stranger.

Coffee?

I was going to bed. I'm tired.

'At your age?' Gérard wanted to say, but only nodded. Paul noticed Gérard's hands, which looked peculiar, the fat little hands of a baby. Anywhere but at my face, Gérard told himself. Paul had never seen him holding anything quite so domestic.

Bin bags?

Come with me, Gérard said, making for his library. Gérard understood that under precise circumstances a paternal command would still be obeyed.

Close the door!

Again Paul did not demur.

Gérard deposited the roll of bin bags on the mahogany coffee table. The dog looked up from the hearthrug and glanced from man to boy.

I had this notion, Gérard said, to junk all this trash. He made a broad gesture at the room.

You can't, Paul said.

I can't?

It's the family's. It isn't yours. You look after it.

Where's my rebel child?

I'm going to bed now. Good night.

Rejoicing in the absence of Fernando and Alphonse, Mathieu's exit, and Bobrán's somnolence – a rare coincidence of circumstances promising a solitary interval – Jean decided to be lenient with himself, indeed, to take all his treats together. Tapping the START button, he drew a spearmint from his pocket, arched his back in a luxurious stretch and plunged into reminiscences of Sylviane, his first girlfriend, a sumptuous natural blonde only slightly taller than himself, with the whitest teeth and bluest eyes. Hired as a clerk shortly after Jean's own relegation to production work, she had answered his gifts of flowers and fine confectionery by agreeing to walk out with him. Throughout the long warm spring of '48, they had strewn with their steps city parks, riverbanks, and vacant lots until Jean's youthful inexperience had led him to urge his ardour both too fast and too far. Of sterner character than, say, Monique – bless and preserve the dear wife! – Sylviane had yet appeared initially inclined (by education rather than by feebleness) to yield to the male. Rather than repine over the lifelong joy he had forfeited through impetuosity, he preferred to dwell upon the pleasures briefly tasted. In particular, he treasured the memory of those moments during their ramblings when, happening upon some stretch of deserted path or patch of park, they would sing – in sweet conspiracy – the old anthem they loved so well. Lulled now by the din of the machinery, Jean sang it through again for old time's sake, his heart swelling at the final verse: 'Exaltons le travail / Et gardons confiance / Dans un nouveau destin / Car Pétain, c'est la France, La France, c'est Pétain. Maréchal, nous voilà . . . !'*

Philippe sat comfortably among his workmates, rocking gently, dimly registering the Sicilian's exposition of labour realities. He was glad he had stepped back. Let the other man steer a while! Philippe pictured sailing boats bobbing. Danielle's comments on his canvas pumps had reminded him where he'd been happiest, growing up near the sea. Each spare moment . . .

Luigi listened to the words issuing from Salvatore's mouth but took scant trouble to consider their meaning. He had heard most of them before, in both French and Italian, uttered with greater urgency. If I had those lips, Luigi thought, that olive skin, straight nose, erect bearing, square shoulders, toned muscle, straight back, firm rump, lean limbs . . . I would be a prime beast, the kind of livestock that falls to the very highest bidder. But if I had those gifts of nature and education, I'd be him not me. Luigi glanced round the table, blushing to see Alphonse staring at him as hard as he had stared at Salvatore. His eyes then fell on Philippe, across whose face there plied the faintest smile. Luigi experienced a moment's irritation as he recalled Marseille's recent attempt – not the first – to grill him about Italy. Somehow Philippe knew of his time at Fiat Ferriere. Another life. You don't look back. Italy is mired in red and black bullshit. They'll lock you up there for a youthful mistake and leave you to rot. Besides, I never believed in anything for more than five minutes. Things that are dead and gone should be left alone.

August 1994, Wrocław, home of Agnes Wiewiorka. *Sztuka i Życie* was interviewing Tomec for its 'Moments in a Life in Art' series. 'For me,' Tomec began, 'there have been five moments. As a child I was always sketching, painting, sculpting . . . but with no subject or technique . . . so the first "moment" – Tomec pulled a face – came in 1944 as these lands plunged into

---

* Let us exalt labour / And remain confident / In a new destiny / For Pétain is France, France is Pétain. Marshall, here we are . . . !

a violence no longer methodical but chaotic, headlong, generalized. Like many, I fled west, choking on ash and traipsing through ruins, resolving to bear witness . . . The second moment was in Paris where, despairing of my primitive skills and faltering vision, I turned to abstraction, using the war's own primary colours, daubing canvases with great slabs of black, red, grey and brown . . . The third moment came as I sickened of abstraction, Paris, artists, intellectuals, my moderate worldly success and dead-alive marriage . . . The fourth moment came in a provincial French city – it could have been anywhere – where I lived at last a solid routine of peace and industry – even after I fell in love. There, with the foreboding that the young woman I loved would soon grow out of me, I put to one side my *Stations of the Book* sequence and began instead to sketch, paint and sculpt her over and over and over until indeed she left. The fifth moment was when I briefly met her again, two years ago, when she read me the opening pages of Leib Rochman's *Mit blinde trit iber der erd*, where S. stands in an emptied ghetto, imagining it vibrant again with all its Jews and commotion. This brought me full circle and to my present work.

Eric's ears, eyes and brain were straining. Salvatore talked of unemployment (Eric recognized the word 'chômage'), spewing numbers and percentages ('pour cent' Eric heard). Philippe was grinning – clearly happy with things; the peasant closed his eyes to concentrate; the African kept saying, 'C'est ça!' The suspense of squaring up for a scrap with 'capitalisme planétaire . . .'

Jacques' thoughts were a long way off – almost forty-seven kilometres up a mountainside, with Jeanne, in Jeanne's bed. He had to think carefully, he told himself. A lot of things were dawning on him in a hurry that evening. Being prescribed medical hooch likely to cut your balls off makes you take rapid stock of things. If his old boy slumped and shrivelled inside her, Jeanne might appear not to be bothered at first, but women can get as attached to love-making as men. Jeanne really mattered to him. He had realized it the moment she hesitated to move into his house. Whereas he no longer missed Edith at all. Except occasionally. That still surprised him. Of course he would always cherish her memory. But he didn't think of her very often any more. Shit, what was this guy going on about now? Get to the damned point so we can all go for beers! Listing our demands. Yeah, yeah. Some substitute for Marseille! The English kid stares at me like he thinks I must be listening because I've got my eyes wide open. Someone should tell him it's the ears that do the listening. Basic anatomy. Where was I?

Jean kept wondering what the little Gypsy's letter said. Written by some Albert Gbenye. Gbenye's brother had apparently mentioned the Gypsy in letters home, suggesting they were friends. Then the letter had been snatched. Maybe he asked others to read it.

Jean hit the START button, slipped off his seat and shouted for Bobrán, who looked put out, as if not expecting interruption. Still, he got to his feet and pulled a chair up close to Jean, who was back ripping cable ties from sprue.

I could teach you to read.

Like when?

While I eat. Or while we wait to clock off.

Bobrán imagined his cousin's laughter, the looks on the faces of the morning shift. It was obvious what Jean wanted. He'd string him the line he gave Marcel.

He disappeared.

Who?

Joseph. Just like that. His brother has come looking.

Really?

Sure.

Jean looked disappointed.

Well, what's that to me? I thought I'd help you learn to read. We could start with easy books. For kids.

No thanks.

Jean watched him walk away, dragging his feet in those plimsolls he always wore. Offer to help them and what do they do? Chuck it in your face.

Mehdi wasn't just listening now, he was speaking, slicing through all the Sicilian's waffle about differentials, conjunctural crisis, inter-sectoral solidarity, and trade-union tactics, sounding again like any normal five-year-old, acting in fact like a good little boy, so well-behaved you might suspect he was making fun of his father, biding his time till he could be naughty again. Rachid had explained to Mehdi how they intended to tell the baby all about him: they would place photos of Mehdi by the baby's cradle, tell funny stories – like the time he cut up his sheets with a pair of scissors – pretend he were still alive somehow somewhere. Mehdi had nothing to say about that. His silence lingered like a shrug. Perhaps he was thinking about it or perhaps he felt his father was trying too hard and that to pretend he was alive somewhere was no better than repeating ancient tales of hell and heaven. As the words 'half-hour stoppages' impinged on Rachid's consciousness, he flicked his eyes briefly into focus. Well, that'll terrify Boucan, he thought, glancing into Salvatore's face, half-expecting to see it fluttering again like speed-shuffled cards through the ages of man from first to second childishness.

November 1976, Grandgobier. After the initial read-through, the director invited responses to the play. 'Vladimir' referred to something he called the phenomenological reduction and said the moods and relationships in *Godot* were what you would get if you bracketed society, history, politics and took some fairly ordinary people and placed them in the resulting vacuum to explore their perceptions: it could be anywhere, anytime. The set designer chipped in with 'universal anomie' and 'Estragon' spoke of reification and the 'eternal return of the identical,' while 'Pozzo' concurred, citing the tramps' inability to tell the time or even to identify the season, let alone recall the previous day's occurrences. Excellent, the director said. Then Alphonse piped up. I don't see that at all, he said. To me this play is European, even French, absolutely rooted in place, time and culture, with its references to Mâcon, to the Rhône, to the Seine-et-Oise, to Normandy. One of the tramps compares himself to Jesus, and they discuss the gospels, don't they? Then there is the enactment of slavery and humiliation and Lucky's speech mentions research, science, Shakespeare and lawyers. We know where we are but we don't exactly recognize it. Excellent, the director said again.

Marcel saw the foreman arrive from the lift, doing that scatting thing again he did in the toilet, thinking he wasn't noticed. Marcel was pleased to see him though: it was weird to have the floor to yourself, reminiscent of prison, now how was that? Don't let your thoughts order you, Martin taught. Easily said. Marcel had to compile a list of girlfriends to lose. Part of his plan: stay decent, keep out of prison, be ambitious. Chantal was a start, but he wanted more: a fine apartment, smart car, the best hi-fi. Factory work was stopgap: the goal was totally legal and reasonably lucrative or maybe vice versa. Landlordship, possibly. 'Property's the future,' Chantal's dumb-as-shit brother said but even dumbshits, like stopped clocks, had to be right sometimes. He'd check property out. In the meantime, he would get skilled up. Electrics, plumbing, tiling, locks – all that shit. His old boss had shown him once how to evict tenants in arrears. They'd taken some sacks down to the river, trapped a couple of dozen rats, then released them on the tenants' landing, pressing their doorbell in the street. If that's what it took for the hi-fi, that's what it took.

To conclude, Salvatore said, the all-factory strike committee recommends we shut down half an hour early next Wednesday and every second Wednesday till our demands are met.

Is that it? Alphonse asked.

Salvatore nodded and Luigi looked round the table.

Philippe nudged Jacques. Fernando looked up and saw the peasant scratching his pate. Eric glanced at Rachid, who placed his forearms in front of his chest so his fists touched, muttered 'grève,' then yanked them sharply apart to a distance of about five inches while whispering 'une demi-heure tous les quinze jours.'

How is that supposed to hurt? Alphonse asked.

The shutdowns will disrupt production for more than the half hour. Machines cool, pressure drops, engineers have to come in . . .

Alphonse turned to Philippe who was sucking his tongue and gazing up at the polystyrene-tiled ceiling.

This isn't Italy and it isn't '68, Rachid remarked.

If we struck for a week or at least a day . . . Alphonse began.

They could bring in agency workers, Salvatore said.

Yeah, Luigi said, you can count on them to scab.

Well, that's what the bosses like to think, Philippe whispered.

This isn't about bringing down the system, Rachid told Alphonse. It's about slow resistance, patient, organized resistance. You fight only those battles you can win.

Said Chairman Mao, Philippe added.

Rachid nodded.

Fernando frowned.

Mao-Tse-Tung? said Eric.

He doesn't work here, Luigi snarled.

He was sacked, Fernando said.

Salvatore coughed. We'd all love to bring down the system, he said. But – and here he glanced at Rachid – some of us have family responsibilities.

That's irrelevant, Rachid snapped. Having people depending on your wage makes you more militant not less.

Where's my mental control tonight? It's not like me to squander attention on pettiness. I weakened and took all my treats at once. (The product's sticking again. Oil it next time. START.) My mind was hijacked by graffiti subversion, strike talk, Monique's reprieve, the Gypsy's letter, the insult to the Vierge: matters to sully the purest mind. (Prime the brush. Just enough!) Twenty-three sixteen! I should be pondering national and international events, staying alive to the world, taking a view, preparing to throw my weight onto the scales, assume my place in history – however small – if the opportunity arises, if destiny calls. You never know when. History alone makes a man a man. (Open guard. Rip cable ties from sprue. Dab ejector pins. START. Could I perform these actions any faster?) Besides, there are events one needs to know about: the Right is raising its head at last. Make no mistake! On the march. As in Spain, to commemorate the anniversary of the Generalissimo's death. And attacking that synagogue in Rome – not that one approves necessarily. Still: straws in the wind. So clear the mental debris! Portuguee? Out! Gypsy's letter? Out! Strike? Out! Graffiti? Out! Monique's reprieve? Out! Out! Out!

What are they talking fucking-about? Revolution? Even back home, that's over, but at least Caetano's gone. The Brit, Arab, Italians . . . even Marseille doesn't have a clue. And Alphonse . . . isn't it enough to be black, without being red too? Fernando suddenly relaxed. Everything was fine. They can't keep a good man down. I'll find my way.

Outside it was spitting. Gérard felt it on his face. A slow-motion insult. He splayed his legs to release some wind. A smelly sigh, hush! He stared at the façade of his mansion. His? His clan's! Like 'his' library. He hadn't expected a lecture on family responsibility from his faggot son. Okay, not a lecture exactly. 'It isn't yours. You look after it,' Paul had said. He'd tried to be open with the boy: sometimes you'd love to scream and stamp as you trash your surroundings, sling out clutter you never asked for, right? Tip it into bin bags and leave it for the refuse men. You issue orders all day long – to managers, employees, secretaries, your chauffeur, mistress, wife – but have no control over your own time, surroundings or life. It takes your rebel son to remind you you're nothing but a caretaker. What does anyone think I am? Gisèle, say? Claude even? A machine? Gérard felt a tightness in his neck. He rotated it, tried to work it loose. Probably strained it standing too close to Raymond, looking up into the tanned and handsome face atop that perfectly honed and proportioned body. Enough to give anyone a pain.

Salvatore looked round. It took an effort to remember the quiet moment earlier that evening when he'd seen this little room empty and admired the table and wondered if he'd ever have such a space for himself. He observed that the men were now talking all at once: Rachid to Eric, Fernando to Philippe (who didn't appear to be listening), Alphonse to Jacques (who was paying more attention to Philippe and Fernando's lopsided exchange), and Luigi, softly, to himself (unless he was singing . . .). Salvatore shuffled his papers. He had covered the ground, explained the situation, canvassed the options. He had expounded a reasoned case for limited strike action, within the framework laid down by the union. He hadn't talked down to them or over their heads: he'd pitched it right. It was part of the union delegate's role to educate and inform, yet to wear one's expertise lightly, never to intimidate. He hadn't wasted time getting down to business either. Straight in. No need to use up the statutory time allowance: that would be infantile. It was nearly time to take the mood of the meeting. Any other questions? he asked, raising his voice. Any other questions? ANY OTHER QUESTIONS?

Mathieu stood in the raw materials area alongside the pallets. His left hand reached beneath the string sustaining his trousers to scratch at his lower back. His right hand picked at a patch of forehead. He had to say something to the union meeting. He hadn't been to one before, though he had every right. He wasn't a man of words. (Nadine . . . Nadine would tell him what he was feeling before he knew he felt anything.) Nor did he like people watching him. He didn't even like looking at himself. Playing jazz was fine because the audience doesn't look *at* you but only *toward* you, and the instrument – the trumpet – is in the way, a mask and a mirror, sending the audience's stare right back at itself. Besides, it's dark. Whenever he risked getting caught in the glare of daylight or neon, Mathieu had an urge to duck and dart, as if dodging bullets or shells. Still, he had to announce the fact that the two Gypsies . . . no . . . the temporary-agency workers . . . had done . . . what? I'll just go in and say it. I'm not a words man. Thing is: they can't strike but nor can they work, it wouldn't be safe.

June 1968, Arles. Yitoune was thirteen, living with her father. She had phoned, left a message. She was being stalked and threatened by a local rapist, a police informer, untouchable. She had nowhere to hide. Bobrán rode the hundred and seventy kilometres on his moped, arriving late afternoon. Yitoune had been dragged away with a knife to her throat. The man's sobbing wife told him to search some farm buildings on the edge of town. Bobrán glimpsed Yitoune through a window as the man slapped her and tore her blouse. The fight lasted forty minutes: sticks, fists, boots, bars, a screwdriver, rocks, finally a serrated knife that passed between them several times. Bobrán was weaker and smaller but younger and more cunning. Each time the rapist got the upper hand, he taunted Bobrán that he would kill him and fuck Yitoune, 'fuck her till she's mine.' Bobrán wore his enemy down till at last he sat athwart him, the knife trembling at the man's throat. Bobrán hesitated for a long minute, panting and thinking hard. He had watched goats die when their throats were cut, had heard pigs squeal. He leaned back to avoid being splattered and carved the jugular.

The men interrupted their conversations and looked toward the Sicilian. As something like silence descended, he stretched his left arm out, leaned back and looked down at his left hand which he splayed on the table with each finger as far as possible from its nearest neighbours. He seemed to be admiring his nails. Any other questions? he said. Everybody looked at everybody else, but they all ended up watching Philippe, who seemed interested in Salvatore's hand until its owner removed it from the table and hid it from view.

Perhaps we could take the mood of the meeting. I've set out the case, Salvatore said.

Fernando had noticed the door silently open and the foreman appear behind the Sicilian. He pushed back his chair to offer the chef d'équipe his seat. All eyes fell on Mathieu.

His face was red. He jerked his head at Fernando to sit back down, then shifted his weight from his left hip to his right and back.

It wouldn't be safe for the Gypsies – you know what I mean – to work on unsupervised. Agency workers. So they turn their machines off at the same time as everyone else. I wanted you to know.

Luigi was furious with Mathieu. It was the second time that evening the foreman had crashed into his thought stream, scattering fantasies of Aurelia-cum-Gilberte, and triggering rapid and disheartening detumescence. And then the stupid Portuguee had offered the man his seat! The chef was still stood there, shifting from foot to foot, everybody gawping like guppies in an aquarium, as if he might say something else. Fucking half hour's strike! What difference did it ever make anyway? They take themselves so seriously. The Sicilian prick is the worst. I learnt my lesson in '69. I'm not going to think about that. The fact is one man has to work and another man has to provide that work. Where would we be without Boucan? If we put him out of business by jacking up his costs, we'd all be on the street, right? You don't get around international competition. It's no good pretending. I'll be safe in my butcher's shop so fuck them all! Except, who'll buy my meat if all the work goes to Yugoslavia or Spain? They don't think of that. Gilberte understands this. I never have to explain a thing. I think maybe I really do love her.

51. Casting characters.

When the clock showed 23.17 on the ninth of November 1976, precisely no one stood by the drinks dispensers, in the lift no one, in the chef d'équipe's office overlooking the shop floor no one, in the toilet no one. The big Gypsy, the sole worker present in the injection-press workshop on the ground floor, lingered close to the end of his press, stroking his belly, his ciggie jutting from glistening lips. In the first-floor workshop, his cousin lounged, his eyes monitoring every control light, while the little guy, hidden behind the press number twenty-three, crooned Vichyist ditties. But the meetings room? Ever more crowded, with the chef twitching on the threshold; Totò (to his moribund mother in Sicily) rising to his feet; then, from left to right: Gilberte's lover; Mehdi's doting mourner; the brunette's would-be boyfriend; Maryse's sweet-eyed Portuguee client; Odile's cuckold spouse; Edith's widower; the budding interpreter of Beckett's Lucky. In the furthest corner of the works, elbows pressed to sketching bench, thoughts circling his girlfriend, the Polish sculptor resisted the urge to lift the for-emergencies-only telephone. In his hillside residence, Gisèle's best-heeled customer reclined, fingering his drizzle-wet follicles, oblivious to the strike being plotted in the city below.

Tomec laid down his pencil. For several minutes everything had seemed easy: his sketching had gone well, his hand darting like silverfish. Yet something was missing. He could tell from the ticklish chafing at the surface of his mind. It had nothing to do with the factory, the graffiti, the men. Nor was it his work, his art. Sarah. Evidently. That too had happened too easily. They had fallen into a liaison, plummeting together with scarcely a word spoken. He hadn't dwelt on it for fear it might dissolve. He recalled Jan's early-morning visit, his request for a disguise and his transparent infatuation with Sarah who had shimmied past him naked and reeking of sex, leaving him with the astonished look of a man struck with lockjaw. All recollections led to Sarah. At his shoulder while he flicked through his sketches, she had picked one out. 'Who's this?' 'The slave-child from Andes – and the younger Gypsy at work – from memory.' 'And it's me, isn't it? The hair.' 'You're right.' 'The nose.' 'And the freckles.' He would have to dwell on her. Otherwise she would slip through his fingers without him noticing she were there and without her knowing he noticed.

Mathieu looked round then dipped his head sharply and withdrew.

What was that about? Fernando said.

Doing the boss's business, Luigi said.

It'd be hard to be more wrong, Philippe said.

Everyone looked at Philippe, who looked at Salvatore.

The foreman is responsible for safety, Salvatore began. Given that he'll be on strike, he won't be responsible for temporary workers, who'll therefore have to shut down their presses.

Neat improvisation from the jazzman, Alphonse said.

Philippe nodded, happy for any imitation of wit.

The Englishman nudged the Algerian for an explanation but got no response. He didn't seem to be listening.

Before putting the stoppage to a vote, I'd like to raise the issue of our night bonus, Salvatore said.

What night bonus? Fernando said.

We don't have one, Luigi said.

Indeed, Salvatore said. The union's own plant-wide survey of wages has revealed that we – the only men in the entire plant who work nights – are by far the worst paid.

How do you like that? Fernando said.

The Englishman studied Philippe's demeanour. He never looked ruffled and always had an answer. He used just enough words and no more. And he wore denim like he was born to it.

Stifling a yawn, Philippe was still listening to the Sicilian's talk of wage variations – the relative pay injustice oppressing their tiny group of night workers. Pompous fucking preacher! As for his compatriot – well, you never trust a man who can't talk about his past. Of course the bonus was a ploy to tie the men into the union, since without it there's no hope of achieving anything. But what was slipping past without comment was rather more significant: the agency workers' refusal to serve as scabs – a small but historic gesture, however unconscious. The Gypsies might even lose their jobs over it. The chef was sticking his nose out. This time Philippe gave in to his urge to yawn. Hell, I've got other things to think about: myself, my wife, my little girl. He took a look at the Arab. He's off somewhere else. Philippe shook his cigarette packet at the man. No response. Leaning across the table, agitating it right beneath the Algerian's nose brought the tiniest answering smile. He's okay, just lost in thought. Can't blame him. Without warning, Philippe got to his feet. You'll excuse me. I have to piss. You've got my vote for the strike.

Downstairs, in a mood of proto-uxorious submission to Chantal, Bobrán's big cousin, slouching across two chairs, a flat hand comforting his groin, had sworn to run no insultingly stupid risks, and from this point on strictly to limit his robust outpourings of libidinal sap to such chicks, natural-born trollops, or lucky lady-bountifuls as would always find it impossibly difficult to withstand his alluring ways, rampant crotch, and known Casanovan bravura, and so rush, crash or fall stumbling (acting plausibly blind but in fact as fully conscious as any Hairy or Curly) straight into his path and down onto his twitching dick. Thus planning to avoid all known pitfalls from both his youthful and his post-prison bouts of rutting, his plan was to spoil Chantal with a modicum – if not of outright chastity – of sturdy will and honour-bound aspirations, to strap on a simulacrum of that traditional loin-shackling contraption for non-conjugal amorous constraint (though not masochism). With his thoughts still running along this ditch, his gaol shrink sprang to mind, in particular how Martin had said that pussy was not all that loving and living could afford a curious man. But was his curiosity up to finding out if Martin was wrong?

Jacques had watched Philippe leave the room, appearing relaxed, but really seething – he knew the man. It was no good him blaming somebody else: he had resigned his union role, nobody had thrown him out. The Sicilian would operate in his own way, to his own agenda, which was natural. Jacques wanted to go and talk to Marseille immediately but he stayed put. Philippe needed time to cool down. Jacques rested an elbow on the chair Philippe had vacated and allowed his legs to splay out beneath the table. His smile inched back. Everything that happened had a reason, such was Jacques' conviction: things always came right in the end. Jacques started listening again to Salvatore. It was hard work keeping up with all those words pouring out. The man was a creep, in every way Philippe's opposite: tying everyone up in knots, conceited, nervy, showy, never using a short word when a longer one was available, looking down his nose at men like me, the Portuguee, the black, the Arab, the English guy – who does that leave? Just a creep. He brought somebody to mind. Who? Jacques laughed right out loud. Salvatore stared. His son-in-law, that was it. Creep.

July 2016, near Montpellier. Eric will awake from a double dream. He will feel far from home, in the country of his childhood where, distracted by friends, work, affairs, he notices in terror that for weeks he has failed to check on his frail father. He phones his father's home, then his sister. In murderous tones, the brother-in-law answers, 'I see you've heard. Jane!' From yelps of anxiety, Eric seems to awake to discover his father alive in some wretched homeless shelter. Then from tears of shame and self-directed fury, Eric awakes anew to his hillside house and wife's slow breath. As briefer dreams break in successive waves and his wife stretches and yawns, a truer memory settles and is rehearsed. Father died in 2005. That afternoon he mouthed he loved me and I replied, 'You could have said so sooner. I never would have known.' Then I bent and kissed him at his hairline. Hours later, as if it were some new experience, he ceased to breathe. He even smiled. I said, 'If you don't care to, you don't have to take another breath.' He breathed twice more, then stopped. I called Jane. My father is dead once more.

Am I not transparent? Can nobody sense or guess at emotions swelling my proud Algerian breast? Too foreign to contemplate? Sitting in my seat, a closed book . . . Can it be possible – let alone good – for us to live as fog-lapped promontories mysterious to our next-at-table? Are our brains locked, our souls gagged, our words stopped? Is fellow feeling to be reserved in France for compatriots – even among persons born or raised beyond France's borders? Foreigners cannot surely be alone in bearing or siring babies or forfeiting off-spring to Grandgobier's roads. Are we – immigrants all, as my self-appointed dance partner maintains – not subject to similar feelings and ideas? I understand my desires. Even as Signor Salvatore waffled, I was consulting my loves and dislikes and longings. Everyone is as profoundly deaf to Algerian silence as to Sicilian noise. A party would be fitting. A party as in former times. Malika will invite anyone close or interested. A feast of food and wine and song. I will dust off my oud. Karim will come, if plenty of notice is given. As day dawns, we will all learn of his latest dreams of revolt. We will celebrate, anticipating new life and better days.

The Arab just got up and left. Alphonse had watched the man go. Not a word, not a gesture. He could at least have told us he wanted to pee! He looked eaten up, Alphonse thought. But by fear, sadness, or bereavement?

Maybe that's all the same. Nobody looked alarmed or astounded when he went. Salvatore shrugged. Everyone knew how he'd vote. Alphonse wondered whether he should go after the man, talk, fool about, play the clown, say sorry once more. He saw and felt too much to look away. That's drama for you. You can't keep empathy roped off. Now he's gone, everyone has to talk at once, as though that gloomy presence had kept us all passably courteous. Nobody cares what Salvatore says. That's the truth. A half-hour stoppage once a week? So that's what we've come to! You can feel the powerful tremble, the system quake. They've got us gagged and bound – between the employers and the CGT. Anyone who speaks up for a tougher stance gets shouted down, called troublemaker, wrecker, saboteur: 'Go talk to the students who flog *Rouge* at the gates!' Alphonse got up, nodded round the room. He needn't say how he'd vote.

February 1990, Grandgobier. With Claude long since departed with another younger, less ugly man, Gérard had withdrawn from involvement in the family business. Recently he had moved into a palatial yet spartan town-centre apartment: no clutter, no dog, no dusty documents, no squeaking stairs. Paul was occupying the mansion with his lover, a man with tinted hair and literary aspirations: they appeared to do nothing but throw parties to raise money for homosexual causes. Paul took little interest in the day-to-day running of the factory, employing a plethora of managers. What could it possibly matter anyway? Why should they spare a thought for posterity? It was not as if they were going to be able to shit children any time soon, despite the best liberal efforts of science. At the plant, the oldest metallurgy departments had been ripped out and retooled and the plastics section was now run by three operatives per shift, tricked out in spacemen's white costumes. Gérard's grandfather would not recognize the place. Gérard – alcoholic, diabetic, and still reliably dyspeptic – remained impatient for his life to improve and his mood to lift. Meanwhile, he acclaimed and marvelled at the thunderous collapse of Communism relayed by his television.

Salvatore performed one of his stage coughs.

Before anyone else leaves, we'd better put the half-hour stoppage to the vote. Anyone against?

Jacques pursed his lips and swung his head from side to side. Fernando shrugged a single shoulder. Eric glanced at Luigi for help.

Tu veux faire la grève, oui ou merde?

Oui! Faire la grève!

Beaming, Salvatore assembled his papers.

There was a lull.

Luigi lit a cigarette and assumed a philosophical air. As Salvatore exited, Luigi turned to Eric.

So you couldn't find a job at home?

Eric squirmed.

At home?

Home. England, right? Who chased you out?

Jacques and Fernando were eyeing Eric now.

I wasn't happy. I wanted to be somewhere else.

Luigi bared his teeth.

Nothing wrong with that, Jacques said.

Luigi removed the cigarette from his mouth and stared at its tip. He recalled something he'd read at Philippe's machine.

Did anyone see that story of the woman who had four children so she could avoid prison?

That's bullshit, Fernando said.

It was in the paper.

Papers are full of bullshit. Nobody has four babies to avoid something.

The other men stared at Fernando, waiting for more, but none came.

All right, Luigi said.

Fancy the foreman poking his head in, interrupting proceedings! Not that he didn't have every right – as a paid-up union member. Yet as soon as he appeared behind me, everyone had eyes just for him. It might have served as a demonstration of how to undermine a union representative or sabotage a gathering. After he went, nobody heard a word I said. Not that his manner was impressive. He's no speaker. Standing there dithering, scratching his head, picking at his skin condition, chewing at his matchstick, meeting nobody's eyes, as if shy or dimwitted. In either case, a pretty strange army veteran! Not that his news wasn't important. If the two Gypsies can't work on during the stoppage, then Jean Herbier upstairs at his semi-automatic is on his own. Taking everything together, my chairing of the meeting went okay for a first time. I can improve on it, make my points stronger, figure out how to communicate authority, make men sit up. I don't have charisma, do I? It doesn't have to matter. Providing I earn their respect. How hard can that be? I just have to consider them and make them consider me. My advantages, my diction, my aptitudes.

At Luigi's press fourteen, the chef d'équipe was losing patience. He jerked the guard back and hoisted the product high. Passable. If it didn't settle soon, he'd shut it down. He couldn't hover there all night. (Nadine, her face as if sleeping, but not snoring. A corpse that was still breathing.) I used to hope she'd rear up in bed one day and shriek, 'Just kidding!' I've grieved long enough. Now I have a notion how to do it, there's nothing left but to kill her – kill the corpse. That student did it with a shot of adrenalin to the leg: no pain, no panic, no trace. There are countries you can buy drugs over the counter, no questions. Practicalities! I've given injections before. Procedure! I can follow protocol. I've killed dozens of people in the coldest of blood first to liberate this country, then in foreign wars. I never lacked resolve, panicked or surrendered, conjuring guilt out of innocence – like that student did – turning kindness to cruelty. If I had no law to fear, I'd press a pillow to her face. Why would she struggle? Corpses have no will to live. What does she have? A dial tone.

Philippe had strode back to the four presses he worked with Jacques, studied the latest pieces as they clattered through their sets of slats, checked the hopper levels, emptied floor trays over their respective tubs – after which he started systematically to thresh the four lots of product. He had to get all this work out of the way before Jacques arrived – so they could go for a coffee together. There were matters they had to discuss. He prepared some words about those tablets that had got Jacques so worried. It was a tricky subject to broach. He thought of how matters stood with himself, all the freedoms he might yet live to relish. Could he do some other sort of work? Must he feel lousy about himself for ever? He could probably meet a girl, a lady. He could still attract females. He would like to figure out who pulled the levers that made society tick, made people jump. Marcel had posted himself at Philippe's paper pile from where he watched Marseille work. Philippe stared straight ahead. Earlier Marseille had said he saw ghosts. Maybe that was true. Sometimes he was so deathly serious it gave you a jolt.

Luigi had tried his very best but gradually the talking had died. Maybe he wasn't a talker and maybe they didn't all like the same subjects. First the peasant, then the Lusitanian, had left him just sitting there. And what earthly subject might he ever raise with the Englishman? Unimaginable. Besides, butchers needn't talk all the time, need they? With ageing clients: greetings, weather, where their fucking children are at, etc. With kids and juveniles: music and film. With the in-betweens: 'Hi, see the match? Really? Amazing! Me? Well, I missed it.' After the Englishman had upped and left, Luigi sat a while watching his cigarette, studying the way it burned, the maize paper turning darker like a scar circling the red-grey tip. It was time he went. He made his way back, past the pallets, a few metres further, barely a minute's walk, with legs as lanky as his. The chef was at his machine, leaning against the guard. Maybe he'd been there all the time, eating matches and waiting. Excluding the minute he had spent telling us the Gypsies had decided they'd strike if we did. Because that's what it means. That's definitely the way management will see it.

December 1988, Ardèche. Cold bright Sunday morning, lunch almost ready, his wife in the kitchen, three children in the yard (two were his!) with bats and balls and a chuckling grandfather, Fernando washing his car, buffing it to a sheen, showing a little fat round the middle these days, his breath coming quickly, whistling an Abba tune featuring his name, recalling a workmate from back when times were harder, before life suddenly went right. Funny the things you think of. A blow, almost gentle at first, starting in the chest, fanning to the neck, breaking his breath. Lurching, letting the cloths fall, sliding against the car's flank, unable to call out, stretched on the tarmac – he'd laid that himself, done a neat job – waiting for someone. Soon they would come. Today would not be the day. He wasn't going to die. He could hear birds singing. He was not alone. Funny your thoughts when you lie dying. Not that he was dying. Not that I am. But won't somebody walk by? Why does no one walk by? His daughter was looking down now, fear on her face, understanding something. Fernando mouthed the words, Meu amor, não me sinto bem. Escusa . . .

Sarah was expecting her daddy's voice.

You said you couldn't phone me.

I'm not supposed to. I was thinking of you.

Tell me where you are, what you're doing. I want to understand. Are you surrounded by those people?

Tomec described the workshop, the light, the bench.

Well, I'm standing on *your* towel, Sarah said, trampling *your* seed. Do you love me?

She had blurted it out in a false voice, sounding like Estella preparing to torment Pip.

There was a long silence.

She sighed, wanting to put the phone down.

I've never wanted anybody so much. I want to hold you, be inside you, hear your endless speeches. I want you to take me again and again by the scruff of the neck and force me between your legs like you did this afternoon, like boys playing at ducking one another in the river. I have a passion for you. But love? Love? Most of the time I think I don't even like you.

Ah!

Silence.

I didn't . . .

Don't apologize. I'm so used to being loved.

I know.

Do you think I've been spoiled with too much love?

No.

You don't love me.

No. But perhaps I will.

Silence.

Maybe you have said the right thing to make me stay.

I'm not interested in saying the right thing. But I do want you to stay.

I don't think I want to see you tomorrow.

If you're not there, I'll miss you.

Me too. I love you.

Me too.

I knew it anyway.

Silence.

I'd like to fuck you now.

I don't like your words.

Then let me hear yours.

Silence.
Till tomorrow then maybe.

Jean hit the button. The mould closed. He waited. It opened. Global competition was on his mind – always savage in times of slump. Employees should unite to pull as one – instead of indulging in divisive stoppages! He tossed the cable ties into the box. He would do his bit. Could he enhance his efficiency somehow? He had ample time to think while he waited. He could shut the machine down a few minutes late, say at 4.50 . . . He analysed his actions in detail. Mould opens. Left hand slides back. Then pull cable ties off mould, dump saleable bit in box and useless chaff in bin. I push machine shut. The way I've always done it. The way we all do it. But wait . . . Hey! What if I shut the machine and hit the button the second I take the ties and, while I wait, pull the ties off and sling them into the box . . . how many seconds could that save? One? Two? He'd use his own stopwatch, given him by Ninique. He would study his motions against time. If he shaved two seconds off each cycle, how many cable ties would that make each shift? He would do the maths.

Bobrán meditated upon the life that chance or fate had given him to lead: here he continued, a quiet man, a peaceable man, craving nothing more than to remain at home alone or with one particular friend and lover, neither meddling in the life of other people nor attempting to rock any boat. Yet trouble infallibly found him out. Bobrán thought about heaven, wondering how quiet it might be, and hoping God might grant him admittance, forgiving every wicked action he had ever committed. He felt certain that God-in-heaven would drop the hard-bitten exterior He generally wore upon earth and waive the rulebook. But what if God demanded even purer behaviour in heaven? Then could He not provide a little help and encouragement? Up there, Bobrán thought, might I not in fact be healed of my love of men? Maybe God Omnipotent would turn Moritz into a woman and let me love him in that new form. A better me would emerge – perfected for heaven. At the notion of a feminized Moritz, a mountain of gloom fell upon Bobrán. He longed to feel pain, but had no idea how to procure it. He longed to atone for being alive.

Eric was yearning for a less radical change, one he could pursue unaided by any paranormal or divine beings: he foresaw a day when finally he would have acquired by his own endeavours every piece and principle of a new mind and manner, affording him a sense of his self and surroundings a million miles from his despised English middle-class origins. Such a change could never begin – scarce even proceed – from his own echoingly void being or mind: wholesale robbery from several sources would be necessary. Like some fussy jackdaw he would chase down each edifying prey, loading upon his shoulders every skill, dodge and granule of knowledge whose possession he so signally lacked: smoke rings, charisma and French-casual dress from Philippe; sullen cool from Rachid; elegance in speech and accessories from Alphonse; non-chalance from Bobrán; insolence from Marcel; insouciance from Jacques; indifference from jazz-musician foreman; and from Fanny – Gallic passion, sexual legerdemain, even romance. Romance – the very concept had pre-viously curled his English lip – now, he reasoned, sensing his burgeoning French lip as squarely aligned as ever – should and could be his, purged of any Mills-and-Boon shame. He closed his eyes and conjured Fanny's body naked alongside his.

Tomec set off to comb the factory for trespassers, his artistic aims distilling in the half-light. Taking fragments of people and lives he had known, he had to find rhythm, pattern, honesty, casting men and women as characters, not actors. These fragments had to cohere, giving the work a clear earthly ethic and aesthetic.

July 1965, Drôme. Jacques saw her as he rounded a bend. Straw-haired, angular, a knapsack at her feet, a thumb in midair. It didn't occur to him not to stop. She got in, spoke little, then nodded off. Jacques stared at the snaking road, its asphalt mirages doggedly outpacing him. At each gear-change, inches from his right hand, he glimpsed a patch of thigh with sunlit blond hairs. Jacques relaxed, happy she was there. After about twenty minutes, without any planning, his right hand lifted from the shift-stick and fell with a gentle squeeze on her thigh. She let out a cry and Jacques replaced his hand on the steering wheel. He was appalled by the terror he saw on her face. Sorry, he stammered, I didn't mean anything. But his fingertips had possessed the secret of her skin, springy and warm to the touch. Sitting almost sideways now, knees to the passenger door, she hugged her knapsack to her tummy. Let me out, she whispered. Jacques stared at the empty road ahead, the scorching plateau. She wasn't carrying any water, and wasn't likely to take his. It was no place to drop a girl. Anything could happen to her.

Marcel felt relieved to see the men dribbling back onto the shop floor, their meeting presumably finished, first Marseille – looking oddly sober – next the Sicilian, the Arab slinking past, then the peasant and the Brit almost together, finally that Italian face-ache, looking sly and mean like he'd been jerking off. Marcel didn't like to be left alone in the section, hated to imagine the consequences of anybody's property going missing – blame had to fall first and last on the Gypsy ex-con – forever suspect, forever the outsider: that summed up his fate. No use complaining, prison had been the same: hanging out at the edge, peering in. Never consulted, never confided in. Informed, if lucky, of decisions others had reached. Even Bobrán never gave him a full story. Meeting Chantal, things had changed. His proposal had been a masterstroke. The line he'd fed her about having a baby some day. She realized she meant more to me than a great lay. She'd already said she didn't fancy kids. God! the thought of a flabby belly and loose cunt! It's alright if you're hung like a mule, but if you're proportioned at all normally, you're bound to end up feeling small. Fuck that.

Philippe and Jacques pulled up wooden crates at the drinks machines and bought coffees.

> Your wife's cheating on you . . .
> You get to the point . . . Why don't you find yourself a male doctor?
> Your sister found out . . .
> A man would understand. Tell him you're not through screwing yet . . .
> Do you know one?
> Down here?
> Jacques nodded.
> They shut in the evenings. Try locally. Ask at the pharmacy.
> Jacques pictured the pharmacist's face.
> So what are you going to do? Jacques asked.
> I've thought of killing her with contempt . . .
> Too slow?
> Philippe nodded and looked away.
> Jacques put his coffee down and pulled his crate closer to his friend.
> Take a hold. Don't drift. Don't make your peace with unhappiness.
Life's brief and you're free.

Have you been reading Sartre?

Sartre? Do I need to?

Clearly not.

You're taking the piss . . .

Philippe raised his eyebrows.

And another thing . . .

Philippe turned a weary face to his friend.

Find yourself a woman to love – or at least to take to bed. You won't feel better till you do. For yourself. Don't tell your wife, just do it. For the sake of your pride. As a man.

I don't need that.

Oh yes you do.

At machine eight, having checked the latest product clattering through the aluminium slats, Rachid emptied the floor bin into the knee-high tub, then trapped the tub between the tops of his thighs and the machine flank, making it easier to thresh the pieces. He recalled the feast he had arranged a week after Mehdi's birth, a glorious affair lasting half the night, most fitting for a firstborn. After Fatima's Caesarian birth, Malika had been too weak and upset to celebrate. This time he would plan something magnificent. Moving on to machine nine, he checked the hopper level before doing the threshing. If he could just sneak out of a window – home was a four-minute walk – astonish Malika, make love to her, then sprint back like the athlete he'd been when he'd first known her. If there was someone to look after his machines like the Marseillais looked after the peasant's, the foreman would ask no questions and the nightwatchman would never notice. Malika would no doubt leap at the intruder's throat as the bedroom door creaked open, but then she'd clasp him to her breast and he'd weep tears of happiness. Much better than tramping home exhausted in the morning.

The union meeting had reached a unanimous decision: to undertake industrial action comprising fornightly half-hour shutdowns, in opposition to the austerity plan promoted by the government of M. Raymond Barre; in coordination with other Établissements Boucan workshops; under the direction of the regional CGT-CFDT-FO federations; in compliance with the civil law code.

The meeting had discussed data on plant-wide wage differentials, highlighting the low wages received by night-shift operatives; it was noted that both temporary-agency workers had been informed by M. Petit (supervisor) that on safety grounds they would need to shut down their machines during scheduled stoppages.

With the exception of the Ivorian, all the workers had returned to their allotted machines, where the extraction of surplus value was proceeding with the discretion and efficiency of blood transfusion.

Alphonse, having wandered through metallurgy, had resolved to speak again to the Algerian. However, on striding through the scratched plastic flaps marking the entrance to the plastics section, he observed the foreman step from the lift. Seated at the end of the machine aisle, Rachid watched him dither. The foreman removed a matchstick from his mouth and jerked it silently upward, upon which Alphonse turned on his heels and headed for the stairs.

52. Envy, Self-Denial and Regrets.

Bending low and squeezing the tub between his tensed thighs and the battleship flank of his machine six, Salvatore threshed hard, forcing the product from the sprue in a whir of gloved hands and crashing, cleaving plastic. On his way back from the meetings room, he had halted at Philippe's pile of papers to pick up *L'Humanité*, which he had held open before him as he strolled down the machine aisle, attempting discreetly to relax his legs, lower his shoulders and impart something of a swing to his overall carriage. Confronted with such confidence and sobriety, nobody could possibly think to address him by either voice or glance. He waded through the din and glare as through treacle-dark silence. Referring to parliamentary by-elections fixed for Sunday 14 November, the front-page headline simultaneously reported and issued a rallying call to voters: 'À vous qui avez tant de mal à vivre, le parti communiste lance un appel.'* Salvatore absorbed the first few lines of text: 'Vous êtes de ces millions et millions de Français et Françaises qui connaissent aujourd'hui de graves difficultés d'existence. La vie chère mange votre salaire insuffisant. Chaque mois, vous vous demandez comment vous allez boucler le budget familial . . .'** The Sicilian had placed the paper on his chair and donned his gloves for work. Straightening up now to remove sprue from the tub, he considered with satisfaction the outcome of the meeting he had just chaired: he had secured the vote in favour of industrial action; he had provided patient and firm leadership while dutifully soliciting questions and comments; those who might have wished for more militant action – the African, the Arab and perhaps the Marseillais (for who might ever guess at that man's mind?) – had been isolated and would cause no further immediate trouble; as for the foreman's surprise intervention, the ensuing distraction could not have been avoided or mitigated by any conceivable action he might have taken. In short, he had done everything right. As Salvatore dropped the sprue into the adjacent bin, his eyes alighted again on *L'Humanité*: 'there but for fortune,' he thought, as if to ward off the goblins of ill luck. In truth, the newspaper's miserabilism left him unmoved: he could not imagine that with all his talents and opportunities, not to mention the openings he was engineering for

* 'To you who are finding life a struggle, the Communist Party launches an appeal.'

** 'You are one of the millions and millions of French men and women who today face grave hardship. The high cost of living is eating up your meagre income. Each month you wonder how your family will make ends meet.'

himself in diverse segments of French society, he might ever represent the party's intended audience of low-paid or jobless supporters-cum-supplicants. In whatever company he moved, it took only a glance at encircling humanity to confirm his distinction and superiority. Not just chez Boucan or at the university, amid (respectively) social misfits and the lazily mediocre, but even, to his recent surprise and elucidation, among Laure's well-groomed and fragrant friends: the moment when Laure and they had risen as a cohort from the table and crept beneath the folds of an opulent curtain to spy on the alleyway commerce of a common prostitute and her momentary client would surely remain stamped in his memory as a marker of his ethical distinction. He tipped the tub of swirling product into the cardboard box behind him and bent to catch the latest piece as it racketed through the aluminium slats. Climbing the stepladder to check his machine six's hopper level, soaring over the machinery to a position of enhanced visibility, he straightened his limbs and furrowed his brow. He caught sight of the big Gypsy idly chewing gum. Idly? Could gum be chewed any other way? He began to recall their conversation that evening, which had introduced to him the philanderer's notion of 'spare pussy,' but he chased the memory from his mind. Life would always present patches of uncertain terrain with crevices and cracks through which one might accidentally – or even at first voluptuously – slip. One could not take too much evasive action. The dramatic case of the tennis-club couple sprang to mind. Salvatore had fielded their stray balls from the neighbouring court, imagined their enviably gilded lives, admired that mixed-doubles easy foursome intimacy. Only now was it evident that the man from the one marriage bed and the woman from the other had always been fated to rattle loose from their dull spouses and spectacularly to collide. Salvatore flipped the hopper lid shut and descended the steps, then went to thresh at his machine seven. As he squeezed the tub and plunged his arms into the tangle of products, beginning to thresh and grind, he surrendered to a sensation of uneasiness regarding his fiancée. Laure was surely perfect in every way, yet she began to bore him. How so? he wondered, offended by the notion. It was not in their conversations or on their evenings out that she became tedious: it was in bed. He blamed himself. Yet he was not especially choosy or demanding. Perhaps the Gypsy's debauched talk of wedding as a final shackle and of last-minute flings and infidelities had affected him, against his better judgement. He shouldn't have listened, but how do you silence a man like that? Obscenities were in any case irresistible: you could no more stop your ears than you can look away at a road accident. It was on sound rational grounds that Salvatore had decided that Laure would have to do: she was as good as any other, probably better than most, and he didn't want to be alone any longer. He had long ago grasped the fact that the troubles that came with living with a girlfriend or wife were substantially less time-consuming and more tractable than those you face alone: the performance of housework, the procurement of sexual relief; the avoidance of loneliness. Was this a bout of pre-wedding nerves? A date hadn't even been fixed. His greatest misgiving about Laure – since he was in the mood to be honest with himself – was that Laure, unlike all his previous girlfriends – oh, it was nothing really, scarcely worth mentioning – had never developed any kind of penchant – any kind of taste, one might say – for bestowing upon him a thorough, whistle-clean, ding-dong – what was the correct term? – 'fellation,' damn it. She had volunteered once and he, feigning indifference, had cautiously accepted, washed himself thoroughly, rinsed the soap away nicely – a delicate touch, he had thought – and prostrated himself to her whim. Sipping a peppermint cordial after the deed was done, she told him she had read in a magazine that 'une pipe' was something for which men were known universally to pine and which she had accordingly been curious to try out – as a token of her love. While preparing to perform the act, however, Laure had let out an enormous sigh before making her approach rather in the manner of a fairground contortionist, for even while her mouth negotiated the morsel she somehow contrived to hold it at arm's length, and only ever really touched it with the tip of her tongue. After a minute or two of fussing (a duration which to her beloved seemed unending), she had coughed slightly, drawn back, pulled a face, picked a pubic hair from her lower lip, then rushed off to brush her teeth, enquiring from the bathroom whether he had enjoyed it. Salvatore had lied and then lied again by saying it really didn't matter and finally stated the sincerest truth by declaring that he didn't care if she never sucked the thing again. Irrespective of this setback, Laure remained an attractive young woman and a fine catch in every way. Salvatore smiled to recall the last occasion, only three Sundays previously, that they had encountered the tennis-club couples playing in the court adjoining their own. The very man who, unbeknownst to them all, was so soon to die, had fluffed a lob, sending it into their court to fall at Laure's feet. As Laure returned the ball to him smartly, the reckless libertine had glanced up the court at Salvatore and smirked. By masculine instinct, Salvatore had grasped the meaning of the memorable look: what kind of man gets to fuck that kind of woman? Salvatore had experienced a warm flush of pride in ownership. It shocked him now to think, as he hoisted a tangle of product-free sprue, that the deceased adulterers were perhaps, in that celebrated overall scheme of things, to be exalted with envy while their hornéd survivors were to be cast down in pity: clearly, the intensity of the illicit pleasures tasted by the marriage-breakers had been worth violent death to at least one of them. As Laure had returned 'post-*pipe*' to bed that time, her breath freshened, her cordial drained, her explanation tendered and accepted, Salvatore and she had executed a swift and vigorous coupling, after which she had petted him to sleep, cooing sweet words: que t'es beau! que t'es bon! que je t'aime! If such blandishments appeared strangely familiar to his receding consciousness, it was because they had once been lavished upon him by his mother: che beddro picciliddro! che buono che sei! quanto ti amo! He had never before wished the two women to meet and now that he began to perceive their startling congruence it was surely too late. If he could but glimpse the two women side by side, frame them in a single eyeful, might he not unravel some personal riddle and perhaps save himself from making a vital mistake? Wiping his brow, he poured the products into the cardboard box at his back and sat down. Soon he would have to make the train journey home to Sicily. He hoped he wouldn't arrive too late. He wondered what it might be like to kiss his mother's cold forehead. Vito would be there of course, and Gianni would presumably fly in from Toronto, Elena from Norway and Berto from Antwerp. They would talk of their distant lives, photos would circulate, then they would go their separate ways. Theirs had never been a close family. Their father had seen to that. Salvatore could not recall ever having kissed a corpse in a coffin – or indeed anywhere else. Just how cold would the skin feel against his lips? He hoped he wouldn't cry. He would steel himself. Could he be alone with the body? He might sit all night with it and talk. He would pretend his mother could hear him. She had never listened to him for very long. She had been content to mutter sweet nothings and to massacre him with kisses and hug him till he gagged; but the instant he started talking she would shrug and yawn and walk away. His earliest memory was of his mother's retreating back and tiptoeing feet, as she cut him down in the prime of a thought, his mouth gaping, his sentence dangling. It would be good to talk to her all night. He could pretend she was interested. He might tell her about Laure. But that wouldn't take long.

↔↔↔↔↔↔

Bruno and Chantal were lying back to back. Are you asleep? Chantal whispered. Bruno breathed heavily. Chantal waited a few moments longer then got out of bed, gathering her clothes and bag from the floor, and went to the bathroom. Sitting on the toilet, she wrote him a note. She told him she had had a wonderful evening and that she would miss him and think of him sometimes in the months and years to come. This seemed a rather cold way of saying goodbye forever and she considered tearing up the note and starting again, but then decided it was all right after all. What more was there to say? 'Avec tendresse,' she wrote at the bottom. She capped the biro and put it back in her bag. She felt that any kind of signature would be redundant, so she left it at that. She slipped the note beneath Bruno's toiletry bag, washed, dressed, and returned to the bedroom to rummage for her shoes at the foot of the bed where she recalled heatedly kicking them off. She thought back to the moment Bruno had emerged from the bathroom, dropped his towel and fallen to his knees between her legs. She had reached her hands down, her fingers in her public hair, pushing down to bring her clitoris up as his mouth had closed over it and he had begun to lap. She had relaxed back and thought of Marcel, the way he'd fucked her slowly into wakefulness that morning. For the first time perhaps she felt true love for a man. But she'd miss her Belgian. She was missing him already. She felt her orgasm closing in. Then he'd climbed up over her, filling her. Yes, Bruno had been fun. He had been good. A dainty morcel. Un très bon coup. Charming too. She found her second shoe at last. Bruno stirred and for a moment Chantal remained bent double, immobile, holding her breath. She heard him turn over and whimper slightly. He might be having a bad dream. It was best to leave them, wasn't it? In a sudden hurry to get away, Chantal grappled her shoes to her side and let herself out of the room.

↔↔↔↔↔↔

However enigmatic Bobrán appeared to others, even to those who might have known him well, there were still two true things that could be said about him without fear of error, let alone contradiction, and the first of these was that he possessed a natural and unreflective urge toward altruism or – to be more precise – toward self-denial: for it was not that he particularly favoured others, it was rather that he acted automatically as if he were always already beholden to them, his own interests and desires being naturally subordinate to theirs.

Thus it was that even as a small child, though as sensitive to cold and hunger as the next person, Bobrán would happily give up his jacket or forgo his portion of bread or soup for any passing stranger, whether adult or child, human or animal.

Later, when confronted with the choice between acting in his sister's interest to destroy a lethal threat to her life or in his own by shirking decisive action and thus eluding the lifelong status of assassin, he had chosen safety for his sister and ignominy for himself.

Now again, with the same self-denying reflex regnant, his path was clear. Albert Gbenye and his family 'needed' to know the truth of Joseph's death, perfectly unaware that its discovery was likely to draw the wrath of the corrupt and powerful down upon the one man in France who had befriended Joseph when alive. Bobrán could speak out or remain silent, help others or protect himself: there was no contest.

The second true thing to be said of Bobrán is that he found his thoughts unruly, his memories mostly unwelcome, his desires often inexpressible, the general run of his feelings so overwhelming that he sensed a mental pressure producing a loss of control over the contents and workings of his own mind. As if to compensate, he had other moments of great torpor, when he felt himself dull and his life flat. Whereas he had never developed any treatment for sensations of emptiness, he had by his early teens found a way of relieving the pressure of super-abundant thoughts, memories and emotions: the self-administration of pain.

By the age of eight, Bobrán had discovered that if he took a fold of skin on forearm or thigh between index and thumb, then pinched and twisted hard, the resulting pain opened a sluice beneath his mind permitting the rapid evacuation of mental lumber. This simple and discreet procedure afforded focus and comfort. He felt he was back in control. When he was twelve, he found that knives with serrated edges worked better than bare hands, and that it was rarely necessary to draw much blood.

In his late teens, Bobrán's private method for checking and briefly diverting his consciousness reached its definitive stage of development as he eschewed pain in favour of danger. From now on, whenever the thread of his mind became frayed and its braiding hard to untangle, his thoughts too jumbled, his feelings hectic, the little Gypsy would engage in some acrobatic or daredevil activity – preferably in public – that placed him in a degree of danger sufficient to simplify his mind by bringing it to bear upon a single shifting point.

His most reckless feat to date had been to walk across the longest river bridge in Grandgobier by its metal handrail. It had not rained, the air was still and he wore his best plimsolls. However, because it was summer and the riverbed was almost dry, he risked not a ducking – bad enough, since he could not swim – but certain death. The traffic stopped, a crowd gathered, and an enterprising radio journalist managed to 'commentate' the concluding moments of the happening from the telephone of a riverside bar.

As Bobrán's shoes touched the safety of the pavement and he ran from the small and babbling crowd, the anguish that had tormented him since being jilted by the first man for whom he had ever conceived a passionate attachment gently lifted and a smile crept over his face. This last detail astonished him so much that he raised the fingers of his right hand to his mouth to make quite sure. Whereupon the smile turned to laughter: it was only then he was sure he had survived.

↔↔↔↔↔

Alphonse strode down the middle of the ground-floor machine aisle toward the Algerian, who was seated in a fog of his own smoke, out of which, his eyes screwed almost shut, he peered at the approaching African. At the office end of the aisle, Mathieu had halted Alphonse with an interrogative look, removing the matchstick from his mouth, ready to speak but saying nothing.

My machines are fine, Alphonse said. I've got to talk to the Arab.

Mathieu nodded and stood aside.

Rachid didn't look surprised. He watched Alphonse walk toward him. Then he rose and went to the hopper end of his machine eight, dragging the chair to the stepladder so the two men could sit in near privacy.

I was watching you during the meeting, Alphonse said as he sat down. There's something not right, isn't there? If you tell me it's none of my business, I'll vanish.

Really? How do you do that?

What?

Vanish.

Alphonse smiled uncertainly.

I'm an actor, a performer of a kind, Alphonse said. I do make-believe.

I can't explain how I feel when I see people looking like you did in that meeting. Something was eating you from the inside out. I'm always looking at people, that's what I do. Besides, you were talking to yourself.

So? Look around. Rachid glanced up at the ceiling.

Sure. We all talk to ourselves. Especially on our own at four in the morning. But you were chatting away in the middle of a union meeting. Well before midnight.

I was talking to the dead.

That's all right then.

Rachid felt Alphonse's eyes staring hard.

I can wait, Alphonse told himself. I can be patient.

Rachid took a decision. He turned round slightly in his chair to poke his bony fingers into the breast pocket of his jacket. He pulled out Malika's note and handed it to the Ivorian.

This is private, Alphonse remarked.

So don't read it.

When did you receive it?

I found it in that pocket this evening.

While Alphonse read, Rachid looked up along the machine aisle. Luigi was standing at the end of his machine fourteen. Marcel was talking to Eric. Philippe and Jacques pushed through the plastic flaps from the raw-materials area, chatting and joking.

Alphonse folded Malika's note and handed it back to Rachid.

It's fantastic, isn't it? A child! A baby! Isn't it wonderful? Alphonse beamed.

Rachid was startled. He hadn't known how to assess the news, certainly couldn't act on it till someone else told him how. He now produced an expression that Alphonse had never seen on the Algerian's face: pure defenceless joy, with no side to it, no squint, nothing held back. Alphonse wanted to clap him on the back.

A few minutes ago I was thinking of breaking a window, climbing out, shinning over the wall and running home to hug my wife. But I wasn't sure.

Alphonse narrowed his eyes and leaned closer to the Algerian.

Do you want me to organize something?

What like? I mean . . . Here?

Sure. A drink at least. Do you remember the foreman's sixtieth? We could at least get some beers. It's only an idea. Someone could say something. Make an announcement.

Rachid looked up the aisle and saw Marcel and then Philippe.

Well, I can't sit here all night as if nothing's happened. I'd end up climbing out that window.

This probably isn't the best moment to lose your job.

No.

I'll see what the chef says.

↔→↔→↔→↔→↔

Seven seals, angels, churches, plagues: Angela was weary of reading. She put her Bible down on the table. She could hear Gilberte snoring. Perhaps that was why Luigi worked nights. Fat people snored. Angela was thin. The right woman would never have flung herself at him like a Jezebel. She would have made him wait.

*

Ricky had woken thirsty, gone for water and seen Angelica's note. He tore it in two and threw it in the bin, then pulled on some clothes, resolving to find her and bring her back. Near the door he saw her key on the floor, looking bare without its ring. He kicked it into a corner, went to the kitchen and swept all the glasses and dishes from the drainer and the shelves onto the floor. Some of them didn't break. He wanted to stamp on them but hadn't got his boots on. He punched a wall, then nursed his fist, surprised how much it hurt. He retrieved the note from the bin and reassembled it. 'Please don't follow me. I did love you once. Hold on to that.' *Hold on to that!* After everything he'd done for her: taken her in, helped her find work, taught her Swedish, really loved her. He'd even apologized and said he regretted hitting her. Anyway, she'd overreacted. He found her key and clenched it in his hand. She might be at Rosa's. His knuckles hurt. He sat against the door and began to rock. 'I loved you, you stupid cow,' he said.

*

Luc was wondering how to tell Richard Müller, his patient employer, that he wouldn't be returning to work. Müller was not going to understand. Nor were Luc's parents or friends. You don't abandon a promising career as an architect because of a passing tragedy. You don't just drop out, they'd say. Besides, what other qualifications did he have? What else could he do? Luc felt he'd been sleepwalking, blind until the accident, living without a care or a thought. His eyes had been opened. People might say he was in shock or depressed or grieving. None of that was true. He could not allow events to be as random as Mehdi's father had implied. It had not been a car or a truck or 'some other young man on a moped': it had been he, Luc, singled out by a thing, a force, that felt very like fate. It had to mean something. He couldn't be an unwitting instrument of slaughter one day and return to designing houses the next. He had to work this out. If necessary, he would withdraw from the world for a while: the truth had to be out there. What could matter more? Of all things, architecture now seemed to Luc the most petty and the most arrogant. The way architects played God! – Müller's hero, Le Corbusier, no less than others – stretching down their fingers, creating nice little spaces in which their creatures can eat, sleep and multiply. How could he, Luc, ever take himself seriously when the real God had singled him out and hurled him at a child? What did God want of him? And whose God? His or Mehdi's?

*

Claude snatched the mask from her face and sat up in the dark, her eyes opening wide. She wished she hadn't pretended to be asleep earlier: she hated deception. She hadn't wanted to hear his troubles, nor to be 'made love to,' supposing, as occasionally still happened, the mood took him. Gérard had lost all real interest in her after Paul was born, not even listening to her when she spoke. He must have thought a child was all she needed. For years she'd hoped his affections would return once Paul was older, but they never did. Sometimes he would come home drunk and apologetic and fumble and prod at her pathetically. She would be patient and grateful, willing their 'life together' to restart properly. To her astonishment, he sometimes accused her of having grown cold and distant. Gradually she had moved beyond sadness and regret: she was thinking she might have him followed. He had been such a goat in his youth she was sure he must have a mistress somewhere. There would be no going back, no forgive-and-forget. She would be settled comfortably. Paul was old enough to understand. She didn't want Gérard anywhere near her any longer.

*

Émile was standing talking to Samuel, ringed by other draftees. They had barely half an hour to go . . . to *Zéro* hour. He had lost sight of the crop-haired blonde. The student type who had talked to them seemed to be following her, but you could tell they weren't together. Émile regretted his shyness. He should have spoken.

*

It was almost half past ten in England. Betty was writing an airmail letter to her 'Auntie Peg in Canada.' She had written a page about gardening – a topic of infinite interest to both women – and had little room left to answer Peg's 'kind questions' about her children. She reported Jilly's promotion and then took a deep breath. 'I don't know if it's something I did or failed to do but I feel we took a wrong turn with Eric somewhere. But, yes, we *do* write. Well, *I* write. Eric phones occasionally. When he does write, his letters are very interesting but I'm not always sure he remembers who he's writing to. When he's home he sneers about our comfortable lives. He calls us "bourgeois" as if we didn't know what that meant. Last time we spoke, he said he'd been "cooped up by that island far too long." Perhaps, in Canada, you can understand that, but I've never lived anywhere else. I don't begrudge him his freedom. If I'd grown up in the sixties, my life would surely be different: for a start, I might not have children! Do you think that ever? Mostly, I just miss my little boy.'

*

Yvonne Labarde regretted messing up her schooling. For years her half-brother beat her with a stick most evenings to make her study. Every night she prayed he would die. He said she was clever and could make something of herself if she wasn't so lazy. At twelve she realized he would never be happy with anything she did so she gave up trying. At seventeen she left school and started chez Boucan. She met Bernard and moved straight in with him. Nine years passed. Now, in bed, she foresaw the boredom the following afternoon would bring, the extinction of thought, the humiliation of having nothing interesting to do and of being constrained to semi-idleness for hours on end. Day-shift supervisors insisted you remained close to your machines, didn't talk, read or play cards. Some of them were younger than her, had worked there less long, had been promoted for nothing more than their ability to lick boots. She snuggled up to Bernard, comforted by his snoring. So far in life she had done everything wrong. Bernard too was wrong for her. He was kind, faithful, patient, generous, faultless. He deserved her love. All Yvonne really owned was her dreams.

53. Interruption . . . Preparation.

Interruption.   Mathieu was leaning against the safety guard of Alphonse's machine eighteen. The Ivorian had vanished again, leaving the tub brimming with sprue and machine nineteen short of raw material. Mathieu heaved back the guard. He brought the product up close. Searching for tiny defects, he considered the fact that adrenalin might just fail to kill Nadine even if he could get hold of any, and heroin had to be administered intravenously. Wouldn't that leave a trace? Who could he ask? Maybe medics had an inevitable monopoly on mercy-killing. Maybe he'd have to practise injecting himself. (No! Nadine shouted, heaving herself sphinx-like onto her forearms. No!)

Alphonse was at Mathieu's elbow.

Chef?

Just wait.

Mathieu looked at the piece from every angle, then hurled it into the floor tray.

Did you come to do some work?

Could we stop the machines and raise a glass – like for your birthday?

What the hell?

Could we . . . ?

Jesus! In whose honour?

Rachid just found out his wife's pregnant.

Happens every day.

Alphonse hung his head.

Mathieu took the burnt-out matchstick from his mouth and looked at it, blinking, then walked to the control cabinet to face the dials. (Nadine, discernibly pregnant, wits flown, head shorn, the first time he saw her. When she miscarried they had grieved for some Nazi rapist's baby and she had never conceived again.)

You know about his son . . .

Mathieu spun round, glaring at Alphonse. He waved his claw at the tub and his right hand at the hopper. He glanced at his wristwatch.

Does the Algerian want this?

Yes.

We'll shut down at 23.25.

But that's . . .

For five minutes. No longer.

Daily. Chuck was shouting into the bar phone. That morning a faculty secretary had given him a message. His brother was in Europe. Chuck had to phone a Paris number after eleven.

Why don't you come home? Bill was asking.

'Why don't you come home?' Chuck whined.

You said you'd come back when Nixon was gone. Now even Ford's gone. Is it a woman?

Oh, sure. I'm looking at her. Want a description?

Shoot.

Chuck had a side view of Julie.

She's well-stacked but not what you'd have to call pretty. Jaws and nose too heavy. Sometimes she's beautiful, sometimes she's ugly. She has a friend called Fanny – no, really! – who's pretty all the time, in a bland kind of way. Right now, most men would probably rather take Fanny to bed, but for the long term you'd want to wake up next to Julie. I can see them both in sepia, you know? In twenty years Fanny will turn unfailingly into a pudding, whereas Julie will be ugly some days and beautiful others, just like now.

Chuck had listened to his last couple of sentences as if on echo. He didn't like his sound. It wasn't his voice. He was stuck in the wrong shape and couldn't wriggle free. He wanted to say something pleasant.

It's good talking to you, Bill. How're things?

I'm fine, Chuck. Just wish I could see you.

Sure.

You could introduce me to your girl.

Yuh.

Just think about coming home. Please.

What would I do back in the States? I've gotten so old so young. I'm not fit for life any more. Not the life the US throws at you daily.

Angles. Luigi was chewing over something the black guy had said toward the end of the union meeting – that since people had fought hard for the democratic right to strike it would be disrespectful not to use it now that we had it and that it needed to be exercised regularly to demonstrate it still worked. Then he'd said that striking was illegal in lots of countries. Luigi had said that lots of countries had nothing to do with anything and the Portuguee had agreed.

Luigi sucked hard to revive his Gitanes Maïs. The Sicilian was walking up the machine aisle, wearing his look of deathly seriousness.

Salvatore wanted to be told he'd managed the meeting well, but couldn't ask.

The meeting went okay, didn't it?

Luigi looked worried.

But we don't want to stick our necks out, he said. We don't want a name as the most militant bit of the factory.

There's no danger of that.

Striking's our democratic right, I guess.

Salvatore wanted to pat Luigi on the head.

That's the way I see it too, he said.

You've got to look at a thing from every angle, Luigi said. You can never see it right the very first time, can you?

Control.   To what extent can you vary the steps involved in doing your job? To what extent [henceforth: TWE] can you move from your immediate working area during work hours? TWE can you control how much work you produce? TWE can you help decide on methods and procedures used in your job? TWE do you have influence over the things that happen to you at work? TWE can you do your work ahead and take a short rest break during work hours? TWE are you free from close supervision while doing your job? TWE can you increase or decrease the speed at which you work?

'Powerlessness Scale' from Jon M. Shepard, *Automation and Alienation*, The MIT Press, 1971.

Tuna.   Marcel had just topped up his hoppers eleven and twelve and was glad to have his feet back on the ground. He removed his gloves and smoothed down his lime-green shirt front, picking recycled fluff from the cuffs. He took his lighter and cigarette pack from the top of the control cabinet, moving to the aisle-end of machine eleven, lodging a cigarette in his mouth. Close by, the two Italians leaned together as doleful as undertakers' mutes, but Marcel was relieved he was no longer alone on the shop floor. Looking around, he felt boredom lapping at his eyes. There was nothing to do, nothing to think, not a lot of 'traffic' to observe. Maybe he'd take another look through Philippe's papers, check out that picture of Concorde. He was sure it looked nothing like a cock. Dumb Polack. Dumber African for laughing. He'd rushed past in a lather, asking where the chef was, while I was teetering on the top step, tipping a tub into the hopper. Damn near lost my foothold. My head spun. Fuck knows! I yelled. Nothing now till our one a.m. meal break. Tuna tonight. Then three and a half hours more. Home to Chantal. Tomorrow afternoon I'll see Paulette. Just to tell her. She must know it's coming. If we fuck first, she'll cry more. Might get resentful. I'll tell her immediately. She'll start crying, reach for my fly and I'll say it won't make any difference and she'll say she knows and I'll surrender gracefully. That's how it'll go. I've known her too long for her to surprise me. I'll miss her. It'll be just fine.

Smiles. Most of the men on the plastics-section night shift possessed a broad repertory of smile-types, yet each man had a clear propensity for one particular type. Jacques, for example – as has already been noted – had a wide-angled all-blandishing smile as his default expression. Salvatore's smile, by contrast, was administered mostly as a reward or encouragement. Eric smiled, it seemed, mainly to disarm: 'I'm innocuous, honest . . .' his smile seemed to declare. Rachid's smile was rarely anything but private and, if accompanied by a direct glance at someone or an explicit greeting, appeared fleetingly to admit his interlocutor into that well-guarded privacy. Alphonse's smile was highly singular yet conveyed many things at once: it was easy, reassuring, generous, warm, democratic. Jean's smile was that of the would-be brave: whistling in the dark, cheering himself up, soldiering on regardless. Shy and too self-absorbed to smile very much, Bobrán's occasional sudden grin might appear as a leer, unsettling, even threatening, to those who didn't know him. Philippe's smile was the hardest to interpret: never a declaration of uncomplicated friendliness, it came layered, revealing itself gradually, like the flavour of a fine cheese: self-deprecating, sardonic, occasionally supercilious, authentically humorous, generous and gentle.

Away. Sarah was pacing up and down Tomec's studio. He had stung her. She was angry. 'Most of the time I don't think I even like you,' he had said. She wouldn't forget that. She had said she loved him. It wasn't the end, but an intimation. She'd have to kick him away. But not yet.

Big Win. Fernando was three minutes into his erection exercise. He was enjoying a daydream that spliced his recollections from that afternoon with a couple of fanciful ideas he was developing for his next session with Maryse.

He flexed his pelvic musculature, making his penis strain magnificently against his zipper, and dreamed on. He was hoping to beat his recent record of nine minutes.

Into Fernando's mind there slithered the questions: Where is she now? What is she doing? Who is she with? Maryse had told him she worked mainly afternoons, so he worried how she spent her evenings and whether she had a boyfriend. He thought of ways to find out. The easiest would be to follow her.

Fernando attempted to recruit his failing manhood by refocusing his thoughts on her body, but the spell was broken. Besides, it was never Maryse's body that worked the trick for him. It was the fleeting illusion of love-making. He sat up and glanced at his watch: four minutes flat. Flaccid.

As Fernando subsided into melancholy, the foreman came alongside, looking serious. He had removed his matchstick from his mouth and was grasping it in his claw. Fernando expected a speech.

We're shutting down for a few minutes, okay?

Tonight? What, now?

Yeah. In a few minutes.

Okay. But . . .

The Algerian's having a baby. His wife just told him.

How?

I don't know. I'll fetch some beers and you see what you can rustle up. Biscuits, anything edible. Tell everyone.

Fernando felt sharply better. If good things happened to others, they could happen to him. How could one big win be impossible? One good tip. One jackpot.

Ikarus. Hört zu, Genossen, Biermann began, causing a silence to descend slowly upon the room. Wolf waved a scrap of paper. I've a new song. I haven't got it off by heart yet. As some of you know, the American poet Allen Ginsberg recently paid me a visit; I showed him round and we walked and chatted – he's a great talker, full of craziness and folklore. On the Weidendammer Brücke, when he saw the Prussian Eagle, he took out his camera and insisted I stood against the railings with the wings sprouting from my sides. Everybody knows the legend of Icarus, right? At first I had to laugh, but he got his photo any-way. He said he'd send me a copy. Anyway, after he left, this song began to take shape.

Wolf sang of a cast-iron Icarus tangled in barbed wire grown deep into his skin, his chest, his brain, his grey cells, stranded in an insular half-nation battered by leaden waves, determined to remain stubbornly put until the bird-beast should dig its talons into his flesh and heave him over the edge. He put his guitar down with the final refrain ringing in his friends' ears:

> *Dann bin ich der preußische Ikarus*
> Then am I the Prussian Icarus
> *mit grauen Flügeln aus Eisenguß*
> With grey wings of cast iron
> *dann tun mir die Arme so weh*
> And then do my arms hurt so much
> *dann flieg ich hoch – dann stürz ich ab*
> So up I fly – and down I crash
> *mach bißchen Wind – dann mach ich schlapp*
> Make a slight stir – then break apart
> *am Geländer über der Spree.*
> On the railings over the Spree.

Unexpected. Philippe had filled his hoppers, checked the product and emptied his floor trays. He put on his gloves and stepped to the threshing tub at machine one. He was glad to do something physical. It was good to sweat. Sweat out the excess alcohol. He marvelled how tonight everyone seemed to have things to tell him he hadn't expected or particularly wanted to hear. Danielle and Jacques mainly. Little Gypsy too, come to think of it. Just now, Jacques had set him straight about the virility of old men. Well, well, there is hope for us all. He says I've got to find myself a woman. I'm supposed to feel humiliated. I don't know why I don't.

Jacques finished his threshing at machine three and needed a rest. He went to stand close to Philippe, laying his huge hairy arms on his friend's nice cool pile of papers. Philippe was working hard, smashing the sprue together till the products fell away. He looked up and grinned. Jacques was glad he'd said his piece, cleared the air. It was too damned easy to disparage old men . . .

The foreman was there now, talking to Marseille. Marcel stepped across the machine aisle and standing alongside Jacques pulled *Le Nouvel Observateur* from the bottom of the pile, thumbing through, searching for something.

Mathieu told Philippe of the planned five-minute shut-down and why it was happening. Philippe seemed surprised and glanced down the machine aisle at Rachid.

Are you sure?

The African said.

Let's check it's okay with the Algerian.

Philippe and Mathieu walked round Jacques and Marcel and down the machine aisle.

What's up? Marcel said.

Beats me, Jacques replied.

Bluff. Barefoot on his carpet, Gérard Boucan, his sleeves rolled up to his chubby elbows, was stuffing black bin bags with a jumble of books, letters, photographs and other inherited paraphernalia hitherto permitted to clutter and crowd his shelves and furnishings. While Gérard – as his son had observed – could not jettison such memorabilia, nothing would induce him to continue living surrounded – nay, suffocated – by them. In the morning he would order Concetta, Jorge or the surly fucking gardener to seal the bags and lug them to the cellar. Then he would call in cleaners and decorators. The room would be his. Strange how the simple act of tidying could galvanize his decision-making faculties. People were going to see some changes. He would love to toss Paul out of doors: it might be the making of him; unfortunately, Paul's mother would never hear of it. Claude, in any case, he would have followed. As for Jorge, he would seek subtly to corrupt the man: with kindness first and then with money. Gisèle he should certainly replace: whether thirty-two or forty, she was running to seed. A younger woman might do him good. As for the plant, he would heed the advice of his auditors, implement a tougher line with strikers, identify and isolate trouble-making ideologues, initiate a productivity drive and launch a process of de-manning, with all savings to be earmarked for retooling. Lastly, should there be any more graffiti nonsense, he would call the cowards' bluff. With his toes caressing its rippling neck, Gérard rocked his ancient mongrel gently awake. You, my friend, he said, can remain just as you are. You're safe.

Split. At the wooden table that filled the far end of the downstairs plastics section, Rachid sat crumpled ant-like, pensive yet relaxed, his left cheek on his left palm. In his head, Rachid heard a voice which he took to be Mehdi's while also assuming it to be the product of his own mind. Just as the sun continued 'to circle the earth' long after Rachid had understood that it was the earth that orbited the sun so Mehdi continued 'to talk to Rachid.' In short, Rachid believed one thing but experienced another.

Mehdi was assuring his father that at death humans become immortal, and thenceforth enjoy the spectacle provided by their erstwhile kin, grateful indeed to those earlier gods who first called humanity into being. 'Just imagine, father, a world devoid of mortals and their labours: a countryside left rough and untilled; the hills uncapped with towns or cities; no burnt offerings to thrill our fine olfactory sense; no playthings to seduce or merely to admire.'

As Rachid sifted these unfamiliar thoughts, he saw before him two pairs of shoes, two pairs of trousers, two shirt-fronts, faces, the foreman and Marseille, approaching slowly from the haze, halting before him, as he exited his reverie.

Imitating Mathieu, Philippe shook Rachid's hand. Mathieu spoke. Congratulations. The African said . . .

Rachid stood up, nodding. He looked away. Again Mathieu spoke.

So we should celebrate. And there's no time like the present. We'll shut the machines down for five minutes.

When?

Mathieu consulted his watch then glanced at Rachid's machine eight. Another ten products. Do you drink? Good. I'll say something.

Mathieu walked away, leaving Philippe at Rachid's side.

Mink. Jean sat stiff-backed at his machine, having shelved for now any effort to enhance his time-and-motion efficiency. After the various distractions of the early part of tonight's shift, it was time to rediscover his discipline and resourcefulness and face the ordinary boredom of the night ahead. Boredom? Peace and quiet within which to resume his review of the day's events. He would eat at one and Alphonse would read at three.

As Jean pressed START and leaned back, poised for profound reflection, he saw Fernando approaching. What could that man want now? Didn't I say our hospitality was in my wife's gift? I only propose: it's the home goddess who disposes.

Fernando told Jean about the imminent brief shut-down.

You're joking, Jean said.

Fernando shrugged.

I don't believe you. Sacrifice output because some Arab's wife's pregnant? Is this a prank? They breed like mink.
Fernando shook his head. He'd seen a picture of mink once. Ugly beasts. Can't you be happy for the man?
Jean hit START, then sat back and looked Fernando up and down. I'll need to hear it from the foreman.
If you have any food or drink to contribute . . . Okay, forget that.

Barely. Thrilling to the Algerian's news, conjuring the life in Rachid's wife's belly, Alphonse threshed the sprue at machine nineteen to a dizzying blur, sweat trickling from his brow and poetry memorized years earlier breaking the surface of his thoughts. He had never felt happier for a person he barely knew. He could have wept.

Dethronement. At a table-booth in the *San Francisco* sat Gilles, Heike, Margot, Moritz and Jean-Pierre. Everyone was absorbed in talk – with the exception of Jean-Pierre, philosophy lecturer, Margot's husband, Gilles' confidant and friend, who listened and watched, while meditating upon the work of Louis Althusser, whose *Lenin and Philosophy* peeped from Heike's shoulder-bag. It was a text he knew well.

Moritz was telling him about Wolf Biermann, whose forthcoming concert he expected to be 'historic.' Jean-Pierre nodded politely. Looking away, he saw Margot kiss Heike's cheek. Heike, however, was attending to Gilles' exposition of the centrality of culture in contemporary revolutionary struggle. Stealing, as Jean-Pierre could not fail to notice, from one of Badiou's recent dazibaos, Gilles discoursed on Mao Zedong's observation that Marxism could be reduced to the single phrase: 'It is right to rebel against reactionaries.'

Margot, stroking Heike's thigh and alluding to Luce Irigary, asked Moritz for a view of the revolutionary dethronement-of-the-penis implicit in homosexuality. Excuse-moi? Moritz said. For boys – Margot explained patiently – since both possess a penis, the goal can only be pleasure, and any oppression, whether reproductive or otherwise, is excluded. For girls, the phallus is simply absent. Consequently . . .

Moritz said he had nothing against heterosexuality in principle; his problem was the act itself. Margot looked perplexed. Well, Moritz said, the thought of sticking one's cock up where babies come out . . . I mean, no wonder you people get so many diseases.

Leaning back, eyes on the ceiling, Jean-Pierre was considering the objectively undialectical approach adopted in *Lire le Capital,* culminating in the conservative-mystificatory vocabulary of later Althusserianism, when Chuck, a university acquaintance, reached his hand over the others' heads and said, Salut, prof!

Perfect.   Luigi was rechecking his product at machine fourteen. There had been no change. The tiny promontory was still there: no bigger, no smaller than before. As he tossed it into the tub, fond thoughts of Gilberte came unbidden to his mind. That didn't often happen. He wondered anew whether he loved her. But how could he tell?

Luigi took a fresh new Gitane Maïs from his pack, looked at it from several angles, then lit it. He recalled his thoughts on bumping into Salvatore and his girlfriend one Saturday evening that summer with Gilberte. Je vous présente Laure, Salvatore had said. Luigi had pointed at his girlfriend and blurted, Gilberte. Enchantée, Laure had said, with a delicate inclination of her head. Salvatore had made a shallow bow. Gilberte had grinned and Luigi had covered his mouth.

Laure was tall and fine-featured, her eyebrows plucked to a pencil-line. Sofisticata, Luigi thought. Like wine. The kind of girl who never farts in bed, gets crotchety when you do, never swears, and employs plentiful vaginal deodorant. Salvatore had made an excuse: they were late for a classic Norwegian film showing at the arts cinema. Oh? Gilberte enquired. Black-and-white, Laure declared.

As soon as they were out of earshot, Gilberte had said, Fancies himself, doesn't he? Luigi liked that about Gilberte: she saw right through people, got straight to the core. He would like to treat her somehow. Maybe he would make love to her in the morning. Surprise her. She liked to be made a fuss over.

Luigi checked the product at machine thirteen. Perfect. Materially identical to all the others.

Mentor.   The storyteller was angry at being humiliated into retirement. He had tried his best, heeding the advice of the three-headed mentor he called John Alfred James, an Irish-Portuguese Berliner, Triestine aesthete, Kreuzberg physician, Chicagoan scribbler. His failing was that he never thought before he wrote, nor even while he wrote: his writing *was* his thought.

Spread.   Mathieu was in the glass-fronted office overlooking the ground-floor workshop. Lifting his hold-all from the floor, he tipped its contents – day-clothes, towel, street-shoes, sandwich in greaseproof paper trussed by a rubber band – onto the nearest chair. He placed the empty bag on the table and rummaged through filing cupboards, discovering paper napkins, white paper plates and cups, transparent plastic cutlery. He started searching for biscuits, water, crackers – anything, however flat or stale, to eke out a celebration. He found a small bottle of mineral water and a newish-looking packet of langues de chat – Nadine's favourite biscuit.

Mathieu looked up as Fernando pushed the door open.

Herbier wants to hear it from you, the Portuguee said.

The foreman moved his burnt-out matchstick around in his mouth. He was staring at the biscuit packet. Fernando tried again.

Herbier says he won't shut his machine down unless you tell him.

Mathieu waved at the biscuits and bottle of water.

This is all we got. Did you find anything?

This and that. Not a lot. The African has some crisps. The peasant has wine and apples. There are biscuits. All we really need is beers.

The foreman looked uncertain.

Marseille is going for the beers. And I've asked him to talk.

Fernando turned to go, then turned back. Mathieu saw a sparkle in his eye.

What is it?

We need a tablecloth. And a flower.

Are you serious?

Any fucking-piece of cloth will do. Provided it's clean. Forget the flower.

Okay, Mathieu said.

A spread has to be spread on something.

I get it. Find something.

The Portuguee was still standing at the door.

I'll talk to Herbier, the foreman said. Two minutes, okay?

Roving.   Eric was feeling nervy about his Saturday cinema date. There were so many things to go wrong, so many ways he could mess it up. He longed to be overwhelmed by a full-hearted passion, no sneering or second thoughts:

surrender. But would he find the words? Could he stop himself blushing, sweating, stammering, ending it all before they got started?

At machine ten, he turned the latest piece over in his hands. He had stared at it long enough. Philippe was walking back up the machine aisle. Like hitching a ride, Eric stuck out his hand with the product protruding from his palm. The Marseillais slowed and took it from him. For a good fifteen seconds, he turned it every which way.

Rien à dire, he said, lobbing it at Eric's bin.

Philippe had noticed *The Grapes of Wrath* beneath the Englishman's chair.

Il faut lire *En un combat douteux.*

Quoi?

En un combat douteux, Philippe repeated.

Eric picked the novel up and showed Philippe the author's listed works at the end of the biographical notes. Philippe flicked through it with his index finger.

C'est pas ici.

Philippe fetched a pencil stub from his trouser pocket and scrawled the words, 'En un combat douteux.'

In a doubtful combat, Eric whispered.

The Marseillais moved off to his own machines. He glided more than walked. Infinitely cool. Between Philippe nights and Fanny weekends, Eric was going to get himself a French education. He flicked the novel open and read the bio. 'He was educated at Stanford University, and afterward led a roving life . . .'

Eric was sure Steinbeck would never have put it like that.

Renata.   Jorge had pulled on underpants and gone to fetch a glass of water. On the kitchen table he found a note from Babette: 'A certain Carmen Valdez phoned the bookshop this evening and left a work number. She's in Hungary. She saw your advert in *Libé.* She says she has news for you and that she's a cousin. Babette.'

Jorge took a glass from the drainer, filled it from the tap. Having drunk it down, he stood in the middle of the kitchen, holding the empty glass. His bedroom door opened and he looked up to see Renata. For a moment he had forgotten her. She was wearing his shirt. She had done up one central button.

He looked at her feet crossing the tiled floor. She came toward him slowly, raising her knees high at each step, a cat padding across snow. Again and again her feet adhered and then peeled themselves from the tiling. He was afraid to look. He wanted to make love to her again. She came to a rest beside him.

Is everything okay? she enquired.

Yes. I placed an ad in *Libé* a few months ago. For information regarding my family. Someone has just seen it. A cousin.

Do you want me to go?

No. Why? Don't go.

Renata wanted to kiss Jorge's cheek. She leaned forward onto her tiptoes but realizing he was still absorbed in thought, she rocked back again onto her heels. She walked away. Jorge saw her ankles and the backs of her knees. I shall love this woman, he thought. I'm glad I didn't lie to her. You must never start anything with a lie.

Maximum Visibility. All men and materials should be readily observable at all times: there should be no hiding places into which goods can get mislaid. This criterion is sometimes difficult to fulfil, particularly when an existing plant is taken over. It is also a principle which is strongly resisted, and special offices, stores, cupboards and enclosures are often requested, not because of their utility but because they form a symbol of office or status. Every piece of partitioning or screening should be scrutinized most carefully, as it introduces undesirable segregation and reduces effective floor space.

K. G. Lockyer, Production and Factory Management,
Pitman, 1974.

Be-ZING. Jacques was standing between his machines, swaying slightly, smiling his automatic smile. Sometimes you don't know what you think till you speak. For someone who didn't talk much, he reckoned he'd made his point pretty well.

When you're young – he had told Marseille – you think old guys don't get them anymore. Well, we do. And here's the big secret – they're just as useful as ever they were to any lady friend we happen to have. It's not like when you're twelve and the February sun hits your trousers and – be-ZING – you have to yank your shirt out at the front. It creeps up on you, builds, takes time. But once it's there it's as solid as ever. Sometimes more so. You think I'm going to let some lady doctor with a mangy dog and unforgiving attitude take that away?

I wasn't thinking, Philippe had said. You're right. Anyway, all I did was shrug! See a man doctor. Someone your age.

As Marseille walked away, Jacques had swung his right arm up and clipped him on the back of the head.

And now Philippe was back again, standing right next to Jacques, frowning.

I've got to say something.

You didn't take offence . . .

What? No. I mean in a couple of minutes when we shut the machines down and raise a cup to Rachid's family. The chef asked me.

He picked the right man. Speak from the heart.

I daren't.

What?

The love of a good woman, the joys of parenthood . . .

Shit. But it's not about you. You'll think of something.

Philippe nodded.

I'll think of something. Of course. Anyway, I've got to go for the beers.

Agreed. Mathieu was standing scowling at Jean's shoulder, tapping his watch.

We're shutting down for five minutes at 23.25.

That's in two minutes. This isn't in the rulebook.

Lodge a complaint.

I'm supposed to turn in less product because Arabs have babies?

I'll work this machine five minutes while you're eating your one a.m. meal.

Agreed.

Committed. Stepping behind Mathieu into the lift, Bobrán said:

I need coffee if I'm going to drink beer.

So you heard . . .

Fernando told me. Lucky Algerian! I'd like kids. Well . . .

Drink it quick, Mathieu said as they stepped from the lift.

The African is shutting mine down, Bobrán replied.

Bobrán liked celebrations and he loved a silent shop floor. Normally, the machines were turned off only on Saturday mornings. He walked fast, rising high on his toes, making a detour – for the sheer love of movement.

Tomec was there, sitting on a wooden crate, fist to chin. He looked up on hearing Bobrán's coin hit the slot. Bobrán told Tomec about the shutdown.

I don't want to miss that, the Pole said, rising and heading off briskly in the opposite direction.

Two decisions came fully formed to Bobrán's mind: he would go to Germany with Moritz; and before he left he would speak to Joseph's brother. The little Gypsy knew exactly what he'd say: I'll help you any way I can. I'll tell you what I know. Some of it you won't believe.

It was picturing Albert's face that had clinched it. The moment he had imagined the man's face, he was committed.

Blink.   While some lives flow at a steady rate, uneventful and happy enough, others lead up to or – in retrospect – take their meaning and purpose from a single moment or experience. For Rachid, until the catastrophe of Mehdi's death, the centre of his life appeared to be fixed forever in his country's war of liberation when, un-coincidentally, he had met Malika. Marcel's watershed moment – with fine symmetry – had been his arrest, concluding three short years of high-on-the-hog gang crime by ushering in a further three of wretched incarceration. Philippe's moment had been the late-sixties, years of revolutionary upheaval and disillusionment, as he came of age in Marseille. For Mathieu, who had lived through war, resistance, imprisonment and anti-fascist liberation, it seemed that his time was yet to come. Alphonse and Bobrán too – though their lives had not been uneventful – awaited some revelation of meaning, some sense of being in possession of their own small histories. The moment to which Eric's life had been circuitously and haphazardly tending and which might – or might not – confer upon it some later post-hoc significance was right here and now before and all around him. Characteristically, however, it seemed that he might well blink and miss it.

Preparation.   Bobrán was finishing his coffee as Philippe approached, his left palm brimming with silvery coins, his right hand hooking a shallow tray by one of its shorter sides.

I shall be needing your lawyer friends, the little Gypsy said.

Philippe placed the tray on the floor and began to feed the beer machine with coins.

I've decided to spill the beans, Bobrán said.

Right, said the Marseillais.

Philippe removed each bottle as it dropped, stacking it carefully in the tray.

Bobrán looked away into the dark, then got up. He dropped his cup in the bin beside him.

As Bobrán walked away, Philippe said, I'll phone them tomorrow.

Having positioned the thirteenth bottle in the tray, Philippe sat on the discarded crate. He rotated his wrist and read the time: 23.24.

Reflecting that Jacques seldom drank beer, Philippe took a bottle, stepped to the machine to uncap it, then sat back down and lit a cigarette. His brain required urgent stimulation.

He stared into the bottle, watching the bubbles rise and burst. He didn't need to feel any calmer. He needed words. Memories of beach holidays wouldn't do the trick. He had to prepare something. It fell to him to announce Rachid's news. He closed his eyes and his head swirled. Parenthood. Children. Right. He liked to think before he spoke. It wasn't about him, Jacques said.

Beer had been a bad idea. He lobbed the bottle, still half-full, but it hit the side of the bin and crashed to the floor. He stared in astonishment. I never miss at this range! Taking a long drag on his cigarette, Philippe contemplated leaving the mess to others but then pictured some unknown hapless morning-shift workmate slipping, stumbling and cutting himself.

He rose and used his feet to create a tidy heap. Dragging the bin close and bending low, he picked up all the fragments and posted them through the bin flap. He was just going to have to wing it.

54. Salvatore purges. Jean sneers. Philippe speaks.

Marcel had shut down his machines eleven and twelve and gone to stand below the glass-fronted raised office at the head of the machine aisle. Feeling cramped in his clothes and clammy in all the creases of his body, he pressed his palms down over his thighs, pinching the trouser material to unpeel it from his skin, while shaking his legs like a sprinter at the starting blocks. He retracted his belly and parted his feet, rocking from left to right till his genitals fell comfortably free between his thighs. He took his packet of Camel from the breast pocket of his shirt and counted nine. Inserting a cigarette between his lips, he fetched a lighter from his left trouser pocket. The smoke shot down to the rear depths of his rib cage which it soothed and swaddled like a blanket. This makes a change, he thought, gazing down the machine aisle. For someone like me, just passing through, soon to be married, with all kinds of choices, it's light entertainment, a break in the routine.

Arriving from the lift, a plastic carrier bag in each hand, Fernando walked round Marcel. Behind the Portuguee, shiny-faced Jean Herbier halted, dithering alongside the big Gypsy, uncertain where to stand. Marcel blew smoke past his head, and turned away, shaking his long lithe legs. Feeling compelled to speak, Jean said, Ça va? To which Marcel replied, Ouais! Jean then enquired, C'est la fête? Whereupon Marcel remarked, Ça casse la routine. Jean resented the physical, downright intestinal, fear that Marcel inspired in him. A tune lurched unbidden into his mind dredging behind it familiar yet incomprehensible words, Rhedurne de Zender! Hahdrresse Hunnohne . . . ! Jean brightened up and looked round, his foot tapping feebly.

At the opposite end of the machine aisle, the Portuguee was placing his bags and a flat cardboard box-to-be against a foot of the table. The Algerian, who had finished his threshing, was whispering, Mehdi, are you watching? Don't miss this, son. His dead son made no audible reply yet there was a distinct rustling and nudging, a sign from the child as unmistakable as a shiver or a burp. The Sicilian glanced up at the grey-cheeked Algerian, folded his newspaper away and got to his feet. He wished somebody had seen fit to tell him what the shutdown was about – common courtesy, damn it. He looked round: the peasant, the Arab, the Gypsies; probably everyone knew what was happening – except him.

Fernando wished to clear enough of the huge wooden table for a celebration spread of drinks and titbits. He pushed away a jumble of tools, little buckets containing dud product, tubs of colour pellets, magazines, a scrunched-up cigarette packet, a metal metre rule. He was fuming again. The titch had fucking-no business objecting either to the Algerian's happy news or the chef's decision to make something out of it: he was out-fucking-of-line and how come nobody told him? Because he's older than most of us? Fuck that! People behave badly and who takes responsibility here? No fucking-body. Chaos can't be healthy: you don't breathe right where there's no respect. Fernando stared at the space he had cleared. How fucking-come he knew what to say only always after the event? It was the same thing with Maryse: he knew what to do with her only always afterward. At least with Maryse there was a next time. What was happening here was a beautiful celebration and nobody could be allowed to wreck it.

Salvatore walked to the end of his machine six. He flicked shut the metal sluice-plate beneath the hopper, cutting the flow of raw material to the melting chamber. As the presses opened and a product clattered through the aluminium slats, he drew back the guard. Stepping to the machine's controls, he switched a knob from automatic to manual. Then, depressing a green button, he caused the main body of the machine slowly to shunt approximately fifteen centimetres into the machine aisle, exposing the injection nozzle. From the flank of an almost empty sack of raw material slumped against the base of the machine, the Sicilian ripped a square of stiff brown paper. This he pushed into the concave space that had opened up between the nozzle and the press. Back at the controls, he leaned on a green button, causing the chamber to spew its contents onto the paper until the nozzle emitted no more than a hiss. He switched the machine off, checking the last product before emptying the rectangular floor tray into the threshing tub. His machine number six now silent; Salvatore turned to machine seven, repeating the procedure.

At the other end of the machine aisle, Luigi had finished shutting down his machines fourteen and thirteen. He was tugging gingerly at the edge of a scrap of paper bearing a smoking gout of plastic waste recently delivered from the nozzle of machine thirteen. Finding it was still too hot to be moved, he let go of the paper and went to stand alongside Jean and Marcel, recalling the latter's notion of bringing girls into the plant. He wondered how Jean would react to such an initiative. Luigi liked the idea of sharing girls in some homely work setting, yet on the whole favoured the discretion and privacy of a butcher's cold room. Regrettably, he could never smuggle any mental image of Gilberte into such an erotic scenario.

Tomec was approaching at a healthy clip from darkest metallurgy, his mind's eye reviewing a gallery of facial and body features fit to furnish a multitude, when a paradox struck him: the closer he came to the plastics section, the more the noise abated – not smoothly, as with a volume knob gently rotated, but in jerky steps, the din ratcheting down. As he stepped through the hanging flaps into the plastics workshop, the Sicilian's machine seven fell silent. Without saying a word, Tomec halted alongside Jean, content to observe the men in silence, unwilling to betray his ignorance of the reasons for the shutdown. At the far end of the machine aisle, Tomec saw Fernando take a rag from one of the bags and begin to wipe the table. Marcel, Jean and Luigi seemed to have moved closer together – a delayed reaction, the Pole supposed, to his earlier enquiries regarding the graffiti. He should have left the matter well alone. An innocent mistake.

Arriving from the lift, Alphonse spotted Luigi stooping beneath the raised office and accordingly slipped discreetly through the gap separating the Italian's machines thirteen and fourteen. He strode down the aisle and stood next to the Algerian and began to discourse on contemporary drama. Rachid, who appeared distracted, removed his glasses and blinked.

Having shut down his machines, Eric suspended his part-anxious, part-lubricious anticipation of his Saturday-night date with Fanny. Noting that the group of men beneath the raised office had swollen further, and inferring that that was the place to be, he shuffled up the machine aisle and into the narrow gap between Luigi and Marcel. Unlike Tomec, Eric had no qualms about revealing his ignorance. C'est pourquoi, tout ça? he stumbled out, jerking one arm around. Marcel took a long look at the Englishman before resolving to decipher his meaning. He saw Jacques bent over his threshing tub at machine four, sweat glinting on his weather-beaten old forehead. What's this all for? Marcel repeated, priming his audience by imitating Eric's arm-jerk. Eh, bien, la femme de l'arabe est en cloque! he announced. Jean and Luigi laughed and Tomec's eyes rolled up and back. Marcel's use of vivid idiom had been nicely calculated to throw the Englishman into a flapping confusion that mandated further elucidation. Marcel slapped his hands to his hips and thrust his belly out, stroking it with his right hand, pointing with his left where he imagined his absent uterus to belong, and saying, La femme de l'arabe . . . Wah! Wah! WAH! Bébé! Compris? Ah! Oui! Eric said, instantly scarlet.

Standing at the end of his silent machines, Salvatore glanced around, catching the big Gypsy's impression of what appeared at first to be an ordinarily overweight person, but who on the repeat rendition – now aimed, it seemed, principally at the Englishman – was clearly in some pain, possibly with appendicitis: Salvatore knew about appendicitis. The Gypsy's audience was laughing ecstatically. No doubt some vulgar joke, Salvatore reasoned, reopening *L'Humanité* and electing refuge in a glowing account of a tractor factory in Omsk. The Sicilian's thoughts, however, skipped again to the deceased tennis-club couple, whose trysts he found himself imagining in some detail, picturing the two as they entered and exited a well-known Grandgobier hotel, first separately then together, with himself located, as his daydream would have it, just across the road, at a brasserie terrace, sipping his menthe à l'eau. Before shaking himself from this compelling reverie, he pondered whether he should share this chance discovery with Laure.

Readjusting his spectacles, Rachid saw the Sicilian fold his newspaper and adopt an easy pose. To the Algerian's left, the Portuguee was stuffing his rag back into one of the carriers while, to his right, the Ivorian had at last fallen silent. At machine four, Jacques had stood up for a rest and a stretch and removed his cap and was fingering his crown. Further up the machine aisle, Rachid saw Marcel, Luigi and Tomec stepping back and looking away from the Englishman, as if to provide him with space for something.

Mathieu left the supervisors' office, descending the metal steps with a hold-all gripped in his left claw. Having carefully circled Marcel and the others, he limped down the machine aisle. He couldn't see the Marseillais anywhere. He was about to plonk his bag in the middle of the wooden table when Fernando requested he place it on the floor, explaining that he wanted to set everything out on a nice neat surface. Mathieu complied, then took a few paces back up the aisle, removed his matchstick from his mouth and jabbed it in the direction of Philippe's machine, addressing Jacques: Où il est? Jacques raised his eyebrows and smiled like an elf. Mathieu, tottering in the middle of the machine aisle, pressed his thumbs to his temples in a struggle to summon words he might employ to mark the joyous occasion – should Philippe let him down. All he could conjure, however, was an image of his beloved Nadine in a state that for all the strenuous mind-voidance exercises he performed during his shop-floor rounds he had never managed to approximate. He shook his head, hoping the new nurse was being nice to Nadine, but reminding himself that carers, even when apparently sensible and sweet-voiced, are not to be trusted.

Sensing belatedly that he could improve on Marcel's answer to Eric's query, Jean extended his right hand at breast level and repeatedly crooked and uncrooked his index finger, entreating the Polack, the big Gypsy, the Italian and the Englishman to draw near. What we're in fact here for, the little man declared with a wink, is to celebrate Arab fertility and the eclipse of the French race. All the men looked amused, though no two of them in quite the same way. Marcel roared his laughter directly into Jean's face as though the man himself, rather than his observation, were the source of hilarity. Noticing Marcel's outlandish laughter, Luigi, who at first had nodded at Jean's observation, suddenly had to cover his mouth. Tomec, after muttering, French race!, cackled briefly at the sight of Luigi aping Marcel; whereupon, the Englishman, even further out of his depth than usual, endeavoured to join in the merriment, imagining he had missed something indispensable. Marcel was the first to stop laughing. He straightened his face and posture so abruptly that the other men fell silent. He glanced at Luigi, Eric and Tomec to assure himself of their attention, then leaned into Jean's face and said, The Arab's all right. The Marseillais says so.

Bobrán ambled in from metallurgy. He avoided his cousin and Jean Herbier, noticing Luigi and Eric breaking away and moving down the machine aisle ahead of him. This was fun time, time off, leisure. He loved this shop floor when it fell silent. Right now it felt like every Saturday morning: release was imminent. But also like being in a big top, before the main number. He supposed that somebody would speak. Bobrán grinned at the old peasant as he walked past, then strode over to Rachid, gesturing to him to put out his hand, then shaking it vigorously, saying, Félicitations! Rachid looked uncertainly into Bobrán's face and thanked him, after which the little Gypsy fell back to stand alongside the African, whose eyes were fixed on the men at the table, and in particular on the Portuguee's preparations.

Fernando, having laid the box-to-be on the table, took a penknife from his trouser pocket and ran the blade down the left-side fold, opening the cardboard out to create a wide, clean, crisp surface. He began methodically to transfer from the carrier bags all the provisions he had collected from the men. Alphonse, Rachid and Mathieu looked on as the items of food appeared. Philippe and Salvatore had contributed biscuits, the former a tube of LU petits beurres, the latter a small packet of chocolate BMs; Jean had reluctantly handed over half a packet of TUC crackers; Fernando had given up his one-a.m. chocolate bar, Alphonse a family-size packet of crisps, Eric two cartons of yoghurt – one strawberry-flavoured, the other dark-cherry.

Rachid had had nothing to contribute, since he was not in the habit of eating sweet things at night and didn't think his homemade sandwiches counted as party fare. Mathieu had handed over a large bunch of red grapes, Marcel a pack of chewing gum and an orange, Jacques a selection of his better windfall apples and his half-full wine gourd. As the Portuguee placed these last items on the periphery of the table's cardboard covering, he shrugged apologetically at the men around him. Non, non, pas mal du tout! Mathieu asserted, with a grin, bending to lift his hold-all from beneath the table, and removing a bottle of Vittel, a packet of langues de chat, a wad of medium-size paper plates and a long curving tube of paper cups. These were followed by transparent plastic knives, forks and spoons. In a voice that under normal circumstances would have been drowned by the machinery, Mathieu said, All we need now is beers. And the Marseillais. He tapped his watch with the broken nail of his middle finger. It was ticking all right.

Philippe arrived from the raw-materials area, a crate of beer grappled to his belly, his face long and pale. What was he to say? He had to keep his marital – not to mention parental – anxieties to himself. When exactly, he wondered, had he stopped talking to his daughter – and she to him? He'd have to make a fresh start there – while separating from Odile. The prospect was numbing. There he went again! The moment called for something thoughtful, yet with a dash of joy and, if possible, wit. It wasn't about him, Jacques had said.

The foreman and the old peasant exchanged glances of relief, while Luigi smirked and Marcel laughed outright at the sight of the Marseillais waddling unsteadily down the machine aisle. Most of the other men watched with variously blank or rapt expressions, but Alphonse and Bobrán frowned as though concerned. Fernando simultaneously tut-tutted and held his breath, afraid the Marseillais might stumble and shed the beers.

As Philippe reached the table and Fernando stepped forward to relieve him of the crate, the uncustomary silence and the sudden emptiness of his hands oppressed the Marseillais. Normally, the roar of these machines just obscures the fact that we talk so little, he thought. We forget how to speak in this place. Every word I say will blast out like a coach horn. Most of these men have never heard me not shouting.

As the Portuguee placed the beer crate to one side of the festive spread, Luigi stepped forward, brandishing a Swiss-army knife and flicking out the bottle-opener attachment. Marcel and Jean had followed Philippe down the machine aisle and others too had taken at least one step toward the table. While Fernando uncapped the bottles, Rachid surprised himself by offering a beer to each man in turn. Bobrán, who had taken a paper cup and served himself some Vittel, was the only man to decline. Eric raised his bottle to his lips, but Salvatore, stepping forward, stayed his arm. Philippe, who had gone to stand beside the foreman, stared down the neck of his bottle, observing the bubbles rise and pop. He tried to gather his thoughts. He wanted somehow to use this exceptional break in routine to illuminate their ordinary nights and days.

All eyes had turned to Mathieu, who glanced at Philippe, then spoke.

The Marseillais has agreed to say some words. The foreman then whispered, Keep it brief.

Philippe looked at the faces – friendly, curious, expectant, indifferent, detached, hostile – and he knew what he had to say.

*

On the fourth floor of the block of flats across the street from Éts. Boucan's plastics section, Goran lay on his back, his hands cradling his head, his brow knit, his eyes drilling into the dark. This was how he fell asleep: wishing Iskra would come to bed, nursing a swarm of worries, and dreading the four-a.m. alarm clang. Back home, he'd lain dreaming of leaving Macedonia; now he lay scheming a way back.

Goran was tormented by the thought that he should have taken his family to Germany or Switzerland, Belgium or the Netherlands. He couldn't have foreseen that they would be arriving in Europe (as he called it) at a time of mass layoffs, or that France would be worse hit than her northern and eastern neighbours.

He saw again the blood he'd brushed from the street below: he would find it tomorrow between the cobble stones, liver-coloured, veining the gutter. He recalled the thugs who had pulled their limousine over, checking the job had been done right, showing no fear or shame. If the police came asking questions, Goran would be quite unable to describe them: you don't put yourself on the wrong side of big-time crime. In fact, he hadn't had a good look at the driver, just noticed his long hair, but the boss guy had had a face he would certainly never forget: ugly, bloated, mean, certainly French – the face of a killer. Iskra was right: they had to get out of this neighbourhood.

Goran noticed how silent it was. Other than Saturdays and Sundays, you always heard machinery noise from the factory opposite, above the rumble of city-centre traffic. Tonight was different somehow.

Jeanne had dreamt that the train on which she and her mother were travelling had careered off the rails. Sabotaged, she thought, turning over. Several of the carriages had borne signs saying, *Nur für die Wehrmacht*, and the sound of boots had been heard at each station. Jacques and Henri had both appeared in the dream, but she couldn't recall whether they had met. She was a hostage to what she knew: she knew too much for her imagination to run altogether free.

The first pages of *Les Amants d'Avignon* had catapulted her back into well-buried history. Memories pressed upward like moles piercing moss. She got out of bed and felt her way to the dresser, where she lit the candle. If she ever saw Henri again, the explaining she would have to do! The future had been so certain: socialism or barbarism. How would she tell him that while the final victory of barbarism had been averted, he had died for something well short of socialism: an explosion of consumer goods, an expansion of welfare, steadily rising wages, and a flowering of unimagined freedoms. Could she convince him that this was *not* nothing? He would say that she had changed.

Nor would her own life be easy to account for: here she was, un-scandalously unmarried, 'seeing' the widower of her lifelong dearest friend. Jeanne lifted a tall jug and poured some water into a large bowl. She splashed her face, driving the drops across her cheeks, behind her ears, to the back of her head. She would read Triolet's story further, but mornings only, before Jacques arrived. She blew out the candle and felt her way back to bed.

Maryse was walking home, stoned on Evelyne's hash. Evelyne had declared: 'sex is sex, whether you get paid for it or not. I'd be having masses of sex with lots of guys whatever happened.' 'Everyone's different,' Maryse had retorted.

To Maryse, there was nothing intimate about sex: it was a transaction whether or not money was involved. Given the choice, she would rather hold hands, yet she could sometimes enjoy it up to a point and knew it mattered to other people.

A draftee stopped her, 'Want a drink?' Maryse declined with such a sweet smile, he almost sobered up.

She had not always lived alone. She had shared apartments with friends – sometimes boys, sometimes girls. She wondered if she could ever live with a man: she dreaded compromise and mess.

A feeling of numbness was setting in. Maybe it's the dope, she thought. It's like I've been switched off at the mains.

A stray misty thought brushed her mind, teasing, then suddenly lifting. Butterflies! BUTTERFLIES! That afternoon her Portuguese client had painted her a word picture: a shady riverbank, crystal-clear water, then around a corner a cloud-spray of butterflies, every colour from black to white and back again.

Giuliana yelled into the half-light surrounding her couch. Vito came from the lounge. 'Is that you, Totò?' she asked. 'No,' Vito said. There was a silence. 'I'm scared,' Giuliana said. 'Scared?' 'Terrified.' 'Of what?' 'Of nothing.' 'Nothing?' 'You're repeating me like a droning echo! I'm terrified of nothing.' Vito's voice was patient and calm: sternly tautological. 'If you're terrified of nothing, Mother, then maybe you're not frightened at all.' Giuliana's nose whistled as she breathed in. 'Get Totò.' 'He's not here.' 'Precisely! That's why I'm asking you to get him. My God, I'm surrounded by halfwits.' 'I beg your pardon?' Vito said. 'I'm scared of nothing-NESS! Understand now?' 'Ah!' Vito said. 'Maybe I'm growing confused,' Giuliana explained, 'stuck in this bed, this room. But if you imagine I mistook you for Totò just now . . . Never!' Vito reached for her hand. She let him take it briefly. 'Do you know what my worst fear is? No?' Vito shook his head. 'That the life I'm living here in this house may be a foretaste of the life to come. If hell is nothingness, I'm in purgatory already – hell's antechamber. Tell Totò to come. Wire him.' 'I did.' 'Wire him again.' 'I will.' 'Good boy.'

Bruno, stirring, travelled his hand across the sheet, first slowly, expecting to encounter Chantal's shoulder or hair, then scuttling his fingers till they met the hard rolled edge of the mattress. He sat up. There was not the slightest glimmer of light beneath the bathroom door. He hugged himself, then switched the lamp on. Picking up the receiver from the bedside phone, he dialled nine for an outside line. He glanced at the clock – 11.26 – fearing his mistress might not be home. He knew her number by heart. On the tenth ring, she picked up. 'So you are there,' he said. 'Where did you think I'd be?' 'I don't know.' 'Have you been drinking?' 'No. Why?' 'You don't often call.'

'I was thinking of you.' 'But it's late.' 'I wanted to hear your voice.' 'Since when?' 'I've been sat here all evening with a lousy detective novel.' 'I didn't ask what you'd been doing.' 'When I closed the book, I thought how much I missed you.' 'You sound odd. Are you sure nothing's happened?' 'Why should anything have happened?' 'I don't know.' 'You have a suspicious mind.' 'What does that mean?' 'Nothing.' There was a silence. Bruno searched for something definite to say. 'Would you like it if I were home more?' 'Sure.' 'Is that all?' 'What do you want me to say?' 'I mean with you. I'd leave my wife.' 'You've always said you couldn't.' 'Well, maybe . . .' 'Look, it's entirely up to you.' 'Okay.' 'What has brought this on?' 'Nothing.' Bruno, abruptly recalling how expensive it was to make international calls from a hotel room, said goodbye, then looked round the room.

Nadine Petit's eyes didn't flicker. Perhaps they can't, thought Marie. Maybe they're stuck somehow. It seems she can't turn her head either. But you can sense something. There's definitely someone there. No wonder Monsieur Petit still cares.

The nurse had been describing her background and the responsibilities she bore her family. She had started rambling about work opportunities, explaining that nursing was a respectable career, whereas secretaries always got propositioned by office lotharios, and factory work was boring as hell and anyway even that was insecure nowadays. 'I wish you could advise me,' Marie said. 'I'd listen to the kind of person you once were. Oh, that sounded awful.' She fell silent, as if waiting for a forgiving word. 'Oh, well,' she said.

She got up to leave the room but turned back at the door, saying, 'I promised I'd sing you "Le Temps des cerises," didn't I?' She stood in the centre of the room and cleared her throat, then thought she should introduce it somehow.

Did I tell you my grandfather used to sing me this? He once asked me, 'Do you know what makes this the greatest song of revolution ever written?' 'No,' I said. 'Guess,' he said. 'The fact that it's beautiful, full of longing?' 'Yes,' he said, 'I think that's it. There is no call to arms, no phrase-making, nothing about victorious dawns or everlasting glories. On one level, it's a plain love song, but the love it celebrates is universal and, quite delicately, it evokes the blood spilled in vain to crush the longing for freedom and love.' Anyway, that's what I remember him telling me. Now. Here goes.

Quand nous chanterons le temps des cerises
Et gai rossignol et merle moqueur
Seront tous en fête.
Les belles auront la folie en tête
Et les amoureux du soleil au coeur
Quand nous chanterons le temps des cerises
Sifflera bien mieux le merle moqueur.

*

Philippe stood between Rachid's machine number eight and the wooden table, far enough back to give everyone a clear view of the makeshift feast the Portuguee had laid out so neatly on the cardboard table-covering.

Philippe drew a breath, then appeared to change his mind, glancing rapidly at each man in turn, guessing at their expectations. He turned to Mathieu.

Brief, you said. How long have I got?

Two minutes.

Well, I won't need *that* long, the Marseillais drawled.

Have any of you noticed, he began, how silent it is? Listen to it. It feels like a moment outside of time. Frozen. What could we possibly mean by halting production? It doesn't feel right, does it? To celebrate not even a baby, but a baby-to-be, a foetus: not hope itself, just the anticipation of hope! It's a moment of pure irrelevance – absolute impertinence – to productivity, capitalism, the Machine itself! From here, from this vantage point, we ought really to be able to peep through the cracks and sneak a glimpse of our everyday normality whereby each one of us stays safely at his machines, paid by the hour, industrially cowed, creeping here while others go off to sleep, abetting the machinery in the manufacture of briefly valuable lumps of tomorrow's landfill trash, then slinking away like ghosts before the sun comes up.

The men had stopped shooting questioning glances at one another, eyebrows raised as if he were crazy. They were listening. Salvatore stared at the floor and flexed his fingers, Fernando scratched his stubble, Marcel smirked and Jean – you could almost measure the effort it took – looked like he was restraining an impulse to spit. The Englishman was looking around for help but he couldn't catch Jacques' eye and Rachid seemed mesmerized. Philippe pressed on.

We have stopped work to celebrate something magnificent that we hope has absolutely nothing to do with this factory or with profit or loss or exploitation or productivity. Isn't that right? It had better be. Because the alternative – that we might be standing on the shoulders of columns of wage-slave generations only to sire more of the same – is unthinkable, isn't it? Compared to most workers – even to others employed here chez Boucan – we have it cushy on this shift. But, is this all there is? Let me put it this way: could anyone here imagine bringing up a child with the loving ambition to see him or her some day trudging into this place in our footsteps? Happily, however, we can be confident that no child born today is ever likely to join us here. For just as these machines didn't exist a generation ago, in another generation they and this entire process will be obsolete and all of us here tonight will either have other jobs or none at all.

So let's savour this moment. It won't last. And it's all we've got. We've downed tools to celebrate the news that our comrade, Rachid, and his wife, are expecting a child. That's a great thing. I should know. A child will give you love. More than any woman. Again, I should know. I can remember. The fact is that this child will not only outlive us, he or she may, we hope, outlive the very way in which we work and live. This child will come of age on the eve of a new millennium, with opportunities beyond our present dreaming – opportunities to grasp or to fail to grasp. While there is no blueprint for the changes to come, surely the energies, intelligence and creativity of working people will not be squandered and denied and mocked forever! So let us raise a glass to the child and to the world that he or she must build anew. To Rachid, his wife and child! To freedom! To the future!

As they raised their bottles and plastic cups, neither Marcel, Salvatore, Eric nor Luigi paused to consider their own fathering prospects; nor did Jacques dwell with any bitterness on the distance and coldness of his only child; nor, for that matter, did either Jean or Mathieu feel regret at not having had any children. Bobrán, alone, wished he could somehow produce a child with a lover, any lover – Moritz, for example, would do fine. As for Fernando, he caught himself wondering, for the first time in his life, what kind of father he might ever make – if only there were a woman clear-sighted enough to appreciate him and give him that chance. And Luigi surprised himself by picturing Gilberte – Gilberte, a matronly butcher's wife! – with bawling babe tugging at her breast. Luigi swigged at his beer bottle and relit his cornpaper cigarette. Nah! he thought.

55. Alphonse, Marcel, Tomec, Mathieu.

Jean glanced round. That'll be that then, he told himself. Oratory is deader than I thought. In its place, a deluge of drivel about a brown baby's future and a paean to the long-awaited millennial revolution. But what can you expect from a Red from Marseille, the home of every imaginable métissage and miscegenation since Greeks and Levantines first buggered and pillaged their way through the city? At least it was brief. I could go back upstairs now. But look at them! They don't know where to turn or even how to stand! They're missing something but don't have a clue what. So they drift to the table and gobble like geese at a pond. Mind you, the biscuits might be worth a try. After all, somebody's bound to eat my TUC crackers.

The nightwatchman, not tempted by any of the food on display, observed the scene from the end of Eric's machine ten. The little guy from upstairs was checking out the food, taking some interest in the langues de chat, while the Portuguee shook the Algerian's hand so hard the poor man winced, and the peasant patted the Marseillais and muttered words that caused him to raise his eyebrows in modest demurral. Meanwhile, the Gypsy cousins stood together, the big one talking nonstop at the little one, who looked away and grinned. Tomec's focus shifted slowly from such complex generalities as attitude and intention to mere bits and pieces of people – their identifiable body parts – and to elements of potentially meaningful behaviour: he was retreating from wholesale interpretation to the examination of anatomical and gestural detail.

For a moment it seemed to Tomec that something resembling Brundisium's quayside had rematerialized right here amid this handful of workers. Knowing each man but slightly, he registered the contrast between, say, Salvatore's sip and Eric's gulp, or between Jacques' posture of splay-legged relaxation and the Ivorian's minuscule spot-dancing movements. Every man held his beer bottle in a unique way, almost a signature; executed the act of swallowing just so, whether whole mouthfuls or minutely minced; granted his body a nuanced permission to rub against others (Fernando, say) or, alternatively, performed brusque evasive action when someone strayed into proximity (Mathieu, say). In the very disposition of the bodies before him, Tomec detected a fine structure of criss-crossing animosities, attractions, affections, revulsions, fears and curiosities that formed a web of spider-silk threads that enmeshed the men as powerfully as steel girders.

Having noticed that the Algerian was not eating, Fernando put down his own paper plate, grasped a clean one and badgered Rachid to agree to be helped. Biscuits? Why not? You don't like them? Then crisps . . . ? No? Some chocolate at fucking-least? Rachid resisted, even when Fernando attempted to reason with him: a biscuit can't harm a man, can it? You're going to need every scrap of strength, aren't you? You do at least bounce your kiddies on your knees, right? You're so rake-fucking-thin, man!

Rachid accepted half a biscuit and nibbled at its edge like a gerbil. He was so accustomed to peering at the floor or at the street that the sight of his fellow workers aligned before him was shocking. He felt he had never looked in their faces before: the Portuguee was grinning like he cared whether or not Rachid ate something; the Ivorian, since Fernando had now backed off, was coming closer and starting to speak; most of the other men were attempting to enter into the celebration; further off, the little man from upstairs was sneering and snarling about something or nothing; and the Sicilian, standing all alone, was picking at grapes as if they were worry beads.

Alphonse had nodded at Rachid; now he opened his mouth.

Listen, he said. I've got this poem I could read.

Sure.

You don't mind?

Show me.

Well, it's in my head. I'd recite it.

Rachid waved a permissive hand.

It's quite short, Alphonse said. Do you want me to ask the foreman?

I don't see why.

Okay then.

Rachid looked round at the men again. The big Gypsy had turned his back on his cousin and had been buttonholed by the Englishman whom he stared right through, while the Italian hovered alongside them. Alphonse rested his backside against the centre of the enormous table and faced up the machine aisle. He cleared his throat then cleared it again more loudly. People noticed him, shushed each another, and fell silent. Jean, who had finished his beer and was making his way to the stairs, halted and turned back round.

I thought I'd recite a poem. Its title is 'Emportez-moi' and it was written by Flavien Ranaivo.

I like the title, Fernando said.

Yeah, take me away from here! Marcel said.

Alphonse closed his mouth tight, as if checking an aching tooth.

This is one of several poems I learned as a child at my uncle's knee in Côte d'Ivoire. I'll recite it twice. I discovered years ago that most poems should be read or heard at least twice. You don't always get them the first time.

Alphonse waited till he could hear nothing but a distant police siren, let that fade, then began. He studied his listeners' faces and turned from man to man as each line fell away from him.

Emportez-moi, – the Sicilian set his jaw;

emportez-moi ô mes pieds miens-ci – the Algerian's eyes continued to look straight ahead but lost their focus;

afin de rejoindre cette route, – the Portuguee's frowning head strained forward but his feet did not move;

cette route là-bas qu'abritent – the foreman bowed his head as if at a graveside;

les feuilles mouvantes et touffues à la fois: – the Englishman spread some rolling tobacco on a paper;

il y longtemps que je n'ai pas vu – the Marseillais looked serious, as if worrying what came next;

mon père et ma mère. – the smaller Gypsy was staring wide-eyed at Alphonse as if he had that instant grasped some matter of importance.

Several men coughed and Eric lit his roll-up; Bobrán took a sip of water and Marcel a sip of beer. Rachid's focus returned and he looked about him. Alphonse began again. Most of his workmates appeared to freeze; some of them seemed to vanish into the middle distance.

Alphonse spoke the words clearly, carefully, evenly, as though they were the most ordinary words in the world and incontestably his own. Rachid noticed for the first time that Alphonse spoke with a slight West African accent. This time, Rachid was prepared for the final lines, the mention of 'father' and 'mother.' His parents were dead and he didn't grieve much for them any longer. But there were those for whom he did grieve and as he again heard the poem's last line his thoughts returned to Mehdi, as if the loss of his son now stood for every conceivable loss – past, present or to come.

'Emportez-Moi' par Flavien Ranaivo

Emportez-moi,
emportez-moi ô mes pieds miens-ci,
afin de rejoindre cette route,
cette route là-bas qu'abritent

les feuilles mouvantes et touffues à la fois :
il y longtemps que je n'ai pas vu
mon père et ma mère.*

Philippe was sunk in thought. For five whole minutes this place becomes quite interesting, just when I'm thinking maybe I've had enough and really what the hell *am* I here for? But Jacques is right: I should do what I want. I'd never look back, he said. Otherwise I'll wake up one day and be sixty and it'll be too late. Odile has done me a favour, shaken me up. Perhaps I don't need this place any longer. I've always wanted to investigate things – crime, for instance, corruption, scams – do some digging. People talk to me. Who knows why? I have contacts. All I need is a notebook and tape recorder. I could start while still working here. If all goes well, I'll give up the factory and go for broke. I don't need much to live on. A bedsit would suit me. If things get tough, I could drive a taxi. Nights. Nights are when you find things out. Tongues wag in the dark. I've always liked nights. This beer's addling my brain. I've been on the edge of drunk all evening.

Okay! the foreman barked, breaking through the coughing. Please finish your food and beer and return to work. In two minutes I want every machine up and running. And let's keep this stoppage to ourselves: box up a little later than usual, around 4.40.

Mathieu took some grapes and headed up the machine aisle. He caught Jean at the stairs.

Didn't hurt, did it? he asked.

It's not what I'm paid to do, Jean said.

Turning away, Mathieu saw Luigi coming toward him, chewing gum. (Nadine, the first time ever I saw your face.)

Mathieu pointed at machine fourteen.

If it doesn't settle, we'll shut it down. The morning engineers can fix it.

Luigi nodded.

The foreman caught sight of the Pole standing at Marseille's paper pile. Mathieu was surprised by a new thought, which he considered briefly. Maybe it was the poem that had triggered it. Or Marseille's little speech. Or picturing how Nadine had once chewed gum. Anyway, there was no harm asking. He

---

* 'Emportez-moi,' by Flavien Ranaivo. From the collection entitled *Le Retour au Bercail* (1962). Carry me, / carry me, oh my own feet, / So that I rejoin that road / That road over there that is sheltered / by the dense and fluttering leaves: / it is a long time that I haven't seen / my father and my mother.

took out his box of matches, struck one, blew it out and placed the unburnt end between his lips.

Gardien de nuit! he called, champing on the wood.

Tomec looked up.

I've got a question for you, Mathieu said.

Tomec followed him round the office front and up the steps.

Shut the door behind you.

Tomec shut the door.

If it's about the graffiti . . .

It isn't.

Then . . .

The foreman looked as though he might change his mind. He leaned against the table, clasping its edge, while he stared at the floor.

I hear you're an artist. You paint, right?

Usually I sculpt . . .

But you can paint.

I used to. Nowadays, I usually make sketches when I'm preparing . . .

I want you to paint my wife.

I don't usually . . .

I never took many photos of her. I don't know why. She's not been well. I'll pay you . . .

I don't usually take commissions.

You tell me how many hours it takes, I'll pay you what you make here . . .

Well . . .

She's not looking her best. You'd better do her – Mathieu pronounced the word like it had a bitter taste – *justice*. Will you do it?

Well, usually . . .

Screw 'usually.'

Both men looked away.

I apologize, the foreman said. Will you do it?

Sure.

Thank you. I'll tell you on Friday when's convenient.

Tomec didn't move.

What is it? Mathieu asked. Nothing? You can go.

Tomec left the office. Mathieu remained where he was.

All the other men were eating, drinking, talking: every tongue unleashed.

The Portuguee was talking to the Ivorian.

'It *is* a long while since I saw my mother and father,' he misquoted. That line spoke fucking-right to me. That's what poems do, isn't it? Tell me, what poetry would you give a woman?'

Depends, Alphonse said. Maybe Sappho.

Sappho?

She was Greek, an Ancient.

Rachid's hand had gone numb in Jacques' from all the shaking.

Marcel saw the Italians return to their machines. He took a biscuit then waved the packet at Marseille.

Just look at that, he said, pulling on Bobrán's sleeve.

What?

How come those two are so keen?

Just doing their jobs, Philippe said.

Marcel felt he had more to say. Salvatore was opening his attaché case. He slipped something inside, then closed it again, flicking the combination.

I'll tell you what he keeps in there.

Let's hear it, Philippe said.

The others moved in closer.

It'll be a blow-up doll, Marcel said.

The case is too small, Bobrán objected.

It's a magic fucking-case, Fernando said.

Then anything's possible, Bobrán said.

He could fit his girlfriend in there, Fernando said, eyeing Philippe, who stood back and nodded.

That's it! Marcel said. I bet she comes out and gives him a blow job when no one's looking. That'll be why he's so careful to keep it locked tight. He doesn't want anyone else taking a turn.

Everyone laughed except Philippe, who blew a smoke ring and turned to talk to Jacques. Then, with the exception of Bobrán, everyone else turned away from Marcel.

I tell you what, Bobrán whispered to his cousin. I'll come to your wedding clean-shaven and in a suit and tie. I'll even make sure my mother behaves herself like a gadgé. They'll never know you're related to dirty gyppoes. But that's it.

What's it? That's all I want.

Alright, then.

Rachid was still attempting to explain to Eric about the Sicilian's attaché case. He pursed his lips and mimed inflating something, while describing with his hands a life-sized doll, yet the Englishman wasn't looking any better informed. Marcel, meanwhile, had stepped over to machine seven's control panel and was talking to the Sicilian.

Alphonse had walked up the machine aisle. There was a story in *Le Monde* he wanted to finish. Bobrán had gone to stand next to him and had picked up *Libération*. He deciphered a word in a headline, 'Barre.' Alphonse lifted his eyes and glanced at him. Bobrán put the paper down.

Jean upstairs says he'll teach me to read.

Terrific.

I'd rather you did.

I'm not much of a teacher.

Forget it.

What do you want to read?

How do I know? If this is going to be complicated . . .

You just want to read . . .

That's it.

Okay, I'll teach you.

Alphonse closed his eyes slowly. Bobrán flicked through *Libé*.

Just bear in mind I'm a busy man, Alphonse said. I have stuff to do, lines to learn, speeches to make, Arabs to hug. Don't look at me like that. It was a joke. A private joke. You weren't supposed to get it. This place is weird. Inside here, my time's not my own. Know what I mean?

Not really.

There was a silence, which Bobrán broke.

Just now with that poem, I watched you read out words that weren't there in front of you. I thought the words had to be down on paper. I want to be able to read like *that*.

Ah . . . well . . . that's all part of it.

Uh-huh.

We'll start on Monday. All right?

Bobrán went upstairs, leaving Alphonse reading *Le Monde*.

At machine seven, Marcel had taken the opportunity to ask Salvatore whether he and his fiancée were planning any children.

It's never come up.

Are you kidding? How green are you?

Salvatore looked down. Marcel whistled.

Me and my fiancée have talked it through and she says she doesn't want any.

Salvatore coughed.

Thank you for going along earlier with the foreman's safety-shutdown non-sense, the Sicilian then said.

Yeah, well. But you sure know how to change a subject. Anyway, do you imagine I care less about safety than you do? Because I'm a Gypsy? I just don't like work, is that it?

I didn't say that.

Boy, you're green though, getting married without finding out whether your lady wants kids.

Salvatore had switched his machine on and pushed the sluice-plate beneath the hopper back open. Now he was checking a temperature dial. He looked worried.

Marcel glanced over at the huge wooden table. Fernando was cleaning up, stuffing rubbish in plastic bags. Rachid watched him for a while then began to help him. Jacques had put an arm on Philippe's shoulder.

Tell me something, Salvatore said to Marcel.

What?

When exactly did you hear we were shutting down production to celebrate the Algerian's new baby?

Why?

Just wondering when you knew. It seemed to get decided pretty quick.

Ah! Marcel said, as if trying to recall. I must have heard about it when I came in. Didn't you?

The big Gypsy was grinning so broadly now that Salvatore figured he must be playing some kind of game.

Sure, Salvatore said. Everyone knew, right?

Of course, Marcel said, walking away laughing.

Fernando had finished wiping the table down and was carrying the bags of rubbish and unused plastic cutlery back up the machine aisle, depositing them inside the foreman's office.

The Ivorian looked up and saw Philippe, Marcel, Eric and Jacques strolling toward him.

I liked what you said about the 'Machine,' Alphonse said.

I'm not sure I remember, Philippe replied, stepping over to machine two's control cabinet.

Rachid laughed. He had taken the bottle of beer Bobrán had not wanted.

You said this was a moment to savour, a moment of insolence to the

'Machine,' Alphonse said.

'Impertinence,' Rachid corrected.

Philippe raised his eyebrows at the Algerian.

Anyway, sometimes I think it's that same Machine that shook us all loose from the places we came from – Algeria, Portugal, Marseille, the mountainside, England, Africa – and has got us all caught up here making these bits of plastic for somebody else's profit. Sometimes I like to imagine what else we could be doing. Thirteen of us – if we include the Pole. There are a lot of possibilities. We could stage a play! I'd like that.

Or a holdup, said Jacques.

Eric looked to Rachid for help.

He's saying we could rob a bank, Rachid explained.

Formidable! Eric said.

Or we could form a football team with two to spare, Marcel said.

We could run a school, Alphonse said.

Everyone fell silent. Alphonse alone could imagine running a school.

The storyteller had taken leave of his three-headed mentor and ceased to rage at his imminent but long-foretold dismissal. His vision had dimmed, his hearing grown blunt, his intuition was shrivelling while his empathy faltered; in sum, his nerve was failing. His mood had turned to resignation in the face of the inevitable, while, in a rare bout of introspection, he detected in his mood a degree of satisfaction at the thought that his chronicler's remit had been exhaustively fulfilled: he had sketched to the height of his ingenuity the lineaments of each new visitor to the draughtsman's plinth; submitted to his superiors each interception of the aquarium fish, reporting their utterances in a near-universal medium. His successor would have to begin where he left off, tracking society deeper into each person's minds and thoughts while, contrariwise, projecting even the tiniest of unique human vagaries onto a magnifying social canvas. One final tour awaited the storyteller, one last patrol of the frontiers of his imploding powers. Then, with no bitterness or anger subsisting, and with his former world shrinking to a vanishing dot, he could lay down all ambition and hope, embrace retirement and be thankful for relief.

Among other things, there remained two inter-continental phonecalls to report: Agrigento-Toronto and Budapest-Havana.

At Giuliana's villa, the nurse sitting alongside Vito muted the TV on hearing the phone ring. Late-night news was giving way to more talking heads.

Vito was speaking with Gianni. The nurse watched the screen but heard Vito. 'I don't know about Totò.' Pause. 'I wired him yesterday. He'll probably phone tomorrow.' Pause. (Vito sipped his beer.) 'I don't think she's dying yet. She has an appetite. The doctors don't seem alarmed, but they never do, do they?' Pause. 'Is that so?' Pause. 'No, she hasn't asked. Just Totò. You know how it is.' Pause. 'Well, he's the firstborn.' Pause. 'Look, if you can't get away right now and . . .' Pause. 'That's what I'm saying. Come at Christmas. Elena and Berto both say they'll be here.' Pause. 'Yeah, won't it just!' Pause. 'Me? I'm fine. You know.' The nurse looked at Vito, who closed his eyes.

Jorge's young cousin Carmen was staying overnight in Buda at the house of a party friend who had international telephone privileges. Carmen had reached Felicia at her modest ministerial post and told her about Jorge's small ad in *Libé*. Felicia sounded pleased but wary. 'I was sure he was alive. Did you speak?' 'It turned out to be a bookshop where a girlfriend works.' 'Girlfriend? Oh. Good.' '*Babette*. She said she was a *copine*. My French isn't . . .' 'Babette.' 'So I gave her my home number. What shall I tell him if he calls?' 'Everything. He'll understand. Tell him I said that life is long and we'll meet again. In Chile. Tell him we did nothing wrong. Say that I'm happy.'

In Malmo, Angelica hugged Rosa then shook hands with Rosa's husband. She thanked Rosa for advancing her what she was owed at work. Nonsense, Rosa said. From memory, Angelica scribbled not only her parents' address in Portugal but also the most recent address she had for Fernando. She left for the depot to catch her lift to Charleroi.

Megan had addressed, stamped and triumphantly posted her final letter to Eric, returning to her student room with Maddie and Anne, three pies, and six cans of Tennents. She didn't want to regret anything the next morning.

The letter that Agnes Wiewiorka had written to her brother that evening lay unsigned on their mother's old escritoire. Agnes had sat up late to peruse a French translation of a Seamus Heaney collection that she had received from Tomec.

Fernando's father had returned from the village bar, fuming about the storekeeper. He had accused his wife of chasing away all their children, and had gone to bed without saying goodnight. Fernando's mother had peeled potatoes for the morning, placed them in a bowl of water, and joined him in the cold. She couldn't think what she had done to upset him.

At his apartment in East Berlin's Chausseestraße, Biermann put down his guitar. 'Be c-c-careful,' Hartmut said, 'history is r-r-running through you now.' 'Don't lay that on me,' Wolf laughed. 'I'm only a singer, a catalyst at most.' 'I suppose we're all Ikarus now . . .' Petra mused. Hans snorted. 'We would all have been Spartakus once. It's quite some regression: from revolutionary hero to over-curious child . . .'

In France, but about as far from Grandgobier as it was possible to be, Karim was putting the finishing touches to the weekly thought piece he wrote for *Rouge*, under the rubric *Dans l'atelier* ('On the shop floor'). This week he was again berating union bosses, appealing for proletarian unity, decrying the 'ever more naked attempts to divide us man from woman, black from white, unskilled from semi-skilled, unionized from non-unionized. Solidarity must begin on the shop floor,' he concluded his piece.

In contiguous Parisian arrondissements, separated by the Seine, Alphonse's maternal uncle Laurent and Laurent's lover Juliette, in their modest bachelor pad and chambre de bonne respectively, got ready for bed, the latter placing Basil Davidson's *Africa in History* on her coverlet, the former at his kitchen table glancing over a lesson plan for his Wednesday afternoon final-year maths class. Neither had any thoughts of the other.

Spiralling closer now, just south of Le Puy, Jules Romanès had fallen asleep over his fan heater in his petrol-station cubicle; Yitoune in her lover's dainty arms in a small cramped town named Romans; Jeanne in her own bed in her own house; while Cécile Chartier, at her husband's family mansion in the hills above Grandgobier itself, rose yawning from her bed and in diaphanous négligée descended to her husband's library, where she found Raymond, his volume of Claudel having slipped from his fingers, simulating alertness at her approach. 'Come to bed,' she cooed, her right hand stealing across his chest. On the stairs, she lamented their evening's company, 'Do we have to entertain such boors?' '*She's* not so bad, surely?' 'Darling! *He* at least had the grace to leave once he'd finished the dessert. I had to remain polite as she bewailed the shortcomings of Concetta.' 'Concetta?' 'Their Portuguese maid.' 'Ma *pauvre* chérie . . .' On the edge of the city, Yvonne Labarde had found sleep at last, moulding herself to Bernard's sturdy round back while weaving a dream of a Latin lover.

Close to the city centre, Fanny arrived home unmolested by the drunken draftees celebrating their impending return to civilian life. She found Kosal's letter, folded it carefully and placed it in her jeans hip pocket. It felt crisp and good there. The apartment was quiet and dark. Her mother had left a completed game of patience spread across the kitchen table. Obligingly, Fanny admired it. She fixed herself a glass of cold water and sat down. She felt the letter hard against her buttock. She thought about Saturday, the gawky Englishman. Well, she had to do something about him. It was getting embarrassing.

A couple of streets away, in the same low-rent neighbourhood, Marie had finished singing the final verse of 'Le Temps des cerises.' She remained standing, her hands folded loosely over her belly, her breathing returning to normal. She hadn't for one instant taken her eyes off Nadine, and now stepped over to the old lady. She felt an impulse to kiss her at her hairline, but at the last moment kissed the middle finger of her right hand instead and touched that to Nadine's widow's peak.

Across the road, behind Établissements Boucan, Iskra had heard the machines starting up again and had wondered what had caused the interruption. It had been pleasant briefly to lose that background hum – a false promise of weekend quiet. She went through to the bedroom, slipped out of her clothes and joined Goran in bed. He grumbled briefly in his sleep, but settled when she kissed the back of his head. In seconds she too was asleep.

Inside the plant, Tomec strode through dark workshops, keenly persuading himself that despite the inward groan with which he had responded to the foreman's invitation to paint his wife, a little light portraiture might in fact be precisely the exercise he required. How everything he saw either waking or in dream now lent itself to his artistic project, bringing, as it were, fresh water to his mill! His encounter with the foreman's wife might prove serendipitous. (His pace quickened.) There was nothing he could not use! Had he not been thinking that very evening that he lacked female sitters for his Virgilian tableaux? In a matter of hours, one was presented! Recalling his earlier dissatisfaction with his sketch of the 'skew-wigged harlot,' he now thought: 'might not the foreman's wife provide the model?'

On the upstairs plastics shop floor, Jean was happy to be back at his machine. He checked the first few sets of cable ties with special care, fearing that evening's ludicrous and arbitrary stoppage might have thrown out his machine's delicately tuned temperature and pressure settings. It felt good to be back doing what he was paid for.

Fernando had restarted his machine sixteen, checked its first product, and was now standing at machine seventeen. He pressed the button to move the injection nozzle toward the back of the press, pushing the sluice-plate back to allow raw material into the melting chamber, and switching the machine to automatic. He was looking for words with which to rebuke Jean for the attitude he had taken to the Algerian's news: he had referred to children as mink!

Bobrán had restarted both his machines and was mixing an oblong armlength tub of raw material for eighteen's hopper. Mathieu came from the lift, approached the little Gypsy and said, 'You didn't take my advice.' Bobrán looked blank. 'To leave Marseille alone tonight,' Mathieu said. 'But, chef, advice is stuff you can disregard, right? Orders are what you have to follow, right?' Mathieu shook his head and closed his eyes. When he opened them again, they fell on Alphonse's machines nineteen and twenty. The clock on the wall showed eleven-thirty. He swore. Nothing he said seemed to count any more.

Downstairs, the conversation between Alphonse, Eric, Marcel, Jacques, Rachid and Philippe was continuing. None of them felt ready to return to work, although the din from upstairs had now resumed and both Luigi and Salvatore had restarted their machines. Rachid mentioned a famous saying that Malika had heard the previous Friday evening on a books programme – to the effect that life had to be lived forward but contemplated backward. Alphonse thought it was Nietzsche but didn't want to show off. Philippe reckoned Rachid was on his third bottle of beer that night. He'd never seen him tipsy before. Who could begrudge him?

Anyway, that's wrong, isn't it? Alphonse was saying.

What's wrong? Marcel asked.

That we can only view our lives backward.

No, it's right, Rachid said. But if it's supposed to imply that meanings can only be grasped after the event *that* would be wrong.

What the hell are they talking about? Marcel said, appealing to Philippe.

I'm not sure, Philippe said. But maybe it's this. An event or a moment – even this one, for example – or, your wedding, say, or a strike, or the birth of a child – can only be viewed retrospectively, i.e. interpreted from the future. Right? In a way that's obvious.

So what? Marcel said.

Well, Rachid was talking about meaning, which is not the same as interpretation, right? Because it isn't the future that gives an event or fact its meaning. The meaning of any event is always to be sought in its past, that is to say in the way it gets produced.

That's right, Alphonse said. Though I was thinking more about *re*-production.

You'd better ask our Algerian friend. He knows all about that, Marcel said.

Rachid and Marcel shared a brief smile, then looked away from one another almost at once.

Alphonse wasn't to be put off his subject.

What I want to know is how come we – like the characters in this play I'm involved in – come back day after day and it's as if nothing ever changes. How are the days reproduced? How are *we* reproduced just the same, day after day? To such an extent that the machine, Marseille's 'Machine,' would never notice that we're ageing, living, falling in love, getting sick, making babies, etcetera. How come we can have at least some rough idea how these bits of plastic get reproduced day after day but no real notion of what brings us back here, always the same, always ready for work? Isn't that a mystery?

Marcel looked round at all the dumb faces.

Are you all kidding me? It's the money!

No, no, no, Rachid said. I see what, er, Alphonse is saying.

We could make money elsewhere, Jacques pointed out.

It's all too deep, Philippe said. You might as well ask what time is for. See what I mean? It's the kind of question that only a shrink can help you with.

A shrink? Marcel asked.

Alphonse wasn't letting go.

What I want to know is what brings *us* and not other people here and also what brings us *here* and not elsewhere . . .

Philippe blew out his cheeks and tapped a cigarette out of his pack.

Just then all the men heard an outburst of shouting and spluttering and turned round. The first few words were entirely incoherent though, with hindsight, it was possible to piece them together as, 'Mais, ça suffit des conciliabules!'

Halfway down the stairs from the first-floor plastics section, the foreman was leaning over the banister and shouting from the top of his trumpeter's lungs at the little group of idle workers. They all turned to face him. Spittle flew in several directions. His face was wine red. He was tapping the side of his head with the knuckle of an index finger. Mais ça va pas, non? Putain!

What do you all take this place for? It's not a circus, not a theatre, not a wrestling ring, not a flophouse. Nor is it a philosophers' salon!

His arm shot out to nail Alphonse where he stood.

You! Get the fuck upstairs and start your machines!

Alphonse broke into a skipping little run.

As for the rest of you . . .

Okay, we got it! Marcel said, moving off.

Eric, Rachid and Jacques also went to their machines, initiating the process of restarting them. Philippe opened the sluice-plate at his machine number one, then glanced back up over his shoulder toward the stairs.

The foreman was still standing there, but his arms had dropped to his side. He had taken out his box of matches but had found it empty and was looking at it in disbelief. Philippe advanced the injection nozzle into the back of the mould and looked again. Mathieu scrunched the matchbox into a ball and sent it spinning out into the middle of the shop floor. Nobody saw it land.

AFTERWORD

Dedication and Disclaimer

This novel is dedicated to the men who worked the night shift at Raymond Boutons in Grenoble (France) from September 1976 to October 1977. While all biographical and personal details relating to the characters in this work are wholly invented, there remain some minor physical attributes and gestures that might enable some of those who survive to identify themselves as the remote ancestors and partial models of the fictional characters featured in this work. However, just as the Englishman Eric has very little in common with the author's erstwhile self – beyond some facial features and a heroic passion for smoking – so also are the characters of Philippe, Bobrán, Luigi, Fernando et al but the most distant descendants of the men alongside whom the author once worked. All the actions, attitudes, speeches and thoughts of the characters in this novel are wholly fictional and any similarity to events or situations in the lives of the characters' original models can be no more than coincidence, the more or less happy fruit of methodical imagination. Indeed, given that the author never came to know any of his fellow workers at all well, it could not be otherwise. By the same token, the factory that is partially described in this novel ('Éts. Boucan') is not intended as a literal portrayal of Éts. Boutons, nor of course is the fictional city of 'Grandgobier' intended to pass for Grenoble.

CHRISTOPHER WOODALL was born in London. Between leaving school in 1971 and starting work ten years later as a jobbing translator, he travelled in Europe, the Maghreb, and East Africa, worked in factories, a restaurant, language schools, a crude-oil facility, and took two academic degrees, acquainting himself along the way with the French, Italian, Spanish, and German languages. Much of his writing springs from a single, at first seemingly inconsequential, year-long encounter with a group of workingmen in France, in 1976. His translations include Piero Camporesi's *Exotic Brew* and Lydie Salvayre's *The Company of Ghosts*. *November* is his first novel.

At present, among other things, he is working on the second novel in the tetralogy initiated with *November*. For further details, please see www.christopherwoodall.org.